YOUNG HENRY OF NAVARRE

YOUNG

Henry

of *Navarre*

by HEINRICH MANN

TRANSLATED FROM THE GERMAN BY
ERIC SUTTON

THE OVERLOOK PRESS
WOODSTOCK, NEW YORK

First published in 1984 by

The Overlook Press
Lewis Hollow Road
Woodstock, New York 12498

Library of Congress Cataloging in Publication Data

Mann, Heinrich, 1871-1950.
    Young Henry of Navarre.

    Translation of: Die Jugend des Königs Henri Quatre.
    1. Henry IV, King of France, 1553-1610—Fiction.
I. Title.
PT2625.A43J813   1984   833'.912   84-42674
ISBN 0-87951-981-9

CONTENTS

BOOK ONE: *THE PYRENEES*

BOOK TWO: *JEANNE*

BOOK THREE: *THE LOUVRE*

BOOK FOUR: *MARGOT*

BOOK FIVE: *THE SCHOOL OF MISERY*

BOOK SIX: *THE PALLOR OF THOUGHT*

BOOK SEVEN: *THE TROUBLES OF LIFE*

BOOK EIGHT: *THE WAY TO THE THRONE*

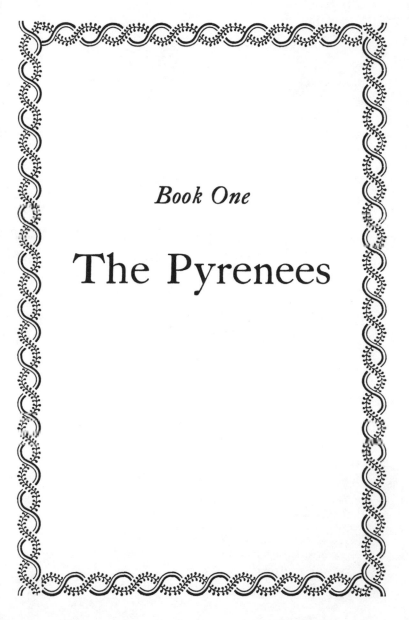

Book One

The Pyrenees

THE BEGINNING

THE BOY was small and the mountains were enormous. He clambered from path to path through a tangle of sunlit, sweet-smelling bracken, with cool lairs in its depths. From behind a jutting rock a waterfall thundered down from a great crag. Two eyes, two sharp eyes, peered across the forest-mantled slopes, and on a far-distant rock between the trees they could see the small grey chamois. How the boy loved to stare into the shimmering blue depths of heaven until his vision swam! To shout aloud from very joy of life; to range the countryside barefooted; to breathe, to soak his body in the warm soft air. Thus the boy grew lissom, and his heart learned joy. His name was Henri.

He had some little friends, barefooted and bareheaded too, but also ragged or half-naked. They smelt of sweat and herbs and smoke, as he did; and although he did not, like them, live in a cabin or a cave, he liked the smell of his fellows. They taught him to snare birds and roast them; to bake his bread between hot stones and smear it with garlic. For garlic made you grow and kept you well. Wine did likewise, and wine they drank from every vessel that would hold it. They were all steeped in wine — these boys, their parents, and that whole land. His mother put him in charge of a she-relation and a tutor, so that he should grow up like the country-folk, though his home was a castle, called

Coarraze. The name of that land was Béarn. The mountains were the Pyrenees.

Here men spoke a many-vowelled, rounded speech, and they rolled their r's. When his mother's labour began, his grandfather insisted on her singing a canticle to God's Mother for help. *Adjudat me a d'aqueste hore.* It was the speech of the country, and as near Latin as need be. So Latin came easy to this boy. He could speak it only; his grandfather forbade him to write it. There would be time and enough for that; he was still a little boy.

Old Henri d'Albret died in his castle at Pau, in the plain, while young Henri was talking Latin at Coarraze, or scrambling through the woods after the little chamois, called *isards*, which he never could catch; and like enough the old man lay in his death-rattle at the very moment the child was shouting as he bathed with the boys and girls in the pool under the great glittering waterfall.

He was oddly inquisitive about girls' bodies. They undressed and moved, they talked and looked in ways so different from his own; but it was the lines of their legs and hips and shoulders that set them more especially apart. One, whose breast had begun to bud, caught his fancy, and he resolved to fight for her. And fight he must, he could see that; he was not her choice, she preferred a taller boy with a handsome foolish face. Henri asked for no reasons, these lovely creatures very likely had none, but he knew what he wanted.

So the little boy challenged the big boy to carry the girl through the pool. It was not deep, but there were eddies in it and smooth stones, that slipped under an unwary foot. His rival toppled over very soon, and the girl would have fallen in, too, if Henri had not clutched her. He knew every step in that pool, but he needed all his strength to carry her across, for she was heavier than a lean little boy like himself. Then he kissed her on the lips, which she in her surprise did not resist, and said, slapping his chest:

"You have been carried across the pool by the Prince of Béarn."

The little peasant girl eyed his small, passionate face and

laughed; his pride was stricken, but his courage did not fail. As she fled back to her unlucky swain, Henri cried: " *Aut vincere aut mori!* " It was one of the sayings that his tutor had taught him, and he had great hopes of it. Alas, the country lads made nothing of the Prince nor of his Latin. Conquest and death were equally unknown to them. There was but one thing for him to do. He stepped back into the pool and purposely fell over even more clumsily than his rival. He aped his oafish face and stumbling gait, spluttered out the very same curses, and he did it all so well that they all roared with laughter. Even the girl laughed.

Then he slipped away. He was only four years old, but he already had an instinct for effect. He had achieved it, but he was not at ease. Vengeance sated did not efface the memory, and a yearning still lingered in that small, bold heart.

His mother sent for him, and at first he could talk of nothing but the girl. His grandfather was dead, he would never see him again. But he was much more cast down to be parted from the girl.

" Let her come, Mamma, I'll marry her. She's taller than I am, but no matter, I shall grow."

The household in the castle of Pau, though barely more than a family grown great, had the trappings of a little court. Old d'Albret had been a country nobleman, and this was his stronghold, which he had lately had enlarged and beautified. From the terrace he looked down on a deep valley rich with wine and oil and forest, the shining curves of the river, and beyond it the Pyrenees.

The mountain range stood up, as did none other, in a closed, unbroken line, mantled with forest to the sky, and gladdened the eye that looked at it, especially the eye of the lord of that country. The old noble owned the nether side of the Pyrenees, the spreading valleys and the hills, and all that grew thereon, fruits and beasts and men. His too was the southernmost corner of western France, Béarn, Albret, Bigorre, Navarre, Armagnac; all that once was Gascony. His title was King of Navarre, and he would have owned allegiance to the King of France had the latter been possessed of his full power. In the meantime the kingdom had for many years been riven everywhere between Catholics and Protestants. That provided such provincial princes as Navarre with their best chance to make themselves independent, and to take what they could from their neighbour by force, were it only a vineyard.

But fire and slaughter ranged over the countryside in the name of the two hostile creeds. The difference of creed was regarded in deep earnest, and it made utter enemies of men whom nothing else divided. Certain words, especially the word " Mass," had so terrible an effect that brother was no longer understood of brother, and became of alien blood. It seemed natural to call in the aid of Swiss and Germans. Let them be of the right faith, and, according as they went to Mass or not, they were better than a Frenchman who thought otherwise and were given leave to burn and pillage with the rest.

The sturdy faith of the peasantry was at least of profit to their leaders. Whether they really shared it or not, they could, in the name of religion, extend their domains by brigandage, or at the head of their little lawless armies lead a pleasant life at little cost. For some the civil war was a profession, though most people lost by it. But even these kept their convictions.

Old d'Albret had been a good but unbigoted Catholic. He had always borne in mind that his Protestant subjects begot children too, that they were useful toilers who tilled the fields, paid taxes, and increased the wealth of the country and its lord. So he let them go to their preachments in peace, and his soldiers protected the pastors as they did the priests. No doubt he reflected too that the growing numbers of these Reformed Protestants, called Huguenots, were more likely to help than hinder his independence, as the court in Paris was decisively Catholic. He was merely one of those feudal lords who from time immemorial had done their best to dam the power of the King of France. Latterly they had made use of the Huguenots, men of a fresh and youthful faith, who knew the true God from near at hand, but were none the kinder for that knowledge.

They were rebels against the temporal as well as the spiritual power. Even in Bearn the peasants had long since asked where there was any mention of taxes in the Bible. If none, then why pay taxes? Well, the old man understood how to manage them, they were men of his own kind. They liked to use large words, but they kept cool heads. They fought well, not forgetting that fighting, after all, was profitable.

He wore a Basque cap like his people, except when necessity arrayed him in helmet and cuirass, and he loved his country as he loved himself, just so much of it as he could compass with his eyes and all his other senses. When his grandson Henri was born he took care that the event should take place in the castle at Pau, whither his daughter Jeanne was summoned for the purpose, while journeying elsewhere. Not merely did he make her sing during her labour the song *Adjudat me a d'aqueste hore* in the language of the country, to guard his grandson from meanness of spirit. He made the new-born babe smell the wine of the country, acclaimed him as his own flesh and blood by the tilt of his head, and smeared his lips with garlic.

Two earlier boys had died, but Henri lived, and the old man bequeathed all his property and his title to his daughter. Jeanne was now Queen of Navarre. Her husband, Antoine de Bourbon, was in the service of the King of France, his distant relative. He was mostly in the field. Jeanne had loved him deeply before he began to go in quest of other women; but she never set her hopes on him, and indeed he was soon to die. Her ambitions were beyond his compass; her mother had been the only sister of Francis I — the King who had been worsted at Pavia by Kaiser Karl V; but he had vastly enlarged the French possessions of the Crown of France.

Jeanne d'Albret was therefore a great lady, and not at all content with the lands of Béarn, Albret, and Navarre, which were in themselves a kingdom. The reigning King of France, of the House of Valois, had four sons alive, so there was little likelihood of the collateral line of Bourbon coming into power. None the less, Jeanne made bold to prophesy a splendid future for her son Henri — as she remembered later with amazement: could she have possessed the gift of second sight? She was merely ambitious. Her ambition hardened and embittered her, and it proved a burdensome inheritance for her son in later years.

When her little son came back, she took particular pains to teach him the history of their House. She ignored his pursuit of the pretty serving-maid, nor did she care when he ran, here too, barefooted after the children of the street, full of curiosity about those strange creatures called girls. Jeanne was no observer of what happened, she was as set upon her dreams as a queasy woman. Henri, who ached to be kicking up his heels like a mountain goat, would feel one of the maternal arms about him; the other clasped his still smaller sister Catherine. Queen Jeanne bent down her flaxen head between her two children. Her face was thin and pale and finely cut, the brows arched sadly above the great dark eyes, the forehead was already faintly wrinkled, and the corners of the mouth had begun to droop.

" We shall go to Paris soon," she said; " our kingdom is too small. I want Spanish Navarre."

" Why not take it? " asked little Henri. And he added quickly: " Papa should conquer it."

" The King in Paris is friends with the King of Spain," his mother explained. " He lets the Spaniards invade us."

" So will not I! " cried Henri. " Spain is my enemy and always will be! Because I love you," he said impetuously, and kissed Jeanne. Tears trickled from her eyes into her half-bared bosom, which her little son caressed while he tried to comfort her. " Does my father just do what the King of France tells him? I won't," he assured her in a coaxing tone, feeling that this was what she liked to hear.

" May I go with you? " pleaded the little sister.

" The serving-maid must come too," insisted Henri.

" Will Father come and see us when we get there? " asked Catherine.

" I dare say he will," murmured Jeanne, and she rose from the high-backed chair to evade any further questions.

THE JOURNEY

Soon after this, Queen Jeanne went over to the Reformed faith. It was a notable event — not only for her little land, which she did her utmost to convert to Protestantism. It raised the spirit and the influence of the new religion everywhere. But she had done so because her husband Antoine still took fresh mistresses at court and in the field. He had been of the Reformed faith, and then lapsed from weakness into the Catholic creed; so she did the opposite. There may have been piety in her change of faith, but it was done mainly as a challenge: to her faithless husband, to the court in Paris, to all who baulked and baffled her. Her son was to grow up to greatness, and that he could only achieve at the head of Protestant armies; so much was already clear to his mother's ambition.

When at last they were setting out for Paris, Jeanne embraced her son and said: "We are going on a journey, but not for pleasure. We shall come to a city where almost everyone hates the Religion and hates us. Forget it never! You are seven years old and a boy of sense. We have been to court once before. You were very little then and will not remember it. Your father might call it to mind, if he had not forgotten and thrown away so much of what has been."

She sank into a sorrowful dream. He twitched her arm and said: "What happened at the court that time?"

"The late King was alive. He asked you whether you would like to be his son. You pointed to your father and said that man was your father. So the King asked you whether you would like to be his son-in-law. You said: 'Yes,' and since then you are spoken of at court as betrothed to the royal Princess, that is how they think to catch us. And this I tell you so that you may not believe all you are told, nor trust these people."

"Bravo!" exclaimed Henri; "so I have a wife — what is her name?"

"Margot. She is yet a child like you, not old enough to hate and persecute the Religion. However, I do not think you will marry Marguerite de Valois. The Queen, her mother, is too wicked."

Henri saw Jeanne's face alter as she named the Queen of France. He shivered, and his imagination received a sudden jar. In his mind's eye he saw a dreadful leering face, claws, and a thick stick. " Is she a witch? " he asked. " Can she cast spells? "

" She would if she could," said Jeanne. " But that is not the worst."

" Does she spit fire? And eat children? "

" Both; but she doesn't get her way. For God, to our good fortune, has punished wickedness by folly. My son, you must not reveal a word of this to any man."

" I will keep it all to myself, Mamma, and I will take great care not to get eaten up." He was quite absorbed in his boyish fancies, and thought that they and his mother's words would be marked for ever on his mind.

"Above all, hold fast to the true faith that I have taught you," said Jeanne, in an eager tone in which there was a hint of menace. Again he shivered, and this time his dread was deeper.

Never before had Henri heard his mother Jeanne d'Albret speak of Catherine de Medici. Then they set out upon their journey.

First came a huge old leather coach, carrying the Prince's tutor, by name La Gaucherie, two pastors, and several lackeys. It was followed by six armed horsemen, stout Protestant gentlemen, then the Queen's coach upholstered in red velvet, with Jeanne, her two children, and three ladies. And some more mounted gentlemen " of the Religion " brought up the rear.

At the outset of the journey all was familiar, speech and faces, countryside and food. Henri and his little sister talked out of the coach window to the village children as they trotted alongside for a little way. It was July, and very hot, so the coach was kept closed. Several nights they spent in their own country, one at Nérac, the second capital; the whole Reformed population gathered there in the evening, the pastors preached, and psalms were sung. For a while their road led through Guyenne, the ancient Aquitania, whose capital was Bordeaux, and here An-

toine de Bourbon, Jeanne's husband, held rank as Governor
for the King of France.

Then they reached a country the like of which no child of
the Pyrenees had even conceived of in his dreams. What strange
garb the people wore! And how oddly they talked! The boy
could understand them, but he could not answer them. The
river-beds were no longer dry, as they surely should have been
in summer. No olives, and scarcely a donkey to be seen. In the
evenings the little company were among strangers, and the Protestant gentlemen kept guard outside the doors, as the Catholics hereabouts were not to be trusted. One day, when the
pastors tried to preach, they were driven by superior numbers
out of the bleak chapel that stood on the outskirts of the little
town; even the Queen of Navarre and her children were forced
to flee in haste. There was all the greater thankfulness at find-
ing in one place a majority of like believers. Jeanne was received
as a herald of the faith, her fame had gone before her, and the
people made her lift her children in her arms for all to see. The
pastors preached, psalms were sung, and a ceremonial feast was
held.

They had already been eighteen days on the way when they
crossed the Loire at Orleans. They fetched a compass round the
town, the armed Huguenot horsemen drew in close to the royal
coach, and so stayed until the envoys of the Queen of France
appeared. They were men from the court, who welcomed
Jeanne with gallantry, but they brought with them a bodyguard
of Catholics, and these claimed to ride closer to the coach than
the Protestants. Jeanne's escort would not give way, and a scuffle
followed. Little Henri leaned out of the window, and shouted
to his people to lay about them, in his language and their own,
which the others could not understand. A shower of rain parted
the combatants, both sides burst out laughing, and all was gallantry once more. A dark sky lowered over the unfamiliar poplars, rustling in the wind. It was August, and, to these Southern-
ers, strangely cool.

"What are those black towers, Mamma, and why are they
on fire?"

" 'Tis the sun setting behind the castle of Saint-Germain, whither we are bound, my child. There lives the Queen of France. Remember all I told you, and what you promised me."

" I do, Mamma."

First Contacts

He behaved at first like a pert and bellicose young cockerel. But his first encounter was with servants, who received him from his mother; only the tutor was allowed to stay with him in his room. And then meat, and such a quantity of meat, was brought; and when next day there was still nothing but meat, he begged for his native melons, which were then in season. He cried, refused to eat, and was sent into the garden to amuse himself. The rain had stopped at last.

" I want my mother. Where is she? "

" With Madame Catherine," he was told; and he shuddered, because he knew they meant the Queen. He asked no more questions.

He was wearing his best clothes, and behind him walked two gentlemen, La Gaucherie, his tutor, and a noble of Béarn. Across a lawn other boys approached him, each attended by gentlemen, but by more than two. Henri noticed at once that they did not look like boys who liked a game; the eldest, especially, walked with a swing of the hips and carried his head erect like a grown-up courtier; and his white bonnet was topped with feathers.

" Sirs," said Henri over his shoulder, " who may that bird be? "

" Have a care," they whispered; " 'tis the King of France."

The two groups stopped face to face, the young King opposite the little Prince of Navarre. He did not move, but waited for Henri, who took full time to look at him. Charles IX not only wore a white bonnet, he was clad entirely in white. A white ruff framed his face, which he held half-averted, so that he was always looking out of the corners of his eyes. There was a bleak and cunning air about him that seemed to say: " I know you already; 'tis pity I must know your fellows."

Henri felt cheerful for the first time since he had arrived.

He longed to laugh, but those behind once more muttered: "Have a care." So a seven-year-old puffed out his chest at a twelve-year-old, bowed till his rump was in the air, and swept his right hand in a half-circle over the grass. He repeated this exercise on both sides of the King and lastly at his back. Some of the gentlemen began to titter. Not so Larchant, the noble from Jeanne's suite. He dropped on one knee and said: "Sire! The Prince of Navarre has never yet seen a great King."

"He is never likely to be one," said Charles; he rapped the words out one by one, then pursed his lips under his great fleshy nose. This was too much for Henri. His kindly eyes glittered, and he cried:

"Take care my mother does not hear you, nor your mother, who really rules your kingdom."

Uncommon words for the ears of a king Charles IX's gentlemen were startled. He merely closed his eyes; but he marked that moment on his mind for ever.

Henri cooled down at once and turned to the other two lads as though nothing had happened. "Well, and what of you?" he asked cheerfully, for they seemed to him oddly awkward, which was because he lacked the education of his rank.

"I am called Monsieur," said the first, who was about the same height as Henri. "'Tis my title because I am the eldest of the King's brothers."

"My name is Henri."

"So is mine!" cried Monsieur, in a more boy-like voice, and the pair eyed each other warily.

"Have you any melons?" asked Henri, by way of getting to the point at once. The youngest of the two royal brothers laughed at this, as though it were a joke. It was clear that the lad scarce knew how to raise his voice and be merry.

The boys were standing beneath a tree, and high up in the leaves a bird was twittering; all three looked upwards. Then they noticed that the King was walking on, and all the gentlemen behind him. Both the Prince of Navarre's attendants had fallen into talk with the courtiers of France and had moved away unheeding. Henri whispered:

"We must take off our shoes."

He did so, and began to clamber up the trunk. When he reached the branches, he said to the other two:

"I'll soon be out of sight. Aren't you coming?"

When he was quite hidden, they felt they could not stay behind; they slipped their shoes into a hedge and followed him up the tree.

"No one can find us here," said Henri. "They'll look for us everywhere, and meantime you must take me to the place I tell you. No! Don't steal that nest. Can't you see that they're birds with yellow beaks? Birds like that come and build under my window at Pau."

Some of the gentlemen turned, peered about them, laid their heads together, and set off in another direction. The three boys clambered down, and Henri at last found the way to the place he wanted, which was the kitchen garden. There on the black earth lay the fruits he longed for; he sat down, plunged his hands and his bare feet in them, chanting in a gleeful whisper: "This is the place for me!"

The air was fragrant with the smell of onions, lettuces, and leeks; he nibbled at them all and licked his lips. "Well?" he said to the Princes; "do you eat nothing?"

They stood and eyed his half-buried feet. "Earth is dirt," said they. But Henri had caught sight of a gardener. The poor creature tried to escape as soon as he recognized the Princes. "Come hither," cried Henri, "or it will be the worse for you!" And the fellow shambled forward. "Out with your knife! Cut me the ripest melon!" It was not until he had gulped down half of it that he proclaimed it watery and sour. "Is that the best you have?"

The man pleaded the heavy rain of late. "I forgive you," said Henri.

And he fell to asking questions about the garden, and how the gardener lived, munching as he talked. "You should come to Navarre," he said at last; "I'll give you proper melons to eat. Don't look so stupid! Have you never heard of Navarre? 'Tis a country bigger than France. And the melons are bigger too."

" Truly a bellyful! " remarked the other Henri, who was called Monsieur. For his odd cousin had eaten the entire melon by himself. " And," said he, " I think I could eat another."

" Guzzler! " cried Henri de Valois, then wished he had not spoken.

" I'll kick your behind for that! " yelled Henri de Bourbon, jerking his foot out of the earth. Before he could stand up, the other had fled, his little brother whimpering behind him. Henri had the field.

A rabbit darted past him, and he after it. It crept into shelter, he started it again, but was soon left behind, breathless from the chase. " Henri! " There stood his little sister, and at her side another girl, taller than Catherine, and about the same age. He guessed who she was, but he was too surprised to say anything at first.

" Margot wanted to see you, so we came."

" Are you always as dirty as that? " asked Marguerite de Valois, the King's sister.

" I've been eating melons," he replied, rather ruefully. " Wait, and I will give you one."

" Thank you. No."

" I see. You might stain your fine dress."

She smiled; the little rustic did not realize that she would spoil her painted face as well as her dress.

Well! Truly he had never seen a girl like this. His little Catherine, whom he adored, looked like a goose-girl by her side, for all her Sunday finery. Marguerite's cheeks glowed with a pink of which roses and carnations might have been proud. Her white dress was close-fitting to the hips, then spread in stiffened pleats, glittering with gold embroidery and precious stones. Her shoes were white too, a little soil was sticking to them. On a sudden impulse Henri knelt and brushed away the soil with his lips. Then he stood up and said:

" My hands were too dirty."

But, as the girl smiled scornfully, he said it in a sulky tone. So he took his sister aside and whispered, but loud enough for all to hear:

" I am going to take her skirt off, I must find out whether she has legs like other girls." The little Princess's smile stiffened. " Her nose is too long," he went on. " Catherine, take her away."

Margot's face puckered tearfully, and Henri promptly grew polite. " Mademoiselle," he said eagerly, " I am but a silly boy from the country, and you are a fine lady."

" She knows Latin," observed his sister.

He addressed her in the ancient tongue, and asked whether she were betrothed to a prince. She answered: " No "; so he discovered that his mother's story was no more than a fairy-tale, and she had dreamed it. But he thought: " It might come true." For the moment all he said was:

" Your two brothers ran away."

" I expect they did not like your smell. No prince should smell so," said Marguerite de Valois, with a sniff. Henri was hurt, and said angrily:

" Do you know the meaning of ' Aut vincere aut mori '? " And she answered: " No. But I will ask my mother."

The two children eyed each other with an air of challenge.

" Take care," said little Catherine anxiously; " someone is coming."

It was a lady, and a lady from the court, perhaps the Princess's governess, for she said with disapproval: " Who is this dirty little boy, mademoiselle? "

" 'Tis the Prince of Navarre, they tell me," replied Marguerite.

The lady curtsied deeply. " Your father is come, sir, and desires to see you. But you must wash your face and hands first."

The Enemies

During this time Jeanne d'Albret had her interview with Catherine de Medici. The Queen was in a highly genial mood, inclined to concessions, and not disposed to touch on any perilous matters. But the Protestant, in her zeal, did not notice this, or assumed the Queen was trying to outwit her.

" The Religion and its foes shall never be at one," said she grimly. " No; were my kingdom upon one hand and my son upon the other, I would rather see them both at the bottom of the sea than yield."

" What is religion? " said the stout, dark Medici to the slim, fair-haired d'Albret. " Let us be sensible at last. This incessant civil war will lose us France, for I must let in the Spaniards to deal with you Protestants. And yet I cannot hate you, and I would gladly buy your religion, if that were possible."

" There speaks the true daughter of the Florentine usurer," replied Jeanne contemptuously. What the Queen had just said to her seemed a far worse insult than this. Catherine went on undeterred.

" Be glad I am an Italian. No French Catholic would offer you such terms of peace. The people of your creed shall be entirely free to practise their religion, and I will give them some fortified towns where they may take refuge and be safe. But they must give up insulting and attacking Catholics."

" The Lord my God is a jealous God."

Jeanne was too agitated to sit in her chair. Catherine remained unmoved, folded her fleshy hands, which were covered with rings and dimples.

" You are angry," she said, " because you are poor. War is your trade. I offer you money, that you may do without war."

This was a climax of misunderstanding and contempt that was more than Jeanne could bear. She longed to batter the great creature with her fists.

" And how much are my husband's women paid," she blurted out, " to persuade him to go on fighting against the Religion? "

Catherine nodded — just as though this, and naught else, was what she had expected. It was out at last. This heroine of the faith was just a jealous wife. Answer was needless; this fair-haired, horse-faced creature would not have heard it, she was so beside herself that she had tottered against the wall and sunk down on a coffer as though she were fainting. In that moment a door opened, a painted, gilded door, but studded with iron. The guard clashed his halberd on the ground, and the King of Navarre entered the hall, hand in hand with his children.

Antoine de Bourbon walked with a mincing swagger, like the

handsome women's darling that he was. He did so as a matter of habit, though he knew nothing of what was going forward here. The windows were set in deep embrasures, so that the room seemed dark to anyone entering it. He thought he could descry a movement by the further wall, and laid his hand on his dagger. Queen Catherine shook with silent inward laughter.

"Fear nothing, Navarre! I keep no murderers in hiding — least of all for such as you."

He might have marked the cool contempt in her voice, but he was too vain for that. He ignored the suspected wall and bowed to Catherine. Then he said decorously:

"This is my son, Henri, and he begs your favour, Madame." The little sister remained unnoticed, and looked shame-faced at the floor.

Henri looked at the woman before him and forgot to salute her. Here in the centre of a great chamber, in the place where most light fell, sat the terrible and wicked Catherine de Medici; this was she. The events of his journey, his new acquaintances, and especially the melons had almost put her out of mind; not till now did he suddenly recall what her aspect should have been: clawed and humped and hook-nosed; then he would have known her for who she was; but the boy was baffled, here was a woman like any other. Against the high straight back of her chair she looked small; and she was fat, with spongy white cheeks, and eyes like burnt-out coals. Henri was disappointed.

So he looked briskly round the room, and what did he see? Ah! He was keener-sighted than his father, and there was love in his heart. He darted to where Jeanne lay huddled on the coffer, and as he ran he thought: "That woman has done her some hurt?"

"What has wicked Madame Catherine done to you?" he asked in an eager whisper as he kissed his mother.

"Nothing. I felt faint. Now let us both stand up and be especially courteous." And she did so.

Jeanne came forward with an arm round her little son, smiled at her husband, and said: "Here is our son," but she kept her arm round Henri.

" I brought him that you may see him with your own eyes, dear lord, for you come home but rarely. And I desire to make him known to the Queen as her little soldier, who would serve her as his father has done."

" 'Tis well," replied Catherine good-humouredly. " But if my will prevailed, we should live together in this realm like a great contented family."

" Then I should have to go home and cultivate my lands? " said the martial Antoine, with a disgusted air.

" You would take more care of your wife. She loves you, and she has fainting fits because you leave her too much alone. Though I know of a little potion that will serve her."

Jeanne shuddered; she knew enough of this poisoner's little potions. " I thank you, Madame, I need none," she hurriedly interposed.

She rose painfully from the coffer and came forward; after that, she found herself as fluent a deceiver as Catherine, who assumed a maternal air.

" I have offered to be your wife's friend, Navarre, and I believe she wishes me as well as I wish her."

Jeanne's mind was working hurriedly: " My son shall grow to be a man, I'll be even with you yet. I will indeed — my son shall grow to be a man. I, the niece of Francis I — and this shop-keeper's daughter! " But her eager, gentle expression did not alter — and whatever may have been in Catherine's mind, she remained benignant. But the Medici betrayed herself by taking barely any notice of the two children, not even the frightened little girl. When a woman apes the mother — !

" With all my heart I am your friend! " cried Jeanne, delighted to have unmasked her adversary.

Dead Love

Antoine de Bourbon was elated by the outcome of the interview. When they were alone, he first kissed his wife and then his son. He took him to the window and showed him a pony which was being led past below: " 'Tis yours, and you may ride it now."

Henri darted out; and the little sister followed to admire him.

The eager expression had now faded from Jeanne's face. Her husband, in his high good humour, had not marked the change. She now looked at him wide-eyed, and said:

" Who is your woman now? Who went with you on your last campaign, and doubtless came here too? "

" You listen to too many tales." But he smiled a complacent smile which she found it hard to bear.

" Have you forgotten everything? " she asked suddenly, in a full deep voice. In certain moments Jeanne, to everyone's surprise, spoke in a voice like an organ, too deep and vibrant for that meagre breast. Her husband heard it and was moved, he remembered all that she meant to bring back into his mind. They had loved each other long and deeply.

He had won her after Jeanne had fought, and fought single-handed, against another marriage. Before she knew him, she had been married by force; she had been carried to church, for she swore she could not walk; and indeed she could not, bent as she was under the burden of her jewel-embroidered robe. But her will was unbent, though she was then no more than a child. They married her by force — none the less, her day came at last, though years lay in between, and Jeanne was happy with the man whom she meant should bring her happiness. The days of glory came and went, and then, all too soon, came the days when she and her happiness together faded. And now nothing was left but her son, but he stood for more than all she had ever possessed in the past. If Antoine could but feel that this was indeed their son!

He was stirred by the familiar voice, but not for long, and his memories of their days of passion were banished by a look at her — poor soul! He lived too deeply in the matters that thronged upon him from day to day, a leaguer, an intrigue, a pretty woman. And yet for a moment after Jeanne had said: " Have you forgotten? " he made as though to embrace her, but heart no longer reached to heart; it was an act of courtesy and she repelled him.

Still, it was clear that Antoine was well pleased with her, and delighted at her moderation. Jeanne explained she had no wish at all to let herself be poisoned. " Indeed you did well, my dear lord, to become a Catholic again and enter the service of the King of France."

" They promised me Spanish Navarre."

" They will not give it you, for they need to use the King of Spain against us Protestants. You will not achieve your petty aims; you have other and greater ones at heart, though these you will not easily avow." She said this because it disgusted her to know him as a man of the common stamp, devoid of high ambition.

He listened in bewilderment, and he forbore to answer; for he thought her no longer wholly mistress of her wits. Jeanne despised his proffered embraces, but there should be confidence between them in the affairs of their house. And she said:

" A Protestant Prince will one day surely rule over France; we must prevail because ours is the true faith. On yonder side they have only an old and bloated woman, who believes in nothing."

" Except astrology," he added, glad to agree with her on one point. And he added: " But her three sons! "

" She had them late, she was barren for many years — and consider the three boys that still live," she went on undeterred. " The fourth is dead, he died at sixteen after a reign of seventeen months. His brother Charles has reigned a few months longer, but his eyes are the eyes of an old, old man."

" There are two others to follow him," he observed.

" Their mother will let them die too. She never looks up when a child enters a room. The kingdom only exists for her so long as she is there. If she had religion, she would know that the Lord's hand had blessed her body, not for today and for tomorrow, but for ever! "

Jeanne d'Albret spoke sternly in a low and steady voice that made her husband shiver, and he marvelled at her. And merely to reach firm ground again, he said:

" You should remind Madame Catherine that the late King betrothed our son to his daughter."

" She will remind me of that," answered Jeanne; " and I shall consider whether my son is not too good for a Princess of a decaying race."

Antoine grew suddenly impatient. " You are hard to satisfy. The late King was a healthy man and fell in a tourney. 'Tis not the fault of the Valois if a Medici neglects her children."

" And what of the evil customs she brought with her to this court? " demanded Jeanne.

Although the man felt a storm was imminent, he could not control his expression. Every inch of him recalled with an up-rush of delight all the favours he had enjoyed from the women of that court; it stood written on his face.

Jeanne, but lately so fastidious and restrained, lost her head and began to storm and preach. The Catholics were worshippers of idols and loved the flesh alone. Those of the Religion were stern and single-hearted, and in their hands were iron and fire, to destroy the evil thing.

LET GOD, THE GOD OF BATTLE, RISE

Like enough she could be heard in the ante-room; the door was flung open, some Protestant gentleman appeared and announced that Admiral Coligny was in the house — he was even now mounting the stair and was at hand. All fell back, and the Protestant commander came in, laying his hand on his heart in token of salutation. The King of Navarre actually bent his head to this old man, and in so doing, to the party that he led. Others might use it for their own ends, but this man possessed the selfless austerity of the martyr; it was written on his grim and melancholy features.

Jeanne d'Albret embraced the Admiral. He came at a welcome moment, an impulse of enthusiasm was what she needed. She signed to her people, her two pastors, and her children. She brought her son up to the Admiral, who laid his right hand on the boy's head, and kept it there as the first pastor was speaking. He spoke in words that no one could misunderstand, of the

kingdom of God that was near at hand. " It is our turn now! "
Those were the words they heard, whether indeed they were
uttered or not. And the company in that crowded chamber all
struggled forward, eager to lay their hands at last upon the power
and the riches, all for the glory of God alone.

The second of the two pastors intoned a hymn: " Let God,
the God of Battle, rise." All sang it, fervent and expectant, with
high hearts, now certain of their victory. For they were chanting
their canticles and standing forth for the Cause in the very house
of the King of France! They could dare so much, and dare they
did. So bold they now could be, and bold they were!

Coligny raised the Prince of Navarre in both his arms above
the array of the heads to imprint the scene and all that company on the boy's memory for his life long. Many heroes of the
faith bore mighty witness to their creed. Henri's mind was
touched, and his heart too, for he saw his dear mother weep and
he wept with her. His father, from fear of what might come of
such an occasion, had all the windows closed, so that the air
became too stifling to breathe.

These were indeed transgressions of the permitted limits;
Jeanne realized that for herself afterwards, she had no need of
her husband's warning. She resolved to make every reparation
that the Queen might ask, for there was little hope that Madame
Catherine would not come to hear of what had passed. But when
the two good friends met again, it seemed that the one knew
nothing of the other's unbecoming conduct, or chose to pass it
by. Far from showing any mistrust of Jeanne, the Queen Mother
asked her help against her enemies.

The greatest danger for the Sovereign House was the Guises,
the Lorrainers who laid claim to the throne. Jeanne realized
that, compared with them, the little family of Bourbon would
be looked on as harmless. The Guises proclaimed themselves
far more Catholic than the Queen, and they were rich. Their
purposes were thus doubly favoured; and they had begun to
make favour with the people of Paris as the saviours of the kingdom. The needy kings of Navarre were here unknown   they

came from a distant and heretic province known to be a strong-hold of sedition. Madame Catherine purred like an ancient cat whenever she set eyes on Jeanne d'Albret, and Jeanne felt de-graded, though she did not show it.

She was astute, and fell in with all the old woman's schemes. Catherine bored a hole in the wall of her cabinet, through which she could see and hear what Antoine de Bourbon and the Cardinal de Lorraine might be devising against her; and Jeanne had to peer and listen too, although one of the two suspects was her own husband. Not that he came into question, for he was but little feared; which Jeanne felt to be degrading too, but she kept a good countenance. The old Medici was afraid of the head of the House of Guise, the wealthy Cardinal, who could bribe all her servants, and even Navarre. Still, she could promise him Spanish Navarre and never give it him; that cost nothing.

Catherine, and with her Jeanne, unravelled many intrigues, for the Cardinal received other gentlemen too in Antoine's room, which seemed to him a place that none would be likely to sus-pect. Jeanne marvelled at her husband's levity; through the hole she watched him, all his mind intent upon a mistress, which was a reason the more for not giving him a hint, nor her friend Catherine. She did indeed resolve never to fall out openly with her husband's lady. So Jeanne schooled herself to forbearance; her son's interest and her faith demanded that she should be friendly with the old Medici.

But it happened: the lady, wife of a marshal of the court, met her, actually dared to introduce herself, and even expected a kiss in salutation. For all her resolutions to be reasonable, this was more than Jeanne could endure. In those arms, and on that bared bosom, in those hours, every one of which aged and withered her the more, lay the only man for whom she had ever fought. Jeanne stared savagely into that face; it was an alluring and even a charming face. The vast treachery of life rose into her throat. She could not help herself, she turned her back on the lady and left her standing.

But the lady would not accept this treatment and held her ground. While the Queen of Navarre was greeting others of the company, she came forward; her face was no longer charming, and she said in no guarded tone:

" So you turn me your backside do you, and won't kiss me? By Saint John! You shall get all the fewer kisses from your husband; I'll have them all! "

Jeanne gathered her friends close around her, so as to retire with dignity. Her foe was a tall and menacing figure, and an encounter might have ended ill. Several gentlemen who noticed what had passed escorted Jeanne on her retreat.

But not until later did it appear that the incident was likely to involve her in peril. Never had she seen her husband in such a fury; he talked of divorcing her, or shutting her up, and she knew that it was not only his mistress who was behind all this. The hole in the wall had convinced her that the Cardinal de Lorraine did as he pleased with her poor Antoine, and his aim was the removal of Jeanne. The House of Guise would then have no rival, and the Protestants would have lost their Queen.

Jeanne knew very well that she could only look for salvation with Madame Catherine. Through the hole in the wall they had both discovered the consent given to Antoine by his friends to a marriage with the youthful Mary Stuart. She was the widow of the Medici's dead eldest son, one of those sons who were successively called King, while she herself ruled the land. Catherine agreed with Jeanne that this alliance should be prevented. She had no use for a man in the house, were it only the amiable Antoine. On this point the women were at one.

The result was that Catherine was actually induced to recall another plan, the betrothal of her daughter Margot to the little Henri of Navarre. She said plainly that it would be to the kingdom's best advantage to take a Prince of the Blood and their nearest kinsman and attach him to the House by such a tie. One of her astrologers had told her that this would be one of her most fortunate strokes. Alas, it was too soon, the children were not old enough. The Queen Mother pledged her sincerity to Jeanne by embracing her; but in the old Medici's arms Jeanne felt herself tremble. A certain rumour about her old friend came into her mind. It was said that Madame Catherine had poisoned a high official to lay hands upon his revenues for someone else. At that same moment Catherine held her more tightly, and said:

"I would do anything for a friend."

Chance words perhaps; but they again impressed on Henri's mother how needful it was to keep this woman's friendship at any price. But in her heart she disliked her own powers of penetration, she never could remain sensible for very long. Jeanne might keep her true feelings locked within her, the truth suddenly broke loose and found utterance. The gentle Jeanne took a high and haughty tone, because she spoke in the name of religion. Even in this very conversation, oblivious of all the terrible rumours about Madame Catherine, she said insistently:

"Margot must become a Protestant! Otherwise my son shall not marry her."

She had no notion how the other would take it; but Catherine remained as friendly as ever, and grew even more confidential. She admitted she was considering whether she and all her children should not go over to the new religion. The Protestants were perhaps the stronger, and with their aid she could defeat the Guises. Of faith she made no mention, and Jeanne upbraided her; but her sermon made no impression on her good friend Catherine. She merely answered that it would be better to keep the game quiet, and her good friend Jeanne must see that the pastors still preached behind closed windows.

So saying, she opened a window and signed to Jeanne to look out. Margot and Henri were playing in the garden. He was swinging the little girl, who was wearing no gorgeous dress that day, only a light frock, which fluttered up round her as she swung. Henri squatted on the ground, and as she sailed over him he cried:

"Now I can see your legs!"

"No, you can't!" cried Margot from above.

"As clear as the sun in the sky," he protested.

"It's not true!"

"And they're fat!"

"Stop this swing!"

He did not, but let the swing come to a stop. Margot took his hand to get down, and then slapped his face as hard as she could.

" I deserved that," said he, with a rueful grin. Then he picked up the hem of her dress and kissed it.

" No more of that! " she snapped. " You have always been so dreadfully respectful and polite. Today is the first time you have spoken to me properly."

" Only because I've found your legs are like other girls' legs, only prettier."

" Oh no, you haven't. Wait till we're both bigger."

After which she was silent; she just looked at him, and the pink tip of her tongue flickered between her lips. Her face was hued like a peach painted on porcelain, not a real peach. The boy never could tell whether she was provoking or repelling him. And so, to find out, he fell upon her and kissed her violently. Margot gasped for breath and gurgled with glee.

" You do it better than — "

" Who? " he asked, and stamped his foot.

" Nobody," said she, loftily.

Catherine shut the window and thus prevented Jeanne from calling out to the children.

" Well, they understand each other," observed the fat Medici, with her good-natured irony. The gaunt d'Albret had grown sickly pale, but she controlled herself.

The result was that she kept her son as close as though she had been at home. It was long since he had had any pious instruction, so his mother plied him with it every day, that he might never forget that he was going hand in hand with her into an enemy domain against all comers, in the cause of the faith; he must defend that faith and strive to spread it, he must despise the Mass and holy images and all the rest. Henri trusted in his mother; what she said took solid shape before his eyes. She had not said a word to him about Margot, Jeanne was probably ashamed of what she had seen from the window and took it ill of Catherine for having shown it to her.

But he understood; his evil conscience betrayed him, and one day he told Margot, with an expression that made her shudder, that he could take no more interest in her legs, they would burn in hell. She said she did not believe it, but she was, in fact, afraid and asked her mother for advice.

THE FIRST PARTING

Madame Catherine learned of Jeanne's manœuvres in another fashion. It was not difficult, for her little son kept little to himself. Though the Protestant Queen forced herself to be secret and forbearing, she made no effort to make Henri so. She trusted in the fact that truth is unassailable when it comes from the mouths of children.

Henri liked to please his mother, especially in a matter that he enjoyed so much as bringing Catholics into contempt. In the meantime he became the leader of a band of youths, and he managed to make them all feel that there was nothing more ludicrous than a bishop or a monk. All the young folk at the court soon joined the band, and even the Queen Mother did not know the extent of the conspiracy, for none dared tell her that her own sons were of it. Henri first secured the youngest of the three Princes for the novel sport of dressing up as clerics and ranging the castle in this guise. They burst in upon serious deliberations and lovers' encounters and forced their victims to kiss their crosses. And they had a merry time, though the season was autumn, and late for such frolics.

The youngest Prince, Alençon, was the most enterprising, though too disposed to run away; and naturally enough the second son, Henri, was soon glad to join; and last of all, the infection caught Charles IX himself, the Christian King, supreme head of all Catholics. He donned a bishop's vestments and belaboured the courtiers and the ladies with his crozier, a performance which they were too respectful to resist. The lad was incapable of laughter; he merely grew pale and paler, his stealthy glance more and more suspicious, until he was almost sick with excitement. And who was it that stood aloof and rejoiced his innocent heart in his successful schemes? Henri of Navarre. The court dubbed the conspirators "little darlings" and made as though to take them lightly. Madame Catherine was for long deceived till, at a sudden uproar that broke forth one day outside her door, for a moment she believed her hour had come. There was no one with her but an Italian Cardinal, and he peered about him for somewhere to crawl away and hide. Then the door opened, and a motley train entered, headed by Henri of Navarre astride a donkey, robed in scarlet and bearing all the insignia of high ecclesiastical rank. He was followed by a mob of boys with peaked cowls and padded bellies and monks' habits of every order. They spurred their donkeys and pranced into the room, chanting litanies the while. Those on foot tried to get a ride by jumping on to the others' backs, and crashed to the floor, bringing the furniture down with them; and the panelled chamber re-echoed with songs and shrieks of pain, the crack of splintered wood, the clatter of hoofs, and shouts of laughter.

The Queen Mother began by laughing too, if only with relief to find she was not to be murdered. But when she caught sight of her own sons, although the Princes did their best to keep in the background, her patience indeed gave way, though she did not show it. She pretended to look grim, warned the lads to respect sacred matters and to confine themselves to other games. And she good-naturedly boxed Navarre's ears, and his alone.

None the less, Catherine's eyes were opened to her good friend Jeanne's true sentiments. This came to pass in the autumn, just when the two friends were boring the hole in the wall. All that was lacking then was proof how dangerous the Protestant woman might become, and that did not appear until January, when she drove openly through Paris, to rouse the zeal of her fellow-believers and stir them to revolt. Catherine had permitted them to preach in public, and the Queen of Navarre at once abused that freedom. Catherine said nothing, and kept Jeanne in her confidence; her habit was to let things work themselves out in their own fashion. And even when the decisive moment came, she did not appear in person; the luckless

Antoine issued her orders, believing them his own. Jeanne was to leave the court, and — what was hardest of all — without her son.

The father kept Henri back, that he might be withdrawn from his mother's influence and grow up a good Catholic. Not yet two years ago that same father had meant to make him a good Huguenot. Henri remembered that well; but had he dared to mention it at all, he would have been too frightened — for his father's sake and for his own. He had begun to realize that there must be stronger motives in life than plain honesty. When his mother Jeanne took leave of him, he wept — if she had only known all the things for which he wept! His heart ached for her; he was by no means so sorry for himself. His highest faith was always kept for Jeanne, and only after her for his religion.

She wept over him and kissed him, she was only permitted to see him once before departing whither her enemies chose to send her; but he, against her will, was to be sent to a Catholic school. She did indeed control herself, and told him in stern and menacing fashion that if he ever went to Mass she would disinherit him. He promised that he would not, wept bitterly, and resolved always to do right — not merely because he thought it safest; he was past that now. His mother was going into exile for the true faith. His father had forsworn that faith, and he indeed did what he must do. His parents no longer loved each other, they were enemies, they each fought for possession of him; all of which was very hard to understand. If Madame Catherine had really had a hump and claws, as well as red eyes and a dripping nose, he would not have felt so baffled. But here stood a small boy, confronting the uncertain and mysterious world, in which he was now to set foot, alone.

He was sent to the " Collegium Navarra," the most aristocratic school in Paris; the King's brother, called Monsieur, and a Guise of equal age were also there. Both had the same name as the Prince of Navarre, and they came to be known as " the three Henris."

" I did not go to Mass again," said the Prince of Navarre proudly to the two others when they were alone.

"You ran away and hid."

"Did they tell you that? Then they lie. I said what I thought, and they were afraid."

"Brave lad!" said they, and egged him on to persevere; but he was too eager to notice that they meant to play him false. "Let us dress up again," he urged; "put on bishops' mitres and ride on donkeys."

They pretended to agree, but betrayed him to the masters (who were priests), and next day he was whipped until he consented to go to chapel. And then for a time he was let alone, for he fell ill; indeed, he intended to fall ill.

While he was ill he was tended by the only man whom his mother had left in his company, one de Beauvois. The man had made haste to go over to his mistress's enemies, and Henri observed that he owed his whipping not only to the young Princes; the spy had betrayed him too.

"Go away, Beauvois, I will not see you."

"Will you not read a letter from your lady mother, the Queen?"

Then the boy learned to his amazement that his dear mother assured the traitor of her satisfaction and her thanks for reporting all that passed. "Strengthen my son in his resistance, and keep him loyal to the faith. You do well to denounce him sometimes to the Rector and get him whipped. He must make the sacrifice, otherwise they would not let you stay with him, and I could not let my dear son know what I am planning."

There was much more to follow, but Henri could not forbear looking up at the man beside his bed; he had never met anyone like this, and yet all he saw was a rather corpulent man with a broad face and a squat nose. It was the face of a toper too, but Henri had always thought him a man of every day. And yet here he was, a guileful, crooked creature, though honest enough to look at, and a faithful servant.

Monsieur de Beauvois read more in the Prince's face than the Prince in his. He said in a mild voice, as a flicker came into his lustreless eyes:

"No need to tell everyone all about yourself."

" Even if you know it," retorted the eight-year-old.

" It skills a man to keep the place he wants to keep," said this elderly retainer.

" I see it is so," began Henri, and was about to add: " But I will never trust you again." The words remained unuttered, for Beauvois suddenly snatched his mother's letter from him — with a movement of uncanny neatness that he could barely see; the paper vanished. Then he said in quite an altered voice:

" Tomorrow you will get up and go to Mass of your own free will. I would advise it, for you are weak and could ill endure another whipping, which is what you will otherwise get."

He spoke with such deliberation that Henri at last caught the sound of creeping footsteps at the door behind his bed. He did not turn his head, but pretended to be crying; and thus they waited until the custodian had passed. Then the man told him in a hurried whisper what was in the rest of the letter, before they could again be interrupted.

Jeanne was engaged in what was no more and no less than open civil war. She had no more mercy on her husband, and therefore on no one else. She needed men and money for her brother-in-law, Condé, a great lord, who confused his own ambitions with the claims of the faith, but that was all one to her; he must lead the Protestant army. In the county of Vendôme, where she had been banished, she gave orders for the plundering of churches. She even raised money for violating graves, and the graves were those of her husband's kin. Nothing deterred her, nothing was allowed to stand against her own will.

All this her son heard in his mother's own voice, speaking passionately at his very ear, although it was but the hurried whisper from the man beside his bed. Henri leapt out of his bed, well once more and ready to endure whatever might befall, so he need not go to Mass. Time and again he forgot it all, became his merry self once more, and romped with the other boys; the tall, dark walls of the schoolyard vanished, he was free, his enemies at his feet. Indeed, he seriously believed that they would come and beg him to intercede with his mother for forgiveness.

The event fell otherwise. Jeanne was defeated and had to flee, but her son did not await the end. On June 1st he yielded, he had held out since March. His father took him to Mass himself, Henri swore to him that he would hold fast to the true faith, tall belted knights saluted him as one of their own Order, which made him proud in spite of all. A few days later his mother broke her camp; Beauvois brought him the news with an air of reproach, although he had himself advised him to accept the true faith before his mother's failure. From somewhere north of the Loire she evaded her enemies and slipped southwards to her own land, always in danger of capture by Montluc, the General whom Catherine had sent in pursuit of her.

In what agony her son's heart followed her on her flight! He had disobeyed her and betrayed her, perhaps he had been the cause of her disaster. He did not dare to write to her; he sent letters to one of her gentlemen, which were outcries of perplexity and sorrow: " Larchant, I am so afraid that something dreadful may happen to the Queen, my mother! "

That was in the daytime; but at night a boy lay asleep and dreamed of play. Even among the hours of day there were always some that made him forget it all, his misery and his own small significance in the world. Then he did something from which no one and no troubles could deter him; he set his knee on a vanquished playfellow, laughed, and let him go. That was a blunder; those who have paid their penalty are less dangerous than those who have been spared; but this was something that Henri never was to learn.

He was not popular among his fellows, though he made them afraid and he made them laugh. He set store by their respect, so his pranks had to be successful, though he never noticed that they respected him no longer when they laughed. He acted a dog for them or, if they liked, a Switzer or a German; for the civil war brought foreign landskechts to Paris, and he had seen them. One day he cried: " We'll have Cæsar's murder! " To Henri Monsieur he said: " You are to be Cæsar." And to Henri Guise: " We are the murderers." Then he crawled along to show how a victim should be tracked. The victim was terror-stricken, he screamed and cursed, but the two pursuers were soon upon him.

"What are you about? " asked Jeanne's boy suddenly. "You are hurting him."

"I can't murder him unless I hurt him," retorted Guise. Meantime the moment's pause was enough to bring Cæsar to his feet; he laid about him savagely, and Navarre had to keep him from doing the other an injury.

He could always drop back into make-believe. The others did not understand that a fight could be taken as a jest. They fell into deadly earnest and yelled with fury, while he exulted in the game.

He was smaller than most lads of his age; his skin was dark, his hair was auburn, his eyes were livelier than theirs, and his ideas came quicker. Sometimes they would all stand round and stare at him as though he had been a dancing bear or a monkey.

In all his wildest flights he could suddenly recognize the truth; they were eyeing each other doubtfully, they had not understood what he said, it was too deeply coloured by his native speech. The two other Henris noticed that he used the wrong gender with the word " spoon," but they did not tell him so, they made the mistake themselves as often as he was by. He was well aware they were trying to take some mean advantage of him. In those days he dreamed — of what did he dream? In the morning it was forgotten. Not until he realized that he was suffering from home-sickness, from deep and aching home-sickness, did he know what every dream had pictured: the Pyrenees.

A FATHER'S DEATH

He saw them mantled with forest to the skyline, the feet of the sleeper swept him up them like the wind, and up yonder he was as tall as they were, as tall as the mountains themselves. He could bend right down to the castle at Pau and kiss his mother on the lips. He fell ill again from home-sickness, as he had fallen ill in the matter of the Mass. It was taken at first for smallpox, but it was not. His father had then carried him into the country, for Antoine de Bourbon was again setting out on a campaign, and his little son could not stay alone in Paris. Henri was no less afraid of being left by himself in the country, and begged to be allowed to go with his father into camp. But Antoine would not take him because he had a mistress there.

When he rode away, Henri rode beside him for a space. He could not tear himself away. He loved this handsome, armed, and bearded man, his father, and he clung to him — as far as the cross-roads — as far as the little stream. " I can ride faster than you, will you wager it? I know a short way round, I'll join you again behind the wood." And so it went on, until his father sent him home in anger. But before six weeks had passed, Antoine was dead. The leaves on the trees were fading when a message came for his son that the King of Navarre had been killed in battle.

The Prince, his son, had almost cried aloud in grief, but he suddenly swallowed down his tears and said:

" Is it true? "

For by this time his eyes were always open for snares and lies.

" Tell me how it happened."

Doubtfully he listened: the King was sitting in a trench where it was his habit to take his food. The page who served him had been wounded by a shot. Another shot mortally wounded a Captain who stood in the open as he relieved himself. The King must needs stand in the selfsame place; and yet another bullet struck him just as he was pissing.

Then Henri burst into tears. From his father's recklessness he recognized the truth. It was a burning grief to him to think that he had been so far away and not a sharer in the battle and the peril, like this servant, whom his father had loved.

" Raphael! " he cried; " did the King love me? "

" When he lay wounded, on the ship that was to carry him to Paris — "

" Who was with him? I must know! "

The man did not answer. He said nothing of the lady in whose arms Antoine had died.

" I was alone with him," said he. " When my lord felt that

the end was near, at nine o'clock in the evening, he took me by the beard and said: ' Serve my son well, and may he serve the King likewise! ' "

Henri stared before him, dried his tears, and himself took the man by the beard. He felt that there could be nothing nobler than to die bravely like his father Antoine for the King of France.

The memory of his father set the course of the boy's next two years. All that time he did not see his mother. Jeanne was sorely beset by General Montluc; Catherine was pressing her, that she might become more pliable at last. Madame Catherine was apt at such designs, for she was no hater like Jeanne d'Albret; she simply acted according as the circumstances might prescribe. The House of Guise was her most powerful enemy, the Protestants were for the time being overthrown. All the easier to use them, and especially their spiritual leader. Thus Madame Catherine laid her plans.

The young Prince of Navarre became, as his father had been, Governor of the province of Guyenne; he was created Admiral; he was given a bodyguard of a hundred men; but he had to stay at court. His deputy in the South was, of course, Montluc, Jeanne's detested adversary. In return Henri could be educated as she pleased, although she would not herself be with him. Bluff old La Gaucherie went back to him as tutor, but Henri's training was really in the hands of the wily Beauvois; and there was no more going to Mass. Henri was a Protestant again, but such matters interested him no more.

He told himself that he was born a Catholic, his mother made him Huguenot, and a Huguenot he could remain, although his father had sent him to Mass again — or really it was Madame Catherine — and the knights had kissed him. But if he went campaigning now with those of the Religion, as well might happen — and the boy's heart throbbed — they would not kiss him any more. Indeed, he might well plead to be kissed, for they might win, and then he would have to become Catholic again. Such was the world.

His heart leapt within him. No! thought he. Conquer or die!

He wrote: *Aut vincere aut mori* on a lottery slip, and Madame Catherine asked him what the words meant. He said he did not know.

A Strange Visit

Henri was in his ninth year when he was taken on the great progress of King Charles IX through France. The Queen Mother considered that the whole kingdom should look upon her son at last, and that the first Prince of the Blood, who was Henri de Navarre, should appear everywhere in his suite, a Protestant and no more than a vassal. But once again Jeanne d'Albret thwarted the plans of the fat and cunning Medici; or plotted to thwart them. Suddenly she rode in the guise of an independent sovereign, with three hundred horsemen and not less than eight pastors, into a town where the court was lying.

She fell upon Catherine with a storm of plaints and wild demands, leaving herself barely time to pray with her son, whom she had put in her good friend's charge, as a pledge of their understanding. But Montluc had forbidden preaching in Béarn, and it was rumoured that something worse was yet to come, a meeting between Catherine and Philip II of Spain, the demon of the South, and the arch-enemy of the Religion. Jeanne demanded the truth; Jeanne claimed her rights.

No one regarded treaties with more indifference than Catherine, as soon as they had ceased to be of any use to her. She shook with her accustomed silent laughter, and she said: "My dear, I have you with me now, and that is what was nearest to my heart."

And indeed it was so, for she had made known to Philip that before he sent his emissaries north of the Pyrenees, the Queen of Navarre must be removed from those territories. So Jeanne got no more than money for her keep, money for her horsemen and her pastors, but she was made to withdraw into the county of Vendôme, as had happened two years ago. And the court moved southwards.

Jeanne was furious at falling into such a trap. One night, when her son was asleep on the bare floor of an inn, in a place where the castle could not lodge the entire company, suddenly, at the sound of splintering glass and someone falling to the floor, he leapt to his feet, dashed upon the intruder, and held him where he lay, shouting the while for help. A scurrying throng appeared with lights, and the man was seized and roughly handled. When Henri caught sight of his face, he knew him, and stood silent and dismayed. And he knew who had sent him, and for what purpose. But he took care never to tell a soul that his mother had tried to get him kidnapped. And his tutor Beauvois never spoke of it. They would eye each other sadly sometimes; the older man wagged his head, and Henri looked downcast.

There is a town in Provence called Salon, where dwelt a famous man whom Henri encountered at this time. It was early one morning, the boy was standing naked, the servant just about to hand him his shirt, when Beauvois entered, accompanied by a stranger. What could Beauvois want? thought Henri. Was that a doctor? But he was not ill.

" Where is the Prince? " the stranger asked, halting five paces away, and saw him not, though he was naked. Beauvois did not answer, but waited watchfully — timidly almost, if Beauvois could ever have been timid. The servant with the shirt withdrew into a corner.

The boy felt strangely alone, naked, exposed, with all his faults and blemishes. He began to fear that the end of this business would be a whipping. And he wished that this gaunt and grey old visitor would look at him at last and go.

Long did the old man look at that slim form and little boyish face; though no one could tell that he was looking, for his eyes were veiled and his vision came from very far away. The watcher marked him in awed silence, as he darted back and forward, stumbled against Beauvois, muttering excuses; indeed, he was muttering all the time; and then, at long last, it came into his mind to make reverence. As he did so he doffed his great hat, so clumsily that he dropped it at the Prince's feet. Then Henri did something that little beseemed his rank. He knew not why, but he picked up the hat and gave it to the stranger — a man who could be nothing higher than a doctor, though too clumsy for such a calling.

They stood confronted, the gaunt stranger peering down upon a small and eager face upturned — but the hooded gaze of the apparition drew a veil as far as the cheeks and neck, and the boy saw only a headless figure with a veil in place of a head. He was afraid, and no longer of a whipping.

The man ceased to mutter, his mind was set on what pronouncement he should make: here was a child. Unfulfilled and limitless, and yet, for all his weakness, with more force and power than all who have come before. A vessel of life, thence comes his greatness. And he marvelled at that bold young face, at the very moment when Henri was most afraid.

"This is he," he said aloud, and turned to Beauvois, who was waiting patiently. "If God in His mercy permits you to live so long, you will serve a King of France and Navarre."

These were his only words — he made another clumsy reverence and went. Monsieur de Beauvois held the door for him.

"I thank you," said he; "farewell, Monsieur Nostradamus."

Henri felt that this was not one of those who are ever seen again. And he marked the old man's aspect on his memory.

The Encounter

And in those days he was beset by rumours and by prophecies; and he could not rid his mind of what was happening all about him. Wherever the Prince of Navarre appeared with his train of Protestant attendants, men of the Religion came forth to meet him with strange secrecy and furtive looks.

"Go no further, my lord. Stay among us, we will die before we give you up." And everywhere the same.

A white-haired Huguenot, who was carried in by his grandsons, raised a trembling hand in blessing, and said in a hollow, quavering voice:

"Thanks be to God that I have seen the Prince. When we

all have perished, you will avenge us, my lord, and lead the Religion to victory."

And then the familiar pleas that he should, in Heaven's name, go no farther on his journey.

Later on, Beauvois replied to Henri's questions:

" Have no fear. Leave these people to their terrors; it will but make them more zealous in the faith. They foretell the worst because the Queen Mother is soon to meet the Spaniards. But we know Madame Catherine. She would sooner cheat than kill."

" But what if she must take orders from the Spanish devil? " said Henri, not waiting for an answer; he knew Habsburg hated him, and in that certainty remained.

Beauvois tried to explain that Catherine's purpose might be to plead before the Catholic power for her policy in not continually attacking against her own Protestants, but in trying to win them by indulgence. At the worst, she might ask Philip for aid, as being the only means by which her Reformed subjects could be mastered.

In vain: Henri was not to be moved by argument, his mind was thronged wholly by images, continually stirred by the whispers of those about him, the muttered fears and the foreboding voices that went with him on his journey. In the end, what filled his mind must surely come to pass. What it was, he knew not, but the unknown stood close at hand; and if it did not befall, he was none the less prepared to see it and to hear it.

And so, in the train of greater persons than himself, he came to the city of Bayonne, not far from his native land, Béarn. Here he must make ready for what might come, for here indeed had been his home with his father and his mother in his early days. Soft as the familiar name, the river Adour slipped through it, and the line of peaks that shimmered in the distance against the dark-blue sky — those were his own mountains, the Pyrenees. But Henri, who had so long been home-sick for them, did not for one moment think of fleeing there for refuge.

The Spaniards came at last, a young woman, Elizabeth of France, Queen of Spain, Catherine's own daughter, and, as the noblest of her suite, the Duke of Alba. With him, in private, Catherine talked.

The chamber was guarded from without. The old Queen first appeared, walked across to the windows, and lifted all the curtains. The opposite wall was hung only with pictures. Then she sat in a tall straight chair, with eyes downcast. Behind her was the fireplace, its huge embrasure filled with green branches. The time was high June.

The Duke of Alba entered, his head poised on his stiff starched ruff. He did not bow nor doff his hat. He scarce bent his knees as he walked; his face, though not a young face, quite unmarked. No experience could leave a wrinkle on that haughty mask.

He stopped — not from respect, but with the air of an accuser — and abruptly told the old woman that his master, King Philip, was displeased with her. She listened and made no reply; the Duke expected none, he went on to speak in rasping tones of her neglected duties towards Holy Church, and towards the secular arm that wielded the Church's sword, the House of Habsburg. She listened in silence until he had finished.

Then she asked in her throaty voice how much the King of Spain would offer her to make her kingdom Catholic. It would cost a great deal, she added.

And the Duke replied: "Nothing — unless you receive our troops and recognize Don Philip as your lord."

Catherine's voice shook as she replied: that could not be God's will, for He had entrusted the kingdom to her charge and caused her to bear sons. But she promised the King that she would no longer provoke his anger by tolerating heresy. Her intentions had been good, but her power had not sufficed, and she had been forced to equivocate.

"What is the cost of a dagger-thrust in this country?" asked Alba.

Catherine's breath came faster; she smiled faintly, and there was a hint of mockery in her tone.

"Ten thousand dagger-thrusts cost just so much as cannon, burnt cities, and a civil war."

"Why ten thousand?" said Alba contemptuously. "I mean

a single one." For the first time he deigned to approach that waxen, bearded countenance a little nearer to the tall, straight chair, and he added:

" Ten thousand frogs are not a salmon."

She understood his meaning, but did not answer. To gain time, she turned towards the door and the tall windows, forgetting the fireplace at her back. Then, dropping her voice so that Alba himself could barely distinguish every word, she said:

" Salmon may mean at least two people."

He, too, whispered his reply, and for a long while that whispering went on. Then the two heads parted, the Duke stepped back, as stiff and haughty as when he had appeared. The old Queen got up painfully, he offered her his finger-tips, and she waddled beside that stalking figure to the door.

The pair had gone for some while: not a sound could be heard save the tramp of the departing guard without. Then the green branches in the great embrasure of the chimney-piece rustled, and a small figure climbed out. He slipped round the momentous chair and eyed it as though those two evil creatures had never left the room. Again he heard what they had whispered to each other, even what he could not catch — the two names that they must have uttered. Henri knew them now, Admiral Coligny — his heart stood still — his mother, Queen Jeanne.

He clenched his fists, and his eyes filled with angry tears. Suddenly he swung on his heel, laughed, and rapped out a curse. He had learned it from the old man at home, his grandfather d'Albret; sacred words distorted beyond recognition. And he shouted till the room re-echoed.

Moralité

Ainsi le jeune Henri connut, avant l'heure, le méchanceté des hommes. Il s'en était un peu douté, après tant d'impressions troubles reçues en son bas âge, qui n'est qu'une suite d'imprévus obscurs. Mais en s'écriant allègrement "Ventre Saint Gris" au moment même on lui fut révélé tout le danger effroyable de la vie, il fit connaître au destin qu'il relevait le défi et qu'il gardait pour toujours et son courage premier et sa gaîté native.

C'est ce jour là qu'il sortait de l'enfance.

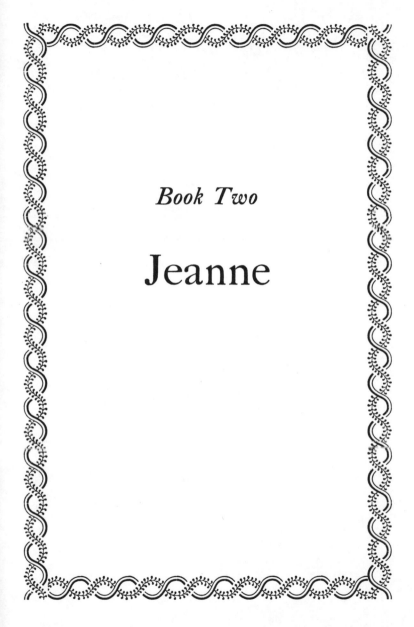

Book Two

Jeanne

"I saw it and I heard it," said Henri to his mother when they were able to meet for the first time alone. And that was not until they reached Paris, though Jeanne had joined him on the return progress of the court.

"Do you think what I think, Mamma? Alba noticed me. The branches in the fireplace were not thick enough, and once I slipped and shook them."

"He will have thought it was the wind. He would surely have dragged you out had he seen you."

"No, not that Spaniard. I saw his face, it was not a man's face; if he had thought it worth while he would just have thrust his sword through the leaves. But he was too proud for that, and besides, he was sure no one could have heard what they were saying. No!" he cried, as Jeanne was about to interrupt. "I could hear. I am your son, I soon found out their plots against you."

Jeanne drew his head towards her and laid his cheek against hers. And she, staring into vacancy, said:

"Men often boast of crimes they never will commit."

"Men, but not monsters!" he retorted. Suddenly he flung away from her. "They looked so funny!" And he promptly stalked like the Duke and then waddled like Madame Catherine. He had a gift for mimicry, as his mother saw; but she barely laughed. Which made him think that his story had indeed filled her with misgivings.

She contrived to leave the court and take her son upon a journey. She went about matters so discreetly that Henri himself suspected nothing; first they visited one of her domains, and guilelessly returned. But the second journey, on which Jeanne carried Henri to view his possessions in various provinces, ended in a flight to the South. It was February when they reached Pau, and the Prince of Navarre was in the fourteenth year of his age when he received his first instruction in the arts of government and war, though these were then identical.

Jeanne treated her own subjects as enemies, because in the absence of the Queen they had risen against the Religion. The good-natured Queen was transformed into a tyrant. She sent her son with a train of noblemen and artillery to take revenge, and it went ill with those rebels.

Her kinsman Condé then engaged in what was no more and no less than an attack upon the King of France and his court. The Queen Mother was of opinion that the flight of her dear friend Jeanne had raised the standard of revolt in the North as in the South; and as always when her affairs stood ill, she was anxious to come to terms. She sent a plausible gentleman with a noble name down into the South; but whatever he might say, Jeanne knew that the object was to lure her once again into the power of the court.

She flatly demanded for her son the actual governorship of all Guyenne, the great province whose capital was Bordeaux; hitherto he had but borne the title. Catherine refused, and the way was clear. Coligny and Condé joined forces and promptly reopened their campaign. Jeanne, for her part, had the impression that an attempt might now be made to lay hands on the person of Prince Henri. The Cardinal de Lorraine in particular she regarded as capable of any crime. He was more dangerous than the Royal House, which already had the power. The Guises craved for it, and Jeanne knew from her own heart what that meant.

So she resolved to shift her quarters within the purlieu of the great Protestant fortresses, to the seaboard of Saintonge, north of Bordeaux. Henri was delighted; not so his mother, who had her doubts.

" Why do you cry, Mamma? "

" Because I cannot tell right from wrong. Satan always stands against the just, and whatever I may do I fear lest Satan may have prompted me to do it."

" But Beauvois says I am big enough to go to the wars and fight."

" And, pray, who is Beauvois? Has Satan never spoken through his mouth? "

" He is now speaking through the mouth of Monsieur de la Mothe-Fénelon." That was Catherine's Ambassador. " I recognize the voice," cried Henri.

Jeanne said no more. She was too glad to find that her lad had an eye for what was right. When she looked at his resolute little face, she scorned the gentlemen about her, who warned her not to break with the court because they feared for their possessions or their lives. She no longer dreaded the promptings of Satan; in her secret self the victory was won. Her son was of an age to bear arms, that settled it!

She merely asked, that no doubt might remain:

" What will you be fighting for, my son? "

" What for? " he repeated in astonishment; indeed, he had quite forgotten, in his glee at being allowed to fight at last.

Jeanne said no more; he would soon find out for himself. The snares of the enemy, and especially those of fate, would teach him that lesson. And the thought that he was fighting for the true faith would keep his head high. Nay, more, his very blood would speak; for he was more nearly kin to Condé than to any Catholic Prince. Besides, their victory would bring a sorely needed peace to France, added Jeanne; for honour must be salved. But God's service always and everywhere came first. Faith would fuse her son's life into one single purpose.

Thus grievously did Jeanne misjudge her young gamecock. She forgot the Princess Margot's legs, though she herself had

seen Henri much intent upon them, when her good friend
Catherine had called her to the window. She forgot too that he
had in the end forsworn his faith at school and gone to Mass.
He had indeed held out for a while, but what could a child do
when so beset? 'Tis ill for even a man to resist, who wants to
keep his friends, enjoy his life, and has no taste for martyrdom.
Turmoils and tribulations leave unmarred the innocence of such
women as Queen Jeanne and teach them nothing. Thus, even
when growing old, they still love and still believe.

Henri knew Jeanne better than she knew him; so he seldom
asked her for money. He was fond of play and of good living,
and found the means for it by serenely sending notes of hand
to the houses of his various friends. Either the notes returned
or the money came; and these little transactions were never
allowed to reach his mother's ears. Only war could pay his
debts, as the young man realized, and his eagerness for civil war
was not wholly exalted or unselfish. His was the case of all the
hungry Huguenots. But his necessity served the cause, for he
spoke and acted with all the greater zeal and conviction.

Jeanne took him with her; but while on their way to the
Protestant fortress of La Rochelle they were again intercepted
by the selfsame envoy of France. He asked the Prince of Navarre
why he was so urgent to join his uncle Condé at La Rochelle.
" To save tailors' reckonings," retorted Henri. " We Princes of
the Blood had better die together, so that none need to wear
mourning for the rest."

The man took Henri for a fool, or he would not have tried
to set him against his mother. Without mentioning names, he
fell to talking about firebrands. " A bucket of water," cried
Henri, " and the fire is out! "

" How so? "

" The Cardinal de Lorraine shall swill it until he bursts! " If
the King of France's envoy was mystified, he was slower-witted
than the boy. It was Jeanne who marked his ready answers. Her
pleasure in her son made her sluggish, and she was near to
being taken by Montluc, who was at her heels again. But at last
they reached the stronghold by the ocean, and her heart leapt

to see none but friends about her again. Some laughed, some wept, but all eyes were aglow. Coligny, Condé, all who were already come and had been anxious for the Queen, greeted her with hearts no less uplifted.

How good it is to come out of the land of hate and persecution into a city of kindliness and safety! Mistrust is banished, caution laid aside, and the fugitive is at first content to breathe and to possess himself in freedom. How good to pour out all his bitterness and torment to those who look at him and speak no otherwise; to be one among a multitude, and to see about him none that he need despise! Deliver us from evil. Guide those I love through all their perils. And behold — they are here.

The boy stood on the seashore. Even in the darkness of the night he could walk without fear of molestation down to the harbour and out upon the mole. The great waves swept shorewards, curled, and crashed, and their roar was the voice of a distant world that knew him not, but in the wind he caught the scent of it. When his mother's heart was high, she conceived that God was nigh. Her son thrilled at the thought that this vast expanse of waters never ceased to roll and thunder until it surged against the unknown coast of the new continent, America. A land that must be wild and solitary and free — he meant free from wickedness and hatred and all the compulsions of the mind that brought men misery or made them mighty. In the blackness of the night on the slippery stones, ringed by the expanse of waters, the lad was very like his mother, and what he called America was really the Kingdom of God.

The stars glittered momentarily out of the dim and scurrying clouds, and for a moment a light flashed through the clouded soul of a boy. Later on, that light would be extinguished; the earth beneath his feet will grow ever more real and more solid, and to it his senses and his thoughts will hold fast.

THE PRICE OF CONFLICT

The Prince of Navarre kept pestering his seniors to attack. He was sick of speeches and debates. When welcomed by the city burghers, he had replied: " I am poor at talking, but — I can do a deed! "

Oh, for a sight of the enemy at last! Oh, to sate his heart with vengeance, prove himself a man, and feel the joy of life at last!

" But it cries aloud to Heaven, dearest Mother! The King of France is stripping you of your possessions, and his troops are laying waste the land. I mean to fight. Do you ask for whom? For you! "

" I see Catherine's hand in this letter to the Bordeaux tribunal," said the Queen; " and the purpose of it is to rob me of my lands. She says I am being kept here as a prisoner, as though she did not intend to make me one! No, this city is a refuge, not a prison, though I may not leave it and am barred from my domains. God exacts this sacrifice. Yes; go. Fight for Him, and prevail over His enemies."

So saying, she took his face between her two slender hands. Its form and features were like her own; high, narrow brows, mild eyes, clear forehead, fair hair, firm, small mouth. The whole lean coltishness of the lad, shadowed, as from the other side of life, her own decay. But he was sturdy and well-knit, his shoulders and chest were opening out, although he did not promise to be tall. His nose was overlong, but the tip of it barely drooped as yet.

" I send you forth with a glad heart," said Jeanne, in the deep and resonant voice that came to her in moments of exaltation. Not until he had gone at last did she allow herself to weep in secret, and she wept like a child.

Not many wept openly in the city of La Rochelle when the army of the Huguenots marched. They were glad because the hour of God and His victory had come. Most of the men had been reft from those they loved, and had left them far away; now they hoped to win them back and keep them. It was a deliverance to enter upon such a war.

But it came about that those of the Religion were defeated. The Catholics beat them twice, and beat them badly, though they were not the weaker force; there were thirty thousand men on either side. The Protestants were reinforced from the North as well as from the South. They could further look for help from the Princes of Orange and Nassau and the Duke of Zweibrücken. The Faith knew no frontiers of land nor speech; who stands for the truth is my brother and my friend. None the less, they were twice heavily defeated.

Coligny was too slow. He should have pushed on more resolutely to join his foreign allies and carried the war into the heart of France. Instead of which he let himself be surprised by the enemy before he had summoned Condé to his help, and saved his army at the cost of a Prince of the Blood. At Jarnac, Condé fell by a shot from an ambuscade. There was great rejoicing in the army of the Duke of Anjou; the corpse was exposed on an ass's back so that all the soldiery should see it and believe that the extermination of the Protestants was now at hand. Henri of Navarre, nephew of the dead man, was better acquainted with God's purposes. It was his turn now; he became a leader of men.

Hitherto he had merely sat his horse and no more; but that was much. It was splendid to ride, with all the fire of innocence and youth, against a treacherous and wicked foe, whose hour of punishment was nigh. Let him look to himself and beware: Henri was in the saddle for fifteen hours on end, exultant, unwearied, and all unconscious of his body. The wind caught him and he flew, his eyes glittered and grew keener, he saw farther than he had ever done before, because there was now an enemy to face. Of a sudden, that enemy was no longer only in the wind and far away. He made himself felt, a cannon-ball came whizzing past. It left only a faint echo behind, but yonder it lay, a great round stone cannon-ball.

At the beginning of that fight Henri was afraid, he was free to confess. " If we knew no fear," said a pastor to him, " we could not overcome it to the glory of God." Henri mastered himself and took his stand on the very spot where the first ball had fallen.

His father Antoine had done so and had fallen. But no ball struck him, his fear faded, and he rode out to encircle the enemy artillery. It would be a stroke indeed if it succeeded.

Now that his uncle Condé was dead, a burden of gravity and responsibility was suddenly laid upon that light-hearted youth. His mother Jeanne hastened to his side and made him known to the troops as their leader, to the cavalry first and then to the infantry. Henri swore by his soul, his honour, and his life that he would never abandon the good cause, and he was acclaimed by all. Now, instead of speeding on the wind, he had to sit in council, which would have bored him had there not been much to make him laugh. He took great pleasure in drawing up a certain letter to the Duke of Anjou. Such was now the title of Catherine's second surviving son, hitherto known as Monsieur, also a Henri, one of the three Henris of Paris schooldays. Now they stood face to face in the field.

This same Henri had written him a proud and pompous screed about his duty, and his obligations to the realm, which might have been passed over, but the affected style! Some alien secretary must have laboured to produce this stilted document, or Henri Monsieur, if it had been he, was as crass with foppery and pedantry as his sister Margot. The Prince of Navarre in his reply derided the whole finical family. The letter, he said, had been written as a foreigner would write, who did not know the speech of common folk. Good French and the good cause went naturally together.

Henri made mention of speech and style, thus betraying something of which he was not conscious: he himself had come from another realm, and his first utterances had not been as these. Meantime he had learned the speech of court and school, and lastly of the soldiery and people, and that was his favourite speech. "French is the language of my choice," he cried in later days, when he knew where he really stood. Now he liked to believe that it had been his first and only speech. He was ready to sleep with his men in the hay, and sleep in his clothes, washed scarcely more than they, and smelled and cursed as they did. There was a certain vowel that he always mispronounced, but he shut his ears, and he had forgotten how the two Henris used to nudge each other in the playground and jeer at

him because he did not know the gender of " spoon." He did
not know it yet.

He was often conscious of the blunders in Coligny's strategy,
when not wholly absorbed in the delights of living and horsemanship. He liked the fighting of the battle better than the
winning of it, for life was long and full of joy. The Admiral, who
was an old man, must be respected, for he had learned the art
of war; and defeats and victories and length of years, all these
together make a man wise. Henri never confided his doubts to
the old war-god with the writhen, mask-like face; he only discussed them with his cousin Condé, son of the dead Prince,
whose life Coligny had thrown away.

They were agreed on the one point that brings youth together: the old man had had his day. He never won any battles
now — and, indeed, was he ever a successful commander? Not
to be unfair to him, he had once, as all the older folk remembered, relieved — what was the name of that town in Flanders?
The Guises then wanted to attack Philip of Spain, the hereditary
foe.

Old, old history, almost forgotten now. The Lord Admiral
was against the campaign; then at the last moment he averted
defeat and shut himself into the unfortified town. The result
was all to the advantage of the Guises, who had planned the
war. Much better have surrendered the town — ah, Saint-Quentin was its name, of course — to the Spaniards. A man who
always fails . . .

Still, the facts of history remain: he did take Boulogne from
the English. Everyone remembers that. He commanded a
French fleet, and when Henri looked from the mole at La
Rochelle across at the New World he recalled that the Lord
Admiral de Coligny was the first Frenchman who planned to
found a French colony. Fourteen emigrants with two pastors
sailed to Brazil; the scheme failed, of course. His was the common destiny: he made the right decision and then lost. When
a man always fails . . .

He has won battles — yes; but they were battles against the

King of France, whom he always tried to reconcile with his Protestant subjects and deliver from the Guises. Hence the Lord Admiral was always forced to make a rotten treaty, and the war began afresh. His moderation should have proved him no rebel against the King — yet he did try to capture Charles IX, and the King never forgot that he had had to flee. Either, in God's name, a man is a rebel against the King, or at least he does not march against Paris and then let himself be led by the nose instead of taking the capital and plundering the whole court. No; as soon as things go ill for the court, a royal edict appears, assuring religious liberty to the Protestants, and a few days after it is cancelled. And even were it kept, what did it profit the brethren? So few chapels were allowed that a Huguenot must ride or walk twenty miles to get to public worship. Small sense in victories won in vain.

A great commander, no doubt, and a hero of the faith. The Huguenots were a minority, and though the court feared them, it was the Lord Admiral that they really feared, and their envoys hint that the Huguenots have no importance for the court save through the Admiral. And now see what he has left after a lifetime of earnest efforts. Until that historic victory at Saint-Quentin, from which the Guises alone drew profit, he seems to have been a man of influence. The late King was alive, he loved and enriched Coligny. Madame Catherine said nothing, and her son Charles was still a boy. Those were his days of glory, before the young men had come forth. But now? The furniture stripped from his château at Chatillon was being sold by public auction in Paris, and the château had been burnt. He himself had been condemned to be hanged and strangled on the Place de Grève as a rebel and a traitor. His estates confiscated, his children proclaimed degraded and dishonoured, and a reward of fifty thousand crowns upon his head, alive or dead. All this, indeed, the Lord Admiral suffered for the true faith, and abased himself to the glory of God. Otherwise it would be unforgivable indeed!

" He murdered the old Duke of Guise. That, at least, he did on his own account, and 'tis what I like the best about him.

A man should revenge himself," observed young Condé. To which his cousin Henri replied:

" I do not hold with murderers — and the Admiral is no murderer either. All he did was not to prevent the murder."

" What does his conscience say to that? "

" That there are distinctions," answered Cousin Henri. " To commit murder is a crime. To cause a man to be murdered is wrong. But not to prevent a murder is perhaps permissible — though I hope I may not be brought to such a pass. Still, the Cardinal de Lorraine ought to be choked. He and his House alone are behind all the troubles in France. They betray the realm to Philip of Spain, so that he may set them on the throne. 'Tis they alone that stir up the King and the people to hate the Protestants. They wanted to have Coligny killed, and they laid their plans; he did no more than strike before they struck. Perhaps he should not disavow it. For my part, I think him justified in the sight of God."

Condé protested, thinking not only of the murder of the Duke of Guise, but also of his father, killed at Jarnac, by Coligny's fault.

" The Lord Admiral disliked my father for his many love-affairs. Otherwise he would not have been killed. But the Lord Admiral knew how to come to terms with his conscience, and I think that you do too," sneered Condé.

" Your father's death was necessary that the Religion should prevail," said Henri gently.

" And that you also should prevail! You are now the first Prince of the Blood."

" I was already so by birth," said Henri hotly. " But alas, that skills nothing when a man is poor and has powerful enemies and must fight like a hunted fugitive. What must we do? Attack? And so I would. I do not forget that 25th of June, the day of my first victory. But can I twit the old man with that? "

" It was indeed a very little victory. The Admiral would answer that you had enjoyed yourself at La Roche Abeille, but that we must creep into our lairs and await the Germans. What if the reiters do come? "

Condé had grown loud and angry.

" We made haste to send all the troops we could to the Queen
of Navarre to clear her land of enemies; and now we pay the
penalty."

" You pay no penalties. You have a different girl every night."

" And so do you."

Both lads dropped their reins on their horses and glared into
each other's eyes. Condé actually raised a clenched fist, but
Henri ignored it. Suddenly he flung his arms round his cousin's
neck and kissed him. And he thought: " Jealous, weak, but at
least my friend; if not, I must make him so."

Condé too embraced his cousin. When they parted, he had
dry eyes, but Henri's eyes were moist.

The dispatch of troops to Béarn was well devised, for they won
a victory there. That would give the gentlemen in Paris something to talk about, thought Jeanne's son; and fat old Dame
Catherine must be shaking on her throne. The main body of the
army in Poitou half-way to the capital. They meant to take it
too; and very soon!

The lads insisted that Coligny should receive them, and he
did so, though he found it hard to show them a steadfast countenance and unwavering faith in God. The Lord's hand had
been too heavy upon him of late. But the Protestant commander
proved a strong man in adversity, well aware of the perils he
still had to meet. No matter if despair laid hold of him in the
solitary night hours, when the face of the Almighty was turned
away. He listened gravely to the two vehement young men.

Young Condé was less restrained than Henri. He brusquely
demanded that Coligny should march on Paris. He called him
faint-hearted because he did not seek a decision, but sat before
Poitiers and could not take it.

The Admiral eyed them both, one so violent and aggressive,
the other watchful and silent. And the old man knew whose
will and ideas were here expressed; so he replied not to Condé
but to Navarre. He explained that too many enemy strongholds
blocked the way; he himself could do no more than keep in
touch with the troops he had sent southwards, and — here he

raised a finger — he had to take care that the foreign reiters got their pay. Otherwise they would desert. He did not tell them that he himself had pawned his family jewels before giving permission for the reiters to take their pay where they could get it. A Christian does not boast of self-sacrifice, nor does a man of any pride. So Coligny let the young Prince Henri talk and do him wrong.

"You let the land be ravaged. My Lord Admiral, I am young and not, like you, familiar with warfare. Yet surely 'tis monstrous that these aliens, instead of fighting at our side, should be let loose to burn our villages and torture our peasants until they give up all they have. Your stragglers are massacred by the country-folk as though they were noxious beasts, and we indeed take a viler vengeance every time on those of our own speech."

"But not of our own creed," replied the gaunt old Protestant. Henri set his teeth, horror-struck at the blasphemy within him that strove for utterance.

"This cannot be God's will," he said.

"What God's will may be, my Prince," said Coligny decisively, "you will learn at the end of the campaign. The Lord has indeed preserved me for deeds to come; the guard have caught another assassin sent against me by the Guises."

Thenceforward he was minded to keep these two young critics at a distance. Before the battle of Moncontour, which he was also destined to lose, he sent the two Princes for their safety to the rear, though one stormed and the other wept bitter tears. Later on came Jeanne d'Albret, and a council of war was held. After this fresh defeat the Protestant army was weaker by three thousand men; nothing was left for it but to withdraw southwards instead of waiting for the smaller force to rejoin it in the north.

Jeanne, as always, brought her pastors with her. She had secret interviews with Coligny, and the Admiral's stricken heart was stirred to victory once more. For the inner victory comes first; the actual victory follows close upon it. Jeanne was confident of that. Then the pastors intoned a hymn, and the army, like its commander, set forth with piety and strength renewed.

There followed a forced march which did in fact unite the two far-severed forces, and the Protestants marched northward to Nevers. From that moment they threatened Paris. The court bestirred itself at once. While the army was still advancing, Dames Catherine and Jeanne were already in treaty. The army was even yet in movement when the peace was signed; then at last it halted. By this treaty religious liberty was guaranteed.

Henri was glad to be with his mother, because he saw her happy. He was indeed happy too, so long as he did not stop to think. But during the advance he fell sick and lay abed in a town; then he had time to remember the horrors of the war and mark them firmly on his memory. It may be that his sickness was merely caused by the brutalities of the Protestant army, as in earlier days he was thought to have caught smallpox because he had had to become a Catholic.

He did not hide his inner conflict from the Admiral.

" Lord Admiral," said he, " do you truly conceive that religious freedom can be enforced by treaties and decrees? You are a great commander, you have outwitted the enemy and menaced the King of France in his own capital. None the less, the provincials whom we have terrorized go on speaking of the Huguenot rebels and will never let us worship in peace where we have robbed and slaughtered."

And Coligny, the conquerer, replied:

" Prince, you are still full young, and, moreover, you lay sick while we were fighting the good fight. Men soon forget, and only God will remember what we were constrained to do in His cause."

This Henri did not believe — or indeed, so much the worse, thought he, if God, like himself, saw visions of wretched men strung up over a fire until they revealed where they had hidden their money. Fearful of what he might say, he bowed and left the presence of the conqueror.

A FAMILY SCENE

Then came a brief space when Jeanne and Henri seemed almost to be living in a world of peace, untainted by guile and hatred. She ruled her little realm, and he the great province of Guyenne. No longer did she need to punish, for her subjects were good Protestants again. But he, in all good faith, stood deputy for the King of France. He honestly did not see why he should be fated to be that monarch's natural enemy; his mother's teachings were not so deeply marked upon his mind. A young man must not be a slave even to ambition. At eighteen, for a few short months, he said: " I have done enough to last me for my life. Women are waiting to be loved, and the reward they bring is richer than the fruits of war, or of the faith, or future kingship."

Those were the days when women were, for him, goddesses in the glory of their youth and loveliness. He might know them and convince himself that they were flesh, but they still were beings of another world, his dreams and his desires transfigured them again. They were indeed for ever changing, he ran no risk of disillusion; he did not keep them long enough. So he never discovered that these were no goddesses, but very mortal ladies, mercenary and jealous. While one was hating him with all her heart, he rode for ten hours to win the guerdon of his exploits from another. She was awaiting him with shining eyes and the countenance of eternal love. He fell at the feet of whoever she might be and kissed the hem of her gown; he had ridden fast and far, but here was his heart's desire. His eyes filled with tears, and, seen through those tears, she grew more beautiful.

But while Henri lived for the favour of young women, several older ladies were busy with his affairs, though he was not aware of it. The first was Madame Catherine. One morning, in her bedchamber in the Louvre, she received a royal visit from her son, Charles IX. He shambled in, still in his nightshirt, and exclaimed even before he had shut the door:

" Mamma, what do you think — ! "

" Your sister has a man in her bedchamber? "

"Margot is sleeping with Guise," snapped Charles, in angry confirmation.

"What did I tell you? She is a bitch," observed Madame Catherine, with the clarity for which the occasion called.

"These are her thanks for all your trouble," yelled Charles. "She knows Latin, and she actually reads while she sits at table. She dances the pavane and has odes written to her." Her iniquities crowded into his memory. "She rides in a gilt coach, and the horses wear plumes as broad as my backside. But I know what she's after, I've been watching her these many years. The slut began it when she was eleven."

"You held the candle," interposed Madame Catherine. But he was not to be deterred. He knew all his sister's lovers and screamed out their names. Then in sudden exhaustion with his own fury he collapsed, flushed and gasping, on to his mother's bed, knocking the pillows on to the floor. His voice sank into a mutter:

"And what do I care? She will always be the same, and sleep with Guise or someone else. Pah!"

His mother looked at him and pondered: "Only a few years ago he was as handsome as a picture on the wall. And now he might almost be a butcher's boy instead of a King." What had she brought into the world? But it was not she it was the Valois. The blood of such barbarians always rose out of their graves and fashioned another of the ancient type. Thus the daughter of the Medici, because her few known forebears had lived in pleasant rooms, and not in stables or in camps.

"Well," she continued, in her calm tones, "if your sister goes on so, I must take Henri Guise for my son-in-law. Who will then prevail, my poor boy, you or he?"

"I!" bellowed Charles. "I am the King."

"By the grace of God?" she asked. "You should have learned by this time that every king by the grace of God must exert himself or he will not be king for long. You are King today, my son, because I, your mother, am at your side."

She said this in a tone he knew of old, which always brought him to his feet. He got up and stood with his nightshirt curving out over his chest and paunch, and faced the little old woman, obediently attentive.

"Margot shall not marry Guise," said she decisively; "his House is too powerful. She shall take a much humbler youth, who is in our service."

"And who may that be?"

"Of good family, but without influence, and unknown in Paris. And I must have him under my own hand. A man I can reach can do no harm. We must keep our enemies in our own house."

"You cannot mean — "

"I am in treaty with his mother to send him here, that I may get him in my power."

"But a heretic! My sister and a heretic! You cannot be serious!"

"And what if your brother Anjou should marry the Queen of England? Elizabeth is a heretic, and a great Queen, too, by her own grace."

"She kills her Catholics," said Charles, with more alarm than indignation. His mother was beyond him. Never did she allow her resourceful spirit to be hampered by religion, and she said the most monstrous things with quite unruffled composure.

"The English Catholics must look after themselves — and so indeed must the French," she added.

Charles dropped his eyes and growled; he dared no more. "There is the King of Spain," he muttered.

"My daughter, the Queen of Spain, is dead," observed Catherine, without a hint of grief. "The only thing I have to fear from Don Philip is that he may make use of my embarrassments. So I need my Protestants." And she thought, but did not say, that when she needed them no more, she would treat them just as the Queen of England treated her Catholics. But that was not to be revealed to her loutish son. Then she came to what was to be his part.

"Your sister must be brought to reason."

" True. This business with the Guise — "

" Who will rob you of your throne," she continued quickly.

" I'll fetch my sister! " he roared. " I'll teach her to dethrone me! "

He was on the point of dashing out of the room, but his mother grabbed his nightshirt.

" Stay! Guise may be with her, and he is armed."

He stopped abruptly.

" And if she sees you she surely will not come. This matter must be dealt with in my presence."

She clapped her hands and said to the woman who appeared:

" Ask the Princess, my daughter, to come hither; I have some important news for her. Assure her it is good news."

They waited — Catherine motionless with folded hands, while her hulking son stamped about in his fluttering nightshirt, gasping with expectancy and muttering under his breath.

At last the door opened to admit an apparition which everyone would have admired except the two persons in that room. Though the hour was early, Marguerite de Valois was already wearing a white silk gown covered with glittering ornament. She wore crimson shoes and a red wig, but she had cunningly painted her face to suit those brilliant tresses.

She swept into the room with all the airs of the beauty she had chosen — graceful, but imperious; a great lady entering a festal gathering. One glance at her mother and one at her brother, and she guessed what she might expect. Her set smile stiffened into fear, and she took one faltering step backwards. Too late; Catherine waved a hand, and the door was slammed from without.

" What do you want of me? " panted the now terror-stricken girl. Charles looked at his mother, and she made no motion; he knew his hands were free. With a yell he leapt upon his sister, snatched the red wig from her head, and her own black hair tumbled all about her shoulders; she could act her part no longer, and, indeed, she was given no chance. Her brother was slapping her in the face, right hand, left hand, again and yet again, no matter how she tried to struggle out of his grasp.

" Sleep with the Guise, would you? " he roared. " Dethrone me, eh? " he spluttered.

Her rouge stuck to his fingers, and her cheeks were streaked and smeared. As she squirmed and twisted, some of his blows caught her plump shoulders.

" Fat Margot! " he roared.

He laughed shrilly and ripped her dress off. The touch of her flesh made him itch to beat her naked body. She, hitherto dumb with terror, found a voice at last. She shrieked and dashed into her mother's arms.

" There, there, my child! " said Madame Catherine, clasping her tight, until Charles IX had hold of her again.

" Across your knee! " cried Madame Catherine, and so he laid her, in spite of all her struggles; one arm held her fast, with his other hand he belaboured her bare and ravishing person. Not content with this, Madame Catherine set about her daughter too, but her fleshy fingers could make but little mark. So she bent down and bit into the lovely flesh.

Marguerite howled like an animal. Her brother, soon exhausted, let her drop to the floor and looked down upon her with glazed eyes, like a drunken man. Madame Catherine too was out of breath, and in her dull black eyes there was a smouldering glow. Once more she folded her hands across her bosom, and said in her usual calm tone:

" Get up, my child. Dear me, what a terrible sight you are! "

She signed to Charles, who helped his sister to her feet. Then she set about arranging her daughter's clothes. When the Princess Margot saw the danger was past, she at once resumed her haughty airs.

" 'Tis torn to shreds, fool! " she shrieked at her brother. " Go and fetch my woman! "

" No," said her mother decisively. " We will keep this business to ourselves."

She smoothed and mended the white silk gown and insisted on painting out the marks of blows and tears on the Princess's face. Charles, at his mother's order, searched for the wig he had torn off his sister's head, pulled it from under the bed, dusted it, and put it on her head again. And there she stood, the imperious beauty who had entered the room a few minutes before.

" Now be off to your Latin books," growled Charles. And Catherine de Medici added: " Pray do not forget this little lesson."

ENGLAND

A second powerful lady was interested in Henri while that young man was intent upon his pleasures. Elizabeth of England gave audience to her Paris Ambassador in her palace in London.

" You are a day late, Walsingham."

" The sea was very rough and stormy. Your Majesty might well have had to receive a drowned Ambassador. And he, I fear, could not have told you all there is to tell."

" And that, Walsingham, would have been to your advantage. Death by drowning is less painful than death on the scaffold. You are nearer to the block and to the axe than you may think."

" Death in the service of so great a Queen should be a man's highest reward, especially when he has done his duty."

" His duty? Ha — his duty. Here is your reward, rascal! " And she struck him in the face.

He saw the blow coming, but did not move, though her little hand could sting, as he well knew. The Queen was tall, of uncertain age, as straight as a suit of mail, and the red hair, which Margot de Valois wore to suit a gown, was Elizabeth's own.

" The court of France draws closer to the King of Spain and you bring me no news. I risk the loss of my country and my throne through this alliance, and you do nothing but look on."

" There is yet another charge against me. It was I who spread that rumour, and it is false."

" You spread false rumours to my damage."

" I had the Spanish Embassy robbed, and made known that letters proving the alliance were found there. All in Your Majesty's interest."

" You are a secret Catholic, Walsingham. Guard! Arrest that

man! I have long marked you down. Glad shall I be to see your head drop."

" Alas, I looked to tell Your Grace one more merry tale," said the Ambassador, with an armed man now on either side of him. " I have promised Your Majesty's hand in marriage, and that to a Prince unknown to you."

" To Catherine's son, Anjou, I suppose." She signed to the guards to stand back. Plans for a marriage — she must hear them first.

" I fear Anjou would be a blunder. I know that you justly think meanly of the Valois. No, a little Protestant from the South, whom the Valois want to catch for brother-in-law, and, indeed, it would be no bad plan. He might cut them clear."

" But they would be embroiled again in Flanders. A marriage between the Princess of Valois and a Protestant Prince — oh, I know who — means war between France and Spain and the invasion of Flanders. A united France — that I will not suffer. We must have civil war in France. And I had a thousand times rather see the Spaniards in Flanders, who indeed else are being slowly wrecked by their own papistry, than a France united under a Protestant."

Elizabeth strode up and down the chamber. She could thus enjoy the sound of her own voice the better. She had waved the guards away, and Walsingham drew back against the opposite wall to leave a clear passage for his Queen. Suddenly she stopped and faced him.

" So I am to marry young Navarre? How looks he? "

" None so ill. If that were all that mattered. He is not so tall as Your Grace."

" I am not averse to small men."

" Truly, they often make more vigorous husbands."

" Fie, Walsingham! What should I know of such matters? And his face? "

" Rather sallow, and oval, Madame."

" Ah."

" His nose is overlong."

" That may be an advantage."

" Its length — truly, but not its shape. 'Tis a pendulous nose. And will grow more so as the years pass, I apprehend."

" A pity. Well, no matter. I'll have no such paltry a loon for my husband. And he — a mere youth, hey? " said the dame whose age it was better not to know. " You raised his hopes? He was enraptured, of course."

" Beauty does indeed enrapture him. He covered Your Majesty's portrait with kisses and with tears," said the Ambassador untruthfully.

" So, so. And you upset his alliance with the Valois? "

" Since I knew Your Grace did not desire it."

" You are not such a dolt as I thought. If so be that you are not a traitor."

Her tone was brusque but gracious. The Ambassador realized that the peril of the scaffold had receded, and made a deep reverence.

" My Lord Ambassador," began Elizabeth, as she sank back on her chair, " pray tell me of the traffic between the two Queens. Look at me, man! I mean Queen Jeanne and Queen Catherine. I know that both have laid their plans for the future government of France."

" I marvel — indeed, I am aghast at Your Grace's understanding."

" Naturally. My ambassadors are my spies, but I keep other spies, to spy on my ambassadors."

Walsingham looked amazed, though he was perfectly well aware of this fact.

" I confess," he answered glibly, " that I was speaking only of the little Prince of Navarre, not of his mother, seeing my mistress is a young and lovely Queen. If I served an aged king, I should have spoken of none other than the Prince's mother. It is Queen Jeanne we have to fear."

He saw from her look that the battle was half won; so his voice grew doubly ardent and respectful.

" I have a sad tale to tell Your Majesty, of human wickedness and guile. Poor Queen Jeanne was betrayed by an Englishman." He seemed quite overcome at the thought and made a gesture of repulsion.

" It was not I; for we must use discretion. It was one of my agents, and he himself devised the plan. I consented, and he made his way to La Rochelle, where all Queen Jeanne's friends forgather; among them, Count Louis of Nassau. My agent prevailed upon the German princeling to take to his bed and feign sickness until Jeanne came to visit the invalid. . . ."

The tale that followed was in the vein of a Shakspere comedy, and his Queen enjoyed it all the more for the grave air with which he told it. When she had laughed her fill, she said:

" Such a simple soul as Nassau should make no efforts to be artful. Will Jeanne give up the French marriage — the only scheme that could help both German Protestants and French? Did she believe the tale! That I would marry her son, quotha! And her daughter Queen of Scots! "

" Such dazzling prospects are apt to impose — just because the vision is blinded," observed the Ambassador. And Elizabeth said amiably:

" So that was why you betrothed me to Navarre? Why not tell me so at once. Must I cut off your head, Walsingham, before you can tell me what I want to hear? "

" It would not have entertained Your Grace so much as now, and my one ambition is to please, even at the risk of block and axe."

" It was a good stroke, and I'll not forget it."

" My agent, one Beel, devised it."

" Not so, man! You try to magnify your service by a show of modesty. But you may draw a reward for Beel. A reasonable reward," she added hurriedly, for Elizabeth knew the value of money.

SNARES, TRAPS, AND A PURE MIND

Jeanne was the third of the older women who were busy with Henri's destinies, and she alone was labouring in his interest. So she stood upon herself alone, setting no store upon the honesty of the two other Queens. She went to visit the Count of Nassau on his sick-bed, having heard for days past that he was lying in sore pain. She found him feverish and flushed, but rather from wine than fever, as she thought. However, she first listened to all the great news brought him by his friend Beel, the Englishman: the raid on the Spanish Embassy, and the proofs there found of the French court's duplicity. She was offered a Princess for her daughter-in-law, while schemes were afoot for reconciliation with Philip of Spain. How could Catherine fulfil Jeanne's condition and use the Protestant army to liberate Spanish Flanders?

Jeanne pondered. From whom could this news come other than from the Englishman who had devised that raid? She stroked the fat Ludovicus's forehead and behind his ears and discovered that he was wholly well. Then she sent for her surgeon to administer certain specifics to the patient, which he had perforce to swallow. The poor man soon burst into a profuse sweat; other symptoms followed which made it necessary for Jeanne to leave the room for a while. When she came back the victim was already more amenable, and he admitted without further ado that all his knowledge came from Master Beel alone, and that the man was indeed one of Walsingham's agents.

"But he is my friend," said the ingenuous Nassau; "and on my faith you may believe his story. He would not lie to me."

"My dear cousin, you are the only good man in a wicked world," observed Jeanne sympathetically. Whereupon the German conjured her not to consent to a French marriage. By such a marriage her son would lapse into Catholicism, the Protestants would lose their leader, and the Prince would gain nothing by a betrayal of his faith. What would he be as the husband of the Princesse de Valois? Certainly not the King of France. "But elsewhere," continued Nassau, after a momentous pause, "he may indeed be a King. And a great King too. His sister, your daughter Catherine — Madame, she too will be a Queen. 'Tis all so greatly to the advantage of the faith that it must be true," added the worthy man; "and I believe that God Himself has charged me to lay it before Your Grace." Jeanne saw he had quite forgotten Master Beel.

He spoke with fervour; then he suddenly collapsed on his pillows, and Queen Jeanne left him, not without commending him to the care of her physician. She grieved to have had to treat an honest man thus to make him tell the truth. Deceit is not solely served by the dishonest.

With his last breath before he fainted, Ludwig of Nassau had expressly told her who were offering marriage and a throne to her two children: Elizabeth of England and the King of Scots — such great and sudden good fortune would have seemed suspect to any other mother. Jeanne d'Albret accepted it with equanimity, when she thought of her high ancestry, the victories of the Protestant army, and the exalted claims of the religion. She had no suspicion that Elizabeth might make her a treacherous offer in a way that carried no commitment, to divert her from an alliance with the court of France. Queen Jeanne's pride would not let her believe that anyone could use her to keep France divided and weak.

Next day she said to Coligny: " I have striven all night to learn from God's will whether my son is to be King in England or in France. What think you, Lord Admiral? "

" We cannot tell," he answered. " But the most zealous Huguenots, your stoutest followers, will surely be affronted if the Prince, your son, allies himself with the enemies of the religion. But I would not dare to say that it may not be God's will," concluded Coligny, cautiously.

" No," said Jeanne decisively. " He has made known to me that I am to treat this matter in worldly fashion, serving only my honour and the advantage of my House, which he conceives of as His own. Such is God's message to me."

Coligny pretended to be convinced. In reality he mistrusted the intentions of England, for he judged them as a soldier would. The Protestant Englishwoman should have helped him to liberate Flanders from the Spaniards, but that she would not do; while the Catholic court of France was very ready with promises of help. Hence he was in favour of the marriage of the Prince of Navarre with Marguerite of Valois, and such objections as he made were such as would strengthen Jeanne's resolve. She pointed out that the English had always been enemies of France. Coligny urged that they were so no longer — as though it was not enough that a Prince who made an English marriage would thereby sacrifice his birthright and his prospects of the French throne.

Jeanne said that Elizabeth was too old to have a son, and her husband could not hope for any share in the business of government. But, said Coligny, there was still his sister, Princess Catherine, who would quite certainly have children by the King of Scotland. He was indeed the lawful heir to the throne of England, in case Elizabeth should die childless. This was a hazardous thing to say to Henri's mother; he could see that from her anger. Her Henri put aside and sacrificed, her joyous Henri to waste his youth in melancholy bondage to an old Queen. For the first time she realized all that would follow if she made the wrong choice.

The gentle Jeanne rose abruptly from her chair, and she too began to pace the room, like Elizabeth of England, when so distraught in her Ambassador's presence by her own conflicting interest. Not so this Queen; nothing shook her self-command until her son's happiness was at stake. And she said, in that rare and ringing voice of hers: " Not another word, Coligny! Send for my son! "

He gave the order at the door. And while they were waiting, the old man bent on one knee. " I did but speak that you might prove me wrong," he confessed.

"Rise," answered Jeanne. "You were also thinking that Queen Catherine has promised you the command in Flanders. But it is not for me to reproach you with seeking your own ends. If my son should go to England and my daughter to Scotland, I should be but a woman unsupported, the burden would be more than I could bear, and the French nobles could neither reverence nor obey me. If that was my true motive, then may God give me my due."

"Amen," said he. Both stood motionless and with bowed heads until Henri entered. He hurried in, rather breathless, and with a light in his eyes; no doubt he had been running in pursuit of a girl. He did not feel called upon to answer before God for the deeds and thoughts of that last hour, like his two elders. None the less, he was not ill at ease in that atmosphere of solemnity.

Queen Jeanne sat down and motioned to the Prince and the Admiral to sit down likewise; she was still bethinking her how she should begin. Meantime Coligny raised his hand in a warning but respectful gesture, in token that he was best fitted to open the matter. She nodded, and he began.

COUNCIL OF THREE

" Prince," said Coligny, " we are now to speak of the future of the Religion, which is also the future of the kingdom. Here and now a great decision must be taken, and through you. God's decree will find utterance in your voice. Listen well to what He shall put into your mind. I am ready to abide by it."

Jeanne made as though to speak. The old man signed to her once more that he had not finished.

" Two powerful governments are courting the favour of the Prince of Navarre, and much, far more than we can foretell, depends for time and for eternity on which of them you shall choose." The pause that Coligny here made was not intended to give anyone an opportunity for speech; its purpose was to make his two hearers hold their breath. Jeanne indeed was deeply stirred. Henri saw the awe-struck alteration in her face; and it filled his eyes with sudden tears. A sob sped upwards quick as a thought into his throat and was there stifled, though his eyes were wet.

He sat, his vision dimmed, an image of emotion, but thinking all the while: " Old babbler! Why not speak out? Long have I known that I was to marry either my fat Margot or the old Englishwoman. As if Nassau had not been at me long enough. But what should I do in England? Now, Margot — she promised I should see those legs of hers some day."

Coligny bent over Jeanne and whispered: " Give him time. He awaits God's fiat." Henri was now conscious of his mother's agonized suspense; and his own mind tautened. With a decision that surprised himself, Henri said:

" I would serve France. I choose the Religion, and therefore I choose France."

At these words Coligny rose. He stretched out his arms as though in welcome to the Lord Himself. But Henri embraced him; and then he kissed away his mother's tears.

The little council did not indeed maintain its solemnity. The three agreed that their advantages lay in Paris, not in London. Henri actually asked whether the English offer could be seriously meant. Perhaps it was merely made to obstruct the French alliance. Jeanne was for long too self-complacent to admit such an idea. But her pride was salved by her young son's shrewdness and intelligence. Henri observed that he was very ready to leave the distinguished rank of Queen Elizabeth's consort to his cousin Anjou. " One less," he added; and they understood his meaning. Jeanne said that they should take care not to provoke Madame Catherine, as she was proposing an English marriage for her second son. And she repeated: " One less! " Then, staring into vacancy: " There were four," she went on. " After Charles two will be left. Charles was a handsome lad, but he has grown corpulent and gross. And from time to time he bleeds."

At this her younger and her older hearer pricked up their ears. But Jeanne did not look at them; she nodded in the fashion of a woman who knows what she is talking about, even in regard to the body and its functions. " They bleed," said Jeanne. " Their blood does not flow, it oozes from the skin. All four sons of the old King suffer thus, and the eldest died of it."

" Must the others die of it too? " asked Henri, with chill emotion.

" The Valois persecute the Religion," said Coligny harshly. " 'Tis their penalty."

" They do not suffer thus because they are Valois," said Jeanne. " They have it from their mother; she was for many years barren."

The two men's curiosity faded; this was more than they could understand. Jeanne had only discovered such connections because she herself had spent so many nights awake and gasping for breath, with that mysterious tickling sensation all under her scalp, all round her head. As no doctor could explain it, she had come to believe that, by God's will, human destinies are fulfilled in men's bodies before they come to fullness. Jeanne was to suffer and go early hence, when she had borne a son who should be God's elect. But her enemy Catherine's fate would be to grow old and to see all her late-born sons go down to death. All this Jeanne foresaw with a clear conscience and without mercy.

" I will inform her envoy that I shall not oppose an alliance with her House, under certain conditions."

" Stern and absolute conditions," said Coligny, insistently. " The court must declare against Spain. The troops must invade Flanders under my command."

" The Princesse de Valois must become a Protestant," said Jeanne, at which Henri was so taken aback that he cried out. Margot and religion! Religion and the amorous Margot! He knew not how to hide his merriment. He slipped behind a curtain into a deep window embrasure and gurgled into his clasped hands.

" My son is thanking God for the salvation of his future wife," said his mother loftily. Coligny felt that this was too much to demand of God, and he was near to saying so; the Princess led a debauched life. Her relations with the Duke of Guise were notorious. As a Christian he should have spoken, but as a man of the world he was silent, and both waited until Henri again joined them. Then Jeanne opened on all the perils of the enterprise.

" Never forget that they chiefly want to make sure of you. It has always been Madame Catherine's policy to hold her enemies at her side; and after her sickly sons, you have the next claim to the Crown of France. I know she means to rid herself of the Guises with your help, for she thinks that House more menacing than ours," Jeanne went on in a scornful tone. " But her main aim is that you shall be lured to her court. I'll prevent that by going there in your stead, and we will see whether she may not have met her match."

Coligny nodded grimly.

" I will follow Your Majesty on foot. All our demands must be granted, or the Protestant army, under the leadership of the Prince of Navarre, will march on Paris. And then no mercy will be shown! "

Henri felt that little mercy had been practised hitherto. He could see the writhen figures of peasants dangling from beams with fires beneath their feet. But it skilled not to protest, when even his mother knew that this was the world's law, and that the true battle for faith and for the kingdom could not be fought in any other fashion. What else, indeed, did Madame Catherine and her Catholics deserve, when his own beloved mother went in peril of her life from them?

" Mamma! " he cried. " You shall not go. They will do you a mischief." He cried out like an anguished child. Jeanne drew him down to her, set his head upon her lap, and said to him, to herself, and to her own heart:

" A woman by herself is safest. God must protect her, since no one else does so. But what am I in the sight of God — now? Once I was beyond all price — the chosen vessel. Now the vessel is empty and can be broken."

She thought she had so spoken, though the words remained in her mind unuttered, but they portended the sacrifice of Jeanne d'Albret's life.

The council was at an end. Her son and the Admiral took their leave.

A WOMAN IN BITTER EARNEST

As he departed, Henri fell in with his cousin Condé and young La Rochefoucauld, also one of those before whom he liked to boast.

" Well," said he, " I am to marry the sister of the King of France. 'Tis the only place at court still vacant. They already have a Chancellor, a secretary, a treasurer and a fool. Only a cuckold is still needed, and I am chosen."

He laughed, and danced a little dance of exaltation, and his

gaiety was so infectious that, for all their secret surprise, they did
so too.

Jeanne went back to her land of Béarn; it was autumn. Catherine's envoy, Biron by name, came to visit her, and she no
longer said him nay; she did but lay down the first of her conditions. Acts of injustice against Protestants must be made good,
one of her Southern cities must be restored, and a blasphemous
cross in Paris removed. She said plainly that she was not to be
tricked, like so many who had gone trustfully to court.

Autumn passed; it was winter before she at last set out. She
had fallen sick of a fever, and her son was thrown from his horse;
it might well have seemed that these disasters were sent to deter
Jeanne from her journey. But at last the day came when mother
and son must part; at Agen, on the 13th day of January, in the
year '72. The blue distance and the sunlit road gave no hint
that this farewell was final. The horses strained at the harness,
the leathern coach lumbered off, the pale Queen and her daughter waved and smiled. The son stood beside his palfrey and
looked from one to the other. The shadows under his mother's
eyes had broadened in those latter days, he noticed, and spread
over her cheeks. Her smile stiffened, and he realized that she
was now too far off and her eyes too filled with tears to distinguish his face.

Brother and sister, keener-sighted, were still for a while in
contact; Henri's eyes said: " Remember." And hers replied: " I
will." " At the first sign of danger, a courier at once! " Her eyes
made answer: " Oh, that you were with us! " From him the
quick appeal: " Take care of our mother, take care of her! "
Then came a turn in the road, and all had vanished, except for
a momentary cloud of sunlit dust from the last of the escort of
noblemen.

For six long months Henri received letters from Jeanne, the
dearest letters of his life; for however many women he was yet
to love, on however many he was to lavish his energies, he would
always feel that only one had fought for him in utter earnest and
drawn her very breath for his sake.

At Tours, in February, she could have found it in her heart

to turn back, but it was no longer possible. From the salutations of the gentlemen sent by Catherine to receive her, she could tell that she was indeed to be tricked. The old Queen and her son the King were at Blois, but came a little way to meet her. So Jeanne took care to waste no more precious days; she insisted that her son's bride should become a Protestant. The peril was that the old Queen would not say plainly, No; she behaved as though she did not believe that it was seriously meant. She treated it as the fantasy of a deluded and excited woman, who had to be soothed by unfailing good humour; the Queen was unweariedly good-humoured. The terrible old woman was in the gayest of moods all through that winter until May; and all that time they haggled in the castle at Blois. But Jeanne, who felt her strength ebbing, had to endure their company and never lose her self-control, for that would have meant more days wasted.

"But, my good friend," said the old Queen in jesting tone, "what does your young gamecock care about the creed of my pretty hen, when he is . . ." She said it loud and clearly, so that others heard it too, and burst out laughing. Even if Jeanne had lost her temper, she was helpless against that laughter. So she pursed her lips into a disdainful smile that hinted of aloofness amid the merriment of all the rest. Still, she tried to keep the serenity of health. Had she betrayed the slightest sign of illness they could have done what they liked with her.

Catherine lied in jest, and that was hard to counter. She roundly alleged that the tutor of the Prince of Navarre had reported that the Prince was quite ready to marry according to the Catholic rite — by proxy indeed, while he was still in the South; and the sooner the better.

"Strange," Jeanne replied dryly, "that I should be ignorant of my son's wishes, while they are known to you, Madame."

"He meant to tell you, but his gallant adventures put it out of his head," laughed Catherine, rocking her large person on her little short legs, as though about to step out in a dance.

Later on, when Jeanne had withdrawn exhausted, the dreadful old woman told her court an exactly opposite tale. It was

Jeanne herself who had begged that her son might be accepted in any event, Catholic or otherwise; but there must be no delay. Then they all beset Jeanne; the Protestant noblemen overwhelmed her with reproaches, and Catherine's many maids of honour sang the praises of the fairy-tale Prince, for whose arrival they were as eager as a pack of children. These maids of honour had no honour left to bestow, but only pleasure, and that they did at every motion from their nefarious mistress. Indeed, they followed her behest in flaunting the licentiousness of the court in the eyes of the sensitive Jeanne, to wear down her resistance sooner. By the evening, or even earlier, the palace was no better than a stews. Only Margot, the bride-to-be, held herself aloof.

A FLORENTINE TAPESTRY

Henri's mother could not deny that the Princesse de Valois demeaned herself well; her figure was faultless, though she was too tightly laced. Her face was dead white, calm and impassive as the sky, as described by a courtier named Brantôme; but Jeanne, of course, could tell how much was affectation and how much was paint. Both were thicker here than in any other country except Spain. The courtiers were as fulsome as idolators. From a safe distance Jeanne watched one of those godless processions, in which the chief personage was not a priest nor even a bishop: Margot, glittering in pearls and precious stones, starred up to the crown of her head, received the adoration of the whole assemblage of nobles and people. The populace knelt by the roadside. Those who followed in her train walked in a kind of exaltation. A murmur, as of prayer, rose from the throng. Plain blasphemy.

When Margot had returned to the palace, Jeanne sent for her, and she came at once, still wearing her robe of state and all her ornaments. Jeanne could not but observe that there were sunken cheeks behind all this triumphant beauty, or at least that those cheeks would begin to droop when the girl was but little older, and then the image of old Catherine would slowly reach the surface.

"Daughter," said Jeanne, more affectionately than she had intended, "you are a beautiful and a virtuous girl. My one desire is that you may so remain. Your husband will be fortunate."

"Mother, I can but hope that you are right in calling me beautiful. For my moral qualities, I must needs confess that they are slighter than my physical ones. I had but little schooling."

"You are eloquent," said Jeanne, stiffening in her manner. Meantime the smooth-tongued Margot was thinking of her late schooling at the hands of her mother and brother as a penalty for her intrigue with Guise. Ah, when would that joy be hers again! He had been dismissed by Madame Catherine as soon as Jeanne appeared. He was to marry; she had lost her sweetheart. Tears began to well up in the poor child's eyes. But she soon thought of her painted eyelids, with the colour trickling off them, and her waxen face marred with streaks of salty tears. And those tears remained unshed.

"My son is a country lad," Jeanne went on, "but a King's son. He is a soldier, with the sense of honour and the simple heart of all true soldiers."

"Virtue and honour are one and the same. I have read in Plutarch — "

"I too read Plutarch with my son: and he looks for his exemplars among the great men of the past. He is not a dull lad, though I called him simple. And his wit comes from the living heart, it is not born of vain conceits and whited sepulchres."

But Margot continued her depiction undeterred: "He has royal blood in him, but 'tis a wholesome blood, and his mind is oblivious of its own nobility." This was the exact opposite of her own case, so she found it easy to conceive. Jeanne, on the other hand, thought, and thought wrongly, that this belauded son of hers had touched the Princess's heart. And all unsuspecting, she went on as she had begun:

"How I wish, my dear daughter, that you both could leave the court after your marriage! 'Tis an abode of evil. Why, the women here even importune the men."

"You have marked it?" sighed Margot; "it is truly shocking!"

" Live in peace and amity far away from here. I have domains in Vendôme where you could rule, instead of displaying a futile splendour at the court of France — as in that procession of today. I saw the gentlemen that walked in it; a hundred thousand crowns would not have paid for the jewels that one of them was wearing. It is not thus that God loved to be honoured, 'tis His will that we should fight His battles, not do Him reverence by outward show. Beloved daughter, we are all sinners; but our Protestant hearts are not set solely on the empire of this world. In this we are justified; we know how to be poor, to risk our lives and wait — for freedom's sake — and freedom is in God."

Queen Jeanne paused, her burning gaze dwelt on Princess Margot's white face, in which the eyes were now quite shut. And Margot was thinking: " These Protestants are dangerous. My mother is right, they are dangerous indeed. They must be mastered, as Mamma intends — at least, I suspect she does. She is but waiting until she has my Henri in safe keeping, my country lad, my noble soldier, with his high heart and yet another possession that will be more to my own taste." So Margot pondered, while Jeanne laid a hand on one of her knees. It was a possessive and yet appealing gesture.

" Come! " she said, in that rare and ringing tone of hers. " Accept the true faith. You will be happier than you have ever dreamed of. So shall this land know unity and freedom."

At whose cost? Charles IX's sister asked herself behind those closed eyes. And she knew that it could never be. At the same time she noticed that this strange woman was about to behave as no queen ever should. The grip on her knee was tightening; the Queen was clearly sinking towards the floor. Unless Margot did something at once, the Queen would be at her feet. So she promptly seized Jeanne by the wrist.

" Madame, you think too highly of me. Perhaps I am no more than what you called a whited sepulchre. My brother is the King of France. My father was so too — both Catholics, and that is my faith also. We cannot change it, even if I would. I, daughter of all the Catholic kings, cannot sit at your pastors' feet. But your son need not go to Mass as yet; I will be patient."

"You will keep him at this abandoned court?" She spoke in a sobered, chilly tone and with a familiarity that now meant no more than contempt. She masked her growing dislike to serve her high unalterable purpose. Who was this girl who smelt so strong of musk? What could her ill will uphold or change?

"Oh!" breathed Margot, her heart full of sorrow and sympathy for this unhappy woman. "Your son will soon learn how to demean himself at court, I shall be at his side. I cannot indeed become a Protestant, but I shall agree very well with my simple Protestant, of that I am sure." And she had much more to say, for the Princesse de Valois was a ready talker. But every word she uttered rang false and embittered Henri's mother against her, though that she could not guess. Suddenly the face of her suitor's little sister flashed into her mind, the insignificant child, of whom until then she had never even thought. She recalled it at that moment because the portal into the next room, or rather the embroidered tapestry before it, stirred faintly. Margot raised her voice and went on:

"If I did not regard your son as my friend and master, Madame, your sweet daughter would surely make me love him. We have no such maid here, 'tis the first time I have met one like her, and — pardon my pedantry — she is surely an incarnation of one of the royal shepherdesses of antiquity."

And at that very instant Catherine came in. Her mother Jeanne, who had not seen the Florentine tapestry move, started back, and for one moment she credited her daughter-in-law with magic powers, Catherine being barefooted in a white nightgown, with her hair about her shoulders. Fair as she was, and innocent of face, Margot's shepherdesses must have looked much as she did. Margot, for her part, feigned a discreet and decorous surprise. She stood up and opened her arms a little, in welcome to so lovely a vision.

Then Queen Jeanne knew her for a whited sepulchre and looked away in indignation at having been so nearly tricked, while her daughter said confidingly to the regal Margot: "I had a cough today and had to lie in bed and drink ass's milk.

Madame, I wish you could see the little ass, my foster-brother, he is so pretty."

" You are much prettier, little one," cried Madame, kissed her sister-in-law, and began to prattle to her in childish fashion, to Catherine's seeming delight. Jeanne, indeed, was no longer listening, she was looking round at this alien and indifferent room. It was the same everywhere. Pictured tapestries, carved coffers, heavy lowering ceilings, the bed darkened by hangings and a tester, and the deep-embrasured windows; all secret and furtive, splendour ominous of evil, when the reality behind it could be glimpsed — and the people! — Jeanne shuddered, she knew not wholly why.

The Princess knew more than the Queen. She had kept her ears open at court and marked the faces of her mother and her royal brother when they whispered together. As she held the innocent Catherine in her arms she felt a strange impulse stir within her; perhaps her conscience. Perhaps the pride and arrogance that scorns any traffic with deceit. " You are so pretty, Madame," quavered Catherine, her voice rising into a timorous little shriek on the final syllables, " my brother ought to see you today. You like him, don't you? "

" I do," replied Margot, but she thought with growing indignation: " This must not be. I must tell them the truth."

" Where is your little dog, Madame? 'Tis the sweetest little dog I have ever seen."

" I'll give it you." Margot put the child down. She must warn these people. " Let me give you some advice." Margot leaned forward and looked Jeanne urgently in the eyes. For the first time, in the stress of her purpose, her calm and presence of mind deserted her. Her breath came in gasps, and her nose looked actually longer. " But you must not say that it was I that gave it you."

Splendour ominous of evil, thought Jeanne. And she said: " I know that I am being tricked, and that there are schemes for my betrayal."

" If it were no more than that! You must leave the court, Madame! " cried Margot, her voice rising to a shriek; the pose of generosity at which she aimed had turned to naked terror. And she went on in a sudden whisper: " Can we be heard? Take this sweet creature and flee to the South while you yet can. If you would win any part of the game you must not be here — nor must your son."

But Margot was met with obstinacy and unbelief at this her noblest moment. Jeanne determined not to believe in any perils. Margot could make no impression on that faded face, so she held out a trembling hand towards Catherine; perhaps the child would help. Her eyes moved from Jeanne's to the daughter's face, but the look in them was meant for Jeanne. She should watch Margot's dark eyes bring into the child's clear eyes a foreknowledge that soon turned to fear.

Jeanne remained unmoved, though she fell into a flush of anger as her daughter grew pale and trembled. " Enough," she said imperiously; " go back to bed, my child." And not until the door had closed behind Catherine, and the Florentine tapestry was still, did Jeanne reply to the Princess of Valois's counsel and warning.

" Madame, I understand. Your purpose is to make me hesitant and fearful, and you have been charged to do so by the Queen, your mother. Tell her — have you found me utterly cast down? And let me tell you that the Lord Admiral has gained from the King all that we Protestants demand. As for your creed, you need take no final resolve until you have seen that this court declare war on Spain. And you shall see it! And my son, your betrothed, will not come to Paris until our party is gathered here in strength."

" Very well, Madame," said Margot. The poor Queen shook and her bosom heaved as she spoke these proud words; but Charles IX's sister, cool as ever, felt no more motions of conscience or any generosity. She thought, as at the beginning of this encounter, that these were very dangerous people; her mother was right, they must be mastered. But they were wreaking their own ruin, quite in classic fashion, reflected that learned Princess.

" Very well, Madame," said Margot. " I will ponder on your

words." A low curtsy. " And when I have decided yours is the wiser party, I must needs make your religion mine. I hope that the Lord Admiral will bring the Prince, my betrothed, that we may all be together." Another deep curtsy, a waft of musk, and Madame Marguerite was gone.

Jeanne went in to her daughter, who greeted her with wide blue eyes. When Jeanne was beside the bed, the child threw both arms round her neck.

" I'm afraid, Mamma — afraid! "

THE LETTERS

Later on, both women wrote to Henri at Pau. Letters were commonly written in different rooms of the castle, and Catherine secretly slipped hers into the hand of Jeanne's messenger. Jeanne wrote: " Hear as many sermons as you can, and go daily to prayer. Brush your hair back, but not in the former fashion. You must come upon the court as young and gay and debonair. But stir not from Béarn until I write again."

And Catherine: " Madame has given me a lovely little dog and invited me to such grand dinners. She likes me very much. If I now tell you, brother, that I am afraid, I know you will not understand. You said to send a courier at the first sign of danger. I see no danger, but I send a courier. Take care! I saw in your eyes when we parted that you were warning me to take care of our dear mother. She will soon be going with the whole court to Paris, where we have many enemies. I shall keep my eyes open, but would that you were here! "

In May, Jeanne d'Albret wrote to her son Henri from Paris, where she was living in the house of the Prince of Condé. She sat at evening by an open window; her lamp flickered in the warm air.

" I have a picture of Madame Margot for you, which I send you with this letter. There is little here that pleases me, save only Madame's face, and that is truly beautiful. The Queen of France rakes me with a dung-fork, and your Margot remains a papist. I strove with her in vain. I have the one satisfaction that

I can tell Elizabeth of England that your marriage is now fixed. My son, I cannot tell whether I shall always be there to shield you from the temptations of this court. Be not led astray, neither in life nor in faith."

In another room the little sister scrawled in secret:

" A word in haste of what has happened to us today. We go to shops here where Mamma buys what will be needed for your wedding. Today we were with Madame's portrait-painter, as we wanted to choose the nicest portrait, and a number of people gathered outside and murmured against us. They grew louder and more threatening until the guards drove them away. Mamma said they were just a mob of Paris idlers, but I am sure they were murmuring against your marriage. The people here are against it, and they try to pick quarrels with Protestants. I made several of our gentlemen admit it was so. I am not the sort of child that people think. The wicked old Queen has a whole regiment of maids of honour, they have many friends everywhere and stir them up against us, but especially against the Lord Admiral. He came here with fifty horsemen. Madame Catherine hates the Lord Admiral because he is such a powerful leader of the Protestants. I must not say a reckless one, for I am only a girl. I have to write all this in haste, as the horseman is waiting in the courtyard below for me to throw this letter down, and my light is going out, so I must seal it up."

While Catherine was dabbing the wax on paper, the flame flared for the last time from the lamp and went out. Jeanne's lamp was still alight, and she went on: " Coligny is more resolute than ever, which brings me comfort. He calls for war in Flanders, and the Queen cannot resist him, although she falsely protests that no one will join us, neither England nor the Protestant princes of Germany. After all, she is no more than an old woman, but the King, her son, is afraid of the Lord Admiral, and loves him for that reason, and calls him father. When they met again for the first time, Coligny knelt, though in thought and purpose he humbles himself before God alone, not before Charles IX; still, the King is indeed at his beck and call, loads him with honours, and does nothing without his counsel. The

King has given the Admiral a hundred thousand crowns to
restore his burnt castle of Châtillon. The Lord Admiral is now
there. But the King has stayed behind at Blois to enjoy the
company of a new mistress. The Lord Admiral is right; this gives
us the chance to force Madame Catherine out of power. So now,
my son, make ready and set forth! "

Thus Jeanne; and the messenger, a nobleman of Béarn, bestowed it safely on his person, thinking to ride off at break of
dawn. In his charge, at least, he believed the letters of the
Queen and her daughter would be safe. Meantime, on his way
back to his lodging, he was assailed by some drunken men; in
spite of the darkness he recognized that they belonged to the
Queen of France's bodyguard. He laid about him, but received
a blow that brought him down. When he got up, his assailants
and the letters had vanished.

They promptly came into the hands of Catherine de Medici,
who opened them without breaking the seals. Alone in her
bedroom she read the self-betrayal of her enemy and her enemy's
daughter, and Madame Catherine was glad. She was glad because she always enjoyed the unmasking of conspiracies. The
wickedness of life and of humanity confirmed her mind and
character and stiffened her to action. She sat rigid in her high
wooden chair and stared over the letters, which she now knew by
heart, by the light of two white wax candles; six had been burning in the room, but the others she had snuffed out with her
stumpy fingers. The candlelight edged the yellow sagging masses
of chin and cheeks; the upper part of her face was in shadow,
through which the eyes, usually dull and black, glimmered like
kindled coals. Whatever passed across the old Queen's inner
vision, in that room she saw, picked out against the darkness,
only certain fragments of the painted panelling — lips parted in
a shriek, a brandished knife. Then, as a gust of air flattened the
candle flame, she caught a nymph's lascivious smile, and the
hand that clutched at her.

Madame Catherine pondered; by her enemy's plain words she
was to be forced from power. This foolish woman already conceived herself as in power; Madame Catherine alone and de-

serted, and her son the King as the tool of a rebel, whom her tribunal had condemned to be hanged on the Place de Grève. That judgment still stood. Did the enemy not know that her son Charles was often a prey to remorse? And though that might not be his better mood, he went in fear of his brother Anjou, who was the old lady's favourite because he hated women. She would threaten the elder with the younger brother. He knew how quickly death came to the Valois. No, whatever her good friend Jeanne might imagine, she would not rouse the King of Spain, and certainly would not support the Dutch Leaguers against him. Otherwise Philip would give her throne to the Guises, and she would in truth be lost. She must deal as roundly with those arch-Catholics the Guises as with these heretics. First these, then those. Yet a little while and her good friend Jeanne should live to see strange things. Did she say — live?

Madame Catherine thought, all unaware that she was thinking. Her spirit revelled in that moment, exalted beyond all fear into a very recklessness of evil. Thought outruns what deeds seem likely to accomplish; and yet thought leads us to that accomplishment.

In the meantime she paid due heed to the present, but was well aware of all that passed in the palace at that hour. The Louvre was bolted and barred at eleven o'clock, and just before that hour there was a mighty scurry of courtiers hastening to get out; the call would be heard for the third time in a moment, and then the gates would close. The King's archers were still tramping along all the corridors to clear them of stragglers. But when they had passed, there would be whisperings at half-open doors, and the women would let in men. Madame Catherine knew and said nothing. The Captain of the King's bodyguard appeared and asked for the password for the night. "Amor," said Madame Catherine.

She gave some further orders to the Captain, bidding him approach her chair and speaking in a low tone. The six yellow tapers in the ante-room were then extinguished, and that night not one of the great linen lanterns shed its pallid reflection upon the stairways. Twelve o'clock had struck when, escorted by a torchbearer, a muffled figure entered the old Queen's bedroom, but did not shut the door until the officer had departed. Then Charles flung off his cloak. His mother was still sitting where she had sat for hours; she turned her fleshy old face towards him, and as the light flickered across it, her son recoiled.

" I have sent for you in good time, my son, and it was needful that you should come at night. Things have reached the pass when we act. Read these! " She put the letters into his hand. Charles spelt them out and then crashed his fist on the table. In his face was fear as well as anger. His suspicious eyes blinked sidelong, as they always did. And Catherine thought: " An ill-conditioned youth. 'Tis fortunate I have two sons left. The next likes boys, and I shall be the only woman in his life. The last is a crack-brain, I must be on my guard against him."

" I am always thinking of your welfare, my son," said the old woman. " You have lain too long in your mistress's arms at Blois; and now you have sore need of your mother's store of strength to save your throne."

" Let the woman die! " panted Charles, as his veins swelled and throbbed. His face was bloated, and covered with a short and straggling beard, which hung in reddish wisps above his upper lip; but his under lip, usually tight shut in token of his hatred of humanity, now sagged and quivered, for Charles was horribly afraid.

As he cried: " Let the woman die! " he thrust his great head out of his starched ruff, and the two pearls in his bulbous ears bobbed and glittered.

" The Lord Admiral," said the old woman, " whom you call Father — nay, pray call him so, if only to deceive him — the old rebel threatens me openly, and that scarecrow Queen of his has told me to my face she does not fear me. She said she knew I did not eat up little children — Pyrenean goat! She knows nothing. I will surely eat her children up. The girl has written such a touching letter, and it shall duly reach her brother, who is a bold and chivalrous lad and will certainly come; and then I'll use

him as decoy for all these poisonous Huguenots. Paris is swarming with them now, but there'll be more of them still when their
gay young Prince arrives."

Her voice had dropped to little more than a whisper. " Then
we have them. That mob of bragging Gascons have but one
head, and that we can easily cut off. Silence! " she added sharply,
for Charles was about to burst out again with his " Let the
woman die! " She could see it from his face. Meantime
Madame Catherine was poised over a spiritual abyss; would the
deed succeed the thought or would it not? " The Duke of Alba
once said to me," she observed, letting her words fall from her
one by one, " ' Ten thousand frogs are not a salmon.' And I
answered: ' Salmon might mean two people.' "

She eyed him long and fixedly, though he would not look her
in the face. " We also are but two," she said suddenly, this
time in her usual smooth and throaty voice. He recoiled in such
a flush of terror, snatching for a chair that was not there, that
he collapsed on the floor at her feet. " Stay," said his mother,
and thenceforward spoke into his ear — and spoke for so long
that the May morning was already glimmering behind the curtains when the King left Madame Catherine's chamber.

Kings Must Not Look Pale

The officer with the torch appeared at the angle of the passage, where he had been waiting all night — if, indeed, he had
not been listening at the door. Charles followed him, possessed
by hate and fear. The Captain escorted him to his bedroom;
he bellowed at the guards in the ante-room until they awoke,
leapt up from their benches, and crashed their halberds to the
floor. Charles peered from the corners of his eyes at every face
as the torchlight laid it bare. Then he went to bed.

But he could not sleep: faces rose behind his eyelids —
enemies all, and among them those last seen, the faces of his
own bodyguard. Once he thought he saw the door open —
slowly, very slowly, until he noticed that his eyes were shut.
Then he blinked cautiously: nothing — only the pallid glimmer

of a wick afloat in oil. Charles could endure the night no longer; he got up, slunk out through a side entrance, and by devious ways returned to his own ante-room; he was still clad in his nightshirt. His bodyguards lay scattered about the room asleep on their benches; in the midst of them stood the Captain, erect with folded arms, and an absorbed look on his face, as Charles was quick to notice. The look of a conspirator! The man at once assumed a vacant air when he knew himself observed; this increased the misgivings of the King, who stopped in the doorway and looked about him to see if help were near. Then he laid his hand to his lips and whispered:

" Amaury, you are my friend, and I trust you. But when I caught sight of your Lieutenant's face in the torchlight I knew it for a traitor's face. Pick a quarrel with him and rid me of the man. Go down into the courtyard, I'll send him after you."

The Captain obeyed; then Charles whispered to the Lieutenant, who had just awakened, and told him to deal promptly with the Captain. " Run him through, then shout out that he drew on you."

He crept back into his bedchamber and did not emerge until he heard the soldiers' cries. " What is this? Make way! " he cried imperiously, although still in his nightshirt. The men behind him were silent, and Charles, trembling with cold and his own excitement, bent over the winding stair. Far below, in a patch of grey daylight, lay a prostrate form. Someone waved a sword and shouted: " Murder! " Then from behind Charles his mother's unruffled voice. " Tell the man to be quiet and come up." Not till then did Charles observe that she had dismissed the soldiers. He signed to the murderer below. Meantime Madame Catherine discovered by a few curt questions what this unruly son of hers had done.

" Ligneroles," she said, when the young man's head appeared above the stairway, " you have done the King a service."

" It was gladly done, Madame," said the young man, and he went on cheerfully: " Captain Amaury was a secret Huguenot. He had guessed your plans against his party and was in a sore bait about them, and he made known to me this very night what is in store. Ha! I'll be there, Madame. 'Twill be a grand and glorious butchery! "

Charles, still in his nightshirt, heard, and shook until he had to lean against the wall. It was well that young Ligneroles stood before him, and Madame Catherine kept her eye upon them both. And she spoke in her rich and throaty voice: " You have proved yourself a true man this day and deserve a cordial; come! " She waddled before him to her bedchamber, opened a low, deep cupboard, studded with huge square nails, and poured him out a glass of wine.

" Now go and sleep," said she, when Ligneroles had drained his glass and looked suddenly exhausted. " You are excused duty for today," she added amiably as the man stumbled out of the room, unhearing. She watched him to the stairway; he stopped, stood rigid, and pitched head foremost down it. Catherine de Medici closed the door with a complacent air.

" He has broken his neck," she said placidly. " I had to do it to bring back the colour to your cheeks, my son. The affair is at an end. 'Tis only grey morning light that makes us both look pale."

The Same Morning Hour Elsewhere

That same dawn rose in a shimmer of pink and orange upon the garden at Nérac, where it found Henri of Navarre, who could not tear himself away from Fleurette, the seventeen-year-old daughter of the gardener.

" You must go, beloved. My father is astir, and if he should see you, what would he think? "

" Nothing evil, dear one. A faithful servant of my mother cannot believe that I would do aught to hurt him."

" You do him none by loving me. You will but hurt me when you go."

" But a Prince must be always riding through the land, to battle or — "

" Or whither? "

" That you need not know, Fleurette. You would be none
the happier, and let us be happy together, until the day when
we must part."

" Is it true? Are you happy with me? "

" I was never so happy! Have I ever seen such a dawn as
this? 'Tis as lovely as your cheeks, never shall I forget it. And
these flowers I shall remember all my life."

" The dawn lasts but a little while, and flowers are soon faded.
I must stay here, waiting. However far you may ride, and whatever may befall you, remember me — and the little room where
we loved, the scent of flowers through the window, and my lips
that you — "

" Fleurette! "

" — Have kissed for the last time. Go, or they will come to
fetch you, and I would not that others should see your last look
of farewell."

" Then let us drown it in the stream. Come, Fleurette — our
arms about each other. Now look down into the water-mirror
and see how our eyes meet. You are seventeen, Fleurette."

" And you eighteen, my dear."

" But when we are old this stream shall remember us, and
even when we are dead."

" Henri, I can no longer see your face."

" Yours too is blurred, Fleurette."

" I heard a drop fall. A tear! Was it yours or was it mine? "

" Ours," said Henri's voice, from a distance now, while she
stood wiping her eyes. " Fleurette! " and he had gone. She knew
too well her image had passed out of his mind; he was flinging
the name of a vanished hour in challenge to many a future hour
of which she knew nothing and where her feeble name must
soon be lost.

Henri mounted his horse. The May breeze blew freshly
against that bold straight brow that dipped slightly at the
temples, and ruffled the auburn hair. He had not smoothed it
before he left the little room, and it lay as it grew by nature.
For five hundred paces his merry eyes still spoke of that farewell,

and then, as he rode on, they cleared. There was a flower between his lips; Fleurette. When he came up with his companions, the flower had gone.

Fleurette, a gardener's daughter, seventeen years old, went about her daily tasks. She did so for twenty years, and then she died; at that time her lover was a great King. She had never seen him again, or only as a mighty sovereign, who once after a disaster came back to his native town of Nérac to find happiness again, but this time with others. Whence came the rumour she died for love of him? As time went on, it was said that she had died on the day he left her, and the story went that she had thrown herself into the stream — that very stream into which the boy and girl had peered down side by side. A strange legend, for there had been none to see that parting.

Jesus

Henri rode onwards as a prince must do, to battle or to marriage. Henri of Navarre was to be married and must ride out of Gascony to Paris; but he was a sinewy youth. He and his little company were in the saddle for fourteen hours and more, if need was, and they minded their horses well, for they had not always money to buy others; unless indeed they carried off a nag or two from the roadside pastures.

In the van, but never without escort, rode Henri, and many horsemen followed in his train. Not for an instant was he, or any man of them, alone; they lived in the clatter of hoofs and the reek of horse-flesh, in the sweat of their steaming clothes and harness. Henri's grey horse carried him well, but in truth it was that whole company of adventurers, men like unto himself, devout and debonair, which carried him forward faster than he could conceive; like a magic chariot that cavalcade transported him from town to town. The trees burgeoned into blossom white and red, soft breezes blew from heaven, the young adventurers laughed, sang, and bickered. Now and again they dismounted, ate enormously, and gulped down great draughts of wine, which to them was as much an element as earth and air.

Tawny girls came unsummoned and sat on the knees of those brown-cheeked lads; and an impromptu catch, or a bold embrace, as lewd as might be, made them blush and scream. Among themselves, while riding onwards, they constantly discussed religion.

Henri's company were all of them in the twenties more or less, rebels to a man, reviling the established order and those in authority, whom they conceived as having turned their backs on God. Such were not God's purposes. He shared the views of youth. Hence they all believed devoutly in their cause and feared not the Devil himself, still less the court of France. On the road, while still in the South, old Huguenots came forth to meet them and conjured the Prince of Navarre to be on his guard. He knew these old folk, they were hidebound in suspicion. " My good friends," said he, " 'twill all be different now. I am to marry the King's sister. You shall worship as you please, my word upon it! "

" Freedom shall be restored! " came shouts from all that cavalcade.

" The sovereignty of the people! "

" Justice! Justice! "

" I say — Freedom! "

That was their most potent word. Thus provided and equipped, the cavalcade rode northwards. Many, perhaps most of them, understood this word to mean that they should dispossess from their power and pleasures those whom they conceived as free. Henri was familiar with such men, knew them in the mass, and liked them and was at ease with them. But they were not his friends. Friends are more difficult; friendship is more tense and less secure and makes demands that these men never made.

" *In summa*," said Agrippa d'Aubigné, as the train of horsemen rode onwards, " you, Prince, are merely what the populace has made of you. You may indeed be more exalted, as the object made is sometimes more exalted than the maker, but if you become a tyrant, woe upon you! Against a public tyrant the humblest occupant of office may claim every right from God."

" Agrippa," replied Henri, " if you are right, I shall seek some very humble office. But these are pastors' sophistries; a king is always a king."

" Be glad that you are but the Prince of Navarre! "

D'Aubigné was short, he did not reach as far as Henri above his horse's head. He gesticulated as he talked — his fingers were long and slender, and the thumbs curiously stubbed. His mouth was large and quizzical, and he had an inquiring eye; a man of this world, indeed, but at thirteen he had stood out against attempts to convert him from the Protestant faith, and at fifteen he was fighting for the Religion under Condé. Henri eighteen, Agrippa twenty, old comrades, who had fallen out and made it up a hundred times.

He rode to the right of Henri. From the Prince's left came a clear and resolute voice chanting:

> " Monarchs, slaves of your own folly,
>
> You with corpses strew the plains
>
> That you may win a hair's breadth more
>
> To add to your domains.
>
> Judges, who in holy places
>
> Sell the common weal:
>
> Shall your son lay up a treasure
>
> For you to steal? "

" Friend du Bartas," said Henri, " how comes it that so cheerful a gamecock crows so savagely? You will frighten all the girls away."

" My words are not for girls; they are for you, dear Prince."

" For the judges too. Pray not to forget the judges, du Bartas. Otherwise only your wicked kings are left."

" Wicked because they are blind like the rest of us. We must reform ourselves. Not in the matter of girls — I'll not give them up as yet, but I'll break myself of lewd verses. I'll compose none but pious verses in future."

" Do you mean to die so soon? " asked Henri.

" I mean one day to die fighting for you, Navarre, and for God's kingdom."

At these words Henri was silent. He never forgot that poem, " Monarchs, slaves of your own folly," and he privately resolved that no man should ever lie dead upon the ground for his sake, nor shed his blood to increase the domains of France.

" Du Bartas," he said suddenly, " stand up in your stirrups." The tall noble did so, and the Prince looked up at him with an air of ironic admiration.

" Can you see anything yet of Madame Catherine and her palace of delights? Her lovely maids of honour are expecting you."

" You too, I fancy," said Agrippa d'Aubigné, with a mocking wink. " Ah, I forgot, you are a chaste bridegroom. Still — "

They all laughed, and Henri most of all.

Came a voice from behind: " Have a care, sirs! Love at the court of France has brought many a man what he has had to carry with him to his death."

More laughter. Then someone thrust his horse forward until he had reached the Prince's side, heedless of the others' furious looks. His was the most vivid face of all, but the high forehead cramped the features and made it seem small. The eyes had read much and were sad, though Philippe du Plessis-Mornay was only twenty-four and was to live until he was seventy-four.

" God has laid His command upon me," he announced. " I have prepared a discourse that will move the King to establish freedom of faith and to defend the cause of the Netherlands against Spain."

" Give your discourse to the Lord Admiral," said Henri. " He will get a hearing for it. They do not fear us yet, but I fancy they soon will."

They spoke unheard by all the rest, who were busy recounting the joys in store for them at court. The perils, too, were vociferously debated, and in detail. The name of the dread disease was uttered. Philippe Mornay, in a sudden flush of fervour, cried:

" I care not if I be infected, so Charles IX grants freedom for our creed."

" You will be a repulsive sight."

" We are all repulsive sometimes; what matter, in the sight of eternity? Is not Jesus, too, repulsive, a God crucified? But we believe in Him. We believe in His disciples, the very refuse of humanity, and even in the Jews. What did He leave behind Him but a woman distraught, a memory scorned, and the reputation of a fool among His own people. If emperors contended against His teachings with the sword and with the law, so too does every man today contend against himself in his own heart. The flesh against the spirit! But the nations have bowed down before the word of these few men, and the empires worship a crucified Jesus. Jesus! " exclaimed Mornay with such vehemence that all listened and looked round to see whence He would come forth. Not one of those men doubted that He would appear among them when the hour struck.

In the minds of every one of them His wounds were fresh and bleeding, and the tears of Mary flowed unstaunched. Golgotha — they could see it with their bodily eyes, a bleak and barren hill looming against darkling clouds. They approached it between their own olive-trees and fig-trees, and they had sat at the wedding of Cana. His story matched the times in which they lived; now for the first time they knew Him as they knew themselves. He was of their company, save that He surpassed them in holiness, and also, as du Plessis-Mornay had dared to say, in repulsiveness of aspect. Suppose the Son of man came forth from yonder cluster of rocks and took command? His steed would, of course, no longer be an ass, but a war-horse. He Himself would be arrayed in doublet and cuirass, and they would gather round Him crying: " Sire! Last time You were defeated by Your enemies and crucified. This time, with us, You will be victorious. Have at them! "

Such would have been the demeanour of the simple Huguenots had Jesus appeared to them in bodily form. The Jews and the soldiery were represented by the papists of their own day, whom their main purpose was to dispossess, to their own en-

richment. But for Prince Henri and his friends the case was not
so clear. They were beset by misgivings over what should be
done if Jesus came. Du Bartas asked the others whether, if
Jesus returned and His story were to start once more, they should
then advise Him to escape crucifixion, since therein lay His
destiny and the salvation of the world. And he shrugged his
gaunt shoulders, for no one could offer him an answer. Du
Plessis drew an even harsher picture of what he called the repulsion of the Crucified. Du Plessis-Mornay was prone to extremes,
in spite of his Socratic air, and liked himself so well that he thus
continued until his four-and-seventieth year. Poor du Bartas
was plagued by the blindness and the wickedness of men and by
the impossibility of bettering the world or even of acquiring any
knowledge at all, so he was fated to go early, though he passed
in the clamour of a battle. As for Agrippa d'Aubigné, his heart
was kindled from the very moment when du Plessis called so
roundly upon Jesus. In that minute Agrippa had begun to compose a poem, and he was pretty well prepared to welcome Jesus
in verse as soon as He appeared. All that Agrippa did was born
of passion and the hour. This made him a cheerful man, and
his Prince liked him for being so. On the other hand, Henri
was drawn to du Bartas and his anxious, faithful heart. But the
violent du Plessis he loved most of all.

Henri knew, far better than any of his company, that the
fellowship of Jesus was not for him or his. They had, in his
opinion, no more prospect of such an honour than if they had
been Catholics. He was not sure the Lord preferred them,
though He probably liked them best. Apart from this attitude
of mind, which was private to himself, he shared all the feelings
of that cavalcade. Since that appeal to Jesus, Henri's eyes had
been filled with tears. He was doubtful whether those tears were
for his Lord. When they started forth, perhaps; but not when
they reached his eyelids. The image of Jesus was effaced by the
countenance of Queen Jeanne, and Henri wept because to his
inner vision Jeanne seemed paler than she had ever been. She
had long been travelling up and down the land in the company
of her preaching pastors, with nowhere to lay her head, like

Jesus, and, like Him, hated and despised; and she faced battle, the hazards of war, turmoil and flight: she, a woman, and his mother. Hard was the road she trod in the cause of the faith. Perhaps indeed she was nearing Golgotha. For, after all, she was in Catherine's hands, as the Lord Admiral had dismissed the Protestant army and contented himself with threatening the old Queen. Until the next campaign imperilled her again, Catherine had the upper hand. This journey that was to end in marriage was really made at her command; on that point Henri did not deceive himself. He commonly held fast to facts; he was not blinded by faith, like Coligny, nor by his own frowardness, like his mother Jeanne.

A FACE TRANSFORMED

He carried the letters under his doublet, aching to read them all again, and his sister's too. But he lived wholly in that company of horsemen, his days were passed under the sun and his nights under the stars, and he was never alone. Week upon week they rode, the country wore the aspect of the North, and Henri cared little for it now. All his life long the kingdom moved beneath his horse's hoofs, for as he rode, it sped beneath him and bore him on his way. He had the sense of an infinite and unending movement, and he was sometimes conscious that the movement was not his alone; the land of France was astir, in whose still dark destinies he was himself to become involved. And so, upon the road ahead of him, night brooded under the tree-tops and awaited his approach.

" Agrippa, what may we really expect at the court of France? "

" Really? " repeated d'Aubigné. " One event is your wedding, which will surely be a noble festival. But, if you would really know: all the tribulations of the saints."

" Say you all because you know not which? "

" Even so, Henri. You too are aware of somewhat at this hour while the bats and fireflies circle round our heads. In the daylight such forebodings vanish."

They spoke in low tones: such talk was not for their companions' ears.

" Are we to sleep in a town tonight? "

" At Chaunay, sir."

" Chaunay in Poitou. Good. There I will decide."

" What? "

" Whether I shall go on. I must consider this quickly, and again read the Queen my mother's letters undisturbed. See that I have a room to myself, Agrippa."

But when they had sat for two hours at the long tables outside the inn at Chaunay, the Prince of Navarre no longer felt disposed for solitude; indeed he had motioned to a long-limbed lass to precede him up the stairs or, rather, up the ladder. As he made to follow her, he heard some yells, mostly from the bass voice of a stout matron, who was dragging a whimpering girl out of the room and down the ladder, while a figure stood below with the butt of a lighted taper: Agrippa d'Aubigné. It was clear that he had fetched the girl's mother and tricked his friend Henri; but far from looking ashamed, he was laughing. Henri whipped out his sword. " Draw! " he shouted in a fury.

What did the poet Agrippa do? He ripped a rung out of the ladder and brandished it in response. The ladder tipped over as he did so, the women shrieked, jumped off it, and fell on the two men, who were hurled sprawling on the ground. When Henri had struggled out of the mêlée, he found himself abandoned in the pitch darkness. What had become of the others — and where was the ladder? However, he was thankful to be able to grope his way out of the inn. Under a bush, through which the stars were twinkling, he fell asleep.

He awoke to the dawn of a June day, the 13th of that month, a day he was never destined to forget. A lark was soaring upwards from the meadows, singing, into the pale blue of heaven. Overhead rustled the scented foliage of an elder-bush, from near at hand came the ripple of a brook, and an avenue of quivering poplars masked the town. The freshness of the morning flung his cares away, he walked back and forward under the poplars, once and yet again — in mere enjoyment of the fresh, sweet air. Then he remembered the letters which he had meant to read and consider. He stopped, took them from beneath his doublet, and shuffled them like a pack of cards. Why read them? The decisive fact was his marriage with fat Margot — "Madame," as his little sister called her. In that regard, both ladies, Jeanne and Catherine, were at one. The rest must be left to fate — whether the Lord Admiral would outwit the old poisoner, and whether his little bride was to remain a papist and go down to hell. He thought it very doubtful. He himself had been a papist more than once and ripe for hell-fire. It was possible, but none could tell. So much was certain: never would his strict Huguenot mother preside over so alluring a court, where the women offered their favours to the men. His mother had written those very words, he knew them by heart.

And then it happened: he saw her — not with the usual vision of the inner eye, but incomparably more clear; he saw the face of Queen Jeanne against a background that was not the greying air. In a flash of harsh and vivid light he recognized his mother as one no longer of this world. These were not the features marked upon his memory when the leathern coach drove off and the son was left standing at his horse's side. Sunken cheeks — and shadows, heart-rending as the desire for all that we have lost, encompassed her, as with the frail integument of something that has ceased to be. Great eyes, no longer proud nor hard nor loving, that knew him no longer — though now they know much that was hidden from this world.

The son flung himself down on a grassy slope; his carefree mood had fled, he was stricken with fear, not only by this strange image of his mother, but because, as he now remembered, it had already come to him in dream. Four nights ago, surely, he reckoned and he pondered, frowning as he sat still shuffling the letters like a pack of cards. But as he looked at them more closely, he observed that two of them had been secretly opened before he had himself broken the seals. Four nights ago? The slit round the seals was dexterously done, and a dab of wax had made the damage good. Four nights ago — and again just now — why?

The last sentence in his mother's last letter ran: "Now, my son, make ready and set forth." Now he knew: Queen Jeanne intended to dispossess Madame Catherine, and the Medici had read that letter. His mother was in peril of her life! — he leapt to his feet and dashed back through the poplars. " Armagnac! " he shouted, catching sight of his servant before the man had noticed him. " Armagnac, to horse at once! There is no time to lose! "

" But, my lord," the man made bold to reply, " no one is afoot yet and the bread is still to be baked."

Henri was always accessible to facts. He yielded: " Very well, but we must be in Paris in five days. I shall go and bathe in the river. Get me a clean shirt, Armagnac."

" I had meant to wash your shirts today, sir. I had thought we should be tarrying here." The young noble who was acting as Henri's body-servant winked at his master. " That little affair of the ladder — shall we not set it up again and make good what was missed? "

" Rascal! " cried Henri in honest indignation. " I'll wallow no more in straw. Every man must be mounted by the time I get back from my bathe." And he dashed off, untying his points as he ran. When he came back they started, but barely a quarter of an hour had passed when a courier galloped towards them, flung himself from his horse, and gasped out, staggering so heavily that he had to be propped up from behind: " From Paris — five days' riding in four days." His face was blotched, his tongue was hanging out, and, stranger still, great tears were rolling from his staring anguished eyes. They could be heard dripping on to his jerkin, so deep was the surrounding silence.

Henri reached down his hand and took the proffered letter; but he made no move to open it. He let his arm fall, bent his head forward, and in the deep silence of the little group of horsemen islanded in that great plain he said in a low tone: " My mother is dead. Four days ago." He was speaking to himself, as the others realized. They feigned not to hear until he spoke to them; even those rude hearts were moved. Then, when the new King of Navarre had read the message, he uncovered; all the rest did likewise; and he said to them: " The Queen, my mother, is dead."

Some exchanged glances, which was all they ventured as yet. This was no common event of every day. It foreboded changes they could not foresee and transformed them into what they could not tell. Jeanne d'Albret meant too much to them, they could not picture her as dead. She had led and fostered them, she had helped them to their daily bread and to the bread of eternal life. Their liberties had been won for them by Jeanne. Their strong places, like the sea-fortress of La Rochelle, it was she who had seized and held them fast. But for her defiance there would have been no chapels at the town gates. The peace of the countryside, where the women tilled the fields under God's guardianship while the men rode forth and fought for the Religion — all this was the gift of Jeanne d'Albret, and what would now become of it?

Then their thoughts changed to horror, turned to wrath, and grasped savagely at the suspicion of guilt and crime. Such disasters do not happen by themselves. The dead woman had baffled great ambitions, they all knew whose. In that isolated company thought and feeling were at one, no words were needed. Vague mutterings like those in a dream grew slowly louder and swelled into a menacing clamour; at last the word that was present to them all leapt out of the scabbard — as though a second courier, this time unseen, had proclaimed it: " The Queen was poisoned."

The words were shouted from a hundred throats, each man echoing the unseen messenger: " Poisoned! The Queen was poisoned! " And the dead Queen's son did likewise; the message had come to him, as to them all.

Suddenly they fell to grasping each other's hands, in an unuttered oath to avenge Jeanne d'Albret. Her son gripped the hands of his friends du Bartas, Mornay, and d'Aubigné. A special handshake made his peace with Agrippa, and that handshake meant: " Yesterday a ladder overturned, and a brawl about some woman, and today — this. No more quarrels nor regrets. This is life, and we face it hand in hand." And Henri shook hands with Armagnac, whom he had abused so heartily just before. Meanwhile, an uplifted voice was heard: "Let God, the God of battle, rise!"

It was Philippe du Plessis-Mornay, always most inclined towards extremes, and at first he sang alone; but as he repeated the first line, other voices joined him, and by the second line they all were singing. They had dismounted, joined hands together, a company unseen by all, save possibly by God, and they sang to Him on high; and the chant was like the tocsin of a storm:

> "Let God, the God of battle, rise
>
> and scatter His presumptuous foes;
>
> Let shameful rout their host surprise,
>
> who spitefully His power oppose."

HER LAST MESSENGER

They sang on until the end; then they awaited a word from their young leader. He had become King of Navarre, here on this alien highway, and he must tell them whither they should go and what they should do. Du Bartas bowed to Henri, and said in a low tone: "Your mother was the first. You will be the second. Turn back."

"Summon all your people," cried Mornay. "Those of the faith will rally round you from all the realm. Then we shall march in might against this murderous court."

"You need not fear for yourself, sir," said d'Aubigné, in a much calmer tone; "so long as one other is yet alive." The rest looked at him and he went on: "He has made the offering of his life, I know it. I heard what he said to his lady at night." And he fell to picturing the scene between Coligny and his wife.

Agrippa was a poet and could present the nocturnal conversation between the pair as though he had actually been there. "'Do you believe yourself invincible?' said the Admiral to his lady. 'Lay your hand on your heart, and ask yourself whether you would stand firm when all desert you and face the jeers that always follow upon failure, when you are driven into exile. The King of Navarre himself deserts us, and is marrying the daughter of our foe.' "

This was too much. Henri burst out at him: " That he never said. Agrippa, your muse is a lying wench. I hold fast to the Religion — and now let us ride on."

This was what Agrippa wanted; he was no man for prudent pauses, and the more perils he foreboded, the more boldly did this poet ride onwards.

So the cavalcade moved forward once more under the darkling clouds; but it was not long before people met them in the roadway, with uplifted hands, who said: " Queen Jeanne was poisoned," though none could say whence the news had come. At last no one asked them who they were and from what town they came. It was enough that they were on the way, how long a way they knew not, to see the new King of Navarre and tell him what they knew. In the weariness of the journey many had forgotten their indignation; they merely stammered out their anguished warnings.

Even a company of carefree adventurers are impressed at last by such encounters; then came a final and decisive one. On the outskirts of a wood they fell in with a Protestant gentleman whom they all knew, La Rochefoucauld, a friend of their King. He too was in the wild state of a man who had ridden a five-day stretch in four. He said but a few words to the King, but Henri at once drew rein and turned his horse. And that whole company, without a question or a word, went back to Chaunay.

Henri took Monsieur de La Rochefoucauld aside, and sought a secluded and shady place; this he found under the poplars, and demanded the whole story of his mother's death. Rochefoucauld told it. As she lay dying, Jeanne's last earthly thoughts had been for her son, before her spirit fled to God. She did not wish him to abandon his journey from fear; of that there had been no question. But her view was that he should not go to Paris at all unless he went in overwhelming force. This she urged in the light of her own bitter experiences of the last four months. She had thought — and in so saying she had dropped into that rare ringing voice of hers — that her beloved son's marriage would open great events, either for him — or for his enemies. Her last thoughts were set steadfastly on all the perils of life and the means to overcome them. She had once known times, or believed she had, when wickedness dared not show its face. Today it walked abroad, she would have her Henri know, and looked down on virtue. Then in the act of dying she offered up to God the words of a psalm. And which psalm was that?

"*Let God, the God of battle, rise.*"

Rochefoucauld had the Queen's Testament upon his person, and he handed it to the King, after touching it with his lips. In it indeed no mention was made of her most secret disquiets, for at the end she dared not put them on paper. One thing only: she commended his poor little sister to his care. At this Henri burst into tears — the first he shed.

Again and again he cried: "Poor little sister! 'Tis what our mother used to call her." And he thought: "She should be here. Whom have we at our side? Brother and sister have nothing and no one in the world, save only each other. The rest is betrayal of the eye and heart. Oh, world of women, the rapture that they bring us, and our fear that we may let but one among them slip. Truly I have let slip one only, and her, alas, too often. From her I never needed to beg for love, nor to seek for sympathy. We were born of one body and have no secrets from each other. She laughs as I do, so they say. At this hour she is shedding the same tears, and yet not even those that she is weeping for our mother are wet upon my hands. She is far away from me, as she always is, and we are wasting the best of all our grief, she mine, and I hers."

The Ambassador told him that his sister Catherine had wanted to accompany him. All preparations had been made, the horse was waiting in the courtyard, the coach at the city gates. Meantime she had been detained, not by force, but merely on various pretexts, until La Rochefoucauld had gone.

There had been attempts to detain him too; he had had to be resolute indeed.

" Is she a prisoner? " asked the brother, with dry and angry eyes, and grim lines about his lips. That, by all appearances, was not so. The court was concerned for her; especially Margot, his future bride, and old Catherine as well. The marriage ceremony, to which everyone so eagerly looked forward, darkened as it already was by the death of the Queen of Navarre, must not be exposed to any further mishaps. It would be fatal if anything befell the bridegroom's sister; she was a delicate girl, perhaps (said they) she had inherited her mother's weak lungs.

Henri leaned forward and asked in a voice that quivered: " Was it only her lungs? "

For a while no answer came, and when it did, it was no more than a shrug of the shoulders.

" Who suspects poison? " asked Henri. " Our friends alone? "

" The others far more. They know of what they are capable."

" I would rather not know," said Henri. " If I did I should have to hate them and hunt them down. Too much hatred paralyses a man."

Such was his natural feeling; life was more important than vengeance, and men of action must look forwards, not backwards at the beloved dead. Meantime there were still his duties as a son, and though he longed to be on the road once more, he forced himself to stay at Chaunay and wait for reinforcements. His Huguenots came in from every side; sometimes he sent men to meet them and guide them on their way. He meant to arrive in force, as Queen Jeanne had wished. He also sent her last instructions to his Governor in his kingdom of Béarn. When the letter was ended, Henri observed that he had laid but little stress on her charges in spiritual matters, and yet these had been nearest to his mother's heart. He was abashed to think how utterly he had forgotten religion, and added a postscript.

The envoy who brought him the news of the death and suspicious illness of the Queen had been four times four-and-twenty hours on his way. Henri took three weeks on his journey from Chaunay in Poitou. When the messenger met the new King, he was a broken man. Henri halted, put up at inns, received his followers, drank, and laughed. Laugh he surely did. The exhausted riders were amazed when they came up with him; he waved to them in welcome and jested with them in their Southern speech. In the very hour when the horseman appeared with his evil news, the son had seen a vision of his mother with a face he knew not — the face of eternity. He saw it no more, and it never returned. Instead, in the days that followed, he recalled the great lady who had guided his boyish years with her will and understanding; and indeed he marked that picture on his mind to give him heart.

Moralité

Voyez ce jeune prince déjà aux prises avec les dangers de la vie, qui sont d'être tué ou d'être trahi, mais qui se cachent aussi sous nos désirs et même parmi nos rêves généreux. C'est vrai qu'il traverse toutes ces menaces en s'en jouant, selon le privilège de son âge. Amoureux à tout bout de chemin il ne connaît pas encore que l'amour seul lui fera perdre une liberté qu'en vain la haine lui dispute. Car pour le protéger des complots des hommes et des pièges qui lui tendait sa propre nature il y avait alors une personne qui l'aimait jusqu'à en mourir et c'est celle qu'il appelait la reine ma mère.

Book Three

The Louvre

EMPTY STREETS

THE DEAD Queen's son on the way to his wedding exulted to be astride a horse, and he looked cheerfully about him. The breeze seemed to waft towards him a faint fragrance of the court, the food, the perfumed people, and the women, who offered their favours without waiting to be importuned. He looked forward to success in that quarter; he knew how to set about a woman, with all the confidence of his good looks and wit. Margot, too, should be well pleased with him; he would entertain her and make her laugh. It was not a matter that a man could tell his friends, but he was not at all repelled by his betrothed's bad reputation — indeed, he found it an allurement. However, in the meantime here were the pretty village girls, and he would often vault from his horse and kiss them. And as they scurried off they marvelled how well a Huguenot Prince could kiss.

The cavalcade had now swelled to a great concourse, and the talk among them was very different from before; the new arrivals were incensed at the murder of their Queen. They were riding to no festal gathering, unless it were a festival of vengeance. They meant to challenge every man at court. The fever of their feelings sometimes swept through the procession and caught the minds of Henri and his friends. Mornay then proclaimed all the perils that awaited them in Paris. Du Bartas bewailed the wickedness of man, and Agrippa d'Aubigné enlarged on the deep purposes of God in the provision of enemies. Henri's lips curled as he answered, and his eyes clouded with anguish and with wrath:

" I never prayed God for one like that old murderess. God might well have spared me such a foe! "

Time and again, when the hate that possessed that whole company seemed clotted in his own heart, he could not but wonder whether he was mad to be riding to his wedding with the murderess's daughter, while his mother's coffin might yet be above the ground. Who would be the next victim? Here was he, pricking forwards to fling away his life and his honour too. How horrible it must be to feel poison working in one's body, thought Henri: he shivered, and grew strangely numb and chill.

So fear and hate lent him ears to hear the voices at the rear that railed against this peaceful progress through the land. The peace was broken! The army must be withdrawn and the Admiral recalled. Paris, which had trembled before them once before, should come to know them in good earnest and find them truly unwelcome guests. Sometimes a halt was called, with much debating and vacillation; and the weeks slipped by. At last they all, even Agrippa, began to waver, but Henri shouted: " Mount! Forward march! " and as they rode onwards, he sang, like a child who has to traverse a dark forest.

At last he came to a place whence it was too late to turn back, for here waited the first envoys sent to carry ceremonious greeting to the Princesse de Valois's bridegroom. Thenceforward that company of wild Huguenots were the prisoners of a red-cloaked Cardinal who rode beside their King. On the next day, the 9th of July, they reached the suburb of Saint-Jacques; there they burst into a roar of joy, though rather savage joy, for at the head of the Protestant gentlemen who had come to greet their King rode Coligny himself, hero of their wars. That weathered countenance was the sole survival from the battles of the faith, now that Queen Jeanne had gone. It was thanks to Jeanne and to the Lord Admiral that they were no longer persecuted sectaries, but a force united, marching on to conquest. They cheered wildly and brandished their hats, and the beards on their tanned faces quivered as they shouted at their two beloved leaders. " Lord Admiral! " they yelled; " Our Henri! " they roared — though they actually called him " Noust Henri," in the rustic Latin that no one in these northern parts could understand.

It was noteworthy that, for all the clamour of their entry, the streets were, but for them, deserted. Before his men became aware of this, Henri himself observed that all booths had been cleared and all shops shut. He had secretly hoped that the city magistrates, or some of them at least, would meet him at the gates. Not one was there, nor even any of the City Fathers or the burghers. A cat darted across the street beneath the horses' hoofs. A sense of uneasiness came over the cavalcade, and they rode on more quietly.

The streets were narrow, and most of the houses small. They were gabled, with wooden supporting pilasters, and many of them had staircases outside. The timber was stained in gay colours; and the image of a saint above the gateway of every house was the sole spectator of the Huguenots. Sometimes a cry of " Brigands! " reached their ears; they could almost have believed those saints had spoken.

Some churches and some palaces stood out in a new-fashioned splendour, a glory that was not of stone, dream-buildings of another world. Some of those horsemen thrilled to see them, and they roared with delight at the heathen gods on roof and portal, and even at the martyrs' statues on the temples, for the very saints had all the air of naked Greek girls. But most of those grim champions of the faith kept their senses shut. They had been trained to cast down the idol and root out the evil works of those who made bold to darken the face of the Lord.

The young King of Navarre, hiding between Cardinal and Admiral, looked eagerly about him at the city of Paris, an alien city which he had never truly seen, for as a child he had been immured in a convent school. He marked the hostile shouts, and he noticed dim figures fumbling at the slats in their impenetrable windows. Curious servant-girls or vagrant drabs were all that could be seen in the street by which they entered, and those lurked in the shadows. In pairs they stood, peering out of the gatehouses, two bright eyes glittering, a shimmer of red hair, and a vague white gleam of bared flesh. Here, he felt, was the secret of this hostile city, and Henri reached out to them as they towards him. Rose-red and white come forth, come forth, O flesh and blood, harbinger of joy, no chilly heathen goddess thou, but bold-lipped and radiant with hues that bloom here alone! The horsemen turned a sudden corner, and there stood one of them in open sunlight; she started and made as though to flee, but caught the eve of the Brigand King — and stood, a-tiptoe, motionless, a fleeing figure frozen. She was slim and lissom as a sapling, her neck tall and slender, her long outstretched fingers curving upwards, softly a-quiver like a woman who is afraid and yet yearns for love. There was a mocking gleam in her eyes as Henri caught them, but when she had to look away at last, they were eyes of surrender, troubled and remote. He, too, was for the moment lost, and then — " She is mine," he thought. " And the others too! Paris, thou art mine! "

He was eighteen. At forty, grey and wise and crafty, he was destined to make that city his at last.

The Sister

At that moment his cousin Condé said: " Our journey is at an end." The royal guards had already enclosed the horsemen and escorted them across the outer yard. Henri and his cousin mounted the broad stairway, but Condé dropped behind, or Henri ran ahead of him, for at the top a figure waited. It was she! His heart throbbed so that he could hardly speak. They clung, and twice he kissed his sister's cheeks, which, like his own, were wet with tears. They said no word about their mother. And when they stood apart and eyed each other, they fell again to kissing as though they could not stop. They did not speak, and armed retainers watched them from the doorways all around.

The old Princess of Condé suddenly stepped forth from one of the rooms and embraced Henri, muttering a prayer. Observing that he was travel-stained and tired, she called for wine. But he would not stay, he was on tiptoe to reach the Louvre and present himself before the Queen. His cousin then told him that the Cardinal, his uncle, and the other gentlemen who had ridden out to greet him had now dispersed with all their following; but before they did so they had insisted that the powerful force of Huguenots should be dissolved. An escort of fifty armed nobles had been permitted to the King of Navarre; he had appeared with eight hundred. "Enough to occupy Paris," said Condé. "It was fear that made them barricade their houses. For one moment the very court was a-tremble at you! What was in your mind?"

"Not that," replied Henri. "But it might well have been, had I thought fit to make the stroke. And now for other matters. I must see the Queen of France."

"Take me with you," whispered his little sister anxiously. "I am yours, and our fates will be the same."

"Indeed I will!" he cried. To the guileless Catherine he showed himself very gay and confident. "Marriage — that will be the fate of us both. Your brother Henri will get you a fine husband, little sister!" He kissed her and dashed away.

THE ROYAL PALACE

More than a hundred of his diminished troop still thronged the courtyard and the street below. He left thirty behind as an escort for his sister. With the remainder he rode off to the palace. When at last he came to a bridge called the Mechanic's Bridge, he glimpsed, as he thought, a vision of a new and sumptuous royal palace. But as he rode down the street called Austria, the vision faded, and he saw before him a grim forbidding building, more like a fortress or prison, so much of it as indeed was visible above the frowning walls: squat towers, humped roofs, and broad deep moats brimming with fetid brackish water. The thought of entering such a place might well bring a man's heart into his mouth, especially if he came from a broad land of far horizons. But he meant to enter, and indeed, whatever might be the issue, he was eager for the venture. His high young heart told him he need fear no magic. The old woman he had dreamed of as a child still lurked in her spider's web, where his unhappy mother had been caught. So would not he!

The horses' hoofs rattled over the bridge; and as he crossed, Henri saw in a flash the river scene he was to leave behind: his last glimpse of a carefree world, bright clouds, the gleam of water between the hay-barges, and on the bank the laden ox-carts lumbering along, and the shouting and laughter of the common folk, who know not what goes on above their heads. But in that place his mother had been murdered! The familiar surge of fury caught him by the throat and blinded him. A hand touched his shoulder, one of his own friends; and he heard a voice say: "They have shut the gates behind us."

In an instant his self-mastery returned. He observed that the Louvre guards had promptly barred the approach to the bridge before his armed escort could cross. His men were clamouring without. He roared for silence, and then thundered at the guards, who were ready with their excuses. There was no room for so many Protestant gentlemen. "Then make room!" "Fear not, my liege of Navarre! There will soon be room enough in the Louvre for all the Huguenots who come. The more the better!" Archers and arquebusiers stood with legs astraddle against the parapets, their weapons in the hollow of their arms.

Henri eyed his scanty followers; then he headed them and rode on, as he reckoned, for exactly twenty paces. The horses' hoofs now hammered upon wood: the drawbridge. A gateway — the gateway of the Louvre, dark and massy, flanked by two ancient towers. Then a vaulted passage, pitched so low that the horsemen dismounted and led their beasts, their free hands laid upon their pistol butts. Henri, alert and tense, counted out another twenty paces. They emerged into a courtyard.

It was a narrow court, but looked peaceful enough, though crowded with people. Only men were visible, armed and un-armed, men of various ranks, all busy in some fashion. Courtiers diced or wrangled, burghers on business came to and fro from the offices on the ground floor of the oldest building. Cooks and lackeys left their stifling labours to take the air. Here it was always chilly, even in July. Towards the centre could be seen the foundations of a tower; its huge walls, the thickest in the castle, had darkened that court for many centuries. King Francis, Henri's great-uncle, had had it demolished. And even now only a fitful light filtered into that courtyard, like the half-light at the bottom of a well; it was, indeed, called the well-shaft of the Louvre.

Newcomers passed unnoticed in that motley throng, and, as it chanced, Henri and his companions found none they knew among the little knots of noblemen. They were indeed held up by the King's bodyguard when they tried to force their horses through the press. "God in heaven, gentlemen, go back at once. The stables are beyond the bridge; Gascons without a lackey among them will find no favour here — be sure of that! "

Such was their welcome. Henri did not reveal himself, he even motioned to the others not to do so; he fell to bantering the young officer of the bodyguard until the youth drew his sword; he was disarmed by the gigantic du Bartas, who shouted in a somewhat too overbearing tone: "This is the King of Navarre! "

This announcement produced much noise and turmoil on either side, and the Lieutenant had to be dragged back, having no intention of relinquishing his enemy. "If he is King of Navarre, then I am King of Poland! " At last an imperious figure pushed through the throng of gaping lackeys, and Henri marked him: it was his own Armagnac, whom they recognized at once. And, though his uttermost persuasion was needed, he convinced them of the truth. The masters hearkened to their men, and the bystanders fell back respectfully before the future son-in-law of the King of France. Henri walked on, between Armagnac and the young officer of the guard, who trembled for this issue of this encounter. At the foot of a stairway he said, in deprecation of his zeal:

" 'Tis not a month back that my Captain lay here with a slit throat. And the former second-in-command, one Monsieur de Lignerolles, fell down those stairs and broke his neck, no one knew how he came to do it."

And then by way of effacing his indiscretion, he added in a fateful whisper: " The apartments of the Queen are over yonder." Abashed by his own words, he stopped and would go no farther.

Armagnac led Henri to his room. The Gascon gentleman who served as Henri's valet had hurried on ahead, put the room to rights, and had provided a tub half full of water, large enough for a king to sit in, unless he were a giant. And clothes were laid out in readiness, the like of which this young gentleman from the provinces had never worn. Silk garments stiff with glittering embroidery; and the finest of all, his wedding garb, was white from top to toe. He bethought him that his mother's eyes had watched over all this, and his own eyes filled with tears again.

Queen Jeanne had had no mourning garments made for him; that proved to her son she had not looked to die, but death had come upon her unawares. Poison, not disease, had killed her; he was now convinced, and in that moment glad to be convinced. For he was about to enter the presence of his mother's murderer.

The Wicked Fairy

He had made his arrival known to the old Queen, and when he was ready, two gentlemen came to conduct him to her presence. He accompanied them through countless rooms and corridors, they uttered not a word, and he knew that caution kept them silent. He, who would commonly have asked them many questions, was absorbed by one sole thought, and that was hatred. At last they flung open the doors of the Queen's audience chamber, bowed deferentially, and left him alone. By each doorway stood two Switzers with legs astraddle, but those at the inner door held their halberds crossed. All four of them might have been hewn from stone, and their bright eyes were fixed on vacancy. They did not look at the stranger, nor did they understand his speech. He might have shouted, had he wished: " My mother was poisoned! "

As he was to be kept waiting it occurred to him to hide behind a window curtain. When the murderess came in she should not be aware that he was there, and thus he could mark her expression unobserved. The noonday sun glittered on the window, and beyond a formal garden he could see the shining river, and the scene to which he lately bade farewell, the guileless noisy people, the swaying loads of hay, and the creaking carts and barges. He could also see the long sunlit façade that ended in this room; beautiful indeed, almost a miracle, a building conjured up by magic from a world of dreams. In the homely city of Paris there was here and there something that seemed alien to the lives of those that lived there. This was beyond the compass of the court of France; forgotten was the well-shaft of the Louvre, where the ruin of a tower stood crumbling above buried centuries. Enough; this was the bright façade that masked some very dark antiquities. Henri of Navarre had realized that the mistress of this palace might well be the old murderess, but she was a fairy likewise. A man must guard against the snares of the Evil One, and such a façade might well be one of them. A delusion of the senses! thought the young Protestant; though it was a dead woman's thought in her own son's living brain. Queen Jeanne knew that room well; here had she treated of the affairs of the Religion and of her son, here had she struggled and spent her strength, and here perhaps she had drunk a glass of water into which something had been dropped by the old fairy's hand.

Henri swung round. He had heard nothing, but Catherine had already waddled into the centre of the room. Dazzled by the light, he could only recognize the shape of her, but she had marked the young man and was eyeing him with care. Her hands were invisible — doubtless hidden in the folds of her dress.

She was in black, and began to speak to him in her throaty voice. "And this woman lives!" thought the dead woman's son with fury in his heart. He sickened as he heard her say how grieved she had been at her dear friend Jeanne's death, and how glad she was to have him here at last. That he did indeed believe, but resolved she should get little profit from it. Meantime his eyes had grown accustomed to the dimmer light. She had indeed hidden her hands! She, who dared to speak of the hand of God, might well do so! The dead woman's son kept his teeth firmly clenched lest he might cry: "Let me see your hands, Madame!" But then she showed them. She slipped the small plump hands that he so longed to see out of her gown, laid them on the table before her, and sat down.

Henri stepped vehemently towards her. Before the old Queen stood the broad and massy table, and behind her the four powerful Switzers with their long pikes. She could well be calm and talk in easy tones.

"I am indeed grieved for you, young man. Eighteen years old — are you not? — and already twice an orphan. I will be a second mother to you, and will guide your footsteps, for young men are prone to walk too fast. You will live to thank me, young man, for I can see you are by nature lively and sincere. We should understand each other."

It was horrible. On the table he could almost see the semblance of a glass; and the old woman's little fingers creeping towards it, while through her lips the abyss found utterance. This was a spell and must be broken! Surely there were words and signs with power to shatter that sagging, leaden countenance and dissolve it into air. Meantime, in that suspended second Henri was conscious of something other than such arts; he became aware that his mother's murderess was an object for compassion — like the ruin of the tower in the well-shaft of the Louvre, which had outlasted the buried centuries. It would soon be cleared away. Perhaps in the end she would do it herself. She herself or her House were indeed fated to raise the lovely façade of the castle in the midday sunshine. But she sat there as the image of the evil and senseless past. Evil, when it is also out of date, is, in the end, absurd, even if it reaches out to murder. Notwithstanding its belated misdeeds, its impotence and its decay are merely piteous.

" You speak true, Madame! " cried Henri in a high and confident tone. " 'Tis very sure that I shall thank you. And may all my doings speak so loudly of sincerity as yours. I long to find favour with so great a Queen."

She could not fail to mark such extravagant irony; he did not care. A glint came into her lustreless black eyes as they searched his face, which revealed nothing but the hardihood of youth. And, under that vigilant gaze, Henri continued:

" I hope to hear from you, Madame, somewhat more than I have yet learned of the Queen my mother's end. She was fortunate enough to be in your confidence, and all my poor mother's letters were full of your praises, Madame."

" I believe it," replied Catherine. She thought of the last of those letters, in which Jeanne d'Albret had flattered herself she could force her out of power — letters which she herself had opened and sealed up again. And Henri thought of that same letter too. The old Queen grew yet more unaffected, and even friendly.

" My child," she said, " it is not mere chance that we are here alone together. It was right and fitting that you should present yourself here, or I would have summoned you: I desire to tell you what I may about your mother's death, my dear boy. Ignorance of the true facts may make a mystery of natural events, and thus cause bitterness."

" A good stroke," he thought, and answered: " 'Tis very true, Madame, I have observed as much myself. None who saw the Queen my mother recently could have believed her life in danger."

" And what of you, my child? " she promptly asked — in the maternal tone of the most upright of old ladies. The moment had come! Now for the word that, he felt, had brought him here! Murderess! Thus in his inner vision had he foreseen the hour of reckoning with Madame Catherine. And yet he faltered; his resolute hatred met with an obstacle he had not yet encountered. " I await what you have to tell me," he was amazed to hear himself observe.

TWO MEN IN BLACK

She nodded with an air of satisfaction. Then, at a slight jerk of her shoulder towards the two Switzers on guard by the inner entrance, the soldiers uncrossed their pikes and flung open the doors. Two black-clad men of different height promptly stepped in, both bareheaded and unarmed, but on their faces an air of somewhat gloomy self-importance. They bowed with extreme formality, first to the Queen of France, then to the King of Navarre, awaited their signal from the Queen, and when she dropped the hand that bade them speak, the men began, with their faces turned towards Henri:

" My name is Caillard, formerly physician to Her Majesty the Queen of Navarre." Thus spoke the taller of the two, a man who clearly regarded his attainments with great respect.

" My name is Desneux, I am a surgeon." Here was a different type, a man who was plainly irked by his professional gloom.

" At Your Majesty's order I, Caillard, member of the Faculty, on the 4th of June, a Tuesday, presented myself at the house of the Lord Prince of Condé, where I found the Queen in a fever and abed."

This was prearranged, thought Henri, and would last some while; he sat down. " And what measures did you take? " she asked the second black-clad visitor. " Did you administer a clyster? "

" That is outside my province," said the surgeon. " 'Tis for my colleague to deal with matters of that kind "; whereupon he thrust his elbow into the other's side.

The physician paled with anger, but controlled himself and proceeded.

" I, Caillard, member of the Faculty, examined the Queen and at once discovered that her lung was deeply affected on the right side. I also diagnosed an unusual callosity and suspected an ulcer that would spread through the body, and cause death. I accordingly noted that the Queen of Navarre had from four to six days to live. That was on the 4th, a Tuesday. On Sunday, the 9th, death supervened." And he produced the notebook in question.

Henri glanced at the scrawled entry. The expression of the second man in black hinted that the first man's observations had no value except as providing amusement. He plainly considered the word with him and began without more ado.

" I am only Desneux the surgeon, and a man unknown. Your Majesty has never heard my name. But you are doubtless acquainted with the illustrious Monsieur Caillard, so great an ornament to the Faculty. He has lain in the bosom of wisdom, while I am but a poor mechanic and labour with the saw. He foretells to his patients the exact hour of their death, if need be by consultation of the stars. I, for my part, cut them up after they are dead, and thus I do indeed find somewhat that can be seen and felt and does not lie. But what I find has indeed always been recorded in the great Caillard's sibylline books, for which reason I can claim to be no more than his humble helper." And he bowed to the physician.

The latter accepted the homage as his due. " It is even so," he replied. " When the Queen had breathed her last, I carried out the charge she left me in her lifetime, and instructed the surgeon Desneux, here present, to open the body."

The dead woman's son leapt to his feet. " You dared to do it! "

Caillard's gloomy self-importance remained unruffled. " At Her Majesty's order I not merely had her body opened; but her head as well. For the Queen suffered from a violent irritation in the head and feared a disease which her children might inherit. And though I reminded her that without God's will no disease can be transmitted in such fashion, she insisted."

" Proofs! " cried Henri, stamping impatiently. " Or I'll not believe a word."

The man produced a scroll, handed it to the dead Queen's

son, and Henri read his mother's name unmistakably written in her own hand. And, in another hand, was her direction, as the doctor had reported it.

"And what did you find? Tell me — quick! "

This time the surgeon spoke. "In the body I found all that Monsieur Caillard had foreseen, the thickening of the lung, and the ulcer, which burst and was the cause of death. And in the head — this."

With the air of a conjurer, faintly smiling at a successful trick, he pointed to the table, where lay a large sheet of parchment covered with lines. A moment ago the table had been clear. Henri approached, looked down at it, and shuddered; it was the drawing of a skull, his mother's skull. The surgeon proceeded:

"When I had sawn through the Queen's head — "

"In my presence," interposed the physician.

"We could not otherwise have opened up the skull. There I found under the cranium certain vesicles which, while the possessor of the skull yet lived, must have discharged upon the inner integument."

"Hence the otherwise inexplicable irritation," observed the physician. The surgeon nudged him in the ribs and chuckled:

"He explained it. That was beyond my power. But the drawing is mine. There — where I have set my finger."

But the tall and grave physician merely brushed aside his colleague's finger; and the little man grew blue with rage.

Henri listened while the doctor indicated the lines and points with particularity and the most intense conviction, but he marked Madame Catherine as well. She too first bent observantly over the parchment, though it was surely not the first time she had seen it. As her dead friend's disease was made most clear, Madame leaned farther and farther back until she was again upright in her straight-backed chair.

"So strange a case," observed the doctor; "and indeed of so suspicious a sort that my predecessor would indeed have talked of magic. But I abide by nature and the will of God."

Madame Catherine nodded and looked at her friend's son; it was the face of a sincere and kindly woman, experienced and astute no doubt, but at the moment baffled, and honestly concerned at the black mischances of life. If he could only penetrate that mask, thought the son of the poisoned Queen — so uselessly poisoned, as it seemed. It was a convincing tale. The physician was as honest, or nearly so, as his knowledge was limited. Those vesicles beneath his mother's skull, were they caused by poison? If he could only fathom that dark gaze and grasp what lay beneath it: certainty.

The Queen Nearly Wins a Victory

His inner struggle could hardly be concealed from the astute old woman, but she paid no heed: she behaved as if her sole aim was to spare a son's grief. First she signalled to the two gentlemen of the Faculty, at which they bowed as before and departed, with the same expression of gloomy self-importance they had worn on their arrival. Then she waited — and indeed she waited just too long; his hatred, which had for the moment been scattered, came back with force renewed. The son remembered those two rifled letters, it was after their dispatch that his mother had died. Unconsciously he began to stride up and down the room. Catherine calmly watched him. He grew uneasy under her gaze, stopped abruptly, and stood before her with arms akimbo, as no man may stand before a Queen. And the word "Murderess" was never so nearly on his lips. She forestalled the outburst and said in slow and quiet tones:

"My dear boy, I am thankful that you now know all that I do. And I was glad to see you recognize the truth. Now let us put away our sorrow and look forward to a happy future."

"But the skull!" hissed Henri, glaring into that large leaden countenance. Then he peered at the table; the drawing was gone. He let his arms drop in amazement. For the first time a faint smile spread over Madame Catherine's face, and it was not a pleasant smile. The meaning of it was: "You should not have let it out of your sight, my young friend."

Strangely enough, his blunder restored his self-command, and Henri became practical again. He was powerless. The advantage was hers. They must come to a compact. So he shed his hatred and suspicion, much as though he had put them in his pocket. And it cost him but little effort. With a feeling of disburdenment he sat down opposite the old woman, and she nodded. "I mean to do you much service," said she.

Henri waited and she went on: "Now that we are friends, I can tell you simply why I am giving you my daughter's hand in marriage. I do so on account of the Duke of Guise, who might become dangerous to my House. He was her school friend; you know well that Henri Guise has been trying to make favour with the people of Paris. He proclaims himself more Christian than I, and yet I am the true defender of Holy Church."

A faint glitter came into her impenetrable eyes; Henri forgot how he had longed to plumb those eyes, and he laughed a silent laugh like hers; she did at least confess her unbelief, and that he liked. In his contempt for hypocritical fanaticism he was at one with Catherine de Medici. In an instant she was grave again.

"But he has managed to win over the Pope and Spain; and with their money he could send a great army against me. Moreover, if he continues thus, he may rouse Paris: and he may hire murderers. His purpose? To make France a Spanish province."

She had forgotten that an unimportant young man happened to be listening to what she said. Madame Catherine was absorbed in her favourite pastime of hovering over a spiritual abyss.

"I too," she said softly, "could come to terms with Spain. He dislikes my clemency to my Protestants." She pondered, while her closed lips moved. And Henri marked her expression rather than what she said. Hire murderers? She could do that too. But there was no need; that plump little hand of hers was so skilled at compounding potions. He watched her, and she soon felt his eyes upon her.

"My Protestants are as near to me as all other Frenchmen," she observed, now calm once more — and added with quiet emphasis: "I am a Queen of France."

"Your son is King," he said, heedlessly correcting her, and really only because he remembered his mother telling him about the King, who had attacks of bleeding. The two surviving brothers of Charles IX were fated to suffer from the same disease; the eldest had already died of it. " Who," thought Henri, " is this lonely old woman, whose sons successively die? All Frenchmen are as alien to her as we Protestants are." And he said:

" Madam, what a lovely palace is the Louvre! But all that makes it so comes from your home. The architecture is Italian " — like the art of compounding poisons, he would gladly have added. She shrugged her shoulders; of the two arts, she knew nothing of the first. She had cared little for her native Florence, for she had been unhappy in her youth and driven into exile. Madame Catherine stood for nothing but herself, and therein lay her power as long as she endured.

She was now eyeing the young man suspiciously. " You speak of the King. Did you see him before you came hither? "

He said No — with emphasis. She dropped her voice yet more. Even the Swiss guards must not hear, though indeed they understood no French. " The King is often not himself," whispered this denizen of the abyss. " I tell no one, but he has attacks of frenzy, when he raves about murder, some fearful murder. 'Tis a symptom of his disease," she hissed.

Henri's sole reflection was that he was allying himself to a most agreeable family; but that was nothing new. The mother of this sickly brood soon recovered her composure. " My other two are excellent lads, especially Anjou. Be a friend to him, dear child. And, above all, side with us against the Lorraincr. You shall command the army; you will make a good general, and do as well as your father did. That is why I give you my daughter. But beware of Guise; women admire him."

" And sleep with him," thought Henri. " Spare me your shifts, Madam! We know each other, and I know the woman I am taking to wife. But my beloved mother did not know " — so his loving heart assured him.

And he said, to provoke her: " So that was why you dismissed Guise before I arrived, Madam."

And the old lady answered with increased complacency: " He will come back for the wedding. 'Tis often well that a girl should not be always seeing a man too greatly favoured. But an old woman like myself has to keep an eye on him. I like to have all my enemies about me in the Louvre." And among them he was clearly reckoned.

He might well have taken offence at her plainness, for all his own early mistrust of human nature. She was inclined to strip life too bare. But he was mastered by the sense of confidence that had gradually possessed him while she spoke. When a youth of eighteen was offered such flattering intimacy, he could hardly be expected to reject it. He, at any rate, had nothing to fear from the old witch, and she had not mixed a potion for his beloved mother. At that moment, had there been a glass on the table, he would have drained it at a draught.

But Madame Catherine signalled to the guards, who promptly flung open the outer doors, and the two noblemen who had introduced Henri stepped into the room. In faint astonishment he made his reverence and departed.

A BAD CONSCIENCE

This time he spoke to his companions. One of them was the King's First Nobleman, de Miossens, an extremely cautious man, who never revealed he was a Protestant. Henri told to his face that he had certain infallible signs by which he could tell those of the Religion.

"Do you not fear the Paris mob?" he asked with a laugh. "Surely they are no friends of ours?"

"If it were only the mob," replied de Miossens mysteriously.

"You should be ashamed! A First Nobleman of the King should show more pride."

He left his two companions standing and strode off; in the palace garden he had caught sight of Charles IX himself, alone, amusing himself with a pack of baying hounds. Henri called to him from a distance. The King did not hear; another thought came into his mind as he found himself standing underneath the room he had just left. Here was the sunlit façade in all its un-believable magic, a lure of the Evil One, no doubt, but a sight to dazzle a man's senses. In a flash he realized that Madame Catherine had indeed dismissed him rather too appropriately — just when he had at last believed she had not poisoned his mother. The moment he was convinced, she had sent him away. She saw through him most uncannily, and he had tried in vain to plumb those impenetrable eyes. He shuddered; once more he felt the prick of the mood that held him when he walked into that room — as a judge and an avenger. Murderess! — Twice had he swallowed the word, not from caution, like a courtier, but because the old woman had really fooled him out of his suspicions. Youth did not avail against such snares, it had but damned him to impotence.

He glanced up at the window. Yes, he had not been mistaken. The face had vanished before he caught a glimpse of it, but he was certainly observed; an eye was on him, watching to see if his boyish trustfulness was still unshaken. Not entirely, Madame Catherine! There were many things he did not know; indeed, he did not really know how the Queen his mother died. But he would never forget that, of her two native arts, poison and fine buildings, she possessed but one. Evil fairy, if indeed she was a fairy. She was to teach him fear, but in the meantime she had made him laugh. She had told him that her fat son was mad.

More slowly this time he walked towards Charles IX. The King did not notice him as yet. Indeed, his shifty gaze seemed more persistently withdrawn, and he pretended to be intent upon his pack. Two of the dogs had flown at each other's throats, and the King was yelling at them to fight it out. His voice suddenly rose above the tumult:

" Nasty brutes. I wish they would kill each other."

Henri regarded this reception rather with more contempt than anger, and he turned to go. Charles left his dogs and followed. " Navarre! What did the Queen my mother say? " He peered at Henri sidelong as he spoke, and the latter then knew that Charles had been awaiting him in great disquiet.

" We talked mostly of skulls, and once about a murder. It was a very pleasant and a very friendly talk."

Charles swayed and shook as he burst out:

" In God's name, Navarre, I'll hear no more of murders! 'Tis not long since two of my bodyguard killed each other, like two of these brutes here. The Queen my mother always has her head full of horrors."

" She says the same of you," retorted Henri; at this the King of France set his lips tight, and the whole shape of the man seemed to shrivel. If he was crazy, as his mother said, his fear was greater than wrath. He paled, and his sallow face looked sicklier still against the white silk he wore. It was in that moment that the dead Queen's son first became suspicious. Charles's conscience was too plainly bad. He and his mother, who both called each other mad, must each be afraid that the other might betray a secret. The warnings of his friends came back into his mind: he would be the next — he must summon the men of the Religion to his side. Indeed, he would have been wise to leave this den of murderers while there was yet time; to fetch his sister and ride forth among his horsemen. But he could not; had he not come hither to learn fear? — and yonder were two girls, behind two resplendent peacocks, that stepped ahead as though they were in harness. One was Margot, own daughter to the murderess; that was the first thought that shot through Henri's head. But it was promptly overtaken by the next thought: Margot had grown pretty!

The Maze

Joy quickened his steps. " Sweet Margot! " he cried. Charles swung round in surprise; then he pretended to go back to his dogs. The Princess of Valois was the first to speak when Henri stood before her; and what she said was: " I hope you travelled hither pleasantly."

" With your portrait before my eyes," he said with prompt assurance. " But it lags behind the truth. Who is your lovely friend? "

" Madame de Sauves," said Margot to her companion, instead of answering him, " take the birds away! " The maid of honour clapped her hands, and the peacocks moved away before her. She had taken the measure of this young man from the country. A mocking glance from beneath her arched eyebrows was enough. Here was an easy and a guileless prey. In the Princess's hands, and in hers likewise; and she tripped away, very slim and elegant.

" Her nose is too long," said Henri when she had departed.

" And what of mine? " retorted Margot, for her friend's nose was not longer than her own, but it was straighter. He noticed that his speech came very readily.

" One thing is sure," said he; " Mathilde's lips are thin."

" Charlotte's," said the Princess.

" Aha, you have told me her name! " he cried, delighted with his victory, for he was conscious that Margot was not to be his for the asking. " I like a softer mouth, and larger, whiter teeth." He looked at hers, then looked her in the eyes — but, for Margot, there was not enough assurance in that look. It was softly ardent, it tried to kiss her with a look, but in all courtesy, honour, and propriety, not as a man might eye a pretty drab at a street corner. The plump-legged girl had grown into rather a formidable young lady. He would not storm her heart, and hers were not the visionless and clouded eyes of self-surrender. Daughter of a murderess! he bethought himself with an inward shudder; growing in beauty amid the dark deeds of her mother.

She thought: " He still has his eye upon my legs! " For she recalled as well as he did, from their childhood days, what she had promised on the swing; indeed, he had then tried to take it without more ado. What now stood between the two of them, that he should be afraid? Meanwhile her waxen face remained as placid as the vault of heaven. Henri could not, like his mother, tell how much was affectation and how much was paint. But Jeanne had thought the girl's figure faultless, and her son thought likewise. She was still too tightly laced, but that he did not mind, nor did he foresee that those cheeks would sag in years to come. Though not so heavily bejewelled as she would have been for a great festivity, here in Henri's eyes was a very sumptuous lady, who promised deep delight to all his senses.

"Aha," thought he; "play the Princess if you will. Soon we shall be in bed together."

Behind that calm brow this was her thought: "Shall I ever sleep with Guise again? I fancy not, for I like this Henri. A country lad and yet a King's son, as his mother said."

And his mind responded: "Margot, Margot, you shall never sleep with Guise again, I will keep you richly occupied."

Meantime she had already launched upon a frigid eulogy in Latin of his campaigns and warlike deeds. He replied in the same tongue, assuring her of his respect for her gifts of mind together with her truly royal bearing. Each laboured to compose the most polished phrases, but their thoughts were elsewhere.

Suddenly the conversation took another turn.

"You have seen my mother."

He recoiled like a man discovered; for whatever passed across his mind, he never forgot that this was the daughter of a murderess!

"In private," said he; "and on a grievous matter, as I think." Her painted eyelids flickered, and at length he caught the glitter of a tear. He seized her hand and whispered: "Come away from here!" For behind them he could feel her brother Charles's peering eyes. Gravely he led her across a broad garden path, but the moment they reached the shelter of a hedge he burst out:

"Did you see my mother before she died? Why did she die? Oh, speak!" For she, of course, said nothing.

"You surely know the tales that are told?" He persisted. "Do you think them true? You will not tell me? Oh, Margot — you are cruel."

Instead of answering she stepped into an alley between two tall hedges, though it led to a maze, where there was little light even on a sunny day. But her feelings warned her they had best not see each other over-clearly at that moment. He walked beside her, brushing against her at every step, and she could feel his breath upon her neck.

"I am distraught. I fumble in the dark and can find no way out." It was even so that they were making their way along

the winding alleys of the maze. " I have never ceased to think
of you! " he broke out; and there was such a quiver in his voice
that she stopped and looked at him; tears stood in his eyes.
They were certainly real tears, but it was also certain that he
hoped they would melt her to reveal the truth.

" I can be sure of nothing," she began; her breath began to
come in gasps and she broke off.

" But you suspect? You have some clue? "

" No — no! " There was that in her voice that begged him
to be silent; but in vain.

" We are to be married. Do you understand why I do not
kiss you and caress you? You have a secret from me, and that
is stronger than all else."

Her only answer was a moan; but he would not desist.

" I adore you as I never did. There will now be only one
woman I can love," he cried, and he believed it. " Margot!
Margot! It may be that you are the daughter of the woman who
killed my mother."

The words died away into a stricken silence, and the girl began
to sob. She realized that for the dead Queen's son she had acquired a new and terrible significance. She had become a strange
and fateful figure, born of tragedy, though she herself was a
kindly and good-humoured girl. Her passions got the better of
her sometimes, and she was beaten for her escapades All she
knew was that men were killed at this court, and those who
thwarted her mother were removed. She lived in such conditions unperturbed, and often enough she had carried on a love
affair while a man was being murdered not far away.

" You may be that woman's daughter," he repeated; but he
was speaking to himself, in answer to the inward horror that
warned him against this rising passion.

" It may be so," she said at last, as nonchalantly as she could.
Proof there was none, but she, like everyone, was convinced that
the Queen's death was murder. She did not share his doubts —
and she pitied him, even more, indeed, than if he had been sure
and flung his accusation in her face. Here was he — a youth
with kindly eyes — defenceless; his mother had been murdered

by her own kin, and he meant, for Margot's sake, to put that murder from his mind. All this, and, most of all, his guileless-ness, stirred her strangely; her heart began to throb, and she waited until he should grow serious at last and seize her in his arms.

Poised and tense he stood, his arms half-raised. Then he burst into a sudden cry of fear, and she too cried out; she had not seen what he did, but there was now a bond between them that made them feel alike. He had chanced to look towards one of the dim green arbours; thence appeared a form that seemed about to step between them. And the youth, his senses all awhirl, cried: " Mother! "

He never knew how long the illusion lasted. Suddenly, in his arms lay Margot — Margot for whom he craved, clinging to him in self-surrender, and between her laughter and her tears, she stammered out:

" 'Tis a mirror set to lead people more astray, and what you saw was I — your Margot. I am here, for now I love you."

Two tears were trickling down her face, and she found her-self wondering whether they would smear her paint. He was thinking that she would now put Guise out of her mind, and his hands strayed towards her panniered skirt. For in their most exalted moments men do not forget the humbler sources of delight.

But these unhallowed fancies rode like driven barks upon the mighty sea of passion. Encompassed by dark life and silent deeds, they had dashed together out into a raging storm. Their hearts urged them to plunge into those waters and never re-emerge. They stood clutched in each other's arms; it was their highest moment, and the only one that never faded from their minds. Even in after years, when they met by chance, and much hatred and much mockery stood between them; in a moment they were girl and lad again and back in that green and shadowed labyrinth.

Margot first broke loose. She was exhausted, never had she felt so deeply. Henri barely knew what seized and held them. He felt somewhat ashamed and was near to laughing at himself and her. Ecstasy was banished by embarrassment as they strayed along the curving paths, for Margot too was lost. When they chanced on the way out, she laid a hand on Henri's arm and said:

" Alas, it cannot be. I shall not marry you."

It was the first time since their childhood that she addressed him in familiar fashion — and then only to say No.

" Margot, we must marry; it is so decided."

" But you saw someone who tried to come between us."

" My mother herself planned our marriage," he retorted, to put an end to any further questions. She was still panting with exhaustion, but she added: " It is not possible."

What she meant was: " A passion so involved with guilt, suspicion, and embroilment, and the face of a poor dead woman thrust between our kisses." Margot, had she wished, could have rendered this in Latin; but her feeling was untouched by vanity, so she left it unexpressed. She humbled herself, which that sceptical Princess had never done before. There awoke within her a Christian sense of duty and of what was precious in humanity. Much that Margot had never yet divined came over her in that labyrinth — so much, indeed, that it could not endure. Meanwhile, she said:

" You should have gone away, beloved."

" Can I hear that word upon your lips and leave you? "

" 'Tis a profligate court. I study, that I may not see what passes. My mother believes in her astrologers alone, and they prophesied the death of Jeanne, no doubt because they had been suborned to do it. But I wonder what they whispered to her of the future."

Margot indeed had a shrewd idea of much that might be imminent. But rather than throw suspicion on her mother she ascribed it to the astrologers. " Go; and go quickly! "

" But I should seem to be a coward." His indignation rose. " How can I pull my cloak over my head and run away, with all Paris jeering at me? "

"That is but foolish pride, sir."

"Ah, my lady, all this time your mind has been intent on another matter. The Duke of Guise, perhaps?"

At this misconception of her purest feeling, Margot flashed a furious look at the insolent youth, and before he could recover himself she had slipped behind him and out of the maze.

A Ballet of Welcome

When Henri emerged, at first a little dazzled by the bright daylight, he saw she had not gone far. Her brother, the King, had caught her, and gripped her by the arm so tightly that her face was drawn with pain. He was snarling at her in a towering passion, though what he said could not be distinguished. However, it was clear that he had overheard their last dispute. He could know nothing of what had gone before. Henri quivered at the recollection; it surged up through his being like a hot spring from a rock. She too must feel so, however much she might resist.

But Margot succeeded in wrenching herself free, and she faced her brother, breathing pride and wrath.

"You will not compel me, Sire, to take a Huguenot to my husband. I never lent myself to your intrigues. My religion was well known, and that I mean to keep."

Charles was at first staggered at such obstinacy. She dared to call the plans of Madame Catherine, her own mother, intrigues! Then his demeanour changed; he had caught sight of Henri. And he said, for all to hear: "Fear nothing on that score, my little Margot. You shall remain a Catholic though your husband be a Huguenot." And he added something in a whisper, probably a threat; perhaps their mother's name, for the Princess threw a quick glance of alarm at the window overhead. Her brother regarded her resistance as at an end, lifted her hand, and led her with measured steps toward her destined lord and master.

"I bring you my little Margot," said Charles IX to Henri of Navarre.

And to cover any embarrassment he added: "Navarre, we exchanged no salutations — I was busy with my dogs. We will make amends for that in proper fashion."

He walked a few paces away and clapped his hands — though he must indeed have given his orders beforehand, and very elaborate orders too; the pair had lingered long enough in the maze to give him the time he needed. But it may well have been another, more far-seeing, who had made the preparations long ago.

From each side of the lovely garden front came two lines of gentlemen in festal garb, one moving towards the King of France, and the other to take their stand behind the King of Navarre. Soldiers filed into position along the wall, Swiss guards to the left and French guards on the right; and they struck up a roll of drums that lasted until all the gentlemen were in their places. Then from the outer hall came a suave and graceful music played by violins and flutes.

In the meantime the centre portal opened, and the ladies of the court stepped forth; many lovely ladies, but, like pearls encircling a diamond, they did but provide the setting of the two costly Princesses, who, well aware of their own costliness, walked hand in hand with pink uplifted fingers and set down their feet as delicately as though they might snap at every step. They were Marguerite de Valois and Catherine de Bourbon, and elaborately as they walked, there was still a touch of antic grace in all their movements. To the rhythm of the music they passed between the two lines of gentlemen. The two Princesses, their gold embroideries, their elaborate headdresses, their fine and delicate skin, glittered in the sunshine from top to toe as they paused and circled for the great act of State ceremonial that was now to begin. In this they had but minor parts; they provided incidental ornament, as indeed they were maliciously aware. Fastidious Valois and girlish Bourbon were equally amused, and shared their feelings in a faint pressure of the fingers.

Henri and Catherine also exchanged glances: and what they said was something like this: "Do you remember our little castle at Pau, and the orchard and the crags above it? . . . Can

I ever get through such a performance as this! . . . Keep your eyes open and all will be well. . . . Where did you get your fine clothes? . . . And yours? . . . From whom else but our mother, of course."

This silent converse lasted but an instant. Charles had already begun the chief ceremony. Henri heard a voice behind him — d'Aubigné or Condé or Rochefoucauld, or possibly young Léran: " Sire," it whispered, " follow the King of France exactly in everything he does."

" 'Twill be for the first time," he answered, but observed that Charles was master of his part. Clad in white silk from head to foot, with a feathered bonnet, short puffed breeches, and long stockings — he took one step forward; it was the signal for his brothers d'Anjou and d'Alençon to stand beside him, just behind each shoulder; but that movement was a symbol: the King, and the House of Valois, in a flash of pride and glory; and for that moment Charles, now brutalized before his time, recovered the slim elegance of boyhood. At that same moment the wood-wind instruments joined and swelled the graceful cadences into rhythms more majestic — until they died away in a fresh roll of drums.

Above the King, above the magic palace and the glittering throng, hung a clear pale canopy of blue. Every sound carried a great way, and especially across the Seine, which was only separated from that royal garden by a strip of rough neglected shore. This was soon invaded by some river folk, and the strongest even tried to storm the wall. The guard promptly thrust them down with the butts of their halberds; but those who caught a glimpse of these high doings were very gleeful, and even those who saw nothing burst into raucous plaudits.

But one window, high up in the garden front of the Louvre, clicked faintly; no one heard it, and through the gap, between the curtains, appeared an old woman's sallow face. With eyes like coals it looked down on the performance of what she herself had prepared and planned: the solemn confrontation of the Catholic and the Huguenot Kings, the presence of the two royal brothers, and the brilliant array of noblemen. That would

make the little Béarnais and his shabby retinue realize that they
were of small account, and heighten their respect for the court
of France. Such were the thoughts behind that leaden countenance with its drawn and sagging cheeks.

From where she stood, Margot alone could see it, and she
found herself growing dizzy. What was she to do? Not that —
not that! It could come to no good end. She must needs take up
with Guise again, though she had finished with him now —
solely to evade a marriage with Henri, whom she loved as she
loved her life.

Margot remained alone with her forebodings and her conscience. All, even her beloved Henri, were absorbed in the event.
Indeed, it soon claimed Margot too, and, as the event usually
does, it prevailed over her inner voice. Henri, for his part, had
his eyes everywhere. Save for the face at the window, he saw
it all: the truly regal ceremonial, the sea of faces, and even the
populace, who in their fashion bore their share in the ballet.
Thus he conceived the whole performance, for his was not an
eye that saw beneath the surface; but he kept his critical wit
undaunted by the event. So all he saw was an array of faces,
which he recognized as bought — ordered, bought, and paid for.

In the meantime he aped every movement of the Valois,
setting his foot down in strict unison, then lifting and poising
it to make their progress slower and more imposing. Beside him,
or rather just behind him, walked his cousin Condé, the only
man of his House and blood whom he had at hand. Whenever
the King and his brothers stretched out welcoming hands, or
laid them against their hearts, or took off their hats, Henri and
his cousin made haste to do likewise — both of them in festal
garb, being indeed almost the only Huguenots thus arrayed. The
two groups moved forward, to the rhythm of the music, in a sort
of sacred dance, all intended to express the office and the sanctity
of kingship. As the two sides drew nearer, more details could
be seen, and the illusion of a moving unit was destroyed. And
the faces, the bought faces, began to stir his curiosity.

("Nançay is certainly no friend of mine. He is the Captain
of the bodyguard. I think I might know more of it when

stripped of that obsequious mask. Well, I must show them so much respect that no more ballets will be needed. They are faces that have marked us; let us mark them too. Surely that smile yonder belongs to a certain Maurevert? ")

"Cousin, is that man's name Maurevert? "

("Smile indeed it might be called; but sure it is that the smiler would sooner kill than dance. I'll not forget Maurevert.")

Meantime the quickest intuition may be darkened by some chance and personal discomfiture such as a man's sense of his own absurdity. And this happened when across the now narrowing space Henri marked the scorn on the faces of those who thought themselves invisible at the rear. Henri knew at once what made these courtiers feel so superior: the shabbiness of his retinue. He had secretly feared this revelation all the time and had indeed gathered about him the best clad among his followers. They were few, and as they approached the opposing ranks, they could no longer conceal the array of worn doublets and dusty boots behind them. The men appeared just as they had come from waiting many hours on the bridge, when a handful of them and no more had at last been admitted into the hated Louvre. These were not the faces of bought men: they were weather-beaten, and compared with the waxen faces of the courtiers, harsh and bigoted. On the one side, vain splendour and ceremonial; on the other, poverty undisguised and importunate. These men made war that they might live, but in thus warring many of them were set upon something nobler, which some called Religion, and some Freedom.

Henri's good humour returned for the first time since he had come. He would gladly have burst out laughing, perhaps with better right than the courtiers had to grin. Instead of which he stiffened, bowed very low to Charles, and swept his right hand in a half circle over the grass. He repeated this exercise on both sides of the King, and would actually have done it to his back had not Charles taken the young buffoon into his arms and given him a brotherly salute on both cheeks, digging him in the ribs the while. Each knew quite well the purport of that per-

formance; it was the selfsame parody of homage as the boy of
seven had offered to the boy of twelve in years gone by.

" Just as much a fool as ever," said Charles, so that none but
Henri heard. Then he ceremoniously introduced him to his
brothers, just as though Henri had not sat beside one of them
at school and later faced him in the field; and played all manner
of foolish pranks with both of them. In the meantime from the
façade of the Louvre came the click of a closing window; the
performance had served its purpose, the stroke was played.
The young man from the country must have had the impression
of a rather strange but not unpleasant family; thus reflected an
old woman, who was not devoid of a humour of her own.

Some crashing chords from the harps gave the signal for the
ladies to begin; but in case they had not heard, the First Nobleman, de Miossens, waved them forward. They duly set themselves in motion, led by the two Princesses, with pink fingers uplifted and barely touching, and feet that seemed to glide over
the sward. When they and their flower-like following of young
women came up to the two Kings, the gorgeous Princesses sank
slowly to their knees — or almost to their knees, for everything
was merely hinted, even to the kissing of the King of France's
hand, whose noble attitude at that point was beyond all mimicry.
He made as though to raise his sister towards him, and then he
led her to her lord, the King of Navarre. And this time he did
not say: " Here is my little Margot."

Charles himself took the young Catherine of Bourbon as his
partner. With her he opened the procession, which to the
courtly rhythms of a dance moved round the garden to
the aviary. Here were displayed the foreign birds " from the
islands "; and they glittered in the sunshine no less brilliantly
than the Princesses themselves. The cages were a marvellous
spectacle, and did in fact make a great impression on the guests.
" Té! " cried a Huguenot; " I should like to take a talking bird
home with me, but only if he can read Mass." At which his
companions burst into a roar of laughter. The others did not
laugh.

These birds " from the islands " had not only the gift of speech; some of them, especially the smallest and most gorgeous, could scream so vociferously that they drowned all other sounds, even the cheerful plaudits of the populace. The wall had been gradually stormed by the river folk; many were astride it, watching the antics of their betters with gleeful shouts. But the ladies, the gentlemen, and the birds were not far from the wall, so the guard became more energetic to keep them from molestation. A youth who seemed about to jump into the garden was thrust back, this time not with the butt of the halberd but with its spike. With a whimper of pain he fell backwards and disappeared. The incident was seen and heard by few, but among them were Henri and Margot.

" First blood! " said Henri to Margot.

She had grown white beneath her paint.

" A good omen! " she gasped.

Then said Henri in ringing tones:

" All these fowls put me in mind of roast chickens, and also of the fact that 'tis a while since many of us breakfasted."

This was greeted with applause by his hungry retinue. The courtiers for their part waited obsequiously until their King should deign to give them their dismissal.

The company then divided. Kings, Princesses, Princes, among them Condé, and the maid of honour, Charlotte de Sauves, made use of a little stairway, the famous little stairway of secret visits, favours, and arrests. The others used the main stairway of the palace.

THE ROYAL BANQUET

Tables had been set out in the rooms on the upper storey, one for the Kings in the audience chamber, and several in the ante-room for their gentlemen. The ladies of the Princesses' escort had vanished; which was barely noticed before the company had dined. But later, when the atmosphere had grown more heated, a gay throng of them trooped back.

The King of Navarre poured a glass of wine into his soup;

which gravely offended the King of France and the Princess of Valois. Whereafter he ate quickly and heavily, nor did he heed the conversation while thus engaged. He did wish he could have heard the talk outside, between his own people and the courtiers. But the music was too loud.

A certain Monsieur de Maurevert, in the outer room, was demonstrating great respect for the shabby doublet of his neighbour, who chanced to be the tall du Bartas. The courtier politely enquired how many campaigns this threadbare garment had survived. The Protestant, unused to either irony or compliment, took the opportunity to grow gloomily philosophic.

" We have been too much a-horse. But though a man rides round the earth, he rides to death. We do not ride together, Maurevert, but we shall be dead together." Whereupon he drained his glass, and compelled the other to do likewise.

Du Plessis-Mornay could infuriate de Nançay, who sat face to face with him, without the aid of wine. " We could have forced this city of Paris," cried Mornay; " but we are virtuous and marry her."

Captain de Nançay lost his head and laid his hand on his sword, but de Miossens and d'Aubigné held him back.

" If you run me through," shouted Mornay across the table, " that will not prove my faith a false one." Whereupon he fell to eating in good earnest. But the fiery, dauntless Mornay was one whose sacrifice was not accepted by the Lord. His was a genial virtue; that was evident when his Socratic countenance blossomed and beamed in the delectation of the feast. The First Nobleman, de Miossens, in self-excuse, pointed to the gorging champion of the faith, when Agrippa d'Aubigné called him to account for his lukewarmness and duplicity. " The dominion of the unjust hangs heavily above our heads, and the enemies of God do judge us. But you, one of our own people, serve them, Miossens. Can a man make a compact with his conscience? " asked the poet, speaking across the infuriated de Nançay, who was not listening. De Miossens merely shrugged his shoulders. This was no company in which he could speak his mind. A Protestant, but First Nobleman to the Catholic King, he did what he could to help his fellow-believers at the court. And he was not surprised by their attacks.

Agrippa proceeded to explain himself. " There are some that betray God and sell us. We lose our goods and chattels and even our freedom of conscience. Naught is left to us but our utter unity with Christ and with the angels. That stands for joy and freedom, life and honour."

This was more than the Captain could endure — the charge of treachery, or the celestial triumph of which Agrippa boasted? De Miossens exchanged his seat with de Nançay and sat down beside Agrippa.

" The Huguenots can do nothing else but preach," snorted the infuriated de Nançay, at a certain Monsieur de Maurevert; who replied:

" Softly, softly! They can also bleed." His nose was long and pointed, and he had very close-set eyes.

In that corner there were none but gentlemen of the court. The mixed assemblage had, in the course of the banquet, unwittingly split once more into two camps. At the lower end of the table clustered those of the Religion. Between them and the Catholics there was now a gap. De Miossens found himself among his old friends, but parted from his new ones. He paled, but his sense of honour prevailed; and he remained.

" After a long sojourn here," he said, " a man grows unsettled and at last begins to doubt whether we alone are justified before God. Be of good heart," he added, hastily, forestalling Agrippa's protest. " You are safe, but there may be danger to your young King, who looks to me as though he did not regard the aim and end of life as unity with Christ and the angels."

" We must not fear death," said Agrippa, refusing to be silenced. " 'Tis our refuge from the tempest — and if we perish in the flames, they will blaze up before us to the throne of the Eternal! "

It was eloquently said — but it was inspired, not by any desire for death, but rather by Agrippa's conviction that he had a long while to live. That was a prospect of which the discreet

de Miossens was by no means sure. He eyed Agrippa so long
and so gravely that the other at last became aware that this had
ceased to be a dinner-table talk on edifying subjects.

"What would you say, d'Aubigné, if the flames that are to
blaze up before us to eternity burst forth, not twenty years
hence, but here and now, in the palace of the Louvre?"

No one interrupted him now; he went on speaking quietly
amid the din of shouts, the clash of cymbals, and the clink of
goblets.

"I know too much. Facts are heavier to bear than faith. The
word is near to going forth, but it has not gone. To what end?
That I would not whisper to my own soul. Still, the wedding
must take place first. Your King and our Princess are so comely
a pair that the sight of their affections might make the vilest
criminals pause. Bid your men provoke no man here, neither
the court nor the people, for the issue stands upon a razor edge.
Otherwise some of us will soon find ourselves before the throne
of the Eternal."

He rose, and added in the other's ear: "I had almost said too
much."

His temples were but touched with grey; but his shoulders
were too deeply bowed for a man of his years, as he rejoined the
gentlemen of the King of France, whose First Nobleman he was.
He was greeted by one Monsieur de Maurevert, a man with
a pointed nose and close-set eyes, who eyed him searchingly
and said:

"You have been with the Huguenots, Miossens, and you
have talked too much."

The two gentlemen were standing in full view by the narrow
passage that joined the ante-room to the audience chamber.
Yonder were the retinue, and here the Kings, and Henri was
placed exactly opposite the little passage; thus he saw them both.
He could get a side view of Miossens, with his greying hair and
bowed shoulders, but the other he could see full face; and what
he saw there made him ponder. He even broke off what he was
saying to the King of France. Charles followed his eyes, and

when he noticed on whom they were set, his brows contracted.

"Cousin Henri," he said quickly, "you have something love-lier beside you than anything you can see yonder."

That was no more than the truth, for beside Henri sat Margot; not merely was she lovely, she thrilled him with a low and husky voice in which she masked lewd talk with learned speech. She and Henri were a match in more matters than one, and what they spoke of between them with such classic elegance should scarce have passed the rosy lips of such a proud and comely dame; but it slipped out smoothly enough. They were, indeed, overheard, a fellow-guest would join in from time to time and lend a stronger savour to a jest. Madame Charlotte de Sauves, with her saucy nose and witty eyes and delicate arched brows, was a lady of no mean audacity and charm. Her forehead was indeed too high and her limbs looked fragile, though they were not. She was like to prove a pretty fighter in the lists of love, and she and Henri had already come to terms, with and without the aid of words.

He had lost his heart to Marguerite de Valois. The sound of that husky, faintly drawling voice sent a thrill up through his body that caught him at the chest and throat and brought the tears into his eyes. Sometimes he saw his beloved as it were half-veiled, like a joy that is as yet a promise. Time and again he was near to slipping off his chair and on to his knees before her, and thus solacing his feelings. But he dreaded what might be said. For Charles IX was drunk and had begun to rally "his fat Margot's" future lord; while his brothers d'Anjou and d'Alençon, having sat too long at table, had begun to quarrel. Henri's re-torts to the King of France had grown notably more brisk. His cousin Condé nudged him in the back by way of warning. At last the two Princes' dispute brought them to blows, and they must needs be parted.

D'Anjou was bleeding in the face; he withdrew to the other side of the table and said to his cousin Navarre: "When we met in battle you were at least an honourable foe, and I usually beat you."

"But only by the aid of your letters, d'Anjou. They were

marvels of pomposity, they might have been written by a Spaniard. Indeed, they left me helpless. Nay, rather they put me into
a fever, and I could not fight. But had you really beaten me, I
should not be sitting here — and not at your sister's side."

At this the other grew calmer, and even showed signs of fear,
though it was still the wine within him that was eloquent:
" Look, Navarre, my cheeks are bleeding. 'Tis nothing. My
brother d'Alençon hates me because he must wait his turn.
My royal brother hates me, his successor; and that is yet more
horrible. Our mother longs to see me on the throne, and
Charles knows it is dangerous to thwart her. Fear makes him
furious. Drink with me, Navarre. We have borne arms against
each other honourably; and I am revealing the family secrets to
you. When I went into my royal brother's room yesterday, he
was dashing round it like a beast, with a naked dagger in his
hand. He looked at me sidelong, you know how. I am a lost
man, all the saints know that. He had scarce turned his back
before I had stepped out of the door, as quiet as a mouse, and
I gave him less of a bow than when I entered, as you can well
believe."

" There is nothing I do not believe," said Henri; and thereby
he included the poisoning of his mother.

And he went on: " You are a family whose charms are hard
indeed to withstand. I found them irresistible." So saying, he
turned, and the face he saw so dazzled him that the blood surged
into his throat; and yet it was the face of the daughter of that
fateful House.

She indeed was intent upon her lewd and learned jests, with
anyone who could return them. He flushed, and was near to
blurting out his indignation to Condé and d'Alençon, when he
noticed the colours of his House upon her dress. She and her
friend had agreed to wear some not too prominent embroidery
in the colours of his House; blue and white and red. The House
of Bourbon — so she had been longing for him, as he for her;
she wore his colours, and when she had refused him, it had been
in truth a stroke to fling him to his knees. For Margot loved
him!

This set him in a frenzy; "Come!" he cried, and made as though to carry her away. She pretended to have heard nothing. But his sister Catherine leaned towards him and said:

"Remember, we are in the Louvre!"

He remembered it at once — and looked hastily about him: the audience chamber, its carved ceiling so richly gilded that it was commonly called "the golden room." There were windows on two sides of it. They had sat so long at table that the twilight was now flooding in, violet and grey, from the south and the river meadows. Through the western window the golden radiance of the dying day poured into the golden room and shone upon a drunken King and on a man in love — himself. He must mind what Catherine said. Her knowing little face was turned to his; it was not their mother's face, but it spoke to him as only hers had done. His sister was right; this was the palace of the Louvre, in it they two were friendless and alone.

Once more Marguerite de Valois laid him under the spell of that voice of hers, and would have won his heart afresh, no matter whether or not her conversation had been modest. But suddenly he found himself intent upon the conflict in the anteroom. The revellers had long been cursing and threatening each other, the drums and cymbals could no more be heard, and the battle might break out at any moment. And Henri realized that Marguerite de Valois had no power upon him now: her voice, her beauty, and — still more — her fragrance were no more than a sham and an illusion to blind his eyes to the plain call of duty. His mother had been poisoned — oh, horror of all horrors! At his back, through the wall of the golden room, and not far away, were the apartments of her murderers. But between her that lurked there and the foes before him, who might attack his followers at any moment, sat a man in love; in love with Marguerite de Valois, and the old Queen was watching through her spy-hole.

("Little sister, you look at me with such great and shining eyes. Nay, be sure I will be prudent, though I be caught in the designs of drunkards and murderers. 'Tis true; whatever be our plight, it cannot prevail against my passion for Marguerite; she is as lovely as her picture, and what she truly is I may discover when I come to be beside her, or perhaps not even then. But, sister, I shall not leave this court. For Margot's sake I love it — 'tis a place of deeds and danger. Corrupt, our mother called it, and it is corrupter than she knew; indeed, she wanted me to take my wife away from it and live in rustic peace. No; that can never be. Here the women are forthcoming with their favours, said Queen Jeanne. Charlotte de Sauves indeed has lost no time, and I — make no claim to chastity. And yet for Madame Marguerite I would give my life. Sister, sister — speak of our mother to me once again, for my heart stands still.")

As though he had actually spoken, Catherine de Bourbon leaned towards her brother and said: " Remember our mother! "

And the youth, swept so soon by all the storms of life, answered in a thrill of understanding: " I never forget her."

Meantime his cousin Condé came back from the outer room. " I have dismissed our people on your authority," said he.

"How dared you! We must not be the ones to yield."

"Then order them to kill Charles's men, not sparing a single one. And do so now: there is yet time."

Then from the outer room came the tramp of the departing Huguenots, cursing as they went; some indeed turned and stood their ground awhile, for their master's order was little to their minds.

Condé fell into a fury: " 'Tis all one to me. I'm the man for a mêlée! Do but say the word! "

Henri was silent. He realized what the other in his wrath forgot: they would have had to begin by murdering Charles IX and his brothers. They could not spare a single enemy within the Louvre, and then they would have to deal with Paris. Pah! What ghastly madness — born of the loaded air in that gilded chamber, or, more likely, hatched by the old murderess behind her spy-hole! Charles stared at the scene with the glazed eyes of a beast. His brothers stood in the doorway and egged on the brawlers. Henri pushed between them, stepped into the ante-chamber, and shouted to his men. For a moment the issue hung in doubt until enough of them had bethought themselves of what might follow. They checked the word that trembled on their lips and withdrew across the great state apartment, where darkness was now falling; thence their voices faded into silence.

At that moment, too, lackeys appeared with torches, followed by a brilliant throng of women; not merely the few who had appeared in the garden, but a whole regiment. Nor were these the only light-armed feminine forces that were under Madame Catherine's command. They dashed to every threatened point, not at all averse from trying their skill on these wild Huguenots as well. Lackeys hastily lit the tapers! Four rows of five chandeliers in each, for the girls were painted to suit just that amount of light. These bandits, as the Huguenots were called, would tell them all they thought and all they purposed, and Madame Catherine would be punctually informed.

" Take care! " said Henri sharply to Agrippa, who passed on the warning.

" How now, gentlemen! " cried the King of Navarre to the courtiers, as debonair as ever; for they were arrayed in the ante-room as though they looked to be attacked. " In the presence of these ladies my rough doublets will be as smooth as silk." He spoke as though in mockery of his faithful lieges — which so much pleased the gentlemen of the court that one Monsieur de Maurevert kissed his hand. Nor did Henri withdraw it, though he shuddered at the contact of those lips.

When he came back, Charles had just been carried by his servants into his bedchamber, which was the nearest of the royal apartments. In the farthest of them Henri had tried to elicit from old Catherine whether she had poisoned his mother. Thither had Madame Marguerite disappeared; and no wonder! — Catherine's daughter! Her brothers and Madame de Sauves had also gone. Beside the disordered table and the King's up-turned chair only his sister and his cousin awaited Henri. Catherine eyed her brother, but said nothing until the door was shut. Even then she whispered. He pondered, did not answer, and gave no sign save a quiver of the eyelids. Then she took her cousin's arm. They preceded Henri into the antechamber, crossed it to the right-hand corner, and made their way down the little private staircase into the courtyard.

THE TAVERN

There they vanished. The "well-shaft of the Louvre" was pitch-dark. Through various windows at different levels in the walls flickered a faint reddish light, which served but to show how narrow was the wedge of blackness in between. Henri stood motionless until he heard a voice whisper: "This way!" He followed it round several buttresses and along an unlighted passage, and again it whispered: "This way." At last they slipped into a room, the King of Navarre and his First Gentleman of the Bedchamber, d'Armagnac, where by the light of a solitary taper shadows flickered across the walls.

Henri's noble henchman bolted the massy door and then observed: "The walls here are three feet thick, and the window is set ten feet high. The folk who lodge here are drinking at the tavern, so here at least we can speak without risk of being overheard."

"Still, let us look into all the corners."

Behold! — in one of them a lovely girl; not dancing in the state apartments under the twenty blazing chandeliers; she had slunk hither in pursuit of the King of Navarre, to discover what might be going forward that evening and report to Madame Catherine, who always graciously received such news. There was nothing for it but to take the lovely creature out and shut her up in utter darkness.

"I'll release her later on," said d'Armagnac. "The immediate business is to get Your Majesty out of the palace unobserved."

"No hope of that, the old Queen hears of everything."

"Not at so late an hour. So there be none who watch me disguise you, Sire, you need fear no man this night. When I have done, no man will know you." Whereupon he set to work. In the end his master looked like the poorest of his people, with his face stained and blackened, and a false beard.

"I have given you some wrinkles," said d'Armagnac. Henri

promptly hobbled like a dotard. He was provided with a sack of faggots. "Why faggots?"

"Because it is the lightest load to carry. Your name is Gilles and you have a sister in Paris."

"Am I bringing her these faggots?"

"No, the ham that is hidden beneath them. If the sack is searched at the gate and the ham discovered . . ."

"My identity as Gilles is proved. An excellent notion. Tell me the password. . . ."

"Ham."

At this the two men laughed their fill behind those massy walls. Then Henri set out, and came safely through the gateway where the guard were playing cards; he merely shouted: "Ham!" On the bridge the guards were more stringent and made him empty his sack; and they impounded the ham.

"Now get along to the tavern, you old heretic, where your so-called sister serves as drab."

Henri limped out, bowed as though under a load of bricks, and as he wanted to avoid any encounter in the street called Austria, he slunk round several dark corners, still limping for enjoyment of his mimicry, until he came upon a dimly lit ground-floor room on one of the darker alleys. Shadows of moving figures and the lilt of a song proclaimed the tavern. The outer door as well as the door of the tap-room stood half-open, to let out the smoke from the chimney where some spitted fowls were turning before the fire. One of the girls was tending them, while the two others filled the glasses or sat on the knees of the guests and joined in their songs. The landlord beat time to the song. He looked like a peasant, with bits of straw sticking to his clothes. The guests were all armed, even a very small man who sat piping out the chorus. It was a cheerful little song about a rash maid, who was beguiled by a Huguenot's handsome beard; and what came of that? A baby, which could not be baptized, for it brought a club-foot into the world, and soon after it was born it tweaked its own mother's head round till her face looked backwards.

The only light in the place came from the burning logs; it

glimmered round the bawling mouths, but slantwise across the foreheads lay a sharp line of shadow. To Henri, who was watching from outside, the scene looked merely bestial and crazy, and he began to loathe the rags of his disguise. And yet it would be rare sport to go alone and unarmed among these six revellers. At this point he was bundled aside by a very tall personage who entered at that moment and loudly wished the company good evening. He recognized the deep voice and especially the figure; the man's back was towards him, but it was unmistakably du Bartas's back. "'Tis a fine song of yours," said he; "I should like to hear it again."

The only one of the six that answered was the small man behind the heavy oaken table, who squeaked: "Ha! You're tall enough — reach me down a sausage from the ceiling."

Du Bartas lifted a hand. "Only if you promise to sing me the song of the Huguenot baby again."

The man refused, but one of the girls clutched the tall Huguenot's arm and said: "The song wasn't meant for you; there's no harm in singing, is there? If you sprung a child on me, I'm sure it wouldn't have a club-foot." At this all three women yelled with glee. The men stayed sullenly entrenched behind the table, and not a muscle of their faces moved as they watched the landlord's manœuvres. The ruffian slunk behind du Bartas's back to the fire, picked up a burning log, and was eyeing the heretic to see where he might best plant his blow. That was the moment for Henri; he darted forward, gripped the fellow by the wrist, picked some sticks out of his sack, lit them at the knavish landlord's log, and brandished them in his blackguard countenance, until the terrified man flung his log back into the fire. Then Henri dropped his sticks.

"Away with you, and draw the gentleman some wine, — good wine if you have any. My money is spent, or will you take more wood in payment?"

"Drink with me," said du Bartas, as to a poor companion in arms. They sat down at the vacant end of the table by the door, and between them and the other drinkers in that squalid room opened the same ominous gap as at the King's table in his palace of the Louvre. The landlord set a jug before them and growled without looking up: "In my village they burnt the folks' feet in their own fires."

He did not say who had done this, but the two Huguenots silently understood. They knew that they had too often behaved like common bandits. Du Bartas assumed the bleak and hopeless air with which he was wont to speak and write of the blindness and the wickedness of men. Henri was near to crying that he had pleaded with the Admiral to refrain from ravages and torture; but the answer was that those of the other faith must suffer. And what came of religious wars was written on the faces of those drinkers in the tavern.

However, this was blasphemy, even the very thought of it, and Queen Jeanne's son recoiled. He hoped, too, that du Bartas had not, in fact, recognized him and had come in by chance. So he bit his tongue and said nothing. But the landlord had not finished:

"Tomorrow morning I must needs go to confession," he snarled, still not looking at them. "The priest forbade me to serve food or drink to those brigands who infest Paris and attack Christians and insult young women. And not one of them has shown the colour of his money. There sits the first who has not left his reckoning unpaid," he said in a voice betwixt servility and scorn. Henri leapt up in anger.

"Be seated!" roared du Bartas; it seemed unlikely he had recognized his King. Henri really felt like the shabby, wrinkled dotard that he looked; and he spoke in a voice to fit the part. "Have a care, sir. The man in red behind the rest is drawing a knife." — "I can see him," replied du Bartas.

The man in red, under cover of the others, began to slip out of his corner. The small man, who could barely see above the table, covered him by squeaking out: "The mercer's wife's son has disappeared."

"The Huguenots slaughter children," said the others in reply, apparently heedless of the strangers. "They are known to practise ritual murder."

Trouble was imminent when some new arrivals entered:

Huguenots, and among them two of his own cavaliers, whose names and deeds were known to Henri. Their two companions looked insolently about them, and might well have passed for highwaymen, had they not been of the Religion. Therewith the position of the parties at the tavern table was equalized; the man in red abandoned his manœuvre, and all weapons on the other side were put away.

The two cavaliers, strangers to Paris, explained to du Bartas they had fallen in with two comrades of the faith in the dark. Otherwise they would never have found a tavern. Their condition indeed appeared to show they had already visited several, and there revelled and drunk deep, for they were in sore disorder. Henri promptly forgot his humble part and cried imperiously: "Thieves and roysterers! Such men as you degrade our party!"

This was greeted with a roar of laughter, and du Bartas nudged Henri briskly in the ribs, by way of reminder that he was talking rather out of character with his attire. Thenceforward he was silent and took no further part in what went forward. The newcomers rattled the money in their pockets, slammed some coins before them on the table, and shouted for the fowls, which were indeed now brown and glistening and ready for the platter. After generously inviting Monsieur du Bartas and his waggish little friend to join them, they proceeded to gulp down their food as fast as they could, listening for distant noises all the while. The girls they totally ignored. When barely sated they made off, both cavaliers and highwaymen. For a time their cautious footsteps could be heard, fading into the distance; and then a patter of men running.

"Now, landlord," said du Bartas, "you can no longer say that Huguenots do not pay their reckoning." Silence answered him; meantime the tramp of marching men and the glare of torches came nearer: the street watch. The officer and a man appeared in the door. "Where are the Huguenots?"

"There!" exclaimed the landlord, pointing to the tall man and his wizened little companion; "eating fowls, and I knew at once their money wasn't Catholic." The man in red, the cripple, the other three guests, and the girls all agreed. Not till after much cross-examination by the officer was it admitted that several others had been there. But those two had paid the score! They had waylaid and robbed someone for sure. And the pair of them were taken away by the watch.

Du Bartas took no further notice of Henri, he walked on ahead with the officer. And the outcome of what he said to him was that the watch altered their direction. They soon reached a house that Henri knew: the Palais Condé. He would indeed have gone straight there had he not been lured into an adventure in disguise. He had been long since expected; lackeys dashed out with lanterns, and they had even been warned of the King's odd attire, for they bowed low before him.

And suddenly du Bartas bowed likewise.

THE LAST HOUR

Henri was first taken to a room where he washed himself and changed his dress, and then into another, wherein sat Admiral de Coligny.

The old man half-rose, but Henri was too quick for him and thrust him back into his chair. The Princesse de Bourbon was also present, and she curtsied to her brother. Then she said: " Brother, I am your devoted servant; permit me to remain and hear what you and the Admiral shall decide in this last hour."

She spoke as insistently as when she had bidden him remember their mother at the banquet in the palace. Her air of ceremonious gravity was intended to stiffen her brother's heart. Catherine knew too well whose face was always in his mind, and all that he was ready to forget on that account. She was but a child still, and her voice quavered; but she had spoken. She withdrew out of the circle of light.

" My Lord Admiral," said Henri, " you wished to see me. I, too, sought this meeting and I gladly came."

" The Queen of France does not suspect? " asked Coligny.

" I am sure she does not," said Henri, though he was far from sure.

" I must tell you what you cannot yet have discovered for yourself; we are not loved in Paris. Your marriage makes no difference, we are hated, because our faith is hated."

" Perhaps, too, because you permitted too much plundering," added Henri to himself, remembering the tavern talk. How bitterly the people of this land must have come to loathe, not the Religion, but its followers, when a common man can pick a burning brand from his own fire to murder a customer merely for being a Huguenot!

" Such hatred is beyond all right and reason," said he; " we are all Frenchmen."

" But we shall go to heaven," replied Coligny, " and they to hell. That is certain — as certain as that the Queen, your mother, lived in this faith and died in it."

Queen Jeanne's son bowed his head. He had no reply, as soon as the old champion brought in his mother as an ally. The old man and the dead woman were arrayed together against him; they belonged to the same epoch and held the same rigid opinions. They had indeed until lately shown themselves so violent and irreconcilable towards the court that disaster was inevitable. How then? Must his mother herself bear the guilt of her own murder? By no means. He would sooner she had died of her disease, and not at Madame Catherine's hands.

At that moment his sister slipped a lamp along the table between him and the Admiral; they must see each other clearly, for much depended on their coming to an understanding. But what Henri saw was a grey old man, not the war-god whom he knew.

Admiral de Coligny had been, in Henri's eyes, a rock-hewn figure, unassailable. Not, indeed, that he had always won his battles; but he was war personified; and he had worn the mask of the noblest of all wars, the war of faith, a more than human mould of features, such as are only found on the statues in cathedral portals. Thus had the boy Henri conceived him all through the years, even when he ventured to criticize the commander. All this was banished at a stroke; and in place of monumental piety and strength, here stood revealed the ultimate failure which is called old age. A man still stood his ground, but the eyes were dim, the cheeks looked sodden, even the beard grew sparse and straggling — only the lines from the nostrils to the clouded brow withstood decay. Whatever were the hopes of victory, the hero remained as prepared as ever to make the offering of his life to God.

Strange old man; but he had been his mother's friend, and sorely stricken by her death — more so in truth than her own son, who had a life to live and had not ended when she died.

" Did she die well? " he asked quietly.

" In God, as I, too, hope to die." There was a faint hostility in his tone. (" I," Coligny meant to suggest, " shall soon join her. You, young man, remain behind, and are deserting us.")

Henri felt this and protested.

" Lord Admiral, you were not of the same purpose as the Queen, my mother. I know it from a letter that she wrote to me. You vainly tried to force the court of France into war against Spain. But my mother made this marriage instead."

" You are not yet married."

" You are against the marriage."

" We cannot now draw back. One thing we can do, and to that end I summoned you here tonight. I presume once more to give orders as a commander, whom even a young Prince obeys."

" I am listening."

" Insist on guarantees — before the wedding. By God, you must make yourself and the Religion safe before these people have achieved their ends and need us no more."

" 'Tis but a week hence," cried Henri, no longer looking at the old man. Over the tapers he could see a vision of Margot.

" Such haste should have made you suspicious. Their purpose is that you should be parted from your following and abjure the Religion."

" Not so. She makes no such demand."

" Who? The Princess? She stands for naught. But her mother? I prophesy that you will be held a prisoner."

" Never! They love me."

" As we Huguenots are loved."

Henri fell suddenly silent, and Coligny was able to continue.

" They will offer you honours and delights beyond all you can imagine, but you will still be their prisoner and never again be free to act as you shall choose. The House of France will keep you aloof and alone, and Queen Jeanne's son will no longer be the Leader of the Faith."

This struck at the young man's heart, and for the moment he was stirred by the mysterious quality of age. What lay behind it? It might be that some store of knowledge came forth from this ancient hero, like a light kindled by strangers in a deserted house.

" Insist on guarantees — before the wedding. Your bodyguard must be wholly of your people, and the guard-posts in the Louvre must be held in equal numbers by your men, and safe places must be assigned to us in Paris."

" 'Tis easy to make demands, Lord Admiral, but hard to get them granted. I have a better scheme; let us strike at once, seize the King of France, disarm his soldiers, and occupy Paris."

" You would do well to be serious," said Coligny stiffly, for here was the turning-point: fate was about to speak to this youth's lips. But the lips were drawn in mockery.

" Must there be bloodshed? " asked Henri.

" A little — to save a great deal more," said the voice of secret wisdom darkly, but this was no more than the babble of senility.

Henri held his face in the light so that Coligny could see that it was fearless and that his jests were not those of a weakling. His profile in those days was that of a Gascon soldier, hawk-like, dark, and keen — the face of a fighter, unmarked as yet by sorrow or by knowledge, and he spoke:

" My mother thought, before she died, that I should not come to Paris at all, or, if so, in overwhelming force. But you have sent the Protestant troops home, Lord Admiral, and rightly; for a man cannot march to his marriage at the head of an army. Here I stand: though I have no cannon I am, as the Queen would have had me be, the stronger. I am unafraid, and I keep a bold front. Ask Madame Catherine and Charles IX; I have compelled them to show me all respect — or ask one Monsieur de Maurevert, who kisses my hand."

This was the speech of a young Gascon soldier, and an old man's mournful silence made him yet more vehement:

" Are the young men eager for a party struggle in the name of religion? Do they not long for a common victory over Spain? It will be for us to unite this land against its foe; in this, we, the youth of France, are all at one," he cried; such a word as youth was his surest counter-stroke, and an advantage that could not be gainsaid. The Youth of France; not those treacherous faces at the ballet in the garden, nor the brawling faces at the King's banquet. A fellowship, with life upon its side, but with small indulgence for old age.

Indeed, Henri of Navarre, later of France and Navarre, in a flush of ardour forestalled the cause that was to be his, and his alone, and conceived as the watchword of the youth of France. But there was no such fellowship: his own young friends were against his marriage to the Princess of Valois — d'Aubigné, du Bartas, Mornay, the cavaliers who rode with him to Paris, and even the Huguenots in his own country. All this he forgot in his mood of self-dedication. In time to come he would often find himself isolated amid the throng, betrayed, and perplexed behind his mask of steadfastness. This he could not know; and he faced this ancient from another age with the bold but yet unminted visage of the future.

Youth and age had spoken, there was no more to be said; it was then that Henri's sister stepped into the light.

" Brother," she began in her soft voice, which she managed to control, save for a faint quaver on the final word or two, " brother, you will be a great King and I shall bow down before your bed." Strange words, but spoken with a faith that shamed his own. This little, clear, arched forehead hid their mother's stubborn faith. Yet more; his sister had indeed a vision of his greatness yet to be, and of herself making due reverence before his bed of state. In the meantime she must tell him the truth about their mother.

" Never, even to the end, did she mean you to marry Madame

Marguerite. No, brother; our mother knew she had been poisoned."

Again that blast of horror. Henri tottered, then swayed forwards on to his sister's shoulder.

" What did she say? "

" She said no more than what you were told by Monsieur de La Rochefoucauld. But I tell you that our mother knew the truth, and that was why she said you were not to come at all, or only in overwhelming force."

He could no longer doubt — at least while he listened to that tense and eager voice and while the horror still possessed his mind.

" Was hers the Admiral's plan? " he asked humbly.

" Nay, it went further." His sister seemed to grow in stature, and her small voice deepened. She pushed her brother from her and stood with her outstretched hands resting on his arms. And gazing into his eyes she spoke: " Away from Paris, brother! Call all the Huguenots together before dawn and go, even if you must use force. Spread the news through France that Queen Jeanne was poisoned! The nation will rise, the very corpses on the battlefields will stand to arms: and then march to your wedding. 'Tis our mother's will. I tell you what I know, and bid you hear."

Catherine then turned away, like a messenger who has said what he was sent to say. It had indeed been an effort, and her bosom heaved. The air in the room was heavy, and Henri had a foreboding of some strange event. They had been speaking in a closed room, and in that stifling atmosphere their sense of reality had faded. The Lord Admiral stood behind his chair, his clasped hands raised and his eyes uplifted, and to Him who dwells on high he recited the words of the Psalm:

" Let God, the God of battle, rise
    and scatter His presumptuous foes;
Let shameful rout their host suprise,
    who spitefully His power oppose.
As smoke in tempest's rage is lost,

or wax into the furnace cast,

So let their sacrilegious host

before His wrathful presence waste."

Henri opened a window into the black night. Lightning flickered across the distant horizon, and a hot wind drove the fiery clouds across the sky. No use to warn Henri that his enemies were enveloping him like wreathing smoke. He would not appeal to God against the wicked. His whole being swept him into the adventure, the name of which was Margot; it was also called the Louvre; and the passion of his senses was the same that urged him forward to his fate.

He turned back into the room and said: " I may not believe you, sister. Our mother knew not whether she was poisoned, and she cannot have wished me to escape and only venture back at the head of an army at my back. Such were not our mother's counsels."

" You deceive yourself, my brother; the same blood runs in our veins, and what I believe, that also you in your own heart believe likewise."

He would not be convinced. " Though she may have said so in her last agony, our brave mother would not say so now — were she to return."

" Would that she might! " cried his sister, looking towards the door; and her brother answered: " Well, if it is so, she will come."

Both, side by side, their eyes upon the door, prayed silently that it might open, and that beloved form appear. A hot gust blew in upon their necks, the thunder rolled, blue interlacing flashes spanned the sky, leaving darkness in their train; and the watchers shuddered. Coligny, behind the other two, had ceased his chanting and stood expectant; then the door swung open. All three gazed at her who had come back to them, the Queen — in the flicker of a lingering lightning flash. The tapers in the room suddenly went out, and to a tremendous crash of thunder, she came in.

" Madam," said Admiral de Coligny, laying his hand on his

breast as though in salutation of a living woman. Brother and sister took one step towards her, Catherine with a faint gasp of joy, while Henri's lips parted to exclaim: " Mother! "

But the word was never uttered: the lady waved to her attendants, and men with torches took their stand beside. And in the glare she stood for all to see — the Princess of Valois, Madame Marguerite; Margot.

The little group could not at once believe their eyes. They had been far more ready to believe that what they saw was Queen Jeanne, and they looked to see the apparition change back into her semblance. But it did not: the lovely painted face of Charles's sister still confronted them, and spoke in her deep and golden voice.

" Sire," said she to Henri of Navarre, " we sought you in the palace and found you not. One of my mother's maids of honour told us strange stories of dark chambers. The guard at the outer gate of the Louvre had marked a man out who might well have been disguised for an adventure. And though your friend du Bartas followed him afoot, we were troubled for his safety in Paris at night."

" Who was troubled, Margot? " interposed Henri.

" I," she said in her clear melodious voice. " I told my mother and asked permission to take a company of guards to fetch you home."

" Margot! The truth is that Madame Catherine sent you out to get me back into her power? "

" I marvel," said Madame Marguerite in crystal accents. " Since the beginning of this day, which has been a long one, you know me as well as I know you " — and she reached a hand to him.

The hand was one that a master might have moulded out of marble, waxen and silken-smooth, with rounded back, and long delicately jointed fingers, upturned at the tips to show the faultless ovals of the painted nails. A bare hand, without rings or jewels.

Henri took it, raised it to his lips, and went out with Margot, without a single glance behind him.

MORALITÉ

$\mathcal{V}$ous auriez beaucoup mieux fait, Henri, de rebrousser chemin tandis qu'il était temps encore. C'est votre sœur qui vous le dit, elle si sage, mais qui ne le sera pas non plus toujours. Il est trop clair que cette cour où règne une fée mauvaise ne se contentera pas de vous avoir tué la reine votre mère, mais que vous devrez payer encore plus cher votre entêtement de vous y attarder et votre goût du risque. Il est vrai qu'en échange ce séjour vous fait connaître le côté plus équivoque de l'existence, qui ne se passe plus qu'autour d'un abîme ouvert. Le charme de la vie en est rehaussé et votre passion pour Margot, que le souvenir de Jeanne vous défend d'aimer, en prend une saveur terrible.

Book Four

Margot

Before Notre Dame

Monday, the 18th of August, is a great day of festival; the King's sister is to be married, and to marry a Prince from a far country, as handsome as the day and rich as Pluto, for gold grows in his mountains. He came here with wagon-loads of gold; his horsemen and their horses, too, were stiff with gold. It was whispered to the Prince in the South that our Princess was a lovely lady and more learned than any daughter of a king. A famous astrologer showed him her portrait in a magic mirror; she smiled, she spoke, he could not resist that voice and those eyes; and he set forth on his long journey.

It was a pity that the windows were closed and the shops shuttered last week when the Prince and his great retinue rode into Paris. Then at least we could have seen with our own eyes how much was true. All manner of stories are about. We hear of assaults on respectable burghers, some of them robbed of their purses by bandits called Huguenots. We go no more abroad after dark, for one never knows. There are sundry other matters that look none too well. Our King is marrying his sister to this foreign Prince, who is said to be a heretic, and indeed the King of all the heretics. Does God permit this? Our priest is furious. But the Pope, they say, has given his consent. Can that be possible? There is something wrong. The Huguenots are said to have threatened and constrained the King and forged a writing from the Holy Father. Their cunning and their deeds of violence are known. For many years now, since we were children, they have made war on the Catholics, plundered and ravaged all the land, and even threatened the King's life; and suddenly — a wedding! No good shall come of this. There have been omens!

This evening I shall bolt and bar my house. Last night the great folks were banqueting, they say, in the palace of our King, and there was a ball in honour of the betrothal. The Louvre looked as though it were lit up by the fires of hell. But the bride, they say, vanished, just as if the Devil had spirited her away. But one cannot believe all the stories that one hears. Belike she slept in the Bishop's palace by the cathedral, where she is to be married and hear Mass today. There will be a gorgeous court procession, and the bridal dress has cost as much as three houses in Paris. It will indeed be a noble sight. Many of the mob and all the burghers are already on the way. The sun is shining. Let us go. . . .

Such were the thoughts and speech of mob and burghers when, after an early dinner, they streamed from all parts of the city towards the church of Notre Dame. They were not wrangling; such were the shifting moods of each and all of that great concourse. They were agog with curiosity; that day, they knew, would bring them many a motley scene of piety and horror, splendour and misery. The mob's own restlessness, as always, cast a shadow on events to come, and each man barred his house against his fears; but in the streets both mob and burghers yielded unresisting to the turmoil.

A mob may not be checked without violation of its being. Its natural impulse is to move onwards, heedless of what may happen. Gradually they surged round the wooden structures that had been erected on the square before the cathedral. The Swiss Guard, posted there as a precaution, with halberds crossed thrust the populace back up the converging streets. These foreigners were impervious to appeals and curses, because they understood no French. They were heavy men, made to look even broader by their club-shaped sleeves, with great flaxen beards masking their slashed doublets. They moved with the gait of bears and were very easy to elude; some of the nimbler citizens merely slipped under the shafts of their weapons. In the end the intruders were always driven back, but they had the glimpse they wanted, and came back to wrangle and air their superior knowledge.

" We of the Carpenters' Guild were naturally first to hear about it all. We built the great scaffolding before the main doorway of the cathedral, on which our Princess Margot is to be publicly married to the King of Navarre by the Pope in person."

" Not by the Pope; a friar I know says he is going to marry them. He foretold the wedding. If only I dared to speak! "

" 'Tis no more than I know already. And I foretell that the King of Navarre will be a cuckold. Eh? I must not say such things? Then 'tis you that are the cuckold — ask your friends! "

" I scorn to answer you as you deserve, I am a man of peace — you will get your answer from the Huguenot gentleman beside you. Mind he doesn't break your head! "

" Good Christians, hear! You see that here, as everywhere in Paris, there are too many heretics. They are preferred before the faithful, the guard makes way for them."

" The bridegroom is a heretic. Which means, good Christians, that you will fall into the hands of unbelievers. Woe upon you! "

" Good Christians, hear! These foreigners infest the city like a swarm of locusts, and some among you they have already beaten, robbed, insulted, burnt, and hanged. Stop this marriage lest worse may befall! "

" Holà! Here be some black-avised ruffians. Ye may well hide your faces beneath your hoods! Spanish monks who mean to stir up mischief and rouse the mob to storm the tribunes during the wedding. That would suit your Spanish Philip's book. How now — whither away? Aha! They vanish when discovered."

" None the less, these bandit Huguenots shall burn in hell, and if justice were done they ought to burn on earth as well."

" I tell you, the Pope himself is coming to celebrate the wedding. We carpenters built the wooden gallery from the Bishop's palace to the cathedral? It will cost the court a pretty penny, and could be for none other than the Pope."

" You carpenters must be doing well just now."

" Not so well as the mercers. They have tapestried the gallery in white and covered all our craftsmanship."

" But the landlords are more thriving than them all."

" Not so — the clothiers — think of the wedding garments for the court."

" No, the girls are doing best, these foreigners have their pockets stuffed with money."

" The Huguenots' reckoning will come. They bring good business for the moment."

" Stand aside there! If you must bleat about your business you need not block our view. Here they come trooping out of the Bishop's palace. 'Tis truly kind of them to march along that gallery for us to look at them; indeed, from the way they walk, not one of them seems to realize he is glittering like a peacock in the sun with the eyes of all Paris on him. That's your true gentleman — never knows what's happening. Here come the ladies! Don't they put the gentry out of countenance! Now the day *has* started. To think that milliners and jewellers and hairdressers can make such marvels! We shopkeepers may indeed be proud."

However, a practised eye would have noticed that the procession, having reached the cathedral, had halted. As though they had been no better than the mob, some of the noble guests tried to push to the front so as to get more quickly to their seats on the platform. A scuffle followed, and the officers of the French Guard had to stop a brawl among the noblest in the kingdom. At last the company were duly arrayed: King, Cardinal, bridegroom and bride, the Queen, the Princes, the Princesses, the retinue of noblemen and ladies, and the priests in attendance on the Cardinal; each in his place, according to his rank, and each distinguished by the colours he wore.

On a tall open platform stood, on a fragrant summer morning, and under a blue sky flecked with white, the flower of the kingdom. The rows of houses that enclosed the square were gay with hanging carpets and thronged with gaily dressed spectators. Below, along the walls and by the outlets to the streets, a silence fell, hats were doffed, hands clasped, and knees bent. Close behind the glittering array upon the platform, loomed the cathedral, a monument to all the generations that had gone before. Its pealing bells were ringing changes to eternity. And the Cardinal of Bourbon married the King of Navarre to the Princess of Valois.

When the ceremony was over and the guests clambered down from the platform, there was much entanglement of swords and trains, unnoticed indeed by the spectators, as the great personages forthwith vanished into the church. Those with claims to a seat had of course been gathered there for hours; nobles, or rich official burghers, all of them too guileful and experienced to pay much heed to any elaborated ceremonial. They did indeed kneel when Charles IX appeared, but that was the extent of their homage; they were much more eager to mark any defects in the performance.

The Cardinal of Bourbon was getting old; Charles IX looked like a butcher peering about him for a victim. His wife, Elizabeth of Austria, was even more richly arrayed than the bride. It was the most that she could do, for she was stiff and speechless, knowing no language save, perhaps, a little Spanish or German; she could certainly speak no French. Too plump for her twenty years, she was ignored on more intimate occasions, while at public ceremonies she served merely as a decoration; and Charles of course betrayed her right and left. So much for Elizabeth of Austria. It was mainly from the lynx-eyed women that these comments came. What of the newly married pair! Nothing against them; a handsome, debonair, sturdy youth, rather broad-shouldered for his height — for all his high heels he barely topped little Margot — who, of course, as always, was a pattern of a Princess!

The men said: "How Navarre keeps dragging her forward! Disgraceful! Scarce any proper interval between them and the

King. The fellow seems greedy for his fate. Well, he alone is unaware of it. We know all about his pretty wife. There are pockets under her skirt, and each contains the heart of a dead lover. Dead of love, if you will. Oh yes, folk die of love, though you need not believe it if you choose. On the other hand, her artful old mother may well have taught her the art of compounding potions. Psst! not so loud! Madame Catherine is not here, but everything comes to her ears."

The women said: "The Duke of Guise! Back punctually for the wedding! Now it will begin again. Nonsense! Don't you know she is now in love with the handsome La Mole. There he is! How many were there before him, I wonder. She had her first lover at eleven. I always remind my husband there's a worse woman at the court than I."

The men were still abusing Henri for not keeping his proper distance. Navarre would soon be elbowing the King and the Cardinal — insolent heretic! How much money could be safely lent on the security of his vast domains? A sack as tall as himself! Sir, you are malicious. If the sack were not taller than the King! And he still a Protestant.

Ladies of the court in their pew whispered: "Why a Huguenot? And the haste, my dear — hardly decent, surely — strange, in any event. The Pope's consent arrived with amazing suddenness; we had always heard that His Holiness forbade the marriage. Let me tell you, no one has actually seen the Papal brief. There was merely a letter from the Ambassador in Rome — if indeed it was written in Rome, and not drawn up under Madame Catherine's eye."

And the gentlemen of the court muttered from their seats near by: "'Tis more than likely the Queen Mother is behind this business. Her schemes are dark, but the purport of them may appear sooner than we think — and then beware! Charles has appointed the Protestant, de la Noue, in command of the expedition to take Mons from the Spaniards. De la Noue will take the best men, and he will take them from the Admiral in Paris. There's something in the wind. Well, we must keep our

mouths shut and know nothing. The wedding festivities will
be magnificent."

On this point the ladies were equally agreed; but ladies and
the gentlemen of all ranks there present fell silent when they
observed what was happening in the choir. Instead of joining
in the Mass, the King of Navarre left his young bride standing
and with his Protestant gentlemen passed out of a postern door.
Although this was not unexpected, the vast congregation was
scandalized. It was common knowledge that at the first word of
the Mass the Devil tucked his tail in, but the fellow might in
decency have stayed. Still, it was just as well that the incident
was everywhere observed. Such provocations could not continue.

DAME VENUS

Henri made his way round the cathedral back to the Bishop's
palace. None were with him but gentlemen of the Religion,
some that he had not seen for a long while, who had come to
attend him on this great day. Among them was his old tutor
Beauvois, who had stood so discreetly by the boy Henri when
he was struggling against being taken to Mass.

"Beauvois," said Henri, in a voice that thrilled with joy, " we
have done well for ourselves, ey? You now have a pleasant
house in Paris, I marry a Princess, and not a word about Mass."

And the fat old gentleman replied: " Sire, I have grown lazy
and no longer care for travelling. So I spend my old age in a
house that's barred and bolted, and on the door of it the mob
scrawl abuse."

He blinked. He would gladly have reminded his old pupil of
much that had been forgotten in the mood of victory and would
not have been welcome now. Many called for wine. Henri
needed nothing to intoxicate him but the vision of Margot. Impatient they are, or think they are, yet time flies with pinions of
joy, and old Chronos speeds the light globe of Fortuna. About
four o'clock it was announced that the ceremony in the cathedral
was over. The bridegroom went forth and fetched the Princess,

who was now his wife. In the presence of the King of France he kissed her; the Huguenot from the South kissed the Princess of Valois. But it was a sight that stopped many slanderous mouths. The court filed through the festal gallery back into the Bishop's palace, and all the onlookers, both mob and burghers, feasted their eyes a second time on this pageant of wealth and beauty. There was a banquet at the palace, and, in the evening, celebrations at the Louvre: a ball that was to last until morning, diversified by a masque of silver rocks. Through the great hall, under the vaulted roof with its twenty chandeliers, moved a procession of ten huge stage machines, invisibly propelled, in the guise of glittering boulders, on the first of which sat Charles IX arrayed as the god Neptune, and indeed almost naked, for he liked an opportunity to exhibit his person. After him came his two brothers and some courtiers, impersonating other gods and sea monsters. As the machines rumbled through the hall, the canvas rocks began to show signs of collapse. However, the display was greeted with much applause, and a group of musicians sang some verses specially composed by the most distinguished poets.

The night was far advanced when the guests sat for supper; more than one couple had met and made a marriage after the fashion of the King of Navarre, who cared little for Mass, but a great deal for his lady. The old Queen's lovely maids of honour did not want for Huguenot adorers. Agrippa d'Aubigné was an easy prey, his heart was soon ablaze. Du Bartas was aloof in spirit, but his flesh gave way. The bridegroom's friend Philippe du Plessis-Mornay was intent on other matters. His was a nature which amid scenes of orgy retired within itself and grew more and more austere. Indeed, he was inclined towards extremes; others exceeded in debauchery, he in virtue. His Socratic countenance wrathfully transfigured, he shouted to the revellers:

"Fools! Art we to be beguiled by a buffoon who plays the King in tragedy — who spreads a golden drugget on the stage, and two hours afterwards must return it to the property-man with the money for its hire? Remember, pray, what rags and dirt and vermin he may hide beneath those regal trappings, and how often his resplendent Majesty itched and had to scratch himself."

This, thought those who heard it, was rather too redolent of treason. But Charles's brother — and successor, if Charles bled to death one day — d'Anjou, clapped Philippe gleefully on the shoulder. " The buffoon in question is my brother," he whispered. " You may say what you think to me, because I think so too. I like you Protestants for your candour, and the faith in God that makes you so."

The Prince was not alone in his affection for these rough champions of the faith, though that affection took various forms. Catholics and Protestants lay about embraced, Monsieur de Léran in the arms of Captain de Nançay. Lévis, Vicomte de Léran, a graceful, handsome youth, looked more like a page than a soldier. The gigantic de Nançay was so ravished that he fairly crushed him to his chest, but the lad slipped out of his embrace and promptly bit his fat admirer in the ear. For a moment the revellers held their breath; but wrath was scattered in a roar of laughter. So passed the night.

It wore the guise of Dame Venus; a few sceptics like du Bartas recognized her yet unveiled. But even they did not observe that all this was Madame Catherine's work. She had sent forth her skirmishers, and her maids of honour did what nothing else could do; they broke down all barriers of faith. God had made no mingling of that blood; Dame Venus, after her fashion, undertook the task that night. She, indeed, of all the heathen deities, is least disposed to fraud and guile; what she promises she forthwith fulfils. And at that court, indeed, which for all such purposes was Madame Catherine's court, love's pledges were discharged at once. Hence a part of the company was always in the apartments of the maids of honour, and even, in the turmoil of that night's encounters, waiting at open doors, as the new arrivals sought their turn, and those actively engaged were encouraged with somewhat jealous though heartfelt applause. Then they went back and danced.

At times the great hall was but half full, and the musicians in their gallery played to a barren echo. The topers stayed, and the philosophers; and, bending affectionately over Margot — Henri.

They were sitting under a canopy of flags, the flags of the provinces of France, of past battles and of distant lands. And, each to each, they were utterly alone. Henri told her that he had always, always loved her. Margot answered for herself and for her heart, and her answer was the same. And they believed it, though both knew better. But it seemed to have become true. . . . This is the lover of my life. . . . I have known none but Margot; with her I shall begin to live. . . . He is the spring; without him I should soon have grown old.

"Henri! Your body is made to the classic norm for a man's body. By my honour, you deserve a reward for that."

"Margot! I am glad and eager to share that reward with you — as often as you will and can."

"The proof will suffer no delay," she cried; it was a Valois Princess who spoke. He had leapt up from his knees — and they, too, went the way the rest had gone. The way of the flesh, indeed, but some flesh is exalted. Outside the great hall Henri picked her up and carried her. Down the corridors he strode, with Margot in his arms. Guards formed front and saluted. Prostrate drunkards peered after them as they passed.

His passionate intent was baffled by the bridal dress; it hung foursquare upon her hips, Margot was fast boxed within it. Here the boy-lover proved himself as discreet as he was experienced. He laid no harsh hand on that glittering shell, but in an instant he had opened it. How unlike Guise, thought Margot! — though Guise indeed was taller and looked more distinguished. Thus was the shell opened and the pearl unveiled. But she, far from proffering her charms, swayed and made as though her knees were giving way; strong hands picked her up and flung her where she wished to be, on her famous bed of black silk. A lover of women, he knew all the less about them! "He is mine," she thought, before her sight and hearing were engulfed, to the great profit of her other senses.

THE HOUSE OF AUSTRIA

Henri went back alone into the great hall. He found it more populous than before; the royal pair was present. Charles had in the meantime covered his nakedness; he was, however, drunk. "There he comes — from the arms of my fat Margot!" he shouted at Henri. And the looks of all the company showed that they, as well as the King of France, knew what had been happening and expected the lucky bridegroom's return. The Queen did not laugh; events were never mirrored in that mind. Her voice was barely known. Elizabeth of Austria sat aloof, enthroned and motionless in an embrasure of the great hall, surrounded by an empty space whence no guards were needed to repel intruders. Erect in her golden dress, rigid and inviolate as the statue of a saint, her face so thickly painted that it, too, looked inhuman, she gazed down on the assemblage. Behind her spreading skirts lurked two Spanish priests; themselves scarce visible, they marked everything that happened.

Charles clung to his brother-in-law's arm: and into his ear, but loud enough for all to hear, he blurted filthy jests about his sister. Henri resolved in disgust to leave him lying if he fell. Indeed, he was half minded to trip him up. But he did not, and under Charles's lurching guidance they gradually approached the empty circle round the Queen.

"Look at her!" stuttered the King; "up above us all. And just you try and throw her down! If she was dead she would stand up like a gilded dummy. The House of Austria is a nightmare, and this woman with whom I have shared a bed haunts my dreams, looking like Medusa, and turns my blood cold. She may be the daughter of the Roman Emperor — but she is no wife for a man, Navarre! My grandfather, Francis I, lay in chains at Madrid, and before the Emperor Charles, fifth of his name, would let him go, he demanded his son as hostage. They tormented my father, and now they use the Emperor Maximilian's daughter to torment me. All Europe is beneath their heels. Their gold, their plots, their armies, and their priests are dividing my people and ravaging my land. Navarre!" muttered the

King savagely, " avenge me! 'Tis for that I am giving you my sister. Avenge me and my kingdom. I can do nothing; I am ruined and I am growing desperate. Remember me, Navarre! — and beware — " and he added in a whimper that could scarce be overheard: " beware of my mother and my brother Anjou. But whatever may befall you, do not blame me, Navarre; for I am but a man who is afraid. I fear all people that walk this earth."

He stopped, with a hissing intake of the breath; fear indeed had come upon him. Behind the Queen he caught the glitter of two pairs of piercing eyes for an instant, and they vanished. Charles tottered and clung to Navarre; the pair stood islanded within a ring of watching faces. His Huguenot brother-in-law was inwardly exultant and thus mastered his rising dread. King Charles had fallen silent, and upon the ring of courtiers silence fell — and gradually Henri felt their eyes upon him in tense and hostile watchfulness. Of course, these fanatic enemies of the Religion could not bear to see him intimate with the King, their master. They had looked askance upon his marriage, that he knew, and they must needs express their feelings. That day, at the bidding of Dame Venus, there had been much strange commingling. But now the throng began to push and jostle. Catholics fell to thrusting Protestants against the walls. But at the invisible barrier around the Queen they stopped and gathered, watching, waiting.

All armed, as Henri saw at once; but for the time, more curious than aggressive. Well, they would not overpower him easily; his Protestants behind him closed their ranks, prepared to strike. The maids of honour had scattered, and eyed the scene from a safe distance, twittering as the storm approached.

Charles, though not yet master of himself, felt the void about him, and the now stifling air put him in a frenzy. " Wine! " he roared. " I'll tipple with the Queen till she drops to the floor. I'll knock that precious gilded dummy over, see if I don't! "

She scarce understood him, and sat motionless as before. But Charles, exhausted perhaps by his debauchery, leaned so heavily on his Huguenot brother-in-law that Henri could no longer hold him up; both would have fallen had not a man leapt forward and clutched the King. Henri found himself looking into the face of one Monsieur de Maurevert; and the face was writhen with hatred. In an instant he was thrust aside by the Duke of Guise. " What are you about, Maurevert? " said the Duke hastily. " A man like you must not be seen here — go! " He steadied Charles. " Bear a hand, Navarre. The throne is in our care, and we must stand by it."

" 'Tis for that purpose that we rode with our noblemen from Lorraine and Béarn," Henri interposed in the same lofty tone, and stood up straight and stiff like Guise, who was tall and fair. They glared at each across the drunken King, heaving him to his feet when he threatened to collapse.

" Put me up beside the Habsburg lady," whimpered Charles, with a sudden gush of tears. " I am a little saint too — which is more than you two are. Both of you have slept with fat Margot. You first, Guise, but she wants no more of you now." Whereat he lurched against Henri of Guise, who thrust him back on Henri of Navarre. " You are hers now, Navarre. She loves you, I love you, and our mother, Madame Catherine, loves you very much."

" Damnation! " he exclaimed — he had caught another glimpse of the two Spanish priests, whom he had, in the meantime, forgotten. But those black apparitions, and the looks they flung at him, cast a sinister change upon the King. " I know what you want of me," he stammered, though they had once more promptly vanished. " I know too well. It shall be done. The will is yours, not mine. I wash my hands of it."

For the moment he was sober and could stand; Lorraine and Navarre released him, and Charles, his hands now free, peered about the room. The throng by the invisible barrier seemed to him altered, no longer merely curious nor watchful. The mass of Catholics now gathered about him with menace in their eyes, heaving to and fro as the Protestants bore down upon them from behind. Some of their leaders had clambered on to chairs. Du Bartas alone was tall enough to give his orders from where he stood. A confused hubbub arose; the presence of a King could no longer constrain them, and it was clear from the turmoil and the shouting that the truce would soon be broken, and blood be shed.

At that very instant the two Spanish priests behind Elizabeth of Austria were seen to move. They vanished, and though no motive forces could be seen, the Queen's dais began to glide away with her. It bumped and jolted as it went, like a stage machine; indeed, it moved in exactly the same fashion as the silver rocks that carried the naked King and the other sea deities when the ball began. But it did move, and with a final heave the seat of Habsburg had safely passed the threshold. Before the door could be shut, the tapestry covering the dais was lifted, and two gasping Spanish priests crawled out and stretched themselves.

The King of Navarre burst in a roar of laughter, so joyous and hearty that not a man in that great hall could have taken it amiss. Evil could not stand against it, and, for the moment, feuds were forgotten. A stocky man standing on a chair right at the back saw this and seized a chance: his name was known to many — Agrippa d'Aubigné. And he chanted in shrill and dulcet accents: " The Queen of Navarre is waiting and weeping on her famous black silk bed. Who can predict the morrow? Up, and let us escort the bridegroom to the bride." The throng applauded, but to deepen the effect, he took refuge in verse:

> " Not far away is death, and then at last
>   Life without death, a life that cannot cheat,
>   For life is saved, death brought unto defeat,
>   Who would not long to see his perils past?
>   Now the glad voyager in harbour lies,
>   And journey's end shall purge his weary eyes."

The connection between this effusion and the matter in hand seemed slight, or merely comic, so they all began to laugh, and the victory was won. Charles proclaimed that he and all his court would escort his brother-in-law Navarre and bed him with his sister; and he took the husband by the hand. On Navarre's other side stood Lorraine. It was a tense moment, the former lover escorting the new husband to his bride. A procession was then formed, without distinction of religion. Those who had been so near to striking were thankful that the hour had not arrived, and the procession started, picking up the throng of maids of honour as it went. Wherever it passed, doors opened, and all manner of great ladies hastened out to join it. Some older gentlemen of the court, who had already gone to sleep, were awakened by the noise and fell in, just as they had risen from their beds. De Miossens, First Nobleman, strode forward gravely in a bed-gown and fur mantle, his legs bare. Guards with torches ran on ahead and lit up the old stone passages; few knew where they were, and the vast concourse trailed back and forward through the labyrinth of the Louvre, chanting as it went:

"*Who would not long to see his perils past?*
Now the glad voyager in harbour lies,
And journey's end shall purge his weary eyes."

"At last!" cried Charles, but it was the wrong door. The whole court had to wind along the cramped alleyways until the right door at length was reached. Here Charles delivered his parting address to the happy husband. "You are a fortunate man, Navarre! A Princess, the first and noblest in the West, has bestowed her innocence upon you; until the moment when you take it from her, she has lived in loyalty to you, and now you are knocking at her door," whereupon he himself crashed his own fist against the oaken portal. Then he kissed his brother-in-law on both cheeks and burst into tears.

The bride made no sign, although no one could have slept through such an uproar. They paused and listened, and the Duke of Guise remarked:

"By all the saints, and especially by Saint Bartholomew! Had it been I, the door would have sprung open of itself; for it knows me well."

So Guise, in spite of his impassive demeanour, was mortified and angry. Navarre's retort was prompt:

" She keeps the door shut merely that there may be no mistake."

" She keeps it shut," retorted Guise, " because she is used to something better."

" One thing after another! " snapped Charles. " We had not come to watch a duel, but to bed the bridegroom."

None the less, outside the Princess Margot's door her two cavaliers faced each other in a truly ominous attitude; one foot out-thrust, erect and rigid, and a wild look in their eyes. The silence spread to the rear of the procession, and women were lifted up to watch the pair — Navarre in white silk, Guise in blue — snarling like two cats. Had he not been the rejected suitor, Guise would have had much in his favour; his tall figure, his icy calm, his clear-cut features, now tense with rage, all the more formidable because of his usual winning air. Navarre met this display with mimicry. On his smaller scale he, too, could impersonate a beast about to spring, but in so doing he made that beast absurd, incidentally and yet beyond gainsaying. He drew himself up, bowed, and crouched — why, his very hair grew fairer, the next moment a tawny beard would come sprouting from his chin as he aped Lorraine's stilted Northern speech.

" I began with village girls, and now I have eyes for none but the Princess. The Princess was content with Lorraine until she aspired to Navarre."

This was more than Guise himself could match, and his haughty airs were countered; he was out of the fight, quite apart from the derision of the bystanders, which, though here and there suppressed, began to break out into laughter. Suddenly the oaken portal swung back, the Princess stood in the doorway laughing: and the whole court laughed too.

" Who is not glad when he at last in harbour lies? " croaked Charles in a stage whisper. A roar of laughter; the Princess dragged her husband into the room and slammed the door; another burst of laughter.

THE SCAR

They stood and eyed each other, while the sounds of the departing court faded down the corridors into the distance. At last they could see it moving through the opposite wing of the palace, as the gleam of torches shifted from one window to the next. And when the river folk rose from their sleep in their barges or their cabins on the shore, again they thought the palace of the Louvre was burning in hell-fire. Who knew what might be toward?

They eyed each other — then Madame Marguerite waved her lovely hand in a fashion that bade him undress himself. She herself did not slip off her bed-gown until the moment she lay down. She knew the faults of her figure, and she knew too that they were more apparent when she stood than when she lay. But, most of all, her purpose was to observe the figure of this new man of hers. For Madame Marguerite was a connoisseur, both of male bodies and of Latin verse. Her new-made husband fumbled at his ruff, he found it difficult to get out of his white silk ceremonial dress. Its puffed sleeves were meant to make him look broad-shouldered, but slim-waisted. His hips seemed firm and sturdy, which made his boyish lanky legs look all the longer. This effect could, to a point, be achieved by art; and it was not without anxiety that this experienced lady awaited the result. Behold! it was better than the promise of the outer envelope. Madame Marguerite pondered and compared, and here she found all the standards of the antique, which she had begun to believe were fabulous, really fulfilled — so much so that for the moment a look of appraising curiosity still lingered on her face. It was the throb of the blood beneath his skin that first stirred hers; and the connoisseur was lost when she had touched his sinewy limbs.

That time both proved themselves, as never yet, unwearied in delight; it was a rivalry in which they were a well-matched pair. When in later years, and engrossed with other women, Henri wished to deny that he had ever been in love with Margot, he described that night, and those that followed, in a word that is

often on the lips of meaner folk when they strive to appear
greater than they are. Meanwhile he could have proved in his
own person that there are times in life when the rapture of the
flesh comes near to death. Indeed, death may then be nearer
than it seems to those in whom life is brimming over: they have
merely forgotten to throw a light into the corners. "Not far
from us is death." Ghostly words that Henri must have heard
awhile ago, and of such were his innermost forebodings. They
were the last words that hovered in a brain now wearied out
with love.

It was but a brief respite, for desire, insatiable, flooded into
his very sleep; it soon awakened him, and with eyes still closed
he fell to kissing the body at his side, when suddenly his lips
came upon a scar. He opened his eyes and fingered it; he was
experienced in scars. They came from blows, and bullet-wounds,
and bites, and happened on battlefields as also upon lovers' beds.
For their proper estimation much depended on the portion of
the body scarred. If a soldier was scarred where Margot bore
her scar, it was clear that he had taken to his heels and fled. He
was perforce a coward on that account; indeed, a King of France
and Navarre, named Henri, was himself fated to be scarred in
that same place. But this was one of the loveliest parts of a
woman's body; it was his, and his alone — but if someone else
had bitten it, it was not his! He seized and shook her, and as
she did not at once respond, he turned her over towards him,
and into her scarce awakened face he snarled:

" Who bit you on the backside? "

" No one," said she, which was just the answer that he wanted.

" 'Tis a lie! " he shouted.

" 'Tis the truth," she persisted, as she sat up and met his
anger with the loftiest composure of mien and voice, while she
secretly lamented he had noticed it so soon. In a week he would
not have cared at all. So thought Madame Marguerite, from
long experience.

" There are marks of teeth," said he.

" They only look like tooth marks," she retorted, and the
more improbable the answer, the more confidently she spoke.

"They are marks of teeth: of Guise's teeth."

She let him say this again and again. He would soon be sick of saying it, she thought, and on her bosom, which she edged towards him until he began to fondle it, he would soon forget her backside.

She did, however, deign to add, with a shrug of her plump shoulders: "No, not Guise's teeth nor anyone else's." Which infuriated him still more. How hard it was, she thought — nay, almost impossible — to refute a false charge. There were many charges he might well have brought against her, and he must needs choose one of which she was innocent. Must she confess how her mother and her brother dealt with her one morning, when they set upon her to give up Guise and take Navarre for a husband? Surely he could recognize Madame Catherine's gnarled old teeth.

"Tell me the truth!" he groaned as he gripped her.

So he was jealous. Suppose she did tell. What would he do? Would he believe she had been beaten and bitten on his account to make her marry him? He would not; and she would also have to confess that she had come straight from Guise. A trying dilemma!

Suddenly he released her and hammered his fists upon the pillows, and vented his fury, not upon her, but on her black silk bed, so famous for all that had happened on it. But the attack was meant for her! And she slipped to her own side of the bed, ready to leap out. It would be her turn soon. So he beat his women, did he? — and Margot thought him a fine fellow and knew her heart was his. In the end she resolved to confess nothing, while he went on wailing: "Confess! Confess!"

Suddenly he utterly changed his tone. "You will never tell the truth. How could the daughter of the woman by whom my mother was — "

There was the word, and there the thought. Until then she had been lying on the bed and he looking down upon her as she lay. At this, she sat up, both listened to the echo of that unuttered word and eyed each other horror-struck. Her next movement was to cover her nakedness, and his to leave the bed.

While he flung on his clothes, they watched each other furtively; he, wondering what this woman could be like who had so dragged him down: she, eager to know whether she had really lost him. She told herself No; he would come back, he was the more securely hers because since that night their bond would be one of guilt. While he called it guilt, he would not know satiety. Beloved Henricus, she thought in Latin.

There he stood, clad in white silk, and fumbled with his ruff and said with military curtness: "I shall join the army in Flanders today."

"Let me give you a saint to keep you safe," said she, leaning towards a chest of books, her companions when no man was by; took one out, detached a page, and gave it to him. A lovely hand, and a most nonchalant gesture. She did indeed hear him gulp down a sob, but she did not again look up — she dropped back on the pillow, and when he closed the door Margot had fallen asleep. Her last thought was that a lady worn out by a night of love was not a convincing tragic figure.

But she had a dream.

The Warning

Henri had left the bedchamber too soon. After the orgy of the night the palace of the Louvre as yet showed no signs of awakening to its usual malign activities. In the corridors and rooms Henri stepped over sleeping forms, who looked paralysed rather than asleep. They had collapsed on the scene of their last encounter, whether their business had been love or drink or fighting. Sprays of roses climbed in through an open window, and beneath it lay a huddle of guests with their gay clothes stained with their own vomit, the sunlight pouring in on them. As he picked his solitary way among them, he caught glimpses of secret chambers, where the night had been spent in every perversity of lust. Against the outer wall leaned sleeping guards, clasping their halberds in their arms. Dogs looked up and blinked, barked feebly, and went to sleep again.

Henri was bewildered by the multifarious scene. In the vast compass of the new building and the tortuous passages of the

old one he lost his direction, if indeed he had ever had one!
Sprawling over a broken stonework balustrade lay a fat man
asleep, and from the tall white cap still poised above his sweating countenance, Henri realized that he was near the kitchens.
The servants too had revelled until they dropped, but the sight
of exhausted flesh is the more repellent when found among
refuse and foul dishes. Navarre, in his white silk dress, recoiled
— last of all he found himself in some dark, cob-webbed chambers, with iron-studded doors, like dungeons, and indeed he
thought he had come upon them once before in the bowels of
the old palace.

As he waited for his eyes to grow accustomed to the place,
he heard an abrupt " Pst! " beside him and looked down on a
young woman. He drew her under a dormer window set high
up in the wall. " Not into the light! " she implored. " I have
not yet made up my face, I must look hideous! "

" What are you doing here? Why — Yes — you are she.
Armagnac shut you up just now because you were spying on me.
Are you spying on me now? "

" Indeed, Sire, I am your loyal and devoted servant, and I am
here to help you and you alone."

He tilted her face back into the light. She was a pretty, fresh-
looking girl, and even her ravaged make-up could not hide her
charm. He kissed her on the lips, and as he did so her responsive
shiver told him she was his. What baffling creatures women
were! Perhaps if he had not routed out the little spy and drawn
her claws —

" Aha — so you like me now? I am glad, for I think you delightful," he said in his most winning tones. And at the words,
whether he meant them or no, her face lit up. But his heart
was touched, for no woman ever failed to touch it. So she had
her moment; he had made her happy.

" And what will you do for me? " he asked, ignoring what
had passed. She was gasping and could not answer for a moment.

" Give my life for you, Sire. I shall lose it, that I know. Madame Catherine will find out that I am here. She too is well
served."

" What can she care? "

" Softly! She is not far away. I caught her just now coming out of her rooms. I lay on a carpet as though I was asleep. I was alone — alone," she repeated eagerly. " I had found my room full of strangers. But she crept past, opened her son Anjou's door very gently, and bade him come with her. She did not open the King's door. On her way she tapped at other doors, and several people followed her one by one, and I crept after them. Oh, Heaven! — a game of hide and seek with life as forfeit! " She shuddered and he could hear the chattering of her teeth.

" You shall see all, Sire," and she took him by the hand and led him on into pitch-darkness. Who was she? Perhaps the mistress of an enemy, and he lurking in the shadows. No. That was the room where she had been shut up by Armagnac, she knew every step hereabouts. What is it, Madam? We seem to be climbing. Ah — rungs — am I to go up the ladder? Hold it steady for me, little lady, it is slipping. Higher — and higher — a glimmer of light at last. Up into an attic, where one can lie flat on a jutting beam that runs through a narrow opening into another room. Not even a child could wriggle through it. However, I see a room; not the sort of room that Madame Catherine is accustomed to, but there she sits. Her high-backed chair is set against the farther wall, the light falls on her from above, and that must be what gives her that leaden look. She is wearing her widow's weeds, as usual; the others have just risen from their beds. Yonder are the Guises, and there is Anjou. " Madam, do you know a certain Monsieur de Maurevert? " It is not he, what should he be doing here? " Silence, the Queen is speaking."

Alas, they are too far below, the words are lost, as in a rocky cleft. She must be scheming against the King her son, or she would not have crept here without him. He is treating with England and the Protestant princes. He calls Coligny his father. She hates Charles. Her son is Anjou, as you can see from looking at him. Mark his twisted ears; thick-lipped, and dark all over like the spirits that haunt him. He shifts uneasily, he cannot wait for what is to happen. He puts a finger to his lips to bid his favourite be silent. Oh yes, one of them must needs be there. "Madam, do you know a favourite who looks like a dancing-master? Is his name du Guast?"

("She does not answer, and, indeed, we must be careful. These people are plotting against someone. Either Charles or myself. Well, let them try; Paris swarms with Huguenots. They have crawled into that cellar to make a murder; how pale they look, especially the Cardinal of Lorraine! Pull down your hat and hide your blotchy skin, you old goat! What was he up to last night, I wonder. Ah, he goes into a corner and talks to Guise. Handsome man, Guise! Will look well when laid out. Guise, my beloved Guise, I am the next Prince of the Blood, after the Valois; they are sickly lads, and I — not you — have married their sister.

"Stay — he is raising his voice, the others cannot stop him, now I can hear him. The other is to be killed at court. Who? Charles? I? Not the Lord Admiral; he is joining the army in Flanders. Anjou is looking greedy; it must be Charles, his detested brother. No, Madame Catherine refuses, she insists on silence, her son's death will come soon enough for her. She whispers; they all lean towards her, and one, especially one — what is his name, with the close-set eyes? I wondered just now what he could be doing here. Absurd, there cannot be any scheme afoot. But Guise takes him carefully aside — I know: Monsieur de Maurevert, of course.

"Aha — Anjou looks strange — is he often thus attacked? What does he say? Means to have the blood of the man who has set his brother so bitterly against him? Who can that be? Coligny? Pah! Anjou is not the man for such a deed. Besides, his good mother shakes her head and gets up. Well, I, too, had better — Guise is going too, he means to see the others safely back. I shall laugh if we meet each other on the way. Back again down the ladder. Why, where is the little dame — gone already? Ah, well, I must find my way myself.")

And he did so, hurrying through the servants' quarters, among the gaping, blinking lackeys; and he stepped out at last on to the

old court opposite the front terrace, behind the famous little
stairway by which favourites and conspirators slipped up to the
royal apartments. At that moment Guise emerged at the farther
end. Henri hurriedly planted himself on the first stair, where
Lorraine caught sight of him.

" Whither away so early, Navarre? "

" Is it early, Guise? My honoured mother-in-law receives me
at any hour, you see."

" Have you been with Madame Catherine? Up yonder? "

" Where else? " Henri laid a hand against his heart, in the
manner of one boasting of an honour he has not enjoyed. At
this the tall Lorraine beamed with satisfied superiority. He had
just left a secret meeting with the Queen herself, and here was
a preposterous little liar who claimed to have been received by
her at that same hour. With his hand on his hip, and on his
fair-complexioned countenance a large complacent smile, Guise
observed:

" Then you have heard the news from her; still, I take pleasure
in repeating it. You have won, Navarre. The court of France
has decided on war with Spain, for as your Admiral wrote in his
memorandum, the nation needs a foreign war; a just but not too
difficult war, and one likely to be profitable. Otherwise our
countrymen will plunder and rob each other. The old gentleman knows us all too well."

" The document was drawn up by Mornay, who always beats
a scheme out to the end."

" 'Tis just what we should have thought. This is your design,
Navarre."

" Yours too, I think? "

" We defend ourselves — no more. You Protestants are planning to destroy us; so much is proved out of the mouths of
Mornay and Coligny. So we prefer to march with you against
King Philip. We'll meet again in Flanders — if ever on this
earth! "

He turned to go — but did not: nor did he mean to go. The
tall, fair-haired figure swung sharply around.

" Navarre! Play fair — as I do! It is true I had concentrated troops in Paris when you were advancing on the city at the head of your nobles."

"I have more of them to come." Henri was the shorter man, but as he was standing on a stair, he met Lorraine's eyes level.

"My men are marching into Flanders this very day. Why not give orders likewise, Navarre!"

"I play your game — 'tis an old game and I like it. Do you remember our schooldays, Henri Guise?"

"You started the game, Henri Navarre. Cæsar was murdered. We all lost our tempers."

"You and Anjou did. You meant to kill me in good earnest. Such passages are never forgotten, my friend."

"An early friendship is the only one that does not die before we do. I am not ashamed to weep," said Guise solemnly, and something like a tear or two did trickle from his eyes, though Henri, on his stair, felt he could have wept in more convincing fashion. But he was conscious of more shame than satisfaction. This man was his deadly enemy, even though he was so only because he had lost the Princess. But both men's voices shook with passion as they stood there lying to each other. Alas! — they had been boys together! In a flush of shame at life as it must needs be, the man on the stair turned his head away, and thus took his eyes off his adversary. As he turned, something, he knew not what, seemed to rustle beneath his doublet, and he raised a hand to his chest. As he did so he heard a sharp cry — "Stop!" looked up, and saw before him quite another face, one contorted with fury, from which the gentler memories of youth were blotted out; here was the naked present, with a dagger in its fist.

Henri laughed, as though the most fearsome revelations were those he most enjoyed.

"But I could make a better show of tears than yours."

"You are a brave man, so I let you live."

"You might be sorry if you did not," retorted Henri, with a glance over Guise's shoulder. The other swung round like a startled beast; there stood a Huguenot with sword unsheathed.

"My lord and master speaks truth," said the tanned and

bearded campaigner in his threadbare leather doublet. " Guise had but to raise his arm, and before he could touch my King, a Gascon gentleman named Armagnac would have had the honour of splitting the Lord Duke of Lorraine into two equal parts."

That strident Southern voice was the first that day to break the brooding silence of the well-shaft of the Louvre. Guards ran out of the bridge gatehouse. Doors opened on every side, and men poured forth. Before anyone could find out what had happened, Guise had vanished in the throng. Armagnac, who had swiftly sheathed his sword, went about asking what was the matter. Then he returned and announced in a loud voice to his master that two chapmen had fallen out over some customs dues.

But he whispered secretly: " We must get out of here at once! " For Armagnac, though a bold man, knew when guile was called for.

He also knew a passage by which they could get back unobserved to his master's room. " But your wedding clothes, Sire — they are covered with dust and cobwebs. A valet would notice it, though a Duke did not; or he might have grown suspicious sooner, too soon, perhaps, before I could arrive."

" Do you follow me everywhere? "

" I watch over you like a nurse — take care! "

At a sharp turn in the corridor they came upon a bundle wrapped in sacking, not quite of human length. Yet stay — a pair of feet in little shoes were left uncovered. A human body. How small they look when they — Master and servant exchanged a glance. The servant's eyes were eloquent of caution. But the master lifted the sacking at a point where he expected to find a strange face. The dead always seem strange, the sight of death always comes as a surprise. With a hoarse cry Navarre started back. His servant clapped a hand over his mouth. " Silence, Sire! Quick — in here, before anyone comes." He dragged his master away, flung open a door, and closed it softly.

" Now say what you will. Here we cannot be overheard. 'Tis a foul deed, like those that live here," observed the Protestant with conviction. His master stood motionless and silent, and he went on: " We do not kill like that. Such a pretty lady, so gentle and so sweet. I know a pastor who was converting her to the true faith."

" Do you know her name? "

" No. Perhaps Catherine, perhaps Fleurette. A poor but noble lady, as I am a poor but noble gentleman."

And Henri thought: " I never knew her name, and now I may not ask it. And none must see my anger and my grief. She died for my sake and she died for love. What did I say this morning to the Queen of Navarre, my wife? That I would join the army in Flanders; I had forgotten it already."

And he said: " We ride today to Flanders."

" Bravely said, Sire. On a battlefield I am at home; I can attack, and if need be, run away. But here — you find a bit of sacking at a corner, and you must step over it and keep your mouth shut."

Armagnac went on talking as he prepared the wooden tub for Henri's bath. While the King was undressing, a little scroll of paper fell to the floor. This was what had rustled: Margot's patron saint — which was it?

It was a page out of the Anatomical Atlas, depicting the interior of a human body. Against every organ was written its Latin name in the margin, in the scholarly Princess's handwriting; and she had herself made a drawing of a dagger — with its point against the diagram; it was clear she knew the vital spot and its Latin name.

That was what the Princess of Valois had meant, and this was her warning. Had he come on it before, would he have drawn the dagger before Guise did so?

" No," said Henri aloud. And Armagnac looked up in astonishment.

A DREAM

But she had a dream.

Margot, in her dream, was Dame Venus, in the guise of a marble statue, standing in a labyrinth of green garden walks, whose cool shadows she could feel on her white back even in her dream. For the figure was endowed with feeling and was conscious of itself. Behind her, to the right and left of the hedges, she espied two warriors, mortal rivals for her favours, although neither of them could so much as lift his naked sword. They too were statues, who, like her, were clad in a rigid garb of marble and fixed to pedestals, as she was. However, her thought would have sufficed to hurl the rejected suitor to the ground in fragments.

With her sightless eyes she gazed forth upon a landscape where the silver stream, the sunlit banks, the palaces and statues, all awaited her behest. Statues stood everywhere, and they spoke, though their voices made no sound. And what they said was: " The choice is yours. Decide ere it is night. The sun still shines upon you from above, warms your smooth flanks and floods your being until your very heart begins to beat. But as the day grows cooler, you will lose your warmth and strength. Darkness will summon all the evil forces, and they will thwart your purpose. You were no more than vain and careless, Dame Venus, for you feel but faintly and your consciousness is dim. Decide! Decide! " cried all the statues suddenly, no longer voiceless, but twittering and screeching like the little birds from the islands. Then suddenly all was still, and a void came upon the created world as upon the world of thought.

Through the utter desolation of the universe rang out a voice the like of which no man had heard; a vast voice, reverberating down the echoing distances of space. The dreamer had to rally all her forces and think more keenly than she ever did awake; at last she recognized the scene. A loggia in the midst of a great palace, and therein stood God. He waited; the great voice was silent for a while, that she might draw her breath and not perish from looking on His face. He appeared in the guise of a statue, His garment hung about Him in clear-cut, classic folds, and did not stir as a gust of wind swept past.

The loggia lay at the front of the Louvre, where there was none as yet apparent. The familiar building dissolved into the ideal image of the palace which mysteriously abides within us all our lives; as if we had seen it on a rapturous journey in our youth, though we shall never see it more with these our eyes, nor ever come upon it again anywhere. But here it stood in imperishable glory, decked with all the master works of art; and the name of that palace was Sinai. In the midst stood God, in stone, not above the middle height — but as His eyelids lifted, a thrill of bliss came upon the dreamer, and she longed to cry: " Yes, Lord! " though she had not even heard His will. For she knew what it would be. *Thou shalt not kill!* His short curled black beard began to move; blood flowed into His lips and they grew darkly red, and the Lord said: " Princess of Valois! " She trembled, she could not answer to her name for very fear, because she had dared to conceive herself in dream as Venus. That was merely madness. This at last was real, this was the holy truth. " Madame Marguerite! " cried the Lord. And she answered: " Yes, Lord! "

She had answered to her name; but she could not now command the deep and ringing voice of Marguerite de Valois. That was now God's voice, He spoke with her voice multiplied. She herself could only babble in God's presence. But God heard her and accepted her. He spoke to her, that she might not mistake Him, in Greek. And He said:

" Thou shalt not kill! "

THE RESCUE

As soon as the Queen of Navarre awoke she dressed and hurried to her mother. She took some of her guards with her, to force an entrance if need were. However, she was promptly admitted, and she could well see why. Her brother Charles was with Catherine, and in a furious rage. He swore and he cursed; he was the King, and orders should be given by him alone, not by conspirators who met in dungeons.

This outburst irritated Madame Catherine, who wanted to reflect. Moreover, she feared for her own safety; her daughter, if no one else, could read that in her mask-like mien. The mother was pleased to see her daughter and pointed to the accustomed stool. Whatever else Margot might be, she was her mother's child; she loved to crouch at the old lady's side, and there, with both hands thrust into her hair, pore over great leathern tomes, of which there were always several piled upon her knees. As her habit was, she took her books from the table and mechanically turned the pages, but her eyes looked beyond them and wandered from her mother to the King.

Meantime Charles was abashed by the strange fact that this outburst failed to impress the old lady, who merely looked at him. Well, he would show her what he knew, and that would shake her complacency. So he thrust his head out at her, with its red and pendulous mustachios, and stood with his hands dangling at his sides; but his hands were fists. Thus from the corners of his eyes he watched his mother, to see how much he had to fear from her.

" Did you sleep well, mother? "

" Your revels made not a little noise, my son."

" None the less you were early abroad, and several others with you, among them my brother Anjou. I am well informed. Your plans are aimed at me — they are dangerous to the State, otherwise you would not meet in a dungeon."

" It could only seem so, my son, to someone who viewed it from a ladder."

" You do well not to deny it, mother; for my witness will gladly tell the story in your presence."

" I think not."

Which, to the son, meant: You are a fool. To the daughter, that whoever saw what happened was no longer alive. For a moment Margot bent over her book, while Charles fell into a frenzy. He would have his brother Anjou arrested. His own mother was plotting to murder him and put his brother on the throne. "But I'll call in my Protestants. None but Coligny shall help me to rule this realm! " he cried boyishly, with a certain horror at his own temerity. The effect was what he had dreaded; his mother burst into tears. Nor were tears the old lady's only demonstration. She waved her stunted little arms; her heavy visage was transformed into the innocent face of an anguished child; she clapped her tiny fingers to it, peering through them all the while, and moaned. But, though her lamentations grew more desperate, not a drop of moisture trickled through those fingers. Madame Catherine could mimic everything but tears. Charles indeed began to waver, but Margot noticed that one failure.

The old lady wailed between her sobs: " Permit me, Sire, to withdraw to my own country. I have long since been in fear for my life. You trust none but my sworn enemies."

This must surely shake him; and it did. He stammered out helplessly that he did but ask to know what had been decided that morning.

" How best to save your kingdom," said she; and she said it in a voice that promptly hardened, and with her usual mask-like mien. The outburst of a moment ago might never have happened. And she went on in a louder and reproving tone:

" And we had to decide without you. It was a matter for measures — drastic measures, such as great rulers have to take upon occasion, but beyond your powers, my poor son "; her imperious air contrasted strangely with her so recent semblance of humility. There sat Madame Catherine, more potent and secure than ever, as though she had never pleaded for permission to go back to Florence — from which city she had, indeed, in former days, been banished.

Charles looked down his feet, bewildered by the conflicts of his mind; he remembered his mother's hints in times when the dreaded hour was still far distant; he had fallen in with these fell designs as no more than the visions of a nightmare. Indeed, at first they were but an indulgence of his mother's taste for peering into spiritual abysses. But Charles well remembered Amaury and Ligneroles, two victims of his fears — at a time of lesser peril. Meantime, to show his independence, he had given his confidence to the Huguenot, Coligny, called him father, and taken his advice on every matter. As a result, he was on the verge of war with Spain. The House of Austria was closing in on him and his beleaguered realm; Austria owned the south and the centre of the Old World; the New World and its gold were under Austrian control. Austria held the Church in fee, and through her all the nations, France included; Austria shared his bed in the guise of an Archduchess, so stiff with gold and power that she was as rigid as a statue!

" What now? " thought Charles in desperation, as he surveyed his feet. " They mean to kill, there's nothing in their minds but killing; Guise and my mother mean to kill Frenchmen and destroy my subjects. The Lord Admiral means to kill Spaniards, which seems the better way. But if he comes back victorious he will be too strong, and I shall be afraid of him. Till then the Guises are strónger than he or I. My mother's scheme is that the Guises shall first attack the Protestants. Meantime I am to bide in the Louvre and wait. My unblooded troops are then to fall on survivors and dispatch their leaders, still warm, into the next world."

He looked up in perplexity. His mother gave him an encouraging nod. Often enough he had heeded her counsel, and he understood her — up to a certain point, no further. Then she grew mysterious, and he began to waver. He might have divined her purpose, her first and decisive motion, but for a contradiction in his thought that kept him baffled. In that dungeon the dread decision had at last been taken. He was not there, and he could not discover it. He shivered and felt sick — where could he look for help?

Suddenly his sister stepped forward. " There shall be no murder; I forbid it." And her voice was clear and full.

Madame Catherine eyed her open-mouthed. What could be the matter with the child? " You? Forbid? " said Madame Catherine slowly; and Charles, in his amazement, cried: " You? "

" I! " said Margot calmly; " and through me Another speaks." By this she meant the marble, red-lipped image that was God.

So Navarre was threatening, thought Madame Catherine. She must strike the quicker.

" Is it permitted to dictate to the King of France? " she asked in astonishment.

The Princess merely assumed a haughty air and made no reply.

" Pray who gives the orders here? " asked the King. It was a foolish and a dangerous question, but his curiosity prevailed. His mother still could not believe her ears. Charming creature!

Poring over books or lying with her lovers. They had had, indeed, some trouble with her over Guise. Did she need another beating?

" If you do not explain yourself," said Madame Catherine, always patient at the outset, " how are we to understand you? "

" You understand me. There is to be no murder! "

" Who speaks of murder? We must, alas, wait daily for the two parties to come to blows: Guise's Catholics and Navarre's Huguenots. I grieve, my little daughter, for your sake, as you have had the best of both of them. But what are we to do? "

But Margot was not to be diverted by this ominous good humour: a charge had been laid upon her in her dream. Behind her mother's pallid face she could see the rich-lipped countenance of God.

" There must be no murder; the parties must not come to blows. 'Tis for us alone to give the signal."

" Us," repeated Madame Catherine, more sharply, and in rising anger. This lecherous little pedant had seen much more than befitted a damsel who clung so innocently to her mother's skirts. And indeed she made that fact quite needlessly plain.

" I am not a fool, mother. I hear much said that has no meaning save in what may happen in the future. You say to the King, my brother, what he himself does not understand. But I have been learning of late; I understand the speech of birds," she added, in a sudden impulse, from the dream vision of those myriad statues, which had spoken to her after a manner she could understand, though their speech was a twitter like that of the little birds from the Islands.

" What think you, my son? Shall we try another of those little lessons that so profited your sister? You remember, Sire, the morning when your fat Margot had slept overlong with Guise." And a stealthy glitter crept into the dull eyes behind the mask.

No, he had no intention of giving Margot a beating. In the meantime he had been clearing the confusions in his mind, and he saw the issue clear. " She is right," he cried; " there shall be no murder! "

" Go! " Her tone was harsh and chill, and she pointed to the door — before which no guards were that day posted. She had cause to fear the worst, and her composure paid tribute to her courage. This scion of Gallic chieftains might simply have her clapped into a dungeon; her favourite son, Anjou, would not then champion her cause; what is done may no longer be recalled. But it was the first time she had reason to dread her daughter's thirst for knowledge. Without a quiver in her voice, she repeated: " Go! " But, alas, they did not go.

" Admiral de Coligny is not to be killed! "

" The King of Navarre is not to be killed! "

Both cried out simultaneously; the two names clashed. The old lady shrugged her shoulders.

" You see! You are not yourselves agreed."

" I want what Margot wants."

" I put my trust in my brother the King."

So she had to deal with allies. As soon as Madame Catherine lost her advantage, it was her habit to use guile.

" We will make a pact, dear children. You have named two persons. I wish no harm to either of them, and I'll not lift a finger to have either of them destroyed. But if one of them falls, I cannot be called on to protect the other. It is beyond my power," she added, in an almost plaintive tone — for this daughter of hers had surely grown. By virtue of her knowledge and her resolution the Queen of Navarre had added to her stature.

" I understand the speech of birds," she said, looking down upon the old lady. " Your Majesty really means that you will first have the Lord Admiral killed, and then the King of Navarre, my husband."

" How can you speak so! "

" She is right! " cried Charles in a flash of realization. " Margot is a clever girl. But the Lord Admiral shall not die. 'Tis my command. He is my father."

" How can you speak so! " repeated the old lady, turning from this clumsy dullard to her quicker-witted daughter.

" Think — who is there to take command — who could master these hatreds, and stem a tide of murder? "

" The King, my husband, shall not be murdered."

" I have as little power as you. They want blood. No one knows how it will begin."

" You know."

" You know! " roared Charles.

The old woman quivered; then with an air of grief — of grief and dignity, like one who must bear a heavy burden and not shrink — there was no more moaning now:

" I bear within my head," she began, tapping her temple with her forefinger, " a vision of the House of Valois. You have none. You are young and heed nothing but your desires. I alone uphold the burden, or it would fall, and with it you and all your House."

It was her noblest moment; and it did not fail of its effect. This time the old lady did not know why the two confederates had no reply to make. She was puzzled, and in her miscalculation she made a false move.

" You have fallen in love, but you are still my daughter. We know what has always survived our upheavals: we ourselves. Little Navarre does, as all your little lovers have done, his best. One morning he will have vanished from your bed. You will ask where he is; and you will ask again. Then you will ask no more, and will not care to know how he perished." But her words were wasted.

Margot answered with the voice of God:

" Thou shalt not kill! "

" I never heard the like! " murmured Madame Catherine with eyes upturned.

" Or I shall turn Protestant."

" Or she'll turn Protestant," roared Charles, and the distracted mother realized that her children had joined hands.

" I demand the life of the King of Navarre."

" I demand the life of Admiral de Coligny."

" Hold, if you will, to this obstinate old ruffian; he is ruining the realm, and you call him father." She would thus rid herself of one opponent, and make her peace with the other.

" 'Tis well. You and Navarre will go to England. The Englishwoman's help is niggardly and slow; but we need Elizabeth and her money, as your brother Charles, and his father Coligny, are embroiling us with the might of Austria. Depart when you will."

Then a faint movement of dismissal; her speech had failed her — or she pretended that it had.

The daughter at once returned to the subjection of a lifetime, bent her head, curtsied, and went obediently out of the room, followed by Charles. His sister, to his surprise, had won, and he forgot he had not made good his own plea — in the very moment when the issue was decided.

SIGNS

Margot sacrificed her pride and went to Henri, although he had left her that morning in anger. She could excuse him because, as a man, he was quite guileless, and she confessed that he had reason for complaint, both in regard to her former love-affairs, forgotten as they were, and in the other matter. That was the worst, and worse for her than for him; for he was not as certain as she was that his mother had been poisoned by hers. Meantime she had made atonement, and the horror that had come between them was banished; she had saved his life. Margot, on the inspiration of a dream, had fought for Henri — she had won, and now she sped on wings to claim her reward.

He had bathed, dressed in fresh attire; and he and his room smelt of fragrant essences. As she came in, there was desire in his eyes and hers. The blood pulsated in their veins, their heads swam, and they were near to falling into each other's arms. But, alas, a third was present, a stocky, genial little poet, Henri's friend Agrippa.

" Most excellent Agrippa," said the Queen of Navarre in a high and forceful tone, " pray leave us; I have an important State secret to make known to the King my lord."

D'Aubigné grinned, but before finally retreating he made three bows instead of two: the first to the King, the second to the Queen, and one more to the bed. Whereupon the pair burst into a roar of laughter, and Henri said:

" Beloved Queen, I burn for that State secret even more than you would have me do " — with a glance at the bed. " But Agrippa had better finish his report. He has seen signs of things to come."

" Indeed, Sire, I did not say so. Some strange events, such as may happen every day in the streets of Paris."

" No more than that, Agrippa? Tell me, my dearest Queen, whether the mob often assemble to hear your priests preach against us Protestants. The parson stands on a curbstone or a flight of steps, and eggs his listeners on to hang and strangle heretics. Suddenly they catch sight of a solitary Huguenot and run in chase of him. The poor man takes to his heels, but they pull him down. Is that a common event? "

She had grown deathly pale. This was more than she had suspected. Time was pressing, the door would soon be closed. Away! They must get out of that city betimes. She spoke without heed to who might be in hearing: " Henri, my beloved Henri, hear me. This night, when the streets are clear, we are to leave for England." And with a wave of her lovely hand she put aside his protests.

" Henri, my beloved lord, you must indeed perceive that peace in Paris hangs on victory in Flanders, and that on English gold. The Lord Admiral's victory will be a Protestant victory, but your troops and ours will be under his command. That will end the feud. After that there will be no preaching from curbstones. Wherefore — we must to England by the fastest ship."

" I thank you. But — "

" This is not an escape. Let me finish, Henri, my beloved lord! We are not escaping, we are sent upon a weighty mission. 'Tis Coligny's desire, for the advantage of the cause."

It was a plea of desperation. From the third person present came a sound like a suppressed whistle, silenced at once by an imperious look from Margot. His King turned to him and said: " What think you, Agrippa? " And Agrippa answered:

" I think that the love of a beautiful Princess is the greatest possession in the world."

Honour is a greater one, Henri heard a decorous voice within him say. And religion is another.

His decision was quick. " I will await my orders from the Admiral."

" So be it," said the beautiful Princess, inwardly determined to do her utmost to prevent any colloquy with the old heretic; she had wiles to hold her lord until they could roll off in their travelling coach, and all else was left behind. Agrippa d'Aubigné at last obeyed her signal and went. And they flung wide their arms in breathless expectation.

They appeared late at the banquet that day; they should have been there at three o'clock, before their guests, whom it was their duty to receive. For the entertainment was given by the King of Navarre in the Anjou palace. When they arrived they found an agitated company which suddenly fell silent. For two or three hours they ate and they drank, meats from all manner of beasts, wines of every growth, but, as at the start, the talk was noisy, in so far as it was no more than the banter of the dinner-table; but cooler or more suspicious guests exchanged no word nor look, they departed at once. Some, too, fell to marking who were present, though not too openly. The First Nobleman, de Miossens, lay abed and was said to be sick of a colic. Several other Protestant gentlemen were no longer to be found; apparently they had left Paris in haste.

" These are signs," said du Bartas to du Plessis-Mornay at one end of the table. " But I'm amazed at the restraint and good humour of the survivors. This is the third evening of festivities; all these poor folk must be too wearied out to jump out of their seats, gather in two groups, and curse each other. Hatred often goes to sleep, or lurks in men's minds ready for a spring."

" We are pausing for a moment," answered Mornay, " before we transform this land and realm into a blood-soaked carcass, at which all the beasts of the earth will come and gnaw; the Goths will take what the Huns reject, and the Vandals will devour the leavings of the Goths."

Thus the austere Mornay, prone, as always, to extremes. And all about him men sat and marked the missing. Catholics too were absent, among them Captain de Nançay. He had been needed at the Louvre, it was heard; but upon what business was not known, or was not mentioned. One Monsieur de Maurevert had not appeared. Many recalled his pendulous nose and close-set eyes. " The dog! " cried the Duke of Guise in a high and haughty tone. " He hid himself under my bed — to ask a favour, so he said; but the dagger he had about him suggested another purpose."

Guise, in his indignation, spoke at the top of his voice, and Charles IX and the King of Navarre, who were sitting face to face, heard him. Charles was himself very boisterous over his fancied defeat of Madame Catherine. " Navarre! 'Tis no matter to talk of here, but you and your beloved should set up a candle in my honour. But for me, your life was going cheap. I am your friend, Navarre."

His sister called for his glass to be filled, to stop his mouth. Otherwise he would have blurted out that she and her husband were leaving for England that evening. The wine made him enlarge on his great love and admiration for his father Coligny, loyalest of subjects, best of his servants. From the way he spoke, peace was signed between the parties, and the past forgotten.

Du Bartas, at his end of the table, observed: " The Lord Admiral believes it too, in spite of the warnings he has received. But he and Charles are the only ones who do. Which troubles me. A man who suddenly and without sufficient reason ceases to regard his fellow-men as blind and evil is running fearful risks; indeed, he has given up the game."

And du Plessis-Mornay answered: " My friend, if Jesus entered the room at this moment, which party would He join? He could not tell; for both are equally ferocious, with not a spark of love left in their hearts, in theirs nor ours. I — indeed I may confess it — I fear my own self; for my thoughts are set on butchery."

" We know you, Philippe. 'Tis but your mind that loves extremes."

" They exist in the world before they come into mind. Think

you, du Bartas, that a man may long preserve his reason in this place? For my part, I am going voyaging, and if I drown, it will be a good end, for the palace of the Louvre will soon see dreadful deeds."

" Do you go by ship? "

" To England, to get money from Elizabeth." An unusually sardonic grin spread over his long Socratic countenance — in contempt for money, or in recognition of his own luck. Self-deception was not his failing, and he realized that luck unsought had marked him and delivered him.

" Madame Catherine summoned me. I am to go in place of my master, who must stay here. What he needs is not a pitching ship but a firm-fixed bed. But truth to tell, he alone can calm men's minds before the outbreak. Only the waters of the sea can cool my mind, and may I be therein engulfed," he cried with resignation; but he was fated to live for fifty-one years more, and many of those who sat around him, for not five more days.

These words, which he made no effort to conceal, were overheard on various sides, and especially by Charlotte de Sauves. And she took the first occasion, when the King of Navarre had left his place beside the Queen, of telling Margot. Her eyes shone as she spoke. She was of an age to welcome the smile of life with an especial grace. Her little face, which, as the years went on, was to grow peaked, was lit by a roguish charm at thought of her news. " Madam, Majesty, and Margot," she rang the changes in addressing the new Queen, and she said not once but many times how brave and wise was the King of Navarre to stay in Paris, and to deceive his wife so that he might do so. For so she put it, in a glow of praise. A man's honour claims the sacrifice of love to duty. And Charlotte thought: " You lie together all day long, but my turn will come — I wonder when. If Margot knows he is deceiving her already, she will betray him sooner, and he'll betray her — with me."

And Margot, listening, thought: " The woman's jealous. 'Tis my overplus of joy — alas that it should be written on my face. I would have done well to hide my joy at a journey, however long and dangerous. We might have come back safe, while here — I don't know my mother's purpose, but she knows. So she can always play another card against me. If Sauves's babble is true, then Catherine has suggested to my dear Huguenot that Mornay can get money out of England better than a King could do. No! It is not that. The pretext was of course devised by Henri alone! " (This she only realized because her friend gently hinted as much.) " He is sending another envoy, so that we can stay here: too brave to look for safety, and too much in love with me to leave our room for long! "

Thus Margot, thrilling in her flesh and in her soul. She half thought of approaching the old Queen again — but she did not; she felt the respite slip away, and indeed she had then and there surrendered all but the joy that night would bring.

" My heart and my love," thought Henri, in words that he could but utter in her ear at fleeting moments. Meantime he drew his cousin Condé aside and talked with him about his sister; leaving his Queen, for a brief while only, as he thought. But it was to be a while indeed. His cousin told him that he had warned little Catherine not to go into the streets. " Paris is restless. The mob is, after its fashion, agog for what may bring it some excitement. I would beat them down, not when the tumult has begun, but while the brutes are still wavering."

" Happily you need not. We are to attack the Spanish dominion, 'tis not our interest that Paris should remain calm. The excitements of a nation can be turned to profit and advantage. Therefore are we Princes. My sister should have been present at the marriage."

Now, this he said because he very well knew why she had really stayed away. He had not been willing to obey what, to her mind, had been their mother's last injunction; he had not left Paris, and he had not led the Protestants against the court. Instead, he flung away his strength and destiny to marry the Princess of Valois. He had failed her as a King and as a brother. The dead Jeanne felt herself injured and despised in Catherine's person. And the little sister was jealous of her big brother, who was kissing other lips. Henri knew Catherine too well not to know all this; he was merely concerned to defend himself to Condé; so he said:

"She is wrong, cousin, and when I am gone I will prove it to her. I am leaving Paris, as she wished me to do and as our mother charged me. But I shall not come back with the army, but with gold from England."

"You? Loaded with sacks like an ass?" asked his cousin, and the doubt that prompted him did at least mask the contempt he felt. At this point Philippe Mornay came towards them.

"I myself am to play the ass instead of you, Sire." He stretched out his neck and brayed. "The golden ass, a magical beast, but too precious a load might lead Heaven into temptation; and Heaven might split the timbers of that ship and drown the ass. I have forebodings how 'twill end. Your life, Sire, is far costlier; a high price is paid for it. You well know by whom," he whispered, and pointed outwards through the wall at a place whither all things including this affair were centred.

"Then I shall stay," said Henri promptly. "'Tis indeed better that I should. I shall be more the master of my decisions. I and the Lord Admiral are stronger united."

"You have Margot," put in Condé, and turned away. This was exactly what was lurking in Henri's mind; he gave a start and was silent.

Philippe Mornay bowed more formally than was usual. "Sire, I would beg of you to dismiss me now. But as a man departing is like a man about to die, pray accept my inheritance. You will be held in this city to stifle suspicion till the hour is come, that our people may not fight their way out in a force too strong to counter. Thus and thus alone could they escape alive, and there is a voice within that bids them beware, as a steer recoils from the slaughter-house. Mark the talk around you; not a man but longs to get away, save that he must await what is fated to befall, Sire."

"Philippe, in the Admiral's name you indited a notable memorandum for the King of France, in which you said that it was in the very nature of his subjects to rob and murder, if not foreigners, each other. This is just such wild talk. Coligny is assured of the King's friendship. He is even less suspicious than I, why otherwise should he stay? "

" He stays because the grave awaits him. A bed awaits you."

They were parted by a bevy of uproarious guests. When Henri sought his friend, he could not find him.

AND WONDERS

For some while past, events had sped onwards in the rising noise and tumult of the now imminent clash. From the Anjou palace the company crossed over to the Louvre, where the ball which had paused that morning would now continue. There was no open brawling that day, the revellers seemed in some strange fashion oblivious of what passed before their eyes. They did not know whom they were jostling out of the way, nor whom they caught and carried with them as they stumbled along. Even when they reached the immediate circle of the King, their demeanor barely changed. Meantime Henri had been swept out of his place, he had lost sight of Margot; he moved through winding viewless galleries like a figure in a dream. And all unconsciously he cried: " Margot! "

A voice replied: " She has left in a coach with her ladies. Come hither, Sire, to me! "

Henri could not see the face of him that called. He had recognized Agrippa's voice, but it did not speak again, " Let me pass! " he exclaimed; " I must go to the Queen! " Then a disguised voice behind him and not far from his ear replied with startling pertness. Which Queen did he mean? Elizabeth of Austria could hardly have sent for him; while with Madame Catherine he would have some dealings soon enough. Henri looked round; the saucy youth had plunged into the crowd and pretended it was not he. It was in fact Le Guast, Anjou's favourite; the boy had been listening to his master, and it might be profitable to hear what he had to say. Henri laughed and beckoned to him. Suddenly the stripling shot with a yell in most surprising fashion across some intervening heads; Lévis de Léran, the Protestant noblemen's handsome page, had abruptly thrust a knee into those admired posteriors. Those on whose heads the favourite fell started back, stumbled into others, and the disorder threatened to develop a dangerous brawl. A gentleman of the court of France, d'Elbeuf by name, grasped Henri without ceremony by the arm and lifted a curtain; suddenly they were both breathing the fresh air, and quite alone in the darkness.

This happened in an instant, without a spoken word, and Henri, taken unawares, did what he had failed to do when he faced Guise alone and unsupported; he drew his dagger. And d'Elbeuf said with boyish vehemence: " If you refuse me as your friend, Sire, strike." And he bared his chest.

Henri leaned forward; he could not recognize the face, but before now, in a clear light, he had misconstrued friendship. But he remained cautious. " Walk on in front. I am on my way to the Louvre. Take not one step aside."

When they arrived, the gate on the bridge was indeed half open, but could not be swung back nor wholly closed, because some were trying to force their way out, while others were crushing them between the two wings of the gate. A wild uproar accompanied the struggle. The reflection from a few torches lit the drawn faces with a flickering glare. Henri caught sight of beards and threadbare doublets; his own men trying to get out. They had not eaten at the royal table; the poorest of the noblemen and common folk had remained unspotted by the allurements of this court — they had indeed cut the purses of a few city burghers of this city and very likely knocked them on the head, but now they were trying to avoid that fate themselves; and to do so, they were cursing and trying to fight their way out, while the Louvre guard forced them back.

Their King called to them; they knew him, and the turmoil came to a sudden stop. A shout was heard: " There's murder afoot, Sire! Come with us! " Henri looked round: d'Elbeuf was still at his side. " Do what they ask you, Sire," he replied to Henri's look.

From behind the gate came a cry: " Navarre is without; bring him in! "

"Let me through!" cried Henri to his men. But they held him fast. "We will not go without you, *Noust Henric*! We have horses in the stables and we will cut our way out and then come back with you and many thousand more." They ringed him in, they even dared to lay their hands on him — they would have swept him with them, all in the utter confidence of simple hearts; they clung to him as to one of the native vineclad hills that guarded and would guard their homes for ever.

He had but to utter his will. "Let me speak with the Captain," he cried, as he now could see who was in command on the bridge. Meantime Captain de Nançay had had the gate flung wide open; all the Huguenots could now withdraw, his eyes were on their King. Beards and doublets surged through and dashed by the now scanty group that surrounded Henri. The wall of bodies around him crumbled and thinned. Someone who still stayed whispered: "'Tis the last minute." The quavering voice of a friend, who had indeed appeared at the last minute, but all too late to take his chance. None the less, he laid hands on Henri and tried to drag him struggling from the gate. Unconsciously they fought until they were parted; they were both bruised and had their clothes torn.

"What is this, d'Elbeuf?" cried the Captain's voice. "The King of Navarre is not to suffer harm. He is to be respectfully escorted back into the palace."

Henri, now himself, could see none of his own people, and Captain de Nançay, with whom he was now left alone, said insolently: "Sire, at the time of your arrival I had the honour to assure you that the more Huguenots we have in the Louvre, the better we are pleased. Unfortunately, a few have just slipped through our fingers, but thanks be to Saint Bartholomew, we still have you." Whereupon Henri, with the promptitude of youth, struck the man in the face and passed on, leaving his victim dumbfounded. But when some armed men started in pursuit of him, he heard the Captain cry: "Halt!" Nançay ground his teeth and muttered: "Wait!"

From the open windows of the palace came the lilt of dance music; under a softened light lines of figures swung forward and then back. Henri stood below and looked for his lady: it was high time to rejoin her. More than one strange event had parted them, and she herself had left no sign nor word behind her. He gazed upwards out of the darkness and at the shifting scene. In the soft and golden light, to the gentle murmur of the music, she moved in all the motions of the dance, her hands and feet poised as though she were gliding upon air, and smiling like a mask of beauty made perfect. We are neither perfect nor noble, Margot, when we are naked. He plunged both hands into a climbing rose and thrilled at the prick of the thorns; that was the pain that Margot made him suffer. He would indeed have clambered up the trellis — but, alas, out of the room below lurched some drunken clowns, Switzers, who were proposing to relieve themselves on the roses and the lover. He slipped into the room, leaving them to their business and their cachinnations.

It was the guard-room, unevenly lit by a few torches, and empty save for two stone figures supporting a dais. Three steps led into the adjoining room, and he stumbled up them, not knowing where he might arrive. He found himself in a high, vaulted chamber; from the ball up yonder came only a faint tremor of violins, not a glimmer of light. " Holà! " cried he, " is there no one here? "

" Indeed there is," two voices answered, and Henri, all his senses on the alert, recognized them and could now descry faint outlines of human forms against the black background. " D'Anjou and Guise," he cried, " the blithest guests at my wedding."

" Is it you, Navarre? " said Anjou, in his usual rasping tone. " You should be dancing or in bed. We are busy with great matters. Lights, ho! " he added, but as he did not raise his voice, there was no response.

" And what may those great matters be? You are my friends — friends as I would have them, without fear or guile."

" 'Tis even so," said Guise. " Therefore are we striving to prevent a riot in Paris that would spoil your marriage."

" They do not like heretics. Where are those lights? " muttered Anjou.

" And that," said Henri, " is why you — and especially Guise — are pouring troops into Paris, and spreading rumours that the city is swarming with the Lord Admiral's soldiery."

" Where are those lackeys with the lights? That is of no moment; Coligny and Guise have been reconciled by my royal brother in person."

This time lights did appear: Condé, Henri's cousin, followed by a posse of retainers bearing tapers. " I was troubled about you, cousin. I am glad to find you in such safe company."

" Did you know, Cousin Condé, that Guise and Coligny have made friends at the King's behest? " The tapers lit the faces of the little group. Henri felt a new, strange yearning to fling just such a glare upon affairs of State. " Your father, Guise, and all your House, meant to have the Lord Admiral put to death; but before you could succeed, he had your father put to death. And each new Guise kindles his vengeance at his predecessor."

" Lights, ho! " repeated Anjou helplessly, though the room was now a blaze of light.

" I am reconciled with Coligny," observed Guise calmly. " He has indeed sent for his regiment of guards, but I trust him."

" He was not guilty of your father's death. He says so on his oath," said Condé.

" My oaths are equally trustworthy," retorted Guise.

" Let us play cards," put in Anjou.

" You want him dead," said Henri, who had not sat down with the rest. The cards were brought and shuffled, no one marked what Navarre had said. Suddenly Condé crashed his fist on the table.

" He is grown credulous because Charles calls him father. His wife has gone to his castle of Châtillon. He should have been in a place of safety long ago."

" Why do you not sit down, Navarre? " mumbled Anjou, his thick lips quivering. He was afraid.

" I am going to the Queen."

" Go, then. Your marriage is a prop of peace. May the wedding last for ever."

" And I mean to see how many are missing — of my people

and yours. I know what business keeps your Captain, Nançay. But where is the man you caught beneath your bed, Guise? Was it not a certain Monsieur de Maurevert?"

"I do not know and have never seen the fellow," shouted Guise, quite oblivious of his lordly airs.

"Sit down or go away," stammered Anjou to Navarre.

Henri's cousin grasped him by the arm. "But, cousin, you are all in disarray. Your clothes are in tatters and your face is blackened. Whence come you?" Henri whispered:

"They are holding our people here by force."

"Let us cut our way out," whispered Condé.

"No." And Henri said to a chamberlain: "Inform me at once when the Queen of Navarre retires." Whereupon he sat down and began to play.

The table was set beneath the great chimney-piece, but the tapers stood high above it on the cornice, and cast a dim and murky light on the faces of the players. Steadfast in their proud and stony shadow stood the two figures of Mars and Ceres, which had upborne that chimney-piece since one Master Goujon put them there many years before. For the figures left by vanished masters do stand steadfast and support their burden, while the passions of the living burn down like tapers and leave nothing behind. A youthful prince does not discover this in a mirror, nor learn it from the moments as they pass. But opposite Henri sat Anjou, his lips quivering, his chin, covered with a straggling stubble, thrust into a carefully crimped ruff, his eyes glaring at his hand of cards. The game stood ill with him, to judge from his lifted brows. Twisted ears, and hair so dressed that the line of the temples and the cheeks was almost ape-like; these and a bloated nose betrayed the nature of a man who loved to kill, but was himself afraid of death. His bonnet glittered with gems, his face was a mask, without the faintest flicker of a soul behind it: a pitiful face because beset by none but evil spirits. Navarre eyed it and thought: here was the very progeny of Madame Catherine; she had meant to bequeath him her genius of darkness. Misbegotten and repulsive, the creature could only kill from beneath the shelter of the old lady's skirts; without her he would lose the game.

"Trump!" cried Navarre, and flung his cards down on a pile of others. The tapers cast a flickering reflection from above. Anjou leaned forward, touched the card last thrown, snatched back his hand, and looked at it. Condé did likewise, with more vehemence. The others did not move, they knew. "Blood!" said Guise angrily, "who is bleeding?"

Navarre held out his hands, palms upwards; there were scratches on them, like the marks of an adversary's nails, or of thorns. Not a speck of blood. Anjou then looked at his own quivering hands, his face turned ashen. Condé and Guise merely glanced at their hands; and both bethought them to turn over the pile of cards. Of a sudden all their fingers were red. It was not just one card, all the cards were wet, they lay in a puddle of blood, and there were bloodstains all over the table. The servants were questioned, the table scoured, and the chamberlain brought fresh cards.

This time the blood was first noticed when Guise flung down a card, but he was not thinking of his hands, nor did any of the players think of his own or other human hands. From beneath the cards, slow and persistent, it trickled, oozed, and spread. They sat and watched it, motionless, they could do nothing but quail and wait for the passing of that blast from the beyond, from the realm of the unknown. Guise first shook off the spell of horror; he leapt up with a curse, white as the cloth with which the chamberlain wiped the table; in the meantime Henri noticed some reddened smears on his left cheek. What mystery was this! They looked like the mark of his own fingers, imprinted by a buffet on another's face, that of the Captain at the gate. Guise could bear no more, he burst out of the room. Condé gripped the now terror-stricken chamberlain.

"You did it. The blood was in your cloth. Accursed juggler, whence have you come?"

"From the cloister of Saint-Germain," came the astonishing reply; and then the man looked yet more terror-struck at the thought that he had confessed. Condé asked no more questions, he flung the man to the ground and stamped on him with both his feet. Henri looked round; Anjou had disappeared. But young Lévis, Vicomte de Léran, the Protestants' handsome minion, emerged beaming from the darkness and announced: "The Queen of Navarre awaits you, Sire."

THE WATCHERS

"You should be dancing or in bed," someone had said to him; and indeed the bed whither he was bound absorbed him utterly, and, he might well have feared — for ever. Margot brought joys that were more than merely joys; they were a refuge, the only one still left, a compensation for all peril, a balm for all humiliation, that shamed him out of what possessed his mind. ("Margot, your mother did no more than kill mine; you deliver me to my foes, as Delilah did Samson. Never warn me, Margot; recite the Latin poets to me in that sleepy, husky voice of yours, as you make love. Margot, I could leave this chamber armed and slay all your people. I have enough men in this palace of the Louvre, they wait upon my word, and we could get to Madame Catherine quicker than her quickest spies. I am master, to do my will; but I kiss your insatiable lips. Margot, more than woman, and never wholly ours. Ah, Margot, the glory that possesses me betrays that you have but little soul. Give me your body, Margot, before it ages! What will be the fate of my *belles amours*! I shall leave you, that is but too certain, and you will deceive me. An evil woman is a dangerous beast! Margot, forgive me — you are more, much more than I, you are the very earth, on which I lie and soar upwards to heaven itself!")

All this swept through his mind, half in ecstasy and half in desperation. For despair is too near akin to rapture, from which despair distils the essence. So in youth. Manhood leaves and forgets the places whence it sprang. But he that continues near them will live and grow into a man like Henri of Navarre, later of France and Navarre.

Eyes open, and behold another day. Would that it were

past! How shall it be made to pass? What are the designs of those for whom the night is not the focus of existence. Oh, they are active, and their schemes and labours not less fruitful than those of love, and they penetrate as far as sleep. The Duke of Guise went into the cloister of Saint-Germain-l'Auxerrois, that lies between the palace of the Louvre and the Street of the Dead Tree. In that street lives Admiral de Coligny, and on his many visits to the palace his way may well lie past the cloister. Behind a grated window someone has stood waiting since yesterday, watching — watching from behind the bars.

Charles IX calls for his Father Coligny and waits for him today in vain. It is the 20th of the month. A watcher stands at a barred window. Guise is playing tennis with Charles, and for all his frank, fair face, he is thinking all the while of men who watch. Since the day before, the chamberlain, who is in his pay, has had a man posted in the cloister. Against the wall beside him leans a musket; and that man, too, is on the watch.

Madame Catherine remains invisible, with guards at her doors, without and within, moving noiselessly along the gallery, from one door to the next. She peers up into every man's face, and the soldier stands and stares over her head into vacancy. On the watch, thinks Guise. And he remembers that behind the barred window in the lodging of the Canon, his former tutor, men stand prepared. A kinsman acts as chamberlain, another provides the musket, and the man who stands watching — watching — has a respite from the gallows.

On that day, too, a masque was given before the assembled court, in which the King of France himself took part. On the right, Paradise; on the left, Hell — all proper and correct. The entrance to Paradise was barred by three knights, Charles IX and his two brothers, never before seen thus united. Hell provided a display of lewd and quaint antics by devils large and small. But the background presented a picture of the Elysian fields, with twelve nymphs as denizens. All of which was as it should have been, but drama demands disorder, and a throng of wandering knights set themselves to storm Paradise. They were driven off by Charles and his brothers and hurled down to

Hell. As it happened, they wore beards and threadbare doublets.

("Margot! Let us get away from here; 'tis high time I undressed you, for your flesh is burning!")

And Guise thought of his watchers. "The gallows-bird Maurevert is on the watch. The Canon, who loathes the Protestant leaders, and my chamberlain, on whom Condé stamped with both his feet — they are on the watch."

"I am the King of France, and I am defending Paradise," thought Charles. To Hell with those beards and threadbare doublets! And yet — my brother-in-law and my father are of your faith. Pah! 'Tis all no more than play-acting. Jupiter would be proud of a chest like mine, and my thighs match those of Hercules."

At this point Mercury and Cupid came down along a very specious rainbow, lit from the clouds above; not merely to display the stage machinery, but to introduce the ballet. The nymphs were seen to plead with the three knights of Paradise, who picked them up and carried them to the middle of the room; and the performance of these immortals, who were in fact actresses, lasted more than an hour; beards and doublets stayed in Hell, exposed to the lewd antics of the crimson devils. ("Margot, would that we could get away from here! 'Tis high time I undressed ẏou, for your flesh is burning.")

Watchers behind bars. Watchers behind guards.

("Margot! If we but could!")

Watchers.

("I, the King, am the strongest. When we swing the nymphs up into the air at the end, I swing the heaviest myself.")

Watchers. Another day passes with its festivals and revels, and let the ladies judge whose is the most splendid motley — Navarre as a Turk, or Guise — of all impersonations! — as an Amazon. At last came the dawn of the 22nd, a Friday; and since the 19th, in the Canon's lodging, between the Dead Tree and the Louvre —

Men have been on the watch.

FRIDAY

Admiral de Coligny, Gaspard, Lord of Châtillon, was so mighty a man that he never went abroad alone. All his life long he was encompassed by his armies, or sat in counsel, if not as a favourite of kings, then as a leader of revolt. As Charles IX now called him father, some hated him, others feared for his safety, though the fear was less insistent than the hatred. On his passage to the Louvre early that Friday, his men moved with him like a moving wall. At a secret meeting with the King, the Lord Admiral talked of money; the pay still owed to the German landsknechts from their mutual wars.

The Lord Admiral then accompanied the King of France to the tennis court. He saw the King begin the game with the Lord Admiral's own son-in-law and a third, Guise, until lately his enemy, but now reconciled by the King's command. Then the Lord Admiral took his leave and made his way back into the Street of the Dead Tree, reading dispatches as he went. Thus it happened that his noblemen fell back a little space, to leave him undisturbed, and he was not covered when he crossed the square by the cloister of Saint-Germain. A shot rang out, and then another. The first, a copper bullet, shattered one of the Admiral's forefingers, the second wounded him in the left arm.

The Lord Admiral showed no signs of agitation. To his distraught retainers he pointed out a window where a wreath of smoke still drifted round the bars. Two gentlemen dashed towards it, while the clatter of galloping hoofs could be heard behind the house. A third was sent by the Admiral to the King to report the matter. The game of tennis was not finished, but Charles abandoned it at once. He was both indignant and afraid. "The murderer shall pay for this," he said, and he was about to add: "Shall I never have any peace?" but his teeth began to chatter, though the Duke of Guise and others made haste to assure him it was a madman's act.

The two noblemen who had dashed off in pursuit of the miscreant came back to the Lord Admiral; he had not moved. They gasped out that the man had escaped them in the maze of alleys and was now far away. But they had recognized him; he was one Monsieur de —

" Stop! " exclaimed the Lord Admiral. " Utter not his name. I am sorely stricken, and I may die. I will not know the name of one whom human weakness might lead me to hate in my last hour."

Some of his retainers supported him as he walked on, for he was bleeding freely. Those that followed whispered over what was still a mystery. " He hid under Guise's bed and tried to kill him. Why kill his greatest enemy? Woe upon us, if Guise is behind this — and 'tis very sure he is."

" God's will be done," said the Lord Admiral, in his house in the Street of the Dead Tree, addressing the people of his household, who had fallen on their knees in horror as he entered.

Ambroise Paré was a clever surgeon, and he was a Protestant. He was exerting all his skill, after recommending his patient and himself to God's favour. Three incisions were needed before the shattered finger fell. The Lord Admiral's agony was fearful, and notwithstanding all his patience and cheerfulness, nature for a space broke down. When the King of Navarre and the Prince of Condé appeared beside his bed, he could not speak. So he listened while his visitors told him what they knew, because all at court and in the city knew it too. The naked truth had risen from its well and ran about the streets, even faster than the murderer on his galloping steed. The murderer had been suborned by Guise.

At last Coligny said: " Is this the reconciliation for which the King was surety? "

He was calling upon God to witness; he craned his neck above his high pillow and turned his eyeballs upwards, and yet further, until only a narrow curve of them was visible outside the lids. His cheeks were sunken, and the harsh, writhen lips parted, as though they meant to utter no more orders, but to stand open waiting for orders from above. The temples were drawn with pain, but on the forehead, pallid in the glare, the lines seemed to strain upwards towards another world. " Better to suffer

martyrdom than to deny myself and lose Thee, O my God! "
That was the message of that resigned yet lofty countenance.

Navarre and Condé could not fail to recall that, in spite of
all, the elder Guise's death stood to the Lord Admiral's account;
at least, it was so reported — though they found it natural that
he did not himself admit it. It was also clear to them that the
murdered man's son had never really abandoned his revenge.
Still, this was enough; Henri would regard an amputated finger
as an atonement for his own mother's death. The sight of the
stricken old man, and the thought of his own like case, brought
the tears into his eyes. IIis cousin Condé, less sensitive and not
notably considerate, said bluntly what he thought:

" My Lord Admiral, the King himself could not go surety
fur yuur reconciliation with Guise. You yourself should have
been on your guard against a man whose father was murdered."

" I had no hand in it," said Coligny in deep tones. He looked
at them and made as though to raise himself in bed; but the
movement made him shriek with agony. His servant and his
chaplain ran to his help. Condé was abashed, and said no more.

" I," said Coligny solemnly, " did not desire Lorraine's death,
nor did I know that it was planned. He himself had schemed
to kill me, and this day, by his son's hand, he has at last achieved
his purpose. But I did not plot his murder. And that is true.
So help me God."

They listened, and it might well have seemed that God was
listening likewise. Navarre and Condé saluted and took their
leave. Condé was overcome, and to his cousin he withdrew his
charge against the Admiral. Navarre said nothing; secretly he
did not believe a word the Admiral had said. Indeed, it seemed
to him certain that Guise had good grounds for his ancient
hatred of Coligny. He had sent a man to murder one who had
caused his father's death. It was much less, or not at all, his
purpose to have the leader of the Protestants murdered. That
had not been in his mind, and the other Protestants thus had
nothing to fear. " Margot! " cried a voice within him; but he
continued his meditations. The old man would not die. It was
his habit to talk in this pompous fashion, and in extremity to

secure God's favour. " Margot! " cried the voice within him yet more loudly, and he hurried on.

Ambroise Paré laid out his instruments to amputate the shattered arm. Cornaton, the Admiral's faithful servant, and his chaplain, Merlin, burst into tears, while his German interpreter, Nikolaus Müss, stood gravely regarding that tall, agonized form which he so loved and honoured. " A Friday likewise, after the pattern of our Lord." He said it beneath his breath, while all stood silent.

Meantime Navarre did what self-esteem demanded. Together with Condé and young La Rochefoucauld, he went to Charles and protested against the attack made on him and his fellow-Huguenots in the person of the Lord Admiral. Charles himself could barely speak; he was in truth more deeply shaken than Navarre. He merely stuttered out that the Admiral's wounds were his; and he brandished a finger and an arm before their eyes in token that he would avenge the crime. But his mother, who had opened the door as soon as she heard of the Protestant gentlemen's arrival, cut him short. " All France is wounded with those wounds! " she exclaimed. " They will soon lay hands upon the King in his own bed." And she seemed so shaken that her poor son shivered with fear. For he would not yet believe that his mother might have conspired with others against himself. Navarre, well aware that she had, found himself wavering; Madame Catherine almost convinced him because, in her own fashion, she had been sincere. The attempt on the Admiral had been, for her plans, made too soon: Guise had acted independently.

Navarre did not indeed ask Charles to allow him and his Protestants to depart on the grounds that Paris was no longer safe for them. He readily accepted the King's promise that he would visit the Lord Admiral. " I too will come," said the old Queen hastily. It would be fatal to let this son of hers talk with his so-called father in her absence.

But two incisions had to be made in Coligny's arm to extract the bullets. And yet he who turns his face away from his own martyred flesh masters his pain and dedicates it to the Lord, keeps his courage better than he who stands at hand and can see no more than a torn and bloody fragment of the perishable body. The Lord Admiral put the others in good cheer until Pastor Merlin bethought him of his office. He addressed a fervent prayer to God, and none too soon, for the sick man had lost so much blood before he was bandaged that his strength began to ebb. The surgeon looked very grave and sent up a silent prayer as he laid his ear on his patient's chest.

When the Admiral at last opened his eyes, his first act was to thank the Lord as loudly as he could for these wounds with which he had been honoured. Had God dealt him as he deserved, how much more must he have suffered! The pastor realized what was hidden from the dying man himself; these avowals really meant to put his murderers definitely in the wrong. This was forbidden, and Merlin breathed a warning. The Admiral at once declared that he forgave them. With all the humility he could then command he confessed his sins to the Lord and commended himself to His mercy.

" O Lord! What would be our end if Thou didst look upon our sins! In Thy mercy account it unto me that I have rejected all false gods and have worshipped none but Thee, the eternal Father of Jesus Christ."

By false gods he meant the saints; but he also meant Mars and Ceres, whose shameless charms were displayed upon a chimney piece in the royal palace, and also Pluto or Jupiter, impersonated at masques and festivals by the half-naked King. Coligny did not love the world, stoutly as he had fought for it; he did not believe in the corporeal, and for him the truth lay in the domain of the unseen. He spoke to God as to an acquaintance: " If I must die, Thou wilt forthwith take me up into Thy kingdom to rest among the blessed." Admiral Coligny had had to fight for a vile world; rest would not have come amiss to the old campaigner.

But one matter was a burden on his mind; of this he must convince the Lord, who might view it otherwise. While his prayer went up to God, another and a silent plea went with them; suddenly he said aloud: " I am not guilty of the death of Guise. Lord, I did not do that deed! "

He had spoken now, his speech was finished; but had those words reached Heaven and been accepted? His anguished look followed them upwards. Then the King of France entered the room.

He had dined at midday, it was now two o'clock; with him came his mother, his brother Anjou, and a throng of gentlemen, among them Navarre and other Protestants. Charles went up to the wounded man's bed and said: " My father, yours are the wounds, but mine the grief. I swear to take a vengeance that will never be effaced from the memory of men."

At this moment Madame Catherine and her son Anjou began to feel uneasy. All eyes were on them; and they did not fail to notice that of that company most were Protestants. Still, they knew that the Duke of Guise had taken his measures outside. Meantime they had to listen to the old rebel commending himself to the King as his only friend. Why all this trouble from a man about to die? "I think it shameful, Sire," Coligny was saying, "that no matter can be treated in your secret Council that does not come at once to the Duke of Alba's ears." Whereat Catherine de Medici reflected that, had it not been so, she would indeed have been to blame. The power above all power was, in the eyes of a petty Italian Princess — Habsburg. The realm of France? She upheld it, and in that anxious hour she swore she would defend it against its heretic destroyers, at whatever cost of blood. For herself she laboured, for her old frail person — but she drew the strength from subservience to that almighty power.

When Coligny had finished — it was all one long tale of grievance, and a plain abuse of his privilege as a dying man, he demanded to speak alone with the now humbled and obsequious Charles. The King actually asked his mother and his brother to stand back from the bed. They withdrew to the centre of the room. At that moment they were hemmed in by Protestants; a group of Protestant gentlemen held the old Queen and her favourite son at their mercy. It was fortunate, she thought, that they were not as she! They believed in the law; and that was their destruction. When she issued her edicts and gave them a mockery of toleration, they believed her again and yet again, and now they were going to take the word of her poor wretched son. They were hopeless, they deserved their fate. They would not lay hands upon her even while they could; and their last chance would soon be gone.

Such were Madame Catherine's reflections, and they quelled her fears; at whiles she threw a quick and crafty glance around her, though her large pallid face remained a mask of gravity and calm. She was listening all the time to the whispers by the bed, but, alas, she could not make out what was said. She promptly decided to cut short this unprofitable colloquy; she walked up to the bed, while the Protestants fell back to let her pass, for she was Madame Catherine, and told her son he had tired the sick man enough. Charles protested; he was master here, and he added much to the same purpose, not at all to Catherine's surprise. The old hypocrite had of course tried to turn him against her on his death-bed. When she had drawn Charles far enough away from the bed, he burst out: "What the Admiral says is true. The kings of France are kings by virtue of their power to help or hurt their subjects. But this power, and all the business of the realm, is now in your hands, Madame." Charles spoke for all to hear; which, once for all, decided the Admiral's fate. His most merciful end would be to die there as he lay.

The royal wrath still blazed while the King had before his eyes the vision of that room, the bed, his stricken father, the surgeon, who showed him the copper musket-ball, the pastor standing among the kneeling, praying throng, and another, muttering to himself: "Also a Friday."

Charles offered the old man a refuge in the Louvre, and more than that in truth he could not do for Coligny. To Navarre he said, grasping him by the shoulder and drawing him to his side: "Next to you, my brother. The room prepared for your sister, with the door between so that she can reach you and Margot — if you consent, I'll give it to Coligny."

Henri thanked the King with a sense of no small relief. The

scene had stirred his fears; during that last hour he first saw the murderous plot in all its nakedness. Charles's offer of little Catherine's room with the intervening door was a blow to the old lady, as he could see; she turned her back and waddled out.

When the King, his mother, and all their following had departed, a council of the Protestant princes and noblemen was held in a lower room. Several insisted that the Lord Admiral should immediately be taken to his castle at Châtillon. These had by chance been standing where they could see the face of the departing Queen; and that face alone, which Madame Catherine had in the end no longer been able to control, convinced them of their master's peril. Téligny, the Lord Admiral's son-in-law, opposed them; he did want to offend the monarch by a show of suspicion. Navarre turned the scale. " The Admiral," said he, " will have a room in the Louvre next to mine, with a door between. My noblemen shall guard his bed by day and night." As he spoke, his heart beat faster. But he went on to the end; and, though he scarce knew whether he had desired or feared their answer, the majority agreed.

Then they mounted to the upper floor. The wounded man was bandaged anew, and the eyes of all were set upon that ravaged flesh. Someone told him what had been decided, and Coligny, his face upturned so that all could see his agony, answered: " Yes."

In one corner stood a man muttering to himself in an alien speech — the same words again, and yet again.

THE EVE

There's no city so gay as one afire with excitement. The wedding festival continued, and each day there was some fresh and yet more stirring spectacle — not only for the court, but for the burghers and the mob. Surprises, strange events — as good as a free performance at the play. Almost every hour someone's wish was gratified, for all men love evil doings though they may tremble as they do them; but here was evil happening all unsought; it was for them to enjoy the horror, and horror was what

they liked. And this, or something like it, was what they said:
" So the Bandit King has married our Princess, and the other
heretic has been shot. More power to them that did it! Per-
dition to the dogs, say I! Come — let us see if 'tis true about
the fifty arquebusiers. Hoho! Put up your hangers and your
muskets, lads! We are Paris citizens, and decent folk. There —
what did I tell you? The old heretic took fright since yesterday
and asked the King for his protection. Mind yourself, King
Charles, when the Guises begin to march. There's our handsome
Duke, bowing to the crowd, with an eye, of course, on the
women. Hurrah for Guise! Nay — what can this be? Is our hero
fleeing before the Huguenots? "

It was even so. On that 23rd of the month matters at first
stood ill for that idol of the people, Guise. That copper bullet
from the arquebus seemed to have hit the Duke. He himself,
his brother, and the Cardinal of Lorraine were suspect, and only
at large on sufferance. Their people in the cloister of Saint-
Germain were arrested, justice took its course, and the King
swore to clap them under guard as well if they were guilty. They
remained away from the court, and actually left Paris at the
head of a glittering train, but this was but a cover for the plans
afoot. They were always within reach of Madame Catherine's
call.

That day the facts showed Madame Catherine at a disadvantage; but Madame Catherine mastered facts by her coolness
and self confidence, born of her conviction that life was evil, and
that she followed life, while her enemies defied it. Moreover,
her astrologer had predicted the events to come.

So long as daylight lasted, she had an eye for all the measures
taken; the strong guard posted in the Street of the Dead Tree,
and not merely that. Her wretched son had filled all the surrounding houses with Protestant gentlemen. Time and time
again he inquired after the sick man's state. His mother did so
too, and not from mere dissimulation. It was a matter of much
moment whether the Admiral recovered. News came that he
was mending, and she thought: So much the worse for him.
And it was by reason of her secret purposes that she sent her

daughter, the young Queen of Navarre, to visit the Admiral.

Margot was not merely a learned lady; of men, too, she knew most of what there was to know, especially in those latter days. And she also knew that the Huguenots, for all their truculence, were as innocent and defenceless as lambs. Their God had so created them in giving them a conscience, and this, to their ill fortune, was their heaviest handicap. Margot obediently did her dread mother's bidding. Madame Catherine she had been used to look on as a person of the daily scene, though one that she could swiftly turn to tragedy. But since Margot had been in love, her mother seemed to change her guise, and a voice — the voice of love — asked her whether she could still approve of Madame Catherine. The voice remained unanswered. " A real little Huguenot! " thought Margot. However, she would go to the Admiral's house and see how matters stood, and then tell Mamma that he was dying; she would say so in any case, as being the safest measure.

She found the sick man better. He even wanted to leave his bed to receive the Queen of Navarre. This she would not allow; but when the pastor lifted up a psalm of thanksgiving, and the bystanders in that bleak room knelt with bowed heads and sang in unison, she too knelt and joined in. Her heart was fluttering. But her escort was below, windows and door were shut; and these blessed innocents would not betray her.

Anjou, by his mother's most particular order, arranged that Coligny's guard should be commanded by his special enemy, one Caussens. Thenceforward, and all that day, the King of Navarre was beset by every sort of difficulty. There was trouble with Caussens over every weapon that the Admiral's men wanted to bring into the house. His demeanour was such that it was again urged that the Admiral had better be removed from Paris. This was opposed by the same persons as before; by the Admiral himself and his son-in-law, by Condé and Henri of Navarre. These still trusted Charles — who, in the meantime, had become involved in strange events.

The night began as usual; the King retired to bed in the presence of his gentlemen. Navarre was in the room, though wearied by his efforts for the Admiral's safety. He then sought his own couch, escorted by his noblemen. His Queen had not yet come; he was promptly told that she was praying in the room she used for study. This indeed surprised them, but especially Navarre; Margot praying in solitude under the great eye of God. Her mind was burdened with foreboding. She had spent the evening with her mother, sitting on a coffer and trying to read, as her habit was.

Her mother had had visitors, of whom her brother Anjou came first, and later several others appeared; one only was a Frenchman, a Monsieur de Tavannes. The other three were Italians; and the Princess of Valois realized that this assemblage was to herald strange events. Suddenly she recalled other such happenings that she had witnessed and banished from her mind. She could not do so now. From where she sat at the far end of the room she listened and tried to catch the whispered Italian speech. It boded nothing good. Admiral Coligny was to die, and all these people, especially her mother, wanted to get the King's consent.

Margot was so aghast that instead of dissembling she tried to catch her mother's eye. When she succeeded, Madame Catherine attacked her with the most venomous abuse. She, who never raised her voice and could strike without much discomposure, upbraided her daughter in Italian, called her a harlot, and ordered her out of the room. Hence the wretched girl's despairing colloquy with the Deity. She knew too much and could only tell it to an All-knowing God. And when her lord sent to know why she tarried, she came and found him in bed surrounded by quite forty Huguenots. Most of them she had not met in the few days of her marriage. They were all talking at once about the attack on the Lord Admiral. Again it was resolved that next morning the King must do them right against Monsieur de Guise, or they would act on their own behalf. So the time passed and not an eye was closed.

WHERE IS MY BROTHER?

Into Charles's bedchamber came those whom no guard would exclude: Madame Catherine, her son Anjou, and the four others with her. The King leapt up, thinking his last hour had come. Then he recognized his mother, who bade him rest. When he had collected his wits she first terrified him by telling him he was lost. His throne and his life were at stake. Then the others took up the tale. They gave him proof that the Admiral had summoned German and Swiss soldiery; and against these he could not stand. " And you call such a man your father! " interposed his mother harshly. The Catholics were now determined to attack the Protestants, but without the King's sanction. " Your weakness has tripped you up between the two parties, and both regard you as their friend," said Anjou, who had never spoken in such fashion. Him Charles could at least understand, as also Monsieur de Tavannes. The French of the three Italians grew more bewildering as they grew louder and more insolent. Then, of a sudden, they all used language that no king should be called on to endure. It transformed the whole face of his existence. A king is, as on his portrait, unapproachable, and stands aloof from men by his attitude and gait and his habit of peering at the world from the corners of his eyes.

Charles IX stood up as straight as he could in his crumpled bed-gown. He peered at the intruders out of the corners of his eyes and said that justice must take its course. " The Guises' guilt is plain. They must pay the penalty. It is my will."

To which Madame Catherine replied: " Not yours. It is the will of your Huguenots, my poor son, whose tool you are. But when you question the Guises, they will tell you they merely did what your mother and your brother bade them do; we, and we alone, gave orders for the Admiral to be shot, that your life might be saved."

She uttered the dreadful words without raising her voice, and even shrugged her shoulders, so that for an instant he did not understand. And he said with a semblance of calm: " You gave the order? Mother, I can't believe it."

She sat down, looked up at him, and held him with her eye. The three Italians were near to bursting out once more. Anjou signed to them to be quiet, and only with an effort could he control his quivering limbs. This was the dangerous moment; in vain had the Queen's favourite son begged her not to blurt out the truth. But the Queen viewed the truth as a sturdy weapon, fit to be used on her unlucky son. " I gave the order," she repeated, as she sat and watched him grow pale, then flush, make an abrupt movement towards the door, and step back again. For a second's space he had resolved to summon the guard and arrest them all, his mother included.

Nothing happened. The blood surged back into his cheeks, and he tottered. " You must sit down, my son," she said gravely, signing to her favourite to cease his trembling, for the peril was past. " The butcher has lost his nerve," thought she of Charles the King. This would please Habsburg, and the stars had willed it so. All was well in every quarter.

He leaned against a chair, and hissed: " You shall retire to a convent, Madame; you have made me the murderer of my best friend and laid me under a curse for all time."

But Madame Catherine did not lose her almost crass composure, which never failed to paralyse an adversary in the end. Remorseless, she persisted: " As the curse is laid upon you, save your life and throne, at least! A single sword-thrust will suffice."

He knew against whom the sword was to be aimed. As though he had himself been struck, he sank on a chair, a fatal blunder; from that moment they could all, severally or all together, talk down upon him where he sat. " A single sword-thrust — give the order, Sire, and you will avert disaster and a massacre."

He shook his head violently and shut his eyes. " The wards of Paris are arming," cried Anjou, with courage revived, crashing his fist upon the table. It was true, but only because of the rumours he himself had spread, that the Huguenots were advancing upon the city. Charles unclosed weary and contemptuous eyes and stared at his brother. Though discouraged and despondent, he held out in his own fashion: behind a barrier of contemptuous silence. Then all the conspirators redoubled their efforts. " You cannot go back now. You cannot go back now. Sire, you cannot." It was a chorus in which each voice took up the theme, and each remained distinct, the deep utterance of the old lady, the shriller tones of two Italians, and one parrot-like screech; while Anjou and Tavannes interrupted with a war-cry of: " Death to the Admiral! "

Charles endured a whole hour. Time and again he said, though they did not hear, or pretended not to hear: " None shall lay hands upon the Admiral." And he also said: " I cannot break my royal word." This he had given to a French noble-man — and then forgot to whom he was speaking. It was indeed as though he had not spoken.

Suddenly he groaned, leapt to his feet, stretched his head and hands in menace towards the door. Could he be going to call the guard? thought his mother in a spasm of uneasiness. But he did something much more strange.

" Where is my brother? " he exclaimed.

An utter silence followed; all looked at him and at each other. What did he mean, and of whom was he speaking? " Your brother is here, my son," said his mother. But as Charles's de-meanour did not alter, she was baffled. Madame Catherine could deal with facts; emotion puzzled her and blunted her wits. Moreover, she had not been there one evening when her poor drunken son whispered savagely into his new brother-in-law's ear: " Navarre! Avenge me! 'Tis for such a vengeance that I gave you my sister. Avenge me and my kingdom! "

It so happened that young Henri was then abed, ringed by forty of his Protestants. He could indeed have risen. They had claims enough upon the King; why postpone them until morn-ing? The whole company could dash forth and storm the royal antechamber. The door flies open — My brother! You are come to save me!

The door did not move, his brother did not come, and the unhappy man felt the end was near. Madame Catherine could see it in his face, here was something that she understood. He knew himself deserted and a prisoner. Quick — the final stroke! She rose and, leaning on her stick, grasped her son Anjou by the hand and cried in a louder voice than ever: " This court is no place for us; let us leave it, save our lives, and spare ourselves sight of its destruction. It could with ease have been averted. But your brother will do nothing; he is a coward."

This flung Charles to his feet. Coward! It was like a lash in the face. The abyss would gape before him if his mother gave him up. He stood with twitching face while honour, fear, and fury, and a vision of what must come, whirled through his brain. He might have fallen on his knees; he might have stabbed any one of them. But he did neither; he fell into a frenzy. His outburst saved him at the last moment from desperation. He dashed about the room, bellowing to inflame his fury. But it was not wholly honour that inspired this outburst, his taste for play-acting entered into it as well. He stormed back and forward, hurling against the wall anyone that barred his way. Madame Catherine grew almost agile; she crouched behind a vast cupboard and watched him, wondering how far his frenzy would go. Even in such a matter she was sceptical of her unlucky son's capacities.

Charles stopped abruptly — a solitary and stricken figure in the centre of the room, which was the effect he wanted to create. The silence was deathly; but he roared: " Peace! " And to whip himself still further into fury he fell to blaspheming the Mother of God. Then his frenzy came to fullness. " You want to kill the Admiral? So do I! " he thundered to such purpose that his own head swam. But all the Huguenots in France " — he rolled his eyes and roared — " must perish too. Not one must survive, not one, who could reproach me afterwards. That I will not endure. And now make haste and give the orders! " He stamped a foot and shouted: " Will it be soon? Or — "

But there was no alternative, as the unhappy man well knew. The others ran to the door, jostling through it as they went in their eagerness to get out first. His mother was left last; on the very threshold she turned and nodded to him with an unwonted air of approval, which meant: " You have done better than I expected." When the door was closed, she stopped and listened for a moment. What would he do now? Silence — a rather ominous silence. Could he have fainted? She would have heard him fall. No; Madame Catherine confessed herself baffled, and waddled busily after the rest. For there was much to decide, and much to be done forthwith.

She had not really thought, when in spirit she used to contemplate the abyss, that she would ever reach the farther edge. Now her patience, boldness, and foresight had carried her across. Wherefore she alone must now take control of this affair. Her son Anjou must be kept aloof. The future King must not appear in a matter that was salutary and just, but might leave unpleasant stains on those who bore a share in it. Twelve o'clock. What night was this? The eve of Saint Bartholomew. Ah well; the world of events may be well served by such enterprises, but they were too often misunderstood; it was unwise to look for gratitude.

THE CONFESSION

They came surging into the courtyard of his house. Admiral Coligny heard the crash of clubs or staves against the door below. Someone rapped out an order; he recognized the high, harsh voice of Guise. And he knew forthwith what stood before him: death. He rose from his bed, that he might meet it standing.

His servant Cornaton wrapped a bed-gown round his shoulders. To the surgeon, Ambroise Paré, who asked what was happening, Cornaton replied, with his eyes upon the Admiral: "God is calling us unto Himself. They are breaking into the house. There is no chance of resistance."

The knocking ceased; Guise was addressing his men. They were soldiers, a great number of them, including the guard which the King of Navarre had posted in the shops opposite for the protection of the Admiral; he had not indeed believed that they would betray their leader from mere hatred. They held the Street of the Dead Tree and all its outlets; and the houses where the Protestant gentlemen were lodged. These were never to reach the Admiral, whose life was dear to them; for they lost their own lives first.

The bell of Saint-Germain-l'Auxerrois gave the signal. All over the city the civic guard turned out. They recognized each other by their white arm-bands and the white crosses on their hats. Every move had been foreseen, and each man from the highest to the lowest had his appointed task. Monsieur de Montpensier had taken charge of the Louvre, and it was his duty to see that no Protestant escaped. The Street of the Dead Tree was allotted to Monsieur de Guise; he had begged the honour of finishing off the Admiral, who was still not dead, but merely wounded and helpless. While the great bell boomed, his voice rang out: " Soldiers! Never in any war have you won such fame as may be yours today! "

These were words they could understand, and they fell heartily to work

" What cry was that? " said Pastor Merlin in the room above. It rang in all their ears. Cornaton knew; it was the dying shriek of the serving-maid. " They have reached the stairway," said Captain Yolet. " But we have barricaded it and will sell our lives dearly." And he went out to his Switzers.

At Coligny's side still stood his doctor, his pastor, and his servant — and a fourth humble personage, who tried in vain to evade the Admiral's eye; such was the glare from the soldiers' torches that the house seemed to be ablaze. The Admiral's expression was placid; what they saw was the cheerfulness of a quiet mind confronting death; and that was all that he would have them see. It was not for them to look upon a matter on which he had not yet made his peace with God. These men must go, and go at once. He took leave of them all and urged them to save themselves. " The Switzers still hold the stair. Climb on the roof and escape. For myself, I have long since been prepared, nor could you give me any help. I commend my soul to God's mercy, which I am certain will be granted to me."

So saying, he turned from them for the last time; and they could but slink from the room. When he believed himself alone, he repeated in a loud tone: " Thy mercy, which I am certain will be granted to me " — and listened; would a confirmation come from Heaven? The Switzers meantime held the stair. Slowly, very slowly, the peace and cheerfulness faded from his features, and what took their place was fear. Here stood an old man terrified and stricken. His God had rejected him. Still the Switzers held the stair. " Before they yield, I must have prevailed on Thee, O God. Surely I am not guilty of the death of old Lorraine! Thou knowest that I gave no order for his death; and Thou canst bear witness that I did not will it. Was I to dissuade his murderers, knowing that Guise had resolved to kill me? Thou wouldst not claim that of me, O Lord, and dost not count me guilty. But I cannot hear Thy voice. Answer, Lord. There is but a brief time left while the Switzers still hold the stair."

Encompassed by the clamour from the street and from the house, he strove and struggled and resisted, shook his bandaged hand at an inexorable Being, towards whom he turned his warworn face. Suddenly he heard the voice for which he waited. And it said: " Thou didst the deed." The Christian shook with the first shudder of redemption — from earthly pride and spiritual defiance. And in a breaking vision of blessedness to come, he cried:

" I did. Grant me forgiveness! "

The Switzers held the stair no more; all five were dead. A howling mob swept upwards; they tried to burst the door, but it would not yield. When at last they broke it down, they saw what had baffled them: a man who had lain, face downwards, on the threshold. They showered blows on him until they thought him dead. But he was dead already, stricken down by awe at the sight of a Christian struggling and redeemed. No one knew him; it was only the German interpreter, Nikolaus Müss. He had been moved by his reverence and love for the Lord Admiral to keep him company in death.

A man called Bême came forward, a Switzer, but in the service of Anjou. Before the chimney-piece stood a commanding figure, such as a man like Bême would commonly approach in servile fashion. But he bellowed out: " You must be the Admiral? " To his surprise he did not feel a murderer's hardihood in the presence of his victim. The figure kept its distance, and Bême stepped uneasily up to him.

" I am," was the reply. " And you have no power to end my life."

A strange reply; not to be understood without the knowledge that here was one who had surrendered himself to God and was already secure from the hand of man. Bême stood abashed, staring at his weapon, while the other eyed it with contempt. It was a rough wooden stave sharpened at the point, fit instrument to break down a door. He had meant to drive it into the Admiral's body — and as the Admiral turned away, he did so. Coligny fell. One of the Switzers who now thronged the room looked down at his face and marvelled at its expression of scornful pride, which, when he told the story afterwards, he called resignation. The stricken man muttered something, but in the tumult none heard his words. They were: " Not even a man, only the common mob." His last utterance was of irritation with his fellow-men.

When the Admiral lay prostrate, the other valiant landsknechts earned their pay. Martin Koch struck him with his battle-axe. A certain Konrad dealt the third blow, but it was the seventh that killed Coligny. The gentlemen below in the courtyard could not wait. The Duke of Guise called: " Bême, have you finished? "

" It is done, my lord," Bême shouted back; and glad he was to say " my lord " again, instead of stabbing at his betters with sharpened staves.

" Throw him from the window! The knight of Angoulême will only believe his own eyes."

They did so, and the Admiral's body fell among the gentlemen outside. Guise picked up a rag and wiped the blood from the dead man's face. " I recognize him. Now for the rest! " He kicked the corpse in the face and said, as he turned away: " Courage, comrades! The hardest task is done."

And the grey dawn broke.

THE NOISE OF MURDER

As the sky grew pale the young King of Navarre said to his wife, who lay beside him, and to his forty gentlemen, who lay about his bed: " 'Tis too late to sleep. I'll play tennis until King Charles leaves his bed; and then I'll put him in mind of what he promised." Which was very welcome hearing to Queen Marguerite, for she was exhausted and hoped to sleep at last, when all the men had gone.

As the dawn broke, almost before the brief shadow of the summer night had lifted, in a room in the Louvre, looking down upon the square and streets, stood Charles IX, his mother, Madame Catherine, and his brother Anjou. They did not speak, they were listening for a pistol-shot. Then they would know what had happened, and they wanted to see what would happen next. The shot rang out — and all three bustled about to send a messenger to the Street of the Dead Tree, with an order for Monsieur de Guise to return home and do no violence to the Lord Admiral. They knew, of course, that it was too late, and they merely sent their envoy that they might plead it in proof of innocence to German princes and the Queen of England afterwards. However, they took their futile measures with a zeal unfeigned, as though there were still hope left. Indeed, Catherine and her son Anjou were near to falling into a panic after the event — lest their scheme had failed. Charles alone shuddered feebly at the notion; nothing could have happened, all this was no more than a dream.

The expected answer came, and Charles promptly took refuge in one of the fits of frenzy he could assume at will. With a roar that made his condition plain to all, he dashed into his bedchamber and shouted for Condé and Navarre to be brought to him — they must be found and dragged into his presence on the spot! But there was no need; they were on their way to him already.

As they approached they heard, through an open window, a bell ringing the alarm. They stopped, and none of that company dared utter what he thought until Henri spoke: " Into the trap," said he; and he added: " But we can still bite." For before him and behind him walked his gentlemen, and the corridor from room to room was thronged with them. He had just bidden them take heart when all the doors, in front, behind, and on either side, opened, and armed men poured forth. The first to be cut down were Téligny, Admiral Coligny's son-in-law, and Monsieur de Pardaillan. This was all that Henri saw before he was carried down the corridor. Someone gripped him by the arm and drew him into a room, and Condé with him; they had in self-defence kept shoulder to shoulder in the throng. When he had them safe inside, Charles closed the door. They were with him in his bedchamber.

The three behind that door listened to the sounds without: the murderous shouts, the clash of weapons, the thud of falling bodies, the gasps of dying men, and the shouting. When the shrieks of the victims just outside were silenced, the shouting moved on. Some yelled: " *Vive Jésus!* " Others: " Death! Death! Kill them all! " And cries of " *Tue! Tue!* " drew away into the distance. To and fro and back and forward the sound of that shouting rose and fell through the rooms and down the corridors. Those that heard it might well have thought the Louvre was occupied by fiends instead of noblemen and their retainers. The deeds here done seemed like a hideous masquerade. The three were sorely tempted to peer out of the door; surely all this was hallucination. The August dawn was flooding through the palace, and the sole sound was the breathing of many sleepers.

But none of them did look out. All three, Charles as well as his captives, were trembling; their teeth were chattering, and they could not face one another. One buried his face in his hands, another turned his to the wall, and the third bowed his upon his chest. " Do you, too, feel that it cannot be true? " said Charles abruptly. He was mad no longer now that madness raged without. " But it is true," he added after a pause, and then remembered what it was his cue to say. " The guilt is yours. We had to strike first; you were conspiring against me and all my House." This was his first utterance, which his mother,

Madame Catherine, had bidden him make, and in that conten-
tion they persisted to the end. " I," said Condé vehemently,
" could have killed you long ago, were I so minded; we eighty
Protestant noblemen in the Louvre had no need to conspire to
slay you all."

And Henri said: " I usually conspire in bed, by your sister's
side." He shrugged his shoulders, as though argument were
futile. He even made a wry face; and, as matters stood, it would
in some measure have eased their dealings had Charles done
likewise. But Charles needed a display of wrath to support him
in what he yet had to reveal to Henri, who did not yet know the
Admiral was dead. In yet louder tones Charles said that Pardaillan, the Navarrese nobleman who lay dead outside, had betrayed the plan too soon. He had been heard to shout that in
atonement for the Admiral's arm forty thousand men should
have their arms cut off.

Charles worked himself into an outburst that he hoped had
the ring of guiltless indignation, and thus they learned of Admiral Coligny's end. They both shivered as they looked at each
other, ignoring Charles, who was left to shout himself hoarse.
He abused the Admiral as a betrayer and a traitor, plotting the
ruin of France and deserving a vengeance yet more terrible.
And as the tirade proceeded, Charles inevitably began to believe
himself. He grew frenzied with rage and fear, till he ended by
brandishing a naked dagger. But the others did not notice; they
saw a vision of far other faces.

They saw the commander step out of his tent, his army all
about him, and themselves astride tight-reined chargers. Then
galloping into battle and down upon the foe, fifteen hours
ahorse in a tireless ecstasy of battle. They rode on with the wind,
their eyes a-glitter, and keener than ever yet because they were
at last confronted with a foe. Oh, to ride against the enemy, in
all the zest of guileless youth — a degraded enemy now due to
meet his doom! Such was their vision of Admiral Coligny in the
hour when they learned of his death. And Henri remembered
that his mother Jeanne had trusted the Lord Admiral, and now

both he and she were dead. Henri let Charles rave on; he sat down on a coffer.

Charles was growing hoarser; again a storm of murderous shouting was borne into the room. When Charles's voice had to drop to its usual tone, he said they must abjure their faith as the only means of saving their lives. Condé at once burst out in a fury that his faith was dearer to him than his life. Henri waved an impatient hand at him and tried to pacify Charles; they would talk of the matter. Meantime his cousin would have no paltering with defiance; he flung open the window and shouted that though the world perished he would be loyal to his faith.

Henri shut the window and then went up to Charles, who was standing, dagger in hand, in front of a vast cupboard, set with cross-beams and hasps of iron and adorned with great black wooden cannon-balls. Henri walked steadily up to the frenzied creature and said in his ear: " That fellow there is mad about his religion. But you, Sire, are not mad." Charles raised his dagger, but Henri put his arm aside: " Nay, there shall be no dagger-play, brother." How did he come upon the word? Charles dropped the dagger, which clattered to the floor and rolled out of reach. And clinging to his friend and cousin, his brother-in-law and brother, the wretched man sobbed out: " It was not my will."

" That I can well believe," said Henri; " but whose was it? " And as sole answer came another burst of shouting, from whence they could not tell. Charles, convulsed as he was, waved towards one of the walls, as though they had ears. They had indeed, and this time too his mother, Madame Catherine, would gladly have bored a little hole, as her habit was, to watch what was passing in that room. But no doubt she was listening to the shouting, for none, not even a hardened murderess, could fail to listen to that sound. She waddled vaguely round her room, picking her way with her stick more uncertainly than was her wont. She felt the fastenings of the doors, she peered up at her massive and imperturbable guards, wondering how far they would protect her. Desperate Huguenots, even the last survivors, might conceive the notion of forcing their way in and taking her precious old life before they, too, had to die. The broad, waxen face remained expressionless, the eyes without a flicker. Once she went up to a chest and made sure that all her little powders and bottles were in their places. She could still use guile, and even men who forced their way in to kill her might be persuaded to take a refreshing draught before they did so.

Henri laughed, and his laughter subsided to an inward chuckle, as irresistible as Charles's sobs. The comic is intensified by horror. In his ears the sound of murder, but before his vision a picture of the guilty in all their brutish ugliness, which is a mercy, for men would choke from hatred if they could not laugh. In that hour Henri learned to hate, and fortunate he was that he could mock what he hated. He shouted to the glooming Condé: " *Hé!* Think of Anjou — shouting ' *Tue!* ' and crawling under a table! " Which did not cheer his cousin, but Charles asked eagerly: " Is that true? Did my brother Anjou crawl under a table? "

That was what Henri wanted; he had counted on Charles's feelings for his heir. It was well to divert him to his detested brother, that he might forget he had his Huguenot relations at his mercy and that he was mad. Laughter is sovereign against pressing peril; a glimpse of absurdity can at least diminish danger. Henri, who in that hour had learned to hate, also began to understand dissimulation. He exclaimed in a frank and hearty voice: " I well know, my exalted brother, that none of you mean harm. You want to pass the time, as you might at a tourney or a wrestling-match. *Tue! Tue!* " And he yelled in a fashion to make the blood run cold.

" Do you think so? " said Charles in sudden relief. " Then I'll confess I am not mad. But what can I do? Remember, my nurse is a Huguenot, and I have known your faith since I was a child. Anjou means to kill me," he shrieked, rolling his eyes, with a sudden outburst that was suspiciously near to madness, whether genuine or not. " But if I die, avenge me, Navarre! Avenge me and my kingdom! "

" We will make common cause," said Henri resolutely. " You shall be mad when you must, and I a fool because I really am one. Shall I show you a trick at once? A very pretty trick? " he repeated slowly, owing to a secret doubt whether it would be a success. At Charles's back the vast cupboard, with its beams, cannon-balls, and iron hasps was imperceptibly opening; only Henri noticed, and at once recognized the two faces that emerged. He signalled to them with a look to wait. Meantime, for Charles's benefit, he began to wave his hands like the jugglers at a fair. " You believe, of course," he said in the braggart tone that such folk use, " that dead men are dead. Not so we Huguenots; we can do better than that. Be comforted, my brother! You have slain some eighty of our noblemen in the Louvre, but the first two have come to life again."

And he swept his hands with a flourish of the fingers from top to bottom of the cupboard, standing back a little, so as not to be too near the forthcoming magic. Charles too retreated, with an expression of mistrust and fear. " Come forth! " cried Henri; the door swung open, and d'Aubigné and du Bartas lay prostrate on all fours before Charles. It happened so rapidly that Charles had no time to utter the first yell of a fresh attack of frenzy; he looked down on them, silent and frowning. They lay on all fours, one backside half as high again as the other, but both with their hands clasped against their chests in the fashion of poor exiles who have ventured to return whence it is not permitted to return. And in hollow tones both said in unison: " Forgive us, Sire, for leaving Pluto's realm. And spare the necromancer who has brought us thence."

Charles dropped the mask of madness. He sat down and said: " So here you are, gentlemen. You may rise, but what am I to do with you? It is too horrible." For a moment his mind was clear; all that had been done, and all that was still to come, shocked and sickened him — as it would have done the monarch in the painted portrait. A scion of an exhausted race, clad in white silk, peering from the canvas with weary and mistrustful eyes, and one foot poised like a dancer in a ballet. Charles turned one hand, palm upwards, in token that he gave them all their freedom.

They promptly took their chance. Du Bartas went to his door and opened it. D'Aubigné waved a hand towards one of the windows, through which the daylight was now pouring in. " We were fortunate to find it open in the night, and the room empty."

Du Bartas looked through the door and recoiled: the door began to move.

THE MEETING

The door opened, and through it came the Queen of Navarre, Madame Marguerite of Valois; Margot.

" Aha, my fat Margot," said her brother Charles; and Henri exclaimed: " Margot! " The first unguarded impulse in both of them was joy. There she stood, inviolate, though an abyss of treachery and murder had opened at her feet; and with her she brought her still peerless beauty, and the splendour to which life had seemed to be reaching out until that night. And, in their joy, both Charles and Henri shuddered to think they had not been with her in her dreadful hour. And yet she showed no traces of it?

Margot had washed much blood and many tears from her face, and from her body, before she could appear once more, clad in dove-grey and rose-pink like the oncoming dawn, her pearls shimmering against her soft translucent skin. It had cost her an effort. One victim had clung to her and gasped his life out on her body. Others, in desperation, besetting her as though she could save them from the uplifted steel, tore at her shift and did not spare her lovely hands with nails that fear had sharpened. One madman had set upon her, defenceless as she was, because he so loathed her lord. " Navarre struck me in the face, I'll kill what he holds dearest," panted Captain Nançay, as he leapt at her — closed his outstretched talons, and thought to have grasped his prey. She could still hear his snarling voice, still smell his greedy breath, and truly she could not tell how she had escaped him in the throng. Even behind the bed they lay and weltered in their blood, some shrieking still, some stiffening into silence. All this was imprinted on her vision, but there she stood, as radiant as the dawn; it was her duty, as a Princess and a woman. She must not imperil her lord's affection.

She tried to look Henri in the eyes — but found she could not. Against her will she looked away before their eyes had met. He, too, shrank from that encounter and looked past her, as she past him. What, in God's name, could be amiss? This must not be. " Henri! " " Margot! " they said, and walked up to each other. " When did we part? Is it so very long ago? "

" I," said Margot, " stayed in bed and meant to sleep, but you got up."

" I went out with the forty noblemen who had been lying round our bed. I meant to play a game of tennis with King Charles."

" I, my dear lord, meant to sleep. But the dawn brought blood and tears, that stained my shift and my face; and I was soaked with the sweat of stricken men. This, alas, was the work of my people. They slew all yours, and as no one is so wholly yours as I, I had done better to have died. But I walked across the dead to come to you, and so we meet again."

" And so we meet again," he repeated gloomily, and this time made no effort at a jest. She had almost hoped he would; such a youth is prone to mock at horrors. Then she remembered; here she herself was the embodied horror. " I, your poor Queen," she breathed into his face. He nodded, and whispered: " You, my poor Queen, are the daughter of the woman who killed my mother."

" And you love me far too much — far too much."

" Now she has killed all my people."

" And you do not love me any more — any more at all."

He would have spread out his arms for Margot, stirred by the magic of her voice alone, for he kept his eyes downcast. Within him, the gesture was already made; one whisper from her — but it did not come. Did she feel she could not, she must not — or that it was useless, she had lost him? She turned away, and passing a hand across her forehead, she said in a tone for all to hear:

" I am come to my lord the King. Sire, I plead for the life of some unfortunates." She dropped on her knees, not unceremoniously, before Charles IX; there was passion in her supplication, but it was arrayed in the grave formality without which kings must not be approached. " Sire, grant me the life of Monsieur de Léran, who dashed into my room bleeding from many dagger-thrusts, as I was still abed, and clung to me in terror until we rolled on to the floor. Also the life of your First Nobleman, de Miossens, a very worthy man, and of Monsieur d'Armagnac, First Chamberlain to the King of Navarre."

She proceeded solemnly until she had ended, though Charles listened with impatience. His joy at her escape had faded; he was engulfed once more in weariness and loathing, and so remained while Henri and Margot exchanged their salutations. They passed into a world of their own; Charles into his. Suddenly he became aware that someone was asking him a favour — it was his sister; she was watching him and spying on him, she would go to his mother and report what he had said and how he had looked. Aha! but he could change his face; he brought the blood into it, until the veins on his forehead swelled and his eyes rolled almost full circle; his head and limbs began to twitch, he ground his teeth, and, all his preparations duly made, he roared: " Not another word so long as a single heretic remains alive! Recant, you villains! " he bellowed at the little group before him; there were four live Huguenots in the room, and his mother would hear that he had saved them.

Henri laid a warning hand on his cousin Condé, but in vain; he made it a point of honour to speak for all to hear, as Charles had done. He was accountable for his faith to none but God, and he was not to be tormented into a denial of the truth. Whereupon Charles, now beside himself, leapt at Condé. Du Bartas and d'Aubigné, on their knees, gripped him by the legs, while he yelled: " Rebel! Traitor, and the son of a traitor! I give you three days before I have you flogged! " The three days' respite showed some caution in a man so frenzied. Navarre, more deeply pledged to all the Protestants than his cousin, did

as he had done already; in dulcet tones he promised to recant —
even in the face of last night's butchery. But he did not mean
to keep his word, as Charles well knew. There was a responsive
gleam in both men's eyes.

"Let me glut my sight upon my victims!" cried the crazy
sovereign of that night of slaughter, and his voice rose again into
a roar. Every bystander — guards, noblemen, prying courtiers or
lackeys, all should be able to bear witness that King Charles
stood by his deeds and was now about to inspect his victims.
But, as he paused in the doorway, his hand brushed as though
by chance against Navarre's, who alone heard Charles whisper:
"How horrible! Brother, let us hold together." Then he became, and he remained, the brutal monarch of the night of Saint
Bartholomew — gloating on his dead, the heap outside his door,
and the corpses scattered down the corridors. He spurned the
now senseless limbs and trod on heads that could resist and hate
no more. He yelled out curses and menaces as he went, though
there were none to hear them save his two voiceless companions.
Not a living creature was about, for murder is a fatiguing business, and after it men sleep or drink. The dead were left alone.

They looked to be more in number than they would have
done alive; the living gather and are scattered. But the dead
abide; theirs is the earth and all that grows thereon of destiny, a
future so immeasurable that it is called eternal.

> Not far away is death, and then at last
> Life without death, a life that cannot cheat:
> For life is saved, death brought unto defeat.
> Who would not long to see his perils past?
> Now the glad voyager in harbour lies,
> And journey's end shall purge his weary eyes.

As he spoke, a shadow came upon his voice, after the semblance of the dead, whose life extends through all time, and thus
must move more slowly and always in deep shadow. Loud are
the curses of a madman. Henri knew the verses; Agrippa had

first recited them on the night of his wedding, before the long procession formed and Charles, with all his court, had escorted him to bed. This was another procession, though leading to the selfsame room. Henri did not look round for Margot. She walked among the others, who did not heed her, and indeed she was actually the last of the little group. Never in her life as a Princess had she felt herself so insignificant as now, walking with a madman and some broken men between the ranks of dead. What a strange look some wore upon their faces: amazement, almost shame, at an overplus of joy! Others were wholly emptied of their souls and had gone once for all to hell; Madame Marguerite marked that sign, and once indeed she marked it on the face of a former lover and grew sick. Du Bartas gripped her, and she tottered on.

By one chimney-piece two men still stood embraced — they had stabbed each other dead. Not all the Protestants had been taken by surprise, and they took whom they could of their assailants with them. One woman lay lifeless across a man whom she had clearly tried to save. Another helpless woman, thought Margot, as she staggered forward in du Bartas's grip. Helpless. She too had been helpless; utterly helpless. Yonder across a balustrade lay a fat cook; his white cap had tumbled off his head and rolled down the stairs. In that very place Henri had found him, or another like him, not long before; that time he was drunk, this time he was dead. These had been indeed two orgies: the wedding, and now this one, six days later; it was more thorough and left behind it wreckage and upturned faces — which often looked the same, but the intention had been different.

Henri slipped in a pool of blood, started out of his dreams, and found himself gazing into the extinct face of young La Rochefoucauld, the last envoy from his mother. At this he could contain himself no longer, and he burst out sobbing. He clapped his hands to his face, like a child, and cried: "Mamma!" His friends paid no heed to him. Charles still played the fiend, and perhaps he had become one after that passage through the underworld. Margot whispered, so that Henri alone could hear:

" I could not save him. I had nearly got him through our door, but they caught him and killed him." She waited; answer came there none. Too long had been the journey to that door where they now stood; he had made it without Margot, and it was never again the same Henri that went with her on any other journey in their lives. Through that door, marked by the corpse of young La Rochefoucauld, came quite another Henri than had stepped so lightly out of it a little while before.

This was a man who knew. He had heard the shrieks of slaughter echo through the palace of the Louvre all night long. He had looked into the faces of dead friends, he had taken leave of them and of the genial companionship of men — of a free and open life. A troop of cavaliers, all friends together, riding side by side, chanting a hymn while the country lasses run towards them from the meadows; gay and carefree, they had sped along beneath the speeding clouds. And now he was to enter that room a beaten man and a prisoner. He would acquiesce, he would live as a man transformed under the deceptive guise of what once was Henri, who had laughed so loud and always loved and never hated, and was never on his guard against any man. " Why, whom do I see there, thank God, safe and sound! Nançay, good friend, what a joy that you at least have taken no harm! Many, you know, resisted, poor fellows, when they had to meet their end. It availed them nothing, and they got their deserts. None but Huguenots would walk into such traps. Not I — I have been more often Catholic than you, Nançay, and now shall be so again. Do you remember how my people tried to drag me through the drawbridge gate? I wanted to get in to my Queen and her marvellous old mother — for that is where I belong. And I had to strike you, Nançay, to make you let me in; and now I'll ask your pardon by embracing you."

And he did so, before the Captain could elude this demonstration. He struggled and he ground his teeth, but he was kissed on both his cheeks. Nor had he recovered himself before the rogue had slipped away.

Henri found himself in the room into which Margot had admitted him. The door, wide as it was, was barred by Charles.

Charles would let no one in; he stood and shouted for men to come and deal the death-blow to the Protestants that had taken refuge there. De Miossens, the First Nobleman, knelt stiffly before the raving King, not like a man about to die, but with the expression of an old official threatened with retirement before his time. D'Armagnac, a nobleman serving as chamberlain, did not deign to bow. He stood with one foot thrust forward, head erect, and a hand against his chest. But on the bed lay a white, blood-stained bundle, from which a pair of young moist eyes peered forth. "Who is that?" asked Charles, and forgot to shout.

The chamberlain answered: "Monsieur Gabriel de Lévis, Sire. I ventured to bandage him. He had already soaked the bed in blood. The others, Sire, were beyond bandaging." With a wave of his hand that indicated both grief and scorn for death, he pointed to the corpses.

Charles eyed them; and they gave him the idea he needed. "The unbelieving dogs," he cried, "abusing the bedchamber of the Princess of Valois, my sister, by being murdered here! Away with them to the common grave-pit! Nançay, remove them!" Whereupon the Captain had to order his men to drag out the corpses. In the meantime Charles covered the survivors with his person. As soon as the soldiers had turned the corner, he rolled his eyes at Miossens and d'Armagnac and snarled: "Go to the Devil." They fled. Du Bartas too and d'Aubigné seized their chance. Charles shut the door behind them.

"I trust the Gascons," he said. "They'll see to Miossens and get him and themselves away safely. Margot, if you meant to tell the Queen that I was saving Huguenots, I can tell a worse story about you. There lies one upon your bed." And under his breath, he added: "There's room beside him — why not? I am no better off than he." And he lay down beside the white bundle on the blood-soaked coverlet. In an instant his face and his breathing were those of a man asleep. But Henri and Margot saw tears trickling from beneath his eyelids. And when young Léran closed his eyes, great drops rolled down his cheeks likewise. There, side by side, lay two victims of that night.

THE END

Margot went to the window and looked through the casement. Her consciousness was blank; she was merely waiting until Henri came. He would take her in his arms and tell her that all this was a dream. He would laugh and jest as usual about everything but their love; on that alone he would be serious. *Nos belles amours*; his own words came into her mind. But she could not efface the fact that their bed was soaked with blood. They had reached this room over the corpses of his friends. By her mother's act, she was now his enemy. He hated her. Madame Catherine had made him a prisoner. He was her man no longer. The end had come.

But while she pondered on the end, hope sprang up anew, not to be denied. He would take her in his arms and tell her they had been dreaming. . . . No! she said firmly to herself: being a man, with his childish pride of men, he could not. He was sitting behind her, with his back turned, waiting for her to come and kiss him unawares. She was wiser and more experienced, and a woman. He would let her manage matters, and she could surely make a boy believe what was not true. She would begin at once.

But before she could turn, she became aware of a tremendous din. All the bells of Paris had begun; one only which had boomed incessantly a while ago was now dumb; its work was done, and it could now be silent. But through the clamour of the bells still came the shouts of murder. " Vive Jésus! Kill them all! *Tue! Tue!* " yelled the mob without. Margot, after a glance at the square and streets, tottered back into the room. Wise she might be, and experienced, but on this she had not reckoned. What was to be done — for her poor beloved Navarre?

She turned; he was not in the room. The pair on the bed were moaning in their sleep, dreaming they were being executed to the accompaniment of pealing bells and roars of execration. The din seemed suddenly to centre in the room, and stunned her brain. She felt as though she were standing stricken in a storm. The explanation was that the window in the next room had been opened. Henri was there. He could not hear and see all this in Margot's company; he must be alone. He had gone through the shattered door into the room prepared for his sister, where the Admiral was to have been safeguarded from his murderers. Margot dropped her shoulders helplessly: she could not bring herself to cross that threshold. She would not go to him again.

He listened and he saw. The square below was swarming with people who had surged out of the alleys — all busy; among all that throng there was not one idle onlooker. Their business was everywhere the same: to kill and to die; and it went forward with a will, as lustily as the bells were pealed and in time with the rhythmic chant of murder. The work was well and truly done, and yet each man did it in his own diverse and special fashion. One soldier had neatly tied a rope to an old man's corpse, and was dragging it to the river-bank. A burgher struck down his man with care and precision, then hoisted him on his shoulders and carried him to a pile of naked dead. The corpses were stripped by the mob; respectable folk would take no hand in that. Each man to his own task. Burghers hurried along with bulging sacks of money; they knew where their heretic neighbours had kept it hidden. Some actually brought coffers for the purpose, and when these were filled, one of the lower orders was laid under service to carry them away. A dog licked the wounds of its dead mistress, and the murderer was so touched that he stroked it before advancing on his next victim. They were not heartless. It was on only one day in their lives that they committed murder, but they stroked their dogs every day.

At the end of one street could be seen a little hill, on which stood a windmill, whose arms turned, and turned, incessantly. The bridge across the river led to freedom, if escape were possible. A throng of fugitives were struck down on the bridge by the guards, who were at their posts under the command of mounted officers, to maintain public order. Footmen and horsemen moved coolly through the gaps between each murderer and the next. Space was needed; even as bees must have it for their labours in the hive. But for the blood and other matters, especially the hellish din, from a certain distance these good folk might well have seemed to have been picking flowers on a meadow. Above them the blue and sunlit heaven smiled down.

Henri marvelled at their circumspection. Why distinguish so painfully between those badged with white and the rest — when the purpose was to kill? Must a man be of the white community to get the privilege to kill? But they were not killing for their own advantage, but for others, under orders, and for the Cause; hence their good conscience. In all their savagery, which indeed looked so mechanical, they remained orderly and industrious. Yonder were some erecting gallows. The slaughter will be over before it is ready, and it will only serve to hang corpses. No matter; it is not their own affair. They never act for themselves; that must always be remembered. How easily they were persuaded into villainy and brutishness; can they be persuaded into any good? Burghers and mob combined form, when occasion favours, a rabble, thought Henri; and those same words were the last uttered by Coligny.

Ha! Here came the very image of madness, stalking across the square without lifting a finger to aid in the common task; but the rasping voice was unmistakable. " Let blood! And go on letting blood. The doctors say that cupping serves as well in August as in May." It was the voice of one Monsieur de Tavannes, though he held aloof. But he had sat in council with Madame Catherine when this business was decided, being, indeed, the only Frenchman who had done so.

At that moment a man was led out of a side alley by a solitary white guard, who was assiduously shouting to himself: " Tue! Tue! " A cry came to Henri's lips, but he did not utter it. He itched to fetch a musket and fire out of the window. Pah! — what was the use? The earth was populous with victims and their executioners. Henri's dear old tutor Beauvois would not be dragged nor kicked; he walked decorously beside his yelling captor. He was a philosopher and conceived of life as only desirable so far as reason may control it. But what was he doing? Kneeling in his pleated robe, calm and clear-eyed, hands crossed, and waiting patiently until the executioner had whetted his blade. Monsieur de Beauvois!

Henri slid to the floor, hid his face in his arm, and so did not see the smooth slash that severed the portly old gentleman's head. Nor did he ever know that a woman ran out of the next house with a bowl, caught the spurting blood, and gulped it down.

When Henri came to himself, he found the door of the marriage chamber locked. Margot had locked it.

MORALITÉ

rop tard, vous êtes envoûté. Les avertissements venant de toutes parts n'y font rien. Les confidences du roi votre beau frère restent sans écho et les inquiétudes de votre bien-aimée n'arrivent pas à vous alarmer. Vous vous abandonnez à votre amour tandis que les assassins eux-mêmes ne voient qu'en frissonnant de peur, autant que de haine, approcher la nuit sanglante. Enfin vous le rencontrez, cette nuit-là, comme vous auriez fait d'une belle inconnue; et pourtant déjà M. l'Amiral avait succombé, presque sous vos yeux. N'est-ce pas que vous saviez tout, et depuis longtemps, mais que vous n'aviez jamais voulu écouter votre conscience? Votre aveuglement ressemblait en quelque sorte à cette nouvelle démence sujette à caution de Charles IX. Il l'a choisie comme refuge. De votre côté vous vous étiez refusé à l'évidence pour établir votre alibi d'avance. A quoi bon, puisque alors vous deviez tomber de haut et qu'il vous faudra expier d'autant plus durement d'avoir voulu être heureux sans regarder en arrière.

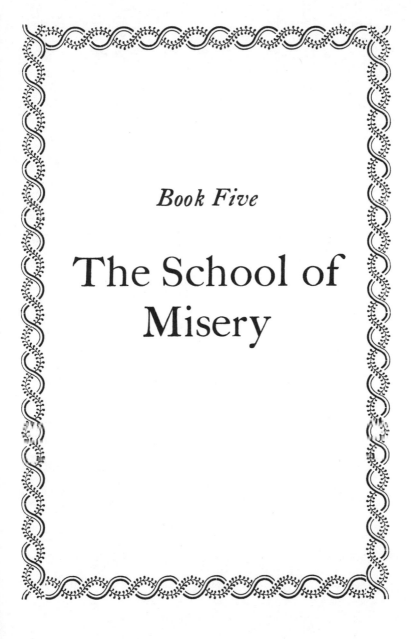

Book Five

The School of Misery

HELL I NEVER KNEW

THE THOUGHT that filled his mind as he fell was the first that came back to him when his senses woke. " My beloved tutor," said Henri, in a tone that was like a plea for succour to a living man. He heard the answer; and it was: " I live in a house that's barred and bolted, and on the door of it the mob scrawl abuse."

These words that had once been truly uttered rang so aptly in his mind that he turned. He was alone, the marriage chamber was locked, and silence brooded on the palace and the city. The clangour of the bells was stilled, the shouts in the square below had faded with the sunshine, and the turmoil and tumult were at an end. Nothing moved except the dangling corpses on the freshly erected gallows. The pile of stripped corpses remained without a movement. Only the dogs prowled over them, licking their wounds. The living denizens of that city, who had been so busy and so eager to show what they could do, had made themselves invisible. And all the openings to the houses were barred and shuttered.

The second thought that came into Henri's mind was that his poor mother was dead, and she had warned him before she died. He went into the farther corner of the room and heard her voice, as he had heard his old tutor's voice a few moments before. And she was saying: "This dissolute court, this evil Queen" — and she was speaking as to a child, to the innocent child that he had been long before all this had happened. For that very reason those soft intonations from the past struck at his heart, because it had now truly happened; with even viler horrors than poor Jeanne could have dreamed of when she lived.

"You were poisoned, mother. Do you know? And since then the Lord Admiral has been slain — has the news reached you? La Rochefoucauld, your last envoy to me, has been murdered. Many are dead who served you, and your nobles are laid low. We were trapped, for all your warning, mother. But I did not heed you, nor the sage old Beauvois, nor — " "My God, how many! " he cried aloud. All those spurned warnings surged of a sudden into his mind — so many, so swift, that he could not think of them apart, and clapped his hands to his temples. Margot — Margot too; that diagram of the human body had been her warning. And that poor girl — her little body huddled into a sack. D'Elbeuf, too: at the gate, when he dragged him out of the throng, there had still been time to fly. Charles himself — "Navarre, avenge me! " Mornay — "Coligny stays because the grave awaits him, but for you a bed is waiting! " Maurevert: sweating death. And d'Anjou: beset by dark phantoms. Guise: his drawn dagger, and his face so suddenly revealed. Madame Catherine: encompassed, always and everywhere, by the brooding secret of that night. "And yet," he thought, "I was minded to be happy — happy with such eyes as those upon me! For I knew not hell."

This was the judgment that burst upon him and flung him on his face once more. He knew not hell. He fell without a sound across the bed, pressed his chest and brow against the pillows, stricken by that judgment, self-pronounced. "I was set on the gaieties of my wedding, while the rest were muttering murder. They recoiled against the walls in two confronting arrays, lest they might strike too soon; while I was escorted to my marriage bed. The Queen, my mother, was the first victim. It was the fate of all of us to follow her, all those omens and those bloody miracles proclaimed our destiny. I was escorted to my marriage bed, and there revelled until the very night of murder. For I knew not hell. All had their vision of it save only I; and that is where I failed. That is my transgression. I acted as though the hands of men might be held back by decency, mockery, or carefree kindness. 'Tis true of me alone — and I knew not hell."

While these thoughts were turning in his head, his body quivered once or twice, as though he were about to leap to his feet, but dared not. First when his sister's words and mien came into his mind. "Dear brother, our mother knew the truth, I tell you truly. Before she died of the poison, she left a charge for you — that you should not come to Paris except with force that would give you mastery. Away from Paris, brother! Send your horsemen through the land! And march to your wedding at the head of your army!" He could still hear Catherine's imploring voice, its shrill, agonized stress of the end syllables. In truth it was his own voice, and this warning was like no other. Those had but stirred him from without, this alone had he confirmed from his own deep knowledge.

Remorse seized and shook him, and he clutched the bed with fists and teeth. "I knew not hell. Where was my true purpose? In my passion for Margot? No, not even there, or I would have snatched her from the court. But I would not leave it, I loved the daring and the danger. I longed to look in the face of fear — and because I was amusing myself like a child instead of keeping my eyes on hell." A second time his very soul was shaken, and the bed beneath him quivered.

This hideous failure made him curse his youth. "I, who set about to teach the Admiral his duty! Who reproached him for waging useless war. But Coligny had the faith that frees men — from Spain or from the passions that bring ruin. He knew hell and fought it. I — plunged headlong into it!" His thoughts were more than he could bear, and dissolved into a storm of emotion, not unlike the ecstasies of his early youth. Thus in the sea-wind at La Rochelle had his heart thrilled at a new world — and now again at another world. Not a large, free world, to be likened to the Kingdom of God; a sorrowful and shameful world, ablaze with sulphurous flames that are leaping nearer to him and will soon engulf him. In the intoxication of despair he leapt up and dashed his head against the wall; again and yet again. His mind was empty save for this self-torment, and he would not, of himself, have stopped. But he was gripped and held.

Faciuntque Dolorem

Two hands thrust him into a chair.

"Peace, Sire. Calm, reason, and equanimity — these are Christian virtues and are also enjoined by the ancient philosophers. A man that forgets them assails his very self, as I caught you doing just in time, my dear young master. I had not expected this — indeed, I thought that you would treat the Saint Bartholomew too lightly, with a kind of scornful mockery, if I may be allowed the words. When I first looked through the door, you were lying on the bare floor, but asleep, and breathing so peacefully that I said to myself: 'Disturb him not, Monsieur d'Armagnac. He is your King, and this was a heavy night. When he awakes he will have mastered it, and like enough dismiss it with a jest.'"

This speech — a long one for Armagnac — spoken with bravado and deliberate variance of tone, allowed the tormented youth time and enough to recover or to transform himself into someone akin to the familiar Henri. "With a jest," were Armagnac's last words; but his master added promptly: "The court was in a brave mood yesterday. Naught more is needed but two pastors and the funeral service. And for love of me, even Madame Catherine will be present." But his laughter stuck in his throat.

"Fair," said Armagnac in an appraising tone. "Good enough for a start; but you must not wear that bitter look when you go abroad once more. Be gay and unconstrained!" He could gauge the tension of that moment. Silently he laid a wet napkin on the forehead that was slightly bruised from its contact with the wall. Then, as his habit was, he brought in the bathtub. "On my way to fetch the water," he observed, as he filled it, "I met no one. Only one door was cautiously opened. While you were sleeping, I was driven by hunger into the streets; there was nothing in the kitchens, more human blood than chickens' blood has been flowing there of late, and those whose business is to slaughter have themselves been slaughtered. The street was empty, save that in the distance two men with white badges were approaching — strange that one had eyes for such a thing. I was looking about me for a refuge — when, suddenly, both turned tail and went. And, as it seemed to me, they ran so fast that I could see their shoe-soles. Sire, what may that mean, think you? "

Henri pondered. " Surely," he observed, " they cannot be afraid of us, having left so few of us alive."

" Do you believe in conscience? " asked Armagnac, with arms raised and motionless. Henri eyed him gravely, as though he had been a pious image. " Your two whites must have thus taken you for someone else," said he decisively. Whereupon he got into his bath.

" It is growing dark already," he remarked meanwhile. " Strange — this was not a day."

" It was a day of shadows," observed Armagnac. " It glided softly into darkness after all that outpouring of blood. Till dusk all stayed within doors, ate nothing, spoke in whispers, and only in one article did they still prove themselves living men. Of the Queen Mother's three hundred maids of honour, not one slept alone."

" Armagnac," said Henri curtly, " I must eat."

" I understand, Sire; you do not say that solely from a bodily need. 'Tis the soul's deep vision that maketh you long for nourishment. With a well filled belly you may boldly show yourself among the starvelings and have the mastery of most. Permit me — " Whereupon the First Chamberlain held out the cloak full spread; and the King, now dry, first observed the table, set with meat and bread.

Henri fell upon it. He slashed and tore and munched and drank, so long as anything was left; meantime two tears rolled from under his henchman's eyelids. " We eat ourselves to death," thought Armagnac — beneath his still raised hand, his guardian hand that day. " Thus we ride through the land, thus we eat, thus we set foot in the palace of the Louvre. Henchmen and yet nobles, but one is King," and he, as Armagnac saw, ate royally. And as the very echo of his solemn thoughts Armagnac burst into a chant.

"Very still — very softly — like an ancient mouse, Madame Catherine, snug behind her spy-hole, peers into her blood-soaked house."

"And what is her design?" asked Henri involuntarily. Having finished all the food, he felt a deeper urge to ask after Margot. And the question he meant to ask was: "Has the Queen, my wife, already left her apartments?" To which the First Chamberlain should have replied: "The Queen of Navarre asked most urgently after you, Sire." And then Armagnac should have added: "Madame Marguerite is eagerly awaiting a visit from her beloved lord" — though Armagnac was not the man for such expressions. Moreover Margot would never have bidden him carry such a message; and Henri, for his part, could never have accepted her summons. That was finished for both of them — and he sighed. Armagnac realized why. He was not the man to carry tender messages, his nimble mind forestalled them.

"Madame Catherine has the Queen of Navarre with her," he said in a quiet but meaning tone — his master looked up in astonishment, and Armagnac paused; when he felt his master's curiosity was stirred, he spoke more rapidly. "I have seen the Queen. She came out to me; a lackey in her mother's room whispered to her that I was at the door. I keep in touch with the Queen Mother's lackeys. This one was carrying in some ink. I asked for what purpose. And he said that her purpose was to write. 'And Madame Marguerite?' I asked, not indeed knowing whether she were within. 'She is sitting on the coffer,' the fool blurted out at once. 'She dare not venture out of the old lady's company.' 'Ha!' says I; 'shall we wager a measure of wine that she'll come out to me?' Thirsty as he was, he agreed, and was soon opening the door for Madame Marguerite; he lost his bet."

"Oh, let the lackeys be, and try the coachmen," snapped his impatient listener. "I thought of that, Sire," said Armagnac. "Meantime the Queen of Navarre imparted to me certain matters — and I hereby report them with the little skill of a man of little weight. The Queen of France is writing letters in her own hand to England, Spain, and Rome. She drafts them more than once, for hers is news not easily conveyed, since she must present last night's events in different fashion for Queen Elizabeth, Don Philip, and the Pope. And in her embarrassment Madame Catherine, against her habit, sought her learned daughter's advice — and in sure knowledge of what is passing, the Queen bade your humble and over-garrulous servant carry you these tidings."

Armagnac bowed; he had finished. Thenceforward he set himself to apparelling Henri, so that his King might have time to think. And Henri thought: " Margot is betraying her terrible mother's secrets to me, her purpose being to let me know that she expects me as before in our bedchamber. No, more than that; her message means: ' Dearest Henricus ' — for a moment he thought in Latin and heard her speak it in that lovely voice: ' Come not, my beloved Henricus; it is forbidden to us now — all the delight and every pain of our murdered love.' "

> *Quid petiere premunt arcte, faciuntque dolorem*
> *Corporis —*

Wild and cruel are lovers' clutches. Came a surge of burning memories of furious embraces and of bitten, clinging lips. " Away with all such joys! Now stands it so, that my beloved surrenders up to me her spirit and her conscience — and this too not without fury and bared teeth. *Faciuntque dolorem animae.* Wounds of the soul. Could we now be reconciled we should weep because we are fated to be enemies and to bring each other grief. It were more expedient to find out together what her folk intend, and how best to escape hence. Whatever may be their purposes, I must swiftly put a hundred miles between myself and this court, and thereby I shall count upon Margot, my enemy, who has betrayed her mother to me none the less."

Here his ruminations halted. And before his mind stood two words only: *Faciuntque dolorem.*

Then Henri found himself saying aloud: " I cannot hold to her nor anyone. I myself must help myself."

CAPTIVE

He looked round. There was only Armagnac, who had heard nothing, or so pretended. The First Chamberlain held his hand on the door-latch, but did not raise it until Henri had plainly returned into the present. In the antechamber stood two nobles by the threshold, ready to carry the King of Navarre with them, not whither he might bid them, but whither they were charged. So waited Monsieur de Nançay, whom Henri had buffeted in the face, and Monsieur de Caussens, one of the Admiral's murderers. Henri stepped up to them with an air of utter nonchalance, and indeed not fully conscious of how matters stood, for he broke into a guileless laugh, which he at once excused by adding in a grave and subdued tone: " Are we going straight to Mass from here? " and placed himself between them. " 'Tis a favourable hour, and we are all most emphatically fasting. Or have you gentlemen found food yesterday? I have not found even a leaf of salad, and hunger is my bane."

As far as the great hall of the Louvre he went on chattering at random, now and again pausing — vainly — for an answer. He was indeed deeply concerned to discover why they were silent. Merely because they were at the moment his guards and he their prisoner? No, they had other reasons, and he must find them out. In that knowledge lay his salvation.

At first all that was visible was a row of backs: people leaning out of every window, and others jostling between them to get a view themselves. The sky had suddenly blackened into night, and an excitement was abroad that at once gripped Henri and his companions. They left him standing. He found himself beside d'Alençon, the youngest brother of the King. The Man with Two Noses, as he was called, owing to an excrescence on that feature, nodded meaningly. His cousin Navarre had expressly to ask him what was happening outside. Alençon answered a single word — and quickly dropped his eyes. " The ravens," was what he said.

Then Henri realized the cause of that sudden darkness: a vast swarm of black birds had settled on the Louvre. An alluring odour had drawn them from afar, while the sun's heat still brought it forth; but they had awaited their hour. And the Man with Two Noses added: "There is provision for them here"; then he slipped away and slunk back in a circle to his cousin, peering to right and left to see who might be marking him. "But for no one else," he blurted out, and vanished for a while behind the jostling throng. A certain handsome fellow, Bussy by name, muttered, as though to himself: "Heed him not. He is rather mad. We all are." Whereupon he too vanished.

Gradually the company drifted back from the windows into the middle of the room, most with pale faces, marred with wounds or bruises; the swelling on Navarre's forehead was not alone. Many an eye revealed the horror within, and a mind self-estranged; and there were hands that seemed to fumble for a hiding place — hands held clutched across the body, and then one hand would glide off the other and wander towards a dagger-hilt. Henri merely laughed aloud at some of those stricken figures. "I have often seen such poultry," said he; "there's never a battlefield without them."

A solitary figure striding across the hall said: "A battlefield is not the well-shaft of the Louvre." It was du Bartas; he did not look at his master and his friend. Henri called after him: "We are neither of us lying in the well-shaft. All hangs on that; there we must not lie." He then burst out laughing, plainly in guileless ignorance of how matters stood; or could good humour go so far? The bystanders turned away to hide their thoughts. Only du Guast, a favourite of the heir to the throne, Anjou, stepped insolently forward: "'Tis a mishap that might easily happen to you, Sire!" Then he, too, vanished through a door. Not a man of them but kept incessantly on the move, and hardly ever accompanied. Did one speak to another, the one so spoken to set his face into a mask and went away alone. The faces of the two murderers, Nançay and Caussens, had in the meantime changed; dark bewilderment stood written on them both; and suddenly they, too, parted company.

All down the great hall, under the array of thirty chandeliers, strode the Duke of Guise, magnificently clad and with a numerous retinue. And then, to the amazement of all that company, Henri Navarre stepped up to Henri Guise, looked him straight in the eyes, and waved his hand; all who saw it held their breath. As they did so, it came about that Guise returned the salutation and actually made way. Then he bethought himself and burst out in triumphant accents: "Greetings from the Admiral!" This put all to flight. Lorraine strode onwards, but his footsteps echoed in the emptiness. Henri, like the rest, slipped into the background until a crowd should gather once again, which seemed likely in a company so stricken by curiosity, distrust, and doubt. At the moment they all shrank back against the walls, and Cousin Condé crept secretly up to Henri: "Do you know what has happened?" he asked.

"I am a prisoner. I need to know no more. A sorry riddle — although I looked Guise in the face."

"Guise trod on the Admiral's face when he was dead. I see you did not know this. For us, I fear the worst."

"Then we shall have deserved it. None may be such fools as we have been. Where is my sister?"

"In my house."

"Tell her that she was right, but that I shall escape."

"I can tell her nothing, for I too may not leave the Louvre. The guard has been strengthened, we shall not escape."

"Well, there seems nothing left for us but to go to Mass," said Cousin Navarre. Cousin Condé, who had burst into a fury at every mention of the word the night before, now bowed his head and sighed. But he was horrified at his Cousin Navarre's frivolity, for he exclaimed:

"The main thing is that we are alive!"

Then he stopped, as the company began to trickle back. "Monsieur de Miossens," he said, "you are alive! Surely it is the greatest surprise of your life?" And: "Monsieur de Goyon!" he cried, "you are alive" — but he was not; he was not in that great hall, he lay in the well-shaft of the Louvre, carrion for ravens. Those that heard Navarre speak so strangely turned away, and in their faces was fear, or guilt, or pity, or merely contempt. Meantime Henri had the impulse to offer this same

congratulation to Anjou, the heir to the throne. By that it was
recognized that he, even after Saint Bartholomew, was still a
mere buffoon; and they made it plain to him by a laugh of relief,
almost of disapproval. But he missed nothing and marked every
man of them, while they thought his mind was bent on mockery.

Anjou then appeared, and in excellent humour; and the air in
the palace, which suddenly seemed to loom up into the August
evening, grew clearer. Here was Anjou in a cheerful gracious
mood of victory. " Do I live? I have never lived before; my
House and my country have escaped a great disaster. Navarre,
the Admiral was our enemy, and he betrayed you. His purpose
was to destroy peace in France and in the world. He planned
war with England and spread the rumour that Queen Elizabeth
meant to rob us of Calais. Truly, the Admiral had to die. All
that followed is but the melancholy consequence, a chain of
mishaps, the fruit of ancient misunderstandings and crass enmities, that we mean to bury with the dead."

These last clumsy words revolted the more sensitive hearers.
Otherwise the speech was welcomed for its aim of reconcilation
and appeasement, which was what all hearts now yearned for.
But the speech had been a long one for Anjou; he felt thirsty,
and all were weary from the tension of the night. But when
wine was called for, there was found to be not one drop within
the Louvre. Supplies were bought for the needs of day to day.
Yesterday's had been drunk up after the slaughter, and that day
had not been a day. No one had recked of wine, or meat either,
and even the common taverns had not dared to open. Anjou
and the court had to endure parched throats. " Still, we need
not flit about like shadows in the dark," observed Anjou, and
commanded that the twenty chandeliers should be lit. It was
strange that this had occurred to nobody before.

The majordomo sent out lackeys, who departed at a run and
came back at a walk, for the most part with empty hands. Only
odds and ends of tapers could be found — after the foregoing
night, in which every taper in the palace had guttered down
during the turmoil of the massacre. For a while it grew yet
darker in the hall. Movements were stilled and voices sank

into a hush. All stood alone, peering at their neighbours, and waited. One woman burst into a shriek. She was carried out, but it was thus made plain that the royal brother's sage utterances had really altered nothing. Henri, as he slipped among the company, heard a whisper: "Last night we did too much or too little."

And he heard a whispered answer: "He is called a King. Had we taken him too, we should have to deal with all kings upon earth." Thereafter the King of Navarre understood somewhat more of his destiny. Better than the others that did no more than whisper, he realized the deep purpose of his cousin Anjou's words and whence they really came. When he entered that hall, Anjou had come from his mother; that was the secret. Madame Catherine sat in her guarded room at her writing-desk inditing letters with her own plump hand, letters that were as straggling as she herself seemed staid; and when she wrote to the Protestant woman in England she wrote after this fashion: "The Admiral betrayed you, dear sister. I am your only friend." Such was the device to evade the stigma of those bloody deeds — it was thrust on a dead man. And the world, which does not care to acknowledge bloody deeds, could rest in peace, as indeed the world preferred to do. All this concerned the dead. "And me!" thought Henri. Under the cover of night and of darkness he suffered his real expression to come upon his face. His lips were drawn, and his eyes gleamed with hatred.

Swiftly he suppressed not merely his expression, but his feelings; for the hall grew light. Lackeys on ladders managed to kindle a few tapers, which threw a feeble glimmer into the centre of the room. From the assembled courtiers came the deep-throated "Ah" that comes from every company which has been waiting in the darkness. Cousin d'Alençon stepped up to Henri Navarre. "Henri," he began. "This will never do. We must talk."

"Do you say so now because the hall is lit?" retorted Henri.

"I see you understand me," observed the Man with Two Noses. He wanted to make quite clear that he was no fool. "Go on dissembling," he pleaded. "I, too, must play the good son and Catholic, though I shall secretly soon go over to your religion. And none can tell how many will do likewise after all that has passed."

"I shall probably become the devoutest Catholic in the Louvre," replied Henri.

"My brother Anjou is puffed up beyond all bearing; he plays the gay and gracious hero whose schemes have succeeded."

"The black spirits that beset him have been banished," added Henri.

"Our lady mother's favourite — now the way is clear before him. All that is now needed is for our crazy brother Charles to die. Will you look on, Navarre, and gnash your teeth in impotence while this comes to pass? Not I! Let us flee and raise the land of France. And there's no time to lose."

"I did indeed once miss the chance of stabbing Guise" — the words fell from Cousin Navarre before he had mastered a sudden flash of wrath. He recovered himself and grew wary. The Man with Two Noses could not be trusted far. If he were not treacherous, he was as shaky as his mother's handwriting, thought Henri. He must build no plans upon Anjou, nor betray himself to that Prince. "But I thank my God I did!" he added by way of conclusion to his remark about the stabbing of Guise.

D'Alençon did not notice that his cousin had now grown watchful. He blurted out his news: "You will not believe it, but they are expecting the foreign ambassadors this evening The Papal Legate and the envoy of Don Philip of Spain are to come and express their high satisfaction at the great deeds of Saint Bartholomew. Lucky criminals always find means to forget what they have done, which does indeed repel them. Madame Catherine is dressed and alert. Ah! Let us move on a space. The walls here have an artificial echo that reaches to my honoured mother's room. She might not care for our conversation."

"Mine is blameless," observed Henri.

"I hate Anjou," was the brother's answer.

"What do you want of him, François? I would merely have

him let me live." Henri intentionally never looked across the room; but he none the less observed that a card-table had been set out under the only lighted chandelier. And Anjou cried: "Brother Alençon! Cousin Navarre!"

"In one moment, my lord brother," snapped François d'Alençon. "We are speaking of a weighty matter." So open an utterance could not be a matter of conspiracy! The cousins drew a little farther apart from the surrounding company. Alençon stressed his words with clumsy, meaningless movements. Once he appeared to be aiming a musket. Once he stooped to the ground, as though unleashing an imaginary pack. "Anjou is mad," said he. "All are mad. Not merely are they expecting the legate, even their meed of praise from Don Philip is not enough. They dream of nothing less than a visit from the Englishman, Walsingham. Those who have not scrupled to strike down a weaker party believe in some strange fashion that England must love them for the deed."

"Cousin Alençon," said Henri, "if you see so much, why do you always overlook the House of Lorraine? They will thrust you Valois from the throne. I am your loyal if humble relative and would offer you a warning. Saint Bartholomew may well have been a Christian deed and may hold the realm together through fear; but forget not that even before it, Paris always looked on Lorraine as the mightier Catholic. What now, when he has kicked the dead Admiral in the face!" Henri said this almost inaudibly, from fear that he might shout it, or that his voice might break.

"Guise kicked the dead Admiral in the face," repeated Alençon, "and he himself is branded by the deed. Handsome Prince, with Paris in the hollow of his hand! How soon is such a face disfigured — even his! By the plague, let us hope!" All this was accompanied by the same clumsy, meaningless gestures.

"Well," said Cousin Alençon, "we are outside the circle of light, and those who cannot be clearly seen are never heeded — except by the paid spies of my lady mother. But this evening she is busy beyond her wont and has actually forgotten to send in her maids of honour."

" I did but venture on a warning to the House of Valois," said Henri soberly. " I meant it well, and none regard the Queen Mother with more respect than I."

His cousin laughed, as at the last jest of a gay colloquy. " You have not betrayed yourself for an instant, Cousin Navarre; of that I bear you witness. I gave myself into your hands, but you did not likewise. However, we now know each other, and there is much matter that you will have learned this evening."

It was true. In the meantime the impish François had vanished from his cousin's side, borne forth by a throng of courtiers surging towards the antechamber. Thence came a flickering torchlight, vast shadows plunged across the corridor, and soon could be heard the unmistakable tones of His Majesty Charles IX coming slowly nearer. He was bellowing and seemed to be in one of his more parlous frenzies. And Navarre, now left alone, thought: " To him too I shall have to lie, and yet he saved my life. I know what threatens me; I looked in Guise's face. And I know the look in the eyes of the old murderess, who will not show herself before the foreign ambassadors wait upon her — and that they will not do. Saint Bartholomew was a failure, but I am their captive. A pretty spectacle it may well be! Madame Catherine and Guise! Ha! I have marked and learned so much this evening that my head is dizzy as though from too much reading."

He bestirred himself and walked through the leaping torch-glare towards the King of France, and as he did so, he assumed his usual carefree mask. Inwardly shuddering with fear and hate, he thought: " In the knowledge of these men is my salvation."

A FAILURE

Charles IX shouted for the torches to be fixed on the chandeliers, whence the pitch dripped on to the white shoulders of the ladies; but he gave no heed to that. Anything was better than darkness; even this red glare of the underworld. Charles and his court had clearly been swallowed up in hell; the thought was in the mind of all that company, and they peered up at the windows to see whether the ravens were still flying past, as a sign that earth was still beneath their feet.

And amid them all Charles raved like a very devil. He, with his own hands, had shot at fleeing Huguenots from the palace balcony. He had indeed missed them of set purpose, but of that he did not boast. " Ha! I have paid my visit to the gallows, where the Lord Admiral is dangling. My father! " he roared, with a burst of demoniac laughter. Then he sobered for an instant and added softly: " The Admiral smells vilely," and recoiled from all that smelt evil in the world, with that haughty sidelong glance pictured in his portraits. Thus too he eyed Condé and Navarre.

" You Protestants conspired against me. What we did we had to do in self-defence. I have so proclaimed it to my Parliament today — it was a judgment that had to go forth in this my realm; thus and no otherwise shall my historians report it to posterity, whether they believe it or no."

Whereupon he called for wine to ease the long burden of that day; and when he heard that wine there was none, he tipped over the card-table. This fresh paroxysm lasted until from a corner of the servants' quarters some kind of vinegarish liquor was produced. Charles gulped it down out of a goblet of chased gold, the body of which was embossed with Diana hunting and her retinue, and the curved handles moulded into the shapes of ravishing sirens. As he swallowed the sour liquor the crazed monarch cast a calculating glance at his Protestant cousins. Sourness stirs a man to jest. " There you stand! " he cried. " Two future luminaries of the Church! On my word, you shall both be Cardinals! " The prospect filled him with huge delight. And this time his whole court laughed too, arrayed in a wide circle round the solitary card-table, under the flaring torches. Charles sat squarely to the table; his brother Anjou, nervous of these paroxysms, contented himself with the edge of the chair. As for the two heretics, they stood with heads bowed before the derision of the company.

The fifth player cried: " Let us begin." It was Lorraine. " Sit down! " he said to the two victims. Then he dealt cards, four to each player; the game was called Prime. The five looked at their hands, and even the wide onlooking circle of the court tried to catch a glimpse. The court clad in silk of every colour, striped and slashed, and begirt with weapons; short men with shining paunches, and tall men, who so towered behind them that they seemed to be standing upon chairs. They bulged like casks over their thin shanks, their sleeves were puffed about the shoulders, and from the great crimped ruffs emerged heads of every species betwixt birds of prey and porkers; and their humps and warts showed up fitfully in the flickering torchlight. All were staring eagerly at the royal game.

" Navarre, what have you done with my fat Margot? " asked Charles, as he played a card. "And why does not my mother come forth, now she has salted the tails of all you Huguenots? Yes — and where are all the ladies of the court? " He had suddenly noticed that there was but little feminine colour in that circle of bystanders.

His brother Anjou whispered in his ear. Charles himself would never deign to lower his voice. " The Queen my mother is just receiving the foreign ambassadors. They appeared in her cabinet — all at the same time. Very well. These gentlemen omitted to pay their respects to me. Moreover, we observed no escort. They made very little noise at their arrival; the ambassadors of the great powers have learned the great secret of invisibility." He threw his second card down with a nonchalant air, and his whole demeanour expressed the silent scorn of one who knew the game, indeed, but hardly cared to play it.

Lorraine dealt four cards. The game was Prime, and the player who had a card of all four suits won a number of points. Navarre turned up his hand and displayed the four different cards. " Henri," suddenly observed the other Henri, of the House of Guise, " you will like to hear that for me the ambassadors have not remained invisible. Indeed, they expressed their surprise that we had left you of all people alive." It was an empty vaunt, as Guise was indeed the last person with whom an ambassador would have appeared that day. Henri's sole reply was to turn his cards up again — one card of every suit.

But when, immediately afterwards, he did it for the fourth time, one player, Anjou, fell into a frenzy of excitement. For all his fear of Charles's paroxysms, he actually crashed his fist on the table in something of a paroxysm of his own, inspired, however, by all the joy and heartiness of victory. The envoys would never come. Madame Catherine was in truth devoured by her impatience for their congratulations. Without some foreign recognition she would not venture forth, nor let Margot appear. Guise, for his part, swaggered with all the airs of a people's darling and dazzled the onlookers even more by the swing of his great limbs than by any of his braggadocios. But Charles IX, far from giving the youth a hint, was delighted. " Pah! — a privy Huguenot," thought his brother malignantly. Anjou felt that the court had at last begun to realize how matters lay. There was uneasiness on all those faces — where should they turn, on what should they lay hold? — traitors' faces all. To think that the city, too, was cowed, and half-inclined to disavow Bartholomew's night, as was the court! The favourite son's flush of glory so turned to bitterness that he burst out sobbing. Such was the recompense for deeds well done. For this had they striven to lift the people from their misery into a better life, and in that purpose had laid aside their conscience and their humanity. For this had they put aside the duties of a Christian and the dictates of truth. He himself had done so; he, Anjou, trained by priests and humanists at the Collège de Navarre, knew himself to the very bone. He was not Guise, whose long limbs blinded him to what he was. He had, of his own purpose, transformed himself into the man of Saint Bartholomew. And that was only pardonable in the event of success. But with the passing of every hour the smell of failure deepened.

The torches had guttered down to stumps; islanded in the encompassing darkness, only the royal card-party was still lit by a lingering glimmer. Anjou was about to beat his fist on the table a second time; indeed, he meant to tip it over as his brother had done in one of his attacks. Meanwhile Lorraine dealt cards, and Anjou's fist remained suspended in the air; yet once more Navarre displayed four cards of different suits. " 'Tis witchcraft! " growled Charles. A long-drawn murmur came from the onlookers, and in that sound there was both satisfaction and disquiet. It is exciting to witness an astonishing event; but a guess whither it may lead is often perilous.

The court was eased of this anxiety. The royal party was suddenly forgotten, every other happening was effaced by another and a new one. In the ante-room appeared pages with candelabra full of lighted tapers — more and more of them, and the palace was suddenly ablaze with candles, where hardly one was to be found a little while before. The court, in infinite relief, thronged towards the doorways, where the noblemen were thrust back by guards; and in the meantime it was plain that this was more of an event than had at first been surmised. On the far side of the ante room could be seen the King's audience chamber, thronged with rows of boys. Their bobbed hair gleamed in the flames they carried before them, and their silver-embroidered tunics glittered. And now the farther door of the audience chamber also burst into a blaze of light. Round the corner were the Queen's apartments, just beyond view; and a mysterious illumination that grew more intense as it approached, a radiance as of paradise and the bliss that cannot be foretold, made the hearts of all stand still; and among the courtiers, with the dying glimmer of the great hall at their backs, there were some, as always happens in a press, who found their voices: " Monsieur le Chevalier, I feel faint." " So do I, madame. I wonder what is toward."

Which was just what Madame Catherine wanted and on what she reckoned. For Madame Catherine found herself in the very state of uneasiness in which her son Anjou had suspected she would be, as a result of the ambassadors' abstention. He was equally aware that disappointments did not perturb his mother, nor rob her of her weapons. Unlike most people, she did not lose her nerve in moments of suspense. She remained calm almost to callousness, and occasional failures served but to enrich her with fresh schemes.

Madame Catherine — Caterina dei Medici — had more than once been notably afraid during the night of Saint Bartholomew;

and her fear was a natural human fear. Long planned and carefully contrived, such unusual enterprises may none the less go
astray. Enough — Madame Catherine, more truly called Caterina dei Medici, had crept round leaning on her stick and
peered up at her stalwart bodyguard, trying to divine how long
these Switzers and Germans could, in a given event, hold her
room and protect her precious old body against an invasion of
Huguenots. But in her own chamber she was intent not only
upon her enemies, but upon her guards likewise. Far better,
perhaps, to give all these sturdy fellows a hearty drink and lay
them motionless upon the floor. Then with a few dexterous
stabs and slashes she would stage a massacre, and everyone would
believe that the Queen had been carried off and murdered.
Meanwhile, in a hiding-place known only to herself, she would
await her hour; and it could not fail to come.

All the mistakes of men, all the blunders of history, arose from
the fact that the destiny of the world and of the land of France
were forgotten; and that destiny was to be ruled, without question or appeal, by Rome and by the House of Habsburg. The
Florentine knew this, and knew it once for all. On occasions
when even her sons resisted her, she threatened to withdraw to
her own city. In the meantime she never dwelt upon the matter;
she looked upon herself as an important instrument of the world
power, her mission being to bring France also under that dominion, for her own welfare naturally, and especially for the
benefit of the ruling House. The French Protestants regarded
this woman in her riper years as in league with the Devil. But
even during the night of Saint Bartholomew she acted with a
perfectly clear conscience — unlike her son Anjou, who had first
to rid his heart of what the humanists had taught him at the
Collège de Navarre.

His mother knew herself on the the right way; and that is the
way of success. It was to be a long while before she, for her part,
convinced herself that Saint Bartholomew had miscarried. Then
her sons lay in the grave, the kingdom was burning, bleeding,
and collapsing; but on the steps of the throne stood the deliverer,

a little Prince from the South. In days gone by she had made him her captive, with her daughter Margot as decoy.

Here he sat for all to see: robbed of his friends and his soldiery, powerless, and a laughing-stock. "Even his Huguenots will despise him when he has recanted, and that he shall do very soon. No longer worthy to be the Queen of France's son-in-law, poor fool. The court shall laugh at him," thinks the astute old lady. "That will be much more sensible than putting him to death. The Queen of England will prefer to hear of him ridiculous than dead." Catherine had sent her the news, convincingly enough; "she will swallow Saint Bartholomew as though it had been some wreck or disaster — if indeed such an act of purification is beyond the compass of a heretic's understanding. What matter if the ambassadors have stayed away? They will yet excuse themselves for not coming. In the meantime — a truce to all doubts! Great successes may well lie beneath disorders at first. Quick — I must take measures. I must get the court in a good humour, that all may proclaim the glory that our great victory has brought upon the palace of the Louvre."

Life came back at once to Madame Catherine, and she sent forth orders. Above all to her daughter-in-law, the Archduchess — an ornamental figure, seldom produced, and usually kept in a quiet ground-floor wing of the palace — really the Queen Mother's apartments, but she occupied the more sumptuous ones above. She herself saw to her daughter Margot's dress. All the pearls, the fair wig, and the diadem, chaplets and lilies of diamonds — chilly burial-place of love, in them all that sumptuous loveliness shall make its progress. No, not the gold-tissue dress. Gold is more fitted for another symbol. As Margot insisted on the finery she wanted, her mother's open hand flew smartly and neatly to her face; the cheek had to be rouged afresh. Then the old lady sent for a hunting-whip — not indeed to be used upon the Princess, who was now in subjection. Another and a strange creature would be called into service and need correction. No time was lost; the two lines of pages with their candelabra had advanced as far as the great hall. But an awesome ray of supremest majesty burst upon the court, from whence they could not tell, and filled them with fear. The oldest noblemen were quite prepared for supernatural events, like country children. This was the moment. Music!

HATRED

Oh, strains of grandeur and omnipotence enthroned! The throng of courtiers fell apart; even the card-players, with the King among them, drew back to the wall; the broad intervening space was fringed by boys, the handsomest in the realm. Lights flickered down their ranks; and between them walked other boys — singing boys, whose soft voices rippled upwards in a pæan of praise. Then came ladies, the most gorgeous of the ladies of the court and the loveliest of the maids of honour. The air was filled with fragrances, and high above them swung a canopy, held up by four dwarfs, clad in red, with long flaxen beards. Beneath it, in her very person, moved that gorgeous presence, so seldom produced, the precious pledge of the world dominion at the court: Elizabeth, Archduchess, own daughter to the Roman Emperor.

Never had she been seen so near at hand, though even now care was taken that the shimmering, dazzling light should not allow her to be too exactly seen. Moreover, only men were given a sight of her; the bolder and more clear-sighted sex were wisely left to imagine something in the procession. The House of Habsburg was here presented by a woman nineteen years old — though who recked of years at the sight of this ageless mask, stiff as the gold wherein she moved? This time she was not rolled forth on a dais by Spanish priests, sweating beneath the hangings. She walked on her own feet, and they were large. Her legs must be long and muscular — had such a venturesome reflection occurred to anyone. It may well be that some that eyed her pierced through the armour of her name and her renown to her legs, and not without irony speculated on those members. She herself was intent upon the rhythm of her progress. She poised each foot before she set it down, and through the rooms, which seemed limitless against the distant-looming darkness, swaying as she went, she carried her array of gold, the burden of the crown, the jewels, the chains, the buckles and the rings, the heavy golden shoes — the gold about her head and breast and feet — swaying, she carried that massy load into the far-off darkness.

Did she long for it? Her back was still a-glitter, and her metallic progress shed a reflection on the floor. Slowly she faded into darkness except for the shimmer of her jewels. A sparkle from the crown was the last seen of them. Then night — and the curtain — fell. All was over and came back no more — which, like the whole spectacle, could be regarded as a symbol. But she who had contrived it, lurking invisible in her silent room, duly reckoned on the effect of that spectacle of splendour. To whom would its passage into darkness suggest its downfall and its end? To an incorrigibly bitter spirit like du Bartas, who had survived Saint Bartholomew and since then had felt little tolerance for men who presumed to be like unto God. So far as he could, du Bartas showed what he thought of the Archduchess's procession; he chanted audibly:

> " Ere time and matter, form and place, were made,
>   In one great whole was God made manifest:
>   Unknowable and infinite, possessed
>   By Spirit, and Light, immortal, undisplayed
>   To mortal eyes, pure, wise, just, and good — "

At this point these truly Christian observations began to be resented; their author was roughly handled on all sides and bidden to hold his tongue. Almost the sole surviver of his fellows after the great purge, who was he to venture on unseemly comparisons with his God, who, in any case, did not walk in golden shoes? The court of France, moreover, saw their victory embodied in an idol, saw the victory move past in splendour, fragrance, and sweet music, and were thenceforward minded to proclaim it through the city and the land, as heartily as Madame Catherine herself could wish.

And who could truly doubt of that same victory? Besides the Christians there were folk whose consciences were over-nice. Young d'Elbeuf was so made that he would act as the moment bade him or at the call of feeling. He had realized that Elizabeth might be any age, for all Charles cared; and he watched the King peering after his wife with the expression that had come upon every face — humility, not without some superstition and a touch of irony. Elizabeth had twice been presented before the King and his court: on the eve of the massacre and immediately after it. And when Elizabeth made her way back again down the dark stairway to her gloomy apartments, d'Elbeuf wondered whom she had to clasp her in his arms, as he watched more maids of honour come in, escorting yet another swaying canopy.

The gorgeous spectacle proceeded; but there was one who saw nothing, heard and smelt nothing of what passed before his eyes. He smelt blood, he heard the shrieks of slaughter; he saw his friends piled one above another, in heaps, like corpses of the common dead. All that evening he had kept guard upon himself and watched the company with wary and suspicious eyes. That could not go on for ever: we are no philosopher nor calculating murderer; it is not cold within us as in an old lady's chamber. Indeed, his breast and lips were burning; and all he knew was that he was thirsty. He peered about him for something to drink. When he found nothing, he was aware of an astonished feeling that the people round him were too many and too near. He had never felt the presence of his fellows irk him, having always lived encompassed. Suddenly he discovered what had happened. He had begun to hate. Hatred had come to birth within him, hatred yet more savage and more ruthless than even on the night of the murder.

How he longed to see them all fall dead! He thrust his chin forward and glared about him from beneath bent brows with a look he had never worn before. Even if he had to perish with them! He would infect himself with leprosy — or ever they saw the first white fleck upon his skin, it would be in their blood

and corroding them into suppurating husks. Every man of them
— with their limbs now taut with triumph over his dead companions. They had spared him that he might witness their
victory at large, and the procession of the golden puppet. In
which of them should he set his teeth? — and he looked about
him seeking out a victim. Not one of those faces, with their
obsequiousness, insolence, and irony, could sate his longing.

Ha! Who was that inquisitive fool blinking at him in so
familiar fashion? That was a shameless cheek where his teeth
might aptly meet. It did not even shrink as his jaws snapped.
In his boyhood days he had once seen a peasant thus bite his
adversary in a fight — and the scene came back to him as he
withdrew his teeth from the other's cheek. But the inquisitive
gentleman, as the blood spurted over his white ruff — why did
he not scream? He had barely groaned. He was speaking now,
in a soft familiar whisper:

"Your Majesty of Navarre. Can you not see my black garb
and my long pale face? You have bitten a fool's face; I am the
Fool."

At these words Henri recoiled from his victim, as far as might
be in the press. The man followed him. He covered his bleeding
cheek and said with a hoarse sharp intake of the breath: " Let
none see what has been done between us. A Fool must be melancholy, he must know unhappiness, and by that very means
awaken laughter. Am I not right? Then you could very fitly take
my place, Your Majesty of Navarre, and I yours. And none
would notice the exchange."

The Fool vanished. Not a soul knew of Henri's encounter
with him. Indeed, Henri found himself in doubt of it. He had
passed through some moments of terrible bewilderment. He
shook himself and set a steady eye upon the pageant still unfold-
ing. Why, there was Margot!

Another swaying canopy approached the watching courtiers.
Beneath it walked the Princess of Valois, Madame Marguerite,
our Margot. She had had to marry the Huguenot; but everyone
among them knew the end and purpose of that marriage, and it
had been well and truly made. Let any doubter look at how the

Queen of Navarre carried her head and set her feet. " That is not world dominion frozen into gold before which they were expected to prostrate themselves. It is the very embodiment of ease — as though it were easy to be beautiful. 'Tis clear enough that our Margot triumphs with ease over every failing, hers and ours. We salute you, Madame! The glory that is fulfilled in you shines also upon us and gives us back a mind unburdened, for it had been sorely stricken by the night that has passed. It must be confessed that our mortal envelope was, in a measure, brimming with blood. We had fallen into it and were bogged. You, Madame Marguerite, transform us into a butterfly, fluttering through clear air, the creature of an hour, yet like unto the immortal soul. We know of two goddesses: Dame Venus and the Blessed Virgin. All women deserve therefor our humble thanks for grace and salvation bestowed. May they be blest! "

If the whole court felt so, a courtier must needs be the first to express it. And he was a certain Monsieur de Brantôme; he ventured to touch that floating hand with his lips. Whereupon others pushed between the bearers of the candelabra and also touched that hand. Margot, as the benefactress of that company, smiled at them, not overweeningly, and indeed with something of compassion. Her feet were small and seemed to be lightly laden, and none fell to appraising how large her legs might be, though several of that company had their very own experience to help them. Before they thought of such a thing, her billowing farthingale had swept past. It was foursquare, tight over the body and very broad at the sides, glittering with many a rich hue, and above it a light lifted hand — then Margot too would have departed into the darkness beyond. But she was by no means so minded; she turned, and her whole train had to swing round with her: the fiddlers, the trumpeters, the noble ladies, the maids of honour, and the rest; and among the rest a monkey.

Margot had almost lost her canopy because she hurried on in search of someone. Him she did not find — but among the kisses set upon that lifted hand one burned in such strange fashion that she abruptly stopped. The whole procession also halted with a jerk; there was much treading on toes; the monkey's too were trodden on, and it screamed. Margot stood and waited. The man with the burning mouth did not raise his face, although she laid her hand upon it and ventured on a soft endearment. But as she was the presiding goddess of that spectacle, she could not linger with someone whose fate looked none too rosy. On, Margot! Before you and behind you are none but your mother's she-spies.

From the King's antechamber, immediately before she vanished, she threw one more look at the spot. He who had been her lover had moved and was no more to be discerned. Margot's heart sank as she turned the corner, but there was a lovely smile upon her face.

As soon as she had gone, the procession, which had only kept together and demeaned itself decorously on her account, began to break up. The girls of easy morals had chosen their companions for the night as they passed by, and carried them along. Jealous noblemen dragged their wives out of the throng amid derisive laughter. Not a stately train, but an unruly mob stumbled across the great hall. The musicians leapt into the air as they played, and the taper-bearers snuffed the guttering lights. No one later could remember what led to the outrage that followed, nor by whom the fateful word was uttered.

To begin with, the person summoned was nowhere to be seen. " Whom do you want for the night? " Then was heard the name: " Fat Bertha." That must mean the dwarf in her cage. " Fat Bertha " belonged to Madame Catherine; she was eighteen inches tall, and in any crowded company was carried in a cage like a parrot. The lackey who carried the caged dwarf at the end of a stave also led the monkey. When the monkey screamed, the dwarf screamed too, and her voice was far more beast-like. She had a great head with a vastly overhanging brow, her eyes protruded, and spittle oozed from her toothless mouth. " Fat Bertha " was clad like a lady of rank, with pearls in her straggling hair. " Fat Bertha! Whom do you want for the night? "

The creature screeched horribly at the question; the monkey was terrified and tugged at its tether, so that the lackey who held it nearly fell down. The door of the cage swung open; the way was clear for the dwarf. Hitherto all seemed to have fallen out by chance. Only afterwards was it observed how the details of the scene were set: the monkey, the clumsy lackey, the open cage dangling from the stave, and, above all, the idiot's shriek when she heard her cue. The old Queen's hunting-crop had taught it her, and in the wildest terror she did what she had been bidden. Her choice fell promptly upon the King of Navarre — or rather it was only subsequent reflection that revealed that accident as prearranged. Now and here it was believed that " Fat Bertha " had herself chosen Navarre when she leapt upon him.

She landed on his neck and, still screeching, scrambled into the openings of his clothes and was not to be dislodged. When he got one foot out of the slash in his sleeve, her hands sank deeper into his neck. In his struggles he swung round and round; the pair were dancing! " She's chosen him for the night and he's delighted! " It was long since there had been such laughter at the court of France.

When Henri saw that all was lost, he naturally fled. Behind him the onlookers bent double as they laughed, with many a shrill cachinnation among the deeper bellowings and gurgles, until they sank exhausted to the ground. Henri dashed up and down staircases and along corridors, with the dwarf at his neck. He no longer tried to shake her off. She had, moreover, wetted herself and him, and to show her attachment to him she fell to licking his cheeks. It was a race through a monstrous dream. He encountered no one; not even were the lights burning in the linen lanterns. Only shafts of moonlight fell from time to time across that mad career.

He was panting audibly when he reached his room; the attentive Armagnac opened the door at once. " What a sight you are, Sire! And how you smell! "

" This is my little friend, Armagnac. There are not many like her." And as she had ceased to lick his cheek he imprinted a kiss on hers. " As for the smell, Armagnac, it is the finest and the best of all the odours and the fragrances that I have smelt this day."

As he spoke the words, a hitherto strange expression, hard and terrible, came over his face. Even Armagnac recoiled. He tiptoed up to his master to relieve him of the dwarf; but she herself slipped down from weariness. Then he disappeared with her. Henri entered his room alone. And he shot the bolt.

A VOICE

At last he lay abed, and round him there were no longer forty noblemen on guard; but thoughts came flying past. They were confused, and connected only as in dream; indeed, they were barely thoughts. It was a scurry through his brain of uncompleted pictures or phrases, halting like the last stage of the procession when Margot had turned the corner. " I'm their captive. Are we going straight to Mass? The ravens. 'Tis all-important not to fall into the well-shaft. How easily, Sire, the same might happen to you. Salutation from the Admiral. He kicked the dead man in the face. For us I fear the worst. Monsieur de Goyon, you are yet alive! " But he lived no longer — as Henri in his half-sleep now knew; for he saw dead men, and they looked on him, though they made way at once for those who had returned to life. " Do I live? Elizabeth meant to take Calais from us. No, the Admiral. *Tue, tue!* That night we did too much or too little. Go on dissembling. These walls have an echo. All that is needed now is for our crazy brother Charles to die. I hate Anjou. Is it your pleasure, Navarre, to look on in impotence? Is it your pleasure? Let us flee. Is it your pleasure? "

The last words were no longer spoken in unconsciousness and were repeated somewhat more clearly than befitted a sleeper. So soon as he began to take account of this, he opened his eyes and firmly closed his lips. None the less, he heard the words again: " Is it your pleasure? Let us flee."

Beneath the image of the Virgin in the corner was set a night-light floating in its oil. In that feeble and uneasy glimmer the image moved — and surely it was speaking. Here was an unhappy man, who could neither understand nor measure his unhappiness, but a voice still spoke within the sleeper; the image of the Virgin might well raise her voice on his behalf.

He was soon to see that illusion vanish. From beneath his bed emerged a head — the dwarf's, of course, who must have crept back into the room. He bent down out of the bed to thrust the head back with his hand. Then said the head: " Awake, Sire! " And in that moment Henri really felt unburdened of his nightmare.

He had recognized the voice and now also he could see Agrippa's face. " Where were you all this evening? " he asked.

" Never far from your side, but never visible to human eyes."

" You were bound to hide yourself on my account, my poor Agrippa."

" We ourselves did our utmost to make our state as pitiable as it well could be."

Henri knew the classic adage and repeated it in the Latin poet's very words. This delighted Agrippa d'Aubigné, and he began something of a speech, which indeed he uttered in a voice too loud for the hour and for such a place. " It cannot be your pleasure, Sire, to look on in impotence while the fury of your enemies — "

" Pst! " said Henri. " Some of the walls here conceal a secret echo; and which they are, one cannot tell. Let us talk tomorrow in the garden, under the open sky."

" Too late," whispered the head, its chin now poised on the edge of the bed. " We must be out of the palace before daylight. 'Tis now or never. What we fail to do at once will miscarry later on. This day the palace of the Louvre is still distracted by the horror of the past night. By tomorrow evening they will have had time to think — and especially about us."

They paused for a moment in silent understanding; Henri had to ponder on what he had just heard, but Agrippa knew that the consent that did not come freely before he had shown his cards — that consent could never be recovered. He trembled, and wagged his head on the bed's edge. At long last he said:

" In ill fortune a neck is better risked forthwith."

This time Henri did not recognize the verse, or at any rate he did not repeat it. He merely muttered:

" They hung the dwarf about my neck. They fell down for

laughing, while I, with the dwarf on my back, dashed through the empty palace of the Louvre."

" That I did not witness," whispered the head. " I had already crawled under the bed. It was then, I understand, that the affair with the dwarf befell you. You are not averse from other such affairs; hence it is not your pleasure to escape."

" Take care — the echo! " said Henri.

Whereupon that cunning head began — why, surely it began to talk in quite another voice! One that was marvellously familiar, except that Henri, when he had heard it used before, had not wholly recognized it. Now he knew — it was his own voice! For the first time in his life he heard himself speak outside his own person.

" It is not my pleasure to wait in impotence until they slaughter me too. Hence I will so utterly subject myself to them that all Protestants shall despise me, and I imperil no one. I'll recant, I'll go to Mass, I'll write a contrite letter to the Pope — "

" No — not that! " implored Henri, addressing, so to say, his own self.

" A letter full of pitiable humility, and the whole world shall read it," replied his very voice. That comedian Agrippa must have practised for a long while to ape it to such perfection.

" No! " cried Henri incautiously, for the words alarmed him, as though he had spoken them himself. How long before he was to really utter them — and, still more, to fulfil them.

" Take care — the echo! " said the head in warning tones, and went on at once in that deluding, dreadful voice: " Or, in ill fortune, shall I risk my neck forthwith? " This in Latin. " But these are no more than poets' counsels! " retorted the voice, in admonition of itself. " Cousin Francis, what is your will? — so that I be allowed to live."

" Did you hear that also? " asked the real Henri. " So crazy a fool — I cannot give myself into his hands."

" But he gave himself into mine," said the mimic voice quickly. " And he is not the only one who would like to escape in my company and rouse the land of France. He goes about saying that he knew nothing of Saint Bartholomew. The others are silent, but their fear is not therefore any less. Why should I reveal to the echo the names of all that have offered me friendship and support? Only two names will I utter, for their bearers deserve no mercy."

"They are —" Breathlessly Henri urged his own voice to speak on.

"They are," said the voice, "de Nançay and de Caussens. They are afraid that the Queen Mother will have them killed, for instruments are often set aside. The two rascals are mine if I will, 'tis but a matter of money."

"*Spem pretio non emo.* I buy no hope for cash," replied the real Henri; but the mimic Henri had also a classic answer ready. "Truth must speak simply and without ornament." And he went on to interpret: "The speech best understood of such people carries coins — coins that dance and clink. I have not been idle, and I have the needed sum. It will be given out before daylight on the bridge before the gate, which will then open wide to let me through. They, too, will come with me, and others in plenty will join with us. I shall be strong, no one shall stop me then."

All this while the real Henri told himself he would not buy hope for cash. But he saw too that too much had already been undertaken and made ready, too many had been let into the secret. So he answered: "Yes," and "I will," and took pains that these same answers should not sound wavering or belated.

The Bond of Hatred

This darkling project ended in sorry fashion, in that Henri and his friend Agrippa were for a while on ill terms. While it was still dark they crept down into the well of the Louvre; there they waited with other muffled figures who preferred to remain unrecognized, for each man mistrusted his neighbour. In the guardhouse beneath the arch of the gateway glimmered a reddish light, and at intervals could be heard the deep reverberant note of a bell, whose echo lingered but too clearly in the ears of all from the night of murder. This time, it may be, its clangour saved the handful of Huguenots, so that they did not show themselves and appear under that portal. Captain de Nançay had to come forth himself when the dawn began to glimmer in the courtyard. His companion de Caussens was with him, and as a first step d'Aubigné slipped his money into their pouches. Then they announced that the horses were standing ready behind the gate; and they bade the others precede them on to the bridge.

But Henri would not walk before them under the narrow archway; he suspected an ambuscade. The pair of traitors had to go first; but a figure barred the way and spoke: " Messieurs Nançay and Caussens, I arrest you. It is evident you have been bribed and mean to let the Huguenots escape." A scuffle followed, though it was uncertain in the half light who were engaged in it, until the King of Navarre dropped into someone's arms — d'Elbeuf's. It was indeed the young noble of the House of Lorraine who had just announced the arrest. And he said to the King, in an imploring tone: " Remember — I once tried to drag you out of the gateway — while there was yet time." And Henri did remember; and he bethought him that the massacre need never have come to pass had he done this man's bidding. This time he had been warned; so Henri put his faith in friendship although offered by a kinsman of Guise, and thrust his arm under that of his new friend. His friend Agrippa hobbled behind; he had received some hurt in the scuffle. Henri pointed over his shoulder:

" That is the crafty rogue that lured me into the trap. He will have shared the money with the other two. I know the Huguenots."

" 'Tis the Huguenot princes who are faithless and ungrateful! " exclaimed poor Agrippa, stricken to the heart by this monstrous suspicion. He stopped abruptly and let the pair move forward.

" Sire," said Elbeuf gravely, while Henri clung to his arm, " let not your anger prevail over your better sense. Your poor Agrippa acted hastily and was over-trusting. It shall be a warning for the future, to you and to your friends, and therefore to me likewise. It will be our daily task to ward disaster from your head. This time we succeeded. Otherwise the pair of traitors would have raised an alarm on the bridge and seized you there. They hoped the Queen Mother would pardon them, they had done such good service on the night of murder — ah, yes, they thought to save their own lives."

" It is true," agreed Henri. " Every man within the Louvre has but the choice how he will secure himself: by flight, or by my betrayal. We must always keep that before us."

" Always," repeated d'Elbeuf.

On that day Henri noticed that Alençon avoided him. An attempt at flight had failed, and the Man with Two Noses had certainly been among those muffled figures in the well-shaft. (" Let each man look to how he stands, and not at my expense.")

The Lords of Montmorency were kinsmen of Admiral de Coligny, but Catholics, and therefore powerful enough at court to urge clemency towards the Protestants, their lives and their faith. And in the face of matters as they stood, what could be done was done. The reason brought forward by the Marshal was the opinion of the world on the events of Saint Bartholomew. This was a reason that could only hold so long as there was no news from Europe, and even so only during the first storm of indignation, which indeed seemed more virulent in the more distant lands, like Poland, and the weaker ones, such as the Protestant German principalities. Elizabeth of England, on the other hand, showed a regard for facts that did credit to her understanding. Madame Catherine soon felt no more disquiet on her account. Half seriously and half in wantonness she counselled her good friend to organize just such a massacre on her island — though there, of course, among the Catholics.

Madame Catherine accordingly began to show herself once more to her whole court. She seemed to lay aside a little of her mystery, she grew confidential. The mother gathered her children about her, all without exception, as she had always so striven to do. " Were but one of you absent I should have no peace," she said in her comfortable voice, in which there was not a quaver of mockery. In how natural and even kindly a fashion she one day eyed Navarre and Condé, whom she had hitherto ignored! Henri was startled and grew wary. She asked the pair

how they were progressing with their instruction in the true
faith. " Well," said Henri. " Indeed, I shall soon know as much
as my teacher. The worthy pastor converted himself to the Catholic faith when he felt that Saint Bartholomew was at hand.
He is fortunate who has learned to calculate aright."

" 'Tis a matter you would do well to learn," observed Madame
Catherine. She looked him up and down and added: " King
Wren." This before her court — and Henri bowed, first to her
and then to her court. The courtiers laughed, partly from mere
folly; but some of them shuddered, for they knew how matters
stood with Navarre, and did but laugh for the sake of their own
skins.

In this, Madame Catherine betrayed herself. She kept King
Wren secretly under her eye day in and day out, although to all
appearances she had not noticed him. This time she waved a
hand, the company about her tall chair drew back, and Henri
stood before her, alone.

" On the very second day you made an attempt to escape. I
have rewarded Monsieur de Nançay and Monsieur de Caussens
for their watchfulness."

" I made no attempt at escape, Madame. But I am glad for
the sake of the two gentlemen." He nodded to them, for he had
caught a glimpse of their leering faces.

" You will give me much trouble yet. As your mother and
your good friend, I warn you." Madame Catherine said this in a
truly maternal tone, as all could hear. But Navarre burst out
sobbing before he could blurt out: " Ah, Madame, never could
I wish to leave a ruler who reminds me of the great women of
Roman history."

So ended this most notable encounter. It had lifted young
Navarre somewhat in the court's esteem, and in that moment
they were more inclined towards him. But a man's estimation
cannot but change from day to day when he must needs have
recourse to too many and too various sorts of subterfuge. By
way of variety he pretended to be docile but unready. He was
told he must write a letter to the Protestant fortress of La
Rochelle, to the Mayor and burgesses, to tell them to open the

gates for the commandant whom the King was sending them from France. He indited something of childlike ingenuousness which, from their knowledge of his character, they would infallibly ignore. Whereupon after a few months there came about a siege of the Protestant fortress, and the whole kingdom could observe the fruits of Saint Bartholomew. 'Tis a simple matter to overthrow the enemy; but take care lest he does not rise up again with strength renewed. This or something like it was what Charles IX said, or stuttered, to himself when bad news came from the distant provinces of France.

Charles was melancholy unto death. Spirits appeared to him by night, again he heard the boom of the bell on the night of murder, and answering groans from the river. His nurse, a Protestant, dried the sweat that burst from him, but the sweat was bloody; so it was whispered in the Louvre. One day the wretched King was visited by his good-humoured cousin Navarre, who gave him words of comfort. "Let not our hair grow grey, dear brother. Here in the palace of the Louvre there is more space than formerly and we live on easier terms. Those who let themselves be caught were fools. I have forgotten them all by now. Your sister will gladly make me a cuckold; but I have occasion and enough to pay her back." He snapped his fingers and swung round on his heels, which he wore rather higher than was usual.

One day he went to bed, on the plea that he was very ill, and he was really sweating and feverish. The doctors who visited him in the name of Madame Catherine agreed that it was so, but with much shaking of their heads. Such fevers come of refusing to go to Mass — "Oh, not yet, in God's name! If it must be one day, let there be some respite, for the love of Heaven! Let me be truly sick, send me bloody sweat, or ghosts to haunt me. I would have my forty dead noblemen standing once more about my bed. Better that than go to Mass!"

But the days passed, and suddenly the dreaded day had come. Then we come forth, and feel the strength we need to meet it. It was the 29th of September, dedicated to Saint Michael, whose knights escorted their fellow-member of that Order, Navarre. on the way to church. He walked with eyes downcast, and even in his own heart he took no heed of the throng that stood about him and mocked and scorned him and may have wept over him. Disguised Huguenots followed his dejected progress, and afterwards they spread about the land the tale of what their beloved leader had been made to suffer. He himself thought all the way of his mother and the Admiral.

And what he thought was this: " My dearest mother, they beset me, and it will not be long before I must send orders to our land of Béarn that they must forswear your creed. I must banish your pastors, and that is as though I were banishing you with mine own hand, my dearest mother. Lord Admiral, your sons and nephews have now fled in disguise. Your lady is held prisoner in Savoy. It cannot be long before the court pronounces your goods forfeit and your memory disgraced. Be not ready to believe, Lord Admiral and dearest mother, that I am betraying you, if I none the less now go to Mass. You know that I have won as many days as were possible — seventeen! My cousin Condé, who at first was much more furious than I, has already gone to Mass, seventeen days ago. You should count it in my favour that I kept them off so long." Thus he spoke to them, as though to living people, which indeed they were. Such eager thoughts do penetrate to those abodes.

When the solemn conversion to the other faith, the fourth in his lifetime, was fulfilled, he was overwhelmed with kisses and caresses, and he returned them in good part. The Queen Mother did him honour; she awaited the youth, who at last stood quite alone, for, as she thought, he had even lost the spirits of his own dead, and his own good name. So she received him with a cheerful smile, and while she had her arms about him she patted him from sheer goodwill, as though he had been a tidbit to be shortly set before her. Why, what was this? All her cheerfulness departed. Beneath his clothes he was wearing a cuirass, he had had it on while he was abjuring his former congregation. A sorry omen; and it was in Madame Catherine's mind to hobble hurriedly away. But he ventured to take her hand and address her with affectionate endearments. But an unwieldly old lady

in a stiff black dress and widow's coif — what is she to do when a
forthcoming youth praises her nose, which is in fact a squat and
ugly one? He made a dab at her — he meant to kiss her on the
nose. In the end she hit him with her stick; only in jest, as it
seemed, out of consideration for the onlookers. He promptly
dropped on all fours and leapt about her like a little dog, barking
and snapping at her heels. Madame Catherine rapped out a
curse. Her small person tried to outspeed her feet; thus self-
divided, she struggled from the room, and the court laughed at
her as she went.

Her vengeance did not tarry. Not only was Henri forced to
write the edict to the Protestants in Béarn, but a letter to the
Pope as well; this surpassed all others in self-betrayal, and she
had it published far and wide. During one of their exchanges of
raillery it suddenly occurred to her to ask after his health. He was
a weakling, was he not, and no true man? His mother Jeanne
had sown the seed of early death within him.

And he opened his mouth to say in tones of mockery: " You,
Madame, shook that seed into her glass." For in those earlier
days there was much confidence between the bird on the limed
twig and the owner of the cage. Hatred is a mutual bond. Then
he heard her say: " I must ask my daughter how you quit yourself." At once he grasped what her purpose was: to declare him
impotent and get the marriage dissolved in Rome. To kill him
would profit her no more. She was all the more eager to be rid of
what could now bring her neither good nor ill — and once more
possess herself of Margot, with all that she could bring. Madame
Catherine always had her head full of marriage schemes for her
children.

That evening he again lay in the marriage bed.

Born of Love

He approached the Queen of Navarre's door escorted by many
gentlemen, of whom only a few would have defended him if the
others had been murderers. But he had taken them all with him
so that they could bear witness later on that he had gone to the

Queen. But as a precaution he carried his dagger in his hand, and with it he tapped on the door — not violently, but it opened at once. " I was awaiting you, my lord and master. You are later today than usual," said the Queen.

He shut the door and shot the bolt. When he turned, she was lying on the bed with her arms outspread to him. He knew what he wanted, and that was to baulk her mother's malignant plan, which he promptly did, and again and yet again. The amorous Margot had to beg him not to forget that they were again united after a long and dreadful parting.

" As I shall now get a son from you, dear heart, pray tell me why you did not sooner think of this means of conquering all your foes? "

" You will give me a son? "

" I feel it," she said; and then she added: " I want to. How I have been longing for you! It was only last evening that I tapped upon your door."

He would have taken her in his arms; this time to embrace his son within her. But even while his heart was throbbing, he remembered that guile was his law. Guile ruled his life. The daughter spends her days on the coffer in her mother's room, and is her instrument. Once already she had herself been oblivious of what treachery she served. " There is no murderer hidden here? " he asked, leaned out of the bed and reached for his dagger. Had she but attempted the faintest movement to hold him — ! No; she stiffened. And she whispered in an anguished voice, so softly that no intruder could have heard: " I had not thought that we were enemies."

" I also had forgotten it," said he. " All this, pleasure and pain likewise, is forbidden to us now." Whereat she quickly gave him her lips, but behind them he could see the glitter of her teeth. And he said, still breathless from the kiss:

" *Faciuntque dolorem.*"

And immediately he heard the whole verse repeated in her lovely voice, and he remembered that she had revealed to him her dreadful mother's secrets, and that very evening she had so behaved before all the noblemen as though it were her habit to receive him every day. He took the risk and said: " My lovely Queen, will you help me to free myself? "

" I admire you, Sire; you are more of a match for danger than any man I know. Virgil had you in mind when he wrote: ' There is no peril of which I am not the master; mine are arms that will bear down all disaster.' "

" Is that your own translation of the lines? " asked the young lover. " You are so learned and so ingenious. But how may I free myself? "

" Above all things, beware of my friend Sauves," answered she, no less loving. " I can see that the siren is luring you. Follow her not, or you are lost! Her lord and master is the Duke of Guise."

" Would you have him back? " he asked; and for very jealousy he forgot to mask the question. But she asked such another: " Do you like Charlotte? "

" No; her face is pinched, and her mind pinched too. And yet was there ever a woman that I did not like? Even your mother, Madame. And that is true, I do not lie. A wicked woman is a dangerous beast. 'Tis glorious thus, two in one. For in nature I love most the woman and the beast — and the mountains too," he added, " and the sea. I love, I love," he moaned, and there lay her body, awaiting him.

After such ecstasy, exhausted and grateful, Margot decided to reveal to her lover everything she might, and even more.

" My dear heart, you must not flee from us; we need you, and we mean to keep you."

For one moment she left him wondering for what purpose. It might be for her body, but that was soon satiated. What, then? For her unappeasable soul? No, the daughter of the wicked Queen, prostrate upon her bed, said: " You must not flee to your Huguenots, Sire. If they had you back again they would be ten times stronger. No, we mean to make use of your person against our enemies, and you are to be with the army of my brother Anjou when he besieges La Rochelle. You must know," she went on softly with her face quite close to his, " that we are not done with your people yet. They marked that your letter to them bidding them yield was not written of your own free will.

Promise me that you will make no attempt to flee meanwhile, or you will be killed. Oh, promise! " she implored in open terror, her forehead upon his and her breath mingled with his breath. But he wanted to see her eyes; he drew back and said:

" Is it truly for you to say what I shall do? "

How crazy a suspicion! She not merely recoiled, she said in icy tones: " I am the Princess of Valois. I will not have you defeat and dethrone my house."

Thus ended the night — and for that reason the next night Henri lay with Charlotte de Sauves, whom he did not yet like — that was to come later. He still had Margot in his blood, and she knew it. Proudly she said to Sauves:

" Madame, you have done a great service, both to myself and to the King of Navarre. You were quick to let the Queen my mother know that you had had him in your bed. Now the Queen believes that her aim is achieved and that I will consent to a divorce. So my dear lord will be allowed to live, for the present."

CONVERSATION BY THE SEASHORE

Charles IX recovered for a time from the burden of his melancholy. The Queen of Navarre was asked by her mother whether her King Wren had shown himself a man. As there were bystanders, Margot blushed, said neither no nor yes, but appealed to a lady of antiquity. " Moreover, as my lady mother married me, there is no more to be said." And this was only allowed to pass because Madame Catherine was wholly engaged in getting her son Anjou elected King of Poland. And she did it against the Emperor's will; so great was her ambition, or her craving for intrigue. At the same time she treated with England to arrange a marriage between her son Alençon and Queen Elizabeth. This might carry a claim to the throne of France. But Elizabeth was a wiser woman than Catherine de Medici, of whom Jeanne d'Albret had said that she was at bottom stupid. Hence the red-haired Queen was not to be drawn into the adventure, but she kept her good friend in play. The army of the Duke of Anjou marched on the Protestant fortress of La Rochelle; and the

King of Navarre and his cousin Condé had to go with it, much against their will.

None the less, they behaved as though they were enjoying the campaign. Henri was always in good humour, always ready to lead his troops against the stubborn city. But, alas, all attempts at storming it failed on every occasion, from February until the summer. And this was because the storming parties shouted so vociferously in their martial ardour that no garrison could fail to observe their coming. The King of Navarre once fired an arquebus with his own hand. A Gascon soldier within caught sight of him and called to some of his fellows to come and watch. " *Lou noust Henric!* " they shouted ecstatically from the walls. He, too, was hugely delighted, and lit the match once more before their eyes. There followed a loud report, and the besieged waved their hats. So did not fare the Duke of Anjou, who was near to being killed by such a shot; the shirt was torn from his back. Navarre was at his side and heard his cousin cry: " I wish I were in Poland! "

This had been his feeling for a long while, and not only because of the troubles that were his; no, before La Rochelle it was clear for all to see that the realm was bitterly beset. It was now plain that Saint Bartholomew had been a fearsome blunder; it had let loose another religious war. Admiral Coligny's plan had been that Catholics and Protestants should fight side by side against Spain. Now, by reason of that accursed slaughter, they were tearing the land to pieces once again, and to every frontier sped the news of the Huguenots holding out in La Rochelle; for they were being provisioned by sea. The army of the King of France, on the other hand, had eaten the whole district bare and was beginning to dissolve. And that was not the worst. Hunger was less to be feared than thought. In the more exalted places, just where there was still food, sat many discontented people, who called themselves " Politicals "; and these people wanted peace.

When anyone says he wants peace, it is always a question — why. In times of peace his corn thrives, and it is first to be discovered whether he is peacefully disposed no matter what may come, or mainly because of his corn. The harvest on which these Moderates or "Politicals" before La Rochelle were set was called "Freedom of Conscience." They desired at last to be able to admit what they believed, and to make known what they knew and what they wanted. Hence they had eyes for the ravaged countryside, the outward consequence of intolerance. But not even the ruin of the land could hold him back who hated human freedom. Indeed, he marked neither ravages nor ruin, if so be he could make all men alike by force. Violated consciences are for him a goodlier sight than smiling fields and peace. He has also the advantage that he can express his mean opinion of peace as openly as Madame Catherine or Anjou or Guise. Whereas to all who merely want to be free, there falls the thankless task of preaching peace.

Such were the thoughts of a captive who actually bore the rank of commander in the Catholic army, but was none the less a prisoner. In truth he came upon such thoughts alone, and especially at his secret meetings with those who were of the movement. But they had not yet, so to say, been clarified or set in order. This only came about in certain talks with a nobleman of no especial importance who was serving in the army.

At these meetings of the "Politicals" there were present, among others, Alençon, or the Man with Two Noses, and one Viscount de Turenne. The former had explicit news from the court regarding a new massacre that was to take place in the very camp among those who had fallen under suspicion; and they were the "Politicals." And this time the King of Navarre would certainly be among the victims. The business had indeed been delayed on his account, for his wife was first to bear a son; the massacre would promptly follow. Yes, his noblemen had received friendly warnings from the Duke of Guise's quarters that they had better keep away from the tents of Navarre; and Anjou's favourite, du Guast, used open threats. A prisoner whose life is at issue must needs be of the Moderate party!

"We are moderate men," say these same Politicals; "and we are wearied and sickened by the state of this realm of France: its government, its court, and its finances. Ruin is at hand.

Only the boldest measures can bring succour. Alençon, Navarre, and Condé must openly break away. The disaffected must unite to form an army. We will get possession of the royal fleet. English ships will bring us reinforcements."

This merely provoked Navarre to jesting, though he was indeed afraid. " Custom," he said, " demands that the Protestants should be expelled from their strong places. Then we shall treat with them and give them back their strong places, whence we shall soon drive them out again. And thus custom continues."

He said this because he was afraid that they would do nothing in earnest, and indeed they only made attempts that failed forthwith, because each of them proceeded in the uttermost confusion. Such were the dealings of that half-wit Alençon. What had the man in mind? To harry his brother Anjou: that was his sole purpose; other conviction had he none. But if Navarre tried to thrust him from the leadership, he would at once turn against Navarre. And Henri reflected that he was the man most threatened; anyone could betray him and deliver him to his enemy.

Hence it was that he despaired of such dealings before the fortress of La Rochelle and betook himself to philosophy. This he did in the company and in some measure under the guidance of a nobleman of no great rank who came out of the South. Shortly before, he had laid down a legal office to try his fortunes at soldiering — in which he had made no particular success. He himself admitted that he had not the talents needed, either for dancing, tennis, or wrestling; nor yet for swimming, sword-play, horsemanship, or jumping — indeed for nothing at all. Even his hands were clumsy, and he could not write legibly, as he freely confessed. And he went on to add that he could not seal a letter, cut a pen, nor, on the other hand, bridle a horse.

All these defects did but increase Henri's admiration for him, as though they had been as many virtues. For they were combined with a mind which Henri, whether he liked it or not, recognized as kindred to his own. In person, too, the nobleman from Périgord reminded Henri of himself — short, compact, and sturdy. He was some forty years old, with a high-coloured face, and a wart on his bald skull. His cast of countenance was genial, but touched with the sorrow of having lived and thought. The youthful Henri's new friend was called Michel de Montaigne.

" Sire," he said, " your condition at the present is akin to that of an ageing man. We are both vanquished: I by years, and you by your foes — which is not a final victory, like the victory of years," added the forty-year-old man. " Enough, in this moment we can understand each other, and you have grasped how matters stand with these dealings between men and men. You bewail their confusion and futility. That, indeed, must be reckoned to the Duke of Alençon's charge."

" He is a half-wit. I in his place could help freedom to victory against force."

"That would be, above all, your own freedom," observed Montaigne, and Henri admitted as much with a laugh.

"You would have your freedom back. But your revolt and the arrival of the English would give rise to even more mortal confusion. Most deeds are done head downwards; and confusion is their essence."

Here they paused in their talk while they were still walking among tents and might be overheard. Then they had left the camp behind them. A solitary cannon lay bogged in the sand of the seashore. A sentry or two, muffled in cloaks against the sea wind, demanded the password, and they cried out into the void: " Saint Bartholomew."

For a while they remained silent, to accustom themselves to the wild uproar of the wind and waves. The beleaguered fortress of La Rochelle loomed up grey against the tattered sky and the sea that thundered towards it from the infinite. What army could aspire to storm this fortress, so visibly established as an outpost of the infinite? The sight of it brought the selfsame thought into the minds of Henri and his companion. With Henri the impulse to thought was a feeling; born in his diaphragm, it sped with lightning swiftness to the throat, which contracted, and the eyes, which moistened. So long as that feeling stirred within him, the youthful Henri grasped the infinite and the futility of all that must have an end.

His companion spoke of the confusion in which the deeds of

men were done. " A great personage hurt the good name of his creed because he wanted to show himself more zealous in the faith than was fitting." Who could that be " *Insani sapiens* — " he said against the wind. Horace had put it into verse, that even wisdom and justice could go too far. By the " great personage " he could not possibly have meant Anjou. The man of Saint Bartholomew in the same breath with wisdom and with justice. But his companion had indeed meant Anjou, and in the fashion of philosophers was merely advancing cautiously on uncertain ground. He recounted yet more examples of such confusion, and as these were taken from antiquity he could mention names. Henri was more concerned to hear what he thought of his present fellows. His companion was not to be moved beyond general observations. But these grow notably transparent, when the matter concerns a man so nearly as his own life. Monsieur de Montaigne thought nothing more alien to religion than religious wars; this he said, monstrous as it sounded. Religious wars were not born of faith, nor did they make men more pious. For some they were the pretext of ambition, for others the opportunity of enrichment. Saints do certainly not appear in religious wars. They weaken a nation and a realm, which then becomes a prey to foreign aggression.

Not a name was uttered, not Madame Catherine nor her son Anjou, nor those of the Protestants. But the words were the boldest that any man could dare to use. Not only the breakers and the storm assailed them; almost all humanity would have howled them down. Henri indeed was amazed that a plain gentleman like this should have uttered what not even a king would have cared to admit aloud. He himself had sometimes felt his doubts of religious wars; but had he wholly despaired of them, he must needs have condemned persons whom he did respect: his mother and the Admiral. The " Politicals " before La Rochelle had indeed conspired, but they would only fight for their creed of Moderation. This was but a fresh cloak for their ambition and their greed. They who thought to attack France with English help would not have welcomed the nobleman from Périgord. For all his Moderation, Alençon would probably have clapped him in the deepest dungeon and there forgotten him for ever.

Henri conceived so great a respect for this man's courage that it dispelled any lingering mistrust.

"What religion is the right one?" asked Henri.

"How do I know?" answered the other.

The words were a self-betrayal and a surrender such as no man would have made had he not recognized a kindred spirit and trusted him without a tremor. And it was so; both men knew that they could trust each other. Henri took the other's hand and pressed it. "We'll go into that deserted house yonder," said he. "The inhabitants have fled, but they'll certainly have left their wine behind."

The house lay near the shore and had been bombarded from the sea. Why? — and by whom? That would never be discovered now, neither from the doers of the deed nor from those who had fled. Inside, the beams had fallen from the ceiling, and the sky could be seen through the roof. But the ladder still stood in the cellar trapdoor, and there was wine below. In what had been the kitchen the two guests sat on a fallen beam and drank to each other.

"Well, we are guests," said Monsieur de Montaigne, "guests upon an earth where there are no abodes that may endure. We contend for them utterly in vain. For my part I have never tried to acquire more than fortune bestowed upon me, and, while I watch the imminent years, I still live in the little castle I inherited."

"There is war in the land," said Henri, "and you might lose it. Let us drink!"

"Drink I will, and drink would taste the better to me if I had lost my all and thus been rid of all anxiety. It is my habit always to fear the worst, and if it really happens, to bear with it in patience. But uncertainty and doubt I find hard to bear. Truly I am no doubter," he added eagerly.

"How do I know?" said Henri, in the words that the other had used a little while before.

"Let us drink!" cried Montaigne. "On the threshold of age

a man should be cautious in every connection; but I often find myself understanding a countryman of mine who, when getting on in years, sought his wife in a place where women are to be had for money. Thereby he reached the lowest level, and that is the safest one."

"Let us drink!" cried Henri with a laugh. Then he added suddenly: "You are a brave man!" and he grew serious. By this he meant his friend's pronouncements on religion; but Montaigne understood him otherwise.

"Yes, I, too, became a soldier. I wanted to prove my manhood. Know thyself! Self-knowledge is the only occupation worthy of mankind. Who even understands his own body? I am idle, sluggish, and have heavy hands; but I know all about my organs, and therefore about my soul, which is free and subject to no one. Let us drink!"

They drank and so continued for a while. Henri joined in when his companion, with uplifted cup, chanted some lines of Horace:

> " I am not borne along with bellying sails,
> Yet neath the stress of adverse south wind's gales
> I drag not out my life: in strength, in brain,
> Appearance, virtue, station, and estate,
> The last, it may be, of the foremost rate,
> But still before the last group of the train."

Then they got up, helped each other to stumble across the shingle, and when they were clear, still stood clutching each other's arms. The fumes of the wine only faded by degrees. And, once more in the turmoil of the storm, Henri said:

"But I am and I remain a captive!"

"Force is strong," observed his companion. "But goodness is still stronger. *Nihil est tam populare quam bonitas.*"

Henri never forgot this, because he had heard it when it was his sole consolation. Goodness is popular, nothing is so popular as goodness. Eagerly he said to his companion:

" Is it true that all deeds are done head downwards, and that confusion is their essence? "

At the sound of the words that Montaigne himself had uttered at the outset of the talk, which had taken so many unexpected turns — at the sound of them, Monsieur Michel de Montaigne recovered himself; he remembered whose arm he was holding and he let it go. Then he turned and faced the ocean.

" Our great Lord in heaven," said he, enunciating every syllable, " seldom deems us worthy of a pious deed."

" Pray, what is a pious deed? " asked Henri, also confronting the ocean.

Montaigne rose on the tips of his toes to utter what he had not — which was for him unusual — discovered from his own rumination. A great breath swept through him and swelled his utterance.

" Conceive of this: an army, a whole army, kneels down, and instead of attacking, prays; being so convinced of its destiny to conquer."

That, too, Henri bore within his mind until a certain day.

It was the end of the talk. A picket in charge of an officer escorted them back to the camp. They had been missed and followed; it was feared that the King of Navarre had escaped.

HEAD DOWNWARDS

In the meantime Paris had been filled with gentlemen in strange furs and of exotic and elaborate demeanour. They were the Poles who had come to fetch their King, for Anjou had actually been elected amid the vast jubilation of the Polish nation, assembled on a field for that purpose. The new King should have made haste; what more had he to expect from that thankless fortress that would not let itself be taken? The truth, if he had dared to utter it, was that he was awaiting his brother Charles's death. Better to be King of France than King of Poland. Charles, who was well aware of this, sent messenger after messenger to La Rochelle to urge him to decide. It is easier for a man to recover when there is no longer someone at hand who, day by day and hour by hour, hopes that blood will burst from out his pores.

Madame Catherine was just to both her sons. She compelled her favourite to depart, that her sick son's mind might be at rest. At the same time she took care, if need should be, that her favourite's rights should be secured. The Polish success, her anxiety about the succession to Charles, and therewith her designs on Elizabeth of England, to whom she caused to be sent much-flattered portraits of the Man with Two Noses, all this kept Madame Catherine mightily engaged. There were indeed moments when she did not know how all these matters stood. But this, as she was very well aware, is all-important for a sovereign who has many she must hold in fee. Had Madame Catherine had her mind free, what followed would scarce have come about.

The very journey to the frontier was made in some disorder. The King of Poland had, of course, to be escorted thither by the whole court; but a court travels with difficulty, even under ordinary circumstances. All the more so when occasion calls for pompous peregrination, and, moreover, every detail will be reported in Warsaw by the Polish envoys who accompanied that great train. Coaches, horsemen, runners, pack-animals, and so forth, ringed by an escort of soldiers and pursued by beggars and inquisitive peasants, rocked and rumbled along the deeply rutted roads. But these causeways of dried clay dissolve in rain. When it rained, the coaches were screened with tarpaulins, and the horsemen disappeared into their cloaks. The great concourse pressed onwards, cursing, in a huddled mass. No more peasants ran up to gape at them or fall on their knees. Vast unsheltered plains on which the rain poured down, and only a few straggling boors appeared in the fields, peered grimly at the court as it moved by, and crouched down again into the sacks that covered them. Decent folk were sitting in their homes or working under their sacks. The court was crawling onwards in the rain like a band of gypsies.

Then the sun came out, and a city could be seen on the horizon; whereupon the court resumed its splendour. The tarpaulins were lifted off the carriages, the gilding reappeared, the crowns screwed into the roofs glittered in the sunlight, and the encircling feathers waved and nodded. All was silk and velvet, gaiety and glory; and with high gallantry of bearing, stern or gracious smiles, the cavalcade entered that city. Reverences and bended backs were graciously acknowledged. The bells began to peal. Salt and bread were tended by the burghers, and the imposts due were paid under the eyes of the armed guard. Charles IX had to drain a bumper of welcome.

It was a draught that went down ill; on that journey the luckless King could bear no brimming goblets, nor the jolting of the wheels, nor the noise and contact of the throng. But most of all he could not bear his memories, and they never left him; they bore him company, though the palace of the Louvre lay far behind. So he said nothing in reply to the ceremonial addresses. He looked sidelong and suspiciously at any attempt to approach him; for thenceforward until the end he must needs be alone. They dragged him onwards through the highways and the byways, through many an anxious hour, though he was sick of them all and they of him. Shrunken and once more very pale, he felt utterly aloof from all that happened, just as he used to feel as a haughty, sallow-faced boy, and as you may see him in his portraits.

He did not reach the frontier of his kingdom. At a place named Vitry they had to leave him behind. They had mishandled him to make their Saint Bartholomew. So they left him sick in Vitry and continued to escort his brother Anjou. Only his cousin Navarre stayed behind with him; but he had his reasons, which Charles could guess. He of course wanted to escape. He had a shrewd idea that there would be no spies haunting that sick-bed. The coach with the maids of honour had gone on, and the old Queen had no eyes for him just then. Why not flee southwards? He had larger plans, indeed, though they were foolish ones. He had let himself be persuaded to withdraw to Germany with Cousin Francis. The Protestant princes would welcome both of them. With their aid the cousins would invade the kingdom, and Cousin Francis should mount the throne before his brother Anjou could get back from far-off Poland. They no longer took account of Charles. Between Soissons and Compiègne it happened; Alençon and Navarre tried to get away, and they were caught.

Madame Catherine suddenly realized that she had been too deep in State affairs abroad to keep due watch on her domestic concerns. To her sick son she said: " All the time I was travelling to the frontier you were alone with King Wren, and you noticed nothing. You were never the master! " Why should she spare him? — his days were numbered.

Charles lay propped on his elbow, his head resting on his hand. He merely peered sidelong at his mother, and answer made he none. He might have said: " I knew it." But he had, otherwise than the travellers, reached the frontier, and he was silent.

Madame Catherine turned no more towards him, she spoke to herself: " I was able to catch the traitors at the last moment, because someone did speak in the end." Who that was, she did not say. At that moment came a knock at the door; Navarre stood without, as though nothing had happened, and asked to be admitted to the King. Instead of which he heard the Queen Mother command that he should be informed that the King was asleep. She spoke in loud tones, not at all as one would speak in the bedchamber of a man asleep. A large number of noblemen witnessed this open humiliation. Navarre with bowed head hurried to his room. There he found that lock and bolt had been removed; officers could come in at any time and look under the bed. And they did so, both to the King of Navarre and to the Duke of Alençon; and these people were among the chief actors on the night of Saint Bartholomew. So matters stood in Soissons at that time.

Armagnac, who slept in his master's room, had to submit to be searched whenever he came back. And not only he — the Queen of Navarre was stopped when she went to visit her husband. At last she was given permission to speak to him through the open door. As there were listeners at hand, she spoke softly and in Latin.

" My dear lord," she said, in gentle and melancholy tones, " I am sore displeased with you. I who did so much to save you! Even the doctors believed that I was pregnant. Alas, I was not, and I fear I never shall be. At what I thought would be due time, I padded my belly. But my mother was not so easy to deceive as the doctors, and I will not speak of what was done to me. While I was set sorely upon your welfare, what was your design? "

" I had none," said Henri lightly. " What should have been my scheme? Surely you must see that your dear mother does but seek a pretext for killing me."

" And rightly so," said Margot — another Margot now: the Princess of Valois. " For you are an enemy of our House, which you mean to overthrow." The other Margot was angered by his want of candour, and her voice was hard.

Henri's tone grew all the lighter: " Ah, so you believe in that conspiracy? They say I called in fat Nassau, do they not? " He blew out his cheeks and made a marvellous mimicry of corpulence. She did not laugh, and the tears came into her eyes.

" You are lying to me even now! " she burst out. He again protested, and went on bantering her until she quite lost patience. " You are a fool! " she cried in a fury, and this time in French; " no better than a fool! To intrigue with my brother Alençon and think he would keep your secret! "

" He kept it strictly," observed Henri, merely to lead her into the trap. Then she quite lost all self-control; she swung her body towards him and shrieked. " He did betray you! " Whereat he provoked her yet again. " At most to one person — whom I know." " Fool! " retorted Margot without thinking, " I know her better. And she promptly carried the matter to her mother."

That was her confession. She herself was the informer. After this self-betrayal she grew tremulous and afraid, and recoiled against the door. But nothing was further from his mind than to lay hands upon her. " Now I know! " he cried good-humouredly. " You had it from La Mole."

This La Mole was one of those handsome men who flaunt their great limbs like Guise. Margot had a weakness for him, she was always destined to go back to the same type. Of this Henri was aware, and therefore he named La Mole — as though Margot were already in such deep relations with him that he might have betrayed to her the secret of his fellow-conspirator Alençon, which she had forthwith passed on to her mother. Such was the purport of what he, laughing, flung at her head when he cried: "You had it from La Mole."

She bit her lips; and she thought: "You have willed it, and you shall be made a cuckold." This once decided, she recovered her good temper. She went up to him, bent one knee, and said: "My dear lord, let nothing remain between us two of this pitiful misunderstanding."

She departed. He watched her go and thought of his revenge, as she of hers.

Thereafter events moved quickly. Conspiracies followed each other without a break, like the days in the palace of the Louvre, and like the months — and like the years. A great stroke was prepared for a morning in February, while the court was at Saint-Germain. Henri and his cousin Condé were to ride out hunting and would return no more. The kingdom would rise in revolt, all the Moderates were ready, Catholics and Protestants as well. Governors of provinces were in the plot and one garrison had been won over. The Princes needed only to ride thither with fifty horses and they would be in safety. Instead of which: arrest, collapse, a forced and pitiful renunciation from Navarre of any such undertakings, and an oath that he would lend no aid to rebels in the future who might be planning to disturb the peace; indeed, he would loyally make common cause against them. All this Henri signed, and did not even believe while he held the pen; and Madame Catherine believed it just as little. King Wren was indeed a troublesome creature, and almost as crazy as her son Alençon, who on the decisive day did not ride out hunting, but lay abed. Her sole safeguard was the dissension among the conspirators, and also the traitor, who never failed. Someone would always be found to betray the whole affair. At Saint-Germain it was La Mole, that long-limbed youth, through whom the King of Navarre had been well and truly made a cuckold. What La Mole suppressed was revealed by the Man with Two Noses, to get himself out of the affair.

Madame Catherine then forgave him in very truth; he was her son, and moreover he was not to be taken seriously. And, from disdain, she was very lenient to the Prince of Condé, and dismissed him to govern the province of Picardy for the King. He fled to Germany instead; but she did not care. No, there was only one person whom Madame Catherine really distrusted, and him, with all the appearance of scorn, she called King Wren. A wren is a small bird, but still not small enough for her. She had abandoned her design of a divorce since her daughter had betrayed him. Let his pious Protestants but hear of that, and he would indeed rise in their esteem! What could they think of him or hope from him? To save his life he had again become a Catholic. He had squandered what remained of his good name in senseless schemes, and abjured them one after the other as soon as they miscarried. Navarre had indeed fallen to the lowest depth when he, to betray the King, forgathered with his wife's lover.

The court then lay at Vincennes; there was there less scope for all those upon whom Madame Catherine's eyes were set. None the less, they were busy with new plans, or rather with the self-same ones as ever: flight, revolt, the help of the German troops — but this time the design was set afoot by the traitor himself. The very same La Mole who had so lately delivered them to the enemy — they now put themselves into his hands. At Saint-Germain they had known him for what he was; at Vincennes it was forgotten. True, Alençon might well be mad, and Henri embittered from having to give these degrading pledges. Still, no one with his wits about him would behave so at a court where every man knows himself to be observed, but especially Navarre and Cousin Francis — quite apart from the fact that they do not trust each other. But there exists a sort of vacant impulse to activity that is very like uneasy slumber. Both young men were well acquainted with La Mole, and what he was: a traitor by nature, and therewith the Princess's lover, who will always stand under the spell of her terrible mother and inform her of everything that may befall. Had Margot actually egged her lover on, and at her mother's orders? Madame Catherine did indeed want to assure herself whence she might expect betrayal, how the forces would be arrayed against her, if she allowed their designs to reach the fullness of blood and judgment.

The forces were these: two young Princes, who for different reasons stood on their heads and ran on all fours, which sends the blood to the eyes and blinds a man. Several great lords also, of the sort that think themselves most notably sensible, moderate, and loyal; men that fancy they understand more than an astute old Queen, and prove it by sitting in the same company with adventurers, an alchemist, an astrologer, and a spy. This last kept Madame Catherine informed from day to day, and those were days as Madame Catherine loved them — days that kept her mind alert and tense and gave her the exultant feeling of an unseen cat stalking a small bird. Its antics must end at last, and it will spread its wings to fly; then the cat strikes.

The Duke of Montmorency, a connection of the late Admiral, and Marshal Cossé disappeared into the Bastille. The two ringleaders, an Italian conspirator, and with him — which was especially gladdening to a connoisseur like Madame Catherine — La Mole himself, her own instrument, though he never knew it, were publicly executed on the Place de Grève. Why, of course, La Mole had been her beloved daughter's admirer, and what a to-do she made when the head fell. Like an Eastern widow at the least. Margot fetched the head and had it embalmed, to preserve it in all its manly beauty; inlaid it with precious stones; and so carried it about with her until another man engaged her heart. Then she had the head carefully buried in a leaden casket.

As for the other conspirators, the task of astrologers is to search the heavens for the destinies of the great; it is for alchemists to determine the future from the fumes of metals. Catherine could not bring herself to take the lives of two such initiates. She calmly assumed that the two wise men had deceived their fellow-conspirators, but that to her they would prophesy the truth.

Quite otherwise she dealt with her son-in-law, Navarre. Her foolish son Alençon was indeed subjected to humiliating cross-examination and confronted with the prisoners. But the old lady took King Wren with her in her own coach. And in high good humour, with her eye upon him, in these hours of exaltation she drove him back to Paris and to the palace of the Louvre. He had supposed he would not enter it again so soon. Now he found the windows of his room barred — and who, who of all men, was put in charge of his person? His good friend Captain Nançay. The prisoner was to be well and truly looked after.

He realized as much and collected himself. This was the shock of sudden surcease after too much disordered movement. Then a shudder of desolation seized and shook his limbs, and his head felt wearier than it had ever done.

" Sire," said Armagnac, " lie not too much abed. Dance, and above all be seen! A man who shuts himself away arouses mistrust, and you have met with enough of that already."

" I am finished," replied Henri.

" You have not yet begun," retorted the First Chamberlain.

" A man can sink no lower," said the unhappy Henri mournfully. " I have reached the lowest level — and that is the safest one," he added, rather strangely. Armagnac thought the remark inconsequent.

Then Henri asked a question: " Was I crazy? " " Why," he went on, " did I do all this? I know what the end must be."

" No one can foretell," objected Armagnac. " Chance decides."

" It was my reason that should have decided, and where was it? Our intrigues confuse our minds the more deeply we are engaged. 'Tis because others are in the business too, and waver; and then I waver also. Believe me, Armagnac, most deeds are done head downwards."

" Those are not your own words, Sire," observed Armagnac in much astonishment.

" I had it from a nobleman I met before La Rochelle. His words struck at my heart, and the strange thing is that scarce had I heard them than I forgot them and was plunged in dealings that confused my understanding."

" Think no more of it," said the First Chamberlain.

" Indeed, I will never forget it." Henri left his bed; he stood and said resolutely: " I'll have no one sharing my command. For the future I will be my own general."

Therewith he drew a highly individual conclusion from the phrase that most deeds are done with the head downwards. The nobleman of La Rochelle would not, for his part, have made any such deduction. But he was only too well aware that all truths are double-faced, and in many an instance from antiquity he could see the image of a youth of twenty whose hands were far from heavy. " He tosses thoughts like balls, he can jump and he can saddle a horse. I — on the threshold of age; he — the image of youth, which, having scarcely known, I now must leave behind." Such were the reflections of Monsieur de Montaigne, away down in his province, for he too had forgotten nothing of that conversation by the seashore.

DEATH AND THE NURSE

In the following month Charles IX would have been twenty-four years old; but on that 31st of May 1574 he lay at the point of death, at Vincennes.

The fact was known to everyone; the whole castle was astir with excitement, which often found a vent in open disorder. The partisans of the King of Poland maintained that he would get back to France in time to punish all traitors; thus they described the adherents of the Man with Two Noses. Hence high voices and the clash of weapons, but that was not all. Orders were shouted down the vaulted corridors, all the egresses were barred, and, more significantly still, the guard tramped heavily back and forth past the two doors on which Madame Catherine kept special watch. Behind them lay her son Alençon and King Wren — who did well to remain there under guard. Once outside, neither of them would have gone far. Any effort at revolt by their friends would have brought them into instant peril. That day death was sovereign, for the King was dying. His mother had, at the last, carried him to Vincennes. The castle was more easily overseen than the Louvre. Here she would be safe from a sudden irruption of the mob, or of the enemies of her favourite son Anjou, when she had him proclaimed King; her third son to fill that throne. The second was that day dying, it was the turn of the third, and she had another yet in hand. If each of them could hold out awhile, Madame Catherine could disburden them of the cares of sovereignty and could remain as she was — for ever, as she thought. For those whose life is action, all time is the present; in it are absorbed both the future and the past. Charles, for example, had never lived, wherefore he had to die. His mother was the last to heed him; and he lay alone.

The doctor had gone, after wrapping the dying man in blankets smeared with balsam to soothe the bleeding sores. But Charles had realized that the doctor had not the smallest hope that the flow of blood would cease. He did but want to spare the sick man the sight of the red patches forming all over his skin, and likewise the smell of his own self. The fragrance of the balsam covered up the reek of blood — for a while only, thought Charles, and even while his bandages were fresh, Charles sniffed, and the smell of that last short hour of his never faded from his consciousness. He had been a strong young man. For the act of dying there remained to him all the strength that life now refused to accept from him: the strength to perceive, and to endure.

"Ambroise Paré," thought he, "my doctor, once bandaged the Admiral. And the doctor would have been murdered with the Admiral had he not escaped over the roof. Who could still escape across the roof? I know, I know; and I should not indeed have known so much had not the Admiral been killed by my fault. I know the meaning of that noise without. I know why I was brought here in my agony; and why I am now left to lie alone and no one asks for me." "I must die," he said aloud.

"That is true, Sire," answered his nurse. She sat upon a coffer knitting. When her charge opened his eyes and spoke, she got up, and she wiped his face. But she did not let him see the napkin.

" It is well, nurse, that you do not talk like the doctor and seek to deceive me. I know, and I submit; 'tis the last occasion that I have to make my courage good. I will not be like others, who leap out of bed at the end and scream and try to run away. Whither then — and why? Though I should certainly have enough strength to get up and astonish my mother and the court with my white linen and my bloody forehead, and set them all to flight."

" You are the King," she reminded him cheerfully, full of a wild hope. She alone had not deserted him. For four-and-twenty years, all but a month, she had, through him, become a person of consequence. She had likewise been able to buy enough land to provide for all her future; and there she stood, beautiful and buxom, a woman of some forty summers. But when your King dies, nurse, you must go with him for a little into the shadows. Yes; his last movements and parting murmurs are kin to his first tears and fumblings as a new-born babe. In those days you held him on your sturdy spreading thighs and to your ample bosom. And thus you think to hold him again for the last time.

He had resolved not to scream nor run away; instead of which he sighed and moaned and cried aloud in fear. He was seeing spirits, now in the very light of day, and he heard wild voices that were not of this world. " Oh, nurse! So much blood from all that murder! I was ill advised. May God pardon me and be merciful to me! "

" Your Majesty! Did you hate us Protestants? No; for you sucked in our faith with my milk. Sire, all the blood of those murdered comes upon those that hated them. You were an innocent child, God will not hold you to account."

" Ay, but what did they make of your innocent child! " he wailed. " Could anyone believe it? I — nothing that I did was really mine, and what has been I may not take with me. In God's presence, when He then asks me about Saint Bartholomew, I can but answer helplessly: ' Lord, I was asleep.' "

His voice sank into a whisper, and the sick man slept. The nurse wiped his face with a fresh napkin, and this time she spread it out. On it was imprinted the blood-stained outline of his face.

As he was breathing deep and loud, she drew the pillow from under his head so that he lay flat and at full length, and then she did something that she must keep from him, like the blood-stained napkin; she measured him. Carefully she measured the body of her King, for by her office and her privilege it was hers to lay him in his coffin, as, at the beginning, she had done in his cradle. One was no more difficult than the other; she was a powerful woman, and he had shrunk, and weighed but little. For a long time she had watched him grow in girth and weight. For a fleeting while he had become high of colour, with an easy lift of limb and a deep full voice. And she looked down upon him, now once more thin and pallid, and so soon to lie without a sound. Between his beginning and his end he had poured out the blood of many men, but his own had gone from him slowly. And she felt that both these things had come about inevitably, and for ends that none could know. Well, one thing remained — she, his nurse, would lay him in his wooden box. She approved all things as they were, and her eyes were dry.

The evening had fallen, the evening before Whitsunday. Charles awoke. The nurse knew it from his breathing alone. She lit a taper, and behold — the bleeding had stopped. But he was utterly exhausted, and it was only with an effort that he raised a hand to make known what he wanted. She did not understand, though she lifted him and laid her ear to his lips. " Navarre," he murmured, and she guessed the name.

She cried out the King's order towards the door, the guards passed it on, and someone ran off to deliver it, not indeed to Henri, but of course to Madame Catherine. She was the first to reach her dying son. The nurse had washed his face, which now looked white as stone, and absolute in its aversion from any

intrusion by the living. Madame Catherine, with the sanguine
nature of the murderess, felt herself here in contact with something alien, something almost sinister. They did not usually die
thus. Too distinguished a performance! Surely, surely, this could
be no son of hers. Still, no matter, since someone else was yet
expected.

Meanwhile Henri Navarre walked the way of fear — through
narrow vaulted passages, bristling with armed men. He shivered at the sight of all that naked steel, the arquebuses, halberds, and partisans. He recognized death, not otherwise than
Charles himself; but he had all his blood in his body, and his
feet to run away with. Once he came to a halt and was on the
point of turning tail. But he went on, entered the room, and
dropped on his knees. From the door to the foot of the bed
Henri advanced on his knees. Here he listened to what Charles
murmured: " My brother, you are now to lose me, but you
might well have been dead yourself long since. I alone would
not fall in with what others planned. In return, you must guard
my wife and my child when the time comes. When the time
comes," he repeated — and softly as he spoke, the words reached
other ears. " Ah," thought Henri, " he knows I am to be King
of France. A dying man sees into the future."

So it is; and hence much uneasiness to Madame Catherine.
Horoscopes and the fumes of metals indeed bore witness against
the dying words. None the less, such words may have grave
issues and are much remarked. Charles struggled to leave yet
another message. It was to be a warning, so much could be
seen from his expression. " Trust not my — " he began, when his
mother broke in: " Do not say it! " But as Charles was now
finally exhausted and fell back on his pillows, it remained undecided whom Henri had most to fear, whether Anjou, who
hated him, or Alençon, his own wavering ally. He resolved to be
on his guard against both.

Madame Catherine left the death-chamber. Henri, still on
his knees, endured until the death-struggle had begun.

At last the nurse was left alone with her charge. Leaning
over him, she marked his sighs — not indeed as though she felt

with him, who himself felt no longer, but quite simply, to determine when the last one should cease. She knew well that
this passing spirit would be haunted only by very early happenings, long since forgotten and known only to them both. It was
so with her too, and at the side of the dying King she too turned
back into old days. Only his short sighs moved his lips; but she
could hear "wood," and "night," and "weary." The child was
lost in the forest of Fontainebleau, and now he was afraid of
the darkness. It had happened a long, long while ago, and now
it happened once more at the end. She hummed the words instead of him. Words repeated in a monotone run together naturally, and she hummed:

> "My child, 'tis very cold,
> It will soon be night, my child,
> Night upon the wold,
> And the wind grows wild."

And as she hummed, drowsiness stole upon her.

> "So small, you find no way — "

Here she secretly observed that a change had come.

> "So weary, and no rest — "

By God, it was the last — his last sigh. She rose at once, and
closing his eyes, she said in a firm voice:

> "But I your nurse shall lay
> You in your little chest."

Moralité

Le malheur peut apporter une chance inespérée d'apprendre la vie. Un prince si bien né ne semblait pas destiné à être comblé par l'adversité. Intrépide, dédaignant les avertissements, il est tombé dans la misère comme dans un traquenard. Impossible de s'en tirer; alors il va profiter de sa nouvelle situation. Désormais la vie lui offre d'autres aspects que les seuls aspects accessibles aux heureux de ce monde. Les leçons qu'elle lui octroie sont sévères, mais combien plus émouvantes aussi que tout ce qui l'occupait du temps de sa joyeuse ignorance. Il apprend à craindre et à dissimuler. Cela peut toujours servir, comme, d'autre part, on ne perd jamais rien à essuyer des humiliations, et à ressentir la haine, et à voir l'amour se mourir à force d'être maltraité. Avec du talent, on approfondit tout cela jusqu'à en faire des connaissances morales bien acquises. Un peu plus, ce sera le chemin du doute; et d'avoir pratiqué la condition des opprimés un jeune seigneur qui, autrefois, ne doutait de rien, se trouvera changé en un homme averti, sceptique, indulgent autant par bonté que par mépris et qui saura se juger tout en agissant.

Ayant beaucoup remué sans rime ni raison il n'agira plus, à l'avenir, qu'à bon escient et en se méfiant des impulsions trop promptes. Si alors on peut dire de lui que, par son intelligence, il est au dessus de ses passions ce sera grâce à cette ancienne captivité où il les avait pénétrées. C'est vrai qu'il fallait être merveilleusement équilibré pour ne pas déchoir pendant cette longue épreuve. *Seule une nature tempérée et moyenne pouvait impunément s'adonner aux mœurs relâchées de cette cour.* Seule aussi elle pouvait se risquer au fond d'une pensée tourmentée tout en restant apte à reprendre cette sérénité d'âme dans laquelle s'accomplissent les grandes actions généreuses, et même les simples réalisations commandées par le bon sens.

Book Six

The Pallor of
Thought

An Unexpected Alliance

WHAT had happened to Margot? Suddenly she declared herself ready to help both of them, the King of Navarre and her brother Alençon, to escape. One of them could sit beside her in her coach disguised as a woman when she drove out of the Louvre. She had the right to take a companion with her, who could wear a mask. But as the would-be fugitives were two and neither would give way, the plan came to nothing, like many others. Moreover Henri had never believed in it, too many had miscarried. He found Margot charming in her zeal and could not say her nay. The sight of his woe made her remorseful for having once betrayed him to her mother. That moved him, although he was well aware of her personal motive. She wanted to revenge herself on Madame Catherine for the death of La Mole.

Even during the solemn funeral of Charles IX, forty days after his death, Henri had nothing else in his head than schemes for escape; and then again, when a boat was to have fetched him from the Louvre and carried him across the river. The failure on that occasion flung him into a blind rage, and he burst into the most imprudent threats — whereby the whole matter was revealed. After that, men might come to him with the most alluring proposals; they were answered by a much more self-contained Navarre. He would hear of no fresh designs. Discussion too prolonged bred doubt, not merely whether a scheme could, but whether it should, be carried out. This applied not only to plans for escape, but to all the affairs of life. Navarre talked a great deal, and he talked to everyone; to women by night, and to men by day; and his hearers might think, as they chose, that they had been entertained, fooled, or listened to with respect. By some he was regarded as the greatest droll at court, others looked to him for exalted sentiments, while he led them by the nose. Indeed, his rare outbursts of candour were designed to be passed on and bring him into favour. To listen to him, Saint Bartholomew was a master-stroke; the sole doubt was where the Queen's genius was most notably displayed; whether in the decision that Jeanne and Coligny must die, or — far more — that Henri should be allowed to live. " With increasing insight," said he, " this also I shall understand. At present I cannot tell why I am alive. My mother and the Admiral were sacrificed for well-considered purposes. A fool would brood upon revenge. I am merely young and eager to learn."

The old lady was informed of all this, and though she may have believed the half of it at most, it was actually his treachery that won her heart. He again was attracted to her, just because she had him in her power. They intrigued and amused each other, in all the special zest of danger. Sometimes she would indulge herself in the strangest confidences when he was by. One evening she frankly told him that he was far from being her only captive. Not even the King was free, her favourite son. She held him by the force of magic potions, said she, and winked.

King Henri, third of the name, had returned from Poland in disguise. In Germany he might have been imprisoned. This had not occurred, but here in his own palace of the Louvre he was the captive of his mother and of her Italians, who had forced their way up to Chancellor and Marshal. Only foreigners — this too she confessed to her friend Navarre, while the night wind of the 30th of January rattled the window-panes — only foreigners should rule a nation. The foreign adventurer never shrinks from shedding its blood. Let it perish if he cannot lead it. That is the law to which nations are subject, otherwise they would grow too light-hearted from prosperity. The French especially are given to writing lampoons. Better that the people should tremble than laugh. "Very true, Madame!" cried Henri with enthusiasm. "And I merely wonder how you could reward your immigrant countrymen with landed estates, but for your excellent practice of having the great French noblemen strangled in prison."

Madame Catherine screwed up one eye, thereby admitting the justness of this charge.

"One of those strangled, whose property you seized, was actually the secretary of your son the King."

"Tell him so! No one yet has dared." Thus spoke the Queen in an ecstasy of confidence to King Wren. She slapped his thigh and dropped into a different tone, that sounded at once mocking and mysterious.

"King Wren," said she, "I approve of you. For long I have watched you and made sure that you would not shrink from a stroke of treason. Men are too prone to prejudice. What is treason? The gift of moving with events. That you do, and that is why your Protestants despise you, in the countryside as within the walls of the Louvre, as many as survive here."

At this Henri shuddered: what must the Lord Admiral and his dear mother think of him for listening to this old woman instead of strangling her. But that would come. His vengeance would be long prepared, and all the more thorough for that.

But none of this was to be read upon his face, which was expressive of docility and the most ingenuous understanding. "It is true, Madame, that I have quite fallen out with my old friends. Hence I shall be the more anxious to do your pleasure, Madame."

"Especially, my young friend, when you thereby earn permission to move about a little. At present you enjoy playing tennis with Guise, and you do well to play tennis with one who kicked Coligny in the face when he was dead. But you are to go with him whenever he leaves the Louvre."

"He goes out a great deal; he rides out mostly."

"You are to go with him and ride with him, that I may always learn where he has been. Will you do that?"

"I may leave the Louvre? Every day? Through the gate? Over the bridge? Indeed, indeed, Madame, your orders shall be obeyed!"

"'Tis not as though I were afraid of Guise," added the Queen. And her new ally answered heartily: "A man so vain as is Lorraine of his own person! He has a fair beard, and is much applauded of the mob."

"He is a nincompoop," said she with equal decision. "He is stirring up the Catholics. He does not know for whom he is working — for me. I shall soon need another massacre, the Protestants give no peace, not even after Saint Bartholomew. So they must have another. Guise shall stir up the Catholics, and you have my leave to rouse the Protestants. Tell them that their arms are defeating us everywhere. Alas, it is not wholly untrue. But to the provinces you may send reports that there will soon be a revolt here; and let it come! Will you duly do my bidding in all these matters, King Wren?"

"May I ride across the bridge? And ride out hunting? Out hunting?" he repeated; and the prisoner burst into a boyish laughter. Madame Catherine smiled at him with a touch of indulgent scorn. Even the wisest old lady cannot always discern the guile that lies behind a genuine rush of joy. A prisoner does well to stoop a little lower than he need, and he who awaits his hour should look all the more irresolute.

When Henri had left his noble friend, he met d'Aubigné and du Bartas outside her door. The pair seldom went forth in company; they were too circumspect for that. But this time they could not resist it, as their master had been so mortally long engaged with the hated murderess. The thing had become a riddle to them. Although they loved him as much as they ever did, they no longer knew how far they could trust him.

He addressed them peevishly: "I did not look to find you outside this door."

"And we would gladly have met with you elsewhere, Sire."

" But that we may not do," put in the other.

" Armagnac will not admit us to your chamber," said his companion. And two hoarse voices pleaded turn by turn. " You put us aside and consort with new friends." " But they are your enemies of old." " Have you forgotten everything? " " To whom you owe gratitude — and even on whom you must take vengeance? "

The tears welled into his eyes when he heard the word " vengeance." And he turned away so that they should not see. " The new court," he said, " is gay, but you would continue in your sadness. Under Charles IX I was indeed a rebel, and how did it help me? Vengeance — what do you know of vengeance? Vengeance long pursued grows deeper and ever deeper, and bottomless at last."

All this was spoken under the eyes of the Switzer guards, who stared into vacancy as though they understood nothing.

And the two comrades of old days muttered: " Make no move yourself, Sire, then the others will act; they who were known to have taken part in Saint Bartholomew. They are none too pleased with the gay court, and there is still less liking for it in the churches. You should hear what is preached there."

" That you should recant, or perish. Well — recant! 'Tis no more than I have done."

At this they were too dumbfounded to reply. And he went on: " But if you will not yield, then strike first. You are strong. Several hundred Protestants are still alive in Paris. You have no weapons, perhaps, but you have God."

Then he departed, and in their perplexity they did not try to follow him. " He is laughing at us," they whispered to each other. Not even the Switzers must hear. And they sought to justify him to themselves. " It may indeed have been a warning that we should not engage in any rising. To make the truth manifest by means of untruth; oh, 'tis no more than he might do. He was weeping just now, though we were not meant to observe it. But he weeps easily. He weeps at the thought of his revenge, and yet he stepped out of that door; from the very room in which his mother took the poison."

They agreed that they could no longer understand their master and that they were truly wretched.

THE SECOND TASK

Henri went to the King, who bore the same name as he and was the third Henri on the throne. They often beguiled the time in company, one Henri with the other. As boys together at Saint-Germain they had dressed up as cardinals and ridden into the hall where Madame Catherine was receiving a real Cardinal. And now they did much the same, as grown men, the King of France and his captive cousin, whose mother and all his friends had lost their lives in that very place. It was on that account that the King of France retired next day to a cloister, to make as quick atonement as he might. He did one penance for his crimes, another for his fleshly aberrations, and yet another for his weakness in regard to his sovereign duties. He was pitiably abused by all about him — intriguers, swindlers, boys, and by one sole woman — his mother. At a certain point he was always aware of what was happening, that he was being robbed and dishonoured — and he relapsed into silence.

They thought the silence ominous and made themselves scarce so soon as the King fell silent. But his speechlessness was no more than the tragic recognition of his own incompetence. From time to time he was stricken by the thought that a dying Royal House could count for little in the world and in the land. "There must be toleration," he said that very day to his cousin and brother-in-law; and the words were wrung from him by his own despair. "Peace is what we must secure. Do I hate the Huguenots? I was one myself when I was nine, and threw my sister Marguerite's prayer-book into the fire. I still remember how my mother beat me, and how pleased I was. To this very day I blush before her when I think of how I felt in those days. She has long forgotten. Where am I now? It was my purpose to make peace between the creeds. But when I ascended the throne I swore I would suffer no religion save the Catholic in my kingdom. What is to be done? I do not banish the heretics as I should, I pray for their conversion. I can but go on praying."

"You can do more than that," Henri Navarre assured him, as the humble hearer of a Henri, who was now called King. "You have an excellent handwriting: be diligent in drawing up proclamations and decrees. Your diligence, Sire, will serve as a noble example for us all."

In his most melancholy times, and so on this 30th of January likewise — the monarch was a notable penman — he seemed to feel he had made good all his failings when he spilt ink with his own hands. But blood always ran into it, and his goodwill remained of no avail. "My secretary Loménie has been a long while ill," he observed. "I will go and see him."

"Do not do so, Sire. He is dead, and his death is still a secret. You were to be spared the news, as you were in the cloister at the time. It is said he had the plague."

This was the strangled nobleman whose lands an Italian had inherited, and that was not the first time the King had wondered at his disappearance. From his ill-shaved face, with its undeniably ape-like profile, two small and cunning eyes quickly marked his cousin's expression and darted back to the paper before him. "This is so noble a life," he murmured, "I could not have waited for my brother Charles to die."

"Was it not worth it?" asked his loving cousin in amazement.

The King huddled himself into his fur cloak and wrote. In the meantime Cousin Henri paced up and down the room, started a monologue with himself, broke it off, and began another.

"The new court is very noticeably different from the old one, as can be felt rather than seen. Under Charles IX we were all madder. There will be just as much sleeping with women and still more with boys. The last is a practice that many are learning for the first time, so as to be in the fashion. I am not, and I regret it; for a certain side of human nature thus remains closed to me."

" You should give thanks to Heaven," interposed the King, still writing. " Boys are even more grasping than women. Moreover, they murder each other. My favourite one was stabbed."

" That did not happen under Charles," observed Navarre, " although the culmination of his reign was Saint Bartholomew. The smell of corpses is more persistent at the new court than the old, that I will admit. But what a friendly life it is otherwise! No one thinks of flight, rebellion, or armed invasion by the Germans. I have learned my lesson, I do not raise a finger."

He waited, heard no sound but the scratching of the pen, and began at another point. " I and Guise have become good friends — who could have thought it in earlier days? If Your Majesty permits, I am to ride out hunting in his company. I shall in any case be watched at every step by those who would like to be, not my guards, but my murderers."

The pen scratched on. " I go," observed Navarre. " It is raining, I do not care to ride out with my murderers behind me. I will go to my room and play with the Fool. He is even gloomier than the King."

As he reached the door the prisoner was called back. " Cousin Navarre," said the King, " I have long hated you. But you are now in misfortune, like myself. This we both owe to the same events — and to our mothers," he said in a strangely emphatic tone. Henri started; he had never looked at matters from that side. His mother blamed for his misfortunes! The virtuous Jeanne named in the same breath with Madame Catherine. It revolted him, and he forgot to control his countenance. But his gloomy companion, in his own uneasiness, noticed nothing. " What abominations is she planning now? " he asked, and his face blackened with suspicion.

" Nothing of that kind, Sire. The Queen is in excellent humour. Why should you not be so too? "

" Because I have another brother," was the surprising answer. Henri could not find words at once. The elder brother's death had brought no good fortune, and here was a wish that the younger one might die! To an Oriental king in his seraglio the world without fades before the fearful peril he must fear in his own palace, from those nearest to his side. Henri divined what was to come. The King indeed despised his mother for her abominations; but his unruly brother Alençon would not let him sleep. Whom would he be forced to despise most in the end — Madame Catherine or himself? It was plain how the King struggled with his impulse. In vain, it had to come out; but his eyes were guarded, even at the moment of his tortured outburst.

"Cousin Navarre! Rid me of my brother Alençon!"

"I am deeply moved, Sire, that you should trust me in such fashion," said Henri gravely and with a bow. Thus he avoided saying no or yes. The King perhaps took it for a yes.

"Then," he said with emphasis, "I shall believe you." Guarded still — though the words could not but sound like a jest.

"Shall I then," said Henri, also in emphatic tones, "be able to ride out without my murderers?"

"More than that. He who rids me of my brother shall be Governor of the kingdom."

That came quite surely from a treacherous heart. "My good Valois," thought Henri, "you shall learn with whom you have to deal." And he leapt into the air with childish joy. "Why, this is beyond all dreams!" he shouted exultantly. "Governor of the kingdom!"

"We will celebrate it at once," said the King.

The New Court

Chamberlains came running up and the palace of the Louvre, which lay asleep so long as the King was melancholy, grew young again at the sight of youth rejoicing. By evening the royal apartments had been transformed into Persian tents. Tapers burned behind embroidered veils, and these with their dim glitter served as roof as well as walls. Pale tense youths with reddened lips, blackened eyebrows, and clad in transparent stuffs, stood motionless, with naked swords, round a tall dais. This was occupied by the spectators, who were but few: several Italians, as well as the Princes of Lorraine. The Duke of Guise, proud of his magnificent limbs, marched about as though he were master of the revels. His brother Mayenne had arrayed his portly person in shimmering silk, girt with a golden dagger — and from the same House came d'Elbeuf, marvellous friend, who never appeared to the King of Navarre otherwise than in the nick of time.

Navarre himself wore his most costly dress, which he had purposely adorned with ribbons in the colours of his House, that all might see how proud he was to be present. The festival was set for men and boys. The boys were to fascinate the men, who were then to single out their favourites. A few graceful creatures were already dancing together. Forms and garb revealed no sex, and their ambiguous charms appealed more especially to the Italians and the portly Mayenne. Navarre gave them best; true it was that there had been no such beings among his cavalcade of buff-coats, who sat their horses for fifteen hours and sang psalms for their entertainment. " If my friends were still alive," he said lightly, " some of them could be transformed into such lovely boys."

" Wait and see what may happen," said Guise. " Some of them yet live."

" I do not know them," said the prisoner. " I take no account of the vanquished. I am always to be found where — " he was about to say: " where life is gay," but he suddenly observed that here was a very particular enemy of his.

Birague, the Chancellor, an Italian, had reached his position through Madame Catherine. With her and several of his countrymen he had made his way one night into Charles IX's bedchamber. This successful foreigner saw in the prisoner Navarre an intriguer against his own power; and he began an actual interrogation of him without more ado: " Are you not on terms with a certain d'Aubigné and his accomplice du Bartas? These people are stirring up the students against a so-called foreign domination, as though there were none but foreigners in the highest places in the kingdom."

" *Sono bugie.* These are lies, my lord! " exclaimed Henri with well-simulated indignation, but in the foreigner's speech. The latter did not believe a word. The Lorrainers could be tricked, but not these sojourners from another land.

" Your friends," burst out Birague, whose rage was choking him, " are nearer the gallows than — "

" Than I am," put in Henri. " You will not catch me."

" I hang quickly and with satisfaction."

" But only little people, *Signore*. You hanged a wretched Captain, who talked of cutting the heads off all Italian rogues. But you would have to bring me before the whole world, sentence me to death, and behead me in grand style. That you will never witness. What shall we wager? "

" I'll wager my best jewel, and it shall stand as pledged."

On both sides the encounter was richly theatrical, as though it had been arranged as an improvised interlude to the music and the dance.

" Sire! " cried Henri to the King of France. The King had entered through a gap in the curtain of the Persian tent, and suddenly stood there resplendent, the Sultan of that feast. Henri dropped on one knee before him: " Sire! Your hardhearted Vizier has nothing in his mind but hangings and quarterings. Was it for this that I escaped Saint Bartholomew? "

" If only the late King had taken my advice! " cried Chancellor Birague. His fury coarsened his utterance and raised his voice into a parrot-like speech. It was that same voice that he had beset King Charles IX, hour after hour, until Charles grew crazy and gave orders for the massacre.

" Listen to him," was all that Henri said at the moment, but he felt that he had Anjou on his side. Anjou that had been, and the man of Saint Bartholomew, now King but only King because his brother had died of his evil conscience; how was he likely to stand as regards his own? He did not like the sight of those who, in hours that were very dark, had helped him to induce Charles to yield. The sight of his mother had grown repellent to him now, like the company of her Italians. He had to endure her, and he had, to his regret, to admit these persons to his most intimate entertainments; for they were indeed susceptible to the charms of boys.

" Stand up! " exclaimed the Persian Sultan, the jewels flashing on his turban. Cousin Navarre bounded into the air as lightly as a ball. " You are my personal captive," the Sultan proceeded, " and no one may lay a hand upon you. And now I would have you friends with my Vizier." Henri heard and obeyed. He performed an actual dance of reconciliation round the Chancellor, who was compelled by his Eastern rôle to look on at all this with dignity, though his eyes were bulging out of his head. " All-powerful Vizier! " said Henri. He touched his own breast, then that of the Chancellor, happening as he did so on an enormous jewel. " There is much thieving in Persia," said Henri. At that moment there were, fortunately, cries of " Hush! " that covered up what might have been overheard. The ballet entered.

It tripped in on tiptoe, waving veils and dipping lovely knees. All were boys, even those dressed as girls, whose eyes sparkled behind their veils more alluringly than women's eyes, as it seemed; and apart from certain awkward marks of masculinity, the movements of their bodies were entirely feminine. The rest — the boys dressed as boys — gave their finger-tips to the sham girls with no less simpering grace, or embraced them with expiring arms of amorous supplication. Muscles never seemed to come into play. When a dancer spun his partner like a top, or swung him through the air, the onlooker could not but feel that it was done not by strength, but by some miracle of gracefulness.

Here du Guast was seen to perfection. Usually a disagreeable and a clumsy lad, stupid, insolent, and venal, here the fellow was in place. In every figure of the dance he rightly slipped into the first row. The onlookers on the dais all had their eyes on him, and he was skilful to make each individual believe that he alone was the object of these allurements. Du Guast knelt before his lady, like all the other boys before their partners, and silently implored her to allow herself to be unveiled. In truth he meant his homage for the King or Sultan, all unknown to whom he was also angling after the Chancellor or Vizier, not to mention fat Mayenne, who had grown so hot that he was sweating. All these gentlemen felt themselves uplifted and actually honoured — just because a giddy boy was attitudinizing for their benefit. Elsewhere they would have given him a kick in the backside or had him strung up. But art remains a power, though it passes and is gone.

At the moment the excitement grew yet more intense. The dancers were unveiled. Who would have thought that human faces could look so fresh and wonderful — unveiled at last after that tense prelude of the ballet. The hearts of hardened men stood still; and for a moment Henri's heart did likewise. He rapped out an oath that all could hear, his usual oath. He could not believe his eyes; indeed, he rubbed them. " Gabriel? " he asked.

" He and none other," retorted the tall Guise scornfully. " Each boy unveils his companion, and our du Guast has unveiled your Léran."

" Come out and fight."

" Gladly, but not over the boy. 'Tis a handsome boy, and his career was made for him at this new court."

Henri's eyes were wet. He wanted to say something to young Léran, but the lad did not look up. And yet his tears had once trickled from beneath a white bandage that hid his face — on the night of Saint Bartholomew. Two of the victims of that night, Gabriel de Lévis de Léran and Charles IX, then lay side by side on the Queen of Navarre's bed. What was to become of them all?

" So," went on Guise contemptuously, " you had some such creature among your cavalcade of buff-coats who sat fifteen hours in the saddle and sang hymns for their entertainment."

'True; there was little left for Henri to say. " Léran is right to disguise himself at need and even turn himself into a girl." Lightly Henri faced what came to him, he swallowed this humiliation after many another, and none knew quite where they were with the volatile Navarre. He laughed at himself as though he were laughing at another. His demeanour was not unpleasant; a just observer found him neither callous nor cringing. But alone of those that watched him, d'Elbeuf pondered what Henri really could be, a child, a fool, or a calculating schemer. And d'Elbeuf's answer was: A stranger — at a school.

D'Elbeuf was an observer, and therefore not much more than

that. Distant kinsman of a great House, without much prospect or expectation — he could only stand among his fellows, of whom perhaps he took but little heed. Thus he discovered the service that his gifts most fitted him to give. D'Elbeuf could have been as fine a figure as Guise, the hero of the mob; but he held himself more loosely, his hair was brown, and he had none of Guise's high and haughty humour. His eyes were good — limpid, loyal eyes which divined in Henri the rising destiny and power that had hitherto been set to serve the lowest aim of self-preservation. He was the friend of doubtful days, that are not yet glorious, and may be indeed far otherwise. When destiny has once decided, d'Elbeuf will be no longer by.

The girls (who are really boys) now hold golden goblets in their hands. These they raise, twirl them on their finger-tips as they pirouette; all without spilling a drop. This is clearly a love-potion, and the boys acting the boy dancers pine for it. Their impish bodies slip into the most languishing poses. The poses grow more and more alluring, lips are parted and grow moist with longing. At least, there is moisture in the mouth of the royal favourite, du Guast; d'Elbeuf could see it clearly. His eyes were intent on what was passing, for he knew that Henri might be concerned. Du Guast knelt and tilted his head backwards; young Léran, as a girl, held the vessel to his lips; d'Elbeuf could count the drops. Several other faces were within his vision, the Chancellor Birague's, strangely watchful, and the eagerly delighted countenance of the King of France. There was a thunderstruck look about the King, as he smiled — at young de Léran. He had not a glance for his former favourite — whence alone it could be surmised that something unusual was soon about to happen. But the way of it was that du Guast, after swallowing the love-potion, bent backwards until his spine seemed like a crack, screamed, and turned up his eyes. Poisoned! It had to happen by the law of things. D'Elbeuf could have prophesied it.

In a moment, as though by order, someone screeched with the voice of an old parrot. "Sire! Your favourite is poisoned. His girl is in Navarre's pay. Hand this Prince over to me and to justice, or you will soon be in fear of him yourself!"

At these dreadful words all held their breath, and every movement ceased. The music broke off, the ballet stiffened into stone, the spectators on the dais sat rigid, awaiting a sign from the King; but he, too, did not stir. Only the stage itself, the Persian tent, was seen to sway slightly. This was caused by the women, the ladies of the court of France, who, excluded from the mysterious festival, had crept behind the curtains and were peering into the room. Noble ladies and maids of honour had there concealed themselves. Even humbler creatures from among the servants had made themselves a gap, while the Queen of Navarre herself tugged at the hangings by their side. What would happen, Margot wondered, in the silence of that spellbound company.

" This," she thought, " cannot but happen as soon as men are left to themselves. First they dress up like us, and act more girlishly than ever girls do. And then it all ends in death and murder. My royal brother will of course want to avenge his poisoned darling. He will deliver up my poor Henricus to the villainous Birague, whose lips are slavering with blood-lust. And to think that not one of these dolts has sense enough to understand the game that is being played! And they believe they can do without us! "

One of them had sense enough. D'Elbeuf of the House of Lorraine leapt from the dais, grabbed the now agonizing du Guast, set him on his feet, and boxed his ears until he stood up straight. " Stop that play-acting! " he growled, " and take care not start it again. And by a twist of the youth's wrist he swung him on to the dais. There he flung him to his knees before the King, and said: " Confess to His Majesty who suborned you to this fraud, and he may spare you from the gallows."

Du Guast's whole body expressed the extremity of terror. It was his best performance that day, ingenious as his previous one had been. Truth beats any impersonation.

His neck had lengthened like one from which the head has just been severed, for necks grow suddenly; and this stretched neck he swung back and forwards from King to Chancellor, and Chancellor to King. Du Guast could feel the fist of his enemy d'Elbeuf gripping the long neck still tighter, and ere it wholly throttled him, du Guast burst forth: " It was the Chancellor." But he regretted the confession as soon as the fist let him go, and tried to take it back. " No, not the Chancellor! It was I alone that pretended to have been poisoned, from jealousy of Monsieur de Léran, because my King smiled at him."

He was not believed, although it was also true. The King regarded the Chancellor merely with all the more disfavour — or, rather, the Sultan so regarded his Vizier, for such was their guise. Navarre was the first to speak.

" Signor Birague, you wagered your jewel! Sire, he wagered that he would have me publicly executed. And he would have succeeded had you not seen through his plot."

The King could not throw the Chancellor into the Bastille nor dismiss him from his office, for Madame Catherine protected her countryman. But the King did what he could and what indeed he was expected to do. He tore the Chancellor's great jewel from his breast. He gazed vaguely about him, as though he had not known what was to happen. In truth he knew quite well. He waved his hand, young Léran stepped on to the dais, and on his knees received the pledge of the royal favour: a blue and shimmering pledge. Stripped of all veils, Vicomte de Léran's head was that of a youthful warrior, advancing in the bloom of manhood to set his foot upon the neck of his vanquished enemy. Which, indeed, du Guast provoked him to do; he laid his face in the dust, and Léran did not hesitate.

When the occupants of the Persian tent saw the scene pass off so pleasantly, they recovered the use of their limbs. They clapped their hands and danced once more, and, lulled by the music, they presented love and joy to onlookers that only believed in such matters when they saw them acted. Far into the night the Persian tent shimmered with its embroidered hangings, through which the light was ingeniously mellowed, so as to shed a glamour on all within. Sultan, boys, and rogues, and many other things, the most precious of which was no more than a blue glitter.

Two of the company were missing. Henri and d'Elbeuf were bidding farewell to each other in a distant part of the castle.

" I will never forget this, d'Elbeuf."

" Sire, you linger here a long time, and must linger awhile yet."

" I have time. Naught else is left to me — save patience and time."

WHAT MAY HATRED BE?

But he that waits a long while discovers that what had been his firmest feelings have become transformed, that they are divided and no longer whole. So it was with his friendship with Guise. Henri had drawn near to him from hatred; because he wanted to know more of him, for such knowledge is a need of hatred. But better knowledge of an enemy may bring the risk of liking him at last. Nay, more; an enemy is more absorbing than one who is taken as he is.

They played tennis, " long tennis," the most difficult game of all, always these two opponents alone, Navarre and Guise; the others had to look on, and what they saw made then often feel uneasy; little Navarre dashing all over the court, and Guise, like a broad-beamed Goliath awaiting his strokes. But that was nothing. Once the ball fell behind the hedge. " Navarre, you are a small man," cried Guise, " crawl through the hedge and fetch it." Instead of crawling, Henri leapt over it from where he stood, to the admiration of the spectators. He crawled back, struck the ball unexpectedly, and the leathern missile hit Lorraine in the chest. He staggered visibly, and cried: " You meant to hit me in the forehead, and then I should have fallen. You are not quite tall enough for that, my little man. Go, bring wine to cool us! "

Another, of course, ran for the wine, but after what had passed, on that same day Guise was taken aside by Alençon and d'Elbeuf and bidden to remember that the King of Navarre was indeed a prisoner and at present without importance; but all who were present, some of them humble folk, had seen the Royal House humiliated in his person. " What do you want? " retorted Guise. " The lad takes nothing in ill part, he never leaves my side. He goes with me into all the churches. He'll soon be more Catholic than I am myself."

They reported this to Henri, and he kept his own counsel. "The vain Goliath," he thought, "knows nothing of my pact with Madame Catherine. His clumsy machinations with the priests and Spaniards — he imagines they will be viewed only from the good side. He does not know me as I know him. No one can take such freedoms as a friend."

At the next game of tennis he did succeed in hitting Guise on the forehead, which was bruised, and the Duke was angered. Henri made a great show of regret. "Truly, I did not want to set your horns growing. Only the Duchess has the right to put them on you." Whereat all the onlookers burst out laughing, and they called each other, louder than was seemly, the Duchess of Guise's lovers. This young lady had quickly and thoroughly learned the customs of the court. Lorraine, who lay on the ground having his forehead bathed, heard all this. He groaned more from rage than pain and resolved to punish these disloyal mockers.

To Navarre he said later: "After all, you have but made me the more watchful, and there is none other who would have dared to do it. I see that I can trust you. Come with me to Father Boucher's sermon."

They rode thither that same day, the Duke of Guise, as always, with a splendid escort; Navarre alone. He did not yet know Paris very well, and listened in vain for the name of the church. As they rode by, a cry passed from mouth to mouth of the mob that watched them: "The King of Paris! Hail!" And this King was greeted with the lifted right hand. The women did so no less than the men, except that they forgot themselves and reached out both hands to the blond hero of their dreams. He beamed down upon just and unjust like the sun itself, in the highest of humour and confident of his cause. Thus they entered the building, and when the clash of the soldiers' harness was silent, Father Boucher mounted the pulpit.

He was a preacher of a new fashion. At his very first words he foamed at the lips, and his rasping voice rose into an almost feminine shriek. He preached hatred against the Moderate party.

Not merely the Protestants were to be abhorred until they were rooted out. In a night of long knives and rolling heads Boucher wanted especially to reckon with those too given to tolerance, even if they called themselves Catholics. To him, the worst in both religions were the lukewarm believers, who were ready for an understanding and wanted peace. That the land should not have, and, cried Boucher, lashing himself to fury, the land would not endure a peace that could but bring dishonour. The peace of shame and the pact extorted by the heretics was hereby torn to shreds. Soil and blood cried aloud for force, force, force, and a ruthless purge of all that was alien to them, a foundering civilization, a corroding freedom.

The masses that packed the church to the back of the altar and the farthest chapels made known by their wild yells that they were not disposed to tolerate civilization, and especially not freedom. Some were trampled to death in the rush to reach the chancel and get a sight of the preacher. They saw nothing but a gaping mouth, for Boucher was a stunted figure that scarce came above the edge of the pulpit. But he could spit a brave distance. His speech easily degenerated into a bellow, and what little that was human in it had not much in common with the sounds familiar to that place; it sounded exotic and artificial. He often looked as though he was about to fall down in a fit, and there were anxious looks for the church officers. Then Boucher clapped his teeth together, and gazed about him with a gracious smile that won the hearts of all. When he recovered his breath, he resumed his bellowing, working his jaws as though he longed to get his teeth into any that thought otherwise, and eat them up.

Freedom of conscience — never! But also no more taxes, no more rent, and especially no serfage — neither the people nor, more particularly, the priesthood were to pay anything in the future. Therein lay the bond between them. The priesthood would hereafter keep the public revenues that were their due, and the people could for their part plunder houses and palaces, rob the Huguenots and all the Moderates, which latter were especially to be destroyed. Boucher heartened his hearers to take no account of the great, not even of the greatest of all — and he launched into barely concealed allusions to the King, a secret Protestant, a Moderate, and a traitor. He pictured to them, from his imagination, the treasures of the Louvre, and the blood bath which he longed to see. Then he abruptly flung them out of their blood-lust into a sick fear of persecution. The people and all that they stood for were in bitter peril, delivered up to secret forces which had sworn their overthrow. Here followed a frantic prayer, plainly a prayer for succour in extremity. The throng listened and then fell to praying loudly too. Above them floated the exhalations of their greed, their fear, their ecstasy, and their hatred.

Henri smelt those exhalations. It was more his senses than his judgment that revealed to him the unclean thing. Otherwise he, in the end, would have fallen a prey to hatred too. To destroy the Louvre and plunder it and murder all within; he, too, had thought of that when he conceived only of flight and return at the head of foreign mercenaries. But the years had slowly passed, and all that was forgotten. Here in this church it came back into his mind as fresh as ever. Once again he realized that a man humiliated and abused carries his vengeance to the very limit. He had more reason than anyone. They had killed his mother, and then the Lord Admiral, and then all his friends, eighty noblemen, his tutor, and the last envoy of the Queen his mother. The survivors were covered with shame, he himself was a prisoner and, in constant peril, subject to daily insult. He knew all this. Vengeance was determined; he had merely put it off and off that he might meditate a better plan. Thus time passes, and hatred passes too.

No; it did not pass, but he came to question it. He lived with these people, they played tennis together, and slept with the same women. Madame Catherine had offered to come to terms with him; had she really poisoned his mother? Anjou would have had him killed on the night of Saint Bartholomew, but now as King he was his protector. Guise had become his good friend; it seemed scarcely credible that he had kicked the Lord Admiral in the face when he lay dead. And yet it was so. All these things they had done in very truth and fact. The sense of it all was that he knew them and they did not know him. He would not deny that he liked them for it all — in a certain fashion. A man can ponder pleasantly upon his enemies, as he does upon a mistress. He must be wary and therefore get more nearly into their confidence.

Thus he justified himself, his hesitation, his forbearance, and he stood aloof from the people, on whom Boucher was urging the blind satisfaction of their impulses. Moreover, Boucher had not finished his agonized supplications, and Henri had long since done with all that had been passing through his mind. Life was short and art was long. Thoughts, too, sped onwards, but when would the time be ripe to act?

Boucher made clear to them that the whole system of the State was criminal, but that God had sent them a leader. Yonder he stood! All knelt down, especially those who stood under suspicion of " moderation." Boldly Guise gazed over those bent heads, and lifted haughty eyes to God — arrayed in silver armour, as though the citadel of power was to be stormed forthwith, and the harness of his armed retainers clashed. The Queen Mother of course had her spies in the church, and they would certainly go and make a tale for her of the terrible Guise. Anyone who had consorted with the man knew that he was a braggart Goliath, and a cuckold into the bargain. One must stand his friend — that was the way to bring him back within bounds and even take pleasure in his company. Did Henri hate him? Indeed, yes. But what was hatred?

And now, after the preacher had finished, the common folk were driven out by the halberdiers; only persons of rank and influence remained. Councillors of the city of Paris, the richest citizens, popular priests, and the Lord Archbishop. He pledged himself that the wrath of Heaven had spoken from Boucher's lips. The morals of the court were beyond what could be imagined; and the Archbishop described a public and shameless performance that the King and his boy favourites had presented in the Louvre, and Christian women had been compelled to look on. This aroused a murmur of indignation. Under cover of the noise someone near to Henri, who was standing far at the back, said: "But the Archbishop sleeps with his sister." And Henri had to laugh — not really at the fact itself, but with his eye on this whole assemblage.

Matters soon took a serious turn, for one of the most important citizens, the President of the Audit Office, disclosed the condition of the country's finances. It was desperate; but as no one had conceived it as much different, it aroused the more indignation among that company. Only in assembly do men grow truly indignant, and only at matters that are already known. Their minds are much more easily whipped up by the utterance of what has long been suppressed than by anything new and strange. The King's dogs and apes and parrots cost him a hundred thousand crowns a year; and that was cheap compared with the vast sums swallowed up by his gang of favourites. One of them was put in charge of the royal finances! The speaker announced this with a shout, and he added: "Everything is permitted in these times except the truth!" But as the speaker was now venturing to tell it, the assembly gained greatly in self-esteem, as though a great revulsion were then taking place, of which that company were at the very centre.

The President of the Audit Office recounted many another wasted million; he bewailed the burden of the taxes, their unjust distribution, the corruption of all those that gathered them, and especially of the royal favourite Monsieur d'O. — just O. On the other hand, the speaker omitted to mention several others, although they had farmed certain taxes and oppressed the people. Among them, indeed, had been members of the House of Guise, and their mention would have been especially unsuitable in the light of what was now to follow. For a number of large sacks were hauled in, and out of them poured gold — much gold, of Spanish coinage. It was distributed, according to the orders of the Duke of Guise, among the councillors, the priests, the influential citizens, officials, and men of war. In recognition of which each man wrote his name upon a list. Lorraine at the top of it, and each man called out the word: "Freedom!"

This was the beginning of the League. Here, with the emptying of those sacks of Spanish pistoles, was it founded, to deliver power and force into the hands of one party. And it was sufficiently endowed with them to bring the land, in many years of terror and misguidance, near to destruction and put back humanity for generations. Here was the beginning, and while the foreign gold was hurriedly packed away, though the recipients did not look at the mintage, shouts of " Hail! " and " Freedom! " poured in from the street.

The betrayed populace were acclaiming their leader; and he had the same right to be taken at his own reckoning as his satellites among the mob. What is betrayal? People are never betrayed so deeply as is afterwards alleged. Only the subordinate leaders had been given a sight of the Spanish gold; the mob sees the blond beard that rouses it to ecstasy. But in their own minds they all know very well that this is no question of the salvation of religion, nor of any fabulous awakening that is to be thus brought about. They want to dispossess others, expel them from the sources of their wealth, and so enrich themselves. They want excitement, self-importance, and they want to kill. Such is the common cause so soon as a band of populace and gentlefolk gather together to found a league for the suppression of the freedom of conscience. They do but shout " Freedom! " all the louder, the betrayed without and the betrayers within, and so prove that if they are indeed betrayed, it is by their own will.

Among the betrayers within, with their fresh filled pockets and their aspirations towards freedom, were Moderates, who, at that time, were not averse from taking part. Even converted Huguenots were not wanting; yes, the presence of Navarre served well enough for their justification. He had been carried there by Guise, that many another might acquire a good conscience. Henri observed this for himself, and moreover it had been made clear to him as well. As before, when someone had dared to whisper, covered by murmurs of indignation at the court, that the Archbishop was no better — so now. The shouts for freedom drowned the avowals of many a worthy citizens. Still, they could be heard muttering: " It was Spanish gossip! Spanish coinage! "

Henri had here no time to question his own feelings; events

had moved too fast. Guise, above all, had shown himself in a new aspect, as a man who could beguile and sway his fellows; no one would have suspected the arrogant puppet of so much artfulness and speed. Behold what the vantage of the game may do! Moreover, they made it easy for him, as they all felt flattered to be sitting in the same society with this great lord. Guise gave them all their duties; the soldiery were to whip up recruits for the forces of the Party, the priests to stir up the common people, and the citizens to resist the State in the matter of all payments. He bestowed on them titles and a claim to the appropriate offices, so soon as they should have been vacated by their holders — by murder, as was understood by all.

As touching what might yet be done, no one would be answerable for his deeds, for here they swore beforehand blind obedience to the Leader. This done, he closed this heartening assemblage. "Navarre," said he, as they broke up, "you have seen how strong we are."

"To my good fortune, yes," replied Henri. "King of Paris, hail!" he shouted with the mob, who had been waiting outside all the time. Before he disappeared, he dug his friend Lorraine in the ribs and, mimicking the throaty accents of the city fathers, he said: "Spanish coinage, gossip! Spanish coinage!" And he was gone.

Faster and faster he went, his guards had to run. He turned into the Street of Austria, over the drawbridge, through the gateway, and across the Louvre courtyard — but saw nothing of it all. He did not notice where he was going, or who watched him, and only recognized his room when he had been in it and pacing up and down it for some while. Then he realized that he now had come to hate. This — this was hatred. Spanish coinage, carried on mules across the mountains, convoy upon convoy of sacks stuffed with pistoles. They were emptied out in Paris — gold flowed unceasingly; pockets were filled with gold, hearts with hatred, fists with force, and mouths with wicked lies. And now all kindness and all reason would be set aside; the mob would burst forth and raven against all faiths, in defence of one. It was no more than he had known all the years of his life. But he had not known the source and origin of these abominations. Spanish coinage, travelling hither across the Pyrenees, his own mountains — he marked the journey in the air; there fell the waterfall, and there stood his house at Coarraze. They meant to steal it from him; Don Philip of Spain had never otherwise intended than to take his slope of the Pyrenees; but he wanted Philip's side. He wanted it because it was his mountain range, and this was his land which Philip's soldiers should never invade, and where his sacks should never travel.

So far for that day. The youth of three-and-twenty seldom thought further, and his hatred was first bounded by the landscape of his home. He hated the Sovereign of the World from love of his little Béarn — though also because France was suffering; suffering like himself, and of all that suffering there was one sole author. Guise and Catherine, forsooth! Each outvied the other in the service of the Sovereign of the World. That was the hated foe. He held Henri prisoner, and he paid for the war of parties in Henri's own land, which Henri was one day to rule.

When, later on, he did come to rule it, his vision and his hatred had mightily increased. He not merely wanted to have freed France, and himself to be the greatest Prince in Europe; he wanted to bring a lasting peace to both, and that meant the end of the House of Austria. He set himself at last to drive that hated House out of the whole continent and to imprison it once for all behind the tall crags of the Pyrenees. That was to be the great plan of his later years, and it was to bring him to his death.

The youth captive hated Don Philip; he took a portrait out of a coffer — an empty face with simpering fair curls. A high and narrow forehead; and the youth stabbed at it with his knife. Then he threw away the portrait and the knife, and wrung his hands. What could this be: hatred? We only hate with all our hearts what we do not see. He was never destined to look on Philip of Spain.

THE THREE HENRIS

He told his good friend Madame Catherine that Lorraine was deep in notable designs. In the interval Henri had collected himself and gave his news no more importance than was wise, having regard to his own position. He gave a comic performance of Lorraine's pact with the portly citizens of Paris. The blond hero's dealings with the mob he only lightly sketched; the Queen Mother could treat it as of no account, or, if she pleased, as a warning. And indeed she heeded it but little. Whereat he stepped up to her side and said abruptly: "Madame, you are lost."

"Do not be uneasy," said she with a maternal laugh. "Guise is, in the end, working for me, for Philip is my friend."

That she indeed believed, and therefore did not realize that King Philip was seeking a governor for himself in France, when he should be sole master of the land, after the kingdom had been destroyed by Spanish gold. Before her stood one who began to understand. But Madame Catherine answered slyly:

"Go away to one of your pretty ladies, King Wren. You as well as Guise shall take your pleasures under my eye, I am not afraid of either of you."

The King of France sat huddled in his fur mantle writing; Henri had awaited just such a time of silent apprehension in order to tell him many things. The worst of all was known to Anjou already; one of his favourites had fallen that day in a duel, Maugion, so handsome a lad, and run through by one of Lorraine's officers. That was going too far; Guise not merely stirred up disorder in the streets, he actually spread terror in the very palace of the King. "Cousin Navarre, we have undervalued him."

"I admit it," said Henri. "A Goliath and a hero of his kind is more than a mere brute. There's malice in the man."

"I shall reply to this in form," observed the King, "but with due calculation. I am setting my royal name on the list of the League."

Which he did forthwith, with a great deal of ceremony and

in the presence of many witnesses of all ranks. The populace and the burghers were to be personally convinced that the King did not need to be reminded by a League of his promise to defend the faith. He set his name at the head, above even that of Lorraine, as a sign that he would oppose the spreading of the Huguenot creed by all and every means. He had no intention of doing so in earnest, and no one else believed it of so feeble a King. His adherence had merely made it easier for the wandering monks to rouse the land against him; lists of the League were covered with names and crosses in every village; every lad pictured a brave Guise, and every maid a handsome Guise; he was the hero of all dreams, in preference to a gloomy Valois, with sudden impulses to revelry, diverting himself with his court of boys.

Henri, third of his name, forgot his position when he disguised himself and became a foreign Sultan or a humble penitent. As King of France he liked bewailing his real state, and as confidant he resorted to his brother-in-law Navarre, later the fourth Henri of the name. One morning he sent for him; it was near to Christmas, snow lay on the ground, and a strange stillness encompassed the palace of the Louvre, which seemed severed from the world. " Henri," said the King, " tell me what you think of me."

" Sire, that you are my master and King."

" No, no, not that — I mean when you reflect."

" I, in your condition, would not provoke the truth. Once you did a deed, and that was the night of Saint Bartholomew. Guise is today much stronger than the Admiral was then. You are a King, and therefore you are a laggard from choice if you let him grow yet stronger."

" 'Tis somewhat different." The King spoke gloomily to himself. " I live in fear of violence."

" Strike before it comes! "

" I am in a sweat of fear," whispered the King, quivering inwardly. He even covered his mouth. " I have had news that Guise intends to abduct me. I shall be his prisoner; and he, the master of my kingdom — and visiting me with a riding-whip."

"He's a head taller than I," said Henri Navarre, "and what then? A tall man has this advantage, that he can pull down sausages from the ceiling, but none other." In his own mind he thought: "The crazy fool wanted me to kill his brother. Because he is not taller than I? All this passes human understanding."

Meantime there was much clattering and clashing at the door, which was flung open, and an officer of Guise announced the Duke's approach. Not that he asked His Majesty to receive his master. The Duke had only to announce himself. Moreover he kept the King of France waiting, and the latter used the interval to hide his cousin Navarre behind a curtain. "You shall hear how he demeans himself towards his King. If he lays hands on me — "

"He might even run his sword through the curtain. I would sooner appear and speak a word with him."

At that moment appeared the third Henri, of the House of Guise. Shouted orders, salutations, and obeisances; a ceremonial entry. King Henri was sitting at his writing-table, wrapped in his fur mantle. Henri Navarre peered out from behind the curtain.

The Duke kept his hat on and made not the faintest reverence. "The weather is good for hunting," said he. "I have come to fetch you, Sire."

The King cleared his throat loudly; it was a signal for his cousin and indicated that this was the scheme for his abduction. "True, my good friend," he replied, "but 'tis very plain you have no parliament, nor edicts to issue because it refuses to record your chosen grants of favour in the register."

"Your Parliament is right," said the Duke, assuming a harsh tone. "Your *placets* enrich your courtiers, while the nation is ruined."

"That is just what was said in the time of my brother Charles. I never did hear of a nation that was not ruined." This was uttered as a challenge, and the Duke behaved as was expected: a stern tribune of the people launched into a tirade of figures and high words. When at last his knowledge was exhausted, the King, huddled in his furred mantle, and with the faintest movement of his thick lips, observed darkly:

" 'Tis just for this reason that I receive you here, Guise, alone and without witnesses, lest you might not speak your mind thus freely."

" Whom have I to fear? " said the Duke, as he stood with legs astraddle and thrust aside the proffered chair. " Which of us really leads the League? " he asked.

" You," said the King fervently. The Duke felt there was something contemptible in the reply, and he interposed: " You may be King, but you are mean of heart and will therefore not be King for long. I — " He paused, and said a second time: " I," and once more he left unuttered what he had in mind — that he would himself be King.

The King, far from dismissing him, encouraged the insolent youth. His cousin in his hiding-place could hardly bear to see the royal blood thus baited. He was, though twenty-one degrees removed, of that blood himself. He shook the curtain folds to attract Guise's attention. But Guise was much too intent upon humiliating the King. " You are the King of many favourites," he snarled. " But money will abate their number. In the end you will be crouching in the farthest corner of your kingdom, without favourites, without money — and even without blood."

Fear seized the King and shook him. His furred mantle slipped up over his neck, and his cousin behind the curtain looked to see him vanish beneath his writing-table. Instead of which he said, in a weak, imploring tone: " Speak on! "

It was too much, even for so insensitive a man as Guise. He broke off the colloquy, turned, and walked to the rejected chair. " Speak on! " he repeated to himself, and shrugged his shoulders. The words could be clearly heard behind the curtain, as the chair and the Duke were near to it; and the tears came into the eyes of the witness behind that curtain. A shameless brute with plenty of blood in his body, and a mob at his back, could enter the King's presence without right or claim and threaten that the last drop of his blood should ooze out of his pores as his brother's had done. What sort of world was this! Henri

Navarre ripped the hangings aside and stepped forth, a naked dagger in his hand. " I could have stabbed you in the back, and you would have deserved it."

" Oho," cried Guise, " so it was a trap. That is why I was bidden to speak on, for Valois was certainly not listening to his own praises. I presented myself here," said that resplendent figure, edging quietly backwards towards the door, " as a loyal servant of the King, and my purpose was to save him and his kingdom by my honest counsel. I did not bring my sword with me, and I would scorn to draw my dagger."

He had probably forgotten his dagger also, for he held his hands as though about to clap them. In a moment the room would have been packed with armed men. But Henri stopped him in time.

" Henri Guise," he cried, " let us play at Cæsar's murder. Do you remember the game? You and I used to act the conspirators."

" A truce to your buffoonery," said Guise; but he was in reality glad to be quit of his quandary in this fashion. He had indeed said and done enough to set a conspiracy afoot. The King's face suddenly altered and grew terrible; he stiffened and stood up like Majesty in judgment. " There is Cæsar! " cried Henri Navarre, in high excitement. " At him! " Guise was about to make a dash — but fell; his fellow-conspirator had seized him by the leg. Henri Navarre promptly fell upon his neck, held him down, and said with the bravado proper to his role: " Sire, what shall I do with a man who insults his King? "

" Cut off his head! " said Cæsar furiously. Perhaps he really was beside himself; or perhaps his mind went back to the Collège de Navarre and the sunless cloister yard where in the old days three boys, and three Henris, had played that same game.

" 'Tis done," said Cousin Henri; he let his victim rise, and sheathed his sword, not before wiping it of imaginary blood.

A pause followed; during the silence and the rising embarrassment the three Henris had to come back from the games of the cloister yard into their lives as men, for enmities have become inexorable facts and we are no longer acting in a tragedy, but in life. What was now to follow? Were they as before once more to play their parts in a masque of tragedy? Life grows very suspect by the repetition of situations which were born long ago of our own fancies, and breeds an impression of unreality — not one on which we do well to linger. Henri Valois breathed heavily and sat down. Henri Guise made his neglected reverence. But in Henri Navarre's face there was still a shadow of doubt or regret. This did not escape the others, they exchanged a meaning glance at his expense and smiled in secret. It was exactly what used to happen in the cloister school.

But other matters fell out differently: on the afternoon of that same day, at tennis, Henri Navarre purposely gave some points away to his good friend Guise and allowed himself to be beaten by him — but at the same hour a very young nobleman, one of his own men, since the lad's father had given him into Navarre's service — Rosny was his name, sixteen years old; he had only survived Saint Bartholomew because the headmaster of his school had kept him concealed — Rosny, later known as Sully, challenged one of the Duke of Guise's noblemen to a duel and killed him. In the meantime the Duke won his game of tennis.

The next time the King saw his cousin, he said: " I have more to fear from you than from the high and mighty Lorraine. You will be my successor. You are a Prince of the Blood, and you are also very clever. Were it no more than cleverness! My suspicions tell me that it is."

STRANGE ADVENTURE OF A CITIZEN OF PARIS

The King, who distrusted his friends, had to listen to his mother, Madame Catherine, when she told him what was most urgently at issue; which was that the evil rumours regarding the royal morals should be silenced. One morning there was a loud ringing of the bell in the shop of a little linen-draper, by the name of Heurtebise. The married pair could hear the sound in their bedroom, though it faced towards the yard. At first they dared not leave their bed, and each clung to the other lest either should be rash enough to make a move. At last the ringing grew so insistent that there was nothing for it but to go and see. The man slipped on his cloak, and the woman took her prayer-book: " Stand out against them, Heurtebise, and deny all that you may have said about the League. Say that it was over the wine, and you had not made your confession until yesterday."

She crept after him and peered out from behind the counter, while he with great deliberation removed all the bars and bolts and chains. The bell pealed and clashed, but voices could also be heard through the thick oak planks. The linen-draper prayed aloud. Suddenly the door was open, and there stood his own brother-in-law, Archambault, of the Louvre palace guard. He crashed his arquebus on the pavement and said sternly: " Monsieur Heurtebise, you must come with us! " Then he saw his sister bobbing up from behind the counter, and he added in a muffled tone: " I know not what we are to do with you, brother-in-law, but we are four. You must come with us."

The other three then appeared, but Heurtebise, instead of praying, spoke up smartly to the soldiers. He threatened them with the League, in whose service and pay he was. And that was a very different matter from the bodyguard of a King who passed his time with boys. There had been sermons in the pulpits against such doings. " All this is well enough, friend Heurtebise," said the soldiers, " but you might oblige us; we may not have to hang you."

" Many a man," said the wife, " who has trusted you has never been seen again. I'll keep you instead of him, brother, and woe to you if anything happens to my good man."

So the arquebusier Archambault was left behind as hostage in the shop, and the three men-at-arms carried the linen-draper Heurtebise to the palace of the Louvre. Gate, bridge, and archway were familiar to the citizen, who had often had to make his way to the well-shaft of the Louvre, the abode of the tax-gatherers, who kept so keen an eye upon his incomings. Moreover, he was a stranger, easily frightened or outwitted, and every native of the place always had the best of him — how, who

could tell? And that morning he did not pass, as was usual, unnoticed. He might indeed on ordinary days be threatened by
the Provost if he did not hurry, but that was all; and on those
occasions he pleaded his position as a burgher, and his brother-
in-law bore him witness. But today he heard whispers of " Heurtebise " on all sides; outside the gate, from the tax offices, and
then in the neighbourhood of the kitchens. Doors opened as
he passed with his armed escort; " Heurtebise," men said in
each other's ears, with a strange expression as they said it. For
a long while he could not tell what these faces recalled, until
a terrified inward voice reminded him that he looked exactly
so when he bared his head before a passing coffin.

At the foot of the outer stairway his guards handed him over
to two Switzers; one marched in front of him, and the other behind. The corridors through which the little procession went
were at first dimly lit, because the day was young, and this was
the western side of the palace. The way led downstairs and
up again, and round corners; to the linen-draper it seemed endless, and his knees began to quake. " Fellow, whither are you
taking me? " he said to the leading Switzer, but he might as
well have addressed a wall. The foreign mercenary did not so
much as move his great poll; he tramped onwards in his great
puffed shoes, his hairy fists carrying the halberd at the slope.
Heurtebise sighed and prepared himself to reach a place at
last where neither moon nor stars would shine. Then his blinking vision caught a glimmer — of gold and silver, many-coloured
marbles, damask, brocade, ivory, and alabaster. All such precious names were awakened in his memory by the light of the
eastern heaven, which shone into a room with open doors. All
the windows beyond were flaming with the dawn — and thus in
dazzlement was a citizen transported to a royal palace. In after
days he would have sworn that in that room which he had so
quickly passed a company of noblemen and ladies had been
disporting themselves in their high and haughty fashion. He
did not reflect that the figures on painted and embroidered
pictures may mimic movement in the flaming hues of dawn.
Indeed, when the room was far behind him, he began to dis-

tinguish voices; and he even caught the sound of harps — though this with silent disapproval. Such barren arts — so early in the day!

Thus prepared, he was for the third time transferred to other escorts, but this time, instead of soldiers, they were elegant young aristocrats, chamberlains or pages; in any case, their cheeks were painted and framed in glossy hair in feminine fashion, and certainly for the same purpose, to be stroked and caressed. Something turned in the head of the worthy citizen, while two comely youths smiled at him and faintly bent their slim necks before none other than himself, Heurtebise. He had nothing in his shop for the likes of them. Crimped ruffs, as light as gossamer, but woven with gold thread — there were none such in his stock. But they walked on either side of him in the friendliest guise, entered a room with him, and talked through their noses at him, as the mode then was. This room indeed so blazed with gold that he now could neither hear nor see. Wide-eyed he gazed at the two comely youths — they were actually thanking him, and speaking in such gay voices. " Monsieur Heurtebise," they snuffled, " we are now about to open two more doors, through which we shall accompany you. Outside the third we remain behind, you will go in alone; thither we may not follow you."

At this the good man shuddered once again. What was to happen now? He had grown accustomed to the company of these polite young men; it was indeed such as to shake certain homely prejudices — regarding the position of aristocrats, and also as touching their morals. He had grown better disposed to the palace of the Louvre, against which the priests had, perhaps unjustly, preached such violent sermons. The court had its good qualities, the King was a man like other men. He, Heurtebise, had come upon nothing unseemly in this place. Through the two succeeding rooms he walked with firmer step. At the sight of a naked statue he nudged one of his new friends. Then they halted outside the third door. " Sir," said one, " you will be bidden to enter and to open your eyes."

" Look, if you please, and mark all that you see," said the

other insistently, while each of the boys flung back one wing of the great door. Heurtebise set one foot within, the door closed behind him. He found himself in a dim room, the daylight prisoned in the window hangings, and near by a guttering night-light. Gradually he began to distinguish outlines of objects, especially of a bed. The curtain was drawn — who was there asleep? He took one step forward — had he not been expressly told he was to open his eyes? They promptly bulged out of his head. His hair stood on end, a shudder seized and shook him, and he dropped on his knees.

The King! No other. So much could be seen from the lips alone; but Majesty turned his sinister eye upon him, though the face did not follow it. Exactly thus did one royal eye fix on those that greeted him when he peered out of the depths of his coach. But this was no coach, Heurtebise, wake up! The King's eye signals to you that you are to notice who is lying at his side. It is the Queen. Pinch your leg if you will, it is still the Queen, with her flaxen hair and pointed nose. You are honoured, Heurtebise, in being thus chosen. The Queen turns her head upon the pillows that you may see the other side of her face. She sleeps beside the King, not otherwise than Madame Heurtebise, whom everyone knows sleeps with her good man in the nuptial bedchamber behind the shop. So simple a matter, though as rare as a miracle. Of many thousands not one has encountered it, save only you.

Reverentially he crossed his hands upon his breast and bowed his forehead, that he might not abuse the honour that had been vouchsafed to him. He felt a touch upon his shoulder. In his awe he had not noticed that the door had opened. Backwards on his knees he shuffled from the room. The two young men each gave him a hand to help him to his feet. They understood his bewilderment and told him a heartening repast awaited him. The table was set in a hall, between an arcade and staircase, and so, in some sort, in a public place. He had to sit down at a solitary cover, a steward raised his staff, and cooks entered, each bearing a dish weighing at least eight pounds of silver, and containing several sorts of fish and flesh and cakes. Wine was poured into his glass from vessels of ruby glass with golden spouts; and a lovely girl sat down at his side. He knew she was lovely, although he did not lift his eyes from his heaped plate.

"Heurtebise," said the onlookers, who appeared from the direction of the arcade or the stairway — halted at a respectful distance from his table, wagged their heads, said "Heurtebise," and went away on tiptoe.

"Monsieur Heurtebise, you are a famous man." It was the girl's wheedling voice. "I should like to ask you a favour, Monsieur Heurtebise. When you come to tell all that you have seen here in the Louvre, do not forget me. I am called Mademoiselle de Lusignan."

At this great and legendary name the linen-draper sighed; it was too much for him. The whole affair had long since been too much for him and filled him with melancholy instead of pride. Heurtebise cast so dark a look at the bystanders that they crept away, some bowing as they did so. It could never come into his mind that they were playing a part. Nor would he ever have believed that the fish which the King of France had caused to be set before him was of yesterday, and the pastry yet older. The wine had been fetched from the tavern, he drank better at home; that at least did not wholly escape his notice. He would not admit it, gulped down several glasses, and found it even worse. There remained Mademoiselle de Lusignan — who indeed was not genuine either. Madame Catherine had sent one of the poor damsels from her "skirmishes" to take in hand this man out of the multitude. And the first thing to dazzle him would be a great name. But after all the glasses of sour wine he took courage, leered at the half-naked girl, and made a grab at her. He did not understand how he thereby came to tip off his chair.

He was short and squat, with a red face and greying hair. Thus he saw himself crawling out from under the table, as reflected in the mirrors. The girl had vanished, which did not surprise him. In that moment he had the indefeasible sense that he had been fooled. He resolved to tell the whole story in his own street. The League and its leaders should profit by his adventure! In the meantime he did not know how he was going to get out of this place. All had left him, the bystanders, the girl, the cooks, the solemn steward — even the elegant young men, who had been so very much his friends. He had to find his way alone; he wandered through deserted halls into a vaulted chamber full of soldiers and was seized by the collar. He had ceased to be Monsieur Heurtebise, they thrust him through the well-shaft and on to the bridge. None of the guards there knew him either; they questioned him roughly, his pockets were turned out, and with a kick he was dismissed from the palace of the Louvre.

He had taken care not to admit to the soldiers what he had seen there. Moreover he began to doubt it himself. The farther he walked through the city, the more fantastic and suspect did his experience seem. It was alien to his nature; his sound sense assured him that the Evil One had had a hand in the game. He would make his confession at once. Meantime he had reached his own street; all the neighbours came out of their houses, he fled into his own and went to bed. Madame Heurtebise brought him a cup of mulled wine.

Not until two hours had passed, for he was a steadfast soul, did his wife discover the story. In the evening it was known to the street, and the next day all over Paris. This was all to the advantage of the kingdom and did harm to the League, wherefore Father Boucher preached against Heurtebise, said he had been bribed, and described him as the instrument of Satan. The little linen draper in the meantime took heart of grace; he grew proud of his experience as time went on, and more certain of it than on the day it happened. "Tell me, Heurtebise, what exactly was it that you saw?"

"The King lying in his golden bed, his golden crown upon his head, and beside him lay the Queen, as lovely as the dawn. And that is true, were I to say it in the hour of my death."

He said it for thirteen years. Then the affairs of the kingdom came to such a pass that the King was murdered, while his successor Henri, fourth of his name, had to win battles over his own Frenchmen if they were not to become the prey of Habsburg. The League at that time enlivened its processions by causing women to dance naked through the streets. A wild and wanton horde, their thirst for blood was nigh to ludicrous. The little linen-draper, known throughout the city for his fairy-tale, was not the first — but the wild women fell on him too as an enemy of Holy Church. "That is Heurtebise, who saw the Valois lying with his whore! "

Heurtebise was trampled to death by many naked feet.

Pleasure

The Queen of Navarre had her own court, several small rooms where she gathered together her women friends of an evening, her poets, musicians, humanists, and her lovers. Here Margot was the goddess and did not need to peer secretly through the curtains, as at the entertainments of her brother the King of France. Her beloved husband Henri found her playing the harp, while a poet recited mellifluous verses in her honour; but in the poetic world her name was Lais, and she was a courtesan, who ruled over men by virtue of her beauty and her learning. Margot-Lais sat, as she had always longed to do, like the central figure of a picture, on a raised chair; turned towards it on the right and left were set two other chairs, with the ladies of Mayenne and Guise. At the divine being's feet and by the seats of the two other Muses were grouped the less important figures, who none the less were needed to complete the picture. It was backed by two pillars, entwined with roses, between which hung a huge, brightly coloured tapestry, embroidered with fantastic creatures of the spring. Apparently a serene and lovely spectacle; all that was needed was for the poet at the centre of the half-circle to celebrate it in song. He did so, swaying slightly to one side and stretching out his other arm as though he were walking on a narrow gangway over an abyss.

In the palace of the Louvre not all was well secured, Henri reminded himself, as he surveyed the court of the Queen of Navarre. And yet he found himself first thinking of the church where Boucher preached. Should he imitate the preacher and give this company a pattern of his eloquence? Should he? No; he assumed the role of poet, but recited what had suddenly come into his mind: " *Adjudat me a d'aqueste hore* — help me at this hour," the words that his mother had spoken while she was giving him birth. It was a rich and ringing chant, and as it was addressed to the Virgin, and to the Queen of Navarre as well, her dear lord had outdone all the homage that Madame Marguerite had received at her court. She offered him her very gracious thanks; to accompany his words she struck the most melodious chords upon the harp, but last of all she gave him her lovely hand to kiss. This done, he assured her before her admirers that he was as eager to please and serve her as he had ever been. She understood him and once more gave him her hand — this time for him to lead her down from her seat and out of the room.

When they were beyond earshot, he began to laugh and he said: " Go and visit the Queen your mother. I am curious to see what you will look like when you come back."

" What do you mean? " replied Margot, much annoyed. " No one treats me in such unseemly fashion, as in the times of King Charles."

" I hope truly it may not be so, though your brother the King is just as incensed against you as your mother."

" What is the matter, in God's name? "

" I shall not singe my mouth with it. Let it be enough for you that I myself do not believe what is charged against you. It is invented by others to embroil us "

He escorted his wife on her way to Madame Catherine. She had hardly left him when another lady met him, the Duchess of Guise, she too in sore distress. It had long been visible from her demeanour; on her raised chair, while all the others looked on so sedately, she turned her head distractedly from side to side. It was the sign of a terror not yet forgotten. " Sire," said the Duchess, helplessly reaching out her open hands towards him, " I am a poor unhappy, persecuted woman, and I deserve all the comfort you can give."

He felt like interposing: " Why not I also, after all the

others?" — but she did not give him time. "As the Duke's best friend, convince him in God's name of my innocence, that he may cease to do me wrong!" She blurted all this out in one breath and had to pause; Henri was able to remark: "I can answer for your innocence, Madame, for you alas have never given me proof to the contrary."

"Conceive of what I have suffered at this madman's hands. This morning I was ailing, and he was put out about some matter, he would not say what. I know indeed what enters into husbands' heads, other than jealousy. Suddenly he would have it that I must drink some broth, and how he spoke! His tone could not but put the worst suspicion into my mind. 'I need no broth,' said I. But he would hear no refusal; 'Pardon me, Madame, you will drink some broth,' and he sent to the kitchen at once."

"Did he mean to poison you?" asked Henri in a low and anxious tone, for it struck him to the heart to recall that he himself had called the Duke a cuckold, perhaps was the first to do so. Since then Guise had found confirmation everywhere, and this was the awful consequence for the poor woman.

"I hope you threw the broth in his face."

"That would not have been seemly. I asked him for half an hour's respite before I drank the cup, and in that time I prepared myself to die."

Henri looked at the poor victim through a veil of his own tears.

"Then the broth was brought. The Duke had in the meantime gone out. I drank it."

Even in his absence his wife had obeyed him, inspired by the hope that her last prayers had wiped out all her fleshly transgressions.

"What do you think!" she said, in a sudden flush of bitterness. "It was just an ordinary cup of broth."

Her anger seized him too. This straw-stuffed Goliath! That was the way he frightened women. That was his revenge when they treated him as he deserved. "Madame," said Henri, with honest conviction, "you are unjustly persecuted, as I can very well see. And you deserve that I should comfort you and make good all the wrong that men, myself among them, have done to you."

He took her finger-tips, and with hands thus delicately poised, they stepped out; their faces turned towards each other with a courteous expression of delight, they trod, not without grace, the path that led to pleasure.

When he saw Margot again, she had come from a stormy encounter with her mother and her royal brother, in the presence of witnesses; it was not the first that had been brought about by the scandal of her conduct. She had not yet recovered her balance. " Was I right? " he asked sympathetically. Her great eyes filled with tears, but she had to be careful that the ink on her eyebrows should not run. So she could not unburden herself then and there. But her dear lord embraced her none the less and assured her that though matters might otherwise be as before, he would protect her, for she was entrusted to his care. That very evening, when the King went to bed, two of his gentlemen would plead with him that he had done her sore injustice.

" Perhaps he will believe it; but you cannot impose upon my mother," said Margot rather too quickly, and shuddered. She tried to discover from her dear lord's expression how much he really knew. For, after all, her outrage against decency had really happened, she had paid a visit to the sick-bed of the lover then in office! But as Henri was impenetrable, she returned to the role of innocence. " If the slander had not been publicly flung in my face! That I will never forgive. No more was needed but that my dear lord should think ill of me and treat me harshly."

" That would never come into my mind, since I know you best of all," said he with a smile that was significant but kindly, and not untouched with amorous intent. All together warmed the poor creature's heart. " 'Tis thanks to your nobility," said she, " that the affair has ended well this time. But now we are warned. Be on your guard: the King will think of other schemes for setting us at odds."

" He shall not succeed," Henri assured her. " And we will take measures in the matter at once." They stayed yet a long while together. In the morning, when he had left her, Margot promptly received a visit from some ladies, who reported that her dear spouse had deceived her only the day before with the Duchess of Guise. For a moment she was taken aback; then she answered: " My dear lord can never endure to see a woman unhappy."

On this she pondered for a long while. For Margot lived for the moment; she was clever, but she did not think. She sketched, to mark them on her mind, two parallel portraits: the Duke of Guise, called Cléon in her narrative, and how he revenged himself and kept the Duchess for hours in fear of death from a bowl of broth; and the King of Navarre, whom she called Achilles: so kindly — and so flighty. " But he was always loyal to his feelings," she wrote. " Achilles never forgot the deep, delightful passion that had bound him to Lais. Neither Lais nor Achilles betrayed it; by their mutual goodwill it was transformed, and out of passion, which often looks like hatred, came a friendship that was very near to love."

Margot laid down her pen and felt truly rejoiced by the aspect that affairs had taken. There was much indeed that she had not explicitly mentioned, much that had been fortunately overcome: the dead, who had thrust themselves between her and her beloved lord, and they were not to be ignored. Then she had betrayed him to her dreaded mother, and he was made captive; and then she had decided to cuckold that young man. Hatred, betrayal, remorse, and pity had their ways until at last Achilles and Lais became the best of friends, and were to remain so for ever, thought Margot. But life is long.

Husband and wife made very free with each other; indeed, they often warned each other of imminent dangers, though always with a certain reserve. " Sire," said Margot on one occasion, " you appear too frequently in the company of my brother Alençon. You had better not conspire with him, you have seen too often how that ends. He remains the heir to the throne. The governorship of the kingdom is indeed promised to you, but the whole court laughs at the very notion."

" Madame, it is never an advantage to be laughed at."

" Suppose you had secret plans. Do you want to be King of France? You will find no one willing to serve you, because they all know you here in this role. They will prefer to serve my brother Alençon, whom I love very much and who certainly will mount the throne. I counsel you for your good."

" Madame," said he gravely. " You shall understand that I am your friend. I often stay in your brother Alençon's company, because I know his life is in danger." His look was so significant that she guessed something of the truth; he had been entrusted with that duty; the King was to use him to dispose of his brother. Margot at once resolved that she would protect her brother Francis. His friend, the brave Buooy, should enjoy her favour. Such being her firm purpose, she turned the talk to her dear friend Sauves.

" Sauves is a pleasant amusement for you," replied Margot. " But she ought not to be more, if you value your safety, my dear lord and spouse. Take care never to let her know what is really in your head. When your heads are side by side you must always bethink you that Sauves carries all and everything to my mother the Queen."

" I don't believe it," said Henri, though he knew that it was true.

" There is more that you will not believe. Sauves loves none but Guise. To him she is utterly devoted." Margot began to work herself up. " Do you need any other proof than her tears since Guise had his face disfigured. I do not grudge it to the siren! " she cried in a shrill fury. " I'll even confess that I had a hand in it. This summer he had to go off to the wars instead of poisoning his wife and sleeping with Sauves. And now he has a deep sword slash half across his face, and is no more the handsome Guise. He is called *Le Balafré*."

" *Le Balafré*," repeated her lord, and they were pleased. Margot suddenly fell back into her wrath. " And Sauves had better take care that no mishap befalls her. It is her intent to set you against me, Sire. Why, she means to marry you! The woman keeps you about her all the day, and actually bids you visit her

when the Queen rises, merely so that I may not have you. Do
you mistrust me more than her? Mistrust, Sire, is the beginning
of hatred! " cried Margot, quite forgetting the existence of a firm
friendship between Lais and Achilles.

Henri tried to embrace her, and as she struggled he smiled in
secret at her agitation, without divining that jealousy would
soon come upon him — of Margot, who was in love with the
gallant Bussy. Pleasure does not always remain pleasure. There
are snares and depths in it. A man can conceal himself within it
and remain unseen. A man can also lose himself in it and meantime miss the most important thing of all. And this was what
happened, especially in the company of Charlotte de Sauves, to
Jeanne's son, the avenger of the murdered Admiral. Many other
ladies of the court fulfilled the same purpose, but he loved her
the most.

Sauves met the smile of life with a charm that was all her own.
Her nature was placid — not stormy and enkindling like that of
the Queen of Navarre. The Duchess of Guise made as though
life bewildered her; not so Sauves, who knew just how far she
meant to go in all matters. Henri understood her — he understood Margot, Madame de Guise, Charlotte de Sauves, and the
rest whom he loved and made happy. They were many, as was
the custom at that court — a prodigal promiscuity — and it was all
too doubtful how long a youthful body would endure. He was
most at his ease with Charlotte, hence his preference.

And that was because they let each other's minds go a-wan-
dering, while they lay awake nights side by side. He knew
whither hers went: to Guise and his ambitious enterprises.
Guise was her only lord, even with his face disfigured. " No matter," thought Henri, " she has so pretty a mouth, when it parts in
thought; and I know no eyes like hers, long narrow slitted eyes
sparkling with wit. It would be disquieting if she, too, never
wondered why I am silent for so long. Perhaps she has already
guessed my thoughts. Her thick eyelashes keep something secret;
then we catch each other's eye and she smiles a pitying smile. I
deserve it too, for what have I achieved, in more than three
years, of all my purposes of hatred and revenge? Nothing. The

King, Guise, and Madame Catherine, all are still alive, and I am their captive and their friend; I think about them more than is good, and I deceive them. The woman beside me is right to look on Guise as the better man. However, his face is now marred — as retribution for having kicked the dead Admiral in his face! "

" My mind often takes me to the mountains," he said to his companion in the stillness of the night. " I like the palace of the Louvre, because of my many good friends and all the lovely ladies here. But always I miss the mountains. Who has not climbed them as a child never knows what it means to carry their name in his heart. The Pyrenees."

Sauves watched him as he dreamed, and tentatively she said: " It is a long way thither."

" I could be there on horseback in ten days. I made the wager with my cousin Alençon," he answered eagerly, and to anyone so sharp of hearing as Sauves, he gave away himself and his abettor. By way of masking the admission, he plunged into fantastic stories about the waterfall that hurtled down the heights. He even told her, quite falsely, that he had once let it sweep him down into the valley, to the feet of his mother Jeanne.

" Whose death is not yet explained after three years," interposed Sauves quickly. And not yet avenged! That she did not say, but he heard it none the less. Oh, he was always conscious of her curiosity. It touched him no less plainly than her skin. Sauves's greatest joy was not in love, but came to her through knowledge and a discerning mind. Before a man was aware, he had betrayed himself to her. Her delicate body was easily fatigued, and on this count Henri made her fearful; and she him, by her sharp eyes.

However, she did not betray him to the old Queen, though it would have been in her charge to do so. There were excuses for her, for the poor gentleman had been guilty of no great matter, save only some secret interviews that led to nothing. Madame Catherine had laughed to think he should have conspired with her son Alençon, who had so often deceived him. The poor gentleman's purposes were paralysed, his thoughts would soon

suffice him of themselves. " He'll do no more," thought Sauves.
" He goes a-hunting, and comes punctually back, full of pride
at the game he has bagged. Moreover, he lies too much with
women." And she meant it well and honestly when she warned
him. Her heart was not evil.

In any event she also wanted to part him from Margot. So
long as a Prince of the Blood was married to a sister of the
King, in spite of everything he had prospects. But the throne
should not be his; her sole lord and master Guise should mount
the throne. So Sauves tried to convince her night's companion
that she had loved him from the beginning — even from the
first encounter in the garden, when her friends Charlotte and
Margot came to meet him arm in arm, and peacocks walked before them. He should be hers, and she would belong to him
wholly; this — so she said — had been her resolve. She was clever,
she was wise, he would marry her, and he would be King. So
much he was expected to believe. In vain; his shrewd smile told
her that she could impose on him as little as he on her. In her
annoyance she dismissed him earlier that morning, though he
would perhaps slip from her arms into her dear friend Margot's.

Such was pleasure. And it so happened that one night he
fainted; the place was fortunately the marriage bed. For an hour
he was unconscious, and Margot was in deep concern about him.
She sat with him and tended him, as indeed her duty was; called
her women and her people; and she did not leave him for a
moment, or he would have died. This attack should be a warning to him, Margot told him. " You have never suffered so before; it comes from too much pleasure with women." Enough;
he was delighted with her, sang her praises to everyone, and she
was the first with whom he took his pleasure once again.

The Turning-Point

Too long delay, too much doubt and calculation. At last the
decision was taken by another. On September 15th of that year
1575 the aspect of affairs was wholly changed; on that day the
Duke of Alençon was no longer to be found. At the hour of

dinner his mother had him searched for all over the palace, for she was highly concerned for his health. She knew from her own experience how quickly death can come. But no corpse was found. Had he then fled, even without confiding in his sister? She held her Muses' court as usual. But King Wren! Madame Catherine was already prepared never to look on him again — and there he came quite innocently from a game of tennis on his way to take a bath. " What do you know, King Wren? Confess! Or you will regret it."

Henri laughed. " Armagnac has just told me that my cousin has fled — in a coach, 'tis said, that appeared empty. Shall I reveal to you, Madame, what will happen now? The Man with Two Noses will summon the country and the people to revolt. And then, Madame, you will come to terms with him and grant him what he asks."

He was angry, she thought, because of the suspicion of complicity that fell upon him; and certainly he deserved it. But she did not tighten the bonds of his captivity. His prophecy was punctually fulfilled; the appeal went forth to land and people. In it the Royal Prince spoke of the general discontent, the longing for peace among so many moderate men of both creeds; but he also demanded justice for himself. For in his brother's palace he was treated with contumely and kept without money. Here the old Queen saw the handhold by which she could get her dear son back again; and hence, in spite of everything, she took the appeal less seriously than her son the King, who was deeply distraught by the affair. And the city of Paris fell once more into a dark mood of foreboding and excitement. What! The brother of the King, called Monsieur, had followed the Lord Prince of Condé to Germany. They would soon return with an army of French and Germans, a hundred thousand men, no less, neighbour! And the citizens of Paris soon began to discover in the reddening evening sky the images of armed men.

Only Madame Catherine kept her sense and reason among all these appearances and rumours. Henri Navarre, as it seemed to her, behaved in more mysterious fashion than her son Alençon, whom she knew and did not fear. One day she suddenly produced the proclamation of his fellow-conspirator and made him read it. After an ordeal of three years Henri could control his features in any situation. Without moving a muscle, he remarked: " I know it all. I wrote such a thing myself when I was with the Admiral and the Huguenots. Monsieur will soon talk in very different fashion. A man may put on airs at first, but in the end he must dance to the tune that has been called. 'Tis naught to me."

His scorn might be real or feigned, nothing could shake his good friend's absolute mistrust of him. Thenceforward she had him still more closely watched, and set new spies about him of whom he had no suspicion. They were, if it might be, to prompt him to indiscretions. Dark webs were woven round him, while he himself delighted the court more than ever with his gaiety and seeming thoughtlessness. It was within him that the heaviest burden lay, and there the shadows fell as they had done in days gone by.

This half-wit had acted while he held back! All had been in vain — all his long dissembling, his meditations, and all his experience of men. Misfortune had taken him to school, and yet he was no more forward than he had been — on the morning after Saint Bartholomew.

Only fifteen days had passed before the half-wit again appeared and fell to treating with his mother, Madame Catherine, as to the compensation for which he would desert his allies. All the worse for Henri! Such a man had boldly grasped at leadership, while he himself had fainted from the consequence of over-many pleasures. How was this? But enough; he would ask no more questions. The school of misfortune must now end, and with it the pallor of thought. He would let his Protestants in the South know that they might soon expect him in their midst. No matter if they meantime despised him for having acted the buffoon at the court of France for three long years. He would show them that he was the son of their Queen Jeanne. No half-wit he! Nor any arrogant Goliath! He knew; his schooling had not been wasted. He would make that kingdom one.

His hot pride assured him in high words that nothing could

prevail against that purpose; not the shame in which he had to live, and still must for a while endure; nor even the further confusion brought upon him by the half-wit, who had stepped into his place and would have gladly wrecked his project. He was confident of his cause. Here, where all seemed lost, his star was rising. A nation awaited a leader; the more false ones that were unmasked and rejected, the more steadfastly would the appointed leader pursue his destined course.

In such case, before the time that still remained had passed, he had to meet a final and a crushing blow; but he endured it. His last chastisement was at his sister's hands. Little Catherine had long waited, and in vain, to see whether her brother would even yet remember their mother Jeanne, the Lord Admiral, and all his dead. Privily in the Palais Condé she said to the old Princess: " I know him, for we are wholly of the same flesh and blood. I was here in the room with him and the Lord Admiral. There was a terrible clap of thunder, the door swung open, and I truly thought that our dead mother would enter and summon him to vengeance. But it was the Princess of Valois, come to fetch him to his wedding. It is never out of my thoughts, and I am very sure that my brother has not forgotten it. I would swear that he has been dissembling before the court all this long time, and even before me, his sister. And when the day comes, he will arise and make himself known for what he is."

She got up from her chair, and as she was excited, she took no care to conceal her slight limp. She was pale, too, and yet half-grown. She had an ailing lung, she had spent those years in seclusion, out of loathing for the court, where the women solicited the favours of the men, in her mother's words. Princess Catherine of Bourbon had remained a Protestant. She could not understand her brother's apostasy, whatever his position. But she approved what he saw fit to do, because he was her brother and the head of their House. And she defended him, his morals, and his dilatory ways, against the Protestant nobility, who came to her in secret from the country, and she sent them home more hopeful. She was weak, she was lonely, she could inspire no more than pity. But many had known Queen Jeanne and were struck by the daughter's high endurance; it was as though the mother herself were speaking, and they bowed once more before her immortal soul.

But no one can defend an idler for longer than three years, especially in the face of rising doubts. He had forgotten nothing, that she knew. Faith indeed was quickly lost where he stood captive. He would, with God's help, recover it. She would deal him a blow that would bring him to his senses. For however matters might then stand, she was his Catherine still. He needed her, because they had both been children together, and in his last extremity he had none to stand beside him but his sister. She would affect to desert him; she would propose to give herself and her cause into a stranger's keeping, and that would be the blow he needed.

It was the innocent reckoning of a generous child. She confessed to one alone, to a certain Theodor de Bèze, pastor in Geneva, author of the canticle " Let God, the God of battle, rise." She asked him whether she could, without sin, so act, and he replied that she could certainly pretend to surrender her cause into a stranger's hands, but not her very body. Just at that time she met her cousin Charles de Bourbon, Count de Soissons, whom she was to love until her early ending.

All is otherwise than you conceive, Catherine. You have always thought that your chastity severed you from a brother who sought his pleasures. You will, like him, plunge headlong into love; you will be well acquainted with all its sorrows, with the bliss and the humiliation of those who love with their whole hearts. He will always desire other women, and even when he is faithful to one, he will desire all of them in her. You will receive, in full measure, at the hands of Charles alone, all that you had looked for — Charles, your kinsman, and a Catholic too, which did not deter you, strict Protestant though you are; and he will betray you in most ordinary fashion. But that you will forget, again and yet again, and after every quarrel your heart will be even more deeply his. That will continue until you are one-and-forty, and there will be much public scandal which you cannot deny, although in the worst extremity your prudery will save your face. The great name of your royal brother is still your safe-guard. He gives judgment, but too late, and marries you to an-other. You obey because you are already broken, but nothing can then avail. In terror of old age you will cling desperately to your beloved; indeed, you will sooner die than grow old — and you die. So will it be, Catherine, and not as you conceived when you sought ghostly counsel from the pastor at Geneva.

Little Catherine appeared unexpectedly at a court festivity. Her brother was told, and he went in vain quest of her in the great hall among the swarm of guests. Wondering whether he had been fooled, he glanced into the King's antechamber, which was empty; but one of the palace guard stood facing towards a corner that was invisible to those entering the room. Henri walked thither and found his sister with a man who filled him with superstitious horror. He had almost turned and dashed from the room — at the sight of his own double. The stranger had Henri's vigorous, curly hair and his narrow cast of face; mouth, eyes, and nose were like his own, and there was no differ-ence in figure; and what shook Henri most of all, the man was dressed exactly like himself.

His sister was resting her arm on the man's shoulder — she had from childhood leaned thus on her brother. And she was speaking with her lips close to the man's cheek; how many, many times had she spoken thus to Henri! But, most horrible of all, she seemed neither to see nor hear him — at ten paces' distance, though he scraped his feet on the floor. He felt his lips to see if he were there in his own person and unchanged. Had he by magic been stripped of his earthly envelope?

"Poor brother," thought Catherine. "Spirits there are indeed, and a man may traffic with them, and magic too does some-times come to pass. But this time I do deceive you, and it strikes me to the heart that I must do so. I have dressed my worthy cousin and put him through his paces, and I pretend that you are no more than air. Truly you have no reason for your be-wilderment. Look at our cousin. Family likeness apart, in his face there is no past, no imprint. He has hunted the wild beasts in his forests. But you — ? Ah, brother, young as you are, sor-

rows and struggles and meditations are written upon yours. Put
off that air of a buffoon and your eyes grow sad at once — watchful and very sad, my brother. Your nose droops still farther over
your lips; not yet much, but a little. You conceive yourself invisible, and your mouth grows wry, because you have so long had
to dissemble. But what I most love are the hollows of your
temples, and those you have had from birth. They alone, my
dearest brother, would have made me yours. Our cousin has
them too. I cannot believe that I shall love him; but if I do,
that will be the reason."

The girl rose and greeted him at last, serene and stern, just as
Jeanne herself would have confronted him. But her wide eyes
were wet with tears, as were his likewise. " Dear brother," said
Catherine, " you have not seen our dear cousin for a long while.
He visits me often, and we speak of you, since we may not hope
that you will desert your companions for our sake."

" I should be marked if I did so," replied Henri, " and you
well know, my dear sister, that I do not frequent Huguenots, of
whom you receive so many. Nor is it prudent that three members of our House should continue to converse alone and secretly
in the King's antechamber."

So saying, he looked at his cousin, who was growing uneasy.
Henri quietly took him by the arm and led him to the door.

" Now speak, Catherine," said he when he had returned. She
first glanced at the man-at-arms. He had taken his stand in the
doorway, as though to bar out any comers, and his back was
turned towards them. Then she spoke:

" They await you at our house."

" I know. But I am a prisoner. The guards are doubled,
there are more spies watching me than ever. They must have
patience still."

" They have none left. They have given you up for lost. They
are now looking to Alençon, I would have you know. And these
are our own people, from the South — blind that you are! The
Governor and the moderate Catholics are there on terms with
the Protestants; they will all give a hand to Condé when he in-
vades the kingdom with his German levies. The provinces that

lie between are also ours. All ripens; all are ready for a stroke, save you. Our mother gave her life, and now another wins the reward, not you."

"I am truly unlucky," he sighed with downcast eyes, sick at heart that he must deceive his own sister likewise. That stricken, trembling voice, quavering upwards on the end syllables — ("Sister! Sister, I am resolved, and I shall strike before you think. Of those that are to help me, not one knows the other. I have learned some lessons in three years. My good friend the murderess has me to thank that Alençon is no longer dangerous. Tonight she journeys forth in secret to get her lost son back. If I told you the first word of all this, Catherine, you would be a party to what may come to pass. And I'll not have you imperilled, Catherine.")

He opened his eyes; they were gentle, patient eyes; there was no stronger light in them.

"You will not?" she asked.

"I cannot," he sighed.

She lifted her hand; they were long, slim fingers like her mother's — and, as in boyhood, when his mother lost her temper, he suddenly felt a smart blow on his cheek. He was not to be outdone; and as though they were still children and still in their own land, where peasants, and princes too, are readier in the expression of their feelings, he swung his sister off her feet, carried her struggling on his outstretched arms, and laid her on the shoulders of the man-at-arms, who still stood planted on the threshold. Little Catherine had to cling to the great warrior to keep her balance. When she was on her feet again, Henri had long since vanished. But now she knew; and she laughed with all her might for joy. And the man-at-arms laughed too.

THE GHOST

Of those who were to help him, not one as yet knew another; only the spies, of course, knew about them all. These were, more especially, Monsieur de Saint-Martin-d'Anglure and Monsieur d'Espalungue, two well-bred noblemen, with a turn of bantering wit that was always in the mode and never went too far. They were good companions, and as Henri had no doubts as to what their purpose was with him, he made the most of their society. His particular confidant was a certain Monsieur de Fervaques — a soldier, no longer young, a bluff, outspoken man. No wit nor word-play here — just a message that Armagnac found in his master's clothes, with a warning not to guess how it had come there; and then perhaps a brief encounter, at which one name was mentioned: Gramont, Caumont, l'Espine, Frontenac. Seven noblemen finally joined the conspiracy in the palace, and each one of them had had to come forward of himself; they had, too, all been tested, for Fervaques suddenly spread a false report that all was discovered and each must save himself. But they stayed; for they thought less of their safety than the honour of marching with Navarre, to bring peace and freedom to the land. Henri recognized the best of them in this — that they did not realize how intent they really were on their personal advantage, or merely on a great adventure.

The new terrace over the river served for these secret meetings. The present King had enlarged the garden in that direction; he had grown tired of his worthy subjects' habit of clambering from the bank on to the balustrade and thence loudly expressing their admiration of his festal gatherings. High above the river, inaccessible from without, stood the long terrace — but no one knew that it had been provided with a trapdoor. A movable flagstone; it lay in the ground at the farthest end, and was besides disguised by several pillars; but anyone who understood the trick of it could get down through the masonry to the water's edge. The plan had been to abduct the Valois in a boat, when it was decided that the Leaguers in the Louvre — for there, too, there were some — should seize his person. Here appeared the ghost of Admiral Coligny.

The first to observe it, on one night of January, was a Catholic gentleman. Although a hearty and convinced adherent of the cause of Navarre, he had no wish to meet the ghost of the murdered Protestant. He expressed his aversion to Monsieur de Fervaques; the dead man was meddling in matters that had occurred after his time, and which he could not wholly understand. The ghost had moreover made a number of ill-considered remarks which the gentleman declined to repeat. This evidence was not to be rejected out of hand. It was much more above suspicion than that of the Huguenots, the ingenious d'Aubigné and the dark du Bartas. These two old friends were still kept by Henri at something of a distance. Here indeed was a bond that needed no special call to make it good, and a devotion that nothing could shake. Their master might do them wrong; they looked for no favour, they needed none, they were content — they understood. The master of a cause must win his enemies to his side, he must buy them, or beguile them, or even convince them he is right. Regard for such tried friends as they were would be extravagance — indeed, an overplus of kindness; a master must know how to be ungrateful.

When, on an early winter evening, he found both men concealed in his dim room, Henri burst out at them in a fury. They merely pleaded that they had a mission from the Admiral; he had returned. They described how and where they had seen him, and Henri had in the end to listen; he had already had the Catholic gentleman's statement. None the less, he told them that he had heard of this from none but them, and such efforts at deceiving him were so much breath wasted. To which they answered: " Sire, our beloved commander! Immortal souls exist no less than we who live, and it should not surprise us that they should sometimes appear."

" That is not the reason for my doubt," replied Henri. " The spirits know that they frighten us, and are therefore well advised not to appear. What have I done to the Lord Admiral that he should haunt me? "

At this, both were silent. Either they did not know or their silence meant that he must answer his own question. " I am much honoured," he went on, " to think that there is talk of me in the world beyond."

" Not more than in this world," said they. " All the kingdoms of the West have heard of a Prince who has for years lived a captive at the court of his enemies. His mother's life was forfeit, his father's friend and commander was killed, and he lost almost all his followers by violence. But he makes no sign, wastes himself in folly, and tarries so long that he seems to have quite forgotten the deed that all expect of him."

"Who expects it? What is expected? "

They told him. "To mention one name: the Queen of England is much intrigued by our affairs, Sire. We know this from Mornay, who has long sojourned there and still has good connections with that island. The Queen questions her Mornay about you, as a truly romantic figure. Will you at last decide to destroy Madame Catherine before she has you murdered? In the land of France the cause of which you are the leader born grows ever greater, while you sit and dream. This must needs stir that middle-aged sovereign's maiden heart. So deep, so impenetrable a Prince! So unlike the windy Alençon, who still has hopes of her hand. But now she has discovered that he has two noses."

Henri bent his head. He had not missed all that was masked beneath these anecdotes. "And he wants me to meet him? " he asked suddenly.

They grasped whom he meant. "Tonight at eleven o'clock," they whispered, and peered through the doorway to see whether they could get away unobserved.

Henri was left uneasily alone; he was afraid. An encounter with a ghost was strange and dreadful — but what of an assignation with a ghost? That was the unlawful thing, for which the priests of both creeds would threaten penalties. And yet it was hard to be dispassionate enough to take a calm and worldly view of such a matter. D'Elbeuf could: that was the name that came into his mind — a man from the opposite camp, a Guise. Henri had not confided to him his scheme for an escape. But d'Elbeuf had warned him of the new spies, who might otherwise have deceived him by their bluff demeanour. He had been silent, and from good counsel. As he lay on his bed, Henri said to his First Chamberlain: "Armagnac, I wish to see Monsieur d'Elbeuf." And that nobleman sent on that perilous errand a very humble chamber-woman of the Queen of Navarre, so that it should not be known from whom the message came. And when at last the friend stood by his bed and had heard the tale, he said:

" The appearance of the Admiral is natural, especially in the light of what accompanied his death. It would rather be a matter for surprise that he has delayed so long. In my opinion, you have nothing to fear from him. Indeed, it may well be his purpose to offer you a profitable warning."

" You are my good spirit, who gives me warnings, d'Elbeuf."

" I am a living man, and there are some things I do not know "; and in the words there was a kindly reproach. Henri, in effect, made use of him, but did not tell him his plans. For an observer like d'Elbeuf this made little difference; he knew how Henri had been stirred to action, and he guessed what was about to happen. But as he was from the enemy camp, he could envisage perils that might escape the doer of the deed himself. Meantime he did no more than hint at what he feared.

" Sire, one thing is certain — you may not make the spirit wait in vain. His case will surely be that of all ghosts; one should not approach them too nearly, for even the kindliest of them might fall into temptation." What that might be, he did not indicate. " Go, and fear not, Sire. From what is known of ghosts, this one will also keep his distance, in dread of that same temptation. But I shall not be far away, though neither you nor the spirit will be aware of me — unless there should be good reason for a living man to interfere," added d'Elbeuf lightly, and smiled, as though the last words were no more than jest.

Henri lay there still undecided; and he sighed: " I must be a coward. I have not noticed it on my campaigns — or only at the beginning of a battle, when I always feel a natural need; but what are ten thousand enemies against one ghost! "

At dinner there was little talk. It was so silent that the King called for music. His black mood was on him, and Henri looked down at his heaped plate. Only Madame Catherine talked on in her slow and throaty tones, and were anyone too distracted to answer, she eyed them as she chewed. And to her King Wren she said: " You are not eating, son-in-law. While there is yet time, you should eat your fill of game and fish and pastry. You will not find it everywhere and always." He made as though he had not heard her above the strains of music; but she had thus hinted that she well knew he was once more thinking of escape. And she wagged her head. King Wren often wanted to be up and away, did he? — let him but try! Upon her son, too, the Queen cast a disapproving eye. "You are pondering some folly," she said to him, leaning across the table. And after a pause: "Your mother, Sire, no longer possesses your confidence." As time went on, Henri felt that the evening would never end. A man cannot take account of women, nor find sharp retorts for men, when he is about to meet a ghost. About eleven o'clock the guards gave their usual signals for the shutting of the gate, and all the courtiers who lodged without departed. Henri tried to mingle among them unobserved, but was called back by Majesty itself. The King presented a picture of misery. Had Henri not been so agitated, he would have recognized an evil conscience. "A cold and stormy night, good cousin," exclaimed the King. "All manner of things may happen in the darkness. Stay here by the fire."

"Someone is waiting for me," answered Henri, and as though it were a lady, he laughed — a laugh that sounded sinister in his own ears.

As soon as he emerged from the shelter of the wall the strong wind flung him backwards. With an effort he reached the terrace, which was plunged in utter darkness. He waited; time passed, but the ghost had not yet managed to become visible. Then, for a moment, the storm parted the clouds — a ray of moonlight flashed and vanished, but in it Henri recognized the Lord Admiral. Black armour, grey beard, and the unmistakable carriage of the head, which had not only marked him among men, but was now with the will of God presented. This was truly he, Henri felt, as he dropped on one knee. He stood at the edge of the terrace, and the spirit far away from him at the farther end, by the pillars, where in summer there was an arbour of vine-leaves. And Henri prayed.

Then the moon shone forth again, and this time its light

lingered on the form that faced him. The face was pallid, like that of a mere apparition, and the eye-sockets were not filled with seeing eyes. And as the figure seemed to move, its limbs slid strengthlessly behind it; no footsteps rang on flagstones of this world. And Henri grew more utterly dumbfounded as he heard a voice that served no mortal throat. Oh, horror — the figure was approaching! Henri's teeth chattered as he prayed. Then — a groan. In muttered words, dismembered by the wind, the Admiral made known that he wanted vengeance on his murderers. Then the moon was hidden; which was well. It was only in the darkness that Henri could find courage to give his answer — that answer being a lie. Confronted by the apparition, he would not have so ventured even in secret. But he made it, and in the darkness and the wind he said: " It is not my purpose to avenge you, Lord Admiral. For your murderers are now my fast friends; and I find favour by my good humour and good dancing, and I mean to stay in the palace of the Louvre." He spoke so as to be heard by any living person lurking near at hand. But an inner voice was whispering all the while: " Lord Admiral, I am what I always have been."

A ghost, of course, can see beneath the spoken word, grasp the truth that is masked by the lie for common usage, since dissemblement became the first rule of life. He could not, and he would not, deceive the Lord Admiral! Suddenly there was a crash on the flagstone, like a falling body, and this was followed by what seemed, to human senses, a scuffle and shouting and the sound of hurrying feet. No ghost could surely thus demean himself, especially such a ghost as this. Henri turned to fly. At that moment the clouds parted, and the moon revealed a living man who dashed towards him and was not to be confused with anyone. " D'Elbeuf! "

" I almost had him! I was astride the vine-stem between the pillars. The ruffian never saw me, but I knew him. It was the Fool; no other than that poor melancholy buffoon — the King's Fool. As soon as I was sure, I jumped — I meant to land on his neck, but, alas, I just missed him. When I got up he had disappeared."

" A man cannot make himself invisible."

" A spirit does not scream like a fool, nor does he feel his way down steps that lead I don't know where. He used a secret passageway."

The terrace lay in the bright moonlight; they could examine every flagstone, but none betrayed its secret. Henri clapped his hands to his brow. " That was it," said he; and he saw a vision of the King's face as he took his leave, a very mask of guilt and evil machination; which might well have succeeded, for he had really believed he was speaking to the Lord Admiral. If, instead of lying he had said: " Ten days more, and I mean to break away "! Or had he said: " I have often meditated vengeance, my Lord Admiral, and the lives of your murderers often lay in God's hands "! But, by good fortune, he had said none of those things; or he would have been found in the morning stabbed to death upon those stones.

He uttered not a word of this to his companion, but d'Elbeuf, so skilled a watcher, understood most of it without the need of words. They returned to the palace and went to the Fool's room. As they expected, he was already abed; they had allowed him the needed time while they were searching the flagstones. He pretended to be fast asleep, but his snores came in gasps, and his coverlet felt cold. So they promptly dragged him out of bed and bound him to a chair. The odd thing was that he did not open his eyes. Armagnac was sent to fetch d'Aubigné and du Bartas. In their presence the interrogation began.

Would he confess that he had come straight from the terrace, asked Elbeuf of the pinioned Fool. Would he confess that he had played the ghost, asked Henri. The Fool, to try to save his skin, behaved like one deprived of speech. He turned up his eyes as though he were dying in good earnest; but his face was set in a grin. Twitches of uncontrollable terror marred the melancholy mien with which he otherwise denied his part. In a linen shirt instead of the dignified black garb, his hatchet face deadly pale, his hair in disorder, and that involuntary grin upon his face — for the first time in his career the Fool was comic. The five spectators roared with laughter at the sight. D'Elbeuf was the first to remind the others that a most malignant treachery to a living man had here been devised, apart from the insult to a ghost, which would know how to avenge itself. At this, the Fool's teeth began to chatter horribly.

Would he confess he had impersonated the Lord Admiral de Coligny that night, insisted Henri; he threatened the Fool with hanging and bade Armagnac take a torch and search the wall for a nail. But the Fool was not deluded by this byplay. The interrogation did not proceed as his accusers intended. *Question:* Was he afraid? *Answer:* Indeed he was afraid. *Question:* Did he repent? *Answer:* Indeed he repented. *Question:* Was he ready to make amends? *Answer:* Quite ready. *Question:* So he confessed that he had been the ghost? *Answer:* He made no secret of it. He had himself been frightened enough already, of the real ghost, who might have wrung his neck at any moment in fury at that sacrilegious mimicry. He was also certain that he would likewise have to pay for his audacity, and this in spite of his honest penitence. Ghosts were known to be merciless in vengeance.

Question: Did he fear nothing else? *Answer:* What should he fear? Nails or ropes? They might spare their threats. If they killed him, the King would know forthwith that the conspiracy which he, the Fool, was charged to discover, had indeed existed. And d'Elbeuf said into Henri's ear: "We had best let him go." Henri then asked whether the Fool had acted out of hatred. Henri had learned in the palace of the Louvre to take close account of any person's hatred. And the Fool replied:

"Hate you, Navarre? Because you played the fool here in my place? I had told you that you were excellently fitted for my part. 'Tis less perilous than mimicking a ghost."

Question: Whether the Fool remembered a certain insult he had suffered during a court ceremony, at which there had been much music and illumination. *Answer:* He remembered. The reference was to a bite in the cheek which Henri had inflicted on the Fool. Neither of them gave a name to so confidential a matter. *Question:* Whether, as a result of this insult, the Fool had taken pleasure in his part that night. *Answer* — which came

with a hollow, rasping moan: He had never yet done anything
with pleasure, but always with befitting melancholy, with an eye
upon the end. His own end was near, and it would be horrible.
Whereupon they unbound him and released him.

And Henri said to his two old friends: " That was the ghost
whose summons you brought to me, and such is my reward when
I follow your counsel." And they were sent upon their ways,
ashamed.

On the third night thereafter a fearful shriek burst from the
Fool's room, and when the door was opened, the Fool was found
huddled on the floor, strangled. The meaning of his death was
understood by all who had had anything to do with the counterfeit apparition; among them the King himself, who perhaps knew
overmuch about that murder — as well as the conspirators, including d'Elbeuf. Henri alone did not learn until later that the
Fool's forebodings had been fulfilled. That evening Henri lay
abed; as often, he had a hot but fleeting fever, the causes of
which no physician could discover, for it was a fever of the spirit.
With him were Armagnac and Agrippa d'Aubigné, who had
been summoned by the First Chamberlain. Armagnac, as he
bent his head over his master's pillow, had caught some notable
words. Now they were both listening; they heard a chant, faint
but distinct: " O Lord God of my salvation, I have cried day
and night before Thee."

The fevered man sang on; they could not distinguish every
word, but it was Psalm lxxxviii; he reached the passage:

" Thou hast put away mine acquaintance far from me; and
made me to be abhorred of them. I am so fast in prison that I
cannot come forth."

Then they took him by the hand, and held him by the hand,
while he chanted the Psalm of the children of Korah on the
weakness of those in misery. Their beloved master must not
think that the Lord abhorred his soul and hid His face from him.
In his weak hour he should know that his friends and those near
to him, and his kinsmen, in no way stood aloof from him because
of his tribulation.

So Henri was reconciled with his old friends and came to a

new understanding with them; and this was the real beginning of his stroke for freedom.

THE HOUR STRIKES

One day he disappeared — at first only as a feint, and to observe the consequences. But great excitement was aroused. The Queen Mother asked d'Aubigné where his master was. Henri was merely in his room, which d'Aubigné did not reveal. A nobleman whose duty it was to keep an eye on him was sent in search of his charge. The search proved naturally vain, for Henri had been warned. The following week he took care to stay late out hunting and not to come back until the court was distracted with anxiety. Two days before he broke forth in earnest, he was missing for the whole night; late in the morning he then appeared in the Sainte Chapelle, booted and spurred, and said with a laugh that the truant had returned; he had merely designed to shame them for their unworthy suspicions: he, whom Their Majesties must expel from the court before he would leave it; he would rather die at their feet! He was afterwards much admired for this stroke — but he had had to serve a long while before that venture.

Matters did not move quickly enough for his friends. Now they could speak freely. Their master permitted it, to ease their minds and practise himself in patience. They did so, and indited a most imposing document; for both Agrippa and du Bartas placed much confidence in the force and endurance of words, which, for resolute souls, are just as good as deeds and, once written, are an earnest of fame. They told their master bluntly that he was sinning against his own good name and was himself accountable for the insults he received. Though he were ready to forget, they would not forget the guilty, nor indeed would they ever believe that he had forgotten Saint Bartholomew. "Both of us, Sire, meant to move without you when you sang that Psalm. Once we are gone, you may be very sure, Sire, that other serving hands will not dare to put aside the poison and the knife, but will use them."

" So you would have deserted me and betrayed me? " he asked, not seriously, but to give them the chance they longed for, to proceed with their virtuous counsels. " You would have done as Mornay did. You old friends are all alike. Mornay slipped away to England, in good time before Saint Bartholomew."

" Not so, Sire. He had not time; but you did not know it, because you have so long ceased to heed your older friends and will not listen when we dare to make our plaint."

" You are right, and I must crave your pardon," he replied; indeed, he was quite touched; whereupon they were allowed to recount the adventures of their friend du Plessis-Mornay, although he knew them all by heart. And he reflected that his friends always wanted to claim advantage over him by knowing something he did not; first about himself, and then about his other friends. So he expressed great admiration of Philippe's dexterity and courage in cutting his way through a band of murderers on the night of Saint Bartholomew, who were just then searching a bookshop for unlawful books and slaughtering the seller. Philippe had, from pride, left the country without a permit and had managed to reach England, always the refuge of exiles, and had there — in what condition was not mentioned — awaited peace and amnesty. Then he joined the German princes, in an attempt to persuade them to invade France: the life of a harried diplomat, if not of a homeless conspirator. Henri, to whom none of this was new, grew more and more meditative. Mornay, Mornay! So restless! So busy! And so virtuous! " I was a captive, and in the end I almost gave myself into captivity."

At last, and all unconsciously, they brought forth what was mainly on their minds. Monsieur de Saint-Martin-d'Anglure and Monsieur d'Espalungue were urging a speedy stroke! His friends, in referring to those agreeable noblemen, did not yet know who they were: the wiliest of all the spies. Nor did he reveal that fact, as they would probably have challenged the traitors to a duel, and the whole scheme would for a time have miscarried. So he took counsel with his own confidant, Monsieur de Fervaques: a soldier, no longer young, a bluff, outspoken man. He gave Henri plain advice to go, and go quickly. Spies, indeed! He was well able to deal with them and put them off the track. This honest man's confidence seemed of good omen. On the 3rd of February Henri went.

There was indeed a previous farewell and a final comedy, both with gentlemen of the House of Lorraine. Henri waited until d'Elbeuf passed by alone; stepped forth and looked him in the face, and d'Elbeuf knew. He had always had an eye for great affairs and recognized them without word or sign. In times of peril he was always to be found at hand, he cleared up doubtful questions, he could read the characters of men and turn an adventure to the best issue. He alone asked for no confidence, no complicity, nor the formality of any compact. All remained un-uttered. D'Elbeuf was there, seemed to give nothing, and demanded nothing. He had indeed kept loyal guard over one whom, in his mind, he looked on as his master, but in doing so he had betrayed no one, and least of all his own House. A Guise cannot ride through the land with Navarre, and cannot fight for him until he is King. That was clear for both d'Elbeuf and Henri. And now, when Henri thus stepped forth, tears came into the eyes of both, and only a few broken words passed between them in that high moment. Then they were parted.

The comedy, on the other hand, was played at the expense of the Duke of Guise, called Le Balafré. The Goliath of the Paris mob must first be kept in play for a whole morning. Henri, in the early hours, flung himself on the Duke's bed, and hailed the potentate as the future Governor-General of the kingdom, by Madame Catherine's promise. How they all laughed in the Duke's room when Guise got up! Nor did the little buffoon leave the hero's side until that hero said: " Let us to the market and listen to the jesters; we'll see if we can find one that's your match! " So off they went, one of them already booted and spurred once more, and he tried to persuade the other to go a-hunting with him; he flattered and caressed him and held him in an embrace that lasted eight long minutes, before the staring mob. But the Duke had business with his League that day; he could not ride out hunting, as Henri was relieved to hear. And he himself rode out at last.

Hunting the goat is a rare pleasure and cannot be too loudly proclaimed. But the forest of Senlis is large, we must spend the night out before the chase and not return until late the following morning. Let no one be anxious for the King of Navarre. It is Monsieur de Fervaques speaking. " I know him well, he takes a boyish pleasure in sleeping in a charcoal-burner's hut. I shall stay here to train his birds." Fervaques was in truth left behind to observe what happened when the flight became known. He was to send messengers to report which road the pursuers had taken. And he did so faithfully, dispatching the first horseman as soon as there were any signs of commotion in the Louvre. The King of France was full of forebodings, of which his mother bade him take no heed. She and her King Wren would not leave each other in the lurch. No matter if he was a little belated. Why, it was only last evening that he had shown such infatuation with Sauves — and not only with her! There was much to keep him in the Louvre.

At the end of the second day, which was a Saturday, Madame Catherine likewise could contain herself no longer. She sent for her daughter, and in her royal brother's presence Margot was called upon to account for her husband. She declared that she did not know where he was, though she was growing disquieted. The scene began to take on the air of the family tribunal, which had been more than once held upon her in the time of her brother Charles. She was sharply told that she could not fail to know; her man had spent the night with her before he had disappeared. True, but she had noticed nothing. Could that be so? No secret talk nor final messages — no hint of a confession as their heads lay side by side? And as she caught the ominous glitter in her mother's lustreless eyes, the poor soul reached out her lovely hands and cried out desperately: " No," which was not, as uttered, a lie. For Margot had not needed any plain disclosures from her beloved lord; she had an inward sense that the hour had struck.

In times gone by she had once without scruple betrayed him

to her mother — to avert disaster, as she thought. But none could now stem the course of what was destiny; why should Margot try? Madame Catherine did not raise her hand against her; and she would surely do so were there here what called for punishment. But this was merely something that had happened, to be faced: something privily permitted, and now been done without concealment. And so it was that, later on, when the King retired for the night, he was shocked, but by no means overcome, when Fervaques confessed the whole matter. It was an auricular confession. For more than an hour and a half Fervaques whispered into the King's ear. The King forgot that he must act, he gave no command, he merely sat and listened, and no longer noticed the flattery disguised in the avowal.

Fervaques had, so far as he knew, meant honestly by Henri. To the King of France he personally owed nothing, for the King did not like him and had never given him any advancement. He was bound to the monarchy by ancient discipline and loyalty, on which he had never lost his hold. By a mere accident he came upon Henri one day in the company of d'Elbeuf, and was at once faced by the necessity of arresting the whole body of malcontents, or joining them, as even a gentleman of the House of Lorraine appeared to have done. He saw that they had much upon their side, mainly their humanity and moderation, which could never endanger anyone, not even himself. Their cause deserved to be heartened by the support of a man of the stout old stock, such as Fervaques; and he thenceforward figured as the trusted agent, privy to their most secret counsels, but always conscious of his own rude manhood — which, indeed, often set him thinking that he and his men would soon dispose of such folk as these: cut them to pieces in a wood or engulf them in a swamp. A soldier, no longer young, a bluff outspoken man, Fervaques could not conceive of any other end for " Politicals " or " Moderates." But, for all that, they did make their stroke at last.

Fervaques then decided that without him they would make a sorry mess of their affairs and merely hurt their country. His main consideration was Navarre's ingratitude towards himself, in simply leaving him behind. He struggled honestly with himself until his ancient discipline and loyalty gained the mastery and moved him to confess. As soon as his resolve was taken, Fervaques forced his way into the King's presence as he was retiring for the night — which his huge bulk made it easy for him to do — besought the royal ear for an important matter, and began forthwith: " Sire, in Your Majesty's service I have become engaged in an affair that runs counter to my loyalty to the throne of France; but I am thereby happily enabled to deliver the criminals into your hands. For myself I ask no reward. But my son has an encumbered estate that could be conveniently increased by the purchase of some adjacent land." Thus Fervaques. Later on, as Marshal and Governor, he was to work for the Guises, only so long as they paid, of course — and, in the end, to sell his province to King Henri Quatre. Before he died he wrote a highly pious testament, designed for public reading, and departed hence with the conviction that, throughout that rugged, honest life of his, he had at all points acted to the best advantage of the nation.

Someone guessed rightly what Fervaques had said in the King's ear, and that was Agrippa d'Aubigné — he too had remained behind so that people should think that Navarre had not fled, without his Huguenots. As the door closed, he caught the traitor outside, tore the mask from his face, and left him to his shame. So at least Agrippa imagined, when a man like Fervaques was stricken speechless and dumbfounded. At last, however, that bluff outspoken soldier did growl out one word, which Agrippa, as he hurried away, did not hear. " Scribbler! " growled Fervaques.

Here were truly minutes lost. But every one was precious, for though the King in his bewilderment might make no sign, the pursuers would even now be saddling their horses. Agrippa hurried to Roquelaure, a Catholic nobleman, whom he trusted, and with justice. The pair of them galloped off beneath the stars. Before Senlis they found their Prince; since dawn he had been hunting the goat. " What is it, gentlemen? "

" Sire, the King knows all. The way to Paris leads to death and shame; anywhere else — to life and glory! "

" Pray, spare me, sir," said Henri to that exuberant poet.

But it was well that he should have heard the matter put thus plainly, and a fortunate stroke of providence that treachery had indeed barred his return. Who can tell? Twenty hours of violent exercise bring much oblivion. The way to Paris would have been the familiar way, and the fetters there were known. The new ones might weigh heavier still. The old companions in arms, to whom he was riding once again, expected to find in Henri the same blind fury that had fostered all those years. But he, in the palace of the Louvre, had learned some lessons. Should he do better to leave the decision to destiny, which perhaps had barred his return? Behold, it was barred! " Gentlemen, we will ride on."

The little troop, ten noblemen, with Roquelaure, d'Aubigné, and Armagnac, was just emerging from a tavern by the light of the landlord's torch. As they came out one by one, Henri spoke confidentially to each: " There are two traitors among you. Watch on whose shoulders I shall lay my hand." He laid it first on Monsieur d'Espalungue's shoulder, and he said: " I forgot to take leave of the Queen of Navarre. Ride back and tell her that no one regrets it who stands by me honestly." He did likewise to the second spy, sending him to the King of France. " I can serve him better in freedom," was the message that the second was to carry. Both, seeing their dishonour unmasked, leapt into the saddle. The rest were frenzled with indignation. " Reflect, Sire! These are dangerous men and will rouse the peasants against us. We are not safe while they are loose. They must die."

Henri held his horse by the halter and answered them as lightly as if they were at a hunting party or a game of tennis. " There will be no more killing," he replied, with his historic and blasphemous oath; and he added: " I have seen enough killing in the palace of the Louvre." Therewith he set himself at the head of his followers, while the figures of the spies vanished into the haze of moonlight, and the hoofs of their horses thundered away into the distance.

At such a moment it was soon decided whither they should make for safety; not this time to the east and to the frontier, which they would have found it hard to reach, but to the west and the strong cities of the Huguenots. The roads in that direction all stood open, they chose theirs at will, galloped along the edge of the forest, and laughed for joy under the starry blue canopy of heaven, or shouted hunting calls, as though their dogs were still pursuing a goat. When they came to an open field and asked the peasants, who were brought out of their beds by the uproar, whether the goat had been seen, none would have believed that these gay cavaliers were on a flight for life and death. They indeed had almost forgotten the possible perils from the spies. One or other of them would be more disposed to reflect that their enterprise had not yet cost a drop of blood, which usually flowed freely when much less was at stake. One — of course, Agrippa — was thereby much exalted. " Sire, there will be no more killing. A new era has begun." He had no notion of flattery. Agrippa was prone to exaggerate his impressions, both those that uplifted him, as well as those that brought him as low as Job.

They rode all through that icy night, direct for Pontoise; but at dawn of the 1st of February, a Sunday, they set their beasts to ford the river — in front and alone, the Prince and his Master of the Horse, d'Aubigné, ahead of the little troop, in token of due precedence. It was indeed Agrippa's demand. Both walked, with their horses' bridles over their arms, up and down the bank of the Seine to warm themselves; then Agrippa asked his master to join him in singing the twenty-first Psalm to mark their gratitude. " The King shall rejoice in thy strength, O Lord; exceeding glad shall he be of thy salvation." Together they chanted it in the mists of dawn.

They were joined not only by their handful of companions; a troop of twenty other noblemen suddenly dashed up. All in Paris had indeed been given the word in secret, but with these newcomers the fugitives were joined by a band of horsemen not to be outwitted by pursuit, and ready to hammer very hard at the city gates in their master's name. Among these first twenty was a sixteen-year-old who slid off his horse on to his knees before Henri. But Henri lifted him and kissed him — in recognition of the keen, clear honesty in that boyish face, a face from the North, from the Norman border. Here was a loyal servant. "Kiss me, Rosny!" And Rosny, later Duke of Sully, was permitted for the first time to lay his lips against his Prince's cheek.

Many destinies were here forgathered on the Seine bank, in a wooded country, under the glancing shadows from the clouds, which — like destinies — do not tarry. All that company were in like case; their King had nothing that was not shared by all — youth and freedom newly won. It so happened, for a while, that the shadows were cast across the foreground and the farther slopes, while, in the midst, lit by a broad shaft of sunlight, stood Henri; and he beckoned each of them in turn to speak with him. With each and all he stood for a while alone, and embraced him, or clapped him on the shoulders, or took his arm. These were the first. Had he had foreknowledge, he would have seen the future written upon every face, the look they would wear at their latter ends, and he would have been as much alarmed as horrified. Some of them were to desert him very soon, more would stay with him until his latest hour. One must be bribed to stay, another would go on serving him for love, when almost all his followers' hearts were weary. But enmity and friendship, loyalty and treachery — all speed the common task of those who are to live their time together.

Welcome, Monsieur de Roquelaure, sometime Marshal of France. Ah, friend du Bartas, must you die so soon, after one of my great battles? Rosny, were we both but soldiers, this realm would never grow. Sully has a love of figures, and I have a heart for men; by both our labours this land of France shall become a great kingdom. My Agrippa, farewell; I shall go home first, but you will go into exile — in your old age, and for your religion, which will again be persecuted as soon as I have closed my eyes. The sunlight shone upon the central scene, but this veil remained impenetrable.

There were smooth young faces there, afire with mere joy to be there and to be riding forth in company. And they soon did so; in the next town they all ate and drank their fill, grew more light-hearted and more venturesome, played all manner of pranks, and actually carried off a nobleman. He had been fearful for his village as the horsemen approached, and tried to persuade them to fetch a compass round it. He took Roquelaure for the captain, as carrying more polished metal about his person than the rest. And it was promised that his village would not be touched if he guided them to Chateauneuf! In their company, indeed, he could not spread news about their progress. On the way, anxious to figure as a man of fashion, he spoke solely of the court; he knew the names of all the ladies' lovers, especially those of the Queen of Navarre, and told the tale of them for her husband's benefit. And when at night they arrived before the city of Chateauneuf, it happened that Frontenac shouted up at the walls to the officer who commanded it: " Open to your master! " The city was in one of the King of Navarre's domains. When that rustic nobleman heard that order, he stiffened with fear; d'Aubigné could hardly move him to fly for safety along a path that led nowhere. " And please God you won't get home for full three days! "

They merely spent the night and then rode on in a column to Alençon, which city lies half-way between Paris and the ocean. And they reached it, thanks to the strength of their own thighs. Their horses endured just as long as they could feel those sturdy thighs supporting them — and thus it was that Achilles no less than Charlemagne with all their famed companions journeyed across their kingdoms.

Prince of the Blood

At Alençon, during three whole days, to the astonishment of all that company, noblemen poured in from every side; there were two hundred and fifty of them in the end. Fugitives had meantime taken the guise of conquerors, to whom cities opened their gates; and rumour went before them. No use stopping the mouth of one rustic nobleman; their progress was already known in Paris. And the newcomers were by no means all of that mean kind who must rush to help in swelling a success; there was many a gay and eager warrior among them, not reckoning those with whom anger was the impulse. The news had brought them out of several provinces, for Alençon lies between Normandy and Maine; and, indeed, some of the later comers were from the court. Whencesoever they came, and with whatever mind, Henri gave welcome to them all.

This angered those who had been first, and so wanted to remain alone first, and especially the older friends. " Sire! This is beyond bearing. Among the new arrivals are murderers of Saint Bartholomew. Sire, treachery is written on their brows! Judas himself is only needed to complete our company! " And Judas did indeed appear. Behold — Fervaques!

The son's estate was now free of debt, and the adjacent land had been bought; Fervaques then bethought him that the time had come to redeem the pledge of loyalty that Navarre had accepted at his hands. He and the King of France were quits, but much was owed him by Navarre, who was now reckoned as a rising power. No sooner thought than done, and Fervaques stiffly lowered his huge person on his knees before Henri, and all the floor-boards in the hall creaked.

Not that Henri failed to wink at his friends. " The man is gold," said he; " he has his price." But the worthy gentleman was conveniently deaf and left it to the younger partner to set the affair on a proper footing. Henri took his resolve and pressed a kiss on the broad grey beard.

Thence the cavalcade journeyed on more slowly. Newcomers were continually joining it, both on the open road and at the brief halting-places. These were four; in the fifth city the King of Navarre and his court sat down because they knew that then and thenceforward they would be in safety. Saumur lies in Anjou. A day's march farther and they would have been in Saintonge, where the fortress of La Rochelle had all that time stood impregnably betwixt land and sea. Henri would not proceed thither yet, because he feared the judgment of those bold, unyielding Protestants. He, who after all this dalliance had appeared at last, and a good half of his following were Catholic! Nay, more; he was so, and remained so, for the whole three months of his sojourn in Saumur, although the pastors expected him at sermon. But he went neither thither nor to Mass. And his noblemen acted likewise, so that at Easter only two of them took the Sacrament. The court of Saumur was "without religion," which was a strange and indeed a dreadful state of affairs.

"What matter — they come!" thought Henri. "They join me in ever-growing numbers, they fill the city and the camp before the gates. 'Tis all one to them whether I am Huguenot or Catholic. I am a Prince of the Blood, it is for me to establish peace and unity in this kingdom. I care little what they otherwise believe; my sovereignty they must recognize. And indeed 'tis no light claim. I come last, after Monsieur and my cousin Condé, each for himself, have stirred up the land by plot and intrigue. My task is all the harder; I cannot be too nice, none must leave me with empty hands, though he be a gallows-bird." So he made haste to beat up a following, that he might not have to stand alone and aloof if the court of France should treat with the rebels. And a rebel he was not; that he denied to all who came; and, from a certain aspect of affairs, he actually believed it. For he rather looked upon himself as the pillar of the kingdom, and possibly the only one.

Monsieur, the King's brother, had his eye on certain provinces as a dowry for himself. Condé wanted to present them to a German Prince of his own faith. Henri sent an envoy to convey to him that as a Prince of the Blood he was concerned solely with the greatness of the kingdom of France; he wanted nothing for himself, and moreover he disapproved of the demands of Monsieur. But rather than deliver the three bishoprics to Johann Casimir of Bavaria and parcel up the kingdom, he would prefer — yes, what would he prefer? Monsieur de Ségur was charged to say what he would indeed have stomached; and it flung Condé into one of his outbursts of fury, such as had seized him after Saint Bartholomew, when he swore to die rather than change his faith; but he became a Catholic seventeen days before Henri did so. " My master," said the envoy, " would prefer to abandon the pursuit and punishment of those who had planned Saint Bartholomew rather than that the kingdom should be divided." Which was so startling that Condé positively bellowed with fury.

This was, too, like enough to raise an outcry in La Rochelle, and Henri was well advised to stay at least a day's journey away from that city. The first answer to such hardihood was of course a charge of forgetfulness and ingratitude. " For whom, then, did they perish, the victims of Saint Bartholomew? You, Sire, were on the way to your wedding, and so led our folk to slaughter. And now our dead are to remain unavenged, so that our master may thus make a better bargain with our murderers. Come back to the faith! Or we, too, shall forget your mother." Such was the voice of the bold and unyielding Protestants, and it carried far enough for Henri to hear it where he had set up his court for a brief space, a court " without religion." Leader of the Protestants? — that was now his cousin Condé, who had long been so. A zealous, hasty man, who saw no further than the strife of parties. Let the good folks of the faith put their trust in the poor nincompoop. He was still living in the times of the Lord Admiral. He did not grasp that it was no better to split the kingdom over a matter of faith than to parcel it out for personal profit, like that half-wit Alençon. Cousin Condé and the Man with Two Noses were alike in that they were men whose schemes were fated to miscarry. They had better have stayed where they were. But a man without a mission is always in most hurry.

It was thus that Henri envisaged matters in his own mind, while he went on rallying supporters, to impress the court of France with their numbers, until that court should be disposed to treat; he would have no dealings with his cousin and former friend, for he was then entering upon relations with the fortress of La Rochelle. Those within it should learn who he was; their friend as always, but a Prince of the Blood. They insisted that he must go to sermon, otherwise he must not reckon on the Huguenots. Cousin Condé had denounced him as a lost sheep. Were he turned out of the Protestant community, he would no longer be a danger to Cousin Condé; the cousin, already a fool, had grown malignant.

On the other side matters stood no better; the court of France made peace with Monsieur, as a result of which Monsieur was crammed with provinces, sinecures, and pensions. Nothing was conceded to the King of Navarre, save that he was to be Governor of Guyenne in the name of His Majesty, and this he already was by title. He had to bide his time, for what else could he have expected? No party, no territory, and — worst of all — no money. Therewith he acquiesced in the partition of the kingdom — only for the time, as he secretly assured himself. But that is of little moment when King Wren must go southwards and take no more share in great affairs of State. For how long none can say. Ten years — who would then have dreamed of such a time? An eternity for a youth of twenty-three.

Patience; and patience we have learned in the palace of the Louvre. In outward dealings he would play for time, he would give way, he would even renounce what was his own, while within him burned the steadfast thought: "We have passed through this school, and none may now excel us. Gentlemen of La Rochelle, so you need a leader for your party and he must go to sermon? I'll go, I'll go forthwith. One who acquiesces in the partition of a kingdom will not recoil from severing two religions: one like the other, merely forced upon me by your obstinacy. Consider my Catholic noblemen, they are the least fanatic. Moreover they could not desert me, they stand too ill with their own court. I hold them, though I go no more to Mass. But I'll go to sermon, just to win you too, since your obstinacy so compels me. I'll not forget this later; stubborn folk were never to my taste, though stubbornness may breed much precious virtue. Still, a man may vaunt his virtue and be no better than a malignant fool — which, I think, explains the enmity between me and my cousin Condé. He brings his pieces into place, but I — with one move I checkmate him, I go to sermon!

"Did you know, good people," thought Henri, when he was pondering long and deeply his reversion to the Reformed Church

— "did you but know that all in the last resort depends on one fact, one will and one man's luck." What he really meant — his birth as Prince of the Blood — he revealed to no man; for even pride may serve to trick a man's true self.

He summoned his sister Catherine to Niort, a town on the borders of the provinces of Poitou and Saintonge, quite near the Mecca of the Huguenots; he would enter it for the first time on his readmission to the faith, that he might not be shamed by that act. On June 31st, at Niort, he solemnly abjured the Catholic faith. As a living proof of which he had at his side the Princess of Bourbon, his sister, a steadfast Protestant when times were worst. On the 28th of the same month he entered La Rochelle. There he had no more need to bow his head; and for him, too, the bells pealed as they had done in former days for his beloved mother, Queen Jeanne, whose fortress and refuge this had always been. He himself had beleagured the city with a Catholic army, as many remembered; they were silent when he passed, and nudged each other with clenched fists. He saw them; but he knew he must be patient. Wherefore no one yet thought of ten years — an eternity.

Catholic gentlemen were with him also, and of set purpose he paraded them within those walls, to show that he had others to back him besides the citizens of La Rochelle. These were attached to no religion, only to himself and to the kingdom, which were one day destined to be one.

This he spoke of to no man, save that one single conversation did lead in that direction, with a nobleman of Périgord, the same indeed who had once walked with him here on the sea shore and had sat drinking with him in a shot-riddled house. Monsieur de Montaigne came in with a throng of courtiers; in the presence of the rest, Henri took no notice of him and did not address him, but he threw him a quick and meaning smile, and Monsieur Michel smiled equally discreetly in response. As soon as he could, Henri dismissed the company; Montaigne, at a sign from the King, remained.

Once alone with him in the cool hall, Henri embraced him and led him by the hand to a table, and with his own hands set a jug of wine upon it and two glasses. The unhappy nobleman pledged him courageously, although the drink would, he knew, do him little good. Since they had met he had been suffering from stone in the kidney. The vision of old age had then stood clear before his mind; now he knew it for what it was. He began to visit watering-places, and did so till the end. The various medicinal springs would have most appealed to him as matter for conversation, as also the customs of the nations in their usage; Italians preferred to drink the waters, whereas Germans more often bathed in them. He had made two important discoveries, both known to antiquity and since forgotten. First, the man who took no baths lived under an integument of dirt, his pores were choked. Second, the neglect of nature had been used by a class of persons to their own advantage. Regarding the position of doctors, the suffering gentleman could have enlarged for hours, with due reference to the Emperor Hadrian, the philosopher Diogenes, and many others. But he put all this aside; and indeed while the conversation lasted he actually succeeded in forgetting his most intimate troubles.

Henri asked him with what purpose he had come, and it did not enter Montaigne's mind to launch upon his travels in search of health. He said that he had wanted to observe this strange novelty of a court "without religion." Henri replied that it would be better to speak of a court with two religions — whereat Montaigne retorted with a quiet smile that that was the same thing. Of two religions only one could be genuine, and only that one should be followed. Anyone who admitted a false one thereby made no distinction, and could really do without either.

"How do I know?" interposed Henri. The remark had never been forgotten since their last conversation and came in aptly here. His companion merely wagged his head and said that it must be conceived as uttered as before God. We did not share God's knowledge with Him; it was all the more our duty to discover all we might on earth, and wisdom was amassed through moderation and through doubt. "I love balanced natures, inclining to neither side. Immoderation, even in virtue, would almost revolt me, though I am baffled to give a name to such a quality." He was about to mention Plato, but Henri said he was heartily glad his guest took pleasure in his company, at any rate. They must pledge each other to good neighbourship at home in the South. Which Montaigne did, oblivious of his kidneys. The wine released him, his cheeks flushed, and he began to talk with the greatest freedom. He expounded to the young man all the issues of his fortunes, his enmities, his failures, his desperate vacillation between two creeds, the peril of departing empty-handed, of isolation, and of rootlessness at last. It is a favoured destiny that carries such ordeals, and it was truly on that account alone that Montaigne had come, as indeed was plain.

He wanted to see whether a moderate and a sceptical mind could fend off the excesses of unreason that threatened it on every side. It is thus that human nature is continually squandered, as history teaches us, and the ancient writers tell the selfsame tale. Bewildered and tormented, and perceiving nothing; such, as a rule, is the race of men. The rare mortals upon whom the Lord has bestowed a sane and healthy soul must be careful to conceal themselves from the brutal creatures whose souls are ailing; or he will not survive for long. The time of humanity mostly passes in outbreaks of these spiritual maladies, and so it will go on. Which is no bad thing; for the diseases of the soul that are at least unburdened are thereby the lighter; *omnia vitia in aperto leviora sunt.*

Thereupon he, too, proposed a toast. He had been in Paris and had seen the "League." And in celebration of this most notable outbreak of a deep-set spiritual malady he asked Henri to raise his glass. Then he added with an air of composed resolve, as though he had matched himself against the League and its Spanish gold, as though he himself had patiently collected a following and was himself heir to the kingdom of France: "The League has before it a peak and a decline; then your time will come, Sire. We will not ask how long it will last and whether it may not be again succeeded by the usual madness. With that we are not concerned. I shall certainly see my King upon the throne."

Here he was actually taken by his accustomed pains of body. Moreover, he thought he could tell from his listener's demeanour that he had said enough, and he rose.

But Henri was merely deeply stirred; all the words of Montaigne seemed to strike upon his inner consciousness. And he cried: " You have it, friend! I am a Prince of the Blood." He strode up and down the hall and cried once more: " Because I am a Prince of the Blood, I shall outdo them all. Hence I draw my right and my capacity."

Montaigne watched him. He himself would indeed have been disposed to enlarge on the health and sickness of the soul of man, and of the times. But he nodded and said: " Such was my intention." For it was becoming plain to him that they had spoken in chorus; the notes were different notes — but the harmony was one. He bowed and as he took his leave he spoke his final word:

" One name may stand for much and explain a hard matter. A Florentine artist, whose great works I was praising, thought to vindicate himself to me for having created them, and he said he could have done nothing had he not had the advantage of being descended from the counts of Canossa. He is called Michelangelo."

Henri hurried after his departing guest, embraced him once again, and said in his ear: " I have created nothing. But I can and will."

Moralité

𝕷e grand danger du penseur est d'en savoir trop, et du prisonnier d'hésiter trop longtemps. Voilà ce captif de luxe, qui a des loisirs et des femmes, retenu par ses plaisirs en même temps que par les amusements désabusés de son esprit. Cependant il voit des fanatiques cupides entamer la moelle même d'un royaume que plus tard il devra redresser. Heureusement qu'il lui reste des amis pour l'admonester, une sœur pour le gifler à temps, et que même un spectre le relance afin de lui rappeler son devoir. Au fond il n'en faut pas tant, et son jour venu de lui même il prendra son essor. C'est sa belle santé morale qui lui donne l'avantage sur tous les immodérés de son époque. Comme un certain gentilhomme de ses amis, l'immodération dans la poursuite du bien même, si elle ne l'offense, elle l'étonne et le met en peine de la baptiser. Par contre, il possède le mot propre par quoi il signale et ses qualités et ses droits. En appuyant sur son titre de prince du sang c'est en réalité sur les prérogatives de sa personnalité morale qu'il insiste.

Book Seven

The Troubles
of Life

A Very Little Battle

NÉRAC is a country town, where the birds fly overhead, sheep patter up to the gateways, and rich, flat fields lie all around the walls; and so it has been for a thousand years. The men sit hammering wood or leather, cleaving stone or chopping meat, or stand beside the green waters of the Baïse, fishing. But let a troop of horse appear in a cloud of dust, goods and chattels are huddled away in safety, and the people come forth with empty hands, hoping they may be spared. They put no faith in walls or ramparts, nor in the captains, Catholic or Huguenot, who may be their momentary masters. Others are already on the way and will kill or drive out these. There is but one salvation for the townsman: to bow his neck; and that he does. At Nérac some go to Mass, and others to sermon, and they change their creed to suit their latest conqueror.

The young King of Navarre, a free man at last, avoided Pau, his capital; it was at Pau that his mother, Queen Jeanne, in her high zeal for the faith, had taught her Protestants intolerance. He chose the country town of Nérac for his dwelling and his court. It lay in the county of Albret, the ancient domain of his maternal forebears, and near the centre of the territory that he was thenceforward to govern. These were his own realm and the·

province of Guyenne, with its capital, Bordeaux. His own realm still consisted of the provinces of Albret, Armagnac, Béarn, Bigorre, and Navarre. His noblemen and Huguenots, while he lay in the Louvre, had beaten off not merely old Montluc, who had marched against them at the orders of the King of France, but Spanish hordes that came down from the mountains. The territory of the new Governor — and King — reached along the Pyrenees and up the coast, as far as the estuary of the Gironde. The whole south-west of France.

The air of freedom is as heady as wine, drunk in the wind and the sunshine; and the bread of freedom is delicious, though it may sometimes be dry. To ride through the land after years of imprisonment! To come home but rarely, and yet be everywhere at home. No guards, no watchers; none but friends. To breathe is a very joy; and every cowgirl looks more lovely than the prisoner ever thought his Princess. Though, indeed, Henri thought, as he eyed these folk of his, that they had withered sadly in his absence. That was the fault of Montluc, the Spaniards, and two religions. None can hold against the zeal of fanatics and the incessant threat of death. He had so suffered, and he knew. Too many of them had left their burnt houses and their ravaged fields and turned footpads; he could understand it, but he meant to end it and bring peace to that land.

It was in his mind that as he himself was starting a new life, the people's lives could be renewed. It was no hardship to be cheerful and good-natured. But the little towns were grown set and sullen from ill usage, they raised their bridges when he came. "Turenne, you have a voice that carries; tell them the Governor will pardon what is past, and we will pay for what we take. They refuse? Tell them to be reasonable. But if we must force this town, it will be sacked. Ha! I see Rosny prick his ears. Well, 'tis the way of the world and was never otherwise."

Then there was plundering and ravishing and hanging, in the good old fashion. The town must learn the measure of its new master. An officer was left behind with a few soldiers, and once again the King's writ ran a few miles farther. The Prince of the Blood upheld it as he rode about the land. He said lightly to his friend d'Aubigné, and even to the youthful Rosny: " You shall be one of my Council." And when one day Mornay appeared, he urged that the Prince's Council should indeed be held at the castle of Nérac: du Plessis-Mornay was a statesman and a diplomat. Such occasions were rare at first. On the way home one day the Prince learned that merchants had been robbed upon the highway; and rode full gallop to the spot! A man whose goods are recovered for him is prompt to pay his taxes — unlike the peasant, who will not dig his money up though the robbers set his farm afire. But he is grateful to the Governor for saving his own life and his daughters' honour. And they are very ready to be kind to one of their young rescuers (who was usually the Governor); as was known to some fathers, but not to others. So Henri set about a petty task, that was at first a great one; but here, within his own small compass, there should be peace, and fruitful fields, and populous villages.

Bright was the sky and silvery the light, and the evenings were like velvet, when the Governor and his Councillors, who wore, indeed, a very martial aspect, rode, after their labours, into the rosy glow of sunset; whither they did not know. But that was joy: never to know where the meal would be eaten, nor whose bed was to be shared. In the Louvre there were always watching eyes, and whisperings in the antechamber. So all the more he loved to visit the poor folk, who often did not know him; and indeed he looked of small account in his shabby corded velvet jerkin, bearded, and wearing a felt hat. Money he did not carry; they asked none for their goose and cabbage broth, nor for their red wine from the cask; but money reached them afterwards from his treasury in Pau. The poor were naturally more akin to him than the rich; he did not wonder why, and would have found it hard to say. Because they smelt wholesome, not like the King of France and his favourites? His own clothes, when he sat among them, reeked of sweat like theirs. Was it their racy speech and the rude nicknames that they used? He, too, was fond of such sobriquets for his most respected followers. He loved, and shared, the easy humours of the poor.

Besides, he could do no other. In a land where four thousand homesteads had been burned and the population brutalized, overweening airs were out of place. There had been one Governor, not, as it seemed, a cruel or an avaricious man, but merely proud; he had shown immoderate pride towards the common man, and the common man had up and killed him. Henri had taken warning, and there was a purpose in his threadbare hose; though the shanks that filled them were thought a trifle lean! It had indeed been said of him that two things he could not do: be serious or read a book. A serious man, in common eyes, is near to being proud; a man that reads books is an alien, and may go his ways, which is what the gentry mostly did. Not so Henri. He lived in the country, he owned not only castles, but a mill as well, which he worked like any other miller; so rumour had it. They called him the Miller of Barbaste — and did not ask how long often he was really there, nor what he did there. Poor folks are not inquisitive. They mistrust learning, but a word is often enough, they do not look behind it.

A King, a true King, is a mysterious figure — but if not in gorgeous raiment, he would be nothing of the kind: unknown and insignificant though he is the very King. The sudden revelation of him makes the heart stand still. Once, while out hunting, he was parted from his retinue and came upon a peasant sitting under a tree. " What do you there? " " What should I be doing? I am waiting to see the King." " Then mount behind me, and you shall have a good look at him." The peasant did so, and as they rode on he asked how he should know the King. " Observe the man who keeps his hat on when the others bare their heads." At that moment the hunting party appeared, and all of them doffed their hats. " Well? " he said to the peasant, " which is the King? " But the other with rustic cunning answered: " Lord! Either you or I, for we alone have kept our hats on."

Beneath the words there was fear as well as awe. The King had gulled the peasant, who therefore, with due caution, quizzed the King; which was a sharp reminder to the King. It chanced that, besides the King, only the boor was covered; he was astride the horse behind the King, but fear and awe must still possess his mind. Such affairs began in careless arrogance and ended in a lesson. One day he rode in high good humour to the city of Bayonne, where he had been invited to a feast. When he arrived, the table had been set in the open air; he had to eat surrounded by the populace, and abide their questioning, while they crowded round him, sniffing at his soup and even at his leather jerkin; and he, laughing and talking in their Southern speech, had to maintain the royal mystery. And he did it because he had a simple heart, though a far from simple mind. Success in such a matter brought him the same sense of deliverance as a battle won. While the issue was in doubt, the peril was forgotten; he was intent upon it and could think of nothing else.

When he visited the poor, he would confide his troubles to them, and with all the indignation and the humour of the poor. They abused his officers for forbidding them to poach; so he took them out hunting. They learned his grievances against his deputy, Monsieur de Villars, whom the court of France had thrust upon him in the place of old Montluc. Villars haunted him as though they were both still in the Louvre. The city of Bordeaux would not admit the Protestant Governor, and as Henri could do nothing, he pretended to be indifferent. Only at the tables of the poor, when faces began to flush, he burst out, and in their company became a rebel, for they were all Protestants. Their creed was their weapon, and became his too. His faith was theirs.

Huguenot marauders, no less than Catholics, laid waste the countryside. First they burnt the church, and then withdrew, but three days afterwards the manor, too, were the ransom not by then raised and ready. The menaced owner dashed to Nérac, but the Governor was not to be found. He was walking in his gardens on the bank of the Baïse, so the petitioner was told. " But there are four thousand paces of them — four thousand of the King's great paces. See if you can find him there, my lord." (A little river and tall trees, all of the same vitreous green, and an arrow-straight avenue, called La Garenne, quite covered in by leaves.) " You will find there is a bridge leading from the park, where you may walk as you will, across to the flower-garden and the orangery. Not so fast, my lord; is your house afire? You might well miss him — look, my lord, by the stone fountains and in every arbour. The King may be sitting on a bench and reading Plutarch. Yonder is the King's pavilion, its white walls and red roof so gaily reflected in the waters of the Baïse. The doors are guarded, and pray, on your life, make no attempt to enter there, my lord! If the Governor should be therein, no one may inquire how he is engaged, nor with whom."

The anguished gentleman left Nérac unsatisfied, and furious with the Huguenot Governor. But when, on the third day, the marauders returned as they had promised, who was it that appeared at the last moment and fell upon them? Henri had their leader hanged, for all he was a Protestant. The men he enrolled among his soldiery on the spot. In the evening he dined at the manor; the nobleman and all his people were exultant and sent to all his kindred and his friends to tell them how the Huguenot Governor had saved him. Truly the first Prince of the Blood! And yet, if we must reckon with him — one day, should there be no other successor to the throne; but that lies far ahead. Meantime may he continue to protect our villages against his fellows in faith. He is above all a soldier, a stern commander and a scourge to all marauding bands and footpads. Those who fail to inscribe themselves in a captain's roll are punished; but those who swear their oath and then desert, commonly with the soldiers' pay, are shot. And the markets are once more under guard.

Henri, as he watched his work bear fruit, took care that all this should be put about in letters and in talk. He set most store by approval from without; for this can even alter facts. If he could but create a semblance that there was but one religion in his provinces! There were men of both creeds in his army, and he was concerned that such a novelty should be marked and properly esteemed. At his court in Nérac he had as many Catholics as Protestants; most of the noblemen served him without pay, for himself and for the cause, and all were pledged to keep the peace — which was not always kept. As for the King, save for Montgomery and Lusignan, none stood so near to him as Roquelaure and Lavardin; he seemed no longer to be conscious that only the former shared his creed.

Indeed, he knew it well enough, and yet he dared, in the face of the compact and reigning truth, openly to say: " A man that does his duty is also of my faith, but I share the faith of all men brave and good." He said this, and he wrote it although the words might well have made a noose to hang him. But behind him were the Louvre, captivity, deceit, and fear of death. It was thus that he might well have learned to hate humanity. Instead of which he still appealed to the two virtues that should unite mankind: bravery and goodness. Brave — of course. Even in the Louvre most men were brave. But good? Almost all were still chary of betraying goodness. For that they needed not merely to be brave, but bold. But he prevailed upon them, though they knew not how; he did so by seasoning his own goodness with a little guile. Men no longer despise gentleness and tolerance when they feel themselves outwitted.

The recent peace had once again miscarried. It had been named after Monsieur, the brother of the King of France. Monsieur had, after his peace, ceased to be Alençon and become Anjou, the richer by a revenue of a hundred thousand crowns. The pay of his German troops was even provided by the King, against whom they had fought. Monsieur, for his part, could now have taken his ease, though in his brief life he never succeeded in so doing. But he betook himself to Flanders, in an ambition to be made King of the Netherlands and reach out from throne to throne for the hand of Elizabeth of England, now forty-five years old. The lanky Queen and her little Italian; so they called the Man with Two Noses; there was much laughter at the pair of an evening in Nérac, when the Governor and his Council discussed the news over their wine. But the peace, called the Peace of Monsieur, had otherwise miscarried. The citizens did not even appear when the King gave a display of fireworks. The shameless Guise and his League were intriguing, and there were few tables in the realm at which a man could sit without fear of question on his creed. So the King of France called an assembly of the Estates at his castle of Blois. Protestants no longer came; they knew too well how they would be betrayed. But the King of Navarre caused Monsieur du Plessis-Mornay to write a letter pleading the cause of peace; and he wrote himself.

The others were merely concerned to damage each other's cause. Protestants as well as Catholics. The ,latter, as the stronger, appealed to force, the former to their pledged security. The weaker party must never cry his just claims, but call for tolerance and kindliness; under shelter of these virtues he will easily increase his power. But virtue allied with power wins more adherents than either alone. Henri and his ambassador were at one upon their purposes, and they went the same ways. Mornay fathered his address to the Estates on a kindly Catholic, though it had in fact been wholly indited by devout and guileful Mornay himself. Henri indeed — so he wrote — personally prayed to God to enlighten him as to which was the true religion. He would then serve it and banish the false one from the realm, and, if it might be, from the world. Fortunately God vouchsafed no message to him on this matter; so he ran no risk of having to surrender his strong places.

What he could truly do to prevent another outbreak of civil war, that he did with all his might — he even hastened to meet the envoys sent to him by the King of France. Their aim was to convert him to the Catholic faith once more, even within the walls of his loyal city of Agen. One of them was the very Villars who would not admit him to Bordeaux, the other an Archbishop of his own House; but the third was no less a person than the Treasurer of France. Henri received them all together, and each in private. There is no knowing what a man will let fall without witnesses, especially in matters where money is concerned. At the open assembly the Archbishop so lamented the sufferings of the people that Henri wept — whereat he reflected that the sufferings of the people were his own, and not the Archbishop's; and for that very reason, too, the kingdom was destined for him alone. This was, indeed, an enlightenment from God. So he promptly sent his soldiery to storm a city which had been stripped of its garrison by Villars, that he might appear before his Governor with a more imposing escort, and Henri exulted secretly over his little battle; he did not cease to weep, but tears of joy looked just like any others. A glorious little battle!

The Marquis de Villars took his revenge, nor was it long before he did so. Henri was playing " long ball " in his courtyard, which was enclosed by a square of tall buildings; the façades were adorned with traceried windows and carved arcades, and a magnificent great double staircase led down to the river and the garden. It had all been built by his forebears two centuries before, and at each of the four corners a massy tower stood guard over all these stone splendours. Sentries are as prone as other men to the charms of pretty girls, and during one such moment the enemy crept from one bush to another, and under cover of one house glided behind the next. In the closed court Henri was flinging the long leather ball. When Henri sat at dinner, there was always a watcher in a niche behind his chair. By an extreme of folly there was no watcher here; and now it was too late. A sudden shriek; the enemy slipped in behind the open wall and gripped someone by the throat. The ball-players were unarmed. Henri, while his friends leapt down the staircase, vanished into the castle; and long as the enemy searched for him, he was not found.

Château de la Grange

He escaped under his pursuers' feet, under the town, and then under the fields. The subterranean passage into which he groped his way was very old, and known to none living save himself. He felt for flint and steel, lit a lantern, and by its glimmer was able to avoid the holes and falls of earth. And the journey seemed shorter than its wont, as he thought of the baffled enemy. The stagnant air began to make him gasp: however, a pair of soft arms awaited him at the far end of the tunnel — very different from those which had so nearly closed about him. At last — steps leading upwards. He blew out the tiny lamp and lifted the trapdoor. " Take care! " cried a woman's voice. " Take care!

My pigeons!" She who spoke had just rung the necks of a few
pigeons and laid them exactly where this grimy, panting figure
emerged. He was dazzled by the daylight, he did not see who
it was: Fleurette, a girl he had loved when he was eighteen and
she seventeen.

She was not alarmed at this apparition out of the earth, but
she also did not recognize him; partly because of his disordered
state, but life, too, had altered him, and he had grown a beard.
His kindly, shining eyes would have indeed revealed him, but
they were half-closed and blinking, so Fleurette did not recognize him. Her own face had broadened, and her figure likewise. She clapped her hands to her hips and upbraided him for
scattering her pigeons. He laughed, flung her some jaunty answer, and went to the pool to wash himself. Another pool had
once mirrored their faces side by side and swallowed up their
parting looks and their last tears. " When we are quite old this
stream shall remember us, even after we are dead." True it is;
in after years people will point to the pool and say: there, because Fleurette so loved him, she drowned herself. Even then
she was conceived of as dead, because so fine a love should
live on for itself, without the lovers, whom time must so surely
transform.

Transformed he was indeed. He had washed his face and
brushed the dirt off his shoulders, without once looking round,
while she watched that dishevelled object change into a fine
gentleman. Now he would mount the stairway to the lady in
her love-nest, where the walls were painted with strange beings,
half woman and half fish, and angels' heads, some smiling and
some stern, peered down from the cornices. In the centre of
the ceiling of that little chamber shone the sun, for Christ is
the sun of righteousness, as it is written and as Fleurette has
read. She picked up her pigeons. At that moment Henri turned,
but she did not look up. The air above them thrilled with words
forgotten. Bright is the sky, silvery the light, and the summer
evenings are like velvet. Once again they stand alone in life, here
among the farm buildings. Who was that strange girl bending
down there? He might pick her up and carry her behind the

barn. But no, he might be noticed from a window. He hurried to the house: she went into the kitchen with her pigeons. The yard remained deserted, but the air still thrilled with words forgotten — "Are you happy with me? " " I was never so happy." " Then remember me, however far you may ride — and the little room where we loved and the scent of flowers came through the window." "You are seventeen, Fleurette." "And you eighteen, my dear." " When we are quite old — "

The voices of labourers approached. And the air thrilled no more.

IN THE GARDEN

It was noteworthy that the attempt on the Governor's castle proved disastrous to his deputy. The King of France was furious and would not forgive him, so it was learned in Nérac. Though it may well have been the failure that in the end cost the unlucky Villars his place. The nobles declared against him — not only in Guyenne, but in the neighbouring province of Languedoc, where the Governor, Damville, made a pact with Henri. Damville was a Moderate, one of the " Politicals," and eager to reconcile the two creeds, though such dealings, if mistimed, might, alas, cost a man his place! Villars was like to lose his, for striking too hard from the other side. He was harassed and hounded down by one of the most powerful men in the province, Marshal Biron, who was working against Villars more venomously than even Henri knew, though he was kept well informed.

Meantime Henri had several matters of concern. He must prevail on the court to recall his deputy; and he wanted his sister with him, and his Queen of Navarre, in whose absence he began to grow uneasy. Indeed, he really yearned for Margot; old love never quite abandons the body that received it. And, of course, he bethought him that Catholic subjects could not fail to mark the King of France's sister at his side; even the gates of Bordeaux would be opened! As for his little Catherine — his heart went out to her! She should marvel at his orangery, teach his parrots to talk, and listen to his birds, such songs as she had never heard: birds from the Canaries! Besides, the little soul was a strict Huguenot and would improve his reputation with his fellows of the Religion; for, alas, it was not very good.

That was, of course, because of his affairs. Ah well, there are many that reward our love, each in her own fashion; one with the sumptuous fragrance of her, and another with her sweetness and her charm. One little lady has a suspicious mother, and Henri must ride through the nights to a meeting-place at dawn. A rustic's lass is easier had. Then there was the charcoal-burner's wife in the woodland hut, where the court hunting parties met. She loved her King, and he loved her so hotly that the whole hunt, masters and men, had to wait in the rain while he lay with her within. These quick fires — they are soon burned out. Are they truly? Twenty years later the King ennobled that same charcoal-burner. He would still remember that woodland hut, he still had the vision of those joys. It was woman that bound him to his people. In her he knew them, in her he made them his; and he was grateful.

To fetch his sister out of Paris he sent no other than his faithful Fervaques. That worthy gentleman had betrayed him, but he had since betrayed the King of France as well, and none is so sure as a man whom no one trusts. Fervaques did actually bring her safely all the long way to Nérac, but she did not stay there long; her brother himself escorted her to Pau, where faith was strict and conduct too — even Henri's when he went there. At Pau, where they had been brought up by their mother, he appeared in his sister's company alone, under the trees of their childhood. There stood a beloved little house embowered in tall foliage; there too had Jeanne often taken refuge, when she longed to sit in the cool shade with her two children, and to her inward ear the breath of God seemed to murmur in the murmuring leaves. Nature was one of the many mysteries of the Eternal. Gardeners served God, no less than priests, though with other rites. Chantelle was the name of his gardener; Henri was much attached to the man, and had built him a handsome cottage in the grounds. But the main avenue in the park was called the Avenue of Madame; which was Jeanne. And there her children were now pacing up and down, arm in arm. The sister was thinking, and these were her thoughts.

"We are late, and it is growing dark. The falling shadows deepen, and lift the dreaming garden outside space and time. Even the stone lady pouring water from her jar is steeped in the colour of the evening foliage, she no longer is a mere white and shining statue. As Christians we are all equal; and more than ever in this hour. I, his sister, must regard him as my lord, but scarcely in this garden. Shall I speak? The world touches me so little, and I fear it. But I am drawn to speak to him about the ball at Agen." "Brother!"

"Well, sister?"

"I hear such evil rumours."

"You mean the ball at Agen."

At this she was taken with such trembling that she stopped. Her lame foot was usually but little noticed, and she could dance. But she could not then have walked without a limp. "Of course I know the story," said her brother quickly — "they spread it to drive me and my Protestant noblemen out of Agen. I had first thought to live there, after escaping from the Louvre. The priests at once made a set at us from the pulpit. And Monsieur de Villars started slanders. But the worst were malicious inventions by the Catholic ladies themselves. You must know, sister, that many of your sex take great delight in matters that really never happened."

"Spare me such reflections, brother, and tell me this: is it true that at the ball at Agen, when the hall was full of ladies, you and your gentlemen put out the lights?"

"No; though there was a time when the hall seemed to grow somewhat darker. I dare say a good many of the candles burned down at once. But candles are sometimes blown out in mere high spirits; the ladies may have blown them out themselves!"

This made Catherine angry. "You lie too much. Deny a little less, and I might believe a little more." It was no guileless, girlish voice that spoke so, with the shrill lift on the final syllables. Henri seemed to be listening to his mother's cold, inexorable utterance: indeed, darkness had now fallen, and for all that he could see, she who spoke might well have been his mother; he stood before her like a boy.

" I dare say most lads of mine wanted to kiss the ladies in the dark. I have heard none boast they outraged them. True, the occasion offered, and they were in the mood. And then, of course, no one would own to such doings when the scandal had begun."

" Indeed! " said Jeanne and Catherine. " Is this the conduct you should teach your countrymen? No, you chose to show them what you had learned in the Louvre among the enemies of the Religion."

He gasped and could not speak. And now she struck at him in person. " 'Tis not only that some of those outraged ladies died of fear and shame — you have other sins upon your soul: what of the women you have debauched as you ride about this land? I will not name them nor reckon their number, you know them too well. Henri, learn to love God, not women."

He stood silent, knowing that he must endure the sermon to the end.

" First, we must learn to exercise our hearts in obedience to the Lord. It is at the end that we must needs begin; but, in fulfilment of the whole duty of humanity, eyes and hands and feet and arms and legs — all must do their part. Cruel hands are the sign of an evil heart, and shameless eyes bespeak corruption."

So she continued, with much eloquence and fervour. Princess Catherine received letters from Geneva and kept them in her mind — though it was not long to be her fate to live according to such precepts. Henri fell to weeping in the darkness. He wept easily, even over what could not be altered and what indeed he had no mind to alter. It was not only the thought of what he was that stirred his tears, but of what might befall his little sister, whose nature was so nearly akin to his. With all her hot piety the poor soul fought against her passion for her cousin Henri Bourbon, who was at that moment hunting the wild boar. But let him appear, and the die would be cast indeed, before Catherine even knew. It was the end of her girlish innocence that struck at Henri's heart. And yet his sister's innocence should some time end. Partly from pity, partly from acquiescence in a woman's lot, he flung his arms about her and stopped her noblest sentiment with a kiss. Then he led her into the house.

Since all affection, even between kindred, and every flush of feeling, have their money value, next morning Catherine was presented by her brother with a little town which had hitherto refused to open its gates; he had to storm it first. Gifts, indeed, she was to receive in plenty — but in after days, when her royal brother was so circumstanced that he could make such gifts. Seven hundred fine pearls on one occasion, and a heart richly set with diamonds; what they cost being known to the Treasury alone. But the hours at Pau were numbered. The rich furniture in the great castle was once more enveloped in its wrappings; Henri always thought it the most splendid he had ever seen. He did not touch the crown jewels of Navarre in times when he had not so much as a spare shirt. To horse! He must ride forth where there was trouble to be met. There was anxious news, too, about Margot. Her brother Francis, who wanted to make for Flanders, she had let down from her window by a rope, then burned the rope in her chimney-piece and nearly set fire to the Louvre. Then she, too, departed to Flanders — where there were some very queer doings at the moment; very queer indeed, my lads! said Henri to his Council.

THE PRIVY COUNCIL

The members of the Council entered the castle two by two. The double flight of steps enabled those who were something less than friends to mount it on opposite sides. Between the two arms of the stairway a spring leapt from the wall into a semicircular basin. The marble balustrade curved so elegantly upwards that none could forbear to lay a hand on it, nor the eye fail to linger over the simple carvings with which a mason's chisel had so lovingly enriched the stone. But half-way up, the arms joined, the stairway broadened into a ceremonial approach to a royal castle. A clatter of young footsteps and a sound of merry voices heralded a throng of Councillors as they dashed across the upper court and turned to the right, up a few stairs, and through a pillared gallery that ran along the whole front of the building, the capitals of which were embossed with images of ancient legends. The doors of the rooms stood open, and the day was bright. All hurried into the largest room, gathered in excited groups, laughed, embraced, or turned contemptuously away — all waiting for their Prince.

In the shot-proof wall, otherwise windowless, was set a niche that served as guard-post for the sentinel. Between his iron bars the soldier looked down into the outer court, and over the ramparts to the countryside. From the town gate a road stretched away into a distance from which enemies might come. Peace and safety dwelt on both banks of the Baïse, on the hither side and beyond the bridges, which were called the Old Bridge and the New Bridge. One led to the placid park of La Garenne, and the other linked the two quarters of the town. Below the castle the townsmen dwelt for shelter. On the farther side the gentlemen of the court had settled, since a court had come to Nérac. Hand-workers, shopkeepers, and servants gathered round the strong houses of the great; thus streets arose, narrow winding alleys, a city in little, through which sped gurgling brooks and where children played. They clambered shrieking up the high Old Bridge, while the older folk plodded down it; and across the mirror of its open arch, deep down in the water, passed the shadows one by one — of all that lived there.

At the top of the castle staircase, on a curved stone bench, sat two gentlemen awaiting Henri. The one in the travelling-cloak was Philippe Mornay, who thought Henri foolhardy to ride abroad alone, in the dusk of evening and in time of war. For it was war once more. The Peace of Monsieur had not held. The King of Navarre had sent his diplomats in search of allies, but most had refused the invitation as best they could. One was a cousin of the murdered Coligny — Montmorency, who had himself lain, nearer to death than life, in the Bastille. But that portly gentleman was too lazy to be vengeful — too lazy, as Mornay put it, to do his duty by the faith. " The Lord spews forth lukewarm service," said the Huguenot — and proceeded to set forth why all those who merely drew profit from the faith and were not great enough to serve its cause must be brought low. Mornay had thrown over the Duke of Anjou, who was heading blindly after kingdoms for himself. Now after many perils and adventures he had encountered a Prince of whom he meant to make a trial, though that Prince had hitherto led an all too careless life. But the issue did not stand on character, it was a man's mission that would make him prevail. God was stronger than the passions of his chosen instruments. The pious Mornay was really not at all disquieted that Henri should be late; for he was under strong escort.

" You were captured on your journey hither? " asked Mornay's companion.

" But I was not recognized," replied Mornay, with a lift of his shoulders, quite convinced that his enemies had been stricken by timely blindness. " It happened thus, Monsieur de Lusignan. We were looking at the ruins of your ancient house, and the moonlight was so magical that fairy-tales seemed true. There in old days your ancestor met the fairy Melusine and had from her those joys and griefs that women have dispensed to men in every age. And that fairy must have bewitched us, for twenty armed men were on us before we could cross the ramparts. However, a man can always announce himself as what he is not, if so be he does not look a Huguenot."

The other could not contain his laughter. A man who looked like Philippe Mornay! It was not only that he wore a plain white collar and dark garments; his whole bearing and expression proclaimed him what he was. There was no challenge in his eyes nor any self-concern. They looked forth calmly and sagaciously from beneath an unclouded brow into the consciences of men. And that brow would remain serene until the end, though the face grew drawn and marred with suffering and sorrow, because Mornay stood in honesty before his God. But that was not yet. Meanwhile he was sitting on a curved stone bench, youthful and high-hearted, awaiting the Prince, whose rising fortunes were to be his also. Mornay had no fore-

boding of the words that in years to come he was to utter in
farewell to his sovereign:

" We have to announce a terrible calamity. Our King, the
greatest King that has appeared in Christendom for five centuries — "

Bright was the sky, silvery the light, and the velvet dusk was
at hand. Henri came out of his garden and crossed the New
Bridge, his arms laden with flowers. The pair by the staircase
rose, and he shouted to Mornay: " What news? " and though
there was no good news, he gave him a flower. " Someone picked
it for me," said he, with an unconscious jerk of his shoulder
towards the pavilion by the river; and they knew who had picked
that flower. At that moment there was a sudden uproar in the
castle above. " My Huguenots murdering my Catholics! " cried
Henri, and ran up into the courtyard.

Monsieur de Lavardin had indeed fallen upon Monsieur de
Rosny, a young gamecock who enraged his Captain by some
outrage upon discipline. The others were shouting too; the
room was in a tumult, though no one seemed to know what the
quarrel was about. Fortunately Henri knew. At a place called
Marmande, Captain Lavardin had sent Ensign Rosny up into
a perilous position. Henri himself had to extricate the young
man and his handful of arquebusiers, and even so, though they
brought off their only cannon and two culverins, they had to
abandon the ammunition. Lavardin could not bear to be reminded that he had made the desperate attempt on Marmande
against the King's advice. And now Rosny had stirred up the
sorry business. " You young nincompoop! " roared his infuriated
Captain. Whereupon Rosny leapt upon him, while some egged
on the combatants, and others tried to part them. It seemed
scarce possible that six or eight people could create such a hubbub
in one room — though it was little more than a riot of high
spirits and good humour. Henri appeared, still laden with his
flowers, and dashed into the mêlée. He bade Rosny stand; and
told him that he would serve no more with the best company and
the best of captains, and that he, the King, would take him in
pity for his youth. Rosny gracefully submitted; indeed, he had

reckoned on that issue. His usual calm and sagacious air returned. The King embraced Lavardin, and he too was pacified. There was then much vehement talk of some little town where it was said there had been outrages committed. The King's army was for ever ranging the country, exacting vengeance and enforcing peace and order. Every member of that Council could speak his mind to the King, and some upbraided him for not pressing on the war. His cousin Condé was much more active and complained of Henri's indolence. " It is my country, not his," said Henri, half under his breath. Only Mornay heard. The Council were talking all at once. But Henri was heeded by them all when he made mention of the Queen of Navarre. He sat on the table with one leg dangling and the other underneath him, chewing at the stem of a rose, and spoke with quick intakes of the breath as though from inward laughter — though his mood was far from one of gaiety.

The Queen of Navarre had first helped her brother Monsieur to escape, and then she hurried before him into Flanders to support his cause. Dangerous work — in a land that the Spaniards held beneath their heels, the heaviest heel being that of Don John of Austria. " The Queen, my wife, tricked them all by feigning illness and saying she needed to take the waters at Spa. Before the Spaniards — who are, you must know, blockheads; they walk like men on stilts and hold their heads as stiff and straight as their own starched ruffs, and never see beyond their noses — before the Spaniards had noticed anything, Her Majesty had got the whole country in a ferment. Whereupon Don John hurriedly removed her, the very day after he had given a ball in her honour. But there was no help for it; her own brother, the King of France, had denounced her to the Spaniards from fear of Don Philip."

This evoked a burst of wrathful laughter and a few curses. Henri added darkly, through his teeth: " No matter. My poor Margot held high state as a Queen — until she was expelled. She rode in gilded coaches and silken litters and bowed graciously to the enraptured Hollanders. She was indeed enraptured with herself. Margot is not happy in her family. She should come to me. I need her here. But, alas, her royal brother forbids her to live with a Huguenot." The last words he spoke for all to hear; but he noticed that, in the general uproar, only Mornay had really listened to what he said.

" Monsieur de Mornay," he said, " sad it is, but the King of France detests his sister, and she may not see us."

Mornay replied that Her Majesty the Queen of Navarre desired nothing so much since her unlucky journey to Flanders. " Her royal brother is merely turned against his sister by the League. The Duke of Guise — "

" Let us go out," said Henri sharply, and he went out of the room in front of Mornay. They walked with great strides, as was Henri's habit, up and down the corridor. The Ambassador, who had just returned from the neighbourhood of Paris, knew the latest murders in the Louvre. Guise kept the King in fear and apprehension. The King now constantly took refuge in a cloister, not merely in dread of the next world. Apart from his own death, he feared the extinction of his House, for the Queen had given him no son.

" And never will," put in Henri quickly. " The Valois will get no more sons." He did not say from whom he had that knowledge and that certainty: from his mother. Mornay looked at him and reflected that God had rightly brought him to this Prince. In a flash he realized what Henri was — no miller of Barbaste, no pursuer of petticoats, nor a captain of soldiery, but the future King of France, and conscious of his destiny. He dissembled, both from guile and because he had time to wait; for youth endures. But he never forgot. At this revelation of his Prince's heart, Mornay bowed low. There was no more need of speech, the bond between them was established. Henri waved a hand towards the park of La Garenne; they would meet there next time unobserved.

At that moment they were interrupted by those veteran friends, d'Aubigné and du Bartas, who used their privilege of breaking in upon their King at any time. They crossed the courtyard at a run, dashed up the steps, and began to talk at once. But their news did excuse their agitation. The Marquis de Villars had been dismissed. The failure of his attempt upon his Governor's castle had brought the deputy into disfavour with the King of France. In his place came Marshal Biron, who most certainly deserved the post, at least in the opinion of Agrippa. He hoped for great things from the newcomer, whose generous soul had led him to use his influence at court against his sinister predecessor. Du Bartas, of a different temperament, expected an even darker intriguer than the last. The Council was divided between these views when the matter was made known.

The more sagacious, such as Rosny and La Force, the latter a Catholic, regarded Biron as little more than an ill-conditioned brute; in a burst of fury he had once slashed off the muzzle of a horse, which spoke ill for him. Lavardin and Turenne, of opposite creeds, agreed in this, that Marshal Biron deserved at least some confidence. He belonged to one of the first families in the province of Guyenne; he would assuredly have to keep the peace. So much might well have been believed. But while the discussion proceeded, Henri read the royal decree, which his old friends had given him. Therein it stood recorded that the Marshal received the power and warrant of supreme command in all the province and land of Guyenne, in the absence of the King of Navarre. " As though I were absent — as a prisoner in the Louvre, for instance! " thought Henri. He shivered and then flushed; and silently he rolled up the document.

MORNAY: OR VIRTUE IN ESSENCE

Very early next morning Mornay went into the park of La Carenne. No guards were yet on duty. If the King came, their meeting would be quite secret, and what they said would be known by none. Mornay hoped that the King would seize such an occasion and come alone. Mornay had no small opinion of his influence, wherever he had made it felt, in England, in Flanders, in the King's business, or in the establishment of peace. And while he waited in the park, while the birds twittered and trilled, he pondered on the glory of God, who has set the innocent domain of nature on the confines of this evil world;

through His Son they were indeed united, for Jesus, like us, departed in sweat and in blood, and, like us, He carried within Him the canticle of earth, though a more exalted one than ours. Mornay noted this on his tablets, to show to his wife Charlotte Arbaleste. For three years they had been married, though often and long parted by the husband's continual missions to raise money — and yet more money, for the princes of the earth. Mornay was more conversant with reckonings of debt and interest than with discourses upon life and death. But he had composed some by the desire of his betrothed, when they met at Sedan in the Dukedom of Bouillon, classic haunt for refugees.

They first met in the stress of life and death, two years after Saint Bartholomew, and each escaped it only to live on, poor and persecuted for the honour of God. Charlotte's possessions were confiscated, as her father and her first husband were Protestants. Mornay's friends counselled him to attempt a more advantageous match; but he replied that money and possessions were the last things that a man should think of in the matter of marriage; the true matters of concern were character, godliness, a reputation. With all these was Charlotte blessed; moreover she had a clear head, a knowledge of mathematics, a steady eye, and skill in the art of painting. She was kind to the poor, and even dreaded by the great for her stern attitude towards evil. Most of all she loved to manifest her burning zeal for God and for His church. All this, not money and possessions, had she brought with her into marriage. Mornay felt indeed rich when she told him that her father had once heard Master Martin Luther dispute with other doctors at Strassburg. Now, Martin Luther never was in Strassburg, as Mornay had discovered. But if something her father had said had become transfigured in her memory, her noble ardour must not be shaken, and Mornay said nothing. Such was his marriage with the Huguenot dame.

" Aha! So you guessed my meaning and have risen early," said a sudden voice — Henri had slipped into the arbour unseen and sat down beside Mornay. And he added quickly: " What think you of my Privy Council? "

" It is not privy enough — and it is far too noisy," replied

Mornay, with the mask-like expression he had learned from Henri.

" Much nonsense was talked about Marshal Biron, eh? He is my friend. Surely you think so? "

" Sire, if he were your friend, the King of France would not have appointed him. And as your deputy he will certainly not long remain your friend."

" Ha! " said Henri. " They told me you were no fool, and they were right. We have had a good deal to learn, eh, Mornay? Yours was a sorry life in exile."

" And yours, too, in the Louvre."

Their eyes hardened. The moment passed; and Henri went on: " I must take care or the court will have me under lock and key again. Read that! " And he gave Mornay Biron's decree of appointment: " Power and warrant for Marshal Biron — "

" In the absence of the King of Navarre," continued Mornay after him.

" Yes," repeated Henri, with a faint shudder. " Never again! " he added. " Twenty horses would not drag me to Paris."

" You will enter it again as King of France," Mornay assured him, with a wave of the hand that no courtier could have bettered. Henri shrugged his shoulders.

" Guise and his League are too powerful. I'll confide in you; he is now too powerful even for the King of Spain, and Don Philip, as a safeguard against Guise, has caused secret offers to be made to me. He wants to marry my sister Catherine, no more and no less. I myself am to have an Infanta. He will have me divorced from the Queen of Navarre — in Rome, where he can make his will prevail."

Mornay eyed him with a look that probed his conscience.

" What can I do? " said Henri gloomily. " I must accept. Is there any other way out? "

" I know but one," replied Mornay, very stiff and stern; " you must never forget what you are: a French Prince and the champion of the faith."

" Shall I then reject this noble offer from the mightiest sovereign in the world? "

"Not merely reject it, but report it to the King of France."

"Just what I have done!" cried Henri with a laugh, as he leapt to his feet. The Huguenot's face lit up; they fell into each other's arms.

"Ha! You are still the old Mornay of those days when we were riding north to Paris. You loved extremes, you were always a rebel, and discoursed of the dust and mould that lurked in kingly purple. But even then you were never imprudent, and you did nòt bid farewell to fortune when you escaped the night of Saint Bartholomew."

He clapped him on the belly, in token of his recognition and delight. "The evasion of death — 'tis the principle of all diplomacy — and also of the art of war." So saying, he took Mornay by the arm and marched him off at great strides, of which that avenue measured a full four thousand.

Henri and his Ambassador often met in the early morning unobserved. The real reason of the King's liking for Mornay's counsels remained unknown, nor could any secret watcher have discovered it. It was that Mornay regarded Henri as the future King of France; but he had more than the mere evidence of his inner consciousness, which was all that Henri saw. The condition of the world made it very plain that this realm, and in all the West this realm especially, must be moulded into unity by a Prince of the Blood. Not France alone; Christendom was "sighing for a sovereign." And this could not be the decaying Philip, with his crumbling empire, in dissolution like himself. Such states can only persist by incessantly striving to break down the freedom of the few remaining free nations. But thereby they do but hasten their own ruin. Mornay foreboded for Philip, before a death that must be shameful, the sternest chastisement at the hands of God. This he merely thought and did not utter. He coolly pointed out that the blind expansion of a power and its lust for dominion could bring no good. The policy of maintaining such a realm as this in tumult was — Mornay called it neither godless nor criminal, though he meant as much. He spoke, indeed, of the logic of events; and of truth, for truth made manifest cannot fail to conquer.

All in all, it was Mornay's concern that not Henri's feelings only, but his reason and his understanding should foretell his destiny. He must know himself in alliance with the truth, the truth of fact and the truth of morals; one neither precedes the other nor can take its place. We are, as men, creations of God, we are the measure of things, and nothing is real but what we recognize by the law within us. Such high thinking, as exalted and profound as any mystic creed, must surely win allegiance from a Prince who was himself its centre point. Prophecies are always alluring, even at six o'clock of a morning in a park with the frost still on the grass; indeed, Henri would commonly have slept full four hours longer, for his light adventures did not usually end until far into the night. But he came, to hear sound commentaries on himself and on his enemies.

His way to the throne, so he was told, was to be made in marvellous fashion as the ally, nay, even as the saviour, of the last Valois, who had heretofore detested him. But Mornay in this matter held to the precept: "Love your enemies," which could not indeed everywhere hold good, as denying human destiny. But it was expedient to mark the cases where it did hold good. Henri was by his own nature prone to love his enemies, to win them over to his cause, and even prefer them to his friends. Perhaps, indeed, the alliance with the last Valois dwelt within his mind as a presentiment, and only later, when achieved, he imagined that Mornay had thus early called things by their exact names. In this wise Henri learned also of the destruction of the Spanish Armada off the English coast ten years before the event. When it happened, he truly believed that it had been actually predicted to him in the park of La Garenne by Mornay. The Ambassador had perhaps used the word, whether he were referring to a fleet or an empire. But the light of his discourse had never been extinguished in Henri's mind. For understanding is a light, and virtue spreads its radiance. Villains know nothing.

Henri took counsel of Virtue in the person of Mornay, which was pleasant so long as Virtue said: "You are young, and you are by nature chosen. Fine opportunities fall in with your fine dispositions; indeed, for you they are created. Until the hour for greater deeds shall strike, make yourself the undisputed master of this province and of your party. Take time; here the sky is bright, ten years are like a day." So far Virtue spoke most pleasantly.

But Virtue began to say, and indeed indited the same in a memorandum, that the King of Navarre should be dressed by eight o'clock at latest and hear his chaplain read prayers. Then he should go to his cabinet and listen to the reports of all his agents. No more uproarious Councils, where the Councillors laugh and quarrel and tell stories. It was Mornay's wish that Henri should only frequent such of his Councillors as were virtuous; but who were they, save Mornay? Henri personally must set an example to his House, and not only to his House but to the kingdom of Navarre — nay, more, to all Christendom. Mornay would not tolerate any faults in his chosen Prince. All must find in Henri what they most desired but had never met with: Princes — good-fellowship; judges — justice; and the people — the will to ease their burdens. The Prince must take care to comport himself with dignity, even with magnificence; but he must be particular to give no opening for slander. Not even his own good conscience must bring him satisfaction; there is always a task ahead. And this member of the Council, who took his title seriously, launched into his Prince's morals.

"Permit your faithful servant yet one more word, Sire. The open amours to which you devote so much time are now ill-timed. The hour demands, Sire, that your affections should be centred upon the whole of Christendom, and especially upon France."

"How like Catherine!" thought Henri. Learn to love God, not women; those were her words. And here was another Huguenot now pestering him on the matter. No, the voice of Virtue was no longer pleasant. It had spoken too soon and claimed from the young Prince a decorum which was then suited neither to his character nor to the state of his turbulent little province. But this point, and almost this alone, always remained Henri's weakness. When he was already the accepted heir to the throne of France, Monsieur de Mornay's obdurate virtue still urged the selfsame counsels, in and out of season, and roused him to mockery and anger; then at last they ceased. Life continued uncriticized, Virtue's task was abandoned, and a man of middle age began to be borne down by passions, by which he tried to cozen himself that he still was young. Thus it will be, Henri. Youth and love will one day have become the delusions of a still insatiate heart; and even Mornay will be silent. Be glad that he speaks today!

Instead of which he took his revenge. In his Council, which he obstinately left unaltered, the King observed, in Mornay's presence, that he owed more thanks to the Catholics than the Huguenots. The latter served him from selfishness or zeal for the faith. But the former got no profit from their service and damaged their own faith to help their master's fortunes. So unjust was the comparison that even the Catholic gentlemen murmured. But Henri flung aside all decency and kindness; in his envoy's presence he mimicked the flappings of a raven. The Protestants were commonly called ravens, because they wore dark clothes, chanted psalms in none too pleasing voices, and had a name for marauding habits. When the king indulged in this visible insult — he continued the performance furtively in a corner — all pretended to have noticed nothing, and even the Catholic gentlemen covered up the matter with loud talk. Whereupon Henri disappeared.

Once outside, he burst into tears — from shame and mortification at his attitude to virtue, as embodied in the Huguenot, Mornay. He indeed hardened his heart, he received the Ambassador no more in private, and especially not in the park of La Garenne at six o'clock in the morning, for he did not rise until ten. But he still thought of Mornay, though he did not see him, and compared him with all the others at the court, mostly to their disadvantage. Thus he pondered: "There are many sorts of friends: d'Aubigné, who used me to escape out of the Louvre. Du Bartas — he saved my life in a common tavern, not to speak of d'Elbeuf — ha! I loved d'Elbeuf, who watched over my every movement. But what were they? Soldiers, brave men by nature; no one made a boast of bravery, nor did it so much as touch upon the confines of virtue. And now take any of the best men on my Council; what is left of them when balanced against Mornay? " All were marred by vices, and many of them ugly vices, which Henri was all the more ready to forgive. Friendship and royalty had power to wipe them away. But none possessed the knowledge, lofty and profound, of the great Huguenot. Doubt was not to be wiped away.

Friend Agrippa was a sore strain, he taxed the King's generosity; his name was best known in the Treasury at Pau. One day he was talking to another nobleman about the King, so loud that Henri could not fail to hear. The other had not listened, and Henri himself repeated what Agrippa had said: " He says I am a stingy brute, and no one upon earth is such a monster of ingratitude." Another day a half-starved dog was brought to the King; he had loved the beast and then forgotten it. On its collar was engraved a sonnet by Agrippa; it began:

> *Citron: once slept he, in a better day,*
> *Upon your bed: now on the hard highway.*
> *Your faithful hound discovers, like your friends*
> *'Tis thus a king's and master's favour ends.*

Henri changed colour as he read. His recognition of a wrong that he himself had done was quick and fierce, though he might soon forget it. He was much more inclined to find an excuse for the transgressions of others. He thought only of poor Agrippa's services and not of his hot poetic temper. Young Rosny was much more fond of money; he never spent it, he added to his store. He had come into his father's estate, was now a Baron, and had entered into possession of lands up in the North on the Norman border. When Henri had to pay his soldiers, Baron Rosny sold a wood, therewith resolving that Henri's victorious campaigns should recoup him tenfold. He built himself a house at Nérac, beyond the Old Bridge, for good business demands leisurely pursuit. Moreover, his Prince had to keep out of his way when blunders had been made; Rosny then became abusive. He was neither vassal nor subject, he told Henri to his face, and he was in a mind to go, of which in truth there was no notion, if only because of the house. Whereto Henri replied that the way lay open, and he himself would find better servants — which was likewise not seriously meant. As Rosny had turned out, he was the best; when he went for a time to Flanders to visit a wealthy aunt, for her money's sake he pretended to be a Catholic.

Of two ladies he chose the less lovely, the richer, and married her. The Baron fetched his young wife out of his castle in the North, while the plague was ravaging the land. The wife sat in a forest in her closed coach, and from fear of infection would not let her husband approach. Nothing perturbed the Baron. The plague and all lurking perils — he marched through them with a kind of tempestuous pride. When the danger was past, he laid aside his cuirass and returned to his accounts. He fought through every battle with his King. But when the kingdom had been established, Henri found a great Finance Minister ready to his hand.

Here they both were, still young and at the outset of their fortunes; together they stormed unruly little towns and risked their lives for a flag or a sodden trench; but the lucky Rosny always covered his outgoings. When at last a place was sacked, who was it that pocketed four thousand crowns for saving the former lord, an old man, from the fury of the soldiery? He loved honour and fame — and money very near as much. One day Henri was cheering Mornay with the prospect of times when they could both be rich. He did so purposely, to tempt him. Mornay merely said: "I serve, and I am already rich."

Whereto Henri replied in a deliberately acrid tone. "I care little for your sacrifices, Monsieur de Mornay. I am thinking of my own."

"They are offered, not to men, but to God." The answer was modest, and withal a reprimand. Henri changed colour.

Shortly afterwards their little troop was ambushed from a wood, and by some cavalry of Marshal Biron, who outnumbered them. The King of Navarre and his handful of men could do nothing but turn and make for the open, raked by musket-shots. When it was safe to draw rein, the sole of one of the King's boots was seen to have been shot away. The King stretched out his foot, which was quite uninjured, for someone to draw on another boot. Mornay did so. Henri did not see his face. Mornay stood with back bent, and blood oozed out of his neck. " Mornay! You are wounded! "

" A mere scratch — when I consider the danger that Your Majesty escaped. If you wish to reward me, Sire, do not expose your life thus heedlessly again! "

Henri shivered. The first reward for which Mornay had ever asked was this. Mornay looked up, his face already covered with blood and very pale. " We agreed upon Marshal Biron's ill intentions, Sire." Not a word more; but Henri could hear what was meant to follow — " when you received me alone and talked with me familiarly in the park of La Garenne "; and his heart beat faster. He said in a low tone:

" Tomorrow, at the same place and hour."

A Secret

Philippe Mornay slept little that night; neither did his conscience sleep. He had for long struggled inwardly to decide whether he should reveal a certain matter. The occasion was at hand, and his duty was by now insistent. While for a time his brain was confused by the fever from his wound, he saw his own self standing before the King and heard himself speak — quicker than his wont, and much more urgently. The King admitted all, even the abominable story about the miller's wife, a disgraceful and indeed a perilous affair. The King bowed his head in token of remorse, but lifted it again, as Mornay in his fevered dream longed to see him do. Far be it from him to shame his King. Even less was he minded to mar the memory of one person whom the King loved most. But, alas, it must be done, if the King was ever to be halted on the headlong path of his own passions. He must be made to see whither they led, and only one person could do that: the possessor of the secret.

" Lord! Deliver me from this duty! " cried Mornay in his fever; and his wandering thoughts at once fulfilled his prayer.

There was no longer need for him to reveal what tortured him so terribly, for the King knew it already. The inexplicable had happened; it was the King and no longer Mornay who was in possession of the fatal papers. He took them from his pocket, gave them to Mornay to read, and assured him that the knowledge of their secret had stayed him and saved him from ruin. He now realized, said the King, that even a dedicated life might be degraded by incontinence, so that the few that knew the secret thought of the dead lady with pity and dismay. Conceive then of the matter when a whole nation regarded its departed Queen as devout and pure. " I," said the King in the fevered man's dream, " will take this as a warning and do better. I pardon all that have followed their earthly nature. I myself have done so overmuch. But now there must be an end of it; that I promise, as the King."

When Mornay had received the King's promise, he fell more peacefully asleep — but awoke when it was time to go to La Garenne. His head was wholly clear, but at first he thought that the two documents, together with the secret, were really in the King's possession instead of in his own. He had to open his portfolio; and there they were. All was as before; the King knew nothing, and this grievous duty was still awaiting Mornay.

As had never happened before, he reached the avenue after the King. Henri was impatiently striding up and down. No sooner did he catch sight of Mornay then he led him to the bench, looked anxiously at his bandaged skull, and inquired as to the wound. A scrap of skin and hair had been carried away by the bullet, explained Mornay. The damage was slight, hardly deserving of the royal interest. " If it is Your Majesty's pleasure, let us speak of business."

" That will, indeed, suffer no delay," said Henri — but he hesitated before opening his financial straits. There was something strange about Mornay, something akin to fear. Henri decided that he must have had a bad night, and talked about the peasants, whose taxes must positively be eased. But how was the loss to be made good? And he cried, with a jesting air, though his heart indeed was heavy: " Would that I could imitate the late

Queen, my mother, who fined herself for the slightest wrong-doing. She paid a hundred pounds to the Treasury when she had forgotten to pray. My fines would come to rather more than those of my dear mother! "

Then Mornay mastered his fear. It had been a fear of men; and trust in God put it from him. He arose, and Henri looked at him curiously.

" The late Queen," said Mornay, clear and calm as ever, " was strict with herself in all matters, except in one alone. Her Majesty secretly contracted an unlawful marriage with Count Goyon, who was killed on the night of Saint Bartholomew. The Queen did so without the blessing of the Church, nor was it granted to her afterwards, as she would not publicly admit her sin. She was then forty-three, and the King your father had been dead for nine years. She had a son by Monsieur de Goyon."

Henri leapt to his feet. " A son! What fairy-tale is this? "

" Your audit-books, Sire, contain no fairy-tales. There you will find an entry of seventy-five livres for the maintenance of a child, named François Goyon, put out to board by the Queen on May 23rd, 1572."

" That was when she went to Paris — to arrange my marriage — and there died." Henri's voice quavered, and his eyes filled with tears. For the duration of a thought he saw a vision of a Jeanne magnified by these strange and manifold vicissitudes. Her son grew dizzy. The thought passed. His mood turned from pride to humiliation. " 'Tis a lie! " he cried, and his voice broke. " A forgery! A slander on a woman that cannot gainsay it! "

By way of answer Mornay handed him the two documents. " What are these! " Henri burst out. " Who dares to write down such a charge? " He looked at the signatures, which were those of de Bèze, the Genevan; then he read some passages, and at last he bowed to the overmastering truth. The most prominent members of the Consistorium certified in the name of the Reformed Church that the marriage had been improperly contracted. The two parties had pledged themselves to each other before two or three witnesses: a marriage of conscience, as it was indeed called, but in fact a marriage against conscience. The claims of good morals were ignored; the marriage was consummated without the knowledge and the approval of the Church — nay, the urgent wish and counsel of the Church had been contemned. The pastors had insisted in the name of the Lord that until the matter had been publicly arranged the parties should not meet, or if they must, but seldom, and for two or three days at most; even so they did but foster the scandal that it was essential to remove if they wished to escape the wrath of God. Failing this, the parties justly deserved to be excluded forthwith from Communion.

There it stood. Queen Jeanne was threatened with the highest penalty of the very Religion to which she had sacrificed everything: her peace and happiness, her strength, and even her life. Why? " If the evil is to persist, which God forbid, then the Church must take extreme measures. So great a scandal may not be tolerated by the Lord's Church." Then followed all the signatures — and they were of course genuine. One single question would have made sure of that. But the son of the humiliated Queen was not disposed to honour the pastors by making any such inquiry. They had acted from worldly considerations and not at the bidding of the Almighty; that was his impression — his first one, and he never lost it. The words of these ecclesiastics were: " Good morals, scandal, public arrangement " — words that proclaimed little of the spirit. Indeed, they did no more than maintain the privilege of those who lived in a society to watch and spy upon each other, to condemn and to acquit, but in all cases to give an overweening majority the power to compel. " We may not love without inspection," thought the son of the admonished Queen. " The comfort is that we are not allowed to die without much fuss and interference! " He made no sign; he had learned her art of silence — in the palace of the Louvre, and there he meant to be once more. The breath of freedom was stilled now that he knew his mother had been admonished in her own land because she loved. He curtly handed back the papers.

" Keep them. Or take them whence you fetched them."

" The papers," said Mornay, " were in the hands of Pastor

Merlin, who was with our revered Queen in her last hours. He had been charged by her to give them to me, so that her children should not read them."

"And now I have read them," was Henri's sole reply.

Mornay drew a slow, deep breath; then came a voice that rasped with the effort at self-mastery. "The Queen confessed to her minister that she could no longer maintain her continence, whereupon he secretly united her to Count Goyon. He knew it was no marriage, but he pitied her."

"Mornay!" shouted Henri — this was too much. What followed came in the toneless mutter of one stricken to the heart. "You are a raven — in a white cap. Your bandage and your wounds protect you, as you well know. I am powerless against a man who was wounded in my service yesterday; that feeling you abuse. I must hear how my mother was possessed by lewdness, as I am — and shall go the same way. That is your resolve, in case I should not heed you now. You bird of ill omen!" he shouted suddenly — turned, and strode away. His head was bowed, and tears were streaming down his cheeks.

Then followed days in which the two heard nothing of each other. The King rode against some turbulent little town, but he did not take Mornay. Between his battles and his labours, which were to make him forget his secret torment, Henri was none the less a prey to thoughts. She had been forty-three years old and could not be continent. And in the thick of the musketry fire her carefree son found himself longing for a bullet that might shorten the time in which he, like his mother, had still to suffer humiliation. But when he escaped the fire unhurt, he rejoiced, and laughed, and jested to himself about his pious mother, who none the less had had her share of what she fancied.

He needed to be always on the move, for on the spot he made the worst discovery — strange it was that he had never marked the sign of it before. The people told tales of how Queen Jeanne dealt with those who offered her resistance. If they did not turn Protestant, they disappeared in her castle at Pau, where there were dungeons, and Henri knew them; they were close by the dining-hall. His mother had been ruthless for the faith; but as she was ready to take any step to keep her marriage secret, like enough she had used these dungeons too to shut the mouths of those that knew of it. Hence, in her son's eyes, her aspect changed, and so remained. He remembered how he had once had a vision of her death-mask wholly altered, on the day when her last messenger had come. " They live on; the dead are but transformed. They are beside us, however fast we ride, and suddenly they turn us a new face: Do you recognize me? I do, mother! "

He recognized that she had grown in stature. This had been his first thought in that moment when he learned of her secret marriage. That thought had now taken a firm shape. Jeanne's stature had really been increased by her manifold vicissitudes — otherwise she was, as always, devout and brave and pure. For all this she had died, and for the passion of her later years. Death is good, death gives us right. " Monsieur de Goyon, you live! " Henri had once shouted in the great hall of the Louvre, after Saint Bartholomew, when he first met the murderers again. In his impotent wrath he had hurled a challenge to the dead, as though they had been present. " Monsieur de Goyon, you live! " — but he no longer lived, he was not in the hall, he lay in the well-shaft, carrion for the ravens. Today he had for the first time arisen, in the company of a woman he had known.

Meantime Mornay, too, fared none too well. He grieved to have given pain to his King; and he came to doubt whether any good had been done thereby. That disgraceful and perilous affair at the mill — he heard that it still continued; and it was this that had finally roused Mornay to make his secret known. He was also troubled to think that the King was now informed of the existence of a brother, whom he could not recognize; which was an offence against practical piety and decency. From such a view, Mornay blamed himself for having resuscitated the Count de Goyon. Henri, on the other hand, was disposed to be grateful. Stirred by very different feelings, they one day suddenly embraced — without a word spoken, for any words would have been ill-timed.

The Mill

But Henri rode to his mill. Often and often he made that journey unattended, along the river Garonne, over a bridge by one of the little old towns, and then across country. He plunged into the woodland, his horse's hoofs sinking deep into withered leaves. As he came out into the open he halted, and gazed at his mill on its wind-swept hilltop; was the miller anywhere about? It was to be hoped that the husband had departed with his wagon, for Henri wanted to be alone with the wife. He had indeed the right to come at will. He himself was the miller of Barbaste, as everybody knew. His tenant had not otherwise shown signs of guile; and yet the boor had settled here with a young and pretty wife. He knew his master and owed him for the rent. Against which was to be reckoned the young and pretty wife, on whom, however, the master was not to lay a finger. The fellow was as jealous as a Turk.

The miller of Barbaste was much in common talk. Older and kindlier folk really believed that he set the sails turning with his own hands and collected the flour that poured from the creaking millstones. He had not, in truth, tied up a single sack; that the tenant did, and with the wife did likewise. Master and husband understood each other excellently well; each knew what the other wanted, and each was wary and alert. In this fashion they had grown well acquainted. As often as the master came, the tenant invited him to dinner. It was never the wife that asked him, she had not the courage; it was the husband. He was aware of his advantage as an upstanding man, possessor of a coveted wife, and had not yet put his superiority sufficiently to proof. If only his master would fall into the trap!

That day Henri waited long at the edge of the wood, in the shadow of the trees; he could be seen from the mill. Its wings were turning heavily — but in the dormer window there was never a sign of the broad white face of the husband, who was usually surveying the countryside. Ah — there she was! She put her head out, peered across, and saw nothing; but on her face there was a sly and anxious look. He was puzzled. How well the dusting of flour on her skin suited those dark eyes of hers, and how slim she was! "Madelon!" He could safely call her name, they were some distance apart, and the wings of the mill were creaking; she did not hear him. Suddenly she started; his horse had whinnied; and before she vanished she made a sign towards the wood, that might mean: Come! I am alone.

Henri tethered his horse, walked across and round the hill, in case the tenant should appear. At last he entered. There before him was the great milling room, two walls piled high with sacks, against the third the millstone circling in its box, while through the fourth the wind whistled in. The milleress turned quickly as the door slammed in the draught; she had been shaking corn on to the millstone, or so pretended. Her wimple had slipped down, and two bright breasts rose and fell as she gasped in her surprise. "My lord!" she said with a curtsy, decorously holding up her dress. She was no peasant wench; she expressed herself in the formal speech and with a touch of irony, as soon as Henri appeared; nor was she to be moved to speak in any commoner fashion. It was a wile with which she kept him in play.

"Madelon," said Henri, glowing with impatience, "that prying man of yours has gone to sleep in a tavern. We have time. I'll tie up your scarf," instead of which he dexterously opened her dress. She did not resist, she merely repeated: "We have time. Why be in such a hurry, my lord? When you have had your desire, you will be up and away and leave me weeping out my eyes for you. But I love your company — because you talk so well," she added, and in her narrow eyes, although her expression remained respectful, there was gathered more mockery than had she been a Marshal's lady. In that moment Henri was adoring the whole sex; so he did not notice what she was at. She laid two flour sacks by the stack of full ones, thus providing a place to sit, or, if need was, to lie. There she disposed herself, and beckoned him to join her, thereby making herself mistress of the situation.

"My friend," said she, "now we can at once set to making love; but that is a business in which I do not care to be disturbed. And at this time of day, customers can hardly fail to come. As for the tavern, it may well be that someone has gone to sleep there; but it is not a thousand yards away, and there's many a man that suddenly awakes." All this was said by the lovely milleress in a high even voice, without a trace of confusion, although he was successfully engaged in slipping off her dress. Indeed, she seemed quite oblivious of all this, and, utterly intent upon her sage reflections, put her plump arm round his shoulder so that he could hear the better, and came to her main point.

"Next time I want us to be alone together from early until late, that we may give each other love and joy without fear that any stranger may interrupt, or anyone intrude on our delights. Shall it not be so, dear friend?"

"As far as I have understood your sermon," he blurted out, trying to push her backwards, but noticed that her arm, which she had laid so affectionately about him, was also her defence. As he had to abandon his purpose he laughed and gave heed to what she had said. "So your husband is to be put out of the way for one day. But how, my pretty Madelon? If that be your purpose, you must arrange it. You are the only one who can!"

"Not so, my lord. You are the only one." Whereupon she had to explain to him how it was to be done. "Only your officers, Sire, can hold a miller fast for a whole day."

"Do you mean — lock him up?"

No, that she did not mean. Documents were to be prepared, discussed at length, drafted several times by the clerks, and then towards evening signed by both sides. Both sides? Well, yes, one of the parties would be Michaud, tenant of this mill. "The other party?" The woman let a few moments pass, while she looked at her young King out of her slitted eyes — would he have the wit to guess? Men are so stupid when they are intent upon something else, thought Madelon. "You yourself, Sire, are the other party," she explained, lowering her voice and nodding gently, in pity for his state of mind. "Your notary will prepare the documents for you, while we two take our pleasure here."

At the last words she raised her voice again, and in it was a ring of blissful expectation — not without a placid touch of quiet scorn. In a flash, he understood; he was to be robbed.

These papers could contain nothing else than a transfer of the mill to her precious husband. That was to be the price for which the woman would forsooth bestow her favours; Michaud vainly hoped to come out of the affair without horns. For she wanted everything, thought Henri — the mill, love, but victory most of all; and victory over both men.

" I understand," he said curtly; and in that moment he desired no more of Madelon than what she had herself already given him: the inexhaustible guile of women, their art of making promises, the sinuous ruthlessness of those sweet hearts.

Next moment he thought: "You thief, I'll beat you yet "; and with this he pushed her backwards. She at once shrieked: "Michaud!" In that pile of sacks one was thrust out of its place, and through the gap crawled the tenant, and dropped sprawling on to Henri. To rid himself of this sudden incubus Henri had to show himself no less sinuous than the wife, while she tried to get him into her clutches. She indeed watched him with an appreciative eye and left her husband to his fate.

When the monarch was safely on his feet and stepped back, the rustic ducked and tried to run his bullet head into his adversary's belly. But the rustic was brought low, and Henri shouted imperiously: " Michaud! " — but without effect. The man's head was broken and he was near to fainting. He dragged himself to his feet by the aid of his master's arm and gripped it fast. Henri did not resist; he wanted the man to recover himself so that there might be no scandal. Wherefore Henri let Michaud drag him where he pleased. The man staggered about in a blind fury, but there was perhaps more purpose in that fury than Henri guessed, for they suddenly found themselves by the deep embrasure in which the millstone screw was turning. Just in time Henri realized what the man meant to do, and tripped him up, or he would have done it. Michaud would have flung him against the screw, which would have caught his hand and arm.

Terror is inventive of expression. Michaud rolled on the floor, emitting feeble howls, like the bray of donkeys in the distance. From time to time he peered upwards, to make sure again that nothing had happened to the King — whereupon he resumed his rolling and his howling. Madelon, more blanched than the flour, her head shaking like a crone's, had knelt down; her hands were trembling too much for her to clasp them in supplication.

Henri felt chilled, but with a burst of laughter he left the pair and ran off, laughing as he went; and with the flour he shook off the adventure. There are events that must remain in the memory just as confused and sudden as they happened; especially surprise attacks in war and love. He was quit of the affair without much honour, but with no more than a fright; he sat up and galloped away with loose rein. There were a great many mills in the land, and countless millers' wives. This mill would not see him again in a hurry. But he might look at it again one day.

The scene changes. Miller Michaud receives the King at his table, a king much aged, with a grey beard and a feather in his hat. The legend of his struggles for the realm has gone before him; and with him have entered all his fabulous love-affairs among his people. Five persons are seated round that table, all eating from a large earthenware dish, with hunks of bread beside them, and wine in tankards. It is evening, and in the draughty mill four flames are flickering above their heads from the spouts of a hanging lamp. Behind them is darkness, the light falls on their breasts; and the figures sit outlined with soft intensity against the night.

The King, with one elbow resting lightly on the table, holds his glass poised. Four people are holding glasses, all except the miller's wife. She, faded now and young no longer, leans towards her King, who has lost himself in dreams. But he sits with her alone at the two front corners of the table. Farther back, at a due distance, two young folks: the daughter and the miller's lad sit clinking glasses, gazing ardently into each other's eyes. At the farther end the miller raises his glass, waves his hat, and sings — the song of the lovelorn King. Grey hair has Michaud, loyally he looks upon his King, gaily sings his song, and well he knows that the King loves the people and the daughters of the people.

The song makes love yet more vivid to the young folks, but for the older ones it sheds a dark transfiguration upon their memories. The King, listening with half an ear, smiles like one for whom the best is over. Madelon of old days — that only you can understand. Was it lovely and delightful, for all the fraud and fury of the end? You both must know. Fleurette indeed, pure flower of the dew and dawn, in later days did not recognize her beloved — and she too has long since lain under earth.

THE ENEMY

The affair of the mill was as generally reported, as had been the ball at Agen. The Governor had then conceived his deputy as having been at the bottom of the story, and he did so now. Biron indeed surpassed his predecessor. It was to be assumed that the miller's wife had kept her mouth shut. Her husband might have got drunk and talked, but it was noteworthy how thoroughly his avowal had been turned to account. He was summoned before a court in Agen, the same town in which the first scandal had occurred. The Governor would have done his best to prevent the court from examining the miller; but the gates were shut in his men's faces, and the defenders took their stations on the walls.

On that day Marshal Biron was not in Agen; he would not so openly commit himself. He always avoided just those cities that closed their gates before the Governor, and the number of them increased. He gave no orders that could be proved against him. Henri would have found it hard to indict him for the armed attack that had cost him a boot sole, and Mornay a scrap of skin and some hair. Marshal Biron was an adept at intrigue, and he understood how to lurk in the half darkness; which seemed unusual for a quick-tempered man. He read a great deal; perhaps books had made him crafty, though reading leaves most people as innocent as when they began. The fact was that he was making a bad reputation for the Governor, and this not only in the matter of women. It was said that Henri did indeed seduce the wives, and also tried to make away with the husbands.

Many a noble trusted him no more, among them those whose property and persons he had saved from the marauders. A man of loose morals easily loses a reputation for justice, in spite of all that the Governor had done to deserve it.

Henri could not but notice his fame diminishing; and not merely the hero of gallant adventures, but the ruler and the soldier was affected. A little more and he would have sunk into a Prince without authority or sovereign dignity, an empty name and title; and Biron would have held the power alone. In the province of Guyenne it was his already, Henri had never succeeded in entering Bordeaux. The deputy, with his superior forces of cavalry and landsknechts, even ventured on incursions into the kingdom of Navarre. At that time Henri lay in his castle at Nérac like a hunted beast. Not once did he summon his Council, from fear of betraying his rage and therewith his weakness. His old friends did their best for him in that issue; to them at least Henri could show himself, and in them he could confide; even his impotent anger and his vain plans for revenge. In their presence he even allowed himself the tears of desperation.

One evening they were all occupied after their own fashion. Du Bartas was mumbling dark grievances, Agrippa d'Aubigné flatly urged that the war against the court of France should be resumed. In any event there was no doubt that Biron was merely acting in virtue of support from the court. It was not for nothing that the King of France had sent envoys to persuade Henri to become a Catholic once more. Even more significant was the demand that he should come to the court to fetch the Queen of Navarre in person. "Sire! My little finger tells me that she will not be seen here again in a hurry." Agrippa brought this out with great effect; from those few words flashed a vision of all the old perils of the Louvre — Madame Catherine bent over her stick, her features ever ominous of doom. These memories heaped horror on indignation, and Henri would in the end have gone so far as to order an attack. He would have advanced against his own deputy at the head of his troops. But the venture would have exploded on the way, as Henri would have recovered his good sense meanwhile. He was spared so false a step, although du Bartas earnestly commended it, in the face of human blindness and iniquity. Then Philippe Mornay spoke:

" Sire! You have an enemy: his name is Marshal Biron. Let us not ask whose orders he obeys, or merely uses as a pretext. Why should he rouse the King of France against you otherwise than the little country noblemen of this land? He slanders you. He slanders you to peasants and to kings, for he would drive you from a province where he wants to be sole master. Sire, you have before your eyes the kingdom. A Biron does not look beyond his province. Catch him here, fight him here with his own weapons! "

" I'll make him a laughing-stock! " cried Henri. " How could I even think of making war on him."

He took Mornay by the arm and led him out on the open terrace, and repeated as he strode back and forward: " I have an enemy once more." He was thinking of Madame Catherine, his enemy of former days.

" We never fail to meet the enemy sent by Heaven," said Mornay. " And it is always the one that we then need." Which is what friends say every time; but it does not mend matters.

" A fine enemy! " cried Henri. " Cuts off the muzzle of his own horse. And he limps."

" He is a crafty man," said Mornay, " and eager for knowledge; he always carries tablets and notes down what he hears."

" He limps " said Henri, " and he drinks. He has a disease of the liver, his bones stand out of his face. Children run away when he looks at them with those hard eyes of his. A terror to children, and an old man — he is at least fifty. Mornay, Heaven has insulted me with such an enemy. I deserved a better one."

" Let us be thankful," replied Mornay, whereon they parted.

The Governor forthwith began a strange campaign against his deputy. Wherever Biron went, the empty bottles left over from his meals were counted, and especially those that he drained between his two meals. The Governor made it his business to spread the news of Marshal Biron's wine. The people soon added of themselves that the Marshal had lain overnight in a wayside tavern, because he was in no fit state to enter the city. As all these shameful details were spread about, all the young nobles turned against Biron; for they no longer drank immoderately, that being a habit of former generations. The young did as Henri did, they drank with both their meals, and at the finish of the day they drank their fill. When Henri entered a peasant's house, he filled his cup with his own hand from the cask; but he did this not only because he was thirsty, but out of good-fellowship. The poor folk never saw him overtaken by wine, and they assumed therefrom that he could carry more than they, though they thought of nothing but drinking all day long. Hence they were more disposed to forgiveness when one of their daughters gave birth to a child.

The young nobles were inclined to lewdness, since tippling went out, and thought thereby to be engaging in more exalted joys than those of drunkenness. They said that though both were vices, in the former the spirit took its share; indeed, it was a pursuit that called for both sagacity and courage. Drunkenness was the lowest of the sins; being wholly and solely physical, it wrecked the reason and brought yet other faculties to a standstill. Biron merely condemned in the Governor what he could himself no longer do. That in which he won distinction, few but his German reiters would conceive of as an honour.

Biron noted such observations on his tablets, and answered them in the castles that he visited; his age had been as chaste as himself, and he had been a virgin when he married. And although it was after dinner he confirmed his discourse by walking round the table on his hands. On a closer view it was observable that he was not using his whole hands, but only his two thumbs. But he did not appeal only to the strength he had so well preserved, but even more to the words of Plato. For this Greek sage had forbidden wine for children until their eighteenth year, and before the fortieth year no one was permitted to get drunk. After that age he forgave it, in the view that the God Dionysos restored to ageing men their former jollity and good humour, so that they even took heart to dance

once more. Whereupon Marshal Biron did indeed step out with
the lady of the house, which did not prevent him leaving a
little later in a towering rage.

Henri, who heard of all this, felt quite drawn to that singular
personage. It was a quality of his to reflect on an enemy until
he came near to loving him. But this was not the view of that
same enemy. He responded to the Governor's friendly overtures, not with insult, but with insinuation. In an effort to win
the old man's favour Henri sent him some fine books which
he had had printed to his order. His printer, Louis Rabier, knew
the latest improvements in the art. Against the will of the city
of Montauban, to which he was under contract, the Governor
had taken him into his own service and given him a house and
five hundred pounds; in return for which the master printed
him a Plutarch, that classic text-book of strong characters. To
the Marshal, Henri sent the *Speeches of Cicero*, a large and
handsome volume, with the arms of Navarre embossed in gold
upon the cover.

The Marshal did not believe that anything so rare and costly
could have been intended as a gift for himself; or so he pretended.
He sent the book back with courteous thanks. When Henri
opened it he found one passage underlined; only one, translated
from Plato; and it ran: " *Difficillimum autem est, in omni con-
quisitione rationis, exordium* " — which simply means: " It is
always difficult to make a beginning." As from an enemy, not
in his first youth, it could also mean: " Cursed little upstart! "

Henri, nothing daunted, had another of his precious books
packed up and sent, a treatise on surgery, and herein also a
passage was underlined, a quotation from Lucretius:

minutatum vires et robur adultum
Frangit, et in partem peiorem liquitur ætas.

Having read this, Biron forthwith abandoned all sense and
decency. In his reply he translated for the Governor a passage
from the poet Martial regarding hair on the human body. He
himself had the bare skin of the bilious subject; whom else
could he mean by the reference to shaggy limbs? Henri realized

that there was no dealing with this enemy; it must come to a fight. And he sent him a further message by means of another book, the author of which was Juvenal:

> *Nec facilis victoria de madidis, et*
> *Blæsis, atque mero titubantibus.*

It was something of a tribute, and really a last attempt to come to terms with the deputy. If the intentions of both were honest — such was the Governor's meaning — then they must both prove it by the good understanding with which they served the King of France in that province of Guyenne. By way of answer Marshal Biron shut himself into the city of Bordeaux and fortified it. He let it be known that at the first opportunity he meant to take the King of Navarre and send him to Paris, where he was urgently awaited; Madame Catherine in particular was pining for her son-in-law's company. Biron had better have kept this to himself. Henri merely called his enemy a windbag, but he had his messengers intercepted; even by the most devious ways not one got through.

Several were caught in succession. One carried nothing save an account of the contest in quotations from the Latin authors; this was represented as an act of treason fortunately detected. The verses were, of course, aimed against the Marshal for his loyalty to the King of France; it was moreover alleged that they admitted of a double meaning. " *In partem peiorem liquitur ætas* " referred, therefore, to the court. To the King and to his House.

The messenger, who was merely to convey these commentaries on the classics, was followed several hours later by a second; and the news he carried was very plainly written. Here was no more talk of niceties of style, but a tale of brigandage, ravishment, fire, and murder, which, it was maintained, must be laid to the account of the King of Navarre. He was ruining a whole province that he might make it more absolutely his. Thus Biron, who in fact had committed all these outrages himself; and when Henri had read the letter he took quite a different view of his deputy's intentions in Guyenne. He saw the whole man with much sterner eyes. No more jesting now. He must act; indeed, he must strike in such a fashion as to inspire that deputy with wholesome fear. Then, perhaps, he might be kept in subjection for a while. " When it is all over, we will laugh once more."

At these words, Agrippa d'Aubigné replied: " And why not while we are in action? I have a goodly notion," he added aside. Henri, for his part, thought that the enemy had not been made ridiculous enough so long as he could meditate onslaughts from his fortress. That very day he had caught another of the Marshal's messengers, and what he carried made up Henri's mind. The message actually promised the Queen Mother the capture of the King of Navarre. For his surrender Marshal Biron demanded, as a price, and for his personal possession, a number of towns, not merely in Guyenne, but in Béarn as well.

Henri was indeed appalled. He was sitting on the lip of a trench, in the falling dusk; in this land which was his home and refuge he was no longer safe, his enemy meant to strike. It is by no means ill to have an enemy and to know him; one may ride against him and do battle, the first fear is soon overcome. But it is ill to discover his schemes and to feel the blast from an abyss not yet suspected. Here was a gulf that sent forth evil exhalations — pah! — it was good to clear the throat of them. " So Biron would lay hold of my cities as his price," repeated the young King.

As he looked up, Henri caught the eye of the captured messenger, who stood before him with fettered ankles. " But you are a Huguenot," said Henri. And the man replied: " Marshal Biron does not look on me as one."

Henri eyed him, then he turned his hand palm upwards, like one that has no choice. " You are ready and willing to betray your master to me in the cause of the faith. You are to carry him a message, and he is to think that you have returned from Paris. Until the day on which you could have come back, you will in fact be lying in the dungeon at my castle of Nérac, where I think you will fare none too well."

But the youth was not at all deterred, and he endured the mishandling that followed. The Governor estimated how much his treachery was worth in money. The Treasury at Pau was to make the payment later. Then Henri rode forth; he had forgotten about the dungeon, and the youth was free. But from that hour he was marked — where he went, and with whom he spoke. He kept quiet and was silent, so that at last he could be trusted. With empty hands and a brief message to be given by word of mouth, the courier reported himself to his master.

As a result, Marshal Biron did actually go to a lonely house, called Casteras, left his escort behind in a near-by copse, and rode alone over the heath, which lay livid under a sky of black and scurrying cloud. The Marshal, who liked to feel the wind, wore no hat, nor any cloak, as the wine within him kept his body warm. He swayed ominously on a nag as raw-boned as himself, but never fell. That was well known. Yellow skull, hard eyes, and the rattle of his hinged cuirass — none could mistake him. Storm and desolation, and Death upon a horse — but there was not one laugh from the Governor's men who lay hidden all about the house. The Marshal had fallen into a trap, as he deserved. Too late now to turn his horse and try to gallop off. He was only a hundred paces from the great gaunt keep, with a narrow balcony beneath the roof.

Upon that balcony something appeared. Marshal Biron promptly halted; this was uncanny — his misgivings had proved well founded. The figure up yonder had not stepped out of the house, it had been too suddenly revealed. It must have risen from the floor, a feat that was scarce to be expected of Madame Catherine. Biron could see quite clearly, the fumes of wine never obscured his vision. He was familiar with the old Queen, her broad, heavy face and the widow's coif. He could also hear her voice, which was all her own. Not in vain had Agrippa studied those suave and sinister accents for four long years; he could now ape them to perfection. "Brute!" he shouted across the heath to the solitary horseman. "You brute! Stay where you are. What have you been at — getting drunk and capping Latin verses! And for that you expect to pocket half a hundred towns and rob the kingdom! I was to wait until you handed over my good son-in-law, the King of Navarre, indeed! I would sooner come myself and make my peace with him, which is easily done if I bring some pretty ladies in my train. What of the mill? Where were you hiding then? Instead of catching him, you were lying dead drunk in a tavern! "

The Marshal listened unmoved to this singular tirade. When it ended, he knew enough — he drew a pistol from his belt and fired. The false Madame Catherine ducked in time, and the sole result was an indentation in the wall. Biron spurred his horse, but another rider appeared round a corner of the house, the Governor, or King, so called; a fellow all too ready to make game of so respected a commander. The old man's eyes were steely, his teeth were still clenched, but unconsciously he raised the pistol. " 'Tis fortunate it has been fired," jeered Henri. " You would extinguish the Royal House of France. I must let the Queen Mother know that you shot at her, Monsieur de Biron."

The man was speechless with rage. At last the words came: " That was a puppet, with a waxen mask and stuffed with rags. But had it been Madame Catherine herself — by my soul, I would not have been sorry to have fired."

" That's my brave hero! " said Henri heartily. " The God Mars in person speaks."

" Mine are the towns! " roared Marshal Biron. " And the whole province shall be mine. King of Navarre or King of France — 'tis all one to me, I've gallows for them all." So he roared. He may sit firm on his horse and look securely into the future; but the thought robbed him of his sense and self-mastery.

" Villain, you have betrayed yourself," said the familiar throaty voice above his head, once more Madame Catherine stood on the balcony, pointing a finger at him. Biron suddenly shivered from head to foot, wrenched his horse round, and fled. But armed men dashed out and stopped him, and kept off his few companions. Then the scuffle was cut short by the Governor's order: " Let him go. We know him now."

So Biron went. Agrippa, in the guise of the old widow, began to dance on his balcony, and the crowd below, who had now crept forth, clapped their hands and fell to dancing too. Tomorrow the whole countryside would tell the story, and laugh as they were laughing now. Laughter was a good weapon against an enemy. Biron would be hid for a longish while, and meantime the matter should be made known at court, as much as was like to serve Henri's turn. The balcony had better not be mentioned.

Eauze: or a Lesson in Humanity

An attack of his disorder made it impossible for the Marshal to send couriers to Paris. He spat bile as the result of his humiliation before the province and the whole kingdom; he thought he could hear the laughter from where he lay abed. Though Henri made no mention of it in his reports, it was very well known at court that Marshal Biron had fired a pistol at a counterfeit semblance of the Queen Mother. The King of France, whom he had threatened with hanging, was minded to call him before parliament and impeach him. But Madame Catherine convinced her son that two of his enemies who had themselves fallen out had better be left where they were. So no measures were taken against the Governor's deputy; Henri received fair words and nothing more.

However, he avenged many an outrage of Biron's, so long as the Marshal was dispirited and ill. But unfortunately he had to allow the most dreadful acts of vengeance, such was his soldiers' rage at the abominations of the other side; and he himself and his men were thought equally brutal by those towns which had happened to surrender to his deputy. On both sides a mere rumour brought a very real retaliation, which again was followed by yet more savage penalties. However men regarded each other, they grew viler still, and there was no end to their brutality.

Once on the way from Montauban to Lectoure, Henri received word of an ambush ahead; he sent on de Rosny and de Meilles with five-and-twenty horsemen to clear the dangerous defile. This done, three hundred of the enemy took refuge in a large walled church; this had to be undermined, which took two days and nights. When the besieged surrendered, the King of Navarre wanted to hang six of them and let the rest go. But he could not be merciful, for it suddenly became known that these same Catholics had done a deed of horror in the city of Montauban.

Not content with outraging six young Protestant girls, some ruffians had "filled the wretched creatures' private parts with gunpowder," set fire to it, and six lovely and devout young girls had been blown to pieces. So three hundred prisoners were now slaughtered without mercy.

While the massacre proceeded, Henri galloped off like one in flight. He was in despair for his good name, which he must tarnish with such deeds of blood merely because his deputy shrank from no outrage. Biron took care to terrorize the towns into keeping their gates shut against the Governor. The justice and strict discipline for which Henri had first been known must for Biron's purpose be made to look like ruthlessness; and indeed he was in a way to get Henri's name as hated as his own. Henri realized this, and on his flight from the massacre of the three hundred he resolved for the future to ignore his deputy's example.

Eauze was one of those turbulent little towns that would not admit him and would not hear of any submission, though the recalcitrants were in fact only the magistrates and a few burghers, who owned more land than the rest, while the poorer folk worked in their service. The common people were for the King of Navarre, who went into the houses of the poor and made love to their daughters, which made him loved also. The poor would certainly have opened the gates; but they could not, in the face of the garrison, in the pay of the rich. But the resistance of the poor made the well-to-do mistrustful of each other, and each prepared himself a cover, in case the town were surrendered. The apothecary said to his neighbour, the saddler: " In confidence, neighbour! Do you know who supplies the King of Navarre with his conserves? His apothecary at Nérac, named Lalanne; but it was I who sold him the receipt."

" Neighbour," replied the saddler, " it is likewise with the leathern case for the royal drinking-cup. The case had to be repaired, but secretly, because a cup that cannot be locked up may easily be poisoned. The case was brought to me from the court," whispered the saddler.

At the same time each took note of what another might unwittingly let fall, in case Marshal Biron arrived before the King of Navarre; for it was every man's intention that all should suffer save himself. A woman dreamed of an angel who told her the Marshal was at hand, and she shrieked out her story on the market square. This would mean trouble for her husband, assuming that the Governor came first. He was a wagoner and had accepted one of Monsieur d'Aubigné's notes of hand in payment from a country tavern-keeper. The King of Navarre had dined there; and this, in the last resort, was to save the wagoner.

The town gates were guarded by a mere handful of foreign soldiery; Henri had been informed of this, as well as of the dissensions among the burghers, and their fears. The garrison was insignificant, and might well be unsteady as a result of Biron's failures. The Governor took with him fifteen chosen noblemen, wearing hunting coats over their cuirasses; they were thus to make their way in unobserved. Scarcely was he himself within than a soldier shouted: " The King of the Navarre! " and cut the rope of the portcullis. Five of them were caught. Henri himself and Mornay, de Batz, de Rosny, and de Béthune. The alarm was rung, the inhabitants rushed to arms and threatened the five companions.

The foremost body of citizens consisted of some fifty men; Henri advanced straight upon them, beginning a speech to his four noblemen the while. " Forward, friends and comrades! " He was speaking less to them than to the good folk of Eauze, whom he hoped to overawe and bring to a standstill. " Forward! Here you must show your courage and endurance, for thereon hangs our salvation. Let every man follow me and do as I do. No shooting," he shouted in a still louder voice. " Leave your pistols where they are! " — as though he were speaking to his own four. But in truth the armed burghers listened open-mouthed to this oration from a King so sore beset, and they did not stir. About three of them did shout: "Shoot at the red coat! That's the King of Navarre! " But before anyone could recover, Henri leapt into the throng, which scattered in terror and fled to the far end of the street.

Thence several muskets and pistols were discharged, but a tumult soon arose, as the poor folk, who loved the King, fell upon the guards. They themselves were utterly bewildered; even during the fight they came to blows with each other; not a man among them really wanted to be discovered to have discharged his weapon. Henri needed only to wait calmly; very soon the magistrates and burghers flung themselves at his feet and said, in the accents of a litany: " Sire! We are your subjects and your humble servants. Sire! We are your — "

" You aimed at my scarlet coat," replied Henri.

" Sire! We are your — "

" Who fired at me? "

" Sire," pleaded a burgher in a leather apron, " I have received the leather case of your drinking-cup to repair. I do not shoot a customer."

" If some people must be hanged," urged another, made familiar by his terror, " Sire, hang poor folk only; there are too many of them nowadays."

" I will not have the town sacked," cried Henri, " although it is the custom and you deserve it. But every man shall give ten pounds to the poor. Fetch your priest at once and pay him the money! "

Whereupon they dragged out an ancient ecclesiastic, but promptly tried to shift the whole disaster on to his shoulders. It was he who had put it into the wagoner's wife's head that an angel from heaven had announced that Marshal Biron was at hand, and not the King of Navarre, which was the only reason why they had, alas, shut their gates. And they pleaded desperately that the old man might be allowed to suffer for the town. If not themselves nor the poor — someone must be hanged; the folk of Eauze would not rid their minds of that idea. Henri was compelled to give express commands: " No one shall be hanged. The town shall not be sacked. But I would eat and drink."

A tavern-keeper promptly seized the occasion; he set out tables in the open market square, for the King, his gentlemen, the burghers, and the well-to-do. Henri demanded chairs for the poor as well. " They have money enough, since you are to give it them." The poor did not wait to be asked twice, but

Henri himself had not yet been able to reach his place for a press of kneeling figures, each of whom wanted a special assurance that his own life and goods would be safe. Others are to be spared — but I? But I? It was a desperate lamentation from creatures who did not grasp what was happening and could not believe it, though it was their salvation. What, in its stead, was so familiar kept reappearing in their bewildered brains and shook the inner equipoise without which poor mortals cannot live.

The wagoner whose wife had seen the angel staggered witlessly about and said to everyone: " What is all this? " And in a more and more eager voice, that rose almost into a wail, but with closed eyes, as though an army of angels had appeared to his bedazzled vision, the wagoner went on: " What is this? What is happening here? " And at last a short man in a green hunting coat answered him:

" It is humanity; and that is what you and I have never seen before."

The wagoner opened his eyes abruptly and recognized the gentleman whose note of hand he had accepted from a tavern-keeper. He produced the paper and said: " Will your worship redeem this? " Agrippa, in dudgeon, turned his back on his creditor. The wagoner departed in the opposite direction, waving his hands above his head and repeating the new word that he had heard but did not understand. It set him doubting his familiar world of notes of hand and reprisals — and, indeed, it plunged him into mortal melancholy. He went away and hanged himself from a beam in his hayloft.

Meantime in the market square there was feasting and good cheer. Girls, with their plump arms and shoulders bared, served the dishes and the wine and got much thanks from guests, who had not otherwise believed that the doings of old days were at an end. As they talked they uttered a new word that had come to their ears, in an undertone, as though it had been a secret. But they drank heartily enough to the young King, who, for no deserts of theirs, had let them live and spared their goods, and ate his dinner in their company. They resolved to be loyal to him for ever, and so pledged themselves with right good will.

Henri recognized that he had done his cause good service. And he looked at the folk about him. Now that he no longer needed to make them his by guile or force, he for the first time had an eye for the faces of his fellow-men — so lately distorted by fear and fury, now boisterously joyful. Henri waved a hand to his Agrippa, for he knew he had his song prepared and ready. Agrippa stood up; there followed shouts of " Silence! " until all were listening. And he sang it — each verse twice, and at the second time they all joined in, to the cheerful chant and quick rhythm of the psalms:

> " Lord, wring Thy hands and veil Thy head,
> The righteousness of men is dead,
>   Here is no place for Thee.
> They kill and kill, and know not why;
> Exceeding bitter is the cry
> Of those that are led forth to die
>   Upon the gallows tree.

> But lo! the Prince of this dear land,
> He cometh, bearing in his hand
> Never a sword, but peace and grace.
> Be not afraid, before his face
> The evil and the good are one,
> Now the dreaded days are done.
> Whatsoever men ye be —
> Cry Hosannah! Ye are free! "

High Guests

The affair of Eauze was remarkable in this, that it infuriated Marshal Biron more even than his discomfiture at the lonely house of Casteras. The King of Navarre was using unlawful means to increase his influence; the deputy had contemned them from the beginning, quite apart from the fact that, in the opinion of the older man, such an intruder deserved no influence at all. Biron was in a torment of jealousy. His letters to Paris had long been complaining of the young man's popularity and his loose morals. But since the day of Eauze they were the letters of a man distraught: Henri was disregarding the laws of war in that he neither hanged nor plundered, and he was undermining the foundations of society by dining at the same table with poor and rich!

So long as the province was merely in disorder, the Queen Mother was in no way troubled. But now she learned from special reports, if not through Biron, that the towns, one after another, were submitting to the Governor. That was not at all to her purpose. So she decided to appear in those parts in person, to put an end to such untoward happenings.

It was clear to Madame Catherine that she must at least bring her son-in-law his wife. The two Queens travelled from the 2nd to the 18th of August, when they arrived in Bordeaux, under the protection of Marshal Biron. They had with them an army of noblemen, secretaries, and soldiers, not to mention the usual noble ladies and lovely women of the court, among them Charlotte de Sauves. She had been invited against the Queen of Navarre's will, but by her mother's orders.

The progress of that gorgeous array was conducted, as always with a magnificence that was interrupted by all manner of shocks. In the South, near the sea, attacks were expected from the Huguenots; several times the whole procession of coaches, horsemen, and foot-soldiers halted in the open country, while armed men gathered round the coaches of the two Queens. When the false alarm was past, the company moved on with much shouting and cracking of whips. However, they basked in their own glory at every larger halting-place. In the town of Cognac Margot had one of the successes of her life; the ladies of the place were utterly overwhelmed by the splendours of her dress. A star rose over that distant province, to the sore loss of the court of Paris, now orphaned of beauty and robbed of sunlight; such were the rapturous words of one of the cavalcade, a certain Monsieur de Brantôme. It would indeed have been better for himself had he had large and shapely limbs like Guise and Bussy and La Mole; for these touched Margot more than any rapturous praise. She herself knew the use of words; on the entry into Bordeaux, which was a triumph, she replied with majesty and grace to all that had greeted her; and chief of those was Biron.

Apart from his other offices, the Marshal was Mayor of Bordeaux, the capital city of the province; and in that city the Governor had never yet been received. Henri flatly refused to meet the Queens there. Then followed negotiations which lasted nearly seven weeks, at the end of which it was agreed, at Henri's instance, that the parties should meet at the lonely house of Casteras, where Biron had been discomfited, and the whole countryside still rang with it. The Marshal did not dare to show himself there. Henri appeared with a hundred and fifty mounted noblemen, and the sight of them inspired the old Queen with as much anxiety as admiration. It was with all the more warmth that she assured her son-in-law of her friendly feelings. She went so far as to name him the heir to the throne — after her son Alençon, of course; but both she and he knew what to think of that Prince.

They then got into the same coach — the escaped prisoner, and the murderess of his mother and his friends. And they did not cease to overflow with cordiality until their arrival at a place called La Réole, where they could at last close their mouths and part. Henri went to another house with Margot. He did not speak again, he merely glared at the candles and muttered to himself, quite forgetful of the fact that one of the loveliest of women was undressing at his back. Suddenly he was aware of a stifled sob, turned his head, and found the curtains of the bed drawn. He took one step towards it, then back again, and spent the night on a couch. He would not recover until after the first encounter with Biron.

The Marshal did not tarry. Hardly had the Queens left the disastrous house of Casteras far enough behind them than he presented himself at their next halting-place. Henri cut short his salutations and assailed him on the spot. In the room were the Queens, as well as the Cardinal de Bourbon, Henri's uncle, who had been expressly brought to make him confidential. All were abashed by the young man's demeanour, and none col-

lected themselves soon enough to stop his outburst. In his very
first words he called Marshal Biron a traitor, whose head ought
to fall on the Place de Grève. Then followed his accusations,
and he made them in no mood of jealousy; he spoke in the name
of the kingdom, which it was his business to defend; he spoke
already from the throne; and the old Queen's face grew more
waxen as she listened.

When Biron tried to answer, he could not utter a word. The
veins in his temples seemed near to bursting. He snapped his
fingers. His rolling gaze chanced upon the Cardinal. And Henri
cried: " We all know you are quick-tempered, my Lord Marshal.
'Tis a good excuse. But if it should come into your mind to
throw my uncle the Cardinal out of the window, then beware
of what may happen. No. You had better walk round the table
on your thumbs; that will calm you." It was no longer a King
who spoke, but the young rogue they all had learned to laugh
at. So saying, Henri took Margot by the hand, and they ceremoniously left the room together.

Behind the door they kissed, like children. And Margot said:
" Now I know what your purpose was, my dear lord, and at last
I am a happy wife again." It was quickly put to proof that she
had yearned for that reunion. "A solitary wife, dear Henricus
— of what use is she? Half my mind fled with you from the
palace of the Louvre. I engaged in crazy enterprises and have
been sorely humiliated." He knew what she meant: her unlucky
journey into Flanders, her royal brother's anger, and her imprisonment. " Yes, my pride suffered. When these cities of your
lovely South received me like some being of a higher order, I
was at pains not to conceive of myself as a travelling actress."

It was too much. Her grief was so spontaneous that this time
she let her tears trickle down over her painted cheeks; Henri
had to remove them carefully with his lips.

Many a town was witness of their talks and dalliances and of
their loves. The gay procession of the two Queens went on and
on. Henri did not accompany it, he merely fell in with it between
two hunting parties, thus avoiding much painful conversation
with his mother-in-law regarding the assembly of the Reformed

Delegates. Freedom of conscience, she would say, lay very near her heart. Madame Catherine had journeyed hither for no other purpose than to discuss with the leading Huguenots the fulfilment of the last royal decree on freedom of conscience. But Henri knew that such decrees never really came into force, and before the conference was over, the next religious war had already begun. Many of his friends thought otherwise, especially Mornay. Henri accordingly consented to choose a place for the conference; but his choice never agreed with that of his mother-in-law. It was not until the evening that he met the travellers as they were just halting for the night. He forthwith retired with the Queen of Navarre, and while she lay in his arms she told him much; which unburdened her mind and was good for him to know.

She was appalled at the violence abroad in the land. Here in the South there was peace — but when she turned her thoughts back! The land was being ruined by violence, under the guise of armed rule. It was the League alone, and not the King, who now gave orders. " My royal brother hates me, but he is still my brother. I am the Princess of Valois — and I remember it the more, now he forgets that he is King. The Guises will destroy us," she burst out between clenched teeth, waxen-pale and with the air of a Medea. Her husband would have sworn that she would never sleep with Guise again — or only, as Delilah did to Samson, to shear his yellow beard.

She ran her fingers over her dear lord's bristly chin, admiring his now graver countenance. For a while she beheld it, doubting, pondering, before she said· " Here in this province you lead a little life. I shall share it with you, my lord and master, and I shall be happy. But one day you must remember that you are chosen for greater destinies — and you must save my House," she added, to his amazement. Her mother and brother had hitherto regarded him as their enemy, who meant to thrust them out of power before it came to him by heritage. Their bodily union had taught the Princess of Valois more quickly than any means by which a human being can test another. She trusted him so long as she was with him; not afterwards. How could she? It was for her to avenge the extinction of her House upon its heir, and to betray Henri once again, before she was at last the only survivor of her race. She remained childless like her brothers. The last Princess of Valois strove all her life long to achieve the peace of those who are happy and secure. She was in truth indifferent to what came after her; therefore she was restless to her very soul. More was to end with her than herself alone; in vain she sought that peace.

In the town of Auch the marriage idyll was stormily cut short. It was not for nothing that Madame Catherine carried her noble maidens about with her. One of them won the heart of an elderly Huguenot, a man of many wounds, so scarred about the mouth that he could hardly speak — and for a girl's sake he surrendered his fortress to the Catholics. Henri first told his stepmother plainly what he thought of her malignant little schemes. He regarded himself as one of the King's servants, and the old villain as one of those that did him mischief. To say this outright brought him satisfaction. But as the old lady pretended that this was the first she had heard of the commander's treachery, Henri saluted her with ceremony, rode forth, and took another little town in pledge. And so the pair baited each other, until they at last agreed that the Council of the Reformed Church should be held at Nérac.

Meantime the year had fallen to December, and the leaves were whirling in the wind; no longer the right season for such state entrances. However, Queen Marguerite of Navarre rode a white palfry, usual steed for a fairy-tale Princess. To the right and left of her curvetted a bay and a chestnut, ridden by the young Catherine of Bourbon and her brother Henri, who had arrayed himself in great splendour in honour of his wife. Old Madame Catherine was not disposed to be observed too nearly by the populace, especially under that clear sky; she looked on from behind a window. The incomparable Margot, radiant in serenity and calm, listened to a recitation by three small girls. They were dressed as Muses, and in honour of the Queen they spoke a prologue written for them by du Bartas. The first talked in the dialect of the country, the second in formal speech, and the third used the language of the olderfolk. Margot understood Latin and French, but a great deal of the Gascon escaped her. However, she felt what the gathered populace expected from her: she slipped off her richly embroidered scarf and presented it to the rustic Muses. Which won their hearts and made hers, too, beat faster.

Madame Catherine narrowly observed all that happened in that little provincial capital. Her old friend King Wren made the most of himself; he entertained her and her escort so far as his resources allowed, and set before them all the delicacies he could provide. At the least, he showed that he was pleased. Madame Catherine was even more critical of the delegates at the assembly, when at last it met. She thought they all looked like pastors or like certain birds, which she refrained from naming in that place. There were sham discussions on mixed tribunals with Reformed assessors, and on the condonation of past offences. But the real matter in hand was, as always, the fortified places of the Huguenots. They demanded an immoderate number, but she did not want to let them keep a single one. She rehearsed before her ladies a speech almost wholly composed of texts out of the Bible, and thought to outwit the good folk in the language to which they were accustomed. But her appearance and her reputation belied anything that issued from her lips; and these were strange encounters.

There was never a meeting at which they believed a word she uttered, and their brows remained as brass until she threatened them with hanging. Queen Marguerite could not but weep, her longing to be loved was imperilled by her terrible mother, who often aroused derision likewise — and this commonly when she went forth into the country. In the assembly hall she occupied a raised throne, which was well enough. Outside, she dwindled into a stain on the bright landscape, an old creature with yellow sagging cheeks who hobbled about on a stick; and anyone that remembered Saint Bartholomew — and had not perhaps laughed since then — laughed now at the contrast. Her very maids of honour really made the spectacle still more absurd. This was not the palace of the Louvre, and the sun shone boldly on both banks of the Baïse and the park of La Garenne. Here war and love were made, openly and without guile. But the old woman reckoned on the secret abysses of sex. Old age enters into a false alliance with vice, and makes itself a laughing-stock.

The most austere of the Huguenots did not then take it amiss of Henri that he engaged himself with several of the ladies that were easily wooed. His Margot was not at the moment distressed by it, she was wholly taken up by her new role as sovereign lady and a being of a more exalted kind. The main fact remained that Henri took only what was offered, but made a face at the beauties when they tried to lure him to the court of France. That was the object of the journey, the assembly, and the visit of these lordly guests; that, and that alone, as he had guessed at once. In the end his mother-in-law had to wait on him in person and set forth what she had in mind. She reproached him because her son, the King, now stood alone in his palace. His brother Alençon would be against him in the rebellion, the Guises and their League were sapping his throne. But no less to be feared was a Prince of the Blood, who had become alienated from the court and was growing gradually too powerful in the province that was his. Had not Henri reflected that he might be murdered? This was his mother-in-law's final trump; she threatened him with murder.

However, he did not fall into the maternal arms, he replied that no promise made him by the court had ever yet been kept. As Governor, it was his care to carry peace from hence throughout the realm, whose service was solely in his mind. Whereupon they soon took leave of each other, with the same lavish expressions of goodwill with which the visit had begun. It had lasted through the whole winter until the joyous month of May. Her two children escorted their good mother for a little way, until she went on alone — on bad roads and through a mountainous land, and among a fickle population. At one place the old Queen was received by maidens strewing roses, from another she had to make a hurried retreat in the face of the general hostility. She merely pulled down her black felt hat over her face — brave she was; indeed, all were brave. Without a tremor she dismounted from her horse and got into her coach, and as it jerked and jolted onwards, her sole discourse was of peace; but what peace was it that the mother of those dying sons meant?

When she had long since ceased to expect him, her beloved son-in-law suddenly appeared from round a corner. He felt he must look on her for the very last time and present her with a lock of his hair. The Protestants had a custom of coiling a thick lock round each ear. The right one he had already bestowed upon his dear mother-in-law at the outset; in the end she was allowed to have the left one too. This happened at a country graveyard, and in confidential mood Madame Catherine confessed that she longed to be lying there. "There are few graveyards in your country." She shook her head. "Do the people grow so old?" Then stopped at several tombs, and muttered: "They must be very comfortable!" She preferred her fellows when they were beneath the earth. Then there was peace, and in her heart too.

Once in after years, as King of France, Henri would go down into the vault of Caterina dei Medici, known in her lifetime as Madame Catherine; he would look at her coffin and say over his shoulder to his retinue — with a troubled smile that none of them quite understood: "She must be very comfortable!"

Moralité

Il a choisi de combattre: s'est-il bien demandé ce que combattre veut dire? C'est surtout endurer, sans les mépriser, des peines multiples, très souvent perdues ou d'une portée infime. On ne commence pas dans la vie par livrer de grandes batailles décisives. On est déjà heureux de se maintenir, à la sueur de son front, tout au long d'une lutte obscure et qui chaque jour est à recommencer. En prenant pierre à pierre des petites villes récalcitrantes et une province qui se refuse, ce futur roi fait tout à fait figure de travailleur, bien que son travail soit d'une genre spécial. *Il lui faut vivre d'abord, et pauvre il paie en travail.* C'est à dire qu'il apprend à connaître la réalité en homme moyen. Voilà une nouveauté considérable: le chef d'un grand royaume et qui sans lui irait en se dissociant, débute en essuyant les misères communes. Il a des ennemis et des amours pas toujours dignes de lui, ni les uns ni les autres, et qu'il n'aurait certainement pas en faisant le fier.

Cela pourrait très bien le rendre dur et cruel, comme c'est généralement le cas pour ceux qui arrivent d'en bas. Mais justement, lui ne vient pas d'en bas. Il ne fait que passer par le condition des humbles. C'est ce qui lui permet d'être généreux et de se réclamer tout ce que dans l'homme il peut y avoir d'humain. D'ailleurs l'éducation reçue pendant ses années de captivité l'avait préparé à être humaniste. La connaissance de l'intérieur de l'homme est bien la connaissance la plus chèrement acquise d'une époque dont il sera le prince. Attention, c'est un moment unique dans l'histoire de cette partie du monde qui va s'orienter moralement, et même pour plusiers siècles. Ce prince des Pyrénées en passe de conquérir le royaume de France, pourrait écouter les conseils d'un Machiavel: alors, rien de fait, il ne réussira pas. Mais c'est le vertueux Mornay qui le dirige et même qui le soumet à des épreuves qu'un autre ne tolérait pas. Les secrets honteux de la personne la plus vénérée, voyez Henri y être initié et en souffrir en silence; vous aurez la mesure de ce qu'il pourra faire pour les hommes.

Book Eight

The Way
to the Throne

It Cannot So Continue

At first, matters went none too well. The royal spouses, Henri and Marguerite, made a solemn entry into their capital city of Pau, which soon proved to be a blunder. Margot was grossly insulted by the jealous Huguenots on account of her papistical worship. She resolved once for all never to set foot in Pau again. Moreover, the King of Navarre fell in love with a girl there, which irked her more than when it had been merely one of her mother's maids of honour. But all this was set aside when Henri fell ill again with one of his attacks of weakness, with a mysterious fever likewise. His headaches never abated day or night, he had to be continually shifted to a fresh bed, and he needed constant cooling draughts as well as comfort. Man is a brave animal. Many endure to have their legs cut off while they are fully conscious. An officer whose foot is damaged beyond cure will himself hack it off so that he can still serve the King of Navarre on a wooden stump. All this men do. What is more than can be borne is a shock to the centre point within, a failure of man's natural self-assurance — fear. Fear.

It was at Eauze, the very town where Henri had with prompt resolve met a mortal peril and where, as a bold experiment, he had dared to be humane. In that same place he lay for seventeen days and thought himself defeated as a man, damned to impotence, and unequal to the fulfilment of those toils and labours for which he usually thought himself a match. Indeed, he thought so to such purpose that he indulged in an excess of pleasures and exhausting passions. And in requital lavish nature lies at times as though defeated and wrecked, and another person must find faith, if that be possible, in what has lost its own. Here, it was Margot, his truly loyal wife, however many lovers she was still to take. All the while he lay ill she never took off her clothes; she watched by his bedside, talked to him, and called him back out of his fears. Afterwards, when recovered, he said something that none had heard him say before: " It stands written up above." What? He and his wife knew; and it was very clear to them since the nights of Eauze.

This eventful sojourn had made the pair into the best of friends. Back at Nérac, the Queen of Navarre could order her court as she pleased, and even educate her master into a fine gentleman — which he became several times in his career, when need was. This time he remained so for nine months. He wore the costliest clothes, all from Holland and Spain, and all of velvet and silk, purple and gold. He bought his Queen ten fans, each more gorgeous than the last. He lavished perfumes on her, and the richest gowns, and even gloves made out of flower petals. He gave her dwarfs, black pages, and birds " from the Islands." She had her chapel in the park of La Garenne, where she heard Mass; there were receptions under the nodding tree-tops, music and poetry, dancing and gallantry — all in glorified simplicity in that lucent air. At the court of Nérac, for a while beneath those nodding tree-tops, there was many a witty languishment and many a fantastic dream. Bright was the sky, silvery the light, and the evenings were like velvet.

Wits were nimble, and weapons might be left to rust. Henri wrote with his own hand a complete translation of Cæsar's *Commentaries* on the campaign in Gaul and also on the Civil War. He got the pens from Holland, the ink from Paris, and the paper was gilded for him by his Chamberlain. He loved to have his books in gorgeous bindings; and he had them so adorned while he himself went about in a threadbare doublet. In matters of the mind he held firmly to form, and in letters, decrees, and even in songs, which in later days he used to make his soldiers chant during his battles, he became all the better writer, according as he learned to deal in greater matters: one in service of the other, and because a man must love clear expression just as he loves a deed well done.

He behaved and indeed he felt during those few months like a man with his fortunes made, an heir to secured possessions, peace, and happiness — which was not at all the case, and the gay phantasmagoria ended exactly as the park of La Garenne fades into the countryside. But he loved to have his Margot for a while to rule over a court and over a gallant King, as indeed he was, for in her honour he soaked himself in perfume and had his teeth gilded. He also ordered the finest furnishings and a silver dinner service for the castle at Pau. Margot herself during her visit there had come upon some old harps; ladies of old days might well have soothed their hearts with them, as Margot did now, she who had never in her restless life known peace, and only found it thus and then.

She often passed a hand across her forehead. " No one poisoned yet? No stabbed corpse behind a door? No one beats me, and even my senses give me rest. I need not lower my brother Alençon from a window, nor set forth on adventures of my own. Humiliation, dissemblement, and fear, the torturing urge within — is all this past? Truly, here am I." Her wondrous hand had passed over her brow; her gaiety returned, and the Queen of that court walked forth to the dance with elegant noblemen and ladies, who bore themselves with dignity and grace. Soft music was discoursed; the flames of the torches flickered faintly in the light airs from the opened windows; gentle as the sounds, the light, and the air were the faces and the hearts of all. They danced and they were charming, and as the night wore away they grew lightly amorous, but no more. Margot might offer lips to many, she kissed none but her lord.

So were they at the court of Navarre; even the King's sister, so strict a Protestant. Though always a little lame, the young Catherine taught the young Rosny a new dance, and all envied him the honour. For this brief while she ceased to heed the passion of her life, forgot her cousin in his forest, banished the torments of her conscience, and allowed the light-hearted Turenne to pay court to her as he pleased. And her dear brother lived and loved, as though it made no matter. It could not so continue.

THE FIRST

Recovered from the malady of his liver, Marshal Biron grew more malignant than ever; he believed the Governor had gone to sleep. He did his utmost to slander him to the King of France. The Chancery of Navarre, and Philippe Mornay, had to labour mightily if his reports were to be countered. It was to be presumed that the conflict could not much longer be pursued in writing. The Queen of Navarre set herself to meet yet further discomposures. A woman who for the first time in her life is happy, and her dear lord has bitter enemies; how shall she help him? She told him all she heard; she made herself indispensable.

Contemptuous words, alleged to have been uttered by the King of France in the privacy of his chamber, Margot knew them; and if she was actually without news, she invented it. She hated her royal brother, who had always been brutal to her; and in requittal Henri too should be roused against him. She was truly wounded by insults offered to her lord. The Duke of Guise had made game of him, even her brother Alençon had entered into the jest, and this in the company of Madame de Sauves, her former friend. Margot could picture the creature's merry smile, and all the less was she inclined to repeat the words herself; especially not to her lord's face.

She had among her women a very young girl, almost a child, quite devoted to her: Françoise, of the House of Montmorency-Fosseux. She was known as Fosseuse. Henri called her " little daughter "; and to please him Margot also addressed her as " little daughter," although she knew that Henri's feeling for Fosseuse was not wholly paternal. The girl did not reveal everything to her revered mistress; rather, she said less about her temptations than her struggles to resist them. Margot sent the shy creature to him

with the most outrageous messages; from childish lips they were
the more likely to stir him up to act. Enough; in the palace of
the Louvre he was laughed to scorn, because he had not even yet
taken possession of his wife's dowry, which included several cities
in his own province of Guyenne. Biron kept them closed against
him. " My dear lord," said the shrinking girl, as she knelt to him
and raised two supplicating hands, " go forth and claim the
Queen of Navarre's dowry. And punish the wicked Marshal."

This he meant to do, but took care not to admit his purpose
to the women. When his army had been mustered and stood
ready, he did not betray himself by a single word; indeed he spent
the last night in the Queen's bedchamber. Then he rode forth
with a rose between his teeth — as though to a rustic festival or a
wrestling match. If his aim miscarried, Margot at least must bear
no blame nor come to harm. All his nobles were as light-hearted
as himself; it was Maytime, and the whole company were in love;
indeed, they called the campaign which was then beginning:
the Lovers' War. D'Aubigné, and even the sage Rosny, seriously
thought that mere chivalry towards the ladies demanded the
storming of Cahors. Henri opened his plan to none that did not
guess it; and none did but Mornay. What was truly of moment
was to keep a steadfast purpose and, though men and things
might fail, hold to the law within; in this there is no presumption, it comes from afar and reaches far ahead. God looks on
many centuries when he looks on one. Hence Henri was unshakable — and inscrutable, for nothing makes a man seem more
enigmatic and mysterious than a deep resolve.

The days were hot; when the town came into view, the army
watered from a well under some walnut-trees. Then it set about
what was to be no mean task. On three sides the city was guarded
by the waters of the Lot, and there most of the garrison was
stationed; the fourth approach was so barred by obstacles before
even the gate could be reached that it would of itself be enough
to daunt an assailant. But the gate was privily inspected by two
of the King of Navarre's officers who were skilled at explosive
devices. Small cast-iron mortars filled with powder were set
against an obstacle and touched off with a match. At eleven

o'clock at night, under a dark and thunderous sky, the army marched unobserved on to the fortified bridge, which was left unguarded. In the van were the two captains with their explosive instruments. These blew the bridge clear of all traps and barricades, and the defenders did not mark the detonations, for the thunder had begun. At a short distance, out of reach of flying débris, followed fifty arquebusiers, then Roquelaure with forty noblemen and sixty guards; behind them came the King of Navarre at the head of the main force of two hundred noblemen and twelve hundred musketeers.

Owing to inexperience, the explosion had destroyed only half the gate. The front rank crawled underneath it and then enlarged the opening with axes, which at last roused the inhabitants, who shouted for the soldiery. The whole town rushed to arms, the alarm was sounded, and in the darkness all manner of missiles — tiles, stones, torches, and billets of wood — whistled round the heads of the assailants. Weapons clashed and rattled and splintered, while gasping, choking throats yelled: " Kill! " In the narrow alleys combatants were locked in mortal grips. After a brief hand-to-hand affray the attackers would have been driven back but for the arrival of Turenne, with fifty more noblemen and three hundred musketeers; with their help the King of Navarre forced his way into the centre of the city.

But farther he could not get. A fortalice wherein all the defenders had taken refuge kept the army at bay. Then the dawn broke, and Henri's men also took cover. The soldiers were not allowed to plunder; the King of Navarre threatened to shoot any offender, and some were actually shot. During the night his men could get no food and had to sleep as they stood, with their weapons and armour piled beside them on the shop counters. The second day came, and with it the task of breaking through the house-wall up to ten paces from the citadel. Again they made no progress, and night fell once more. But the third day was the worst; a relieving force appeared and had to be intercepted and destroyed. Yet one more day to prepare the storming of the citadel, and on the fifth, when it fell at last in flames and ruin, fourteen separate barricades in the streets had to be forced, one by one.

That was the storming of Cahors, a tremendous feat. It had been made more arduous, with neither sense nor profit, by the headstrong citizens, merely from party hatred and jealousy of Henri's rising fortunes. For that very reason the achievement brought him more glory than was its due. It was the defeat not merely of a garrison, but of Marshal Biron and all his other enemies — and this in spite of reverses that did not fail to come. When Henri attacked the Marshal he was worsted, fled to Nérac, and thence dashed under fire on horseback down the great stairway of his castle and forced his way through the encircling troops.

His feet were torn and bleeding. At Nérac Margot had to change the bed-linen when he had lain with her for half an hour; his body was sore stricken. But his mind had never been more eager and alert. Henri led his army — which was more like a rabble of armed bands — out of his own domains towards the north, where the Protestants hailed his new glory and only awaited his arrival to break out in revolt. The court in Paris learned of this, and Biron was hurriedly recalled.

An admirable stroke. Alençon, now Anjou, made overtures to his successful brother-in-law; hastened southwards, and they concluded a pact of peace and amity. Cousin Condé, once a friend, remained obdurate. But a man is irked by always having to take second place, though he has done his duty loyally — fought as hard as his rival, and in obedience to the Party, which was justly suspicious of Henri's zeal for his Religion. 'Tis a great achievement to rise above envy; none can do so without deep insight, and a firm grasp of the doctrine of selection by grace. And pride in a man's own destiny, after the fashion of the ancients, is likewise a stand-by. From Mornay both were to be looked for; virtue was his, and understanding also.

Condé was a poor man — a kindly man, of honourable impulses that were not maintained. His hatred of Henri really began at a battle years before at Jarnac, where his father's life had been thrown away, so that young Navarre thus became First Prince of the Blood. As a prisoner with him in the Louvre, his sufferings had been equal, but not so deep. He escaped, but in all matters he showed less of a touch for what was policy and for the movement of events. He engaged himself with foreign princes while Cousin Navarre was able to establish and strengthen himself in his native land, admittedly with the help of many papists.

So Cousin Condé was the more disposed to stress the sanctity of the party creed, and he that possessed it or preached it was his friend. He thought more of Johann Casimir of Bavaria than of Henri of Navarre; the German (who was a dwarf) detested depravity. The dissolute life at the court of Navarre so disgusted him that at the bare mention of it he spat upon the floor; at which the Prince of Condé did not protest. And he joined a plot against his cousin. A messenger was sent to Henri, urging him to lead his troops to the aid of the Archbishop of Cologne. That prelate had become a Protestant, and there was good occasion for a blow against the House of Austria. The House of Austria was indeed the enemy, but an enemy for later years; the greatest and the last. An advance into Germany would mean that Henri must surrender what he had achieved, break his upward course, with the risk of losing the kingdom also. He would not heed them, as they knew. They could, however, thereby wreck his reputation among the Protestants, not all of whom trusted him; and with the news that he had marched, they raised alarm at the court of France and stirred a dark resolve in the mind of Philip of Spain.

Philip sat spinning plans for the domination of the world. How should he be concerned with a turbulent heretic, a buffoon like Casimir, a crazy Archbishop, and a jealous cousin? But Don Philip beyond the mountains guessed that an enemy to him and his schemes of empire was arising — oh, a puny enemy as yet — but what mattered was not his petty conquests, but the name and fame that he had won. Philip could not look on while Fama set the trumpet to her lips and spread her wings. In years to come there must be only one sovereign in France —

Philip. The House of Valois would die out, and even before it did so, the vainglorious Guise's League would destroy it with those golden pistoles which came rocking on muleback down the mountains. Navarre was troublesome, and Navarre must go. That was the resolve in the mind of Philip, and what else could the jealous cousin wish for?

Henri was now a man of knowledge; his life in the Louvre had acquainted him with hell. He had learned from Montaigne that goodness is what men most love. Mornay had instructed him in the power of virtue. But honour had not shaken his gaiety and good sense. None the less he knew there were men that rejected such a rule of life, and them he was to encounter everywhere until the end. Not Protestants, Catholics, Spaniards, or Frenchmen; but a race of men that live for violence and torment, and love the cruel orgies of the senses. These were his adversaries; he is the champion of reason and of joy. His policy was that of sanity and sense — to pacify a province first, then a kingdom, and last of all a continent; then, by a peaceful alliance with the princes and the nations, to break the House of Habsburg. And after that it will be time for the haters of life, when their murder-plots have failed for thiry years, to plant a dagger-thrust at last. Many a blow and a bullet miscarried in those years; Henri evaded them all, as he now did the first.

The King of Navarre was awaiting reinforcements. The officer commanding them was ordered to bivouac in a place called Gontaud; and Henri was heard to say that he would ride thither next day. But he had been warned that among them was a murderer, which was why he announced his purpose with such apparent heedlessness. Soon after dawn the King of Navarre rode out attended by three of his noblemen, d'Harambure, Frontenac, d'Aubigné. They were met half-way by a solitary horseman, whom they recognized as a nobleman from near Bordeaux. While Henri's three companions edged the stranger's horse between their own, a twitching fear came upon the King — more sinister than any he had felt in fight, when a bold purpose always mastered fear. He longed to gallop off; however, he asked the stranger in a cheerful tone whether his horse was a good one, and upon the answer — Yes — he rode up and looked at it and offered to buy it. Gavarret — such was the man's name — paled and looked embarrassed; but, loath or not, he dismounted. The King of Navarre swung himself into the saddle and promptly drew the pistols; one of them he found to be cocked.

"Gavarret," he said, " I know you meant to kill me. Now I can kill you if I wish." And he fired into the air.

"Sire," replied the murderer, "your generosity is well known. You will surely not take away my horse; it is worth six hundred crowns."

That the King already knew, and he also knew that it was to be the murderer's reward for murder. So he turned and galloped to Gontaud, and there he left the horse. He ordered his officer to dispose of the man as might be convenient, which was done. The man then returned to the Romish faith. When he contracted to kill the King of Navarre in return for a good horse he had belonged to the Reformed Church — but he was neither this nor that. He was a hater, and he hated Henri; Henri knew it, and came to understand that vengeance was unprofitable. There is always another murderer ready to hand.

This was only the first.

FAMA

The second soon appeared, a Spaniard this time; it was no hard matter to guess whence he came. He squinted, he had gaping nostrils and a bulging forehead — not a prepossessing man. This Loro, as his name was, offered to betray a Spanish frontier fortress to the King of Navarre, or so pretended, in order to get within striking distance of him, in which attempt he failed. The same noblemen who had protected the King against Gavarret took the Spaniard to an open gallery that ran round all the castle of Nérac. There each of them planted one leg against the wall, and over this living barrier Loro had to address the King. But as he had nothing to say for himself, apart from some traitorous babble, and nothing on the next day either, he was shot. It is not easy to dispose of one whom destiny upholds, and destiny had for fleeting moments begun to show her face. The two attempts at murder bore witness, more than all else to Henri's rising fortunes.

He was careful to confine himself to the limits of his own land, which indeed he ploughed up with his horses' hoofs until every clod was his and offered him its harvest. And the towns, too, were all won and welcomed him, turn by turn, and the people were conquered once for all — but not by force: walls should be stormed, not people. They have eyes and ears for kindness when they know they might be hanged. They hear the call of reason and humanity, which indeed is the purpose of religion. At the start they were inclined to hang themselves, but in the end they grasped what served them best, if only for a while and here and there.

The new deputy of the Governor of Guyenne was not his enemy; indeed, he had now no chance to be so. Damville, Governor of the neighbouring province of Languedoc, was his friend. Unassailable beside the ocean, at the centre point of the long coastline, stood the fortress of La Rochelle. Thence the line ran slantwise downwards towards the south; beneath it the King of Navarre had a majority upon his side; their hopes of him were very various, but there were many that hoped.

The common folk merely called him *lou Noust Henric* and thereby they now meant much: his daily toils and labours which they had seen for years past; the money that he spent, the arms he carried; and the man himself, the horseman in his pleated velvet doublet, with cheeks as brown as his kindly steady eyes, and his short sturdy beard. When he passed by, their perilous lives grew safer; the peace of that land, always in such peril, was for that time established. Others, men of learning or merely men of sense, fell to discussing what manner of man the King might be in mind. And they began to say that here was a man of quick intelligence, who bore himself with distinction and did what he meant to do in truly forceful fashion. Of such stuff are the greatest princes made, said they, and really so convinced themselves — not without some prompting from the Chancery of Navarre.

Behind these ruminations was Mornay, and in his reports on the position of his Prince he wrote that all good Frenchmen began to have him in regard. Many, indeed, first looked towards him in those days, especially abroad, for Mornay sent his insinuating screeds to England. Thence Elizabeth and her court drew highly favourable tidings of Henri of Navarre. There was little left to hope, so Mornay said, from the King of France, nor indeed from his brother, who was still a suitor for the Queen's hand and was at that moment her guest. Mornay actually went to England in person; he outdid the efforts of his own party and stopped the English marriage of the Man with Two Noses. This only by making the half-wit known for what he was. Diplomacy should abhor mystifications and, if it be skilful, hold fast to the truth.

Another opinion also began to spread; first in its place of origin, then more widely as it passed from mouth to mouth. The new Mayor of Bordeaux was said to have remarked to another humanist: " It is becoming clear that the sole end of these religious wars is to be the dismemberment of France."

Past were the times when Monsieur de Montaigne had agreed upon such a view in secret with Henri of Navarre. He now professed it openly, and not only in the library of his castle or the Town Hall of Bordeaux, which had chosen him chief officer with the Governor's encouragement. He had also written it. From the tower chamber of his little castle a book had appeared, now read by all the humanists in France, who were thereby much fortified in the moderation and the doubts that were natural to such minds, but might have proved their ruin, had the humanists merely learned to think, and not to ride and fight as well. As indeed they did. Montaigne, for all his clumsy hands, had done his duty as a soldier — a duty, because it would otherwise have been left to fools. A man must have this knowledge; he who thinks, and only he, must act. On the other side stands the moral horror beyond the confines of the reason: the deeds of ignorant men, of men violent through excess of folly. Their temptation and their opportunity is force. Behold the kingdom! Left to itself, it will become a morass of blood and deceit, and no upstanding, wholesome race could grow to fullness on such soil, if we humanists cannot also ride and fight. Aha! Be very sure that we shall ride and fight! And to lead us, on a cloud not far above our heads, Jesus of Nazareth Himself, and not a few of the gods of Greece move with us over the land of France.

Monsieur Michel de Montaigne, well aware of his own merits, sent his book to the King of Navarre by a messenger, bound in leather, and stamped with that nobleman's arms in gold, though only on the back. On the front were displayed the arms of Navarre; the arrangement being intended to indicate: " Fame has made us equal for a moment. Sire, I give you precedence."

The haughty gift brought yet a further message. The book was printed in Bordeaux, whence the ships voyaged through storm and calm to the far islands. "It may be that this book will ultimately voyage yet further than those ships, through the centuries into immortality. Certain it is, Sire, that your name will hasten thither first. I hope earnestly that we may both achieve it, for I am your comrade, and, like you, I uphold the law within me, as a man, through battle and through service. Sire, you and I are more than anyone dependent upon fame; and he who would write books for posterity, or aims to hit the taste of men by what he does, must not take glory lightly."

One sentence in the book was specially marked in script:

" *Toutes actions hors les bornes ordinaires sout subiectes à sinistre interpretation, d'autant que nostre goust n'advient non plus à ce qui est au dessus de luy qu'à ce qui est au dessous.*"

MARGOT DEPARTS

Her most troublous time was now at hand, and yet Margot strove to avert disaster when she saw it on the way. Some while passed before her eyes were opened; she had grown accustomed to happiness in Nérac, and no longer reckoned upon any change. She would not at first believe, when Rebours brought her news of what had actually happened between Henri and Fosseuse. Fosseuse — the " little daughter," for Margot as for Henri, a shy little soul, the very pattern of devotion. Rebours, on the other hand, was consumed with envy of any woman who attracted Henri; he had liked her at the start, but she fell ill, and the favoured moment passed.

Now she took her revenge and purloined the accounts of Lalanne, the apothecary, and showed them to her mistress. There stood the entry: " For the King, when he was with the Queen's ladies in their room, two boxes of marzipan. After the ball, glasses of sugar-water and boxes of marzipan for the Queen's ladies." This referred indeed to all the ladies, but the next to Fosseuse alone. " For Mademoiselle Fosseuse, a pound of sweet-meats, forty sous. For the same: bonbons and rose confect, pre-serve, fruit-juice, marzipan " — for Fosseuse alone. " She will ruin her digestion," said Margot in a tone of concern; Rebours was malicious, must not be allowed to report that she had seen the Queen jealous. But Rebours had not yet shown the worst. The last entry ran: " For the King, taken to the room of Mademoiselle Fosseuse, one and three quarters of a pound of marzipan, with four ounces of fruit-juice; two crowns, three livres."

From these accounts poor Margot could see what in fact had happened. Her practised face betrayed no sign of her dismay to the malicious Rebours; she treated the wicked little Fosseuse all the more familiarly, and, as before, she begged her good offices with the King. " Fosseuse, my dear, pray fetch my lord. Tell him I have some news for him about my royal brother of France. I'll tell you what it is. My brother had a bad dream, so my mother writes. He dreamed of savage beasts, lions and tigers that were devouring him, and awoke in a sweat. So he ordered all the beasts in his cages to be slaughtered. Go, tell that to our beloved lord, and tell him the other news as well."

Margot purposely said: " our lord " — Fosseuse was to believe that she suspected nothing, had none but friendly feelings for her, and was very ready to grant her a daughter's freedom. But Fosseuse did not come back this time, she stayed with the King; nor did she give him the message, so he did not visit Margot that day. It was the girl's confession; thenceforward she avoided the Queen, became abrupt and impudent, and set the King against her. Margot, bethinking her of happy years that were never to have ended, was careful to do nothing beyond recall. She hoped her lord would tire of Fosseuse too, as he had of all the others. Meantime she amused or annoyed him with her news from the Louvre. He also got news thence through Rosny, who had two brothers at the court of France. The spouses met to compare and exchange what they had heard, which was then the safest way for them to meet.

" The King of France keeps levying new taxes for his favourites," said he. Said she: " The common people always call him Tyrant." Then both together: " It cannot last for long. The favourite, who is now named Joyeuse, has been given the King's sister and a dukedom: the nobles cannot forgive the King for that. And the people, too, never forget that such a fellow was dressed as gorgeously as the King himself at the wedding, which was paid for out of the taxes. Such a display has never yet been seen in France. Seventeen banquets, all at the public cost; masquerades, tournaments, and on the Seine gilded ships full of naked heathen — no sight for people whom it is dangerous to remind of its burdens."

" Indeed," said Henri, " we must ease those burdens. It does not cost much to tap wine out of a cask; less than getting blood from men."

The luxurious Princess of Valois, once famous and celebrated in song for the insolent splendour of her processions, modestly bowed her head. Her sole ambition was to remain the sovereign lady of that land. For her lord she wanted more; she had long agreed with him regarding his mission — save that she would gladly have postponed it. Her royal brother, whom she did not love, might have an heir; then her House would not die out. Margot often sided with her brother, not with Henri; she could understand why he was as lavish to the noxious little adventurers he favoured, as though they had been his own sons. He wanted to think of them and make them such, that he might not be quite deserted among the ravenous creatures of his dream. Margot understood him at times; chiefly when she sat alone and pondered. Now, he had created Joyeuse's brother a Duke and

given him the Queen's second sister as a wife. He no longer
paid his soldiers; he said: "When all my children are married I
will be sensible." His children! thought Margot; she heaved a
long sigh and went on brooding in the candlelight, not noticing
that a breeze from the window was turning the pages of her book.

One day she was much excited at some news and sent promptly
for Henri, but he had ridden out. Instead, Fosseuse appeared;
she seemed ill and pale, and there was a drawn and peevish look
upon her face. It flashed into Margot's mind that all would soon
be over between him and her; but she could not resist the impulse to confide, even in the girl who had lain in his arms as she
had. "Fosseuse!" cried poor Margot, flinging her arms round
her — no longer a learned lady, nor a Princess, but a woman all
forlorn.

"Fosseuse, it is absurd, though dreadful too. They mean to
shut up my brother, the King of France, in a cloister, because his
marriage is still barren. He has taken to dressing like a monk, he
has shed his ribbons and his feathers, sent away his favourites,
and gone on pilgrimage with the Queen, that she may conceive
and give him a dauphin. His feet were all blistered at the end
of it, but the Queen was still barren. Is it not absurd? Indeed
it is — to be incapable of something so simple as bearing a child.
'Tis a spectacle for the whole court; they all eye the Queen with
insolent curiosity. And they see the King yawning from his vain
efforts to become a father, so they all yawn with him. A cheerful
court — haha! "

During her feeble effort at laughter, her hands had slipped
over Fosseuse; and Margot discovered by a chance contact what
she could have realized sooner, had she wished. This girl was to
have a child by Henri. And she herself was not; she had been
incapable of something so simple as bearing a child. Now she
mocked, not the King and his Queen, but her own destiny. She
went on fingering the other's body until the girl grew angry.
"What would you be at, Madame," snarled Fosseuse. "I'll tell
the King that you mishandled me."

"Little daughter, how could I harm his child?"

"So you would insult me too, Madame!"

The once pleasant child was choking with rage, and her throat grew purple. " If he had not ridden out, he would soon stop these horrible suspicions. Madame, I'll not have such lies told. You do not like me, Madame, and you mean to ruin me! " shrieked Fosseuse when she got her breath. Margot lowered her voice.

"We must not be overheard. Little daughter, trust in me. I'll be a true mother to you. We can both go away together, and I will help and comfort you."

"Madame, you mean to have me murdered. What you imagine is not true."

"Listen. We can pretend we are going because of the plague, which has really broken out in one of the King's houses near by."

"The King! " screamed the now frantic child, as she heard the clatter of hoofs; she turned to dash out of the room, stumbled, and would have fallen. Margot caught her, for the child's sake. But soon afterwards Henri appeared, very angry with the unlucky Margot. He did not believe her explanation. He believed the foolish little liar. Thereby Margot first recognized that her happiness was ended. She lost the high self-confidence of those years at the court of Navarre. Her hopes of a sure future gone, she grew slovenly and dissolute, as she had been in the palace of the Louvre, and there alone.

Her beloved brother Anjou, once Alençon, arrived to negotiate with Henri, and with him his handsome master of the horse. Margot was captivated by him at first sight, and became his slave. Before her brother she did not dissemble. As a man, and as ugly a man as he, she would have become much as he was, a half-wit, and would have flung her whole life away instead of merely parts of it. " Champvallon is the handsomest man since the heroes of antiquity! " said Margot.

" Cut his head off," suggested her brother. " Embalm it, set it with jewels, and carry it about with you; that is the safest way, as you know from experience, dear sister."

" He is the sun of my soul! My heart, my all, my Narcissus! "

" I'll tell him — every word," said her brother, and did so with relish. " It will be a lesson to that cuckold of yours, Navarre. He slandered me to the Englishwoman; she used to bring me my chocolate every morning with her own hands, called me her little Italian, and always wanted to feel whether I had a secret hump. Ha ha! " He had a laugh like that of his graceful sister — soft as a touch on muted violins. But from that stunted body the melodious sound had a sinister ring.

" There is a certain Queen, heartily sick of her court, whom I fancy I shall soon see back in Paris," he said later, when he departed, and took with him that hero of antiquity, who served him as master of the horse. But Margot went off to take the waters, accompanied only by her ladies and her noblemen, not by Henri. He was taking Fosseuse elsewhere. He first strove to persuade both women to visit the same place. He hoped that their love of him would reconcile them — an error that they both took in ill part, though it is one of the commonest of errors. Henri really committed it from kindness, because he saw Margot so constantly in tears. She was weeping because Fosseuse was to bear a child and she could not, she was weeping because her barrenness had robbed her of her happiness — and she lamented her renewed restlessness and the love adventures that had begun afresh. But she also wept in recollection of her partner in the last one, her classic hero; but she was comforted to think that this affliction at least she had brought upon herself and not suffered at the hands of others.

" If you only knew! " she thought in her agony, when Henri was urging her to take the waters with him and Fosseuse. " I hate you, and love none but Narcissus! " It was not true; Margot did not yet hate Henri; but by such endeavours, themselves not seriously meant at first, she might be made to hate him in the end. As Henri had to choose, he decided for his mistress instead of his best friend, and took Fosseuse up into the mountains above Pau, to a place called Eaux-Chaudes. It was solitary and hard of access. Before reaching the baths, one of the most dangerous places in the Pyrenees, called " the hole," had to be negotiated, and this with a woman in Fosseuse's condition.

The malicious Rebours soon discovered what was forward; hitherto she had still believed that the symptoms were of queasiness from too many sweetmeats. She kept her knowledge to herself, and only used it to terrify the hated favourite when they were alone. Margot could desire nothing better. It was indeed for that purpose that she had sent Rebours with the others; and she brooded in solitary vengeance while she bathed alone at Bagnères. The little town lies on a gentle slope in the Bigorre country, not in Huguenot Béarn, where Margot had sworn never to set foot since she had been insulted at Pau in the matter of the Mass.

Poor Margot strayed from her retinue among the woods, and as she carried a dagger for safety's sake, she scratched inscriptions on the rocks. At first it was the name of her lost Narcissus, adding an outline of that handsome figure. Then she wept and wept until she could not see out of her eyes. When she had dried her tears she read the letters she had last written, and they spelled: "Henri." Poor Margot was furious, and set a mark above it. Then she wept more bitterly than ever.

But at Eaux-Chaudes all were eager in the enjoyment of nature and her marvellous powers. Baths in the hot springs were sure to bring a fortunate confinement. And the water was sovereign in healing wounds, and against the ills caused by spending nights on the cold ground, and all other toils of war. Both Fosseuse and Henri used the bath for many hours a day. Round the edge were leafy arbours in which the bather could lie, for a payment of six livres to those who made them. Each was occupied by a sick officer or a guest, whose charges were all paid by Henri, to make the Pyrenees springs famous in the world. Poets like du Bartas composed verses on them, and they too had their reward. Many people made that perilous journey; and the King of Navarre was always attended by a concourse. His sister, who during his absence administered the country, sent him messengers on mules. Mules, too, with swaying skins of wine picked their way up the steep paths. The little mountain town was filled with life and gaiety.

Margot, far below, was living in the pleasant town of Bagnères, where the baths were excellent; the ladies and gentlemen of ancient times had bathed there and drunk from that gushing spring. The best houses were bespoken by the Queen of Navarre's retinue; and she was always beset by a buzzing, perfumed throng, eager to offer her homage. But she thought incessantly of her beloved lord up in the mountains, and all the kindness and the care and the patience he must be lavishing — on Fosseuse, who carried his son. The barren Margot was deserted. Perhaps those waters might at last make her conceive. But her beloved and hated lord lingered with the other, who already bore the child within her womb.

When she drank from the hot spring and lay down in it, she felt as though she were drinking to the void, lying in her stone cell like a sleeper. She called for her people to talk loud and cheerfully through the open doors of the bathrooms and down the whitewashed corridor. She wanted to hear verse, and also her own rich voice. And there was something else to which she listened and which she drank in every day even more fervently than the healing waters; and that was Holy Mass, the exhortations of the priests, and the prayers for a child. " Now I feel it will be so. I shall carry his son; then he will not leave me for Fosseuse. I must not hate him. He is to be King of France and I his Queen, and the Dauphin will be born from my womb. Joy is fulfilled and peace is come. Our love, and all the blood guilt, and our tribulations — these were not in vain. Peace, peace, and joy! "

When poor Margot came back to Nérac she firmly believed that she was prepared. But one morning her beloved lord drew the curtain of her bed; with a face of fear and of confusion he asked her help for Fosseuse. She must forgive him for having hitherto concealed what had happened. Whereat she said: Indeed, however much was due to her from him — and could not continue. But she went into the midwife's room, having dismissed everyone, for Fosseuse had deceived them all until the end; and Margot, whose cup of humiliation was there filled up, helped to bring a girl-child into the world. Not a son; that danger was overpassed; Fosseuse would never take her place. Henri even let Margot take the girl, whose day was over, to the court of France when she set out thither. Which was a convenient way out of the affair for Henri, and set his mind at rest.

For Margot it was more. She went firstly because her dignity bade her go; for were she not the sister of the King of France, who had stooped to Henri, before she learned to humble herself for him — she was still a woman. She was barren, she hoped no longer for a son, nor for peace. She departed so that war might not break out between herself and her beloved lord, while they were still together; nor hatred, while they still lay bed to bed. These were her sole motives at the outset; but Margot would certainly be used for the accustomed plans, to lure the King of Navarre to the court of France — as though the perils of that court had been less known to her than to him. But she lied about them all, and in her letters she described his enemies as quite broken down, Guise aged, and his brother Mayenne grown monstrously fat. Why did she do this?

She wrote: " Were you here, all would offer you their services. In a week you would get more friends than all your life long in the South." And she wrote it because she wished it might be true, proud as she was of her lord. It might even be the truth, or one facet of the truth. The other was that her lord was hated by the Guises and not beloved by her royal brother. As Saint Bartholomew had not been prevented by Charles IX, there was little that his successor could oppose. He was a weak man; no King of France had ever been so vacillating and bewildered, so harried and so desolate. The lords of Lorraine in truth wore a very different aspect from what Margot had described. The city was packed with their soldiery: it was they, and not the King, who appointed officers of State, levied taxes, and issued decrees. Had Henri entered that familiar den of murderers, the King of France might indeed have hailed him as his saviour; but the Guises? Navarre, the only man that blocked their plans, as they reported in those very words to the King of Spain — how would they have dealt with Navarre? They did not kill with their own hands, now that the throne was within reach. That was well enough in the time of Admiral Coligny. In these days Guise and his League arranged, as often as they wished, a riot; and in one of these, as if by chance, Navarre would have lost his life.

At Nérac there was no doubt upon the matter; the Council considered it, and Mornay drafted a reply. When Henri read poor Margot's letters, he took them for treachery, how could he otherwise? — and so they were, in part. Still, there spoke in them an honest heart's desire for her lord's future greatness. But in this her present pass, Margot herself confused and belied what she had done, and Henri heeded it no more.

He answered her sinister invitations with an open insult. He insisted that she should not send Fosseuse away, but keep the girl about her person; thereby purposely putting an end to any friendly intercourse. Moreover, he was no longer thinking of Fosseuse in those days. In the meantime he had found ecstasy in another woman's arms. This was no light love, and even less a passion, dark as destiny or blood. When Henri grew more nearly acquainted with this lady from Bordeaux, he was delighted with her self-chosen name of Corisande, which likened her to some exquisite figure from a romaunt. He was dazzled by her fantastic retinue, a little jester, a tall Moor, parrots, apes, and so on, that escorted her to Mass. The Countess of Gramont was clever, she was eloquent, and above all she was rich. In place of other beauties she had a dazzling skin. As she had been a friend of his sister from childhood, Henri had seen much of her before. Then, suddenly, a great love, or what he took for such.

It was certain, from the very outset, that the lady loved the more deeply of the two. She had indeed dreamed of him in secret, and her retinue had been meant to catch his eye. He haunted her nights since fame had cried his name, and she resolved to be his Muse. The Muse of a great Prince and soldier will raise him regiments from her own resources, and after battles won and cities taken she will enfold him in her white arms. And she will make him write to her, letters in plenty; under her guidance he will become an incomparable author. That will last the whole year, until the fire in that ambitious heart was

out. Then it will stop, and partly too because the Muse's countenance grew a little coarse. She will, like all the others, be dis-
illusioned and bitter, unmindful of the task fulfilled, self-chosen,
like the name of Corisande.

All was very different with Margot. He wrote her no fine
letters. She was there, when there in person. She was not indispensable, no woman is so; but she had moulded his very
youth with all the magic and the curse of her; and they lay
hold of a man's life otherwise than a stately Muse can do. She
will raise no regiments for her only beloved lord, she is more
likely to send troops against him. She is barren, and the last
of her race, and will try in vain to stop him on his way to the
throne. Indeed, at long last she will ally herself with the League
of Guise, and of the Devil himself, against her own House, from
mere hatred of her lord. When her crazy brother is dead, she
will range the country in his place, like one whose House is
soon to perish; and harried by the hatred of her brother King,
she vanishes at last, forlorn and helpless, utterly alone.

She was still in the Louvre trying to lure Henri thither with
descriptions of its gaieties. Of course she knew that he had a
new mistress; she said nothing, but she took her revenge. Unfortunately Narcissus took a wife, but she replaced him soon and
lavishly. Her royal brother at a court ball flung the names of
all her lovers in her face. Next day she departed, dishonoured
and desolate; even on her journey south she was held up by
King's officers and searched like a thief. But who rides to meet
her, who entertains her in his castle and appears with her at
the window? Who is kind to Margot, embraces her in silence,
that she may know there is one who suffers with her and shares
her shame?

In the evening she sat beside Henri, who made a show of
listening to his noblemen; merely that he might not have to
talk, especially to Margot. She was seen to be weeping quietly,
and her voice would have broken had she tried to speak. They
were tears of joy at his kindness to her; but tears of bitterness,
too, at her own impotence. He was in love and this time seriously!
She was in the way — of his mistress with the foolish name,

who was like enough to poison her yet; and therefore in his
own way too. What was the use of kindness? She was not
really there.

At that very moment he groped for her hand under the table
and pressed it. She shivered. Beset by her fears, she thought:
" Farewell to Margot! " Then she shivered again, this time for
joy, because that time had not yet come and the evil hour had
been delayed. The blood surged into her heart; quick, and unobserved, she bent over his hand and kissed it. Then she sat
very erect, wept no more, and looked at no one — within herself she felt that her departure had begun. She struggled to
come back, but could not. Ah, Margot — Margot! Must you
fade and vanish? — Margot!

The Funeral

The last King of the House of Valois loved dancing, and for
his sole amusement, as children do, but always with the darkling
face that he could not change. He felt suddenly impelled to
put aside the document he was so laboriously engrossing and
take off his fur mantle. A slim, still boyish figure, in a white
silk doublet, he moved back and forward before a mirror which
his servants promptly placed in position. To the strains of distant music the King began to step in formal measures, posturing
in all manner of graceful attitudes and figures. From beneath
his drooping eyelids he surveyed himself in the shining mirror,
as though the image had been that of a stranger. That was not he.
Alas, he never conceived of himself as a gay dancer, ungraced by
heaven, an airy being innocent of memories. They dogged him
everywhere; but that entrancing figure in the mirror had none —
nor a head either, for the frame had cut it off. His head, beset
by dark spirits, was ever thinking of the end.

His brother Francis was mortally sick; the blood was oozing
out of him, as it had done from his brother Charles. In Flanders
he had squandered what remained of his strength, as had been
his habit, and now he lay dying. The King was childless, and
no longer had any hopes of a Dauphin, for nothing had availed,

neither the Queen's baths, nor the pilgrimage with blistered feet, nor a solemn procession of the whole court through the church of Notre Dame. All had been done; fear and restlessness and the torments of uncertainty should have been left behind by one who approaches the end alone. But a man does not suddenly and finally reconcile himself to the ban of barrenness and the heavenly decree that his House must perish — Valois could not. For two centuries his race had wielded sovereignty, and he was to bring it to a close. Only at times did the sacrifice seem to him already made; unperturbed and undeceived, he kept his mind set upon the end and exercised himself daily in quailing at it, until fear too might pass and death be stripped of terror. After all, death would not be more terrible for the span of an age, and of a dying Royal House, than for a man alone in his own weakness.

So it was with such a purpose that the King danced alone, or for hours together played at cup and ball, or carried, from a blue ribbon round his neck, a basket of squirming, whimpering puppies; they lived for him and cared for him, he did not need to lift a hand. When the news of his last brother's death was brought, he stood like a dead man himself; he did not stir, he did not answer. The intruders were stricken dumb at the sight of him and were tempted to prod him with their fingers.

The court expected that he would once more play the monk, sing in the choir with the brothers, amid the golden candlesticks and censors which he himself designed, from the longing to bring something into being. No; he ordained funeral ceremonies as gorgeous as a wedding. The people had to take part in them, and indeed they were mulcted for them as heavily as for the weddings of the royal favourites. The whole priesthood was arrayed for the funeral procession, among them that very priest who had preached against the King. They were followed by the coffin, borne aloft by the dead man's noblemen, and behind it walked the King; of his House, now all in coffins, only he was left. The people watched and wondered; Valois behaved as though he wished to display the solitude in which it was his fate to live. The streets were hung with black, and in the procession he walked alone, without his barren Queen, and aloof from all others, who indeed were solely strangers. Before him his brother's coffin was swathed in standards from the campaigns in which the dead man had fought with doubtful honour, many of them against his royal brother. He had wished that his brother would die, and now his wish was granted; he walked alone in the procession, between the coffin and a throng of strangers.

In the King's own retinue the favourites Joyeuse and Epernon took precedence; he had bestowed dukedoms on them, and both the sisters of the Queen. Immediately behind them came his enemies, who thought to succeed him on the throne against his will: the Guises.

They made a greater show than the King himself, their splendid retinue was larger, they rode finer horses, which were led by grooms. They themselves were figures of might and mastery. The face of the Duke of Guise had hardened. He no longer beamed upon the mob and the burghers as in old days; he was no longer the dream hero of the women; he had no need. Smiles and gifts were over. This was the season of command. Citizen and peasant were not asked for their suffrages; those that did not join the League and swear blind allegiance to the Leader were lost. For him they must toil and they must fight; to him they must pay taxes, stand all day long on aching legs at all pronouncements of the Party, when he calls a gathering of his masses! If not, they would have no work nor leisure, they would be outlaws at the mercy of the spy and traitor.

A murderous secret society is spreading, battening upon the State and swallowing it up, while law has come to look as impotent as this King beneath his canopy at his last brother's funeral. Today half the funeral procession — priests, soldiers, courtiers, burghers, and populace — are all discussing his successor, just as if they were burying the King himself. Tomorrow his own favourites will go over to the Guises, the League will drive him living from the earth and force him into some last refuge, until someone kills him in the end. He knows much of what must come — as he stiffens himself to walk upright beneath his canopy of cloth of gold and hears what is not meant for him to hear; they are dividing his provinces among themselves and pleading their claims to offices, finances, and the power of war. He does not really hear, he is too far away; but what he cannot hear, he feels. His inner self quivers with forebodings that seem like utterances. He closes his eyes and sees himself walking by night through a dark forest. To whom can he look for help?

He started — at a sudden uproar. On the steps of a church near by a mob was shouting: " Down with Valois! " — which, to him, was nothing new. Men of their sort were hired, he knew by whom. The watch appeared, the brawlers fled, and in the turmoil the procession wavered. The canopy drooped and gradually collapsed on to the King, who crouched, fell on one knee, then both, and at last was lying prostrate on the stones.

When he was up again and had collected himself, he was encompassed by the Guises. They covered him against the populace, which had eyes and cheers for them alone. The Cardinal of Lorraine flaunted his large and evil countenance. The second, Mayenne, displayed more circumference of body than crafty men may have; which is a matter proved and known. The Duke — as he passes, the paid chorus shouts applause. " Hail! " yell his murderous secret league; indeed, he means to turn the whole nation into one huge murderous league, and there is but little to prevent him, as he thinks. The Duke — another volley of cheers, and roars of " Hail! " — wears the mask of sternness now, no longer of goodwill; a mask tautened with hard muscles, in token of resolve. He will divide the kingdom between twelve of his most exalted bandits, after the King has been thrust out of sight, and all subordinate bandits shall have power to steal and kill; themselves, of course, always in stern subjection, or they will be found prostrate, stiff instead of stern. That is the decree — observe the tense muscles round the Leader's mouth. Kill and be killed — an endless night of Saint Bartholomew, such will be the Leader's kingdom — Hail!

As they clustered round him and he could walk aloof no more, all that he had sensed and felt to be upon him slipped from the forlorn monarch's mind. He laid a hand on one of

Guise's boys — for the Duke had sons, he was not barren — and drew him to his side as though the boy were his. Thus he stood during the ceremony in the cathedral, and on the way back to his palace he walked amid his murderers and the murderers of his country, who did at least still offer him protection. The procession was swelled by their noblemen and retainers, who fell in with it on every square. And what the procession gradually presented to the onlookers was no longer the funeral of a Valois, but the rising power of Guise. The last Valois had his arm round one of their children, he walked to the drumbeats of their troops. His music, under the broad and brazen heaven of that realm, was the solitary tinkle of a little passing bell, now fading into the distance.

THE MUSE

The League, in its zeal for the Romish Church and for Guise, but really, whether wittingly or no, for the dissolution of the kingdom and for Spain — the Holy League had still one, though no very significant, matter of concern. And that was the King of Navarre, though he offered but a paltry obstacle. When so glorious a movement sped through an awakened people, it must surely reach its goal. It was everywhere proclaimed, especially by the honour of the nation, which scorned to truckle any longer to admitted infamy, in the shape of heresy. In such cases it also appears that the " infamy " has little money, and the " honour " a great deal. So indeed the soldiers felt. Almost all took the side of " honour " ; it is not known by any other name.

No time was to be lost, the King of Navarre was too much in men's mouths. The League decided to act. They had the King of Navarre watched, and learned that he constantly visited the Countess of Gramont at one of that wealthy lady's castles. They lay in Guyenne; and the King of Navarre was there more easily to be caught. The League posted pickets of horse at every place where he might pass. Unfortunately he never appeared; he suspected traps and evaded the bandits. He was better served

with news than was the League — by the Countess herself. It
was the perils of the journey that made her the centre of his
news service. When she had to warn him not to come, he
wrote her letters — and he acquired his more admirable style
just as he was advancing on his larger object. One day, when
she was in Bordeaux, he wrote to his Muse.

"My soul!" the letter ran, "the servant whom they caught
at the mill, thinking to catch me, was back yesterday. They
asked him whether he had letters with him, and he said yes; one.
He gave it to them, they opened it and gave it back. It was a
letter from you, my heart."

Here the stylist laughed. He bethought him how agreeable
it could be to write love letters; in them beat the pulse of nature.
They were ashamed of their churlish suspicion; they gave the
paper back and let the lackey go. As a result, it still escaped
them that the dame's money was provided for the equipment
of Gascon soldiers: twelve thousand hitherto, but that was not
all. She owed him double, and he would get it. The woman was
ambitious. She loved a King without money, land, or soldiers.
She was the first mistress that had not merely cost him nothing,
but had given him money. She should not repent it. The blood
sped through him, in that moment he forgot the soldiers and
the money, and he scribbled on: "Tomorrow at noon the troops
will move — I with them, and will cover your hands with kisses.
Farewell, my treasure. Never cease to love your adorer."

Yes; the adorer wrote to his protector and his Muse. He
only mentioned her hands, no other part of her, while the
blood sped through his veins. She had taught him reverence
and a new and nobler expression of his feelings — which, for
the rest, remained the same. Next day at noon he rode out to
Bordeaux, as intended, excited to know what she would say
about his absurd skirmish with some of the King of France's
men. The losses were two dead, the spoil consisted of five horses;
she would scold him for so unworthy an encounter. None the
less, the issue, then as always, had been his life; never less.

He reined in his horse. Blue woods behind broad meadows,
watered by the Garonne. At the edge of the woodland appeared

a lady on a horse. Seated side-saddle across the beast's great back, her white dress handing down to near the ground and glittering in the sunshine. She bent forward from the hips and lowered her brow a little as she peered at Henri. The movement was effortless, the whole appearance seemed unearthly — a messenger from heaven with promises of fame and greatness. "A fairy!" cried he, slid from the saddle and dropped on his knees. She waved her hand, and the rings on her fingers flashed. He galloped across; she half stretched out her arms. She quivered a little as he clasped her, and upturned a blissful face. He covered her hands with kisses, and she pressed her lips upon his head.

The scene was worthy, and both made the most of it — Henri chiefly from a devout desire to live up to the lady and her name of Corisande. This impelled him to display exalted feelings. On the river-bank beneath the poplars they sat down. He was not without concern for the two horses, but they stood quietly cropping the grass. "My greatest friend!" he said ecstatically; and she answered in a pleading and yet gracious tone: "Sire!" Her wide eyes, full of an incredulous joy, strayed over the still landscape, the whispering trees and murmuring water. "You and I alone! We know naught of the war, the terror of the plague has never reached our ears. It must be somewhere in the world, but here it may not penetrate. And here we are safe from treachery, far from the haunts of men."

He jerked a shoulder towards the thicket where he had left his escort; hers were waiting in the copse, he could distinguish several. All were to emerge when the idyll had been savoured to the end. Henri grew eloquent, he described to his beloved their island of the future. He had just discovered it. The lovely isle of gardens was encircled by a stream, where their boat would glide while countless birds sang above their heads. "Here, my soul, are plumes for you. Would that I could have brought you fish. 'Tis marvellous what fish there are there for next to nothing, a huge carp for threepence, and five pence for a pike." Unwittingly he slipped from his emotions into facts. So she too thanked him for a magnificent pie that he had sent her. As for the tame boars, they were kept in the park of her castle at Hagetmau, and she had quite lost her heart to the great bristly beasts. " Sire, you never fail to guess my taste. I shall owe you gratitude all my life." This the lady said with more than a touch of quite maternal irony. As was natural. Of the same age as he, but really more mature, the woman of two-and-thirty watched him meditatively as his hands caressed her body. As though it were not she, the surface of her face remained dead white, her eyes cool and kindly. She knew what she wanted, and believed that she could lead him thither. In that moment, to spare his royal self-complacency, she spoke of his gifts and her gratitude, though with a hint of mockery. Not till then did she mention her own benefactions; they were larger and placed him in her debt — for ever, as she hoped.

The lady clapped her hands, and two horsemen bounded out of the wood; officers he did not know. Not until they dismounted did Henri notice that they were wearing his colours on their scarves. They swept off their feathered hats, bowed deeply, and asked the Countess Gramont's permission to introduce her new regiment to the King of Navarre. She waved a hand in consent. Another sweep of the hats, and they galloped off; Henri had scarce collected himself. No one could surprise him, and transport him into a realm of miracles, as could Corisande.

" Sire, I am ambitious," said she, to cut short his thanks. " I would see you great."

To which he answered: " You may lose your money over me. Not even as King of France should I be able to repay you for what you are doing now.

He was seized with ardour for his " greatest friend." Tears welled into his eyes; and whether he would or not, he had to render homage. Women are the measure: whether they enrapture him or whether he despises them. They are life itself, and change in value with it. That day the Countess Diane reached her highest point, and she knew it. It was to her credit that she would not suffer him to utter what he would regret afterwards, and she checked him cleverly.

" Say not so, Sire! When you enter your capital, you shall look up at a balcony. That will suffice me."

" You shall enter it at my side, Madame."

" How should that be possible? " she asked in anxious expectation — and, alas, cleverness is forgotten when the heart begins to throb.

" You will be my Queen." He raised her ceremoniously and looked round as though for witnesses, there were so many near at hand. His own men did actually come out of the thicket, and hers appeared at a little distance off. Suddenly his face darkened, he stamped a foot, and said with a deliberate snarl:

" Who betrays me to my enemies, though they did but trap my servant? I know: she who was Queen of Navarre! "

So bitterly he hated Margot that he spoke of her as dead. She had left him, shut herself up in Agen, and was working for his overthrow; and he hoped for hers. The woman facing him shuddered; this was a natural force that faced her. What was she? His letters — mere words, directed to himself. Only a solitary man talks to a Muse. For the moment of one breath she knew it all. She saw a vision of the endless bitternesses of years, always betrayed, and never married; and in the end he would be ashamed of her too, because she was losing her figure, and her skin was no longer stainless. The breath passed and the vision faded. Drums rolled, and the regiment marched up.

At a light and cheerful quick-step it marched along both sides of the wood, formed up on the broad meadow, and closed its ranks. The two officers reported to the Countess Gramont. She, in token of invitation, curtsied slightly to the King of Navarre, gathering up her long dress as she did so. He took her finger-tips, lifted them, and led the lady up to the line. Here she curtsied again, and this time deeply; then in a ringing voice she cried across those two thousand heads:

" The King of Navarre is your commander! "

The King of Navarre kissed the Countess Gramont's hand. He ordered the colour-sergeant to step forth and asked her to dedicate the colours. This she did, and laid the heavily embroidered fabric against her lovely cheek. Then the King walked alone along the front, recognized a soldier here and there and grasped him by the doublet, and suddenly embraced one who had already served with him. What he said to each was passed from mouth to mouth. Then he fell back and addressed them all.

" I and you," he shouted, " are all spick and span today, but we shall not long remain so. 'Tis the lot of men like us to go covered with blood and powder. Serve me well and do not budge by so much as a halberd's length, and you will come to no great harm. I have always worsted those rascals of the League. Narrow is the way to salvation, but God leads us by the hand."

Thus the King of Navarre to his two thousand new recruits, who believed every word. The drums rolled, the colours were hoisted, and the King of Navarre mounted. There was no time for him to set his hand beneath the Countess's foot to swing her into the saddle. She had mounted by herself, and cantered away at the head of her ladies and her gentlemen.

Henri did not look after her; he had his regiment.

AT FULL GALLOP

Scarcely had he led his regiment on to the road than a mighty cloud of dust could be seen approaching in the distance — what could it bring save an enemy? The beat of hoofs could now be heard. Henri disposed his troops in the ditches and concealed them in the wood until the enemy could be descried. Meantime the leading horsemen dashed forth from the ochrous clouds; they would soon be on him. Henri himself and his noblemen slewed their beasts across the road and grabbed the reins of the galloping horsemen. One of them fell at the impact, but from among the trampling hoofs he shouted — and there was a ring of terror in his frantic voice:

" The King of France."

At that moment the dust unveiled its secret: a six-horsed coach, outriders, escort, and retinue, all approaching at full gallop. Henri had no time to clear the road; suddenly the swaying coach pulled up. The horses, wrenched on to their haunches, quivered, the driver cursed, the escort stood up in their stirrups, some brandishing their weapons.

" Friends here, gentlemen," cried Henri. He pointed to the

ditches and the wood. " I have brought a regiment to protect the King."

" The fellow expects us! " They eyed each other in amazement and fell back. " We travelled at one stretch from Paris, no one can have overtaken us, unless he flew."

Henri dismounted, approached the window of the coach, and bared his head. The glass was coated with dust, and the window remained shut. None of the servants that stood by thought of opening the door for the King of Navarre. Amazement had stricken them dumb and motionless. Henri himself held his breath. Alone in that utter silence he became aware of what was happening behind those beclouded windows; and he listened to the King's convulsive sobs.

In that moment many thoughts swept across his mind. But he did not move a muscle of his face, mounted his horse and lifted his hand. The cavalcade moved on — the coach with its six horses, the outriders, escort, and rear-guard, and the regiment of Navarre, marching at a light and cheerful quick-step. It kept up on foot, for the procession had ceased to gallop. There had been an air of flight about it — as though the King of France was fleeing headlong from his capital into his farthest province. Which indeed was the fact, as Henri realized, for all his amazement. " Has he come to me? Has it gone so far that he must seek protection here? Well, Henri Valois, you shall not repent it " — such were Henri Navarre's thoughts, and on that journey his heart thrilled with high compassion.

It was evening when they reached the town. The warders at the gate did not discover who was in the coach, and the inhabitants who looked out of the windows could descry but little in the darkness. The cavalcade moved without lights; the King of Navarre had the street lanterns put out. At the Town Hall he gave the signal to stop. As he dismounted, the door of the coach swung back, and the King stepped down. He embraced his cousin and brother-in-law, nor did he say anything then or afterwards. He had, more than he himself had known, longed to clasp a man of his own race, if only at the twenty-first remove.

But the King was perturbed by what he saw about him, the

great building, and the troops that thronged the square and street. A lamp was brought, and Henri noticed an expression of fear and mistrust come over the King's face. " I would see the Marshal de Matignon," said the King. He once more remembered that he must play off the deputy against the Governor. The good old plan!

" Sire, he is not in Bordeaux, and the garrison of his citadel will certainly not admit us. But I am well liked at the Town Hall. Your Majesty will be welcomed here, and safe."

At these light-hearted words the King grew yet more gloomy. He scented purpose and premeditation, and in this indeed he was right; for on the way thither Henri's emotions had not prevented him from reflecting how and where he should best get the Valois into his power. And that was in the Town Hall, his friend Montaigne's domain. He followed the King's eyes, and said: " My regiment is solely here to protect Your Majesty."

And the King answered haughtily: " I myself have regiments."

" Your horsemen, Sire, are out with Marshal de Matignon over hill and valley seeking to attack mine."

The King quivered. In that moment he was convinced this was a trap. Henri was filled with pity at the sight of him; he bent down quickly and whispered urgently into the King's ear: " Henri Valois, why did you come? Have faith in me."

A shadow of relief then appeared on that tormented face. " Let your troops withdraw," said the King in a similar undertone. Henri promptly gave the order; but, for his officers' benefit alone, he added that the regiment was to remain within the walls, isolate the citadel, and look out for attacks. Neither Valois nor he was safe in each other's company. Fortunately he was able to announce:

" Sire! The Mayor with some members of the Council."

Four men in black knelt down before the King. The wearer of the golden chain greeted him in Latin, the purity of which the King could well recognize, and then in French, which seemed the more worthy of regard, since classic style ill befits the common speech, and especially a Southern mouth. The King was gratified and for a while almost forgot to be afraid.

He bade the men get up, and in the end he entered the Town Hall. It was afterwards said that only Monsieur Michel de Montaigne's ingenuity could have made him do it.

Heir to the Crown

The Mayor first ushered the King into the largest chamber. It had not been possible to light this fully, owing to the sudden arrival of the King. The distant shadows made him nervous, and he asked for a small and better-lighted room, so the Mayor's library was thrown open for him. The King of Navarre ordered his noblemen to share the guard with those of the King of France. The latter turned in the doorway and said loudly: " I'll have none but my own men at the door! " Said Henri, loudly too: " My men to hold the outer door."

Thus secured, the pair stepped into the room. Montaigne was about to stay outside with the rest, but the King bade him enter. He smiled darkly as he said: " Monsieur de Montaigne, you are a nobleman of my Chamber. There is little space here. If murderers get in, we shall all three fall in the struggle. Will you warn me in good time of any peril? "

Montaigne's face twitched; in his obsequious expression there was a hint of irony. " *Omnium rerum voluptas,*" he began, and rendered it: " All things give us pleasure by the very danger that was to spoil them for us."

" You have a great many books," observed the King by way of answer; eyed the walls and sighed. He thought of his writings, his comfortable fur mantle, the monk's hood with which he deluded himself that he had finished with the world. Now for a struggle.

" Shall we deal frankly by each other? " he asked; but his tone was not hopeful. His cousin answered: " Such at least is my purpose "; so saying, he began to bend a knee. The King reached out a hand, raised him, and said: " Nonsense, man; I want no ceremony. Say what you want."

" Sire, I ask for nothing but your orders."

" Come, come; begin."

The King was eyeing the walls and wondering whether one of the bookcases in the corners could be moved. As he could not discover the secret that he feared, with his own hands he set a chair in the exact centre of the room. It was done too quickly for the others to do it for him; he had something of the litheness of a boy.

" Sire, would it not serve you best for me to offer a proposal? " asked Henri. " I shall gladly discuss all matters with my friends."

" There has been much discussion. 'Tis for you alone to decide," said the King, grown suddenly formal, and even ceremonious. Henri guessed what was intended: his return to the Catholic Church. He ignored it for the moment and worked himself up into a savage onslaught against his deputy in Guyenne. According to him, Marshal Matignon was no better than Biron. Henri even drew the King into it. "You, who should have treated me like a father, hunt me down like a wolf." The King reproached him for his disobedience, to which Henri retorted: "You can sleep quietly in bed. But you have so harried me I have not lain in my own bed for eighteen months."

" What reports have you sent to England by your envoys? " asked the King; and Henri dropped his eyes. Mornay indeed had written that all good Frenchmen were looking towards Henri; they disliked their present government, and they expected nothing from the Duke of Anjou, they knew him far too well. And now he was dead, and was the King's last brother.

" I ask Your Majesty's pardon," said Henri, and once more began to bend the knee, but as he was not stopped he did so of his own motion. After the advantage that the King had won, he was not disposed to graciousness.

" Do you mean that these disorders shall continue and the kingdom be brought to ruin? "

" There is no ruin where I rule," replied Henri shortly. The King returned to the main issue.

" You know my condition, and your duty. Do you not fear my anger? "

Again the change of creed, all turned on that; Henri understood the King at once. The kingdom might be wrecked if so be that the heir to the crown were Catholic.

" Sire! " said Henri firmly, " that was not your true self that spoke. You are wiser than your words."

" It is intolerable," complained the King angrily, " that you should sit on the edge of the table and the next moment take down a book at the end of the room. I hate movement, it destroys lines."

Henri answered with a verse of Horace: " *Vitam qui sub dio* — no roof shall he have except the sky; and he shall live in eternal unrest! " As he spoke he looked at Monsieur de Montaigne, who bowed to the two Kings indiscriminately. Then he again took his stand by the door, standing rigid like a guard.

The King of France began afresh: " Your sole obstinacy, against such a noble life? "

" Are you then happier in the Louvre? " retorted Henri. " Sire," he went on solemnly, " let me say what must be known to you already, that despite much injustice I have suffered, I do not hate you, for you were as wax in the hands of others. I hate the others, but you are my master and my sovereign. Your throne has always been held by the rightful heir, no usurper has ever seized it, not for seven hundred and fifty years, since Charlemagne."

All this was said to give the King time to nerve himself to say why he came thither at such speed. His purpose was to spite the Guises by installing his cousin Henri as heir to the throne. What else could be in his mind after his brother's death and after the shocking spectacle of the funeral, as the King's escort had described it. And whether Henri was a Catholic or a Turk, Valois must do it. So thought Henri, while he watched the King's face change — tense, then twitching, then contorted in the inevitable fit of fury, strangely provoked by the mention of Charlemagne. The King's face suddenly changed from grey to purple, as Charles IX's did, when his chest was still broad and his voice loud. He leapt from his chair, stood choking for a moment before he cried: " The ruffians! " And again in somewhat clearer tones: " That ruffian Guise! Now he claims descent from Charlemagne. No more was lacking. He has it written down and published among my people. He is the true successor, the Capets never had any right to the throne! 'Tis not to be borne, Navarre! A low-born impostor from across the frontier dares to call us bastards, and himself heir to the crown of France."

" It has come to this because you have given way to them too long," interposed Henri, in the tone of a man trying to bring another back to reason. The King had left reason far behind. He began to gabble in his fury.

" I got away and came at full speed southwards. But I left my marshals Joyeuse and Epernon behind." Marshals of five-and-twenty, reflected Henri, and in what fashion had they become so!

" They will do what they think best to rescue me from Guise. When I come back, perhaps he will be dead."

But here the unhappy Valois observed that he had gone too far before his cousin Navarre, and in the presence of another, whose eyes looked much too shrewd; surely a traitor. Where was his dagger? The thought was to be read in the poor King's face, which grew very dark and ugly. Fear, together with the impulse to kill, merely to get rid of someone — his mother's blood, his long training in the Louvre, all combined, brought the face of the last Valois to what it looked like at its worst. Monsieur Michel de Montaigne, though not unafraid of the dagger, was deeply sorry for the King, as nothing makes a man so helpless as the collapse of reason. Only an obscure nobleman of the royal chamber, he here stood forth the superior of the King, for he never lost his power of thought, even in sleep. He permitted himself to step forward and to speak.

" Sire! We should never raise a hand against a servant in anger. So Plato enjoined. It was in virtue of that principle that a Lacedemonian named Charillos said to an insolent Helot: ' By the gods, if I were not in a fury, I would kill you.' "

Monsieur de Montaigne knew well why he had mentioned just that instance. It reminded the King of the great gulf fixed between himself and all men, whether a simple nobleman or the Duke of Guise. Master and slave: one cannot insult the other, nor can that other take revenge. If the instance was flattering, it scarce offended against truth, and it pleaded for restraint; which was its purpose. It was indeed more effective than the humanist surmised. The King swung round, laid his forehead against the high back of a chair, and his heaving shoulders showed that he was weeping. His grief was silent this time — and not merely grief, it was a breaking of the barriers of his soul, it was resignation and relief. And he turned his back to the pair who could have killed him, that he might weep in silence. His fear had gone.

When he turned at last, he had reddened eyes and the expression of an eager child. " Cousin Navarre, do you know it is ten years since we met? "

" Since I slipped out of your fingers? Is it truly ten years? " asked Henri quickly, recovering, like his cousin, the face of innocence.

" Ten years, and like a day," said Cousin Valois. " I begin to wonder how they have passed. How have you spent them? "

" Surely in the troubles of life? " was the answer; there was a quaver of doubt in his voice, and he shook his head as he spoke.

Cousin Valois reached for his hand, pressed it, and whispered: " It was all a blunder. Surely you understand? A blunder, a delusion, and an unlucky accident." For in such fashion a man excuses the failure of a life, and this is the moment of astonishment.

" Cousin Navarre! Was it fated? Think only of this: she — she would never have planned the night of Saint Bartholomew."

Henri, also with astonishment, remembered: " She herself knew that the Guises could only become dangerous after Saint Bartholomew. They will sell the kingdom to Spain; that was her prophecy to me. But she had to do a deed against her better knowledge." And folly can go no further, he added, but not aloud. " I admit," he whispered in his cousin's ear, " I hated her, for what she made me suffer and for the ruin she has wrought in the land of France."

" Look what she made of me! " muttered Cousin Valois. " I always despised her for that."

They paused suddenly, aware that they were speaking of

Madame Catherine as of a person dead. But she still lived, or a semblance of her did, and the evil that had been her handiwork moved on. The cousins were again faced with the fact that they were enemies and must so confer. After this amicable colloquy they grew contentious.

"Recant, Navarre, and I'll proclaim you as my heir."

"I would offer you alliance if I knew that you would keep it, Henri Valois."

"But you — how do you come to be so resolute, Henri Navarre? 'Tis your faith that makes you so. What is the secret? — tell me," insisted Valois, eager to know how in all the world a man managed to pursue his purpose undeterred.

"Sire!" began Henri, and then changed his tone. "It shall be my care that you receive due allegiance; I will destroy all those that conspire against you, and what I am and have shall serve you as you shall command. Nothing concerns me so nearly as the protection of your throne. After you, Sire, I stand next to it."

This was no more than the truth. Henri knelt, the King did not raise him, nor did he kneel merely for form's sake. He rose when the King stood up, with a foreboding that the word would now be spoken; and he must hear it on his feet. The King spoke, as though to an assembly:

"I hereby recognize the King of Navarre as my sole and only heir."

So saying, he clapped a hand to his heart, stumbled back a step, and almost fell. He had named a Protestant to succeed him on a Catholic throne. He had roused the hatred of the League against his person, even to the point of murder. He had done the bravest deed he ever did.

The King then addressed the Mayor of Bordeaux, bidding him mark what he had heard, lest some mishap should overtake him before he could announce his decision to his court and Parliament.

Monsieur Michel de Montaigne promised to do so — and this time he quoted no classic instances. He had forgotten them in all that he had newly learned from that encounter with the King and his heir. Much, indeed, he knew already; but what he had witnessed brought new life to ancient knowledge.

A TEMPTATION

In Paris a few days later the King sat staring into the fire, seemingly oblivious of what his gentlemen were saying. His favourites, Joyeuse and Epernon, were not present. They had not killed Guise, they had come to terms with him, while the King was travelling through France. But among those present was the corpulent Mayenne, known as the Duke du Maine, brother to the Duke of Guise. Since morning the King had been nerving himself to tell a Lorraine of the decision he had proclaimed in Bordeaux. Time was running out; yet another hour or so and the Guises' own messengers might bring the news. The noblemen were talking of the King's late brother, his sickness and the strange fashion of his end, being the third of the royal brothers who had died thus. This although they could well surmise that the King's own end would be the same. But some seemed to think of him as no longer in the room. The others went on talking in this fashion to curry favour with the Duke du Maine.

Suddenly the King looked up from the fire, with one of those quick, boyish movements, which were a consequence of fear; and in an airy, deprecating tone, he said: " I hear you speaking of the dead."

He surveyed them all, only avoiding the fat Duke, whose corpulence had grown repellent. " I have the living in my mind. This day I recognize the King of Navarre as my sole successor. He is a gifted Prince, whom I — " He spoke in one breath, and without a pause, so that the perilous words about the succession might perhaps pass unobserved. In vain. They roused a mutter of indignation. A shining silken belly was thrust towards the King, who went on in a frantic gabble: " I have always had a liking for him, and I know he regards me with affection. He is sharp-tempered, and something of a jester, but he has many virtues. As man to man we are much alike and shall do well together."

" He is a Protestant," observed Mayenne in a scornful voice.

" I would go to my cabinet," said the King, rising, and the company made way for him. The door stood open, and his receding back was still visible when Mayenne said loudly: " A Huguenot as heir — that will do you little good, Valois. He has nothing more to give away but crowns, I suppose."

All this the King heard while he slowly crossed the next room, that he might not appear to be making his escape, which was why they did not close the door. Many peered out of it, in case the King might be planning to retaliate; indeed, the more cautious followed him. Mayenne was beside himself.

" We'll set the Pope to work and have the Valois excommunicated! " he piped in his high falsetto. And added, with scant consistency: " He shall be tonsured and shut up in a monastery."

They bowed even lower than their wont to the corpulent Duke, and addressed him as " Master of the Faith," a title he had himself assumed to get some advantage over his brother Guise with the mob and with the burghers. The lords of Lorraine held together while the victory was yet to win. Afterwards each hoped to cheat the others of its fruits. Mayenne took no counsel with his brother, who was not indeed in Paris, but with the Duchess of Montpensier, their sister, and the League promptly gathered the people in the streets. There they listened to frenzied speeches, gaped at placards, and scribbled their own excited commentaries upon the walls. Valois had lost the game, no matter what he did. Without Navarre's help he was ruined; with Navarre's help, all the more so — why, the fellow was a Huguenot himself, it seemed. A monk, that was all he was ever fit for — so they wrote, and so they yelled.

All this while the Duke of Guise was away on a hunting trip. He had left the city of set purpose. On the way home he heard the news, but he could not ride fast enough to prevent his sister haranguing the students from her palace balcony. When he arrived, she had just enacted one of her passionate scenes and was in the thick of the next, this time with the King.

The Duchess of Montpensier swept into the Louvre in her litter as though her reign had dawned. The guards scattered at the sight of her — her wild hair, hawk-like nose, and blazing eyes, and her brandished riding-whip, but covered with jewels, even the riding-whip was jewelled. She called for the King, and as his servants had fled, he at last appeared alone. "Madame, I could have you flung into the Bastille." Suddenly he wrenched the whip out of her grasp and hurled it into the corner of the room.

"I still have my scissors," screeched the fury, clutching them. They were gold, and hung from her girdle. "They will serve," she said to him, with a murderous look.

He knew what she meant: to cut his tonsure. And he said: "Madame League is more of a termagant than you, madame. But she will not cut my tonsure."

She laughed hysterically. "Sire, you cannot satisfy a woman. Neither France, nor Madame League, nor I have ever yet been yours." As she brandished the scissors under his nose, he grabbed them, and in an instant held between his fingers a severed lock of her lovely dishevelled hair. While she stood petrified, he said:

"Madame, I shall keep this as a memento of your visit."

"Whence do you get your courage?" asked the Duchess, now herself again, and looking at the King. Until that moment she had had but a distorted vision of her adversary. "What has befallen you?" she asked.

The King did not reply. He swung sharply round into his room. But as the doors stood open he could see the Duke of Guise dashing towards him through the long line of rooms. The King felt faint; but he held his ground, stamped, and called for his guard in the manliest tone he could command. People hurried in from all sides, and at last Marshal Joyeuse. Guise was out of breath, and frantic in asseverations of his loyalty. He had set his soldiers on the mob, he said, posing as the great retainer.

"I marvel how many casks are being floated up the river. Are the people always to be thus regaled? Empty casks build excellent barricades!" Valois's voice was ominous, none recognized the weakling. The casks would indeed build barricades; Guise knew that, but as he looked at Valois he felt the occasion was ill chosen.

The Duke was more decorous than his sister, and more astute than the Cardinal of Lorraine, who claimed to reduce the King's prerogative in his own favour, as a Prince of the Church. His sister, who, following the mention of the casks, was again brandishing her scissors, was sternly reprimanded by the Duke. Moreover, her too frequent outbursts were making her ridiculous, especially compared with the King's now majestic attitude.

" Madame," exclaimed the Duke, " your zeal for Holy Church has distracted your mind. We are servants of the King, who will take the field against the Protestants; he is already levying the taxes that are needed. We are threatened with invasion by the Germans, the Huguenots have called them in again." And turning to the King. " Sire, I offer you my sword, and I will pledge the overthrow of all your enemies."

He stressed the last words, and repeated them: " All your enemies, Sire! " Thus Guise made Valois hear whose overthrow he pledged. " Including the King of Navarre," he said heavily, and marked the effect on that detested face. The brow cleared, and the lips were firmly closed. Guise understood. He took his leave and led his sister from the room. " A truce to your buffoonery," he hissed into her neck.

Henri Valois's meditations followed them. " Henri Guise, I was mightily intent upon you once. I was your prisoner, and you would enter my presence with a riding-whip. A somewhat sickly temptation, I confess, but it lies far behind. Take care, Henri Guise, I have a friend." He eyed the back of his departing enemy and thrilled as he thought of his friend with admiration; he longed to ask, as a woman might have done: " Navarre, did I quit myself well in that encounter? Was I worthy of you? "

The enemy's back dwindled. Then the poor King suddenly became himself again, after so long aping his new friend. " Joyeuse! " he hissed. " Rid me of that man! " Whereat the young Marshal paled, and turned in silence to the wall. The King had as yet had no proof of the favourite's guilt; and now a half-hearted treachery, more repellant than complete betrayal, stood here revealed. The King went, and once in his chamber, he

fainted, because his feelings had been many and too violent —
too violent for what he could bear, and too much for the hour of
evening.

When they heard the tyrant was sick they all proclaimed him
dead, and there was dancing in the streets for joy. Now there
would be an end of comets and the plague and all the ills they
ascribed to a bad King; and, above all, of taxes. The people and
the burghers had been savagely mulcted, that the Holy League
might at last destroy the Huguenots. And the consequent discontent was set by the League to the account of Henri Valois.
The King struggled as best he could. He again approached Navarre on the matter of recantation, which would, for both, have
been a death-blow to the ravening League, though somewhat
damaging to Navarre; but the King would at last have been sole
ruler of his kingdom.

Valois did not really understand why his friend was so obdurate in so trifling a matter as this change of faith. Passionately
desiring it, he did not grasp what it would have cost the other:
his self-respect, and the confidence of his most loyal followers.
The party which he joined would have mistrusted the betrayer
of his own and would have served him ill; Valois himself would
soon have treated him as a man degraded. He had offered him
money and little else but money for his recantation, which was
not unwonted, as principles have their price. But virtue, em-
battled with knowledge, is not for sale. This turned the scale in
the Council at Nérac. " If we arm, the King will regard us; and
then he'll offer us alliance. Together we shall destroy our
enemies." " So shall it be! " cried Henri.

In a last attempt Valois sent his second favourite, Epernon,
from whom he still expected obedience, and even love. Joyeuse
was nothing more to him — Joyeuse, whom he had called his child
and to whom he had given a dukedom together with the Queen's
sister. There are some weak people who do not cling where they
have lost — indeed, they hurriedly abandon the offender, and for
ever. Even if he would, the sinner cannot make amends. They
have dropped him as yet unsuspecting. Joyeuse, gay and brilliant,
went his way, glorying in his growing army; more noble names and

great escutcheons, more magnificent chargers and cuirasses of real silver, than ever yet in any royal army; but the commander of that army was to be a youth of five-and-twenty, whom fortune had made her own.

The King smiled and thought: " You may preen yourself for yet a little while. Navarre is the stronger. I know for certain that his good wife, my sister, is very ready to betray him. I must give her money and men against her lord, whom she hates with a hatred only I can understand. We are of the same blood. I do well to keep Navarre at bay; but I must guard against the League as well. I'll send troops against both alternately, and the same marshals, Matignon and Mayenne, in turn. I would willingly send Guise, to get him beaten by Navarre; but I fear he is too wary. He prefers to deal with Germans — Devil take his soul! Well, at least he cannot hurt Navarre; I'll have no harm done to my friend Navarre. Nor shall he destroy my army. Ha! I am bewildered — my kingdom is all awry."

So thought the poor King, and sent his marshals turn by turn against the League and against Cousin Navarre. As for Navarre, Henri would much sooner have backed him than opposed him, but in that distracted condition of affairs he had to consent to his excommunication. Strangely for a Protestant, Henri replied by placarded pronouncements on the walls of Rome, the city of the Pope, who admired him for it, and he was much talked about in Christendom. On the other hand, the poor King wanted the League weak, not strong — and yet, he barely knew how, he made a new treaty with the League. When Henri, in his city of Nérac, heard the news, for the whole of one night he held vigil alone.

He pondered on what was now at hand, as imminent as the dawn. It was war, real war for existence, no more gay and fleeting encounters, but a bitter struggle to the end. His head cupped in his hands, by the light of guttering candles he surveyed the passage of his life, his joyous little victories, defeats so soon forgotten, long rides, rebellious towns, bold adversaries, and what had often made him weary and haggard, ten years of toil and care.

All this had been, and vanished; Henri pictured his ultimate foe as a great dragon-army circling the earth. He must stay it, or himself be slain. His enemies had marked him down; but for him they could settle their affairs in peace. He should not step up to the throne save across ten thousand corpses. He himself would scatter them on his own kingdom!

Cousin Valois had not kept his word, as indeed he had expected. He yields to the League before the League kills him. Victory won, it will be yet more sure to kill. Cousin Valois had been relying on Henri defeating him and the League as well. Which would be salvation to both him and Henri. That faithlessness fortifies the alliance. Perilous faithlessness, desperate alliance — and Henri could have found it in his heart to pray that this ordeal might be spared him, or that it were past and he lying on the soil of France.

This temptation came upon a man of four-and-thirty towards the end of a night in late summer, at the hour exhaustion is deepest after such a vigil. All the candles had gone out. Soon afterwards the dawn began to glimmer through the window, and he could see that his moustache had gone quite grey.

DAY OF DAYS

But this was no figure of tragedy, standing up defiant at the centre of events. Others are at their tasks and think themselves at least of equal consequence. Guise, who means to beat a German army coming out of Switzerland to help the Huguenots; victories in the field are as yet lacking to his fame. Joyeuse, the young Marshal, is as gleeful as a boy at the thought of beating the King of Navarre with his chosen chivalry. He lingers for the moment in one of the cities he has taken on the way, and after his gorged life at the court he is following a cure to cleanse his inward parts. A commander must be properly purged before riding into battle.

Nor was this the sole adversary awaiting Henri: Biron, the same who had been his bitter foe during their encounter in Béarn, now made punctual appearance yet farther afield. Henri had moved from Guyenne into Saintonge, for his salvation lay in attack: in extending the war, carrying it northwards, and threatening Paris — with fame winging ahead of him and trumpeting his glory. His old friend Biron bethought him of attacking a certain island: Marans, by the sea, of which Henri had described the charms to his lady Corisande. The ribbon of water that entwined that garden islet was but a trench scooped out of the marshes, and there the army of the enemy was caught. He had to raise the siege, he himself was wounded, and the money from the court gave out. How could a King who squandered his people's taxes on his favourites — what was left by embezzlers or the League — how could he pay three or four armies at once? The money for Biron failed first. Henri captured some of it, only a few thousand crowns, but they decided the Marshal's downfall; his troops deserted

Thereby Henri disposed not merely of Biron, but also of his cousin Condé; his successes stood out too plainly over that rival's failures. Henri's victory on the island won him the stern Protestants of La Rochelle, who would otherwise gladly have preferred Condé, a good party man though a poor commander. But his countless blunders could not be ignored, and provoked much head-shaking even in the strictest houses. Above all, he became a laughing-stock in the castle at Nérac, and that he could not forgive.

Next Joyeuse, purged at last. Then Henri rose into a tragic role, when he met the largest and most splendid of the royal armies, in open battle, on the day of destiny. Nay, more: he became the champion of the faith, the hero of Holy Writ. All doubts of him were stilled. This man was not fighting for money and possessions, nor for the throne; he was offering it to God. He sided with the weak and the persecuted, and was thus unshakable, blessed by the Lord of Heaven. His eyes are clear — the eyes of a warrior of religion. The stories told about his love-affairs and his buffooneries — they could not be true. From all sides men flocked to their hero's standard.

Already uplifted by his fame, all were enraptured when they saw that simple, kindly figure with their own eyes, shovelling earth out of the trenches, eating as he stood, sleeping in his harness — and always with a laugh at hand. It was that laugh that

made men love him, whether there was money or whether there
was none, whether they were full or fasting. He even made the
pastors merry, but at night he sat with his captains, Turenne and
Roquelaure, watching, with slow matches ready to their hands.
" Sire, why be so careful not to be taken by surprise? By day
you expose your person as though it were valueless; you wade
through open marshes, with bullets splashing in the water all
about you."

" And I may fall tomorrow," Henri answered. " But my cause
will endure because it is God's cause."

This he said beneath the stars, and he believed it — just as a
man should believe, for his confidence was quite unfounded, and
his cause would have fallen with himself. If God meant to save
that realm, He must save Henri.

There were, indeed, times of exhaustion. Fourteen days without taking off his clothes, his concern for his own troops — and
his concern to lure the enemy whither he was wanted. When at
last the Duke of Joyeuse and the King of Navarre did meet, the
latter found himself between two rivers and parted from his
artillery. But he retrieved matters by speed, mobility, and good
luck; and by the same good luck, the enemy was cumbersome
and slow. The Huguenots were singing psalms before their tents
while dawn was breaking, and the enemy camp awoke. Then
they began to hurl insults and abuse at the foe — effeminate
courtiers, gluttons, thieves who batten on taxes and the poor.

" Are you purged at last, Lord Duke? Here are we, and fear
does more than clysters. You are all crammed with places and
pensions — you'll never fight a battle. We can smell your scents
from over here. You will smell very different when we have done
with you."

While threats of slaughter were bandied back and forward the
silvery array of Joyeuse began to gleam and glitter under the rising
sun. It was an army of the rich: resplendent with precious
metals, many a golden dagger, and many a golden helmet.
Weapons were studded with jewels, pockets were stuffed with
money, and brains intent on reckonings and possessions. Beneath each silver cuirass it was not a heart alone that beat; it was

power — the power of tax-gatherers and usurers, who grow fat on widows and on orphans. " Villain! " roared an old warrior, whose eyesight was still keen. " I know you: it was your landsknechts that burned my castle. You are of the League."

The word fanned the wrath of the Protestant army. The most hated foe was not the royalists, but the assassins of the Holy League. They had destroyed chapels, roasted pastors, and filled women with gunpowder. There they stood, the men who would rob the Protestants of their homes and faith, their existence, and their freedom to meditate on the purposes of the Creator. But it was His will that those men should die that day. So the Huguenots were assured by the pastors pacing back and forward between their ranks, also in doublet and cuirass, that the Word might be preached until the last moment. Before the pastor had finished, the Captain was drawing up his company in battle array.

The King of Navarre was conspicuous everywhere, although clad simply in grey leather and steel; nothing escaped him, and, above all, no movement of the Duke of Joyeuse. Each allowed his adversary time, before the blow should fall in earnest. One of those two was to appear in God's presence that day, while the other was left master of the field. A high destiny for each; and so, from due respect, they allowed each other such advantage as could be won before they struck. Joyeuse performed some intricate manœuvres with his all too brilliant cavalry, and did so undisturbed. Meantime Henri hurried his remaining culverins across the river. He also reminded his two cousins of their kindred blood. Condé and Bourbon Soissons, his sister Catherine's lover.

When Henri believed the moment was at hand, Philippe Mornay appeared with two pastors, and, since battle and perhaps death were imminent, he bluntly reproached Henri with having had another mistress in La Rochelle, which was, in this extremity, enough to stain the purity of the Huguenot cause. Henri admitted his transgression. And he said: " A man must humiliate himself before God, as deeply as he defies his enemies." Whereon he galloped off, for he had caught sight of a deserter — an officer moving doubtfully with his men among some hillocks, half-way between both armies. "Fervaques!" shouted Henri, while still far off. "Join us if we win!"

He swung round at once without waiting for what might happen; but that bluff old soldier's men gave him no choice, they dashed after the King of Navarre. Henri saw from the position of the sun that the time was nine o'clock, and the two armies had been manœuvring for two hours within sight of each other. The month was October, and the light fell slantwise from the clouds, which hung low and drifted slowly over the plain, so that every detail could be clearly seen: two great armies and their commanders dwindled into insignificance under those vast clouds, and behind them a heaven that might be hostile — who could tell!

Henri stood up in his stirrups and shouted to his serried ranks, an instant before he meant to order the advance: "Comrades, we are fighting for God's fame!" He shouted, in defiance of those lowering clouds: "We must conquer for our honour's sake, or at least we must win eternal life. The way lies before us. Forward, in the name of God, for whom we fight." As he shouted this along the lines, he bethought him of the orders that were to follow; but they did not. The whole Protestant army, by no command nor agreement, knelt down and prayed. Its prayers were as the noise of multitudes, or thunder, or pealing bells; and the words were those of the hundred and eighteenth Psalm: "O give thanks unto the Lord, for He is gracious; and His mercy endureth for ever."

Then Henri's heart throbbed with a shock of exaltation, and he remembered a prophecy on a seashore long ago: A whole army kneels, and instead of attacking, prays, convinced of its destined victory. He too, with brow uplifted, and hands clasped upon his chest, murmured as they prayed: "All nations compassed me round about; but in the name of the Lord I will destroy them. This is the day which the Lord hath made: we will rejoice and be glad in it!"

Henri's heart was full of joy, as it had never been. The day that the Lord hath made is that on which we ride and smite our enemies, without fear or pause. His moustache would not go grey from treachery, or doubt, or grief. The day that the Lord hath made, suffers no doubts, for yonder stands the enemy. To-day we are strong in the faith, for we have no choice, we must conquer.

When the Duke of Joyeuse saw these strange things happen-ing on the other side, he cried: " 'Tis a panic! " To which Jean de Montalembert replied: " Lord, you and your courtiers have never rubbed knees against the Huguenots. When you see them with such faces, beware! " Whereat many rich persons in silver armour made more merry than ever. For they knew nothing, and understood nothing.

Yonder is the army of the poor. Yonder is the army of those persecuted for righteousness' sake. The army wherein virtue may at times be found, and sometimes knowledge. Its King's face has grown very haggard since this last campaign; he is wearing a grey helmet and cuirass like all his men, and his sole shirt is still damp from washing. He has spent all that he and his little land possesses on this army; and each of his followers has come for-ward with all that was left of fortune, present and future. This battle lost, all would have been at an end. They would have to go forth into strange lands. There they knelt upon their native soil, crying aloud to heaven, pealing celestial bells with ropes in-visible. " In the name of the Lord I will destroy the heathen. This is His joyful day."

Now it happened that, at the first collision, the royal cavalry broke deeply into the ranks of the Huguenot arquebusiers. They even drove part of Navarre's cavalry before them as far as the city of Coutras and began to plunder the baggage. There were shouts of " Victory! " and Joyeuse thought it not too soon to advance his infantry. Then came the surprise. The Protestants, from con-cealed positions, poured a murderous artillery fire on the flanks of the royal army, which returned it wildly, the cannon being set too low. The infantry fled, and the cavalry were huddled into a helpless mass: a savage mêlée followed, and the King of Navarre found himself embracing an enemy nobleman. " Surrender, Philistine! " Himself as Samson; but he had better have shot the Philistine out of his saddle, for his chivalry nearly cost him his life.

When the Duke of Joyeuse saw that the day was lost, he rode with his young brother, Monsieur de Saint-Sauveur, into the thick of the fight and there perished, as indeed he meant to do. He had been but a royal favourite, and his beginnings were far from honourable. But his pride, since he had grown so great, taught him to go down with honour.

Scarce had he breathed his last when his army broke in pieces. The Huguenots pursued it for two or three miles, each intent on catching some gay horseman whom he could strip and hold to ransom. Behind, on the battlefield, lay two thousand dead, almost all Catholics; else it was desolate. The dead lay among their horses and their weapons, and they lay as they had fallen, in little hummocks, that seemed as natural as those of sand and grass. Among sand and grass and corpses moved one single crouching figure; peered into the faces, shuddered at what it found and recognized, and so moved on, in the falling light and under the lowering clouds.

At the White Horse at Coutras there was feasting in the upper chamber, but on a great table below lay the corpses of the Duke of Joyeuse and his brother. The King of Navarre came in, no one knew whence; in the confusion of the victory none had marked his absence. He found his own lodging full of wounded prisoners, and he went across to the inn, where a few noticed that his eyes were red. First he knelt before his two defeated enemies; then, with an effort, he changed into another man and hurried up to join the laughing, feasting throng and celebrate the victory. One so great had never been won before by those of the Religion, certainly not in the time of the Lord Admiral, as his old campaigners indeed admitted. When the King of Navarre appeared, all leapt from the benches, stamped their feet once upon the floor, and then held their breath in utter silence.

Henri dashed among them with a laugh and cried: " Ha! We've not yet won eternal life — we must be content with this one." He picked up the largest tankard and clashed it against the others held out to him by his bold captains. They gulped down the heaped viands, Henri with the best of them, prated of their deeds in the battle, and Henri of his own, in a voice that rang out like a trumpet. The air in the long room was thick with the smoke of torches, fumes from the great roasting hearth, and the hot reek of human bodies.

Their leathern garments were covered with dark stains, some from their own blood, some from the blood of slain enemies — none could tell which; nor did any observe that Henri had been weeping. And Henri's thoughts were these: "Enough of mourning for my countrymen, slain by my own hands, who would have served me well in later years. There from the roof hang their banners, all that are left of them. It is well — but I will not take the banner of the King of France, and he himself shall not lie on the table below while I feast above. No, that I swear — " And all that while he gaily pledged his friends. "Valois stands along the Loire with his last army, covering his kingdom. I'll not harm you, Valois, I fight my battles for your kingdom. But we must finish with Guise, we both know that. Let him drive the landsknechts into Switzerland; you, not he, are to march into your capital victorious, my Valois. For I'll not harm you; we are good friends."

So thought, so done; and next day Henri mounted his horse to ride through all Guyenne down into Béarn; he had with him a troop of cavalry and two hundred captured banners, as an oblation to the Countess Gramont. Which, in the eyes of all, was truly romantic behaviour. Instead of following up his victory and defeating the King himself, he indulged his tender feelings and carried captured flags to lay them at his mistress's feet. There was much disgust among the victors of the day before; Henri was even accused of treachery by foreign Protestants, whose speech grew freer as they got beyond the frontiers.

He came; there upon the great staircase of her castle, arrayed in white and loaded with pearls, stood the fairy Corisande, as divine as he had only seen her in his dreams. The banners were waved and dipped before her; then, as though he had now earned that honour, Henri mounted the steps to her, took her lifted hand, and led her into the castle. She was happy beyond all speech. So happy was his Muse that she forgot all but his victory and the great destiny before him. No thought of bitterness or any claim upon him; tenderly and trustfully she listened. Motherlike, she bewailed his troubles and rejoiced at their reward; though in truth she should have wished they would endure, as indeed they did. When fortune wavers, then is the Muse's opportunity. But this was her day of days.

MORALITÉ

mperceptiblement il avance. Tout le sert, et ses efforts, et les efforts des autres pour le refouler, ou le tuer. Un jour on s'aperçoit qu'il est fameux et que la chance le désigne. Or, sa vraie chance c'est sa fermeté naturelle. Il sait ce qu'il veut: par cela il se distingue des indécis. Il sait surtout ce qui est bien et sera admis par la conscience des hommes ses pareils. Cela le met franchement à part. Personne, parmi ceux qui s'agitent dans cette ambience trouble, n'est aussi sûr que lui des lois morales. Qu'on ne cherche pas plus loin les origines de sa renommé qui ne sera plus jamais obscurcie. Les contemporains, d'alors et de quelques autres époques, ont pour habitude de s'incliner devant tout succès, même infâme, quitte à se récuser aussitôt traversé ce passage ou soufflait un vent de folie. Par contre, les succès d'Henri n'étaient pas pour humilier les hommes, ce que n'évitent guère la plupart des chefs heureux. Ils devaient plutôt les rehausser dans leurs propre estime. On ne voit pas d'habitude l'héritier d'une couronne, que le parti dominant répudie violemment, gagner à sa cause, par des procédés d'une honnêteté pathétique, le roi même que force lui est de combattre. Combien il voudrait aider ce roi, au lieu de devoir le diminuer, lui et son royaume. Il a eu ses heures de faiblesse et la tentation d'en finir ne lui est pas restée inconnue. Cela le regarde. A mesure qu'il approchait du trône il a fait comprendre au monde qu'on peut être fort tout en restant humain, et qu'on défend les royaumes tout en défendant la saine raison.

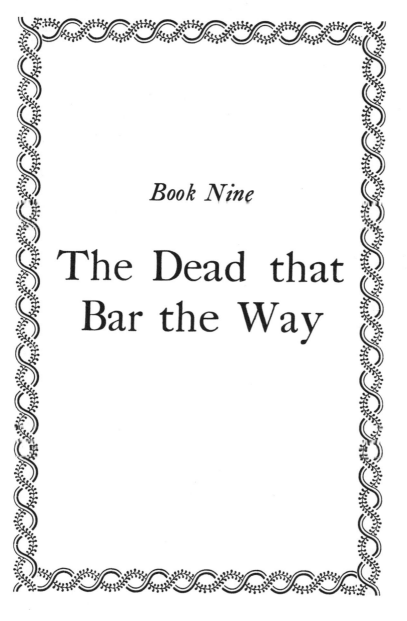

Book Nine

The Dead that Bar the Way

Who Will Dare?

On May 9th, 1588, the Duke of Guise entered Paris secretly with but a small escort. The King had sent to ask him — nay, beseech him not to come. Valois knew that his mere presence would lead to his own end, or decide the other's end. Which of the two would dare, and dare first? Guise had destroyed the foreign army of the Huguenots, but the royal army under Joyeuse had been defeated by Navarre. None the less, the King tried to pose as conqueror; despised equally by the mob and by the burghers. The members of his Parliament, the great magistrates of the realm, were almost alone in inclining to the King: being men accustomed to reflection. Amid such turmoils it was unwise to deviate from the law, and the law was the King. But who could share that understanding? Not the rich, to whom Guise, not the mouldering Valois, stood surety for their money; nor the frantic populace, who cried out that they were starving — a common cry, though they were not like to suffer beyond the usual suffering of the poor. But a mob, having made a false choice, grows besotted. They are for Guise, an unscrupulous adventurer and a demagogue in foreign pay. This unnatural alliance makes them quick to fury and to fear — it is their outraged conscience that is plaguing them, but that they do not understand. Paris, half distraught, is imagining a famine.

Guise, with his five or six horsemen, reached a populous street as yet unrecognized, his face muffled in a hat and cloak. The city, especially the numerous monasteries, was thronged with his troops — there were many within call wherever he might be. But he liked to pose as a man of mystery, above all alarms. Nearly forty, and the father of several sons, he never laid aside the showmanship by which such an upstart gets upon the stage. His own squire, drilled for the purpose, swept, with an impudent flourish, the hat and cloak off the mysterious horseman, and shouted: " Noble lord, reveal yourself! "

Meantime, in the presence of the King in his palace of the Louvre, the old, old Queen, Madame Catherine, said: " Guise is the support of my old age." Her son glowered at the schemer of Saint Bartholomew, the last results of which were now to come upon him, as he knew, though no report had arrived. It came, and when the Duke of Guise came too, his victory was known. " We are saved! " was the first salutation to the Duke from a handsome lady as she slipped the mask down from her eyes. " Sir, we are saved! " Whereupon the whole street fell into a riot of exultation. They forgot that they were starving; the Leader would banish the spectre of famine. They wept for joy, and kissed the jackboots of the passing horsemen. Rosaries were held out to the hero for his blessing; and a number of people were crushed to death.

While the Corsican Colonel, Ornano, was reporting all this, the King did not look at him; he kept his eyes fixed on his mother, who grew uneasy under that dark and heavy gaze. She muttered thickly to herself: " Guise is the support of my old age," but she so spoke to fortify herself in her folly, even against herself; for like enough she glimpsed what was to come. Her face was the colour of graveyard earth; it was to her last resting-place she seemed to be departing as she shuffled off, tottering and tapping feebly with her stick, more and more sunk within herself, and so bowed that she was nearly bent double.

The Corsican Colonel gave his verdict because he was assured such was the King's own view. The Duke must be murdered; and a priest backed this opinion with a suitable text from Scripture.

Several resolute men agreed, and the King made no protest; his silence seemed to mean that he acquiesced. They fell to discussing what forces were at the King's disposal, and whether, when the deed were done, the other side would be too aghast to move before reinforcements could arrive. Suddenly the King's mother appeared once more, and with her Guise in person. Handsome no longer: no proud hero this. On the way to the King's chamber his gracious salutations had been ignored, and the Captain of the guard, Crillon, had clapped his hat more firmly on his head. Whereby the Duke knew what awaited him. He entered and stood pale and daunted. But the old woman was beside him; and the King would make no sign because she was there. Of his House, who were all else dead or in revolt against him, only she was left in the palace of the Louvre; and to her all his life had been subjected. In her presence, against her will, there could be no thought of beckoning for the blessed dagger. He upbraided the Duke curtly and turned his back on him.

Guise sank down on a coffer. The eye nearest his scar was watery, he appeared to be shedding tears. He had marked the whole scene, and how afraid the King had been; as much so as himself, thought Guise. But the look on the King's drawn face had not escaped him: the resolve to kill was only for the time withdrawn. In the far corner of the room the old Queen was trying to pacify her son; and Guise managed to slip out. He was met with cries of "Hail!" Well, he was still alive, and here were his people, in the very courtyard of the Louvre, come to see him safe. Still the hero! — "Hail!" And now to work.

Such are the thoughts of one taken unawares. A Guise did not seriously intend to set up barricades and give battle to the King in his own capital; he had only dealt in intrigues that must lead to such embroilments. When he shrank before the final deed, and would have sooner gone to bed, Mendoza, Don Philip's Ambassador, came to see him and spoke to him in very peremptory fashion. The Duke had a real master who would brook no disobedience. Within three days France must be at open civil war; such was the will of the Ruler of the World. It was not thought necessary to inform Guise of the reason, but he was in fact well served with news. The Armada lay ready at last to set sail for England. The fleet had been equipping for a long while and was now supplied for a space of years, though the voyage was not a matter of more than fourteen days. On the way, it must be able to use the French ports in safety. The Ruler of the World, by nature precise and circumspect, wanted no encounters on the coast of France. Wherefore, within three days, casks filled with sand must be piled up in the Paris streets. The King, from his palace of the Louvre, had long ago seen them floating up the river. And as, in his anxiety, he had brought some Swiss and German soldiery into the city, here was the final pretext for revolt. The foreigners, overwhelmed by numbers, knelt and lifted up their rosaries. The King had to plead for his soldiers, as many as were left alive. He appealed to the Duke of Guise, whereby the Duke had no more heart to kill the King; which was what Mendoza had bidden him do.

As neither Valois nor Guise dared to kill the other, the people knew not what to think, and the streets remained for days together in possession of the monks, who preached a massacre while the bells pealed the alarm. Even Guise's sister, the Fury of the Holy League, played her part: she looked down from her balcony upon a tempestuous throng of youth and stirred it up to murder. She flattered them, she called them generous and high-hearted; and these budding lawyers, preachers, and plasterers were very ready to believe her every word. In times when events move overfast, young blood is always much in favour. The Duchess of Montpensier, in all the exuberance of her fury, still had an eye for faces; down in the throng of her votaries she noticed one that she had noticed several times before. A man that looked so was a man that could be used. She sent a lackey to fetch the young novice.

She did more; she arrayed her buxom person in a gossamer dress and sprinkled her bedchamber with perfume. Raven hair (though dyed), bared bosom powdered with silver stars — she eyed herself not without approval, ravaged though her face was by her passions. Six-and-thirty — for any other it might easily be too late, thought the great lady; but not for a boorish novice, who sees a Duchess's bed for the first time in his life. What should she do, and how far should she go? And a shrug of her opulent shoulders was the answer.

When she had a purpose, she held on until the end. That was where men failed, even the great Guise, who should be the next to mount the throne of France. But one stroke was needed, and from it he recoiled. Not so his sister. She would indeed strike with her own hand. Her hand was strong, her limbs no feebler than her brother's, her shoulders broad. She could herself be the hero of the family, save for the trifles that made her woman; and by that aid she would do this deed.

She gave the signal; lackeys hurried up with the monk and pushed him through the door, which was immediately closed. A goddess was left alone in the room with a coarse and odorous brown creature from the underworld. The perfume was powerless against the reek of dirt, which quite filled the room; but the lady was not daunted. She spoke to the little monk, who glared at her with piggish eyes, smacked his thick lips, and thrust his hands coolly up the crossed sleeves of his habit; he longed to slip them out and lay them on that shining flesh. Of shyness not a trace; in those days the barriers of class were gone, and all were accounted equal within the Holy League. Observe the casks in the street below; and the huddled bodies of the captains and the men-at-arms whom we, even we, have slain. And their women shall be ours. Ho-ho! High-hearted youth, says she.

" What is your name? " asked the Duchess in such a tone that the lad recoiled. " You know it," he muttered. " You called my name from up above: ' Jakob, where are you? ' — that is what you cried. Well, and how's it to be, hey? "

" Kneel! " said the Duchess thunderously. " And say your rosary." She had him at her mercy, that she knew from his crazy words. She unlocked his dreams, as she had done when she was speaking from the balcony. Once on his knees, he had to confess all his sordid, salacious little life: the sins of the flesh, for which he had been banished from his cloister to Paris, to do a certain deed. His director here had impressed it on his mind; sins of the flesh — they could only be amended by a deed. " What deed? "

asked the Duchess. That he did not know. The monks who
trained him left that in the dark. The monks were always training murderers of the King, but in the end they never used them.
This one was hers. "You are mine," she said sternly. "I shall
use you as I choose. I can make you invisible. Stand up and face
the wall." She went to the end of the room and looked about
her. "Jakob, where are you?" He heard her ask several times
before he answered. "So I am invisible, am I?" said he to himself; otherwise his mind was empty. His heart beat none the
faster.

"Jakob, come and touch the hem of my dress, and you will be
visible again."

"I won't," he grumbled, "unless I may touch more than the
hem."

However, he shuffled towards her on his sandals; but before he
could lay hold of her transparent garment, she said, this time in
an awesome whisper: "Jakob! You are to kill the King."

Crass as the creature was, he shook, and his jaw fell; for a while
he stood without a sound, then burst into a moan of fear. And
the terrors of damnation, like visible flames, poured forth from
the fiendish woman's mouth. Beneath her dress he could suddenly see — and clearly too — a hoof!

"Obey me, Jakob, and your fortune is made. If you kill the
King, you will be granted three wishes. A Cardinal's hat; as much
money as you want; and the third shall be mine to give you."
Whereat she coolly displayed her charms. She had spoken in a
cooing voice that quite bemused his senses; she watched him
quiver like an aspen, and his lips begin to dribble; and then the
poor idiot heard her say that a king is no more than a man. Let
him but die and he is dead for ever. "And if they look for you —
why, you are invisible. Jakob, where are you?"

"Here, beside you," he answered, gurgling with satisfaction,
for now he had understood, his fear had passed.

"Nay, not until you have killed the King, and are a Cardinal.
None but a Cardinal may share my bed." This in a chilly and
condescending tone, while she looked at him with a quick, appraising eye. The oaf was much too fat to thrust a dagger dex-

terously through the Valois. He must first be given powders for his easement, though he already can be made to see and hear just what he is told. They must frighten him with fiery devils in his cloister, in case the donkey ever stiffened his hind legs. But that he would not do; she had him fast. And she rang the bell. " Away with the brute and fumigate the room! "

As she went to the window, half naked as she was, many a high-hearted youth below dashed up for a sight of her. Complacently she displayed herself, for the window reached down to the floor. And in the passion of her pride she gazed up at the orb of heaven; it did not dazzle her.

" I — even I, will dare the deed! "

A Night with a Murderer

When the last Valois fled from his palace of the Louvre he thought of his cousin Navarre and longed for his company. " If I had him here, Paris should dwindle a little, we would lop so many heads off. Paris needs to be let blood. I am the only King that always lived and held my court there and made the city rich. The public execution of Guise shall be a popular festival."

Hot and ill-humoured, the poor King could none the less pursue his thoughts at leisure. Guise had quietly left an outlet open; he was escaping by his enemy's consent, who thus got rid of him and seized the government in the capital. The King's coach, headed by his guards, was driving at a walk towards the next halting-place, but his thoughts never wandered far from his cousin Navarre. " Had I sent him Joycuse and my finest army, not to be defeated, but to join him and march on Paris to deliver me! "

But as his thoughts deepened, he realized that this could never have been. His Catholic army would not have obeyed the order. And if that Protestant cousin of his had got to Paris — " Then my throne would have been in peril," decided Valois. This he doubted, but was too wretched not to cling to a suspicion that alone could bring him comfort. " And my life as well," he added in defiance.

Henri himself was much afraid of poison, and had been so for two months past, since his cousin Condé's death. The Prince of Condé had been poisoned; by his own wife, as Henri believed. He at once conceived a like suspicion of his unhappy Margot, distraught as she then was, and a prey to her insensate hatred. Henri, who loved eating and had sat down heartily to table wherever he was invited, promptly had all his food cooked in a locked kitchen, under guard. Cousin Condé had vomited all night long. On the second morning he ate his breakfast standing, started playing chess, and again felt very ill; his skin was already blackening as he died. Henri mourned him for the ally that he should have been; not at all for what he was.

Four-and-twenty murderers were sent to dispose of the King of Navarre. What the unhappy Valois so longed for, aid and comfort from his cousin, others feared and were determined to prevent. He was reported dead, as such reports are spread by those who would profit by the event, and some actually gave details of his death. The Duke of Guise hastened to the King of France to ask whether it was so. The King could only hope that his cousin Navarre yet lived; after Condé's death he had sent envoys to him, of whom the most notable was Montmorency. This was indeed his last attempt to induce the sole surviving Protestant leader to become a Catholic once more. Henri was now undisputed heir to the throne. No one believed it possible that his Protestants could forsake him, now that his rival had departed. But it was possible; Henri knew them all too well. He also knew that he must move straight forward so long as any deviation would wear the guise of weakness. He scorned to draw advantage from disloyalty, and rejected a fulfilment that should come too soon. When the kingdom had been conquered and united, after all the toils that remained to be confronted, when his hair was grey and his power and strength were proved; when, to gain his ends, it was no longer necessary, then, of his own free will, he would go to Mass. Not before. Merely to win acceptance, never.

But Henri feared poison and the knife; against these none may fight, as a soldier and a man's conscience can. The knife is worst — an ever-present threat, not only at the table. Often and often,

in a press of people, Henri felt himself shiver, lest someone behind him might be drawing something from his sleeve. A knife
could very conveniently lurk in the broad sleeve of a monk's
habit. One day a very imposing gentleman appeared who could
not speak the language nor even Latin, and carried a petition with
him on a rolled-up parchment in a little case; as he drew it forth,
a dagger slid into his hand. It was only just in time that Henri
seized and wrenched his wrist away. Captain Sacremore had
been caught with proofs upon him; not a doubt but that he had
been set on Henri, who would otherwise never have believed it
of such a bold, upstanding officer. Murderers, thought Henri,
were cowards; was he to live in fear of them? He would drink a
glass of wine with one of them at last, and make acquaintance
with his kind.

That was at Nérac. In the evening he dismissed his people,
had the prisoner brought in and unfettered, and was left alone,
with only a table between himself and a murderer.

"Captain Sacremore, pray tell me what it feels like to kill. I
fancy I shall one day know what it feels like to be killed — but
not by you. As a soldier and a brave man, what think you of the
coward's deed called murder, eh?"

The man's eyes were evil, otherwise he was well-looking
enough in a ruthless, mercenary fashion. He sat gracefully and
at ease — he was, indeed, of a noble Italian house; his deep ironic
air would alone have made him notable. He did not answer.
Henri pushed the wine across to him; the man thanked him
courteously and drained his glass "There might be poison in it,
Captain Sacremore."

"Sire," said the murderer, in a tone of polite surprise, "you
have many ways of putting me to death."

"And which, think you, shall I choose?"

"Sire, the most honourable — single combat," said the murderer, masking his guile as a jest.

"Monsieur Charles de Birague, I am serious. You came to this
country with the former Chancellor, who had our barons
strangled in prison that the old Queen might lay hands on their
estates. You have been promised, if you murder me, many

pocketfuls of Spanish pistoles. You won the name of Sacremore in the field, as a soldier of fortune, but, for all that, you are a Birague."

" Sire, you would insult me. I propose a duel, as between men of honour; as your murderer I can claim to be your equal, which is why you are sitting with me here at dead of night."

" I know," said Henri. " For this hour you are my equal. Suppose you had succeeded? "

" I would have continued to serve the King of France, who sent me."

" You lie — and you would lie even if the gold in your pockets had not been Spanish."

" Well," admitted Birague, " but I would have stayed here none the less. A weak country is best for men of my kind: one where the people are at odds with the world and with each other, that's where a man like me can thrive. If, Sire, you survive, you will change all this — which is why I tried to murder you, and I would have done so without pay."

So Henri learned a new lesson — a villain can be a man of purpose and resolve. " Sacremore, you have earned your nickname — or nearly." And he laid his dagger between them on the table. " Who gets it first, Sacremore — ! "

In a flash, the murderer's hand shot out, but struck the King's. Both hands withdrew beneath the table edge. But with set, unmoving eyes they watched each other, each quivering with the zest of combat and ready for a pounce. Meantime Henri bethought him of what would give his adversary a shock.

" Sacremore, there will be no more money from Spain. They believe you have betrayed them and will work for me in the future."

The murderer gnashed his teeth, and in his hatred he grew hideous; so foul a mask struck terror, which was perhaps how he had earned his name; and in the instant's pause he grabbed the dagger. Henri could only overturn the table, which he did. The table was heavy; to prevent it crushing him, the murderer needed both his hands and dropped the dagger. Scrambling to his feet, he dashed through the door and fled down the open passage, light-footed as a girl.

" Sacremore! Stop! I'll pay you well! "

Came the crack of a musket-shot and the sound of a body crashing down the stairway. The sentry in the courtyard had fired; Sacremore had ceased to be.

" Pity," said Henri to himself. " A stout fellow, and I would have made an honest man of him. Killed by accident — and after such a night! " Henri forgot that he himself had survived the night and the ordeal. A man must not tremble even at his murderer.

The Call

Valois consorted equally with the would-be murderers of his country and himself; he sat with them at table, and he lived in fear. At that time he was holding an assembly of the Estates at Blois. The King had fled there; Guise promptly followed him, and the Heads of the League also hurried off, sixteen of them, each governing one of the wards of Paris. And common folk from the capital were convoyed thither, to overawe the more intelligent deputies from the provinces, on whom Valois could always count. Intelligence is in ill repute and must be terrorized. A band of flagellants invaded the King; he had to receive them, and his fondness for disguises drew him to join in their performances. A brother of his dead favourite, Joyeuse, impersonated the Crucified, and a frantic presentation of the Passion burst into the poor King's place of refuge; Christ shed real blood, the Roman soldiers rattled their rusty weapons, and dashed when least expected among the excited mob. The holy women were really Capucins, well skilled at howling and wailing and prostrations. Then, under the scourging, the Son of Man fell too. There were shrieks to Valois to lift him up — and threats to murder him as a heretic if he refused. But in truth they went in terror of themselves and their own blasphemous frenzy.

What could a learned jurist and a member of the Royal Parliament think of such events? — for such indeed were pressed into these affrays. Learning is not easily forgotten, and a clear intellect may not confuse itself to order. But a movement of the masses can engulf a man and change him before he is aware; and he who would have been too much given to thought learned from mass emotion and mob-fellowship to bellow "like a calf." Indeed, the President of Neuilly did so to such purpose that even the tyrant Valois was moved; and against that monarch he stirred up the populace by his lamentations, just as Boucher the preacher had done by foaming at the mouth. Each in his own fashion; the Duke of Guise, for his part, did it, with much loathing in so doing, by shaking many dirty hands.

Indeed, most things filled the Duke of Guise with loathing in those days — his role as popular hero, his subservience to Spain, and the very life he lived. Beset by villainous Spanish spies, he must without shame sacrifice his own Prince to Don Philip's imperious Ambassador. He had to beg for help from Spain, should the Valois fall back on the Huguenots. Pah! He would sooner become a Huguenot himself than endure much more of such humiliation.

Vanity and a taste for admiration, undeserved, though little more than weaknesses, had led him astray. And he knew it, for his blood was good. Only very little people conceive themselves as great when a vile and besotted movement of the masses carries them to a peak where they do not belong. When a Duke of Guise was greeted with cries of " Hail, Leader! " he wanted to hide his head, or, better still, to chase the rout back into their dirty lairs. His inmost longing was for a reconciliation with the King of France. The King was to appoint him Constable for the whole kingdom, before the Armada returned victorious from England, and the Spaniards were too flown with insolence. By then Guise meant to have brought them to a stand. But to that end one thing was needed; and indeed it was for that sole purpose that the Estates had met at Blois.

The King had had to promise he would extirpate the heretics; he was further pestered to declare that the King of Navarre had forfeited his rights as successor to the throne. The King tried evasions. Navarre himself sent an address to the assembly, which thereupon solemnly pronounced his claim as lapsed. He was also stripped of his prerogatives as First Prince of the Blood.

At the news of this, Henri forgot his murderers and his Muse, and with his fantasies his fears went too. He marched forth to war. What? King and League, all unloosed against him alone, and so defiling the name of man by their frenzies that he instinctively despised them as he had never done the like of Sacremore. Men must kill and work injustice — that was life; but they need not therefore play the hypocrite nor abdicate their reason. He marched northwards into Britanny, through the land of France, whose rulers were then engaged in dispossessing him. He fought against the royal troops and the Leaguers, not caring which, for he had grown embittered. The throne was in sight — and again he had to plunge beneath the surface as he had done at the outset, when he was unknown. He had won the field of Coutras — and here he was campaigning in the marshes and storming little towns: an ambush, one poor nobleman slain, a hundred unreluctant prisoners, hail and a storm, the capture of a fortress by the sea. Where were those guns? 'Tis folly to contend against sea and wind!

In the ardours of the fight, however, he forgot his disgust and wrath: glad to be there and drawing breath, although even that they grudged him, and winning a little ground, though very slowly. One day alone under a tree at noon, gasping from exertion, having just escaped from death, he prepared to eat; and he looked about him with very wistful eyes. The land stretched out to far horizons, listening in silence to the roaring of the sea. It does not want him, it does not even know him, and had he not felt in his heart that all would be well, he might well have feared that his whole task lay before him still. The same pictures eternally recurred: marshes and an ambush, a hundred prisoners, a poor nobleman slain, storm and hail, and a castle by the sea that must and shall be taken — if only the guns had come up! In his powder-blackened hand he holds his meal, a crust of bread and an apple.

He is hungry, but he will not be daunted. Hither has he come upon life's journey — once he strode in sunshine on the mountains and plunged laughing into shining streams. While still a boy he was put to the school of unhappiness and learned to think, until the turns of thought set strange lines about his lips from time to time. Home once more, he met all the daily troubles of life, as a lad with a hungry belly and sensitive skin may do. The troubles were but trifling; face them heartily and wait — there will be greater ones to come. Now he is famous, soon to be hated, courted, feared — and discovers how the troubles of life may be again what they have been; and standing beneath a tree, he devoured his meal.

At that same hour the King of France was receiving the Ambassador, Mendoza, who had had reports of the victory of the Armada, which he caused to be printed on leaflets. Then he set off from Paris to Chartres; his first act being to offer thanks to the Virgin in the ancient cathedral of that place. Then he waited upon the King, who was lodging in the Bishop's palace. " Victory! " said the Ambassador loftily, at the sight of anyone he knew. He was admitted to the King's presence and produced his dispatch. But the King handed him a later one: the English had attacked the Armada, sunk fifteen ships, and killed five thousand men. An invasion of England was now out of calculation.

Mendoza tried to bluff; whatever were the facts, his haughty attitude remained unassailed. Fifteen ships! — but there were a hundred and fifty in the Armada, the most gigantic vessels that this world had ever seen. Five thousand killed — that would not hurt the landing army, not to mention reinforcements on the way.

Except that they were not on the way; they were blockaded in Holland. The King of France expressed courteous admiration of the floating castles constructed by Don Philip, but unfortunately their height was such that their guns could only fire from a certain distance; a weakness which, unfortunately too, Admiral Drake had been quick to grasp. His shallops had dashed out from Plymouth right up to the giants' hulls and holed them. Heaven had also been so ill-advised as to support the wrong side, and at that very moment storms were scattering the Spanish ships, some as far as the Arctic Ocean, where they were lost.

Spaniards do not laugh, otherwise the Ambassador could not have forborne his laughter at the puny efforts of England and the tempests against the power that ruled the world. He stood in a scornful silence, which the King did not break; and the pair faced each other in that great stone hall, each with his hat upon his head. But two gentlemen of the court were not indisposed to provoke the Spaniard. "The Queen of England has triumphed," said Crillon in a trenchant voice. And another added: "Elizabeth appeared before her people on a white horse."

"A great nation," said Ornano sagely.

"A happy one, now safe and free, and devoted to its glorious Queen. Five and forty years cannot avail against the beauty of a conquering Queen."

Biron, Henri of Navarre's old friend, observed: "A united nation. We should be united." A movement ran through the assemblage, and a name was passed from mouth to mouth, at first in secret.

The King left the hall, followed by the Ambassador. As the King made his way along the vaulted passages, his bearing was majestic, such as Valois knew how to assume. At a rear window he stopped and pointed downwards into the courtyard. The Ambassador recognized about three hundred Turkish convicts, such as were carried on Spanish ships as galley slaves. He asked whence they came. From an Armada wreck, replied the King. The Ambassador demanded their delivery. By way of answer the King drew himself up to his full height by the window. The slaves fell on their knees and cried: "Misericordia!" The King eyed them and turned away. "This must be considered."

Some gentlemen of the court dared to say: "The matter has already been considered. There is no slavery in France. Whoever sets foot on French soil is free. Our King will give these people back to his ally, the Sultan."

The King pretended not to have heard, and ceremoniously escorted the Ambassador to the staircase; and there the haughty Spaniard had yet more to swallow. Before him and behind him there was talk of the prisoners from many nations whom Spain had forced upon her fleet as oarsmen; even Frenchmen had fallen under the common yoke. " Soldiers and our countrymen! What does Spain then mean to make of us? What she has made of all the peoples of the earth: slaves! " The first time that such words were uttered at the court of France was on the day when it was known the Armada had been defeated.

The Ambassador had gone, but the King did not return; he seemed to be waiting, no one knew for what, and many believed him fallen into his former vacancy. So they talked more freely still and repeated yet more vehemently that all Frenchmen must unite in defence of their freedom, as the English had done. What had that country not escaped! All the Inquisition's implements of torture had been put on board the Spanish ships. There were Protestants, declared and hidden, at the Catholic court of France, and none knew which of them presumed to say: " Freedom of thought, all hangs on that; it is the bulwark of our justice and our unity." None protested; a name was passed from mouth to mouth, the same name as before, but boldly now; and Biron once again addressed the King.

" Sire! The King of Navarre — he is a better man than I thought him. It is seldom that we see our own injustice, but in this matter I see mine."

At that moment Guise appeared; Mendoza had sent him to intimidate the King. He talked with ready menace of the thirty thousand Spaniards now in Flanders. A voice: " And where stands the King of Navarre? " Guise waited vainly for Valois to intervene. He ought himself to have done so, but disgust begets despondency and leaves a man indifferent. A voice:

" Sire! Send for the King of Navarre! "

Not one voice was raised in protest. Guise and his League were soon to surrender to the Spaniards a fortress on the Flemish coast; they would further serve the cause of Spain and harry the King. This was the day of destiny for Guise, for the defeat of the Armada gave him knowledge of himself. A voice cried:

" The King of Navarre! "

A little distance from his army stood Henri, under a tree. The land stretches away to far horizons, listening in silence to the roaring of the sea. Henri heard a voice call his name.

DANCE OF DEATH

His thoughts are wandering, and his ears are quick to hear. His daily affairs go forward, but a greater task is soon to be proclaimed. He deals with business, his feet firm set upon the wonted heavy earth. But he awaits his task, inwardly uplifted and expectant. In that tense interval Henri's heart was indeed set upon his war, but also elsewhere — nearer unto God. He said with David: " God, who hath given me victory over my enemies until now, help me still." Thus he spoke, and even: " I am better than ye think me ": strange words in his mouth.

At La Rochelle a church assembly was sitting on his sins: he was patient, listened humbly to the pastors, and did not answer as he might have done: " My little friends, who was it that endured, through the School of Unhappiness, the Troubles of Life, and also mastered the temptations of the soul? Only what was revealed about my mother could have sapped the courage of her son, but I preserved the inborn hue of resolution! " This he neither said to the pastors at La Rochelle, nor did he so boast to his friend the Countess Gramont. He told her none but facts accomplished, his victories over the army of the King of France — and the murder of the Duke of Guise by the King; yes, the King had done it in the end.

Henri had long expected this, he was well served with news from the court, and he well understood his fellow-men. He saw Valois in the Estates Assembly; almost all the members were supporters of the League, as a consequence of savage terrorism at the elections: all haters, insolent and brutal, and whither that hate would carry them they no longer knew. They abolished all the taxes levied by the King in his fourteen years of reign; they robbed him of the remainder of his power, and thereby robbed the kingdom and themselves. Such was the result of fourteen years' incitement and a mob movement whipped up for the purpose. At last that purpose is achieved and needs but to be ham-

mered hard enough into those skulls; then reality dissolves and
is transformed into embodied madness, and a lie preached long
enough sheds actual blood. Withal, these are common citizens,
crassly ignorant of religion, politics, and all affairs of men. For
them the complaisant Valois was a tyrant, and his cultured State
an infamy. The League, that plundered and betrayed the kingdom — they swore on their very souls it stood for "freedom."
Only the abolition of the taxes was needed to fulfil the promises
trumpeted throughout the land for fourteen years.

The wives of these chosen and enlightened druggists and
tinsmiths danced naked through the Paris streets. It was an idea
of the Duchess of Montpensier, sister of the Guises, Fury of the
League, whose demonstrations were to gain attraction from this
obscene buffoonery. This was too much; little citizens are many,
and are not inclined to dash upon destruction, nor let their crazed
wives skip into it. They began to shut their purses; and in other
matters they grew daily more intractable. Hence a fleeting revolt
against the marauding bands which had brought Paris to her
present pass. Guise had to realize that he must do a deed that
would commit his followers beyond recall; the King must die.

At that time the King was very poor, poorer than even Henri of
Navarre had ever been. His court had broken up, his last five-and-
forty noblemen were looking for masters who could pay them.
Valois had nothing to eat, Henri was told; in his kitchen the fire
was out. "Did I," thought Henri, "put it out when I destroyed
his best army at Coutras? I must come to his help. He is appealing to Guise now; and Guise to the League, on his behalf.
The mob is hopeless; only an unscrupulous leader looks for
backing from such folk. But he should be careful. He believes
the King has ceased to be a man; but Guise is not a king, he does
not know kings. When the ambassadors report our approaching end, the strength of the centuries floods our veins. I'll bring
help to Valois."

Guise was growing shameless, so Henri learned. He flung aside
all caution — lodged in the royal castle that he might hold the
King more securely in his hands, forgetting that he himself
might be in Valois's hands. Guise had all the keys; but he got no

news, for all too late the King grew suspicious of his mother and dismissed her intimates, thus extinguishing all the spying and the treachery that were her very life. And Henri silently wished him good luck and admired his solitary courage. Guise stopped his ears; in spite of many warnings, five on one day, he would not budge. There were several reasons for this, which Henri knew. Guise was arrogant; he surrounded himself with his usual splendid retinue and refused to admit of any danger. His arrogance would bring him down — and not only because it made him careless. He thought himself above his part. Henri knew his old playfellow to the bone. Poor Guise, his pride was beginning to make his gorge rise, he could no longer endure his own people's breath. And Henri thought if he were Guise and were a villain, he would like the smell of them — garlic, wine, and feet as well. But he did not like the smell of Spain, so it would be no use. Moreover, Guise had become ridiculous.

In his meditations, by the camp-fire at night, or alone beneath a tree, Henri's spirits began to rise. Guise was spending money. He would not suffer boredom, he sent for the court, he feasted and entertained the whole splendid company, and Valois too — instead of murdering him. He had many women, more than was good for him, and we know all about pleasure, we ourselves have discovered that it favours doubt and swells satiety. A man grows wearied by it, especially such a Goliath as Guise — he most of all. Pride, satiety, and pleasure, all combined, might in the end lure a man to close his eyes and await the stroke. We ourselves escaped the temptation not so long ago.

When the messenger rode up at last, with the news that the Duke of Guise had been killed in the King's bedchamber while the King had looked on from behind his bed-curtains, Henri was not surprised, nor was he sorry. To all the details of the deed, how each dagger-thrust was dealt by a different murderer, all frenzied and dazed like men who could not credit their own act, Henri listened unperturbed. He shed tears on the field of battle, not at the like of this. They had clung to the dying man's legs, while he dragged himself across the room to the Valois, who shuddered and then raved, then burst into ghastly glee and kicked the dead man in the face, as Guise had done to Admiral Coligny. God forgot no deed of theirs, thought Henri. Were all laws broken, His remained.

Guise had spent his last night with Sauves; and Henri had lain with that very woman not long before his flight. Him, whom she did not love, she had merely comforted in loneliness. Her one lord and master she must needs be the last to weaken; so that he stood shivering in his grey silk bed-gown in the dawn, until others came and made him cold for ever. Farewell, Guise; salutations to Sauves. The King has won. He caused the Cardinal of Lorraine to be strangled in prison, and was still searching for the third brother, Mayenne — and he would find him yet! The Dance of Death went on all through that year '88, and the highest officers of the realm were overtaken only one day before Christmas. Hang them in Paris, Valois! For four-and-twenty hours the President of Neuilly, who could bellow " like a calf," and the Warden of the Merchants, have been a-hanging. A nobleman whom Guise had favoured had dealings in human flesh. Hang him up, Valois! The Dance of Death began with the poisoning of our cousin, Condé, and there are dead killers that lie in wait for both of us, for you as well as me. But we have had no dealings in human flesh. Hang them up, Valois.

Such were the thoughts of one who had let many of his " killers " go, and indeed wanted to get used to sitting up with them at night. Away with this subservience to the evil in men's nature! There's good there too, as well they know; which makes their wickedness all the less forgivable. From the beginnings of the race, the nobler sons of men have waged their thankless struggle for reason and for peace. Eauze, and the advent of human kindness — that had been a sorry jest; a phrase like " champion of the spirit " had a merely mocking ring when men were brutal and stupid and so wanted to remain. But here was a King called Henri, who could break his fellows on the wheel or hang them, no less than you can; and you have merely jeered at him for his sense and sanity. All his life long you have requited his goodwill with brutality and madness. Dance of Death — go on! The year has yet a week to run. I await the hour when I hear the Queen of Navarre has been strangled. And that her mother is dead; then I shall lift up my voice in the thanksgiving of Simeon: "Lord, now lettest Thou Thy servant depart in peace."

Thus he spoke, and thus he wrote, and so he was minded, after the killing at Blois. He hoped that Valois would also murder his sister Margot, and, better still, his old mother, Madame Catherine. She, in the meantime, did die — without extraneous aid; she was old and shaken, and Guise's death, and the common belief that there could be no murder in which she had not had a hand, were more than she could bear. It is hard for an old murderess to be blamed for what she can no longer do. Nothing was left for her but death. Could she be really dead? The news roused Henri from the mood that had come upon him. He had prophesied too well, and he did not love to kill. He grew fearful for his Margot of old days. Dance of Death — be still!

HEART REACHES OUT TO HEART

But time for stopping it was long since past. Henri, in his little war, rode through a savage frost, until he was quite numbed in his cuirass; he had to dismount and swing his limbs to warm himself. Later, when he had dined, he was seized by a strange extremity of cold; and he realized that his turn had come to be drawn into the dance. It was an attack of inflammation of the lungs. It took him in a little town, and so violent was the malady that they had to leave him lying in the manor-house. The frost crackled on the window-panes, his fever rose, until there seemed no hope left; he alone never gave up hope. He murmured to himself: "I'll do it yet. It shall not all have been in vain." And he thought to say aloud, but his voice was still a whisper: "Thy will be done!" The will of Heaven was assured that Henri would fight and do what it was his task to do — though he were that day turned over in his grave-clothes like Lazarus; and the crisis that might yet save him was a matter of hours.

And while he caught a glimpse or two of heaven, it seemed as though, before the dawn of a nobler age, the land of France were presenting a panorama in little of all the horrors of the past: Dance of Death, St. Vitus's dance, the Children's Crusade, the plague, the thousand-year-old Empire, and white upturned eyes, so often blinded by visions of what was not there. And this was the way of it. " Ha ha! " says high-hearted youth, after the fashion of Jakob the monk. " At last we hold the whip. There's no matter for laughter in this land. Those folks that made so merry on Carnival Tuesday — they'll laugh no more. Mind how you stay away from church. But if the priest names you, you'll not get home alive. Hoho! We'll mark them down and hunt them out and bring them to the gallows! " A man's accuser is rewarded by his office or his business; such is the admirable custom. Many men grow vile in those days — many who would be decent folk were the times they lived in different; 'tis not to be laid to their account. They are, what none could then fail to be, villains. Not from themselves, or from their own hearts. Though where, indeed, do their hearts now lie?

What a mob especially detests is ordered thought. A raw student, but with the desired opinions, marches into the professor's lecture-room, stamps both his feet, has him locked up, and is appointed in his place. The young doctor replaces his elder rival; the professor not having given his laundress the correct salute. The young official, so obsequious in time past, now grows all the more insolent to the judges of the royal Parliament. They must come with him and deliver judgment in the name of the united people, for a people can only be united when thinking has been stopped. And, very fittingly, their wives dance through the streets in their shifts.

The President of the Court in Toulouse was murdered. Barricades first, then a gallows for the dead judge — and up with the King's puppet. He had opposed the King's deposition, for which many men were hanged. The last Valois had been a feeble man, and not unstained by crime. But near his end he had the honour of men's hatred, not for the evil that he had done, but because of their loathing for reason and human dignity, whose embodiment in their eyes, though but a sorry one, he was.

He flitted spectrally about in his violet cassock, which he wore

in mourning for his brother and his mother. But he seemed in
truth to be wearing it for Guise, whom he himself had killed. He
was no match for the dead man. His deed, the only one he ever
did, had left him utterly disarmed. Any other than himself, the
last of his race, it would have nerved to action. This was the
high moment, now he must spread fear, lest fear should master
him. Courage? — reflection? — the choice was no longer his.
Troops were what he needed, and before his enemies had recovered from their dismay they must be struck down. Hither,
Navarre!

Valois, in his violet cassock, pale and silent, was ever thinking
of that name. He haunted his castle at Blois, alone and deserted,
deposed by Church and people too, now released from their
allegiance. The members of the Estates had departed. He would
not have been admitted to his own capital; indeed, he would
have been imprisoned and murdered; but this, as he very well
knew, was a consequence of what was really weakness. Such
violence, as Valois understood from his own self, is not to be
confused with healthy energy. That was found in another camp.
Navarre, he thought, behind that mask-like face; but he made
no sign, he did not dare. The Huguenots marching on his
capital, and he the man of Saint Bartholomew! Navarre would
indeed have brought him back into the Louvre, but that would
have meant war with the Ruler of the World, who remained as
formidable as ever.

When the Armada perished, only a lightning flash rent the dark
heaven of the last Valois. He was past realizing that the power
that ruled the world had been dealt a mortal blow. That was
a matter for his heir. The heir to his throne would, at the beginning of his rule, be without land or money, and almost without an army; he needed but to win one paltry battle over the
mercenaries and slaves of Spain; and then? A gasp of relief from
all the nations of the world.

Over Valois darkness brooded, every sound was choked. There
was no one now about him who would summon Navarre. None
without that trembled at Navarre's approach; how otherwise
could they have dared to cut off his last revenues, and that after

his one monstrous deed? The room was growing cold, and the King slipped into bed. He was suffering pain — a pain that made him ludicrous — from hæmorrhoids; and his few remaining noblemen laughed at him because he wept.

"Navarre! Come! No, do not come. I am not weeping for pain, but because the one deed I did was futile. Now show what you can do. Never again. And yet — you are the man to whom I mean to yield. I recognize you as my heir, had I forsworn you ten times over. There is none but you, and I have paid for knowing it. Behold me, Navarre, in my misery. It was never so deep nor so bitter as since my vain attempt to free myself. When the deed was done I cried: 'The King of Paris is dead, at last I am King of France!' Call me not so, for I am not. Call me Lazarus when you come, Navarre. No, do not come. Yes — come."

Both Kings, with nearly the whole kingdom between them, were very sick. Henri survived his crisis and was soon himself — never again did he let his mind stray among those murderous fantasies that heralded his malady. He spoke with restraint of Monsieur de Guise's end: "I saw from the first that the gentlemen of Guise could never master such an enterprise, nor bring it to an issue without peril to their lives." Such was his epitaph, and his attitude concurred; more circumspect than ever, and many thought it too restrained. Why not make one of his bold strokes and cut out Valois from among his enemies, who indeed held all the country in between? His friends had always known him as a breakneck, and that in small affairs. So cautious, Sire, in this great one?

He divined his old friends' disapproval. The oldest Huguenots, accustomed from father to son to die for the Religion, the same who had knelt in prayer at Coutras and brought Joyeuse to his end, murmured now, although they did not well know why. They wanted to rescue the Catholic King, though they would barely have believed it possible. But Henri's opinion was that the men must be ripe before the occasion could be so. With Valois matters stood unchanged, as he had learned. The last Valois had left his former refuge and was then in Tours, which lies among cornfields on both banks of the Loire, a haven of peace and order in the heart of his turbulent realm. There he hoped to hold out until enough of his noblemen had bethought themselves of their King. His surviving favourite, Epernon, was in the meantime recruiting infantry. Even so his enemies might well fall upon him first and take him prisoner. Navarre alone was safe; where could he be? And Valois also reflected that he, the Catholic King, who could barely raise a troop of horse, might well see his army disperse if he sent for the Huguenot.

Henri reflected that the King would send for him when his people were so minded, before when it would be too soon. And his heart went out to Valois. He said nothing, but it was on that account alone he summoned Mornay, on the first day in March, in a little town which had lately opened its gates without the need of an attack. There they paced up and down an avenue in the spring sun, which had never seemed so fresh and full of hope.

" Something has changed," said Henri; " I am needed everywhere, and all the towns make haste to open their gates. Have the good folk gone mad, or is it the spring? "

" Sire, it may be a scheme to make you waste your time."

" Why so much haste? " asked Henri, and his heart beat quicker; because he well knew what lay to his hand, and in the last moment he quailed. Long had he striven: step by step, and in the sweat of his brow, he had toiled towards the goal. It was in sight and reach; but now he wavered, the last movement was not made, his old assurance suddenly seemed to waver. Success seemed less a matter of course than when it was still distant and viewed from an entanglement of perils. Prince of the Blood he may be, but his feet are clogged with earth. Now for another voice; Monsieur du Plessis-Mornay shall exercise his virtue and his craft.

" Sire, you have no longer two months to waste in pleasant diversions. Now save France, or it will perish. You must advance upon the Loire with all the forces that you can raise."

" There the King stands," said Henri, with a leap of his heart.

" For that very reason."

" Am I to attack him, Mornay? "

" Sire, you are his friend, and he will be yours, now that ten of his armies have not been able to destroy you."

" Was it ten, Mornay? So much toil and trouble? Well, and now Valois has not one, the League will swallow him whole. I should come to his rescue, Monsieur du Plessis? I may choose to do it. I will consider of the matter."

The result of the conversation was that he proposed to buy a town upon his way, to ease his progress through the kingdom; he who had exposed his life a thousand times when there was little to be won by doing so. Now the kingdom was to be won. But — must he storm walls, burn houses, scatter corpses in the streets? The King that he means to be has too much of this behind him, too gladly would he turn his eyes away from all such doings. He buys cities that will not submit, and later he would even buy provinces, but first he must win more battles and grow old in harness. For otherwise his kingdom is not to be made peaceable, prosperous, and strong, for money.

Such melancholy truths moved in Henri's cheerful mind, whether consciously or merely as forebodings. He was indeed full young for them, but they were not beyond his compass. Fortunate, truly, that he had the excellent Mornay at his side. This in good earnest was a man who remained devout in all his cleverness, and for all the wickedness of many he encountered. He believed in the power of the Word, that is from God. Let us but uphold it, as it came from Him, in all purity and truth; then it cannot fail. And so, in the name of his Prince, Mornay drew up an appeal to all in the kingdom. Frenchmen must be united and at one.

He asked what had been achieved by all these pitiable wars, these deeds of violence, these million dead, and more gold squandered than a mine would yield? And the answer was — he really left his readers to make it for themselves: The ruin of the nation. The State lay fevered to death. Misery without end. And what would be the outcome? First he asked the nobles and the burghers, and forthwith gave the answers that their own judgment would put into their mouths. Then he raised his tone, he spoke to the people — the granary of the kingdom, the garden, the State; their labour fed the princes, their sweat slaked their masters' thirst. With whom will you take refuge, O people, when the nobles tread you down?

Mornay, and through him Henri, used those words: " Tread you down." As for the burghers of the cities, he urged that they would batten on the people. From those two classes could come no help; the people could look only to the King. Peace and security could come from the King alone — and from which King might be guessed. The King of the persecuted and the poor, the victor over silver knights and tax-farmers. But as the appeal went forth in his Prince's name, Mornay did not fail to enter a pledge of loyalty to the King of France. When once Henri of Navarre had, under God's blessing, fulfilled his plan, he would then render obedience to the King of France. His own reward should be his good conscience. He would be content to have delivered all men of goodwill.

So ran the appeal, purposely passing over one class of the population, striving indeed to placate them, with little hope of doing so. The priesthood would be obdurate, and the blind force of hatred, here called the League, could not suddenly be bridled, even by the truth. And yet far and wide the truth was recognized in these words of Navarre. Mornay's faith was wholly justified. And from that truth shone a light that few had hoped to see, and scarce to be believed. Was the nation to be united and at peace? Never yet had that been permitted. What had come about? Even the two Kings were astonished at their eagerness to join hands. There were matters that still parted them; Navarre had no notion of changing his religion, he thought only of inheriting a kingdom. Valois was, as always, in negotiations with the League. None the less, he made known to Mornay that he was ready, and to Navarre he sent his natural sister, Madame Diana.

An armistice for a year was agreed upon between the two Kings, but both meant it to be final. Meantime Henri was on the march, and as the cities on his way threw open their gates, he advanced rapidly towards Tours, where the King had assembled his Parliament. These jurists were men of mind, and as Navarre approached, the more courageous they became; at last they recorded the treaty among the laws of the kingdom. That was done on the 29th of April. On the 30th Navarre appeared.

It was a Sunday, bright and clear. Valois felt as though he had risen from the dead. For the first time he was rid of the fear that the League would capture him and carry him off. The King was at Mass when both armies met, on the bank of a stream, three miles from the city: the noblemen of the King of France with their troops of horse, and yonder the hard-bitten Huguenots. Wisely, they did not halt, but they at once broke ranks, unbridled their horses, and watered them side by side. Thus employed, there was no occasion for idle talk, or looking into each other's faces. They would have seen faces aged, and bodies scarred; they would have recognized the marks of anguish in them as in themselves, and called to mind too many a burnt house and murdered family, and twenty years of civil war. During that first peaceful encounter they could scarce forget the night of Saint Bartholomew — neither the doers of the deed nor those that suffered it; and they did well to slip the horses' halters and ride them into the stream. The King of Navarre watched at a distance and let them be; ahead of him he sent the commander of his infantry.

From the waterside came shouts of " Monsieur de Châtillon "; they could not believe their eyes. And on that bright, clear Sunday Admiral Coligny's son walked alone up to Marshal d'Aumont and embraced him. A space was left round the two generals, and heads were bared. This done, and taken to the hearts of all who saw, the two armies fraternized.

The Kings followed their example. Wisely, too, the Kings let the armies encounter each other first and feel due astonishment at these unwonted freedoms. At the castle of Plessis, on the farther side of the river, the King of France awaited the King of Navarre, whom he had invited to meet him there. This was a presumption which showed that Valois had learned little from misfortunes, and he was suspected of evil designs. At the castle of Plessis the Cher joins the Loire. The crossing at that point is

exposed to a treacherous shot from every side; and on the tongue
of land Henri would be wholly in Valois's power. Several of his
retinue were insistent that he should not go; but he was not to
be daunted, got into a boat with a few noblemen and bodyguards,
and even wore his white plume and short red cloak, which made
him conspicuous from afar.

He went with joy in his heart, because it was God's will, and
also because of Valois's yearning for him; he was assured of it by
what he felt himself. Once across the river, the King's gentlemen
escorted him to the castle, where the King awaited him in the
park; he had arrived an hour before, a prey to every sort of fear,
but outwardly like a man asleep; not daring to ask why Navarre
lingered, and whether some mishap had befallen him. Surrounded by courtiers once more, he uttered nothing of what
was stirring within his mind. But when he heard that Navarre
had come, he ran a few steps, then he remembered his majetsy and
hurriedly displayed it. The park was thronged with courtiers
and curious country-folk. Each King had covered half the space
that parted them before they met.

Navarre had walked down the flight of steps from the castle
into the park. He was dressed as a soldier, his doublet much
rubbed on shoulders and sides by constant wearing of a cuirass.
His breeches were of russet-coloured velvet, his cloak scarlet, and
to his grey hat was buckled his great white plume and a glittering
medal. All this was clearly to be seen by court and people.
Some, too, remarked, though less eagerly, that his beard was
growing grey. Tears there may have been in Henri's eyes, none
could see; but his tears came very easily, as those who had known
of old could still recall. But they too could barely recognize that
thin, drawn face, against which the drooping nose, with the deep,
curved wrinkle at the root, looked all the larger, below tense and
lifted brows. It was not a simple face; and only its determination
made of it a soldier's face. The sickly prisoner of the Louvre had
vanished. Such was the Navarre who strode towards the King.

Half-way they were held apart by a press of people. They
stopped, peered at each other through the gaps in the throng,
waved salutations, and stretched out their arms. Both were pale

and deadly serious. In that moment their hearts went out to each other; in the next, the world was to begin anew. Peace! Peace! — and the solemn moment when justice and humanity shall come into their own.

" Make way! The King! " shouted the guards. The crowd fell back; the King of Navarre presented himself before His Majesty, bowed, and the King embraced him.

Second Book of Samuel: Chapter I, Verses 19 and 25

One lovely morning came Mayenne, the only surviving Guise, with array of horsemen, in pursuit of the King, who was of course guided by traitors, of whom there was never any lack about his person, to a place where he would have been taken. A miller recognized the violet cassock and said: " Take care, Sire! Look yonder! " Mayenne's men had already charged. Crillon could not hold his ground and had to retreat within the town with such a handful of men that he shut the gates with his own hands. The King of Navarre had gone, but was not yet far away; and a messenger was sent after him. Fifteen hundred Huguenot arquebusiers saved the King. The Leaguers thought to bring the attack to a stand by a ruse; they shouted: " Huguenots, we have no quarrel with you, only with the King, who is betraying you." The answer was a salvo.

This scanty force had at last to withdraw; this they did slowly, step by step, firing as they went, and a third of their number fell. Crillon, the soldier of the King, ever afterwards declared his " passion for the Huguenots." The King's new friends put fresh heart and valour into the royalists — in such fashion that Valois himself went under fire. But the League retreated, and did so solely out of fear. Henri was overjoyed to be no longer fighting against the King, but only against his enemies. It eased his spirit, which means more than many a captured fortress. He presented his troops to the King; rode across a bridge at the head of twelve hundred horsemen, four thousand arquebusiers, and when they were drawn up, the King observed: " They all look so fresh and cheerful — are we not at war? " And Henri answered: " Sire!

Though we are never out of the saddle day or night, this is a cheerful little war." Valois understood; and he laughed from his heart, as Henri did, and as he himself had never done before.

The King, with this new courage, had by the summer collected fifteen thousand Switzers, though he had no money. With his own troops and Navarre's he had five-and-forty thousand soldiers, a powerful army; it was to have reconquered his capital — and it could have done so. In the meantime Mayenne's army melted away, until he was left with five thousand men, and among them not a single Spaniard or a German; because a movement of the masses that is counterfeit and base is blown away by a gust of courage, and behold — there are no masses left. In the enclosed city of Paris talk grew frank and free. Brown cowls could only show themselves if armed. Where was the League? Where was the ruling Party? Truth to tell, the monster consisted of at most a fifth of the population, and half of them crazy and half cowards. Between these — nothing.

The King's veteran commanders did not rightly know whether the siege of Paris was to be pressed or not. It might last a long time; and the army of the League would certainly fill up again if the siege came to nothing. But the King of Navarre insisted, with the offer of all his influence. " The kingdom is at stake. But remember — we have come to embrace this lovely city, and not lay violent hands upon it." And he said yet more, to enhance the glory of that enterprise. Boldness wins belief; and so, on the 30th of July, Saint-Cloud, both town and bridge, were taken by the royal army. This approach was held by the King, while Navarre attacked at another point.

Two days later he and his gallant troop had just mounted when a nobleman galloped up and whispered in his ear. Navarre turned at once. Five-and-twenty noblemen he took with him to Saint-Cloud. " Sire, why to the King? " — " Friends, because he has been stabbed in the belly." The answer struck them dumb with consternation, but they soon fell to talking in undertones. Here was the very handiwork of the League, said they. The Party and the movement were not made for war, but murder. The monks of Paris had preached a miracle, and they very well knew what that miracle would be. It had happened, and it was a murder. " Why, three lads came to our master sworn to do the deed of Judith. Yes; but he knows how to deal with murderers. Poor Valois does not. Who was it that stabbed him? "

A little monk, a thick-lipped lad of twenty, no doubt a very pattern of high-hearted youth; but when the King of Navarre's noblemen arrived they found what was left of him in the court-yard: a huddled brown heap. After the deed he had, strangely enough, not fled; he had turned his face to the wall and whis-pered: " Jakob, where are you? " — apparently speaking to him-self: his name was Jacques Clément.

The heir to the throne went to the dying man, who did not at first seem to be mortally hurt. But the last Valois passed, while his heir was elsewhere. When Henri came back, unknowing, the first to greet him were the Scotch guards, who made their obei-sance and cried: " Ha! Sire! Now you are our King and master."

For the first instant Henri did not understand — he with all his faith in his destiny. He shuddered, and he thought: " All this while I have been fighting my own fight, but now I step into the place of a beaten man who lies up yonder murdered, and how shall I lie? " With bowed head he mounted the stairs, entered the death-chamber, and looked at the dead man. We look, while we are here, at many dead — and with the eyes of the spirit at in-comparably more dead than living; and in consciousness of this we conceive ourselves as denizens of the same world as they, and speak to them. Henri spoke to the dead Valois: " The beauty of Israel is slain upon thy high places: how are the mighty fallen! How are the mighty fallen in the midst of the battle! O Jonathan, thou wast slain in thy high places."

Meantime two monks were praying by the corpse, and a cer-tain Monsieur d'Entragues was holding up its chin. With that gentleman the new King was to have many dealings; also with all the others who burst into the room as though they had been summoned. They set their hats more firmly on their heads, in-stead of doffing them in the presence of the new King, or flung them on the floor and swore to die a thousand deaths rather than endure a Huguenot King. Which was meant to ring like the utterance of faith and of conviction; but it rang false, especially as some of the same gentlemen pledged their loyalty to the heir immediately after the murder. They had then been troubled as to what might be their fate; they had not yet agreed among themselves to betray the kingdom and support the League. That, after they had reflected on the matter, seemed the safest plan. Philip of Spain still owned more gold than anyone on earth.

But in thinking that Henri did not take their measure they were sorely self-deceived; not for one moment did he imagine them as zealous for the faith. He had his mourning garments made from the dead man's violet cassock; he was in haste and had no money to buy cloth. The violet cassock was cut down, but it was recognized, and they nudged each other in contempt for the poverty of so unprofitable a King. Promptly they sent to the King's lodging a deputation bidding him recant at once and that forthwith. There could be no King of France without anointment from the sacred ampulla and coronation by the Church. He paled with anger. They might well have thought it was from fear; for in that moment he was plainly in their hands, and they could not know that he was well accustomed to dealing with murderers.

With unsuspected majesty he rejected the demand that he should sacrifice his soul and heart to enter on his kingdom. Whereupon he marked their company with an appraising eye. There were great gentlemen among them; but whom did they put forward as their spokesman? D'O — just O and nothing more — and he looked it: a corpulent young man, who by the favour of the late King had become an idler and a thief; one of those who had battened on the land and its revenues — and here was another King to be so served. This infamous fellow dared to dictate opinions to a man who had borne the burden of the fight, and talk of the common weal, as is the habit of such vermin. Henri fixed him with an eye under which the youth quailed, and said incisively: " All Catholics that are true friends of the people and men of honour are on my side." At this open insult there was silence, both because that stern face uttered it and also because it was true.

But men like these are best persuaded by a clash of weapons outside the door, which was indeed flung open. A soldier — Givry — stamped into the room and cried: " Sire, you are the King we need. Only cowards flee." Whereupon all those he spoke of fled. Then came Biron, to assure Henri that the Switzers, at least, would remain loyal. The Switzers alone — they were not many, and would not have sufficed. But here was Biron, a stout old veteran, who even at his age could walk round the table on his thumbs; he had been Henri's enemy, and was generous enough to confess his blunder. And he came when things looked blackest. " Biron! To my heart! With men like you I cannot fail."

On Earth and in Heaven

In the next five days the new King saw his army melt away, as the army of the League had done. Marshal Epernon, lately a pillar of the kingdom, picked a quarrel with Biron, so that he could say that he disdained to fight like a footpad under such a King. Upon which he withdrew to his kingdom of Provence. Each magnate had his little kingdom, that he had hewn out of the greater one; thither he departed, and took with him his noblemen and all his troops. The new King had no means of stopping them. By a change of faith? They would have been all the more certain to desert him. He would but have earned the contempt of his own companions, his fellow-believers, and his foreign friends. There would be no more money nor soldiers from England or Germany.

In those desperate days, with Mornay at his side, he drew up a declaration guaranteeing each creed the rights then held. For himself, he reserved the choice to adopt the faith now shared by the majority of his countrymen. He did not say when; but he well knew. When the kingdom and its turbulent capital were firmly in his hands, only then, and only of his free will. As undisputed master of the kingdom, he would give his old comrades of the Religion full liberty of conscience; such was his intent, whether for their sake or from self-respect, that he might not trample on all that he once had been. This was the King who would issue the Edict of Nantes and strive hard to safeguard freedom. Upon all this he resolved, and all this he foresaw in those five days when he was well-nigh deserted; and any other than himself would have joined the fugitives and deserted his own destiny.

Meantime the capital, still besieged, plunged into the abysses of unreason. Indeed, the few sober citizens remaining wished their dead leader back. For what came after him exceeded every outrage of his lifetime. Compared to his sister Monpensier, Guise had been a man of wisdom. In an ecstasy of jubilation she flung her arms about the messenger who reported the "Tyrant's" death. Her only regret was that Valois, as he lay dying, had perhaps not realized who had sent the little monk. Guise had stretched a hand forth from the grave and struck Valois down!

At the Duchess's entreaty, her mother, the mother of the two murdered Guises, addressed the people from an altar and fairly shrieked them into frenzy. And in that old woman's shrieks spoke the very soul of Lorraine — its savagery, its recklessness, and the hidden madness that impelled its deeds. The Duchess wanted her brother Mayenne proclaimed King forthwith, but in this she had to deal with the Ambassador of Spain. His master, Don Philip, conceived of France as a future Spanish province, and his troops held Paris. The League, backed by its master, could plunge into excesses. The mother of the monk murderer was fetched out of her village and worshipped like the Virgin. An image of the cowled youth was set up on an altar, between the two Guises, and exposed for public adoration. Seldom in history had mob and burghers, and especially high-hearted youth, revelled in riot thus uncurbed. The religion they had so abused could not avail, for no true faith was in them; nor was there any power of thought that could bridle men's folly and frenzy.

In those very days, before the closed gates of the city, Henri, by all abandoned, held fast to his resolve that he would come to reason's rescue and stand champion for freedom. First the kingdom should be delivered from the Ruler of the World. Henri would neither withdraw to Gascony, nor retreat across the German frontier. There were voices that counselled him to do one of those two things; and they sounded like the voices of sane reason in what seemed a desperate issue. But there was no despair in his heart — he meant to hold fast. Boldness wins confidence, confidence gives strength, strength is the mother of victory, and thus we save our realm and life.

On August the 8th he broke camp. He went but a short way with the body of the dead King; at such a moment there could be no ceremonial funeral. Then he split his army. Of five-and-forty thousand men, but ten or eleven thousand were left. He sent Marshal d'Aumont and his Protestant La Noue with three or four thousand to various points on the eastern frontier, to cover the kingdom against another Spanish invasion. He himself with his three and a half thousand arquebusiers, seven hundred horsemen, determined to lure the enemy's whole army, so much of it as then stood on French soil, to give battle where it would advantage him most.

He marched northwards, towards the Channel, setting his hopes upon the Queen, who had dealt the first blow at the Ruler of the World. But for the possibility of aid from Elizabeth, Henri could not have counted on the surrender of Dieppe. On the 26th he was before Dieppe, which opened its gates at once. This promptitude was born of apprehension. Here appeared, in sudden foray, from a dim distance, the captain of a robber band — for what else was he? A King — without a country; a general — without an army. Even his wife had run away from him. Meantime no one knew when the great Mayenne's regular army might arrive and what might happen before that. English ships might bombard the unlucky city from the sea, and on the land side it was already beset by the Huguenots. The men of Dieppe submitted to what they hoped might prove the lesser evil, and opened their gates. Kneeling burgesses, offering the huge keys of the city, together with salt and bread, and the cup that could at need be poisoned — the scene of surrender was complete. But the Robber King lifted a fat old gentleman from the pavement as though he had been a featherweight, and said to them all: " Good friends, no ceremony, pray! 'Tis enough if we are merry. Good bread, good wine, and friendly faces! "

He did not drink from their cup, which they did not notice, in their astonishment to find him so cheerful and so affable. They were Normans, with heavier blood than his. Their city was perilously placed, and these burghers had met many threats of doom with steadfast courage. But they were baffled by such good humour, as they watched him snatch a rose out of a girl's hand, laugh and jest, and fling a promise to everyone. What had such a man to give? They counted his scanty array, his handful of horsemen, and his straggling infantry. They pondered, and they said: " It cannot be that he means to conquer the Dukedom of Normandy with such rabble? " But indeed it was with just that rabble that he meant to conquer France. The citizens did not even listen when he proclaimed his purpose: to those crass heads the contrast was only too plain.

Such, too, was the demeanour of most Frenchmen at that time — in so far as they foresaw nothing, not even the reality now imminent, though they flattered themselves they were men who could see beyond their noses. Not until the very last did they observe that what their minds were set on was a fantastic dream and not the truth. The League, for all its guise of greatness, moved like a spectre of the night, prompt to vanish when the sun rose. Strange it was that this escaped them; and it was with anxious eyes that they marked the rising truth, embodied in their new King. There was indeed more distrust than hatred, not only among the men of Dieppe, but everywhere. Fear too: a secret and persistent inner voice, that might actually be conscience itself. What? Did he mean to conquer the Dukedom of Normandy with that rabble? Impossible. But when he was victorious — only a single battle won — suddenly they knew: the kingdom was his. And unto the uttermost ends of France men know that the long-expected day is here.

" Dieppe, indeed! " exclaimed Agrippa d'Aubigné, who was pondering a poem. " We are not only before Dieppe, on this misty plain between the woody hills and the river Béthune, where we have to take our boots off to dig these cursed trenches. Here, indeed, we are in person — earthworms, burrowing naked through the clay, in our efforts to make two redoubts, one behind the other, in case it shall occur to our malignant foes to attack us across the plain. We think to protect ourselves by all the arts devised of man, and hold fast to this spot of earth. In our rear lies the town of Arques, and above it the citadel. Still farther back the town of Dieppe shall receive us, if we must retreat, and there is even hope of ships from England."

"What's in your mind, Agrippa?" asked Rosny. "We shall not retreat."

And du Bartas interposed: "Perhaps we shall not be able — because our feet lie still upon this plain."

"Gentlemen!" It was Roquelaure's warning voice. Agrippa was intent upon his thoughts, or his poem. "We are indeed here in person upon this plain of Arques, on the left of the river, and on our right the wooded hills wreathed in mist, and in a hollow of those hills the hamlet of Martinglise."

"Where there is a tavern and good wine. I am thirsty," announced Roquelaure.

"Because our feet lie still upon this plain," repeated du Bartas, stressing the syllables.

And Agrippa: "But where are we in spirit? Not in a tavern, nor dead among the dead. In spirit we are on the foughten field, when the victory is won. Is there a man among us that does not know that we shall conquer? Even the enemy knows that. Why, Mayenne and his army are even now advancing — all eager to be beaten!"

"Would it were so!" observed Rosny, with a calm, judicial air. "What Mayenne means to do is to take the King; he has said so; and he thinks he has the force and skill to do it."

To which Agrippa retorted: "And yet in his secret heart he wants what is wanted by the whole world, not only here and by this distracted land. We are to save them from Spain and from themselves. We stand for deliverance from the Ruler of the World. 'Tis not with them we are at war."

"But with their blindness and their wickedness," added du Bartas.

Whereat Agrippa, in solemn tones: "Friends, the whole world awaits our victory, all eyes are upon us from the farthest lands where men are persecuted. With us are the prayers of the oppressed and the despised, and the conscience of all thinking men speaks for us."

It was Rosny who here eagerly agreed: "We are supported by the humanists in Europe. Which would be little to the purpose if they had merely learned to think, and not to ride and fight as well."

"But that they can do," said Roquelaure and du Bartas, heartily. And Rosny went on:

"Mornay has made it known in all kingdoms and republics that we are destined to bring down the Ruler of the World. He sends Fame to fly ahead and blow her trumpet and tell the nations we are fighting for justice and freedom — these are our saints; that we are champions of virtue, reason, and moderation — these are our angels."

"Don't you believe it, Monsieur de Rosny?" asked Roquelaure in a challenging tone. And Rosny answered:

"Yes — and more. I only wish I had a few thousand crowns from that fat villain Mayenne's baggage."

Then du Bartas, secure in his steadfast vision, began to speak — and his voice struck upon the ears of all: it was that of a guest who brings news from far away, whither he must soon go forth again. "Not upon this plain shall my feet lie still. That is very sure. From these earthly mists we shall all look up and catch a glimpse of heaven. Shattered is the tenfold array against us. I hear the peoples breathe again, and the ambassadors of the republics have set forth to pay homage to our King and offer him alliance."

Rosny was near to protesting; this was beyond all warrant. A trifling victory, four thousand soldiers, and they standing on the outermost edge of Europe and this kingdom; in all human estimation, they could bring no decision. Could it make the King any more than a King without a country? Ambassadors were on their way? Well, what of that? But Fame, pleaded an inner voice. The eager expectation of the world. And the man who was their King. His eyes met those of Monsieur de Roquelaure, who nodded, but did not speak; he had no doubts. For all of them, earthworms, as they had called themselves, toiling at earthworks, barefooted in the mire, the truth had been made visible, though their eyes could not pierce the gathered mists. Alone and before all others these men saw the great reality to come.

Agrippa had but to utter what had meantime been forming in his mind; his audience was prepared.

> " The clouds roll back, and to our yearning sight,
> Almighty God stands forth, cuirassed in light;
> While angel voices chant their Master's praise,
> With angel eyes the heavens are ablaze."

At this point the speaker broke off, for in very truth the mist above them parted and a patch of sky appeared, egg-shaped and very bright, and with their own eyes they saw — none ever confessed what they saw. A vision of the saints and angels whom they had lately named, all standing in the egg of light. In visage, garb, and armour like the great gods of old. And in their midst stood forth unveiled the Son of Man Himself.

PSALM LXVIII

In the trenches before Arques, Henri complained to Marshal Biron that they had now been waiting a week for the enemy to attack. Mayenne lay immovable behind the wood, no skirmishing would lure him forth; in that mist he did not mean to fight. But the mist was to the advantage of the smaller army. Henri wanted to force a battle. This the older man opposed. " Sire, by my advice you did not fortify yourself in Dieppe. 'Tis a noxious little place." " And swarming with spies," said Henri. The Marshal continued: " You know men, as I myself have learned from my own case. But I know war, and have known it longer. Let no such mist tempt you from this excellent position where you are covered on every side. You are certain you can hold it, with all the natural features on your side, the citadel behind you, and on your left the river, and its banks too marshy to be crossed by the enemy cavalry, and still less by his guns. And he cannot aim from any distance in this mist."

"But our guns," muttered Henri, "where are they? That is the mystery. And that will be our surprise."

Biron looked about him, and for a moment they did not speak. Then the Marshal shrugged his shoulders. "Nor can Mayenne attack from the right; the hills are covered with undergrowth and the ground too broken up. All that he can do is to march out from the wood across the open plain. Sire, wait for him between your two excellent redoubts. In the first stand five hundred of your veteran Huguenots; I myself have rubbed knees with them in time gone. And there is also room for you to launch your cavalry, fifty men abreast."

"You have considered everything, Biron, as the troops well know. They are few enough, and every man of them can use his wits. Their martial ardour is full of understanding. 'Tis to our advantage that we are not too many."

"Sire, the mist is so thick I cannot see whether you are laughing."

And Henri whispered in his ear: "The mist will prevent the enemy seeing how few we are. And how skilfully we are disposed," he added — and he moved an arm in a half-circle, pausing at several points, where the troops were posted: six there were, he knew them and could find them in the mist.

Neither Henri nor Biron had mentioned what was plain enough; the mist was a protection, but a danger too, and to both sides. Spies crept all day long back and forward unobserved. Time and again a commotion broke out in the vast army of the League. In the royal ranks men laid their ears to the ground and listened. Next morning Mayenne would wait no longer for the mist to lift; he attacked. Mayenne was astute; he made a move that he expected to deceive the enemy. He did not at first advance across the plain, but sent a small force, not more than three hundred German landsknechts, through the hilly ground on his flank. If he were rightly informed, the King in person had taken his stand on the right of the second redoubt. Mayenne's plan was to work round him under cover of the bushes and the mist, take him prisoner, and so win the day. The King taken, the Germans would at once seize the second redoubt, carry the first from the rear, where they would find that the League cavalry had already broken through. All the fortifications thus taken, nothing would be left of the royal forces but a few handfuls of disheartened men on an open plain. Such was the battle as the enemy planned it; but it fell out far otherwise.

By the first redoubt stood Biron; Henri by the second. Biron was based upon a chapel which that obstinate veteran meant to hold against all comers. He had only sixty horsemen; but he had eyes good enough to see a landsknecht creeping through the bushes and the mist. He sent a trooper to the King. When the three hundred Germans, panting from their passage through the mist, reached the position, they were expected, and they did well to put their hands up and look as pious as they could. They swore they preferred the royal cause, so they were helped across the trenches, allowed to keep their weapons, and greeted by the King. Time passed, and their new beliefs began to waver; as indeed appeared when the League cavalry and infantry swept in overwhelming force against the defenders of the first line. But these were the five hundred arquebusiers of the Religion, grim foes who stood immovable. Some light horsemen of the enemy did reach the enclosed space between the two redoubts. But six-and-twenty of the King's mounted noblemen, who in the mist looked to be many more, dashed at the enemy horse and drove them to the chapel, where they were met by Biron and his sixty.

The landsknechts on the second redoubt were growing less royally inclined as every minute passed. They saw the League force their way into the intervening space. What then happened they did not see, or saw it just too late; they were suddenly transformed into enemies once more, and in the resulting turmoil Biron, who dashed up, was flung from his horse. The same German who had unhorsed the Marshal held his pike to the breast of the King himself and bade him yield. Such a prisoner would have meant a life-pension for the worthy fellow. But, alas, he was too late; in his ardour he had not noticed that the Leaguers between the redoubts had been worsted. Suddenly he saw himself surrounded by horsemen, with lifted arms to cut him down. His face grew vacuous once more; the King laughed and bade his life be spared.

At this, Biron was furious. Stiff from his fall, he clambered into the saddle; none had ever seen him fall from his horse before. Now the King had seen it, and he merely laughed. Little he heeded the German or his pike. " Sire! " cried Biron. " Thank God, I am neither kind, nor clever. Give me that man! "

He was as hard-bitten as his steed, and the iron look had come back into his eyes; indeed, it was by that look that Henri recognized his enemy of old. The tall, lean figure sat swaying in his saddle; all the noise and turmoil of the fight could not shake his sense of justice and revenge. " Such a man are you, Biron," said the King calmly as he turned away. " And such another man is the landsknecht. But I must live with many men." Henri was on foot, in the trench behind the redoubt; the horseman, from his eminence, looked down upon a small, slight, steel-clad figure, with a white plume streaming from his helmet. And in that instant he realized the gulf set between them, far deeper than one of rank. A waft of power from a world he did not know came upon him whom they called Death on Horseback. That buffoon? A gambler upon any stake — a man who weeps as easily as any child? No, Biron, the King, and never so much a King as now: one before whom Marshal Biron is accounted equal with a landsknecht. He is said to be good. A merry fellow too. Well, well. Thus do bright birds fly over a dark abyss. All have their place — kindness, cleverness — and especially, be it said, the just contempt of men.

Biron turned and galloped off to his chapel; the fight was raging round it, and he meant to hold it more obstinately than before — for such a King.

The great army of the League had made no impression on the entrenched camp in the centre. Through the hills on the right it was driven back as far as the hamlet. Biron held the chapel, so long as the battle swayed, while on the left the enemy floundered into the marshy ground. There more royal troops bore down upon them than they had ever thought existed. It did not enter their minds that they might be the same troops every time. A squadron of the King's men, led by the King himself at a hand gallop clear across the battlefield, cut down whole companies and their commanders — and promptly vanished into the mist. The retreating enemy lost their direction. They groped about, still looking for the King; but he had long since dashed off to bring aid elsewhere. Fresh attacks surged against the enemy, though the attackers were the same. Masses of the Leaguers were exhausted piecemeal, before they could recall that they outnumbered their enemy tenfold. Then an entire division drifted on to the soft ground, which gave way beneath the weight. They swung round and retreated in confusion, but many stuck fast in the swamp. The leading ranks fell in with the Switzers.

In a hedged ravine along the river-side stood the King's Switzers, barring the way to Arques, and they would have fallen as they stood, man by man, sooner than let any of the King's enemies break through. Alone and forlorn on a patch of foreign ground, they were men from Solothurn and Glarus, under their own commander, Gallaty. They levelled their halberds and so stood, firm set and foursquare; not an inch would they yield to overwhelming force, though every man of them should fall. Once in the midst they caught sight of a white plume, worn only by the King. " My brave Switzers! " he cried. " This time you fight my battle. Next time I'll help you in your need." They understood him, although he spoke in a strange speech, and even in a French they did not know. He called them *Souisses*. He was their friend and had promised their commander, Gallaty, that, once master of his kingdom, he would pay his debt by delivering Switzerland from her oppressors. It was a pledge for him and them. In time to come he meant to offer his alliance to none but the free nations. They were men like their compatriots who on the day of Admiral Coligny's death had held the stair as long as any of them lived.

The Switzers held the ravine. The King's cavalry, fifty abreast, charged again and again from the redoubts, his infantry fought at six separate points; Biron clung to his chapel — not a man of them was ever relieved, while their enemies fell back exhausted and others took their place. They struggled hand to hand, fired pistols flat into the enemy's face the instant they glimpsed the colour of his scarf. Lance-thrusts beneath horsemen's saddles flung them headlong. A great lord of the League jeered at the young Protestant who had brought him down, and shouted: "You need flogging, boy!" as his neck snapped. By the chapel fell a La Rochefoucauld, called Josias, from Holy Writ. Rosny and Biron had their horses killed. But there were horses and enough that day whose riders lay between their hoofs with a groan that only earth could hear. Above the dying, life thundered on, and the noise of it was like a battle.

The King and his plume were sighted by the chapel in the ravine beside the river, on the redoubts, in the open field — everywhere, by each and every man and by all at once. He shouted out to them, in the mist and in that hour of peril, that they might hold fast and quit themselves like men. He called aloud the great names whose bearers had joined his destinies, and if a name were not yet great, he made it so. He rode past the young commander of his light horse, a son of Charles IX and a peasant girl. "Valois! I know you and I'll not forget you, neither you nor your House. You are my man now and always!" And he was gone. "Montgomery, Richelieu! There's a surprise for you at hand." "Rosny, La Force! When need is greatest, God is nearest." "Biron! The mist is lifting. It will lift, must lift, as truly as God is with us and we shall conquer." "La Rochefoucauld, take heed! — you shall hear the sound of thunder very soon."

Leaning from his horse, he grasped the other's shoulder, but the man fell, and not as a living man falls. A dead man in his armour had been propped upright against the chapel. "Josias? You?" said Henri silently, scarce believing his own question. Alas, when that thunder rolls, La Rochefoucauld will not hear it, nor ever again. "The guns from the citadel of Arques shall save us when the mist lifts and they can aim. I have a Norman pirate behind the redoubt who will tell me to the minute when the mist will lift. Such be my farewell, Josias! La Rochefoucauld lies lifeless by the way, as once lay another of his name in the palace of the Louvre, at the end of the night of murder. So lie the dead by the way." The King passed on.

Now he is with the Switzers. Stand fast this last time! In vain, they are overwhelmed. The ravine by the river is now abandoned, and in the end the chapel too. Remnants of the royal army hold the bridge-head only, and there are those that meditate retreat to Arques and Dieppe. " Friend," says the King to the Swiss commander, " friend, here am I, and I would die with you or win honour at your side." And as he spoke, he saw how all were watching and waiting until the deep ranks of the enemy should roll forward, one by one, and close like a gravestone on him and on his kingdom. And he shuddered. Then, in a flash, he flung his fears aside. " My Huguenots! " he cried. And those steadfast defenders of the first redoubt, his veterans of Jarnac and Montcontour, comrades of the Lord Admiral, who had seen two decades of fighting for conscience' sake, the men of Religion — they heard his cry, they saw his plume, and they left the front redoubt, where they had stood like iron since the dawn.

They had been five hundred, and as they approached there seemed to be five hundred of them still. Beside them marched the dead. Ahead of them came their pastor, one Damours. " Now for the Psalm, Pastor," said Henri; and they sang. It had always been their habit to fall upon the foe in the very flush of what he boasted as success, and this they had done at Coutras too. Never yet had it boded good to any foe; the mighty one now facing them shuddered as that Psalm broke forth; halted, and began to waver.

" Let God, the God of battle, rise
    And scatter His presumptuous foes,
  Let shameful rout their host surprise,
    Who spitefully their power oppose.

As smoke in tempest's rage is lost,
Or wax into the furnace cast,
So let their sacrilegious host
Before the wrathful presence waste."

Then the mist lifted; and the guns thundered from the citadel
of Arques. The cannon balls spread havoc, and the ranks that
had ventured nearest were utterly mown down. This was victory, and France was saved. God gives not at all, or He gives full-
handed of that which is His — the kingdom, the power, and the
glory. All was made clear that day to Henri, possessed as he was
by the fear of God. Coligny, the Admiral's son, appeared, bringing from Dieppe, which was now in safety, seven hundred men
— and beside the veteran arquebusiers of the Religion now stood
seven hundred more. " God hath sent you, Coligny! "

Henri had uttered no plaint nor prayer so long as the issue had
seemed dark and desperate. He called upon God in joy, and in
joy he was eager to bow down. Through many hours of peril he
had galloped over that battlefield, appearing everywhere, so that
each worn battalion thought him always at hand. Now he halted.
Into the mist and turmoil he had shouted many names and made
them greater. Every struggling company, wherever his white
plume flashed forth, he had heartened in courage and resolve. To
the Switzers he had offered his loyalty for theirs. He had spoken
with dead men by the way. He had taught Marshal Biron what
manner of man he was. His day had been a long one, but it was
not until the mist lifted that his day first rose in glory. He was
soon to be six-and-thirty — still no more than young. His face,
transfigured rather by the zest of battle and the agonies he
had endured than by his joy, was wet with tears as well as
sweat.

From both flanks his ancient warriors, champions of freedom
and of conscience, bore down upon the foe, whose strength was
broken; but they sang, full-throated and exultant. Storm-bells of
heaven swung from ropes invisible, by these, the servants of His
will.

" But let the servants of His will
    His favour's gentle beams enjoy.
Their upright hearts let gladness fill
    And cheerful songs their tongues employ.

To Him your voice in anthems raise,
    Jehovah's awful name He bears.
In Him rejoice, extol His praise,
    Who rides upon high rolling spheres."

MORALITÉ

Le triomphe final ne sera pas seulement acheté par ses propres sacrifices: Henri assiste à l'immolation d'êtres qu'il aurait voulu conserver. Déjà il avait dû faire ses adieux à sa compagne des années difficiles. Il faut encore que le Valois, son prédécesseur, s'en aille, et pourtant Henri, l'ayant sauvé de la main de ses ennemis, l'affectionnait d'une manière très personnelle. Son esprit y était plus content, préférant se mettre d'accord avec le passé, que de le renier. Avec le sens de la vie, on se plie à bien des nécessités. La moins acceptable, pour un esprit bien fait, est celle de voir s'accumuler les désastres. Trop de personnages ayant été mêlés à son existence viennent d'être emportés par les catastrophes, et la mort a voulu trop bien lui déblayer le chemin. Sur le champ de bataille d'Arques le roi Henri, en nage d'avoir tant combattu, pleure pendant que résonne le chant de la victoire. Ses larmes, c'est la joie qui en cause quelquesunes. D'autres, il les verse sur ses morts, et sur tout ce qui finit avec eux.

C'est sa jeunesse qui, ce jour là, prit fin.